Francis Bacon, William Rawley

Sylva Sylvarum

A natural history, in ten centuries. Whereunto is newly added the History natural

and experimental of life and death, or of the prolongation of life

Francis Bacon, William Rawley

Sylva Sylvarum
A natural history, in ten centuries. Whereunto is newly added the History natural and experimental of life and death, or of the prolongation of life

ISBN/EAN: 9783337780784

Printed in Europe, USA, Canada, Australia, Japan

Cover: Foto ©Andreas Hilbeck / pixelio.de

More available books at **www.hansebooks.com**

SYLVA SYLVARUM,

OR,

A Natural History,

IN

TEN CENTURIES.

Whereunto is newly added,

The *History Natural* and *Experimental* of LIFE
and DEATH, or of the Prolongation of LIFE.

Published after the Authors Death.
By WILLIAM RAWLEY, *Doctor in Divinity*,
One of His Majesties Chaplains.

Whereunto is added *Articles of Enquiry*, touching *Metals* and *Minerals*. And the *New Atlantis*. As also the LIFE of the Right Honorable *Francis Bacon*, never added to this Book before.

Written by the Right Honorable

FRANCIS

Lord *Verulam*, Viscount St. *Alban*.

The *Ninth* and *Last Edition*,
With an *Alphabetical Table* of the *Principal Things*
contained in the *Ten Centuries*.

LONDON,
Printed by *J. R.* for *William Lee*, and are to be sold by *George Sawbridg*,
Francis Tyton, *Thomas Williams*, *John Martin*, *Thomas Vere*, *Randolph Taylor*,
Henry Broom, *Edward Thomas*, *Thomas Passenger*, *Nevil Symmons*, *Robert*
Clavel, *William Crook*, and *James Magnes*; and other Booksellers in
London and *Westminster*. 1670.

TO THE

MOST HIGH AND MIGHTY

PRINCE CHARLES,

By the Grace of God,

KING of *Great Britain, France,* and *Ireland,*

Defender of the Faith, &c.

May it pleafe Your Moft Excellent Majesty.

THe vvhole Body of the Natural Hiftory, either defigned or vvritten, by the late Lord Vifcount S. Alban, vvas dedicated to Your Majefty, in his Book De Ventis, about Four years paft, vvhen Your Majefty vvas Prince: So as there needed no nevv Dedication of this Work, but onely in all humblenefs, to let Your Majefty knovv, it is Yours. It is true, if that Lord had lived, Your Majefty, ere long had been invoked to the Protection of another Hiftory, vvhereof, not Natures Kingdom, as in this; but thefe of

A 3

Your

Your Majesties, (during the time and Reign of King *Henry* the Eighth) had been the subject; vvhich since, it died under the Designation meerly : There is nothing left, but Your Majesties Princely goodness, graciously to accept of the undertakers Heart and Intentions ; vvho vvas vvilling to have parted for a vvhile vvith his darling Philosophy, that he might have attended Your Royal Commandment in that other VVork. Thus much I have been bold, in all lovvliness to represent unto Your Majesty, as one that vvas trusted vvith his Lordships VVritings, even to the last. And as this VVork affecteth the Stamp of Your Majesties Royal Protection, to make it more currant to the VVorld; so under the protection of this Work, I presume in all humbleness to approach Your Majesties presence, and to offer it up into Your Sacred Hands.

Your Majesties most Loyal

and Devoted Servant

W. RAWLEY:

READER.

H*Aving had the Honor to be continually with my Lord, in compiling of this Work; and to be employed therein, I have thought it not amiß, (with his Lordſhips good leave and liking) for the better ſatisfaction of thoſe that ſhall read it, to make known ſomewhat of his Lordſhips inten-tions, touching the ordering and publiſhing of the ſame.   I have heard his Lordſhip often ſay; That if he ſhould have ſerved the glory of his own Name, he had been better not to have publiſhed this* Natural Hiſtory *; for it may ſeem an indigeſted heap of Particulars, and cannot have that luſtre which Books caſt into Methods, have: But that he reſolved to prefer the good of* Men, *and that which might beſt ſecure it, before any thing that might have relation to himſelf.* And, *he knew well, that there was no other way open to unlooſe Mens mindes, being bound; and (as it were)* Maleficiate, *by the charms of deceiving* Notions *and* Theories; *and thereby made impotent for* Generation of Works: *But onely no where to depart from the Senſe and clear experience, but to keep cloſe to it, eſpecially in the beginning.   Beſides, this* Natural Hiſtory *was a Debt of his, being deſigned and ſet down for a third Part of the* Inſtauration.   *I have alſo heard his Lordſhip diſcourſe, That* Men (no doubt) *will think many of the* Experiments *contained in this* Collection, *to be Vul-*

oar

gar and *Trivial*, mean and fordid, curious and fruitleß; and therefore he wiſheth, that they would have perpetually before their eyes, what is now in doing; and the difference between this **Natural Hiſtory**, and others. For thoſe *Natural Hiſtories* which are extant, being gathered for delight and uſe, are full of pleaſant *Deſcriptions* and *Pictures*; and affect and ſeek after *Admiration*, *Rarities*, and *Secrets*. But contrariwiſe, the ſcope, which his *Lordſhip* intendeth, is to write ſuch a **Natural Hiſtory**, as may be fundamental to the erecting and building of a true *Philoſophy*: For the illumination of the *Underſtanding*; the extracting of *Axioms*, and the producing of many noble *Works* and *Effects*. For he hopeth by this means, to acquit himſelf of that, for which he taketh himſelf in a ſort bound; and that is, the advancement of *Learning* and *Sciences*. For having, in this preſent *Work*, collected the materials for the *Building*; and in his **Novum Organum** (of which his *Lordſhip* is yet to publiſh a Second *Part*) ſet down the *Inſtruments* and *Directions* for the *VVork*; Men ſhall now be wanting to themſelves, if they raiſe not knowledge to that perfection, whereof the *Nature* of *Mortal Men* is capable. And in this behalf, I have heard his *Lordſhip* ſpeak complainingly, That his *Lordſhip* (who thinketh, that he deſerveth to be an *Architect* in this *Building*) ſhould be forced to be a *VVorkman*, and a *Laborer*; and to dig the *Clay*, and burn the *Brick*; and more then that, (according to the hard condition of the *Iſraelites*, at the latter end) to gather the *Straw* and *Stubble*, over all the *Fields*, to burn the *Bricks* withal. For he knoweth, that except he do it, nothing will be done; Men are ſo ſet to deſpiſe the means of their own good. And as for the baſeneß of many of the *Experiments*, as long as they be *Gods VVorks*, they are honorable enough: And for the vulgarneß of them, true *Axioms* muſt be drawn from plain experience, and not from doubtful; and his *Lordſhips* courſe is to make *VVonders* plain,

and

and not plain things VVonders; and that experience like-
wise must be broken and grinded, and not whole, or as it
groweth; and for Use, his Lordship hath often in his
Mouth, the two kindes of Experiments, Experimenta Fructifera, *and* Experimenta Lucifera.
Experiments of Use, *and* Experiments of
Light : *And he reporteth himself, whether he were not*
a strange Man, that should think, that Light hath no Use,
because it hath no Matter. Further his Lordship thought
good also, to add unto many of the Experiments *them-*
selves, some gloß of the Causes, *that in the succeeding*
work of Interpreting Nature, *and* Framing Axioms, *all things may be in more readineß. And for the*
Causes herein by him aßigned ; his Lordship perswadeth
himself, they are far more certain, than those that are ren-
dred by others ; not for any excellency of his own wit, (as
his Lordship is wont to say) but in respect of his continual
conversation with Nature *and* Experience. *He did*
consider likewise , That by this Addition of Causes,
Mens mindes (which make so much haste to finde out the
causes of things ;) would not think themselves utterly lost
in a vast Wood of Experience, *but stay upon these*
Causes (such as they are) a little, till true Axioms
may be more fully discovered. I have heard his Lordship
say also, That one great reason, why he would not put these
Particulars into any exact Method, (though he, that look-
eth attentively into them , shall finde, that they have a se-
cret order) was, Because he conceived that other men would
now think that they could do the like ; and so go on with a
further Collection, which, if the Method had been exact,
many would have despaired to attain by Imitation. *As*
for his Lordships love of Order, I can refer any Man to
his Lordships Latin Book , De Augmentis Scien-
tiarum; *which, if my judgment be any thing, is written in*

B

the

the exactest order, that *I* know any writing to be. *I* will conclude, with a usual Speech of his Lordships. *That this Work of his* Natural History, *is the* World, *as* God *made it, and not as* Men *have made it; for that it hath nothing, if Imagination.*

W. RAWLEY.

A

A TABLE
OF THE
EXPERIMENTS.

Century I.

Century II.

Century III.

Century IV.

Of

Century V.

Century VI.

Century VII.

Of

Century VIII.

Century IX.

of

Century X.

I.

THE
LIFE

OF THE

RIGHT HONOURABLE

FRANCIS BACON

Baron of Verulam, Viscount St. Alban.

BY

WILLIAM RAWLEY. D. D.

His Lordships first and last Chaplain, and of late his
Majesties Chaplain in Ordinary.

LONDON,

Printed by S. G. & B. G. for *William Lee*, and are to be sold at the sign
of the Turks-Head in *Fleet street*, over against *Fetter-Lane*, 1670.

THE
LIFE
OF THE
RIGHT HONOURABLE
FRANCIS BACON
Baron of *Verulam*, Viſcount St. *Alban*.

FRANCIS BACON *the Glory, of his Age and Nation; The* Adorner, *and* Ornament *of* Learning; *Was born in* York-houſe *or* York-Place, *in the* Strand, *On the 22tb, Day of* January; *in the* Year *of our* Lord,*1560. His* Father *was that famous* Councellor *to* Queen Elizabeth; *The ſecond* Prop *of the* Kingdom *in his* Time, *Sir* Nicholas Bacon, Knight, Lord *Keeper of the* Great Seal *of* England; a Lord *of known* Prudence, Sufficiency, Moderation, *and* Integrity. *His* Mother *was* Ann, *one of the* Daughters *of Sir* Anthony Cook; *unto whom the* Erudition, *of* King Edward *the* Sixth, *had been committed:* A choyce Lady, *and* Eminent *for* Piety, Vertue, *and* Learning; *Being exquiſitely skilled, for a* Woman, *in the* Greek, *and* Latine, Tongues. *Theſe being the* Parents, *you may eaſily imagine,*

 what

what the Iſſue, was like to be;   Having had whatſoever Nature or Breeding could put into him.

His firſt and childiſh years were not without ſome Mark of
Eminency; At which time he was indued with that Pregnancy,
and Towardlineſs, of wit;   As they were Preſages, of that
Deep, and Univerſal Apprehenſion, which was manifeſt in
him, afterward : And cauſed him to be taken notice of, by ſeveral Perſons, of Worth and Place; And eſpecially, by the
Queen; who (as I have been informed) delighted much, then,
to confer with him; And to prove him with Queſtions; unto whom, he delivered Himſelf, with that Gravity, and Maturity, above his years; That Her Majeſty would often term
him, The young Lord Keeper. Being asked by the Queen,
how old he was ? He anſwered with much diſcretion, being
then but a Boy; That he was two years younger than her
Majeſties happy Reign; with which anſwer the Queen was
much taken.

At the ordinary years, of Ripeneſs, for the Univerſity; or
rather, ſomething earlier; he was ſent by his Father, to Tri-
nity Colledge, in Cambridge; To be educated, and bred under the Tuition of Doctor John White-Gift, then Maſter
of the Colledge; afterwards the renowned Arch Biſhop of
Canterbury; a Prelate of the firſt Magnitude of Sanctity,
Learning, Patience, and Humility; Under whom, He was obſerved, to have been more, than an Ordinary Proficient, in
the ſeveral Arts and Sciences. Whilſt he was commorant, in
the Univerſity, about 16 years of age, (as his Lordſhip hath
been pleaſed to impart unto my ſelf;) he firſt fell into
the Diſlike, of the Philoſophy of Ariſtotle: Not for the
Worthleſſeneſs of the Author, to whom he would ever aſcribe
all High Attributes; But for the Unfruitfulneſs, of the way;
Being a Philoſophy, (as his Lordſhip uſed to ſay) only
ſtrong, for Diſputations, and Contentions; But Barren, of
the production of Works, for the Benefit of the Life of Man.
In which Mind he continued to his Dying Day.

After he had paſſed, the Circle of the Liberal Arts; His
Father thought fit, to frame, and mould him for the Arts of
State; and, for that end, ſent him over into France, with

Sir

Sir Amyas Paulet, *then Employed Ambassadour Lieger,
into* France ; *By whom, he was, after a while, held fit to be en-
trusted, with some* Message, *or* Advertisement, *to the*
Queen ; *which having performed with great Approbation, he
returned back into* France *again ; with intention to continue,
for some years, there. In his absence, in* France, *his* Father,
the Lord Keeper, *died ; Having collected, (as I have heard,
of Knowing* Persons) *a considerable sum of* Money, *which
he had separated, with Intention, to have made a competent*
Purchase *of* Land , *for the Lively-hood of this his youngest*
Son ; (*who was onely unprovided for ; and though h: was
the youngest in years, yet he was not the lowest, in his* Fathers
affection ;) But the said Purchase, *being unaccomplished, at
his* Fathers *Death, there came no greater share to him, than his
single Part, and* Portion, *of the* Money , *dividable amongst
five* Brethren ; *'By which means, be lived, in some* streits,
and Necessities, *in his younger years. For as for that pleasant*
Sc:te, *and* Mannor *of* Gorhambury, *he came not to it, till
many years after, by the Death, of his Dearest* Brother, Mr.
Anthony Bacon ; *a* Gentleman, *equal to him, in* Height *of*
Wit ; *Though inferiour to him, in the* Endowments *of* Learning *and* Knowledge ; *Unto whom he was, most nearly conjoyned in affection ; They two being the sole* Male-issue *of a second* Venter.

Being returned from Travail , *he applied himself, to the
Study of the* Common-Law ; *which he took upon him to be
his* Profession. *In which, he obtained to great* Excellency,
*Though he made that, (as himself said) but as an accessary,
and not as his Principal study.* He *wrote several* Tractates,
upon that Subject. *Wherein , though some great* Masters,
of the Law *did out-go him in* Bulk, *and. Particularities of*
Cases ; *yet, in the Science, of the* Grounds, *and* Mysteries,
of the Law, *he was exceeded by none. In this way, he was after a while, sworn, of the* Queens Counsel Learned , *Ex-*
traordinary ; *a grace, (if I erre not) scarce known before.
He seated himself for the commodity of his studies, and. Practise ; amongst the* Honourable Society, *of* Greyes-Inn ;
Of which Houſe ; *he was a* Member ; *where he Erected,*
that

that Elegant Pile, *or* Structure, *commonly known by the* Name *of the* Lord Bacons Lodgings; *which he Inhabited by Turns, the most part of his Life,* (*some few years onely excepted,*) *unto his Dying Day.* In *which* House *he carried himself, with such Sweetness,* Comity, *and Generosity;* That *he was much revered, and beloved, by the* Readers *and* Gentlemen *of the* House.

Notwithstanding, that he professed the Law for his Livelyhood, and Subsistence; yet his Heart and Affection was more carried after the Affairs *and* Places *of* Estate; *for which, if the* Majesty Royal *then, had been pleased, he was most fit.* In *his younger years, he studied the* Service, *and Fortunes,* (*as they call them,*) *of that* Noble, *but* unfortunate Earl, *the* Earl *of* Essex; *unto whom he was, in a sort, a Private and free* Counseller, *and gave him Safe and Honourable Advice, till, in the end, the* Earl *inclined too much, to the violent and precitate* Counsell *of others, his Adherents, and Followers; which was his* Fate *and* Ruine.

His Birth *and other* Capacities *qualified him, above others of his Profession, to have ordinary accesses at* Court; *and to come frequently into the* Queens Eye; *who would often grace him with private and free* Communication; *Not onely about* Matters *of his Profession, or Business in* Law; *But also, about the* arduous Affairs *of* Estate; *From whom she received, from time to time, great Satisfaction.* Nevertheless *though she cheered him much, with the* Bounty *of her* Countenance; *yet she never cheered him with the* Bounty *of her* Hand; *Having never conferred upon him, any* Ordinary Place *or Means of* Honour *or* Profit, *Save onely one dry* Reversion *of the* Registers Office, *in the* Star-Chamber; *worth about* 1600 l. *per* Annum; *For which he waited in* Expectation, *either fully or near twenty years; Of which his* Lordship *would say, in* Queen Elizabeths *Time;* That it was like another mans Ground, buttalling upon his House; which might mend his Prospect, but it did not fill his Barn. (*Nevertheless in the time of* King James, *it fell unto him, Which might be imputed; not so much to her* Majesties *averseness and* Disaffection, *towards him;*

as

as the Arts *and* Policy of a Great Statesman; *then*; *who laboured by all induftrious*, *and fecret Means, to fupprefs, and keep him down*; *left*, *if he had rifen, he might have obfcured his Glory:*

But though; *he flood long at a ftay, in the Dayes of his Miftrefs* Queen Elizabeth ; *Yet, after the change, and Coming in of his New Mafter*, King James, *he made a great progrefs*; *by whom he was much comforted*, *in* Places of Truft, Honour, *and* Revenue, *I have feen, a* Letter *of his Lordfhips, to* King James, *wherein he makes Acknowledgement*; That he was that Mafter to him, that had raifed and advanced him nine times ; Thrice in Dignity, and *Six* times in Office, *His* Offices (*as I conceive*) *were* Counfel learned extraordinary, *to his* Majefty, *as he had been*, to Queen Elizabeth ; Kings Solliciter General ; *His* Majefties Atturney General ; Counfellor of Eftate, *being yet but* Atturney ; Lord Keeper *of the* Great Seal of England. *Laftly,* Lord Chancellor : *which two laft Places, though they be the fame, in Authority and Power*; *yet they differ, in Patent,* Height, *and* Favour *of the* Prince. *Since whofe time*, *none of his* Succeffors, until this prefent Honourable Lord, *did ever bear the* Title *of* Lord Chancellor. *His* Dignities *were firft* Knight, *then* Baron of Verulam; *Laftly,* Vifcount Saint Alban : *Befides other good* Gifts *and* Bounties *of the Hand, which his Majefty gave him*, Both out of the Broad-Seal, *and out of the* Aleniation-Office, *To the value, in both of eighteen hundred pounds* per annum : *which with his Mannour of* Gorhambury ; *and other* Lands *and* Poffeffions, *near thereunto adjoyning, amounting to a third part more, he retained to his* Dying Day.

To wards his *Rifing years; not before, he entered into a married Eftate, and took to Wife*, Alice, *one of the* Daughters, *and* Co-heirs *of* Benedict Barnham, Efquire, *and* Alderman *of* London, *with whom he received, a fufficiently ample, and liberal* Portion, *in* Marriage. Children *he had none : which, though they be the means to perpetuate our* Names, *after our* Deaths; *yet he had other* Iffues *to perpetuate his* Name; *The* Iffues *of his* Brain, *in which he was ever*

ver happy, and admired ; as Jupiter *was, in the production of* Pallas. *Neither did the want of* Children *, detract from his good usage of his* Consort *, during the* Intermarriage *; whom he prosecuted, with much* Conjugal Love, *and Respect ; with many* Rich Gifts, *and* Endowments *; Besides a* Robe *of* Honour, *which he invested her withal ; which she wore untill her* Dying Day *; being twenty years and more, after his* Death.

The last five years of his Life, being with drawn from Civil affaires *, and from an* Active Life, *he employed wholly in* Contemplation *and* Studies. *A thing , whereof his* Lordship *would often speak, during his* Active Life *; as if he affected to dy in the* Shadow, *and not in the* Light *; which also may be found in several* Passages *of his* Works. *In which time he composed, the greatest part of his* Books, *and* Writings *; Both in* English *and* Latine *; Which I will enumerate, (as near as I can) in the just order, wherein they were written. The* History of the Reign of King Henry the Seventh *;* Abcedarium Naturæ *; or a* Metaphysical *piece ; which is lost ;* Historia Ventorum *;* Historia Vitæ & Mortis *;* Historia Densi & Rari, *not yet printed ;* Historia Gravis & Levis, *which is also lost ;* A Discourse of a War with Spain *;* A Dialogue, *touching an* Holy War. *The* Fable of the New Atlantis. *A Preface to a Digest of the Lawes of* England. *The Beginning, of the History of the Reign of King Henry the Eighth.* De Augmentis Scientiarum, *Or the* Advancement of Learning, *put into* Latin, *with several* Enrichments *and* Enlargements. Counsels Civil, *and* Moral. *Or his* Book of Essayes, *likewise* Enriched *and* Enlarged. *The* Conversion of certain Psalms, *into* English Verse. *The* Translation into Latin ; of the History *of* King Henry the Seventh. *Of the* Counsels Civil *and* Moral. *Of the* Dialogue of the Holy War. *Of the* Fable of the New Atlantis, *For the Benefit of other Nations. His Revising of his* Book, De Sapientia Veterum. Inquisitio *de* Magnete, Topica Inquisitionis, de Luce & Lumine *; Both these not yet Printed, Lastly,* Sylva Sylvarum, *or the* Natural History. *These were the*

Fruits,

Fruits *and* Productions, *of his laſt five years. His* Lordſhip *alſo deſigned upon the Motion and Invitation of his* late
Majeſty ; *To have written the* Reign *of* King Henry *the*
Eighth ; *But that* Work *Periſhed in the* Deſignation *meer-*
ly ; God *not lending him Life, to proceed further upon it, then*
only in one Mornings Work : *whereof there is Extant, An,*
Ex Ungue Leonem, *already Printed, in his* Lordſhips Miſ-
cellany Works.

There is a Commemoration due ; As well, to his Abilities,
and Vertues, as to the Courſe *of his* Life. *Thoſe Abilities,*
which commonly go ſingle in other Men, though of prime, and
Obſervable, *Parts, were all conjoyned, and met in Him.*
Thoſe are, Sharpneſs *of* Wit, Memory, Judgment, *and*
Elocution. *For the Former Three, his* Books *do abun-*
dantly ſpeak them ; which, with what Sufficiency *he wrote, let*
the World *judge ;* But *with what* Celerity *he wrote them,*
I can beſt teſtiſie. But for the Fourth, his Elocution ; *I will*
only ſet down, what I heard, Sir Walter Rawleigh, *once ſpeak of*
him, by way of Compariſon ; (whoſe Judgment may well be
truſted ;) That the Earl of *Saliſbury,* was an excellent
Speaker, but no good Pen-man ; That the Earl of *North-*
ampton, (the Lord *Henry Howard,*) was an excellent
Pen-man, but no good speaker; But that Sir *Francis*
Bacon, was Eminent in both.

I have been enduced to think ; That if there were, a
Beam *of* Knowledge *derived from* God *upon any*
Man, *in theſe* Modern Times, *it was upon Him. For*
though he was a great Reader *of* Books ; *yet he had*
not his Knowledge from Books ; *But from ſome* Grounds,
and Notions *from within Himſelf. Which notwith-*
ſtanding, he vented with great Caution *and* Circum-
ſpection. *His* Book, *of* Inſtauration Magna, (*which,*
in his own Account, was the chiefeſt of his Works,) *was no*
Slight *Imagination, or Fancy, of his brain ; but a* setled,
and Concocted Notion ; *The* Production *of many years,*
Labour, *and* Travel. *I my Self, have ſeen, at the leſt,*
Twelve Coppies, *of the* Inſtauration ; *Reviſed, year by*
year, one after another ; And every year altered, and amended,

in the Frame thereof; Till, at last, it came to that Model, *in which it was committed to the* Press; *as many* Living Creatures, *do lick their young ones, till they bring them, to their* strength *of* Limbs.

In the Composing *of his* Books, *he did rather drive at a* Masculine *and clear* Expression, *than at any* Fineness, *or* Affectation *of* Phrases, *and would often ask, if the* Meaning *were expressed plainly enough: as being one that accounted* words *to be but* subservent, *or* Ministerial, *to* Matter; *and not the* principal. *And if his* Stile *were* Polite, *it was because he could do no otherwise.* Neither *was he given, to any* Light Conceits; Or Descanting *upon* Words; *But did ever, purposely, and industriously, avoid them; For he held such* Things, *to be but* Digressions, *or* Diversions, *from the* Scope *intended; and to derogate, from the* Weight *and* Dignity *of the* Stile.

He was no Plodder *upon* Books; *Though he read much, and that with great* Judgement *and* Rejection *of* Impertinences, *incident to many* Authors; *For he would ever interlace a* Moderate Relaxation *of His* Minde *with his* Studies; As Walking, Or Taking *the* Air *abroad in his* Coach; *or some other befitting* Recreation; *and yet, he would* loose *no* Time, *In as much, as upon his* First; *and* Immediate Return, *he would fall to* Reading *again, and so suffer no* Moment *of* Time *to* Slip *from him, without some present* Improvement.

His Meales *were* Refections *of the* Eare *as well as of the* Stomack: *Like the* Noctes Atticæ; *or* Convivia Deipno-Sophistarum; *Wherein a* Man *might be refreshed in his* Mind *and* understanding, *no less then in his* Body. And *I have known some, of no mean* Parts, *that have professed to make use of their* Note-Books, *when they have risen from his* Table. *In which* Conversations, *and otherwise, he was no* Dashing Man, *as some men are; But ever a* Countenancer, *and* Fosterer, *of another Mans* Parts. Neither *was he one, that would appropriate the* Speech, *wholy to* Himself; *or delight to out-vie others; But leave a* Liberty, *to the* Co-Assessours, *to take their* Turns. *Wherein he would draw*

a Man

ıre him, to ſpeak upon ſuch a ſubject, as
liarly Skilful, and would delight to ſpeak.
he contemned no Mans Obſervations,
orch at every mans Candle.
d Aſſertions were, for the moſt part, Bin-
ıdicted by any ; Rather like Oracles, than
may be imputed, either to the well weigh-
by the Skales of Truth, and Reaſon ;
rence and Eſtimation, wherein he was
no Man would conteſt with him : So
umentation, or Pro and Con (as they
ıle : Or if there chanced to be any it was
bmiſſion and Moderation.
ved, and ſo have other Men of great
d occaſion to repeat another Mans Words
uſe and faculty to dreſs them in better
ıarel than they had before : So that the
! his own ſpeech much amended ; and
it ſtill retained : As if it had been Na-
od Forms ; As Ovid ſpake of his Fa-

ntabam ſcribere, Verſus erat,

ılled him, as he was of the Kings Coun-
e any Offenders, either in Criminals,
never of an Inſulting, or Domineering
But alwayes tender Hearted, and carry-
owards the Parties ; (Though it was his
home :) But yet, as one, that looked up-
h the Eye of Severity, But upon the Per-
Pitty, and Compaſſion. And in Civil
Counſellor of Eſtate, he had the beſt
t engaging his Maſter, in any Precipi-
ourſes, but in Moderate and Fair
ing, whom he ſerved, giving him this
be ever dealt, in Buſineſſe, Suavibus

Modis ; Which was the way that was most according to his own heart.

Neither was He in his time lesse gracious with the Subject *than with his* Soveraign. *He was ever acceptable to the* House *of* Commons, *when he was a* Member *thereof.* Being *the* Kings Atturney, *and chosen to a place in* Parliament ; *he was allowed and dispensed with to sit in the* House ; *which was not permitted to other* Atturneys.

And as he was a good Servant *to his* Master ; Being *never, in nineteen years service (as he himself averred,) rebuked by the* King *for any Thing relating to his* Majesty ; *So he was a good* Master *to his* Servants, *And rewarded their long attendance with good* Places, *freely when they fell into his* Power. *Which was the Cause that so many young* Gentlemen *of* Blood *and* Quality, *sought to list themselves in his* Retinue. *And if he were abused by any of them in their* Places, *It was onely the* Errour *of the* Goodness, *of his* Nature ; *but the* Badges *of their* Indiscretions, *and* Intemperances.

This Lord *was* Religious ; *For though the* World *be apt to suspect, and prejudice,* Great Wits, *and* Politicks *to have somewhat of the* Atheist ; *Yet he was conversant with* God : *as appeareth, by several* Passages, *throughout the whole Current of his* Writings. *Otherwise he should have crossed his own* Principles ; *which were ,* That a little Philosophy, *maketh* Men *apt to forget* God ; As *attributing too much to second* Causes ; *But* Depth *of* Philosophy, *bringeth* Men *back to* God *again. Now I am sure, there is no* Man *that will deny him, or account otherwise of him, but to have him been a deep* Philosopher. *And not only so,* But *he was able to render a* Reason *of the* Hope *which was in him ; Which that* Writing *of his, of the* Confession *of the* Faith, *doth abundantly testifie. He repaired frequently, when his* Health *would permit him, to the* Service *of the* Church, *To hear* Sermons, *To the* Administration *of the* Sacrament *of the* Blessed Body *and* Bloud *of* Christ ; *And died in the true* Faith *established in the* Church *of* England.

This is most true; He was free from Malice ; *which,(as he said Himself,*) He never bred nor fed. *He was no* Revenger *of* Injuries ; *which, if he had minded, he had both* Opportunity *and* Place High *enough, to have done it.* He was no Heaver *of* Men *out of their* Places ; *as delighting in their* Ruine *and* undoing. *He was no defamer of any* Man *to his* Prince. *One Day, when a great* States-Man *was newly Dead, That had not been his* Friend ; *The* King *asked him,* What *he thought of that* Lord, *which was gone?* He answered, That *he would never have made his* Majesties Estate *better ; But he was sure he would have kept it from being worse.* Which was the worst, *be would say of him.* Which I reckon, *not among his* Moral, *but his* Christian Vertues.

His Fame is greater, and sounds louder *in* Forraign Parts *abroad, than at* home *in his own* Nation. *Thereby verifying that* Divine Sentence , A Prophet is not without honour, save in his own Country, and in his own house. *Concerning which I will give you a* Taste *onely, out of a* Letter, written from *Italy (* The Store-house of Refined *Wits) to the late* Earl *of* Devonshire , Then, *the* Lord Candish. I will expect the New Essayes *of my* Lord Chancellor Bacon, *as also his* History, *with a great deal of* Desire, *and whatsoever else he shall* compose. *But in* Particular *of his* History, *I promise my self a thing* perfect and *Singular ; especially in* Henry *the* Seventh ; Where *he may exercise the* Talent *of his* Divine understanding. *This* Lord *is more and more* known, *and his* Books *here, more and more delighted in ; And those* Men *that have more than* ordinary Knowledge *in* Humane *affairs, esteem him one of the most capable* Spirits *of this* Age; *and he is truely such.* Now his Fame doth not decree with Dayes since, but rather increase. Divers of his Works have been anciently, and yet lately, translated into other Tongues, both Learned and Modern, by Forraign Pens. Several Persons of Quality, during his Lordships Life, crossed the Seas on purpose to gain an Opportunity of seeing him, and Discoursing with him : whereof one,* carried *his* Lordſhips Picture, *from Head to Foot, over with him into* France ; *as a Thing which, he foreſaw, would be much deſired there* ; *That ſo they might enjoy, the* Image *of his* Perſon ; *as well as the* Images *of his* Brain, *his* Books. *Amongſt the reſt,* Marquis Fiat ; *a* French-Nobleman ; *who came* Ambaſſador *into* England, *in the beginning of* Queen Mary, *Wife to* King Charles, *was taken with an extraordinary Deſire of Seeing him* : *For which, he made Way by a* Friend : *And when he came to him, being then, through weakneſs, confined to his Bed* ; *The* Marquis *ſaluted him with this* High-Expreſſion ; *That his* Lordſhip, *had been ever to* Him, *like the* Angels ; *of whom he had often heard, and read much of them in* Books; *But he never ſaw them.* *After which they contracted an intimate Acquaintance* ; *And the* Marquis *did ſo much revere him* ; *that beſides his Frequent* viſits ; *they wrote* Letters, *one to the other, under the Titles and* Appellations, *of Father and Son*; *As for his many Salutations, by* Letters *from* Forraign Worthies, *devoted to* Learning ; *I forbear to mention them* ; *Becauſe that is a* Thing *common to other* Men *of* Learning, *or* Note *together with him.*

But *yet, in this Matter of his Fame, I ſpeak, in the Comparative, onely, and not in the* Excluſive. *For his Reputation is great, in his own* Nation, *alſo* ; *Eſpecially amongſt thoſe, that are of a more Acute, and ſharper Judgement* : *Which I will exemplifie, but with two* Teſtimonies, *and no more. The Former* ; *When his* Hiſtory *of* King Henry *the Seventh was to come forth* ; *It was delivered to the old* Lord Brook, *to be peruſed by him* ; *who, when he had diſpatched it, returned it to the* Author, *with this* Eulogy : *Commend me to my* Lord ; *and bid him take care, to get good* Paper *and* Inke, *for the* Work *is incomparable. The other ſhall be that, of* Doctor Samuel Collins, *late* Provoſt, *of* Kings Colledge, *in* Cambridge, *A Man of no vulgar Wit, who affirmed unto me,* That *when he had read, the* Book *of the* Advancement *of* Learning, *He found himſelf in a caſe to begin his* Studies *a new, and that he had loſt all the* Time *of his ſtudying before.*

It hath been desired; That something should be signified, touching his Diet; And the Regiment of his Health: Of which in regard, of his Universal Insight into Nature, he may (perhaps,) be to some, an Example.   For his Diet; It was rather a plentiful, and liberal, Diet, as his Stomack would bear it, then a Restrained; Which he also commended in his Book of the History of Life and Death.   In his younger years, he was much given to the Finer and Lighter sort of Meats, as of Fowles; and such like: But afterward, when he grew more Judicious; He preferred the stronger Meats; such as the Shambles afforded; As those Meats, which bred the more firm and substantial Juyces of the Body, and less Dissipable: upon which, he would often make his Meal; Though he had other Meats, upon the Table.   You may be sure; He would not neglect that Himself, which He so much extolled in his Writings; And that was the Use of Niter: Whereof he took in the Quantity of about three Grains, in thin warm Broath, every Morning, for thirty years together, next before his Death.   And for Physick, he did, indeed, live Physically, but not miserably; For he took only a Maceration of Rhubarb; Infused into a Draught of White Wine, and Beer, mingled together, for the Space of half an Hour; Once in six or seven Dayes; Immediately before his Meal, (whether Dinner, or Supper,) that it might dry, the Body, lesse: which (as he said,) did carry away frequently, the Grosser Humours of the Body, and not diminish, or carry away, any of the Spirits, as Sweating doth.   And this was no Grievous Thing to take. As for other Physick, in an ordinary way, (whatsoever hath been vulgarly spoken;) he took not. His Receit, for the Gout; which did, constantly, ease him of his Pain, within two Hours, Is already set down in the End, of the Natural History.

It may seem, the Moon, had some Principal Place, in the Figure of his Nativity. For the Moon, was never in her Passion or Eclipsed, but he was surprized, with a sudden Fit, of Fainting: And that, though he observed not, nor took any previous Knowledge, of the Eclipse thereof; and assoon as the Eclipse ceased, he was restored, to his former strength again.

He

He died, on the 9th. *Day of April, in the year* 1616; *In the early Morning, of the Day then celebrated for our Saviours Resurrection, In the* 66th. *year of his Age ; at the Earle of* Arundells *House in* High-gate, *near* London ; *To which Place, he casually repaired, about a week before, God so ordaining, that he should dye there, Of a Gentle Feaver, accidentally accompanied, with a great Cold ; whereby the Defluxion of Rheume, fell so plentifully upon his Breast, that he died by* Suffocation : *And was buried, in* Saint Michaels *Church, at* Saint Albans; *Being the Place, designed for his Burial, by his last Will, and Testament; Both because the Body of his Mother was interred there; And because, it was the only Church, then remaining, within the Precincts of old* Verulam : *Where he hath a Monument, erected for him of* White Marble; (*By the Care, and Gratitude, of Sir* Thomas Meautys, *Knight, formerly his Lordships Secretary; Afterwards* Clark *of the Kings Honourable Privy Gounsel, under two Kings :) Representing his full Pourtraiture in the Posture of studying ; with an* Inscription *composed by that Accomplisht* Gentleman, *and Rare Wit, Sir* Henry Wotton.

But howsoever his Body was Mortal; yet no doubt his Memory and Works will live ; And will in all probability, last as long as the World lasteth. In order to which, I have endeavoured, (after my poor Ability,) to do this Honour to his Lordship by way, of enducing to the same.

SPEECHES

NEW ATLANTIS.

A VVork unfinished.

Written by the Right Honorable,

FRANCIS

Lord *Verulam*, Viscount *St. Albans*.

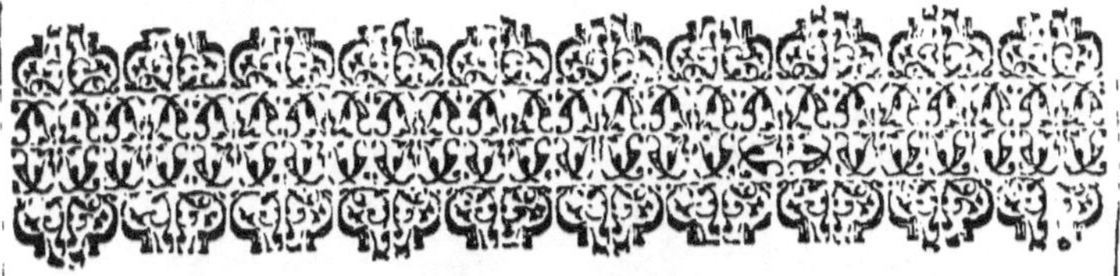

TO THE
READER.

His *Fable* my Lord deviſed, to the end that he might exhibit therein a *Model* or *Deſcription* of a *College*, inſtituted for the Interpreting of *Nature*, and the producing of great and marvellous *Works* for the benefit of *Men*, under the name of *Solomons* Houſe, or, *The College of the Six days Works*. And even ſo far his Lordship hath proceeded as to finish that Part. Certainly, the Model is more vaſt and high, than can poſſibly be imitated in all things, not-withſtanding moſt things therein are within Mens power to effect. His Lordship thought alſo in this preſent Fable to have compoſed a Frame of Laws, or of the beſt State or Mould of a *Commonwealth*; but fore-ſeeing it would be a long Work, his deſire of Collecting the *Natural Hiſtory* diverted him, which he preferred many degrees before it.

This Work of the *New Atlantis* (as much as concerneth the *English Edition*) his Lordship deſigned for this place, in regard it hath ſo near affinity (in one part of it) with the preceding *Natural Hiſtory*.

W. Rawley.

 NEW

NEW ATLANTIS.

E failed from *Peru* (where we had continued by the
space of one whole year) for *China* and *Japan* by the
South Sea, taking with us Victuals for Twelve Moneths,
and had good Winds from the Eaft, though foft and
weak, for Five Moneths fpace and more ; but then the
Wind came about, and fetled in the Weft for many
days ; fo as we could make little or no way, and were
fometimes in purpofe to turn back : But then again,
there arofe ftrong and great Winds from the South, with a Point Eaft,
which carried us up (for all that we could do) towards the North ; by which
time our Victuals failed us, though we had made good fpare of them: So
that finding our felves in the midft of the greateft Wildernefs of Waters in
the World, without Victual, we gave our felves for loft men, and prepared
for death. Yet we did lift up our hearts and voices to God above, *Who
fheweth his wonders in the deep* ; befeeching him of his mercy, That as in the
Beginning he difcovered the *Face of the deep*, and brought forth *dry-land* ; fo he
would now difcover Land to us, that we might not perifh. And it came to
pafs, that the next day about Evening, we faw within a Kenning before us,
towards the North, as it were thicker Clouds, which did put us in fome
hope of Land ; knowing how that part of the South-Sea was utterly unknown, and might have Iflands or Continents that hitherto were not come
to light. Wherefore we bent our courfe thither, where we faw the appearance of Land all that night ; and in the dawning of the next day, we
might plainly difcern that it was a Land flat to our fight, and full of Bofcage,
which made it fhew the more dark ; and after an hour and a halfs failing,
we entred into a good Haven, being the Port of a fair City, not great indeed, but well built, and that gave a pleafant view from the Sea : And we
thinking every minute long, till we were on Land, came clofe to the Shore
and offered to land ; but ftraight-ways we faw divers of the people with
Baftons in their hands, (as it were) forbidding us to land, yet without any
cries or fiercenefs, but onely as warning us off by figns that they made.
Whereupon being not a little difcomforted, we were advifing with our
felves, what we fhould do. During which time, there made forth to us a
fmall Boat with about eight perfons in it, whereof one of them had in his
hand a Tip-ftaff of a Yellow Cane, tipped at both ends with Blew, who
made aboard our Ship without any fhew of diftruft at all : And when he
faw one of our number prefent himfelf fomewhat afore the reft, he drew
forth a little Scroul of Parchment (fomewhat yellower then our Parchment,

A 3

and

and shining like the Leaves of Writing-Tables, but otherwise soft and flexible) and delivered it to our foremost man. In which Scroul were written in ancient *Hebrew*, and in ancient *Greek*, and in good *Latine* of the School, and in *Spanish*, these words, "Land ye not, none of you, and provide to be "gone from this Coast within sixteen days, except you have further time "given you: Mean while, if you want Fresh-water or Victual, or help for "your Sick, or that your Ship needeth repair, write down your wants, and "you shall have that which belongeth to Mercy. This Scroul was signed with a stamp of *Cherubims VVings*, not spred, but hanging downwards, and by them a *Cross.* This being delivered, the Officer returned, and left onely a Servant with us to receive our answer. Consulting hereupon amongst our selves, we were much perplexed. The denial of Landing, and hasty warning us away, troubled us much. On the other side, to finde that the people had Languages, and were so full of Humanity, did comfort us not a little; and above all, the Sign of the *Cross* to that Instrument, was to us a great rejoycing, and, as it were, a certain presage of good. Our answer was in the *Spanish* Tongue, "That for our Ship it was well, for we had rather "met with Calms and contrary Winds then any Tempests. For our Sick, "they were many, and in very ill case; so that if they were not permitted to "land, they ran in danger of their lives. Our other wants we set down in particular, adding, "That we had some little store of Merchandize, which "if it pleased them to deal for, it might supply our wants without being "chargeable unto them. We offered some reward in Pistolets unto the Servant, and a piece of Crimson Velvet to be presented to the Officer: but the Servant took them not, nor would scarce look upon them, and so left us, and went back in another little Boat which was sent for him.

About three hours after we had dispatched our Answer, there came towards us a person (as it seemed) of place: He had on him a Gown with wide Sleeves of a kinde of Water-Chamolet, of an excellent Azure colour, far more glossie then ours; his under apparel was green, and so was his Hat, being in the form of a Turbant, daintily made, and not so huge as the *Turkish* Turbants; and the Locks of his Hair came down below the brims of it: A Reverend Man was he to behold, He came in a Boat gilt in some part of it, with four persons more onely in that Boat, and was followed by another Boat wherein were some twenty. When he was come within a flight-shot of our Ship, signs were made to us, that we should send forth some to meet him upon the Water; which we presently did in our Ship-boat, sending the principal Man amongst us save one, and four of our number with him. When we were come within six yards of their Boat, they called to us to stay, and not to approach further; which we did: And thereupon the Man whom I before described stood up, and with a loud voice in *Spanish*, asked, *Are ye Christians?* We answered, *VVe were;* fearing the less, because of the *Cross* we had seen in the Subscription. At which answver, the said person lift up his right hand tovvards Heaven, and drevv it softly to his mouth, (vvhich is the gesture they use vvhen they thank *God*) and then said, " If you vvill svvear (all of you) by the Merits of the *Saviour* that ye are no "Pirates, nor have shed blood, lavvfully nor unlavvfully, vvithin forty "days past, you may have License to come on Land. *VVe said,* "VVe vvere "all ready to take that Oath. VVhereupon one of those that vvere vvith him, being (as it seemed) a *Notary*, made an Entry of this Act. VVhich done, another of the attendants of the Great Person, vvhich vvas vvith

him

him in the same Boat, after his Lord had spoken a little to him, said aloud, "My Lord, would have you know, that it is not of Pride or Greatness that "he cometh not aboard your Ship ; but for that, in your Answer, you de-"clare, That you have many sick amongst you, he was warned by the *Con*-"*servator of Health* of the City, that he should keep a distance. VVe bowed our selves towards him, and answered, "VVe were his humble Servants, "and accounted for great Honor and singular Humanity towards us, that "which was already done ; but hoped well, that the nature of the sickness "of our Men was not infectious. So he returned, and a while after came the *Notary* to us aboard our Ship, holding in his hand a Fruit of that Countrey like an *Orenge,* but of colour between *Orenge-tawny* and *Scarlet,* which cast a most excellent Odor : He used it (as it seemeth) for a Preservative against Infection. He gave us our Oath, *By the Name of Jesus, and his Merits*; and after told us, that the next day by six of the clock in the morning we should be sent to, and brought to the *Strangers House,* (so he called it) vvhere vve should be accommodated of things both for our vvhole and for our sick. So he left us ; and vvhen vve offered him some Pistolets, he smiling, said, *He must not be twice paid for one labor ,* meaning (as I take it) that he had salary sufficient of the State for his service ; for (as I after learned) they call an Officer that taketh revvards, *Twice paid.*

The next morning early, there came to us the same Officer that came to us at first vvith his Cane, and told us, "He came to conduct us to the *Strangers* "*House,* and that he had prevented the hour, because we might have the whole "day before us for our business: For (*said he*) if you vvill follovv my ad-"vice, there shall first go vvith me some fevv of you, and see the place, and "hovv it may be made convenient for you; and then you may send for your "sick, and the rest of your number which ye will bring on Land. *VVe thanked* *him, and said,* "That this care vvhich he took of desolate Strangers, *God* "vvould revvard. And so six of us vvent on Land vvith him ; and vvhen vve vvere on Land, he vvent before us, and turned to us, and said, *He was* *but our Servant, and our Guide.* He led us through three fair Streets, and all the way vve vvent there were gathered some people on both sides, standing in a row, but in so civil a fashion, as if it had been not to wonder at us, but to welcome us; and divers of them, as we passed by them, put their arms a little abroad, which is their gesture when they bid any welcome. The *Strangers House* is a fair and spacious House, built of Brick, of somewhat a bluer colour then our Brick, and with handsome Windows, some of Glass, some of a kinde of Cambrick oiled. He brought us first into a fair Parlor above-stairs , and then asked us , "What number of persons "we were, and how many sick. *We answered,* "We were in all (sick and "whole) One and fifty persons, whereof our sick were seventeen. He desired us to have patience a little, and to stay till he came back to us, which was about an hour after ; and then he led us to see the Chambers which were provided for us, being in number Nineteen. They having cast it (as it seemeth) that four of those Chambers, vvhich vvere better then the rest, might receive four of the principal men of our company , and lodge them alone by themselves ; and the other fifteen Chambers vvere to lodge us, tvvo and tvvo together ; the Chambers vvere handsome and chearful Chambers, and furnished civilly. Then he led us to a long Gallery, like a Dorture, vvhere he shevved us all along the one side (for the other side vvas but Wall and Windovv) seventeen Cells, very neat ones, having Partitions of Cedar-vvood. VVnich Gallery and Cells, being in

all

all forty, (many more then we needed, were inftituted as an Infirmary for fick perfons. And he told us withal, that as any of our fick waxed well, he might be removed from his Cell to a Chamber; for which purpofe, there were fet forth ten fpare Chambers, befides the number we fpake of before. This done, he brought us back to the Parlor, and lifting up his Cane a little (as they do when they give any charge or command) faid to us, "Ye are to know, that the Cuftom of the Land requireth, that after this "day and to morrow (which we give you for removing your People from "your Ship) you are to keep within doors for three days: But let it not "trouble you, nor do not think your felves reftrained, but rather left to "your Reft and Eafe. You fhall want nothing, and there are fix of our "people appointed to attend you for any bufinefs you may have abroad. We gave him thanks with all affection and refpect, and faid, *God furely is manifefted in this Land.* We offered him alfo twenty Piftolets; but he fmiled, and onely faid, *VVhat, twice paid?* and fo he left us. Soon after our Dinner was ferved in, which was right good Viands, both for Bread and Meat, better then any Collegiate Diet, that I have known in *Europe.* VVe had alfo drink of three forts, all wholefome and good; VVine of the Grape, a Drink of Grain, fuch as is with us our Ale, but more clear; and a kinde of Sider made of a Fruit of that Countrey, a wonderful pleafing and re-frefhing drink. Befides, there were brought into us great ftore of thofe Scarlet Orenges for our fick, which (they faid) were an affured remedy for ficknefs taken at Sea. There was given us alfo a Box of fmall gray or whitifh Pills, which they wifhed our fick fhould take, one of the Pills every night before fleep, which (they faid) would haften their recovery. The next day, after that our trouble of carriage and removing of our Men and Goods out of our Ship, was fomewhat fetled and quiet, I thought good to call our company together, and when they were affembled, faid unto them, "My dear Friends, let us know our felves, and how it ftandeth "with us. VVe are Men caft on Land, as *Jonas* was out of the VVhales "Belly, when we were as buried in the deep; and now we are on Land, "we are but between Death and Life, for we are beyond both the Old "VVorld and the New, and whether ever we fhall fee *Europe,* God onely "knoweth: It is a kinde of miracle hath brought us hither, and it muft be "little lefs that fhall bring us hence. Therefore in regard of our deliver-"ance paft, and our danger prefent and to come, let us look up to God, "and every man reform his own ways. Befides, we are come here amongft "a *Chriftian People,* full of Piety and Humanity; let us not bring that con-"fufion of face upon our felves, as to fhew our vices or unworthinefs be-"fore them. Yet there is more; for they have by commandment (though "in form of courtefie) cloiftered us within thefe VValls for three days; "who knovveth vvhether it be not to take fome tafte of our manners and "conditions; and if they finde them bad, to banifh us ftraight-vvays; if "good, to give us further time? For thefe men that they have given us for "attendance, may vvithal have an eye upon us. Therefore for Gods love, "and as vve love the vveal of our Souls and Bodies, let us fo behave our "felves as vve may be at peace vvith God, and may finde grace in the eyes "of this people. Our Company vvith one voice thanked me for my good admonition, and promifed me to live foberly and civilly, and vvithout giving any the leaft occafion of offence. So vve fpent our three days joyfully and vvithout care, in expectation vvhat vvould be done vvith us vvhen they vvere expired: During vvhich time, vve had every hour joy
of

of the amendment of our sick, who thought themselves cast into some divine *Pool of Healing*, they mended so kindly and so fast.

The morrow after our three days were past, there came to us a new Man that we had not seen before, cloathed in blew as the former was, save that his Turbant was white with a small Red Cross on the top; he had also a Tippet of fine Linnen. At his coming in he did bend to us a little, and put his arms abroad. We of our parts saluted him in a very lowly and submissive manner, as looking, that from him we should receive sentence of Life or Death. He desired to speak with some few of us; whereupon six of us onely staid, and the rest avoided the room. He said, "I am by office Go-"vernor of this *House of Strangers*, and by Vocation I am a *Christian Priest*; "and therefore am come to you to offer you my service, both as Strangers, "and chiefly as *Christians*. Some things I may tell you, which I think you "will not be unwilling to hear. The State hath given you licence to stay on "Land for the space of six weeks; and let it not trouble you, if your occa-"sions ask further time, for the Law in this Point is not precise; and I do "not doubt, but my self shall be able to obtain for you such further time as "shall be convenient. Ye shall also understand, that the *Strangers House* is at "this time rich and much aforehand, for it hath laid up Revenue these Thir-"ty seven years; for so long it is since any Stranger arrived in this part: And "therefore take ye no care, the State will defray you all the time you stay, "neither shall you stay one day less for that. As for any Merchandize you "have brought, ye shall be well used, and have your Return, either in Mer-"chandize, or in Gold and Silver; for to us it is all one. And if you have "any other request to make, hide it not, for ye shall finde we will not make "your countenance to fall by the answer ye shall receive. Onely this I must "tell you, that none of you must go above a *Karan* (*that is with them a mile and* "*an half*) from the Walls of the City without special leave. We answered, after we had looked a while upon one another, admiring this gracious and parent-like usage, "That we could not tell what to say, for we wanted "words to express our thanks, and his noble free offers left us nothing to "ask. It seemed to us, that we had before us a Picture of our *Salvation* in "*Heaven*; for we that were a while since in the Jaws of Death, were now "brought into a place where we found nothing but Consolations. For the "Commandment laid upon us, we would not fail to obey it, though it "was impossible but our hearts should be inflamed to tread further upon "this happy and holy Ground. *We added*, "That our Tongues should first "cleave to the Roofs of our Mouths, ere we should forget either this Re-"verend Person, or this whole Nation, in our Prayers. We also most humbly besought him to accept of us as his true Servants, by as just a right as ever Men on Earth were bounden, laying and presenting both our persons and all we had at his feet. He said, *He was a Priest, and looked for a Priests reward, which was our Brotherly love, and the good of our Souls and Bodies.* So he went from us, not without tears of tenderness in his eyes; and left us also confused with joy and kindness, saying amongst our selves, *That we were come into a Land of Angels, which did appear to us daily, and prevent us with comforts which we thought not of, much less expected.*

The next day about ten of the clock the Governor came to us again, and after salutations, said familiarly, *That he was come to visit us,* and called for a Chair, and sate him down; and we being some ten of us (the rest were of the meaner sort, or else gone abroad) sate down with him: And when we were set, he began thus, "We of this Island of *Bensalem* (*for so they call it in*
their

" *their Language*.) have this, That by means of our solitary situation, and of
" the Laws of Secrecy which we have for our Travellers, and our rare
" admission of strangers, we know well most part of the Habitable World,
" and are our selves unknown.   Therefore, because he that knoweth least,
" is fittest to ask Questions, it is more reason, for the entertainment of the
" time, that ye ask me Questions, than that I ask you. *We answered*, That
" we humbly thanked him, that he would give us leave so to do, and that
" we conceived by the taste we had already, that there was no worldly thing
" on Earth, more worthy to be known, then the state of that happy Land.
" But above all (*vve said*) since that vve vvere met from the several Ends of
" the World, and hoped assuredly, that vve should meet one day in the
" Kingdom of Heaver, (for that vve vvere both parts *Christians*) vve desired
" to knovv (in respect that Land vvas so remote, and so divided by vast and
" unknovvn Seas, from the Land vvhere our *Saviour* vvalked on Earth)
" vvho vvas the Apostle of that Nation, and hovv it vvas converted to the
" Faith. *It appeared in his face, that he took great contentment in this our Question. He*
said , " Ye knit my heart to you by asking this Question in the nrst place,
" for it shevveth that you *first seek the Kingdom of Heaven*; and I shall gladly and
" briefly satisfie your demand.

"   " About tvventy years after the Ascension of our *Saviour*, it came to
" pass, that there vvas seen by the people of *Renfusa* (a City upon the
" Eastern Coast of our Island) vvithin night (the night vvas cloudy and
" calm) as it might be some mile in the Sea, a great *Pillar of Light*, not sharp,
" but in form of a Column or Cylinder, rising from the Sea a great vvay up
" tovvards Heaven, and on the top of it was seen a large *Cross of Light*, more
" bright and resplendent then the Body of the Pillar : Upon which so
" strange a spectacle the people of the City gathered apace together upon
" the Sands to wonder, and so after put themselves into a number of small
" Boats to go nearer to this marvellous sight.   But when the Boats were
" come within (about) sixty yards of the Pillar, they found themselves all
" bound, and could go no further, yet so as they might move to go about,
" but might not approach nearer; so as the Boats stood all as in a Theatre,
" beholding this Light as an Heavenly Sign.   It so fell out, that there was in
" one of the Boats, one of the wise Men of the Society of *Solomons House*,
" (which *House* or *College* (my good Brethren) is the very Eye of this King-
" dom) who having a while attentively and devoutly viewed and contem-
" plated this Pillar and Cross, fell down upon his face, and then raised him-
" self upon his knees; and lifting up his hands to Heaven made his Prayers
" in this manner.

L Ord God *of Heaven and Earth, thou hast vouch-
safed of thy Grace to those of our* Order, *to know thy
Works of Creation, and true Secrets of them, and to*
discern (*as far as appertaineth to the Generations of Men*)
between Divine Miracles, VVorks *of* Nature, VVorks
of Art, and Impostures and Illusions of all sorts.   I do here
acknowledge and testifie before this People, that the Thing
we

we now see before our eyes is thy Finger, *and a true Mi-*
racle. And forasmuch as we learn in our Books, that thou
never workest Miracles but to a Divine and excellent End,
(for the Laws of Nature, are thine own Laws, and thou
exceedest them not but upon good cause) we most humbly be-
seech thee to prosper this great Sign, and to give us the Inter-
pretation, and use of it in mercy, which thou dost in some part
secretly promise, by sending it unto us.

"When he had made his Prayer, he presently found the Boat he was
"in, moveable and unbound, whereas all the rest remained still fast; and
"taking that for an assurance of leave to approach, he caused the Boat to be
"softly, and with silence, rowed towards the *Pillar*; but ere he came near it,
"the *Pillar* and *Cross of Light* brake up, and cast it self abroad, as it were, into
"a Firmament of many Stars; which also vanished soon after, and there was
"nothing left to be seen but a small *Ark* or *Chest of Cedar*, dry, and not wet
"at all with Water, though it swam; and in the fore end of it, which was
"towards him, grew a small green Branch of Palm. And when the Wise-
"man had taken it with all reverence into his Boat, it opened of it self, and
"there was found in it a *Book* and a *Letter*, both written in fine Parchment,
"and wrapped in Sindons of Linnen. The *Book* contained all the *Canonical*
"*Books* of the *Old* and *New Testament*, according as you have them, (for we
"know well what the *Churches* with you receive;) and the *Apocalypse* it self,
"and some other *Books* of the *New Testament*, which were not at that time
"written, were nevertheless in the *Book*. And for the *Letter*, it was in these
"words.

I *Bartholomew*, a Servant of the Highest, and
Apostle of *JESUS CHRIST*, was warn-
ed by an Angel that appeared to me in a
Vision of Glory, that I should commit this
Ark to the Flouds of the Sea. Therefore I
do testifie and declare unto that People, where
GOD shall ordain this *Ark* to come to Land,
that in the same day is come unto them Salva-
tion, and Peace, and Good Will from the
FATHER, and from the *LORD JESUS*.

"There was also in both these Writings, as well the *Book* as the
"*Letter*, wrought a great Miracle, conform to that of the *Apostles* in the
"Original *Gift of Tongues*. For there being at that time in this Land *Hebrews*,
"*Persians*, and *Indians*, besides the Natives, every one read upon the *Book*
"and

" and *Letter*, as if they had been written in his own Language. And thus
" was this Land faved from Infidelity (as the Remain of the old World
" was from Water) by an Ark, through the Apoftolical and Miraculous
" Evangelifm of S. *Bartholomew.* And here he paufed, and a Meffenger
came and called him forth from us. So this was all that paffed in that
Conference.

    The next day the fame Governor came again to us immediately after Din-
ner, and excufed himfelf, faying, " That the day before he was called from us
" fomewhat abruptly, but now he would make us amends, and fpend time
" with us, if we held his Company and Conference agreeable. *We anfwered,*
" That we held it fo agreeable and pleafing to us, as we forgot both dangers
" paft and fears to come, for the time we heard him fpeak, and that we
" thought an hour fpent with him, was worth years of our former life. *He*
bowed himfelf a little to us, and after wwe were fet again, he faid, " Well, the Quefti-
" ons are on your part. *One of our number faid, after a little paufe,* " That there
" was a matter we were no lefs defirous to know then fearful to ask, left we
" might prefume too far; but encouraged by his rare Humanity towards us,
" (that could fcarce think our felves ftrangers, being his vowed and profeffed
" Servants) we would take the hardinefs to propound it: Humbly befeech-
" ing him, if he thought it not fit to be anfwered, that he would pardon it,
" though he rejected it. *VVe faid,* We well obferved thofe his words
" which he formerly fpake, That this happy Ifland where we now ftood
" vvas knovvn to fevv, and yet knevv moft of the Nations of the World;
" vvhich vve found to be true, confidering they had the Languages of
" *Europe,* and knevv much of our ftate and bufinefs; and yet vve in *Europe*
" (notvvithftanding all the remote Difcoveries and Navigations of this laft
" Age) never heard any of the leaft inkling or glimpfe of this Ifland. This
" vve found vvonderful ftrange, for that all Nations have interknovvledge
" one of another, either by Voyage into Forein Parts, or by Strangers
" that come to them: And though the Traveller into a Forein Countrey,
" doth commonly know more by the Eye, then he that ftaid at home can
" by relation of the Traveller; yet both ways fuffice to make a mutual
" knowledge in fome degree on both parts: But for this Ifland, we never
" heard tell of any Ship of theirs that had been feen to arrive upon any
" fhore of *Europe,* no nor of either the *Eaft* or *VVeft-Indies,* nor yet of any
" Ship of any other part of the World that had made return for them. And
" yet the marvel refted not in this; for the fituation of it (as his Lordfhip
" faid) in the fecret Conclave of fuch a vaft Sea might caufe it: But then,
" that they fhould have knowledge of the Languages, Books, Affairs of
" thofe that lie fuch a diftance from them, it was a thing we could not tell
" what to make of; for that it feemed to us a condition and propriety of
" Divine Powers and Beings, to be hidden and unfeen to others, and yet
" to have others open, and as in a light to them. At this Speech the Governor gave a gracious fmile, and faid, " That we did well to ask pardon
" for this Queftion we now asked, for that it imported as if we thought
" this Land, a Land of Magicians, that fent forth Spirits of the Air into all
" parts to bring them news, and intelligence of other Countreys. It was
anfwered by us all, in all poffible humblenefs, but yet with a countenance
taking knowledge, that we knew, that he fpake it but merrily, " That we
" were apt enough to think, there was fomewhat fupernatural in this
" Ifland, but yet rather as Angelical then Magical. But to let his Lord-
" fhip know truly what it was that made us tender and doubtful to ask this
" Queftion,

" Queſtion ; it was not any ſuch conceit, but becauſe we remembred he
" had given a touch in his former Speech, that this Land had Laws of Se-
" crecy, touching Strangers. *To this he ſaid*, " You remember it right; and
" therefore in that, I ſhall ſay to you, I muſt reſerve ſome particulars which
" it is not lawful for me to reveal, but there will be enough left to give you
" ſatisfaction.

" You ſhall underſtand (that which perhaps you will ſcarce think cre-
" dible) that about Three thouſand years ago, or ſomewhat more, the Na-
" vigation of the VVorld (ſpecially for remote Voyages) was greater then
" at this day.   Do not think with your ſelves, that I know not how much
" it is increaſed with you within theſe threeſcore years, I know it well ; and
" yet I ſay, greater then then now.   VVhether it was, that the example of
" the Ark that ſaved the remnant of Men from the Univerſal Deluge gave
" men confidence to adventure upon the VVaters, or what it was, but ſuch
" is the truth.   The *Phœnicians*, and ſpecially the *Tyrians*, had great Fleets ;
" ſo had the *Carthaginians* their Colony, which is yet further VVeſt : To-
" ward the Eaſt, the Shipping of *Egypt* and of *Paleſtina* was likewiſe great ;
" *China* alſo, and the *Great Atlantis* (that you call *America*) which have now
" but Junks and Canoaes, abounded then in tall Ships.   This Iſland (as
" appeareth by faithful Regiſters of thoſe times) had then Fifteen hundred
" ſtrong Ships of great content. Of all this, there is with you ſparing memory
" or none, but we have large knowledge thereof.

" At that time this Land was known, and frequented by the Ships and
" Veſſels of all the Nations beforenamed, and (as it cometh to paſs) they
" had many times Men of other Countreys that were no Sailers, that came
" with them , as *Perſians, Chaldeans, Arabians* ; ſo as almoſt all Nations of
" might and fame reſorted hither, of whom we have ſome Stirps and little
" Tribes with us at this day.   And for our own Ships, they went ſundry
" Voyages, as well to your *ſtreights*, which you call the *Pillars of Hercules*,
" as to other parts in the *Atlantick* and *Mediterranean Seas* ; as to *Peguin* (which
" is the ſame with *Cambalu*) and *Quinſay* upon the *Oriental Seas*, as far as to
" the Borders of the *Eaſt Tartary*.

" At the ſame time, and an Age after or more, the Inhabitants of the
" *Great Atlantis* did flouriſh.   For though the Narration and Deſcription
" which is made by a great Man with you, of the Deſcendents of *Neptune*
" planted there, and of the magnificent Temple, Palace, City, and Hill,
" and the manifold ſtreams of goodly Navigable Rivers, which (as ſo many
" Chains) invironed the ſame Site and Temple, and the ſeveral degrees of
" aſcent, whereby men did climb up to the ſame, as if it had been a *Scala*
" *Cœli*, be all Poetical and Fabulous ; yet ſo much is true, That the ſaid
" Countrey of *Atlantis*, as well that of *Peru* then called *Coya*, as that of
" *Mexico* then named *Tyrambel* ; were mighty and proud King'doms in
" Arms, Shipping, and Riches ; ſo mighty, as at one time (or a leaſt with
" in the ſpace of ten years) they both made two great expeditions, they of
" *Tyrambel* through the *Atlantick* to the *Mediterranean Sea*, and they of *Coya*
" through the South-ſea upon this our Iſland. And for the former of theſe,
" which was into *Europe*, the ſame Author amongſt you (as it ſeemeth) had
" ſome relation from the *Egyptian Prieſt* whom he citeth. for aſſuredly ſuch
" a thing there was.   But whether it were the ancient *Athenians* that had
" the glory of the repulſe and reſiſtance of thoſe Forces, I can ſay nothing ;
" but certain it is, there never came back either Ship or Man from that Voy-
" age. Neither had the other Voyage of thoſe of *Coya*, upon us, had better

B

" fortune,

" fortune, if they had not met with enemies of greater clemency. For the
" King of this Island (by name *Altabin*) a wife Man, and a great Warrior,
" knowing well both his own strength, and that of his enemies, handled the
" matter so, as he cut off their Land forces from their Ships, and entoiled
" both their Navy and their Camp, with a greater power than theirs, both
" by Sea and Land, and compelled them to render themselves without
" striking stroke; and after they were at his mercy, contenting himself one-
" ly with their Oath, that they should no more bear Arms against him, dif-
" missed them all in safety. But the Divine revenge overtook not long
" after those proud enterprises; for within less then the space of One hun-
" dred years the *Great Atlantis* was utterly lost and destroyed, not by a great
" Earthquake, as your *Man* faith, (for that whole Tract is little subject to
" Earthquakes) but by a particular Deluge or Inundation, those Countreys
" having at this day far greater Rivers, and far higher Mountains to pour
" down Waters, than any part of the Old World. But it is true, that the
" same Inundation was not deep, not past forty foot in most places from
" the ground; so that although it destroyed Man and Beast generally,
" yet some few wilde Inhabitants of the Wood escaped: Birds also were
" saved by flying to the high Trees and Woods. For as for Men, although
" they had Buildings in many places higher then the depth of the Water;
" yet that Inundation, though it were shallow, had a long continuance,
" whereby they of the Vale, that were not drowned, perished for want of
" food, and other things necessary. So as marvel you not at the thin Popu-
" lation of *America*, nor at the Rudeness and Ignorance of the People; for
" you must account your Inhabitants of *America* as a young People,
" younger a thousand years at the least than the rest of the World, for
" that there was so much time between the Universal Flood, and their par-
" ticular Inundation. For the poor remnant of Humane Seed which re-
" mained in their Mountains peopled the Countrey again slowly, by little
" and little: And being simple and a savage people (not like *Noah* and his
" Sons, which was the chief Family of the Earth) they were not able to
" leave Letters, Arts, and Civility to their Posterity. And having likewise
" in their Mountainous Habitations been used (in respect of the extream
" Cold of those Regions) to cloath themselves with the skins of *Tigers*,
" *Bears*, and great *Hairy Goats*, that they have in those parts; when after
" they came down into the Valley, and found the intolerable Heats which
" are there, and knew no means of lighter Apparel, they were forced to
" begin the custom of going naked, which continueth at this day; onely
" they take great pride and delight in the Feathers of Birds : And this also
" they took from those their Ancestors of the Mountains, who were in-
" vited unto it by the infinite flight of Birds that came up to the high
" Grounds, while the Waters stood below. So you see by this main
" accident of time, we lost our Traffick with the *Americans*, with whom,
" of all others, in regard they lay nearest to us, we had most commerce.
" As for the other parts of the World, it is most manifest, that in the
" Ages following (whether it were in respect of Wars, or by a Natural
" revolution of time) Navigation did every where greatly decay, and
" especially far voyages (the rather by the use of Gallies, and such Vessels
" as could hardly brook the Ocean) were altogether left and omitted.
" So then, that part of entercourse which could be from other Nations
" to sail to us, you see how it hath long since ceased, except it were by
" some rare accident, as this of yours. But now of the cessation of that
" other

"other part of entercourse, which might be by our sailing to other Nations;
"I must yield you some other cause: For I cannot say (if I should say truly)
"but our shipping for number, strength, Mariners, Pilots, and all things that
"appertain to Navigation, is as great as ever; and therefore why we should
"sit at home, I shall now give you an account by it self, and it will draw nearer
"to give you satisfaction to your principal Question.

"There reigned in this Island about One thousand nine hundred years
"ago, a King, whose memory of all others we most adore, not superstitiously,
"but as a Divine Instrument, though a Mortal Man; his name was *Salomona*,
"and we esteem him as the Law-giver of our Nation. This King had a large
"heart inscrutable for good, and was wholly bent to make his Kingdom and
"People happy: He therefore taking into consideration, how sufficient and
"substantive this Land was to maintain it self without any aid (at all) of the
"Foreigner, being Five thousand six hundred miles in circuit, and of rare
"fertility of soil in the greatest part thereof; and finding also the shipping of
"this Countrey might be plentifully set on work, both by Fishing, and by
"Transportations from Port to Port, and likewise by sailing unto some small
"Islands that are not far from us, and are under the Crown and Laws of this
"State; and recalling into his memory the happy and flourishing estate
"wherein this Land then was, so as it might be a thousand ways altered to
"the worse, but scarce any one way to the better; thought nothing wanted
"to his Noble and Heroical Intentions, but onely (as far as Humane fore-
"sight might reach) to give perpetuity to that which was in his time so happily
"established; therefore amongst his other Fundamental Laws of this King-
"dom, he did ordain the Interdicts and Prohibitions which we have touch-
"ing entrance of strangers, which at that time (though it was after the cala-
"mity of *America*) was frequent, doubting novelties and commixture of
"manners. It is true, the like Law against the admission of strangers, with-
"out licence, is an ancient Law in the Kingdom of *China*, and yet continued
"in use; but there it is a poor thing, and hath made them a curious, igno-
"rant, fearful, foolish Nation. But our Law-giver made his Law of another
"temper. For first, he hath preserved all points of humanity, in taking or-
"der and making provision for the relief of strangers distressed, whereof you
"have tasted. *At which Speech (as reason was) we all rose up and bowed our selves*
He went on. "That King also still desiring to joyn Humanity and Policy to-
"gether, and thinking it against Humanity to detain Strangers here against
"their Wills, and against Policy, that they should return and discover their
"knowledge of this State, he took this course. He did ordain, that of the
"Strangers that should be permitted to Land, as many (at all times) might
"depart as would, but as many as would stay, should have very good con-
"ditions and means to live from the State. Wherein he saw so far, that
"now in so many Ages, since the Prohibition, we have memory not of one
"Ship that ever returned, and but of thirteen persons onely at several times
"that chose to return in our Bottoms. What those few that returned, may
"have reported abroad, I know not; but you must think, whatsoever they
"have said, could be taken where they came, but for a dream. Now for
"our travelling from hence into parts abroad, our Law-giver thought fit al-
"together to restrain it. So is it not in *China*, for the *Chineses* sail where they
"will, or can; which sheweth, that their Law of keeping out Strangers, is
"a Law of pusillanimity and fear. But this restraint of ours hath one onely
"exception, which is admirable, preserving the good which cometh by
"communicating with strangers, and avoiding the hurt; and I will now

"open

"open it to you. And here I shall seem a little to digress, but you will by
"and by finde it pertinent. Ye shall understand (my dear Friends) that
"amongst the excellent acts of that King, one above all hath the preemi-
"nence: It was the erection and institution of an Order or Society which
"we call *Solomons* House, the noblest Foundation (as we think) that ever
"was upon the Earth, and the Lanthorn of this Kingdom. It is dedicated
"to the study of the Works and creatures of *God*. Some think it beareth
"the Founders name a little corrupted; as if it should be *Solomons* House;
"but the Records write it as it is spoken , so as I take it to be denomi-
"nate of the King of the *Hebrews*, which is famous with you, and no stranger
"to us ; for we have some parts of his Works which with you are lost,
"namely, that *Natural History* which he wrote of all Plants, from the *Cedar*
"of *Libanus* to the *Moss that groweth out of the Wall*, and of all *things that h ve*
"*Life and Motion*. This maketh me think that our King finding himself to
"symbolize in many things with that King of the *Hebrevvs* (which lived
"many years before him) honored him with the Title of this Foundation.
"And I am the rather induced to be of this opinion, for that I finde in an-
"cient Records this Order or Society is sometimes called *Solomons* Hou'e,
"and sometimes *The Colledge of the Six days VVorks*; whereby I am satisfied,
"that our Excellent King had learned from the *Hebrevvs*, that *God* had
"created the World, and all that herein is within Six days; and therefore
"he instituting that House for the finding out of the true Nature of all
"things (whereby God might have the more glory in the workmanship of
"them, and Men the more Fruit in their use of them) did give it also that
"second name. But now to come to our present purpose.

"When the King had forbidden to all his People Navigation in any
"part that was not under his Crown, he made nevertheless this Ordinance,
"That every twelve years there should be set forth out of this Kingdom
"two Ships appointed to several Voyages; that in either of these Ships,
"there should be a Mission of three of the Fellows or Brethren of *Solomons*
"House, whose errand was onely to give us knowledge of the affairs and
"state of those Countreys, to which they were designed, and especially of the
"Sciences, Arts, Manufactures and Inventions of all the World; and withal
"to bring unto us Books, Instruments, and Patterns in every kinde. That
"the Ships after they had landed the Brethren shou'd return; and that the
"Brethren should stay abroad till the new Mission. The Ships are not other-
"wise fraught than with store of Victuals, and good quantity of Treasure,
"to remain with the Brethren for the buying of such thing', and rewarding
"of such persons as they should think fit. Now for me to tell you how the
"vulgar sort of Mariners are contained from being discovered at Land,
"and how they that must be put on shore for any time colour themselves
"under the names of other Nations, and to what places these Voyages have
"been designed, and what places of Rendezvous are appointed for the new
"Missions, and the like circumstances of the practick, I may not do it, neither
"is it much to your desire. But thus you see we maintain a Trade, not for
"Gold, Silver, or Jewels, nor for Silks, nor for Spices, nor any other com-
"modity of Matter, but onely for *Gods* first Creature, which was Light; to
"have Light (I say) of the growth of all parts of the World. And when he
had said this, he was silent, and lo were we all; for indeed, we were all astonish-
ed to hear so strange things so probably told. And he perceiving, that we
were willing to say somewhat , but had it not ready, in great courtesie,
took us off, and descended to ask us Questions of our Voyage and Fortunes;

and

and in the end concluded, that we might do well to think with our
felves what time of ftay we would demand of the State; and bad us
not to fcant our felves, for he would procure fuch time as we defired.
Whereupon we all rofe up and prefented our felves to kifs the skirt of
his Tippet; but he would not fuffer us, and fo took his leave. But when
it came once amongft our people, that the State ufed to offer conditions to
ftrangers that would ftay, we had work enough to get any of our men to
look to our Ship, and to keep them from going prefently to the Governor
to crave conditions; but with much ado, we refrained them till we might
agree what courfe to take.

We took our felves now for Freemen, feeing there was no danger of
our utter perdition, and lived moft joyfully, going abroad, and feeing
what was to be feen in the City and places adjacent within our *Tedder*, and
obtaining acquaintance with many of the City, not of the meaneft quality, at whofe hands we found fuch humanity, and fuch a freedom and
defire to take ftrangers, as it were into their bofom, as was enough to
make us forget all that was dear to us in our own Countrey, and continually we met with many things right worthy of obfervation and relation: As indeed, if there be a Mirror in the World, worthy to hold mens
eyes, it is that Countrey. One day there were two of our company
bidden to a Feaft of the *Family*, as they call it; a moft natural, pious and
reverend cuftom it is, fhewing that Nation to be compounded of all goodnefs. This is the manner of it. It is granted to any man that fhall live to
fee thirty perfons defcended of his body alive together, and all above three
years old, to make this Feaft, which is done at the coft of the State.
The *Father* of the *Family*, whom they call the *Tirfan*, two days before the
Feaft taketh to him three of fuch Friends as he liketh to chufe, and is
affifted alfo by the Governor of the City or place where the Feaft is celebrated; and all the Perfons of the *Family* of both Sexes are fummoned to
attend him. Thefe two days the *Tirfan* fitteth in Confultation concerning the good eftate of the Family; there, if there be any Difcord or Suits
between any of the Family, they are compounded and appeafed; there,
if any of the Family be diftreffed or decayed, order is taken for their relief and competent means to live; there, if any be fubject to Vice or take
ill courfes, they are reproved and cenfured. So likewife, direction is
given touching Marriages, and the courfes of life which any of them
fhould take; with divers other the like orders and advices. The Governor affifteth to the end, to put in execution by his publick Authority, the Decrees and Orders of the *Tirfan*, if they fhould be difobeyed,
though that feldom needeth; fuch reverence and obedience they give
to the order of Nature. The *Tirfan* doth alfo then ever chufe one man
from amongft his Sons to live in Houfe with him, who is called ever
after the *Son of the Vine*; the reafon will hereafter appear. On the Feaft-
day, the *Father* or *Tirfan* cometh forth after Divine Service into a large
Room where the Feaft is celebrated; which Room hath an Half-
pace at the upper end. Againft the Wall, in the middle of the Half-
pace, is a Chair placed for him, with a Table and Carpet before it:
Over the Chair is a State made round or oval, and it is of Ivy; an Ivy
fomewhat whiter then ours, like the Leaf of a Silver Afp, but more fhi-
ning, for it is Green all Winter. And the State is curioufly wrought with
Silver and Silk of divers colours, broiding or binding in the Ivy; and is
ever of the work of fome of the Daughters of the Family, and veiled

over at the top with a fine Net of Silk and Silver: But the substance of it
is true Ivy, whereof, after it is taken down, the Friends of the Family are
desirous to have some Leaf or Sprig to keep. The *Tirsan* cometh forth with
all his Generation or Lineage, the Males before him, and the Females following him.   And if there be a Mother, from whose body the whole Lineage is descended, there is a Traverse placed in a Loft above on the right
hand of the Chair, with a Privy Door, and a carved Window of Glass,
leaded with Gold and Blew, where she sitteth, but is not seen.   When
the *Tirsan* is come forth, he sitteth down in the Chair, and all the Lineage place themselves against the Wall, both at his back, and upon the
return of the Half-pace, in order of their years, without difference of
Sex, and stand upon their Feet.   When he is set, the room being always
full of company, but well kept, and without disorder, after some pause
there cometh in from the lower end of the room a *Taratan*, (which is as
much as an *Herauld*) and on either side of him two young Lads, whereof one carrieth a Scroul of their shining yellow Parchment, and the other
a cluster of Grapes of Gold, with a long foot or stalk : The Herauld
and Children are clothed with Mantles of Sea-water-green Sattin, but the
Heraulds Mantle is streamed with Gold, and hath a Train.   Then the
Herauld, with three Courtesies, or rather Inclinations, cometh up as far
as the Half pace, and there first taketh into his hand the Scroul.   This
Scoul is the Kings Charter, containing Gift of Revenue, and many Pri-
viledges, Exemptions, and Points of Honor granted to the Father of
the Family ; and it is ever stiled and directed, *To such an one, Our wel-
beloved Friend and Creditor,* which is a Title proper onely to this case : For
they say, the King is Debtor to no Man, but for propagation of his Subjects.   The Seal set to the Kings Charter, is the Kings Image imbossed or
moulded in Gold.   And though such Charters be expedited of course,
and as of right, yet they are varied by discretion, according to the number and dignity of the Family.   This Charter the Herauld readeth aloud ;
and while it is read, the *Father* or *Tirsan* standeth up, supported by two
of his Sons, such as he chuseth.   Then the Herauld mounteth the Half-
pace, and delivereth the Charter into his hand, and with that there is an ac-
clamation by all that are present in their Language, which is thus much,
Happy are the People of Bensalem.   Then the Herauld taketh into his hand
from the other Childe the cluster of Grapes, which is of Gold, both the
Stalk and the Grapes ; but the Grapes are daintily enamelled: And if the
Males of the Family be the greater number, the Grapes are enamelled
Purple, with a little Sun set on the top ; if the Females, then they are
enamelled into a greenish yellow, with a Crescent on the top.   The
Grapes are in number as many as there are Descendants of the Family.
This Golden Cluster the Herauld delivereth also to the *Tirsan*, who presently delivereth it over to that Son that he had formerly chosen to be in
house with him ; who beareth it before his Father as an Ensign of Honor
when he goeth in publick ever after, and is thereupon called *The Son of
the Vine.*   After this Ceremony ended, the *Father* or *Tirsan* retireth, and
after some time cometh forth again to Dinner, where he sitteth alone
under the State as before ; and none of his Descendants sit with him ; of
what degree or dignity soever, except he hap to be of *Solomons* House.
He is served onely by his own Children, such as are Male, who perform
unto him all service of the Table upon the knee ; and the Women onely
stand about him, leaning against the Wall.   The Room below his Half pace

ath

hath Tables on the fides for the Guefts that are bidden, who are ferved with great and comely order; and toward the end of Dinner (which in the greateft Feafts with them, lafteth never above an hour and a half) there is an *Hymn* fung, varied according to the Invention of him that compofed it, (for they have excellent Poefie;) but the fubject of it is (always) the praifes of *Adam*, and *Noah*, and *Abraham*; whereof the former two peopled the World, and the laft was the *Father* of the *Faithful*; concluding ever with a Thankfgiving for the Nativity of our *Saviour*, in whofe Birth the Births of all are onely Bleffed. Dinner being done, the *Tirfan* retireth again, and having withdrawn himfelf alone into a place, where he maketh fome private Prayers, he cometh forth the third time to give the Bleffing, with all his Defcendants, who ftand about him as at the firft. Then he calleth them forth, by one and by one, by name, as he pleafeth, though feldom the order of age be inverted. The perfon that is called (the Table being before removed) kneeleth down before the Chair, and the *Father* layeth his hand upon his head, or her head, and giveth the Bleffing in thefe words; *Son* of Benfalem (or Daughter of *Benfalem*) *thy Father faith it, the Man by whom thou haft breath and life fpeaketh the word: The Bleffing of the Everlafting Father, the Prince of Peace, and the Holy Dove be upon thee, and make the days of thy Pilgrimage good and many.* This he faith to every of them; and that done, if there be any of his Sons of eminent Merit and Vertue, (fo they be not above two) he calleth for them again, and faith, laying his arm over their fhoulders, they ftanding, *Sons, it is well you are born; give God the praife, and perfevere to the end.* And withal delivereth to either of them a Jewel, made in the figure of an Ear of Wheat, which they ever after wear in the front of their Turbant or Hat. This done, they fall to Mufick and Dances and other Recreations after their manner for the reft of the day. This is the full order of that Feaft.

By that time fix or feven days were fpent, I was faln into ftraight acquaintance with a Merchant of that City, whofe name was *Joabin*; he was a *Jew*, and circumcifed: For they have fome few ftirps of *Jews* yet remaining among them, whom they leave to their own Religion; which they may the better do, becaufe they are of a far differing difpofition from the *Jews* in other parts. For whereas they hate the Name of CHRIST, and have a fecret inbred rancor againft the people, among whom they live: Thefe (contrariwife) give unto our SAVIOUR many high Attributes, and love the Nation of *Benfalem* extreamly. Surely this Man, of whom I fpeak, would ever acknowledge that CHRIST was born of a Virgin, and that he was more then a Man; and he would tell how GOD made him Ruler of the Seraphims which guard his Throne; and they call him alfo the *Milken way*, and the *Eliah* of the *Meffiah*, and many other high Names; which though they be inferior to his *Divine Majefty*, yet they are far from the Language of other *Jews*. And for the Countrey of *Benfalem*, this Man would make no end of commending it, being defirous, by Tradition among the *Jews* there, to have it believed, that the people thereof were of the Generations of *Abraham* by another Son, whom they call *Nachoran*; and that *Mofes* by a fecret *Cabala* ordained the Laws of *Benfalem*, which they now ufe; and that when the *Meffiah* fhould come and fit in his Throne at *Jerufalem*, the King of *Benfalem* fhould fit at his Feet, whereas other Kings fhould keep a great diftance. But yet fetting afide thefe Jewifh Dreams, the Man was a wife man and learned, and of great policy, and excellently feen in the Laws and Cuftoms of that Nation.

Nation. Amongst other discourses, one day I told him, I was much
affected with the Relation I had from some of the company, of their
Custom in holding the Feast of the Family, for that (me thought) I had
never heard of a Solemnity wherein Nature did so much preside. And
because Propagation of Families proceedeth from the Nuptial Copulation,
I desired to know of him what Laws and Customs they had concerning
Marriage, and whether they kept Marriage well, and whether they were
tied to one Wife: For that where Population is so much affected and
such as with them it seemed to be, there is commonly permission of Plu-
rality of Wives. To this he said, " You have reason for to commend
" that excellent Institution of the Feast of the Family ; and indeed we
" have experience, that those Families that are partakers of the blessings
" of that Feast do flourish and prosper ever after in an extraordinary man-
" ner. But hear me now, and I will tell you what I know. You shall un-
" derstand, that there is not under the Heavens, so chaste a Nation as this
" of *Bensalem*, nor so free from all pollution or foulness ; it is the Virgin
" of the World. I remember I have read in one of your *European Books*
" of an holy Hermit amongst you, that desired to see the *Spirit of Fornication*,
" and there appeared to him a little foul ugly *Æthiope* : But if he had
" desired to see the *Spirit of Chastity of Bensalem*, it would have appeared to
" him in the likeness of a fair beautiful Cherubin ; for there is nothing
" amongst Mortal Men more fair and admirable, then the chaste Mindes
" of this People. Know therefore, that with them there are no Stews,
" no dissolute Houses, no Courtesans, nor any thing of that kinde ; nay
" they wonder (with detestation) at you in *Europe* which permit such
" things. They say you have put Marriage out of office ; for Marriage
" is ordained a remedy for unlawful concupiscence, and natural concu-
" piscence seemeth as a spur to Marriage : But when Men have at hand
" a remedy more agreeable to their corrupt will, Marriage is almost ex-
" pulsed. And therefore, there are with you seen infinite Men that mar-
" ry not, but chuse rather a Libertine, and impure single life, then to be
" yoaked in Marriage ; and many that do marry, marry late, when the
" prime and strength of their years is past ; and when they do marry,
" what is Marriage to them, but a very Bargain, wherein is sought Alli-
" ance, or Portion, or Reputation, with some desire (almost indifferent)
" of issue, and not the faithful Nuptial Union of Man and Wife that was
" first instituted ? Neither is it possible, that those that have cast away so
" basely so much of their strength, should greatly esteem Children (be-
" ing of the same matter) as chaste Men do. So likewise during Marriage,
" is the case much amended, as it ought to be, if those things were tole-
" rated onely for necessity ? No, but they remain still as a very affront to
" Marriage ; the hunting of those dissolute places, or resort to Courtesans,
" are no more punished in Married men, then in Batchelors : And the de-
" praved custom of change, and the delight in meretricious embrace-
" ments, (where Sin is turned into Art) maketh Marriage a dull thing, and
" a kinde of Imposition or Tax. They hear you defend these things as
" done to avoid greater evils, as Advowtries, Deflouring of Virgins,
" Unnatural Lust, and the like : But they say this is a preposterous Wis-
" dom ; and they call it *Lots* offer, who to save his Guests from abusing
" offered his Daughters : Nay, they say further, that there is little gained
" in this, for that the same Vices and Appetites do still remain and abound,
" Unlawful Lust being like a Furnace, that if you stop the Flames altogether.

"gether, it will quench but if you give it any vent, it will rage. As for
"Masculine Love, they have no touch of it, and yet there are not so faith-
"ful and inviolate. Friendships in the World again as are there ; and to
"speak generally (as I said before) I have not read of any such Chastity in
"any People as theirs. *And their usual saying is,* That whosoever is unchaste,
"cannot reverence himself. *And they say,* That the reverence of a Mans self
"is, next Religion, the chiefest Bridle of all Vices. And when he had said
"this, the good *Jew* paused a little. Whereupon, I far more willing to hear
h.m speak on, than to speak my self; yet thinking it decent, that upon his
pause of Speech I should not be altogether silent, said onely this. "That I
"would say to him, as the Widow of *Sarepta* said to *Elias,* That he was
"come to bring to memory our sins ; and that I confess the righteousness of
"*Bensalem,* was greater than the righteousness of *Europe.* At which Speech, he
bowed his Head, and went on in this manner. "They have also many wise and
"excellent Laws touching Marriage ; they allow no Polygamy ; they have
"ordained, that none do intermarry or contract until a moneth be past from
"their first interview. Marriage without consent of Parents, they do not
"make void, but they mulct it in the Inheritors ; for the Children of such
"Marriages are not admitted to inherit above a third part of their Parents
"Inheritance. I have read in a Book of one of your Men, of a Feigned
"Commonwealth, where the married couple are permitted before they
"contract to see one another naked. This they dislike, for they think it a
"scorn to give a refusal after so familiar knowledge ; but because of many
"hidden defects in Men and Womens Bodies, they have a more civil way ;
"for they have near every Town, a couple of Pools (which they call
"*Adam* and *Eves* Pools) where it is permitted to one of the Friends of the
"Man, and another of the Friends of the Woman, to see them severally
"bathe naked.

And as we were thus in Conference, there came one that seemed to be
a Messenger, in a rich Huke, that spake with the *Jew* ; whereupon he
turned to me, and said, *You will pardon me, for I am commanded away in haste.*
The next morning he came to me again, joyful, as it seemed, and said,
"There is word come to the Governor of the City, that one of the Fathers
"of *Solomons* House will be here this day seven-night ; we have seen none of
"them this dozen years. His coming is in state, but the cause of his coming
"is secret. I will provide you and your Fellows of a good standing to see
"his entry. I thanked him, and told him, *I was most glad of the news.* The
day being come, he made his entry. He was a Man of middle stature and
age, comely of person, and had an aspect as if he pitied men : He was
cloathed in a robe of fine black Cloth, with wide Sleeves, and a Cape ;
his under Garment was of excellent white Linnen down to the Foot,
girt with a Girdle of the same, and a Sindon or Tippet of the same about
his Neck ; he had Gloves that were curious, and set with Stone, and Shooes
of Peach-coloured Velvet : his Neck was bare to the Shoulders ; his Hat
was like a Helmet or *Spanish Montera,* and his Locks curled below it de-
cently, they were of colour brown ; his Beard was cut round, and of the
same colour with his Hair, somewhat lighter. He was carried in a rich
Chariot without Wheels, Litter-wise, with two Horses at either end,
richly trapped in blew Velvet embroidered, and two Footmen on each
side in the like attire. The Chariot was all of Cedar, gilt and adorned
with Crystal, save that the fore-end had Pannels of Saphires set in borders
of Gold, and the hinder-end the like of Emeralds of the *Peru* colour.

There

There was also a Sun of Gold, radiant upon the top in the midst; and on the top before a small Cherub of Gold, with Wings displayed. The Chariot was covered with Cloth of Gold tissued upon blew. He had before him fifty attendants, young men all, in white Sattin loose Coats, up to the mid-leg, and Stockins of white Silk, and Shooes of blew Velvet, and Hats of blew Velvet, with fine Plumes of divers colours set round like Hatbands. Next before the Chariot, went two men bare-headed, in Linnen Garments down to the Foot, girt, and Shooes of blew Velvet, who carried, the one a Crosier, the other a Pastoral-Staff like a Sheep-hook, neither of them of Metal, but the Crosier of Balm-wood, the Pastoral-Staff of Cedar. Horsemen he had none, neither before, nor behinde his Chariot, as it seemeth, to avoid all tumult and trouble. Behinde his Chariot went all the Officers and Principals of the Companies of the City. He sate alone upon Cushions, of a kinde of excellent Plush, blew, and under his Foot curious Carpets of Silk of divers colours, like the *Persian*, but far finer. He held up his bare hand as he went, as blessing the People, but in silence. The Street was wonderfully well kept, so that there was never any Army had their Men stand in better battel-array, then the people stood. The Windows likewise were not crouded, but every one stood in them, as if they had been placed. When the show was past, the *Jew* said to me, " I shall not be able to attend you as I " would, in regard of some charge the City hath laid upon me for the en-" tertaining of this great Person. *Three days after the* Jew *came to me again, and said,* " Ye are happy men, for the Father of *Solomons* House taketh knowledge of " your being here, and commanded me to tell you, that he will admit all " your company to his presence, and have private conference with one of " you that ye shall chuse; and for this, hath appointed the next day after to " morrow. And because he meaneth to give you his Blessing, he hath " appointed it in the forenoon. We came at our day and hour, and I was chosen by my fellows for the private access. We found him in a fair Chamber richly hanged, and carpeted under Foot, without any degrees to the State: He was set upon a low Throne, richly adorned, and a rich Cloth of State over his head of blew Sattin embroidered. He was alone, save that he had two Pages of Honor on either hand one, finely attired in white. His under Garments were the like, that we saw him wear in the Chariot; but instead of his Gown, he had on him a Mantle with a Cape of the same fine Black, fastned about him. When we came in, as we were taught, we bowed low at our first entrance; and when we were come near his Chair, he stood up, holding forth his hand ungloved, and in posture of Blessing; and we every one of us stooped down and kissed the hem of his Tippet. That done, the rest departed, and I remained. Then he warned the Pages forth of the Room, and caused me to sit down beside him, and spake to me thus in the *Spanish* Tongue.

GOD

"**G**OD Bless thee, my Son, I will give thee the greatest Jewel I
" have; for I will impart unto thee, for the love of God and Men,
" a Relation of the true state of *Solomons* House. Son, to make
" you know the true state of *Solomons* House, I will keep this order.
" First, I will set forth unto you the End of our Foundation. Secondly,
" The Preparations and Instruments we have for our Works. Thirdly,
" The several Employments and Functions whereto our Fellows are assign-
" ed: And fourthly, The Ordinances and Rites which we observe.

"The End of our Foundation, is the Knowledge of Causes and Secret
"Motions of things, and the enlarging of the Bounds of Humane Empire,
" to the effecting of all things possible.

" The Preparations and Instruments, are these. We have large and
" deep Caves of several depths; the deepest are sunk Six hundred fathom,
" and some of them are digged and made under great Hills and Mountains:
" so that if you reckon together the depth of the Hill, and the depth of the
" Cave, they are (some of them) above three miles deep: For we finde that
" the depth of an Hill, and the depth of a Cave from the Flat, is the same
" thing, both remote alike from the Sun and Heavens Beams, and from the
" open Air. These Caves we call the Lower Region, and we use them for
" all Coagulations, Indurations, Refrigerations, and Conservations of
" Bodies. We use them likewise for the Imitation of Natural Mines, and
" the producing also of new Artificial Metals, by Compositions and Mate-
" rials which we use and lay there for many years. We use them also some-
" times (which may seem strange) for curing of some Diseases, and for pro-
" longation of life in some Hermits that chuse to live there, well accommo-
" dated of all things necessary, and indeed live very long; by whom also we
" learn many things.

" We have Burials in several Earths, where we put divers Cements
" as the *Chineses* do their Porcellane; but we have them in greater variety
" and some of them more fine. We also have great variety of Composts
" and Soils for the making of the Earth fruitful.

" We have high Towers, the highest about half a mile in height, and
" some of them likewise set upon high Mountains, so that the vantage of the
" Hill with the Tower, is in the highest of them, three miles at least. And
" these places we call the Upper Region, accounting the Air between the
" high places, and the Low as a Middle Region. We use these Towers,
" according to their several heights and situations, for Insolation, Refrige-
" ration, Conservation, and for the view of divers Meteors, as Winds, Rain,
" Snow, Hail, and some of the Fiery Meteors also. And upon them, in some
" places, are dwellings of Hermits, whom we visit sometimes, and instruct
" what to observe.

" We have great Lakes, both salt and fresh, whereof we have use for
" the Fish and Fowl. We use them also for Burials of some Natural Bodies;
" for we finde a difference in things buried in Earth, or in Air below the Earth,
" and things buried in Water. We have also Pools, of which some do strain
" Fresh Water out of Salt, and others by Art do turn Fresh Water into Salt.
" We have also some Rocks in the midst of the Sea, and some Bays upon
" the Shore for some Works, wherein is required the Air and Vapor of the
" Sea. We have likewise violent streams and cataracts, which serve us for
" many Motions; and likewise Engins for multiplying and enforcing of
" Winds, to set also on going divers Motions.

We

"We have alfo a number of artificial Wells and Fountains, made in
"imitation of the Natural Sources and Baths; as tinÆted upon Vitriol, Sul-
"phur, Steel, Brafs, Lead, Nitre, and other Minerals. And again we have
"little Wells for Infufions of many things, where the Waters take the vir-
"tue quicker and better then in Veffels or Bafins: And amongft them we have
"a Water which we call *Water of Paradife*, being by that we do to it, made
"very fovereign for Health, and Prolongation of Life.

"We alfo great and fpacious Houfes, where we imitate and demon-
"ftrate Meteors; as Snow, Hail, Rain, fome Artificial Rains of Bodies, and
"not of Water, Thunders, Lightnings; alfo Generations of Bodies in Air,
"as Frogs, Flies, and divers others.

"We have alfo certain Chambers which we call Chambers of Health,
"where we qualifie the Air, as we think good and proper for the cure of di-
"vers Difeafes, and prefervation of Health.

"We have alfo fair and large Baths of feveral mixtures, for the cure of
"Difeafes, and the reftoring of Mans Body from ArefaÆtion; and other, for
"the confirming of it in ftrength of Sinews, Vital Parts, and the very Juice
"and Subftance of the Body.

"We have alfo large and various Orchards and Gardens, wherein we
"do not fo much refpeÆt Beauty, as variety of ground and foyl, proper for
"divers Trees and Herbs; and fome very fpacious, where Trees and Berries
"are fet, whereof we make divers kindes of Drinks, befides the Vineyards.
"In thefe we praÆtife likewife all conclufions of Grafting and Inoculating, as
"well of Wild-trees as Fruit-trees, which produceth many effeÆts. And we
"make (by Art) in the fame Orchards and Gardens, Trees and Flowers to
"come earlier or later then their feafons, and to come up and bear more
"fpeedily then by their natural courfe they do. We make them alfo (by Art)
"much greater then their nature, and their Fruit greater and fweeter, and of
"differing tafte, fmell, colour and figure from their nature; and many of them
"we fo order, that they become of Medicinal ufe.

"VVe have alfo means to make divers Plants rife, by mixtures of
"Earths without Seeds, and likewife to make divers new Plants differing
"from the Vulgar, and to make one Tree or Plant turn into another.

"VVe have alfo Parks and Enclofures of all forts of Beafts and Birds;
"which we ufe not onely for view or rarenefs, but likewife for DiffeÆtions
"and Tryals, that thereby we may take light, what may be wrought upon
"the Body of Man, wherein we finde many ftrange effeÆts; as continuing
"life in them, though divers parts, which you account vital, be perifhed
"and taken forth; Refufcitating of fome that feem dead in appearance,
"and the like. VVe try alfo all poyfons and other medicines upon them,
"as well of Chirurgery as Phyfick. By Art likewife we make them greater
"or taller then their kind is, and contrariwife dwarf them, and ftay their
"growth: VVe make them more fruitful and bearing, then their kind
"is, and contrariwife barren, and not generative. Alfo we make them
"differ in colour, fhape, aÆtivity, many ways. VVe finde means to make
"commixtures and copulations of divers kinds, which have produced
"many new kinds, and them not barren, as the general opinion is. VVe
"make a number of kindes of Serpents, VVorms, Flies, Fifhes, of Putre-
"faÆtion; whereof fome are advanced (in effeÆt) to be perfeÆt Creatures,
"like Beafts or Birds, and have Sexes, and do propagate. Neither do we
"this by chance, but we know beforehand of what matter and commixture
"what kind of thofe Creatures will arife.

"VVe

" We have also particular Pools where we make tryals upon Fishes,
" as we have said before of Beasts and Birds.

" We have also places for Breed and Generation of those Kinds of
" Worms and Flies which are of special use, such as are with you, your
" Silk-worms and Bees.

" I will not hold you long with recounting of our Brew-houses, Bake-
" houses and Kitchins, where are made divers Drinks, Breads, and Meats,
" rare and of special effects. Wines we have of Grapes, and Drinks of
" other Juice, of Fruits, of Grains and of Roots; and of mixtures with
" Honey, Sugar, Manna, and Fruits dried and decocted; also of the Tears
" or Woundings of Trees, and of the Pulp of Canes; and these Drinks are
" of several Ages, some to the age or last of forty years. VVe have Drinks
" also brewed with several Herbs, and Roots, and Spices, yea, with several
" Fleshes, and VVhite-meats; whereof some of the Drinks are such as they
" are in effect Meat and Drink both; so that divers, especially in Age, do
" desire to live with them with little or no Meat or Bread. And above all, we
" strive to have Drinks of extream thin parts, to insinuate into the Body,
" and yet without all biting, sharpness, or fretting; insomuch, as some of
" them put upon the back of your hand, will, with a little stay, pass through
" to the palm, and yet taste milde to the mouth. VVe have also VVaters
" which we ripen in that fashion as they become nourishing; so that they
" are indeed excellent Drink, and many will use no other. Breads we have
" of several Grains, Roots and Kernels, yea, and some of Flesh and Fish
" dried, with divers kinds of Levenings and Seasonings; so that some do
" extreamly move Appetites; some do nourish so, as divers do live of them
" without any other Meat, who live very long. So for Meats, we have some
" of them so beaten, and made tender and mortified, yet without all cor-
" rupting, as a weak heat of the Stomach will turn them into good *Chylus,*
" as well as a strong heat would meat otherwise prepared. VVe have some
" Meats also, and Breads, and Drinks, which taken by men, enable them to
" fast long after; and some other that used, make the very Flesh of Mens
" Bodies sensibly more hard and tough, and their strength far greater then
" otherwise it would be.

" VVe have Dispensatories or Shops of Medicines, wherein you may
" easily think, if we have such variety of Plants and Living Creatures, more
" then you have in *Europe,* (for we know what you have) the Simples, Drugs,
" and Ingredients of Medicines, must likewise be in so much the geater
" variety. VVe have them likewise of divers Ages, and long Fermenta-
" tions. And for their Preparations, we have not onely all manner of ex-
" quisit Distillations and Separations, and especially by gentle Heats, and
" Percolations through divers Strainers, yea and Subitances; but also exact
" Forms of Composition, whereby they incorporate almost as they were
" Natural Simples.

" VVe have also divers Mechanical Arts, which you have not, and
" Stuffs made by them; as Papers, Linnen, Silks, Tissues, dainty works of
" Feathers of wonderful lustre, excellent Dies, and many others; and Shops
" likewise as well for such as are not brought into vulgar use amongst us,
" as for those that are. For you must know, that of the things before re-
" cited, many are grown into use throughout the Kingdom; but yet, if
" they did flow from our Invention, we have of them also for Patterns and
" Principals.

C

" VVe

"VVe have also Furnaces of great diverfities, and that keep great di-
"verfity of heats, fierce and quick, ftrong and conftant, foft and milde;
"blown, quiet, dry, moift, and the like. But above all we have heats, in
"imitation of the Suns and Heavenly Bodies heats, that pafs divers Inequa-
"lities, and (as it were) Orbs, Progreffes and Returns, whereby we may
"produce admirable effects. Befides, we have heats of Dungs, and of Bel-
"lies and Maws of Living Creatures, and of their Bloods and Bodies; and
"of Hays and Herbs laid up moift ; of Lime unquenched, ànd fuch like.
"Inftruments alfo which generate heat onely by motion; and further, places
"for ftrong Infolations; and again, places under the Earth, which by Na-
"ture or Art yield Heat. Thefe divers heats we ufe, as the nature of the ope-
"ration which we intend, requireth.

"VVe have alfo Perfpective Houfes where we make Demonftration
"of all Lights and Radiations, and of all Colours ; and out of things un-
"coloured and tranfparent, we can reprefent unto you all feveral colours,
"not in Rainbows (as it is in Gems and Prifms) but of themfelves fingle.
"VVe reprefent alfo all Multiplications of Light, which we carry to great
"diftance, and make fo fharp as to difcern fmall Points and Lines ; alfo all
"colourations of Light, all delufions and deceits of the Sight, in Figures,
"Magnitudes, Motions, Colours, all demonftrations of Shadows. VVe
"finde alfo divers means yet unknown to you of producing of Light origi-
"nally from divers Bodies. VVe procure means of feeing objects afar off,
"as in the Heaven, and remote places ; and reprefent things near as afar off,
"and things afar off as near, making feigned diftances. VVe have alfo helps
"for the Sight, far above Spectacles and Glaffes in ufe. VVe have alfo
"Glaffes and Means to fee fmall and minute Bodies perfectly and diftinctly,
"as the fhapes and colours of fmall Flies and VVorms, grains and flaws in
"Gems, which cannot otherwife be feen, obfervations in Urine and Blood,
"not otherwife to be feen. VVe make Artificial Rainbows, Halo's, and
"Circles about Light. VVe reprefent alfo all manner of Reflexions, Re-
"fractions, and Multiplication of Vifual Beams of Objects.

"VVe have alfo Precious Stones of all kindes, many of them of great
"beauty, and to you unknown ; Cryftals likewife, and Glaffes of divers
"kindes, and amongft them fome of Metals vitrificated, and other Materi-
"als, befide thofe of which you make Glafs : Alfo a number of Foffiles
"and imperfect Minerals, which you have not; likewife Loadftones of pro-
"digious virtue, and other rare Stones, both Natural and Artificial.

"VVe have alfo Sound-houfes, where we practife and demonftrate all
"Sounds and their Generation. We have Harmonies which you have not,
"of Quarter-founds, and leffer Slides of Sounds ; divers Inftruments of
"Mufick likewife to you unknown, fome fweeter then any you have, with
"Bells and Rings that are dainty and fweet. We reprefent fmall Sounds as
"great and deep, likewife great Sounds extenuate and fharp. We make
"divers tremblings and warblings of Sounds, which in their original are
"entire. We reprefent and imitate all articulate Sounds and Letters, and
"the Voices and Notes of Beafts and Birds. VVe have certain helps, which
"fet to the Ear, do further the hearing greatly. We have alfo divers ftrange
"and artificial Echo's reflecting the voice many times, and as it were toffing
"it ; and fome that give back the voice louder then it came, fome fhriller,
"and fome deeper, yea, fome rendring the voice differing in the Letters or
"articulate Sound from that they receive. We have all means to convey
"Sounds in Trunks and Pipes in ftrange lines and diftances.

"We

" We have also Perfume-houses, wherewith we joyn also practices of
" Taste ; we multiply Smells, which may seem strange ; we imitate Smells,
" making all Smells to breath out of other mixtures then those that give them.
" We make divers imitations of Taste likewise, so that they will deceive any
" Mans taste. And in this House we contain also a Confiture-house, where
" we make all Sweet-meats, dry and moist, and divers pleasant Wines, Milks,
" Broths, and Sallets, far in greater variety then you have.

" We have also Engine-houses, where are prepared Engines and Instru-
" ments for all sorts of motions. There we imitate and practise to make
" swifter motions then any you have, either out of your Muskets or any En-
" gine that you have ; and to make them, and multiply them more easily, and
" with small force, by wheels and other means ; and to make them stronger
" and more violent then yours are, exceeding your greatest Cannons and
" Basilisks. We represent also Ordnance and Instruments of War, and En-
" gines of all kindes ; and likewise new mixtures and compositions of Gun-
" powder, Wildefires burning in Water and unquenchable ; also Fireworks
" of all variety, both for pleasure and use. We imitate also flights of Birds ;
" we have some degrees of flying in the Air ; we have Ships and Boats for
" going under Water, and brooking of Seas ; also Swimming-girdles and
" Supporters. We have divers curious Clocks, and other like motions of
" Return, and some perpetual motions. We imitate also motions of Living
" Creatures by Images of Men, Beasts, Birds, Fishes, and Serpents ; we have
" also a great number of other various motions, strange for quality, fineness
" and subtilty.

" We have also a Mathematical-house, where are represented all Instru-
" ments, as well of Geometry as Astronomy, exquisitely made.

" We have also Houses of Deceits of the Senses, where we represent
" all manner of feats of Jugling, false Apparitions, Impostures and Illusions,
" and their Fallacies. And surely, you will easily believe that we that have so
" many things truly Natural, which induce admiration, could in a world of
" particulars deceive the Senses, if we would disguise those things, and labor
" to make them more miraculous : But we do hate all Impostures and Lies
" insomuch, as we have severely forbidden it to all our Fellows, under pain
" of Ignominy and Fines, that they do not shew any natural work or thing,
" adorned or swelling, but onely pure as it is, and without all affectation of
" strangeness .

" These are (my Son) the riches of *Solomons* House.

" For the several employments and offices of our Fellows ; we have
" twelve that sail into Foreign Countreys under the names of other Nations,
" (for our own we conceal) who bring us the Books, and Abstracts, and Pat-
" terns of Experiments of all other Parts. These we call *Merchants of*
Light.

" We have three that collect the Experiments, which are in all Books.
" These we call *Depredators*.

" We have three that collect the Experiments of all Mechanical Arts,
" and also of Liberal Sciences, and also of Practices which are not brought
" into Arts. These we call *Mystery-men*.

" We have three that try new Experiments, such as themselves think
" good. These we call *Pioneers* or *Miners*.

" We have three that draw the Experiments of the former four into
" Titles and Tables, to give the better light for the drawing of Observations
" and Axioms out of them. These we call *Compilers*.

             " We

" We have three that are induced themselves, looking into the Experiments
" of their Fellows, and cast about how to draw out of them things of use
" and practice for Man's Life and Knowledge, as well for Works, as for plain
" demonstration of Causes, means of Natural Divinations, and the easie
" and clear discovery of the Virtues and Parts of Bodies. These we call
" Dowry-men or Benefactors.

" Then after divers Meetings and Consults of our whole number, to
" consider of the former Labors and Collections, we have three that take
" care out of them to direct new Experiments of a higher Light, more pene-
" trating into Nature then the former. These we call Lamps.

" We have three others that do execute the Experiment so directed,
" and report them. These we call Inoculators.

" Lastly, We have three that raise the former Discoveries by Experi-
" ments into greater Observations, Axioms, and Aphorisms. These we call
" Interpreters of Nature.

" We have also, as you must think, Novices and Apprentices, that
" the succession of the former employed Men do not fail; besides a great
" number of Servants and Attendants, Men and Women. And this we do
" also, We have Consultations which of the Inventions and Experiences,
" which we have discovered shall be published, and which not; and take all
" an Oath of Secrecy for the concealing of those which we think meet to keep
" secret; though some of those we do reveal sometime to the State, and
" some not.

" For our Ordinances and Rites; we have two very long and fair Gal-
" leries. In one of these we place Patterns and Samples of all manner of the
" more rare and excellent Inventions; in the other we place the Statues of
" all principal Inventors. There we have the Statue of your *Columbus*, that
" discovered the *West-Indies*, also the Inventor of Ships; your Monk that
" was the Inventor of Ordnance, and of Gun-powder; the Inventor of
" Musick; the Inventor of Letters; the Inventor of Printing; the Inventor
" of Observations of Astronomy; the Inventor of Works in Metal; the
" Inventor of Glass; the Inventor of Silk of the Worm; the Inventor of
" Wine; the Inventor of Corn and Bread; the Inventor of Sugars: And
" all these by more certain Tradition, then you have. Then we have divers
" Inventors of our own of excellent Works, which since you have not seen,
" it were too long to make Descriptions of them; and besides, in the right
" understanding of those Descriptions, you might easily err. For upon every
" Invention of value we erect a Statue to the Inventor, and give him a libe-
" ral and honorable reward. These Statues are some of Brass, some of Marble
" and Touch-stone, some of Cedar, and other special Woods gilt and adorn-
" ed, some of Iron, some of Silver, some of Gold.

" We have certain Hymns and Services which we say daily, of *Laud* and
" and *Thanks* to God for his marvellous Works; and Forms of Prayers, im-
" ploring His aid and blessing for the Illumination of our Labors, and the
" turning them into good and holy uses.

" Lastly, We have Circuits or Visits of divers principal Cities of the
" Kingdom, where, as it cometh to pass, we do publish such new profitable
" Inventions, as we think good. And we do also declare Natural Divinati-
" ons of Diseases, Plagues, Swarms of hurtful Creatures, Scarcity, Tempest,
" Earth-quakes, great Inundations, Comets, Temperature of the Year, and
" divers other things; and we give counsel thereupon, what the People shall
" do for the prevention and remedy of them.

" And

And when he had said this, he stood up: And I, as I had been taught, kneeled down, and he laid his right hand upon my Head, and said, *God bless thee, my Son, and God bless this Relation which I have made: I give thee leave to publish it for the good of other Nations, for we here are in Gods Bosome, a Land unknown.* And so he left me, having assigned a value of about Two thousand Ducats for a Bounty to me, and my Fellows; for they give great largesses where they come upon all occasions.

The rest was not perfected.

Magnalia

Magnalia Naturæ præcipue quoad usus Humanos.

The {
Prolongation of *Life.*
Restitution of Youth in some degree.
Retardation of Age.
Curing of Diseases, counted *Incurable.*
Mitigation of Pain.
}

More easie and *less loathsome Purgings.*

The {
increasing of Strength and *Activity.*
increasing of Ability, to suffer *Torture* or *Pain.*
altering of Complexions, and *Fatness,* and *Leanness.*
altering of Statures.
altering of Features.
increasing and *exalting of the Intellectual Parts.*
}

Version of Bodies into other Bodies.

Making of new Species.

Transplanting of one Species into another.

Instruments of Destruction, as of *War* and *Poyson.*

Exhilaration of the Spirits, and putting them in good *disposition.*

Force of the Imagination, either upon another *Body,* or upon the *Body* it self.

Acceleration of {
Time in Maturations.
Time in Clarifications.
Putrefaction.
Decoction.
Germination.
}

Making rich Composts for the Earth.

Impreſsions of the Air, and raiſing of Tempeſts.

Great alteration, as in Induration, Emollition, &c.

Turning Crude and Watry Subſtances into Oyly and Unctuous Subſtances.

Drawing of new Foods out of Subſtances not now in uſe.

Making new Threds for Apparel, and new Stuffs, ſuch as are Paper, Glaſs, &c.

Natural Divinations.

Deceptions of the Senſes.

Greater Pleaſures of the Senſes.

Artificial Minerals and Cements.

FINIS.

NATURAL HISTORY:

Century I.

Ig a Pit upon the Sea-fhore, fomewhat above the High-water Mark, and fink it as deep as the Low-water Mark ; And as the Tide cometh in, it will fill with Water, Frefh and Potable. This is commonly practifed upon the Coaft of *Barbary*, where other Frefh Water is wanting. And *Cæfar* knew this well, when he was befieged in *Alexandria* ; for by digging of Pits in the Sea-fhore, he did fruftrate the laborious Works of the Enemies, which had turned the Sea-water upon the Wells of *Alexandria*, and fo faved his Army, being then in Defperation. But *Cæfar* miftook the caufe ; for he thought that all Sea-fands had Natural Springs of Frefh-water. But it is plain, that it is the Sea-water, becaufe the Pit filleth according to the Meafure of the Tide : And the Sea-water paffing or ftraining through the Sands, leaveth the Saltnefs.

I remember to have read, that Tryal hath been made of Salt-water paffed through Earth ; through ten Veffels, one within another, and yet it hath not loft his Saltnefs, as to become potable : But the fame Man faith, that (by the relation of another) Salt-water drained through twenty Veffels, hath become frefh. This Experiment feemeth to crofs that other of Pits, made by the Sea-fide ; and yet but in part, if it be true, that twenty Repetitions do the effect. But it is worth the note, how poor the Imitations of Nature are, in common courfe of Experiments, except they be led by great Judgment, and fome good Light of *Axioms*. For firft, there is no fmall difference between a Paffage of Water through twenty fmall Veffels, and through fuch a diftance, as between the Low-water and High-water Mark. Secondly, there is a great difference between Earth and Sand ; for all Earth hath in it a kin'e of Nitrous Salt, from which, Sand is more free : And befides, Earth doth not ftrain the Water fo finely as Sand doth. But there is a third point, that I fufpect as much, or more than the other two ; and that is, that in the Experiment of *Tranfmiffion* of the Sea-water into the Pits, the Water rifeth ; but in the Experiment of *Tranfmiffion* of the Water, through the Veffels, it falleth : Now certain it is, that the Salter part of Water (once

2.

ſalted throughout) goeth to the bottom. And therefore no marvel if the draining of Water by deſcent, doth make it freſh: Beſides, I do ſomewhat doubt, that the very daſhing of the Water that cometh from the Sea, is more proper to ſtrike off the ſalt part, than where the Water ſlideth of her own motion.

3. It ſeemeth *Percolation* or *Tranſmiſſion* (which is commonly called *Straining*) is a good kinde of *Separation*, not onely of thick from thin, and groſs from fine, but of more ſubtile Natures; and varieth according to the Body, through which the *Tranſmiſſion* is made. As if through a Woollen-bag, the liquor leaveth the fatneſs; if through Sand, the ſaltneſs, &c. They ſpeak of ſevering Wine from Water, paſſing it through Ivy-wood, or through other the like porous body, but *Non conſtat.*

4. The Gum of Trees (which we ſee to be commonly ſhining and clear) is but a fine paſſage, or ſtraining of the Juice of the Tree, through the Wood and Bark. And in like manner, *Cornish Diamonds*, and *Rock Rubies*, (which are yet more reſplendent than Gums) are the fine Exudations of Stone.

5. *Ariſtotle* giveth the cauſe vainly, Why the *Feathers* of Birds are of more lively colours than the Hairs of Beaſts; for no Beaſt hath any fine Azure, or Carnation, or Green Hair. He ſaith it is, becauſe Birds are more in the Beams of the Sun than Beaſts, but that is manifeſtly untrue; for Cattle are more in the Sun than Birds, that live commonly in the Woods, or in ſome Covert. The true cauſe is, that the excrementitious moiſture of living Creatures, which maketh as well the Feathers in Birds as the Hair in Beaſts, paſſeth in Birds through a finer and more delicate Strainer, than it doth in Beaſts: For Feathers paſs through Quills, and Hair through Skin.

6. The *Clarifying* of *Liquors* by Adheſion, is an inward *Percolation*, and is effected, when ſome cleaving Body is mixed and agitated with the *Liquors*; whereby the groſſer part of the Liquor ſticks to that cleaving Body; and ſo the finer parts are freed from the groſſer. So the *Apothecaries* clarifie their Syrups by Whites of Eggs, beaten with the Juices which they would clarifie; which whites of Eggs, gather all the dregs and groſſer parts of the Juice to them; and after the Syrup being ſet on the fire, the whites of Eggs themſelves harden, and are taken forth. So *Ippocraß* is clarified by mixing with Milk, and ſtirring it about, and then paſſing it through a Woollen-bag, which they call *Hippocrates Sleeve*; and the cleaving Nature of the Milk, draweth the Powder of the Spices, and groſſer parts of the Liquor to it, and in the paſſage they ſtick upon the Woollen-bag.

7. The clarifying of Water, is an experiment tending to Health, beſides the pleaſure of the Eye, when Water is Cryſtaline. It is effected by caſting in, and placing Pebbles at the head of a Current, that the Water may ſtrain through them.

8. It may be *Percolation* doth not onely cauſe clearneſs and ſplendor, but ſweetneſs of ſavor; for that alſo followeth, as well as clearneſs, when the finer parts are ſevered from the groſſer. So it is found, that the ſweats of men that have much heat, and exerciſe much, and have clean Bodies and fine Skins, do ſmell ſweet, as was ſaid of *Alexander*; and we ſee commonly, that Gums have ſweet odors.

9. Experiments in Conſort, touching *Motion of Bodies upon their Preſſure.*

Take a Glaſs, and put Water into it, and wet your finger, and draw it round about the lip of the Glaſs, preſſing it ſomewhat hard; and after you have drawn it ſome few times about, it will make the Water friſk

and

and fprinkle up in a fine Dew. This inftance doth excellently demonftrate the force of *Compreffion* in a folid Body. For whenfoever a folid Body (as Wood, Stone, Metal, &c.) is preffed, there is an inward tumult in the parts thereof, feeking to deliver themfelves from the Compreffion: And this is the caufe of all *Violent Motion.* Wherein it is ftrange in the higheft degree, that this Motion hath never been obferved, nor enquired; it being of all Motions, the moft common, and the chief root of all *Mechanical Operations.* This Motion worketh in round at firft, by way of Proof and Search, which way to deliver it felf, and then worketh in Progrefs, where it findeth the deliverance eafieft. In *Liquors* this Motion is vifible; for all Liquors ftrucken, make round circles, and withal dafh, but in *Solids* (which break not) it is fo fubtile, as it is invifible; but neverthelefs bewrayeth it felf by many effects, as in this inftance whereof we fpeak. For the *Preffure* of the *Finger* furthered by the wetting (becaufe it fticketh fo much the better unto the Lip of the Glafs) after fome continuance, putteth all the fmall parts of the Glafs into work, that they ftrike the Water fharply; from which *Percuffion* that fprinkling cometh.

If you ftrike or pierce a *Solid Body* that is brittle, as Glafs or Sugar, it breaketh not onely where the immediate force is, but breaketh all about into fhivers and fitters; the Motion upon the Preffure fearching all ways, and breaking where it findeth the Body weakeft.   10.

The Powder in Shot being dilated into fuch a Flame, as endureth not Compreffion, moveth likewife in round (the Flame being in the nature of a *Liquid Body*) fometimes recoyling, fometimes breaking the Peece, but generally difcharging the Bullet, becaufe there it findeth eafieft deliverance.   11.

This Motion upon Preffure, and the Reciprocal thereof, which is Motion upon Tenfure; we ufe to call (by one common name) *Motion of Liberty*; which is, when any Body being forced to a *Preternatural* Extent or Dimenfion, delivereth and reftoreth it felf to the natural: As when a blown Bladder (preffed) rifeth again; or when *Leather* or *Cloth* tentured, fpring back. Thefe two Motions (of which there be infinite inftances) we fhall handle in due place.   12.

This Motion upon *Preffure* is excellently alfo demonftrated in *Sounds*: As when one chimeth upon a Bell, it foundeth; but as foon as he layeth his hand upon it, the *Sound* ceafeth: And fo, the found of a *Virginal String*, as foon as the Quill of the Jack falleth from it, ftoppeth. For thefe founds are produced by the fubtile Percuffion of the Minute parts of the Bell or String upon the Air; All one, as the *Water* is caufed to leap by the fubtile Percuffion of the Minute parts of the Glafs upon the *Water*, whereof we fpake a little before in the *Ninth Experiment.* For you muft not take it to be the local fhaking of the Bell or String that doth it. As we fhall fully declare when we come hereafter to handle *Sounds*.   13.

TAke a *Glafs* with a *Belly*, and a long *Neb*, fill the *Belly* (in part) with *Water*: Take alfo another *Glafs*, whereinto put *Claret Wine* and *Water* mingled. Reverfe the firft Glafs, with the Belly upwards, ftopping the Neb with your Finger; then dip the mouth of it within the fecond Glafs, and remove your Finger. Continue it in that pofture for a time, and it will unmingle the Wine from the Water; the Wine afcending and fetling in the top of the upper Glafs, and the Water defcending and fetling in the bottom of the lower Glafs. The paffage is apparent to the Eye; for

14.
Experiments
in Confort,
touching Se-
parations of
Bodies by
weight.

you shall see the Wine, as it were, in a small vein, rising through the Water. For handsomness sake (because the working requireth some small time) it were good you hang the upper *Glass* upon a Nail. But as soon as there is gathered so much pure and unmixed Water in the bottom of the lower *Glass*, as that the Mouth of the upper *Glass* dippeth into it, the Motion ceaseth.

15. Let the upper *Glass* be Wine, and the lower Water; there followeth no Motion at all. Let the upper *Glass* be Water pure, the lower Water coloured, or contrariwise there followeth no Motion at all. But it hath been tryed, that though the mixture of Wine and Water, in the lower *Glass*, be three parts Water, and but one Wine; yet it doth not dead the Motion. This separation of Water and Wine appeareth to be made by weight; for it must be of *Bodies* of unequal weight, or else it worketh not; and the heavier *Body* must ever be in the upper *Glass*. But then note withal, that the water being made pensible, and there being a great weight of Water in the Belly of the *Glass*, sustained by a small Pillar of Water in the neck of the *Glass*; it is that which setteth the Motion on work: For Water and Wine in one *Glass*, with long standing, will hardly sever.

16. This *Experiment* would be extended from mixtures of several *Liquors* to *Simple Bodies*, which consist of several similiar parts : Try it therefore with *Broyn* or *Salt-vvater* and *Fresh-vvater*, placing the *Salt-vvater* (which is the heavier) in the upper *Glass*, and see whether the fresh will come above. Try it also with Water thick Sugred, and pure Water ; and see whether the Water which cometh above, will lose his sweetness : For which purpose, it were good there were a little Cock made in the Belly of the upper *Glass*.

17.
Experiments in Consort, touching *Judicious* and *Accurate Infusions*, both in *Liquors*, and *Air*.

IN *Bodies* containing *fine Spirits*, which do easily dissipate when you make *infusions* ; the Rule is, A short stay of the *Body* in the *Liquor* receiveth the Spirit, and a longer stay confoundeth it ; because it draweth forth the Earthy part withal, which embaseth the finer. And therefore it is an Error in *Physitians*, to rest simply upon the length of stay for encreasing the vertue. But if you will have the *Infusion* strong, in those kinde of *Bodies*, which have *fine Spirits*, your way is not to give longer time, but to repeat the *Infusion* of the *Body* oftner. Take *Violets*, and infuse a good Pugil of them in a Quart of Vinegar, let them stay three quarters of an hour, and take them forth, and refresh the *Infusion* with like quantity of new *Violets* seven times, and it will make a *Vinegar* so fresh of the *Flovver*, as if a Twelvemoneth after it be brought you in a Saucer, you shall smell it before it come at you. Note, that it smelleth more perfectly of the Flower a good while after, then at first.

18. This Rule which we have given, is of singular use for the preparations of *Medicines*, and other *Infusions*. As for example, the Leaf of *Burrage* hath an excellent Spirit, to repress the fuliginous vapor of Dusky Melancholy, and so to cure Madness : But nevertheless, if the Leaf be infused long, it yeildeth forth but a raw substance of no vertue : Therefore I suppose, that if in the Must of Wine or Wort of Beer, while it worketh before it be Tunned, the *Burrage* stay a small time, and be often changed with fresh, it vvill make a soveraign Drink for *Melancholy Passions*. And the like I conceive of *Orange Flovvers*.

19. *Rubarb* hath manifestly in it Parts of contrary Operations : Parts that purge, and parts that binde the *Body*; and the first lay looser, and the latter lay

deeper ; So that if you infuse *Rubarb* for an hour, and crush it well, it will purge better, and binde the Body leſs after the purging, than if it ſtood Twenty four hours : This is tried, but I conceive likewiſe, that by repeating the Infuſion of *Rubarb*, ſeveral times (as was ſaid of Violets) letting each ſtay in but a ſmall time , you may make it as ſtrong a Purging Medicine, as *Scammony*. And it is not a ſmall thing won in *Phyſick*, if you can make *Rubarb*, and other Medicines that are *Benedict*, as ſtrong Purgers, as thoſe that are not without ſome malignity.

Purging Medicines, for the moſt part, have their *Purgative Vertue* in a fine Spirit, as appeareth by that they indure not boiling, without much loſs of vertue. And therefore it is of good uſe in *Phyſick*, if you can retain the Purging of Vertue, and take away the unpleaſant taſte of the Purger ; which it is like you may do, by this courſe of infuſing oft with little ſtay. For it is probable, that the horrible and odious taſte is in the groſſer part.

Generally, the working by *Infuſions* is groſs and blind, except you firſt try the iſſuing of the ſeveral parts of the Body, which of them iſſue more ſpeedily, and which more ſlowly ; and ſo by apportioning the time, can take and leave that quality which you deſire. This to know, there be two ways; the one to try what long ſtay, and what ſhort ſtay worketh, as hath been ſaid ; the other to try, in order, the ſucceeding *Infuſions*, of one and the ſame Body, ſucceſſively, in ſeveral Liquors. As for example, Take *Orange-Pills*, or *Roſemary*, or *Cinnamon*, or what you will ; and let them infuſe half an hour in Water ; then take them out, and infuſe them again in other Water; and ſo the third time ; and then taſte and conſider the firſt Water, the ſecond, and the third, and you will finde them differing, not onely in ſtrength and weakneſs, but otherwiſe in taſte, or odor ; for it may be the firſt Water will have more of the ſent, as more fragrant; and the ſecond more of the taſte, as more bitter or biting, &c.

Infuſions in *Air* (for ſo we may call *Odors*) have the ſame diverſities with *Infuſions* in *Water* ; in that the ſeveral Odors (which are in one Flower, or other Body) iſſue at ſeveral times, ſome earlier, ſome later : So we finde, that *Violets*, *Woodbines*, *Strawberries*, yield a pleaſing ſent, that cometh forth firſt ; but ſoon after an ill ſent quite differing from the former. Which is cauſed not ſo much by mellowing, as by the late iſſuing of the groſſer Spirit.

As we may deſire to extract the fineſt Spirits in ſome caſes ; ſo we may deſire alſo to diſcharge them (as hurtful) in ſome other. So Wine burnt, by reaſon of the evaporating of the finer Spirit, inflameth leſs, and is beſt in Agues : *Opium* leeſeth ſome of his poiſonous quality, if it be vapored out, mingled with Spirit of Wine, or the like : *Sena* leeſeth ſomewhat of his windineſs by decocting; and (generally) ſubtile or windy Spirits are taken off by Incenſion, or Evaporation. And even in Infuſions in things that are of too high a ſpirit, you were better pour off the firſt Infuſion, after a ſmall time, and uſe the latter.

BUbbles are in the form of an Hemiſphere ; *Air* within, and a little Skin of Water without : And it ſeemeth ſomewhat ſtrange, that the *Air* ſhould riſe ſo ſwiftly, while it is in the Water; and when it cometh to the top, ſhould be ſtaid by ſo weak a cover, as that of the Bubble is. But as for the ſwift aſcent of the *Air*, while it is under the Water, that is a motion of Percuſſion from the Water, which it ſelf deſcending, driveth up the *Air*; and no motion of *Levity* in the *Air*. And this *Democritus* called

20.

21.

22.

23.

24.
Experiment Solitary, touching the Appetite of Continuation in Liquids.

called *Motus Plagæ*. In this common *Experiment*, the ca
of the *Bubble* is for that the Appetite to resist Separa
ance (which in solid *Bodies* is strong) is also in *Liquors*
weaker : As we see in this of the *Bubble* ; we see it all
Spittle that Children make of Rushes ; and in Castl
they make by blowing into *Water*, having obtaine
Tenacity by Mixture of Soap: We see it also in th
which, if there be *Water* enough to follow, will dra
small Thred, because they will discontinue ; but if
then they cast themselves into round Drops ; which
saveth the Body most from Discontinuance: The
Roundness of the *Bubble*, as well for the Skin of *Water*
in : For the *Air* likewise avoideth *Discontinuance* ; and
self into a round Figure. And for the stop and arr
while, it sheweth, that the *Air* of it self hath little
Ascending.

25.
Experiment
Solitary,
touching the
making of
Artificial
Springs.

THe Rejection, which I continually use, of *Exper*
peareth not) is infinite ; but yet if an *Experiment*
Work, and of great use, I receive it, but deliver it
reported by a sober man, that an *Artificial Spring* may l
out a hanging Ground, where there is a good quick Fall
a Half-Trough of Stone, of a good length, three or
in the same Ground ; with one end upon the high Gro
the low. Cover the Trough with Brakes a good thic
upon the top of the Brakes: You shall see (saith he) tha
are past, the lower end of the Trough will be like a *Spr*
is no marvel, if it hold, while the Rain-water lasteth ;
continue long time after the Rain is past : As if the W
self upon the Air, by the help of the Coldness and
Earth, and the Consort of the first Water.

26.
Experiment
Solitary,
touching the
Venomous
quality of
Mans Flesh.

THe *French* (which put off the name of the *French D*
of the Disease of *Naples*) do report, That at the si
were certain wicked Merchants that barrelled up *Man*
had been lately slain in *Barbary*) and sold it for *Tunn*
that foul and high Nourishment, was the Original of
may well be ; For that it is certain, that the *Canibals*, in
Mans Flesh ; and the *West-Indies* were full of the Pox
discovered : And at this day the *Mortalest poysons*, practi
ans, have some mixture of the Blood, or Fat, or Flesh o
Witches, and Sorceresses, as well amongst the *Heat*
Christians, have fed upon Mans flesh, to aid (as it seemeth
with high and foul Vapors.

27.
Experiment
Solitary,
touching the
Version and
Transmutati-
on of Air in-
to Water.

IT seemeth that there be these ways (in likelihood)
or *Air*, into Water and Moisture. The first is *Cold*
testly Condense ; as we see in the contracting of the
Glass ; whereby it is a degree nearer to Water. We se
ration of *Springs*, which the *Ancients* thought (very prob
the *Version* of *Air* into *Water*, holpen by the *Rest*, whic
those parts, whereby it cannot dissipate. And by the col

there *Springs* are chiefly generated.   We see it also in the Effects of the *Cold* of the *Middle Region* (as they call it) of the *Air* ; which produceth *Dews* and *Rains*.   And the Experiment of turning Water into Ice, by Snow, Nitre, and Salt (whereof we shall speak hereafter) would be transferred to the turning of Air into Water.   The second way is by *Compression* ; as in *Stillatories*, where the Vapor is turned back, upon it self, by the Encounter of the Sides of the *Stillatory* ; and in the *Dew* upon the Covers of *Boiling Pots* ; and in the *Dew* towards *Rain*, upon *Marble*, and *Wainscot*.   But this is like to do no great effect ; except it be upon Vapors, and gross *Air*, that are already very near in Degree to Water.   The third is that, which may be searched into, but doth not yet appear ; which is, by Mingling of moist Vapors with **Air** ; and trying if they will not bring a Return of more Water, than the Water was at first :   For if so, That Increase is a *Version* of the Air :   Therefore put Water into the bottom of a *Stillatory*, with the Neb stopped ; weigh the Water first ; hang in the Middle of the *Stillatory* a large Spunge ; and see what quantity of Water you can crush out of it ; and what it is, more, or less, compared with the Water spent ; for you must understand, that if any *Version* can be wrought, it will be easily done in small Pores :   And that is the reason why we prescribe a *Spunge*.   The fourth way is probable also, though not appearing ; which is, by receiving the *Air* into the small *Pores of Bodies* :   For (as hath been said) every thing in small quantity is more easie for *Version* ; and Tangible Bodies have no pleasure in the consort of Air, but endeavor to subact it into a more *Dense Body* :   But in *Entire Bodies* it is checked ; because, if the *Air* should Condense, there is nothing to succeed :   Therefore it must be in loose Bodies, as Sand, and Powder, which we see, if they lie close, of themselves gather Moisture. .

IT is reported by some of the *Ancients*, That Whelps, or other Creatures, if they be put young into such a Cage, or Box, as they cannot rise to their Stature, but may increase in breadth or length, will grow accordingly, as they can get room ; which, if it be true, and feasible, and that the young Creature so pressed, and streightned, doth not thereupon die ; it is a means to produce *Dwarf Creatures*, and in a very strange Figure.   This is certain, and noted long since, That the Pressure, or Forming of Parts of Creatures, when they are very young, doth alter the shape not a little :   As the stroaking of the Heads of Infants, between the Hands, was noted of old, to make *Macrocephali* ; which shape of the Head, at that time, was esteemed.   And the raising gently of the Bridge of the Nose, doth prevent the Deformity of a Saddle Nose.   Which observation well weighed, may teach a means, to make the Persons of Men and Women, in many kindes, more comely and better featured, than otherwise they would be ; by the Forming and Shaping of them in their Infancy :   As by Stroaking up the Calves of the Legs, to keep them from falling down too low ; and by Stroaking up the Forehead, to keep them from being low Foreheaded.   And it is a common practice to swathe Infants, that they may grow more straight, and better shaped ; and we see young Women, by wearing straight Bodies, keep themselves from being Gross and Corpulent.

ONions, as they hang, will many of them shoot forth ; and so will *Penny-royal* ; and so will an Herb called *Orpin* ; with which they use, in the Countrey, to trim their Houses, binding it to a Lath, or Stick, and setting it against a Wall.   We see it likewise, more especially, in the greater
Semper-

28.
Experiment
Solitary,
touching the
Helps towards the
Beauty and
good *Features*
of *Persons*.

29.
Experiments
Solitary,
touching the
Condensing of
Air in such
sort as it may
put on
Weight, and
yield *Nourishment*.

Semper-vive, which will put out Branches, two or three years : But it is true, that commonly they wrap the Root in a cloth besmeared with Oyl ; and renew it once in a half year. The like is reported by some of the Ancients of the stalks of *Lillies*. The cause is, for that these *Plants* have a strong dense, and succulent moisture, which is not apt to exhale ; and so is able, from the old store, without drawing help from the Earth, to suffice the sprouting of the *Plant* : And this sprouting is chiefly in the late Spring, or early Summer ; which are the times of putting forth. We see also, that stumps of Trees, lying out of the Ground, will put forth Sprouts for a time. But it is a noble tryal, and of very great consequence, to try whether these things, in the sprouting, do encrease weight ; which must be tryed, by weighing them before they be hanged up ; and afterwards again, when they are sprouted. For if they increase not in weight, then it is no more but this , That what they send forth in the sprout, they leese in some other part ; but if they gather weight, then it is *Magnale Natura* : For it sheweth, that *Air* may be made so to be condensed, as to be converted into a dense Body ; whereas the race and period of all things, here above the Earth, is to extenuate and turn things to be more pneumatical, and rare ; and not to be retrograde, from pneumatical to that which is dense. It sheweth also, that *Air* can nourish ; which is another great matter of consequence. Note, that to try this, the Experiment of the *Semper-vive*, must be made without oyling the cloth ; for else, it may be, the Plant receiveth nourishment from the **Oyl.**

30.
Experiment
Solitary,
touching the
Commixture of
Flame and
Air, and the
great force
thereof.

FLame and *Air* do not mingle, except it be in an instant ; or in the *Vital Spirits* of vegetables, and living Creatures. In *Gunpowder,* the force of it hath been ascribed to rarefaction of the earthly substance into *Flame.* And thus far it is true ; and then (forsooth) it is become another Element ; the form whereof occupieth more place ; and so, of Necessity, followeth a Dilatation : And therefore, lest two Bodies should be in one place, there must needs also follow an Expulsion of the Pellet, or blowing up of the Mine. But these are crude and ignorant speculations : For *Flame,* if there were nothing else, except it were in a very great quantity, will be suffocate with any hard body, such as a Pellet is, or the Barrel of a Gun ; so as the *flame* would not expel the hard *body* , but the hard *body* would kill the *flame,* and not suffer it to kindle, or spred. But the cause of this so potent a motion is the *Nitre* (which we call otherwise *Salt-Peter*) which having in it a notable crude and windy Spirit, first by the heat of the *Fire* suddenly dilateth it self ; (and we know that simple Air, being preternaturally attenuated by heat, will make it self room, and break, and blow up that which resisteth it.) And secondly, when the *Nitre* hath dilated it self, it bloweth abroad the *flame* as an inward Bellows. And therefore we see that *Brimstone* , *Pitch* , *Camphire,* *Wildfire,* and divers other inflamable matters ; though they burn cruelly, and are hard to quench, yet they make no such fiery wind, as *Gunpowder* doth : And on the other side, we see that *Quick-silver* (which is a most crude and watry Body) heated, and pent in, hath the like force with *Gunpowder.* As for living Creatures, it is certain, their *Vital Spirits* are a substance compounded of an airy and flamy matter ; and though Air and Flame, being free, will not well mingle ; yet bound in by a Body that hath some fixing, they will. For that you may best see in those two Bodies (which are their Aliments) *Water* and *Oyl* ; for they likewise will not well mingle of themselves, but in the Bodies of Plants,

and

and *Living Creatures,* they will. It is no marvel therefore, that a small *Quantity of Spirits,* in the Cells of the Brain, and Cannals of the Sinews, are able to move a whole *Body* (which is of so great mass) both with so great force, as in Wrestling, Leaping; and with so great swiftness, as in playing Division upon the *Lute:* Such is the force of these two *Natures, Air* and *Flame* when they incorporate.

TAke a small *Wax-Candle,* and put it in a Socket of Brass or Iron, then set it upright in a Porringer full of Spirit of Wine, heated; then set both the Candle, and Spirit of Wine on fire, and you shall see the flame of the Candle open it self, and become four or five times bigger then otherwise it would have been, and appear in figure *Globular,* and not in *Pyramis.* You shall see also, that the inward flame of the Candle keepeth colour, and doth not wax any whit blew towards the colour of the outward flame of the Spirit of Wine. This is a noble instance, wherein two things are most remarkable; the one, that one flame within another quencheth not, but is a fixed *Body,* and continueth as *Air* or *Water* do; and therefore flame would still ascend upwards in one greatness, if it were not quenched on the sides; and the greater the flame is at the bottom, the higher is the rise. The other, that Flame doth not mingle with Flame, as *Air* doth with *Air,* or *Water* with *Water,* but onely remaineth contiguous; as it cometh to pass betwixt *Consisting Bodies.* It appeareth also, that the form of a *Pyramis* in Flame, which we usually see, is meerly by accident, and that the Air about, by quenching the sides of the Flame, crusheth it, and extenuateth it into that form; for of it self, it would be round: And therefore Smoak is in the figure of a *Pyramis* reversed; for the Air quencheth the Flame, and receiveth the Smoak. Note also, that the flame of the Candle, within the flame of the Spirit of Wine, is troubled, and doth not onely open and move upwards, but moveth waving, and to and fro: As if Flame of his own Nature (if it were not quenched) would roul and turn as well as move upwards. By all which it should seem, that the *Celestial Bodies* (most of them) are true Fires or Flames, as the *Stoicks* held; more fine (perhaps) and rarified, than our flame is. For they are all *Globular* and *Determinate,* they have *Rotation,* and they have the colour and splendor of Flame: So that Flame above, is durable and consistent, and in his natural place; but with us, it is a stranger, and momentany and impure, like *Vulcan* that halted with his fall.

31.
Experiment
Solitary,
touching the
Secret Nature
of Flame.

TAke an *Arrow,* and hold it in Flame for the space of ten Pulses; and when it cometh forth, you shall finde those parts of the Arrow which were one the out-sides of the Flame, more burned, blacked, and turned almost into a Coal; whereas that in the midst of the flame, will be as if the fire had scarce touched it. This is an instance of great consequence for the discovery of the nature of Flame, and sheweth manifestly, that Flame burneth more violently towards the sides, then in the midst: And, which is more, that *Heat* or *Fire* is not violent or furious, but where it is checked and pent. And therefore the *Peripateticks* (howsoever their opinion of an *Element of Fire,* above the *Air,* is justly exploded) in that point they acquit themselves well: For being opposed, that if there were a sphere of Fire, that incompassed the Earth so near hand, it were impossible, but all things should be burnt up; they answer, that the pure *Elemental Fire,* in his own place, and not irritate, is but of a moderate heat.

32.
Experiment
Solitary,
touching the
Different force
of Flame in the
midst, and on
the sides.

It

IT is affirmed constantly by many, as an usual Experiment, That a lump of *Ore*, in the bottom of a Mine, will be tumbled and stirred by two Mens strength; which if you bring it to the top of the Earth, will ask six Mens strength at the least to stir it. It is a noble instance, and is fit to be tryed to the full: For it is very probable, that the *Motion of Gravity* worketh weakly, both far from the Earth, and also within the Earth: The former, because the appetite of Union of Dense Bodies with the Earth, in respect of the distance is more dull. The latter, because the Body hath in part attained his nature, when it is some depth in the Earth. For as for the moving to a point or place (which was the opinion of the *Antients*) it is a meer vanity.

IT is strange, how the *Antients* took up *Experiments* upon credit, and yet did build great Matters upon them. The observation of some of the best of them, delivered confidently, is, That a Vessel filled with *Ashes*, will receive the like quantity of Water, that it would have done if it had been empty. But this is utterly untrue, for the Water will not go in by a fifth part; and I suppose, that that fifth part is the difference of the lying close, or open of the Ashes; as we see, that Ashes alone, if they be hard pressed, will lie in less room; and so the Ashes with Air between, lie looser, and with Water closer. For I have not yet found certainly, that the Water it self by mixture of Ashes or Dust, will shrink or draw into less room.

IT is reported of credit, That if you lay good store of *Kernels of Grapes* about the *Root of a Vine*, it will make the Vine come earlier, and prosper better. It may be tried with other *Kernels*, laid about the *Root* of a *Plant* of the same kinde; as *Figs, Kernels of Apples*, &c. The cause may be, for that the Kernels draw out of the Earth Juice fit to nourish the Tree, as those that would be Trees of themselves, though there were no Root; but the Root being of greater strength, robbeth and devoureth the nourishment, when they have drawn it; as great Fishes devour little.

THe operation of *Purging Medicines*, and the causes thereof, have been thought to be a great Secret; and so according to the slothful manner of Men, it is referred to a *Hidden Propriety*, a *Specifical Vertue*, and a *Fourth Quality*, and the like shifts of Ignorance. The Causes of Purging, are divers, All plain and perspicuous, and throughly maintained by experience. The first is, That whatsoever cannot be overcome and digested by the Stomack, is by the Stomack, either put up by *Vomit*, or put down to the *Guts*; and by that Motion of Expulsion in the Stomack and Guts, other Parts of the Body (as the *Orifices* of the Veins, and the like) are moved to expel by Consent: For nothing is more frequent then *Motion of Consent* in the *Body of Man*. This Surcharge of the Stomack, is caused either by the Quality of the Medicine, or by the Quantity. The Qualities are three, *Extream Bitter*, as in *Aloes, Coloquintida*, &c. *Loathsome*, and of horrible taste, as in *Agarik, Black Hellebore*, &c. And of *secret Malignity*, and disagreement towards *Mans Body*, many times not appearing much in the taste, as in *Scammony, Machoacham, Antimony*, &c. And note well, that if there be any *Medicine* that *Purgeth*, and hath neither of the first two *Manifest Qualities*, is to be held suspected as a kinde of Poyson; For that it worketh either by *Corrosion*, or by a *secret Malignity*, and *Enmity to Nature*; and therefore such Medicines are warily to be prepared and used. The quantity of that which is taken, doth also cause Purging, as we see in a great quantity of new Milk from the Cow, yea, and a great quantity of Meat: For

Surfeits many times turn to *Purges*, both upwards and downwards. Therefore we fee generally, that the working of *Purging Medicines* cometh two or three hours after the *Medicines* taken : For that the *Stomack* firft maketh a proof, whether it can concoct them. And the like happeneth after *Surfeits*, or Milk in too great quantity.

A fecond caufe is *Mordication* of the *Orifices* of the Parts, efpecially of the *Mefentery Veins*; as it is feen, that Salt, or any fuch thing that is fharp and biting, put into the Fundament, doth provoke the part to expel, and *Muftard* provoketh fneezing ; and any fharp thing to the eyes provoketh tears. And therefore we fee, that almoft all *Purgers* have a kinde of twitching and vellication, befides the griping which cometh of wind. And if this *Mordication* be in an over-high degree, it is little better than the *Corofion of Poyfon*; and it cometh to pafs fometimes in *Antimony*, efpecially if it be given to Bodies not repleat with humors ; for where humors abound, the humors fave the parts.

The third caufe is *Attraction*: For I do not deny, but that *Purging Medicines* have in them a direct force of *Attraction* ; as Drawing-Plaifters have in *Surgery*: And we fee *Sage*, or *Bittony* bruifed, *Sneezing-powder*, and other *Powders* or *Liquors* (which the *Phyfitians* call *Errhines*) put into the Nofe, draw Flegm and Water from the Head ; and fo it is in *Apophlegmatifms* and *Gargarifms* that draw the Rheume down by the Palat. And by this vertue, no doubt, fome *Purgers* draw more one humor, and fome another, according to the opinion received : As *Rubarb* draweth Choler, *Sena* Melancholy, *Agarack* Flegm, &c. but yet (more or lefs) they draw promifcuoufly. And note alfo, that befides Sympathy between the *Purger* and the *Humor*, there is alfo another caufe, why fome *Medicines* draw fome humor more than another ; and it is, for that fome *Medicines* work quicker than others ; and they that draw quick, draw onely the lighter, and more fluid humors ; they that draw flow, work upon the more tough, and vifcuous humors. And therefore, men muft beware how they take *Rubarb*, and the like, alone, familiarly ; for it taketh onely the lighteft part of the humor away, and leaveth the Mafs of Humors more obftinate. And the like may be faid of *Worm-wood*, which is fo much magnified.

The fourth caufe is *Flatuofity*: For wind ftirred, moveth to expel ; and we finde that (in effect) all *Purgers* have in them a raw *Spirit* or *Wind*, which is the principal caufe of *Tortion* in the Stomack and Belly. And therefore *Purgers* leefe (moft of them) the virtue, by decoction upon the fire ; and for that caufe are chiefly given in Infufion, Juyce, or Powder.

The fifth caufe is *Compreffion* or *Crufhing*: As when Water is crufhed out of a Spunge : So we fee that taking cold moveth loofnefs by contraction of the Skin, and outward parts ; and fo doth Cold likewife caufe Rheums and Defluctions from the Head, and fome *Aftringent Plaifters* crufh out purulent Matter. This kinde of operation is not found in many *Medicines*: *Mirabolanes* have it, and it may be the *Barks* of *Peaches*; for this vertue requireth an *Aftriction*, but fuch an *Aftriction*, as is not grateful to the Body (for a pleafing *Aftriction* doth rather binde in the humors, than expel them :) And therefore fuch *Aftriction* is found in things of an harrifh tafte.

The fixth caufe is *Lubrefaction* and *Relaxation*: As we fee in *Medicines Emollient*, fuch as are *Milk*, *Honey*, *Mallows*, *Lettuce*, *Mercurial*, *Pellitory of the Wall*, and others. There is alfo a fecret vertue of *Relaxation of Cold*; for the heat of the Body bindeth the Parts and Humors together, which

Cold, relaxeth: As it is ſeen in *Vrine, Blood, Pottage*, or the like; which, if they be cold, break and diſſolve. And by this kinde of *Relaxation*, Fear looſneth the Belly; becauſe the heat retiring inwards towards the Heart, the Guts, and other parts are relaxed; in the ſame manner as Fear alſo cauſeth trembling in the Sinews. And of this kinde of Purgers are ſome *Medicines* made of *Mercury*.

42.   The ſeventh cauſe is *Abſterſion*, which is plainly a *ſcouring off*, or *'nciſion* of the more *viſcuous humors*, and making the *humors* more fluid, and cutting between them, and the part; as is found in *Nitrous Water*, which ſcoureth Linnen-Cloth (ſpeedily) from the foulneſs. But this *Inciſion* muſt be by a *Sharpneſs*, without *Aſtriction*; which we finde in *Salt, Wormwood, Oxymel*, and the like.

43.   There be *Medicines* that move *Stools*, and not *Vrine*; ſome other *Vrine*, and not *Stools*. Thoſe that *Purge by Stool*, are ſuch as enter not at all, or little into the *Meſentery Veins*; but either at the firſt, are not digeſtible by the Stomack, and therefore move immediately downwards to the Guts; or elſe are afterwards rejected by the *Meſentery Veins*, and ſo turn likewiſe downwards to the Guts; · and of theſe two kindes, are moſt Purgers. But thoſe that move *Vrine*, are ſuch as are well digeſted of the Stomack, and well received alſo of the *Meſentery Veins*; ſo they come as far as the Liver, which ſendeth *Vrine* to the *Bladder*, as the *Whey of Blood*: And thoſe *Medicines*, being opening and piercing, do fortifie the operation of the *Liver*, in ſending down the Wheyey part of the Blood to the *Reins*. For *Medicines Vrinative* do not work by rejection and indigeſtion, as *Solutive* do.

44.   There be divers *Medicines*, which in greater quantity move Stool, and in ſmaller, Urine; and ſo contrariwiſe, ſome that in greater quantity move Urine, and in ſmaller Stool. Of the former ſort is *Rubarb*, and ſome others. The cauſe is, for that *Rubarb* is a *Medicine*, which the Stomack in a ſmall quantity doth digeſt, and overcome (being not Flatuous nor Loathſome,) and ſo ſendeth it to the *Meſentery Veins*; and ſo being opening, it helpeth down Urine: But in a greater quantity, the Stomack cannot overcome it, and ſo it goeth to the Guts. *Pepper*, by ſome of the *Ancients*, is noted to be of the ſecond ſort; which being in ſmall quantity, moveth wind in the Stomack or Guts, and ſo expelled by Stool; but being in greater quantity, diſſipateth the wind, and it ſelf getteth to the *Meſentery Veins*, and ſo to the Liver and *Reins*; where, by Heating and Opening, it ſendeth down Urine more plentifully.

WE have ſpoken of *Evacuating* of the *Body*, we will now ſpeak ſomething of the filling of it by *Reſtoratives* in *Conſumptions* and *Emaciating Diſeaſes*. In Vegetables, there is one part that is more nouriſhing than another; as *Grains* and *Roots* nouriſh more than the *Leaves*, inſomuch as the Order of the *Foliatans* was put down by the *Pope*, as finding Leaves unable to nouriſh Mans Body. Whether there be that difference in the Fleſh of Living Creatures, is not well enquired; as whether *Livers*, and other *Entrails*, be not more nouriſhing than the outward Fleſh. We finde that amongſt the *Romans*, a *Gooſes* Liver was a great delicacy; inſomuch, as they had artificial means to make it fair, and great; but whether it were more nouriſhing, appeareth not. It is certain, that *Marrow* is more nouriſhing than *Fat*. And I conceive, that ſome decoction of *Bones* and *Sinews*, ſtamped and well ſtrained, would be a very nouriſhing Broth: We finde alſo, that *Scotch Skinck* (which is a Pottage of ſtrong nouriſhment) is

made

made with the Knees and Sinews of Beef, but long boiled : *Jelly* also, which they use for a Restorative, is chiefly made of Knuckles of Veal. The Pulp, that is within the Crafish or Crab, which they spice and butter, is more nourishing then the flesh of the Crab, or Crafish. The Yolks of Eggs are clearly more nourishing than the Whites. So that it should seem, that the parts of *Living Creatures* that lie more inwards, nourish more than the outward flesh ; except it be the Brain, which the Spirits prey too much upon, to leave it any great vertue of nourishing. It seemeth for the nourishing of aged Men, or Men in Consumptions, some such thing should be devised, as should be half *Chylus*, before it be put into the stomach.

 Take two large Capons, perboil them upon a soft fire, by the space of an hour or more, till in effect all the Blood be gone. Add in the decoction the Pill of a Sweet-Lemmon, or a good part of the Pill of a Citron, and a little Mace. Cut off the Shanks, and throw them away; then with a good strong Chopping-knife, mince the two Capons, Bones and all, as small as ordinary minced Meat ; put them into a large neat Boulter, then take a Kilderkin, sweet, and well seafoned, of four Gallons of Beer of Eight shillings strength, new as it cometh from the Tunning; make in the Kilderkin a great Bung-hole of purpose, then thrust into it, the Boulter (in which the Capons are) drawn out in length ; let it steep in it three days and three nights, the Bung-hole open to work, then close the Bung hole, and so let it continue a day and a half, then draw it into Bottles, and you may drink it well after three days Bottling, and it will last six weeks (approved). It drinketh fresh, floureth, and mantleth exceedingly, it drinketh not newish at all, it is an excellent drink for a Consumption to be drunk either alone, or carded with some other Beer. It quencheth thirst, and hath no whit of windiness. Note, that it is not possible, that Meat and Bread, either in Broths, or taken with Drink, as is used, should get forth into the Veins, and outward Parts, so finely, and easily, as when it is thus incorporate, and made almost a *Chylus* aforehand.

 Tryal would be made of the like Brew with *Potado-Roots*, or *Bur-Roots*, or the Pith of *Artichoaks*, which are nourishing Meats : It may be tryed also, with other flesh ; as *Phesant*, *Partridge*, *Young Pork*, *Pig*, *Venison*, especially of *Young Deer*, &c.

 A *Mortress* made with the *Brawn* of *Capons*, stamped, and strained, and mingled (after it is made) with like quantity, at the least, of *Almond Butter*, is an excellent Meat to nourish those that are weak, better than Black-Manger or Jelly : And so is the *Cullice* of *Cocks*, boiled thick with the like mixture of Almond Butter : For the Mortress or Cullice of it self, is more favory and strong, and not so fit for nourishing of weak Bodies, but the Almonds that are not of so high a taste as flesh, do excellently qualifie it.

 Indian Maiz hath (of certain) an excellent Spirit of Nourishment, but it must be throughly boiled, and made into a Maiz-Cream like a Barley-Cream. I judge the same of Rice, made into a Cream ; for Rice is in Turky, and other Countreys of the East, most fed upon, but it must be throughly boiled in respect of the hardness of it ; and also, because otherwise it bindeth the Body too much.

 Pistachoes, so they be good and not musty, joyned with Almonds in Almond Milk, or made into a Milk of themselves, like unto Almond Milk, but more green, are an excellent nourisher. But you shall do well, to add a little Ginger scraped, because they are not without some subtil windiness.

46.

47.

48.

49.

50.

51.

    Milk warm from the *Cow*, is found to be a great nourisher, and a good remedy in Consumptions : But then you must put into it, when you Milk the Cow, two little Bags; the one of *Powder of Mint*, the other of *Powder of Red Roses*; for they keep the Milk somewhat from turning, or crudling in the Stomack; and put in Sugar also for the same cause, and partly for the tastes sake : But you must drink a good draught, that it may stay less time in the Stomack, lest it cruddle: And let the Cup, into which you milk the Cow, be set in a greater Cup of hot Water, that you may take it warm. And *Cow-milk* thus prepared, I judge to be better for a Consumption, than *Ass-milk*, which (it is true) turneth not so easily, but it is a little harsh: Marry it is more proper for sharpness of Urine, and Exulceration of the Bladder, and all manner of Lenifyings. *Womens-milk* likewise is prescribed, when all fail; but I commend it not, as being a little too near the Juyce of Mans Body, to be a good nourisher; except it be in Infants, to whom it is natural.

52.

    Oyl of sweet Almonds newly drawn, with Sugar and a little Spice, spred upon Bread totted, is an excellent nourisher; but then to keep the Oyl from frying in the Stomack, you must drink a good draught of Milde-Beer after it; and to keep it from relaxing the Stomack too much, you must put in a little *Powder of Cinnamon.*

53.

    The *Yolks of Eggs* are of themselves so well prepared by *Nature* for nourishment, as (so they be Potched, or Rear boyled) they need no other preparation or mixture ; yet they may be taken also raw, when they are new laid, with *Malmsey* or *Sweet Wine*. You shall do well to put in some few slices of *Eringium Roots*, and a little *Amber-greece* : For by this means, besides the immediate faculty of nourishment, such drink will strengthen the Back, so that it will not draw down the Urine too fast. For too much Urine doth always hinder nourishment.

54.

    Mincing of Meat, as in *Pies*, and *Buttered minced Meat*, saveth the grinding of the Teeth ; and therefore (no doubt) it is more nourishing, especially in Age, or to them that have weak Teeth; but the Butter is not so proper for weak Bodies, and therefore it were good to moisten it with a little Claret Wine, Pill of *Lemmon* or *Orenge* cut small, Sugar, and a very little Cinnamon, or Nutmeg. As for *Chuets*, which are likewise Minced-meat ; instead of Butter, and Fat, it were good to moisten them, partly with Cream, or Almond, or Pistachomilk, or Barley, or Maiz Cream ; adding a little Coriander-seed, and Carraway-seed, and a very little Saffron. The more full handling of Alimentation, we reserve to the due place.

We have hitherto handled the Particulars, which yield best, and easiest, and plentifullest, Nourishment; and now we will speak of the best Means of conveying, and converting the Nourishment.

55.

    The first Means is to procure, that the Nourishment may not be robbed and drawn away ; wherein that which we have already laid, is very material, to provide, that the Reins draw not too strongly an over-great part of the Blood into Urine. To this add that Precept of *Aristotle*, That Wine be forborn in all Consumptions; for that the Spirits of the Wine do prey upon the Roscide Juyce of the Body, and inter-common with the Spirits of the Body, and so deceive and rob them of their Nourishment. And therefore if the Consumption, growing from the weakness of the Stomack, do force you to use Wine; let it always be burnt, that the quicker Spirits may evaporate, or (at the least) quenched with two little Wedges of Gold, six or seven times repeated. Add also this Provision, that there be not too much expence

of

of the nourishment, by Exhaling and Sweating: And therefore if the Patient be apt to sweat, it must be gently restrained. But chiefly *Hipocrates* Rule is to be followed, who adviseth quite contrary to that which is in use: Namely, That the Linnen or Garment next the Flesh, be in Winter dry and oft changed; and in Summer seldom changed, and smeared over with Oyl: For certain it is, that any substance that is fat, doth a little fill the Pores of the Body and stay Sweat in some degree. But the more cleanly way is to have the Linnen smeared lightly over with Oyl of sweet Almonds, and not to forbear shifting as oft as is fit.

The second Means is to send forth the nourishment into the parts more strongly, for which, the working must be by strengthning of the Stomack; and in this, because the Stomack is chiefly comforted by Wine and hot things, which otherwise hurt, it is good to resort to outward applications to the Stomack: Wherein it hath been tryed, that the Quilts of Roses, Spices, Mastick, Wormwood, Mint, &c. are not so helpful, as to take a Cake of New Bread, and to bedew it with a little *Sack* or *Alegant*, and to dry it, and after it be dryed alittle before the Fire, to put it within a clean Napkin, and to lay it to the Stomack: For it is certain, that all Flower hath a potent Vertue of *Astriction*, insomnch, as it hardneth a piece of Flesh, or a Flower that is laid in it. And therefore a Bag quilted with Bran, is likewise very good, but it dryeth somewhat too much, and therefore it must not lie long.

The third Means (which may be a branch of the former) is to send forth the nourishment the better by sleep. For we see, that Bears and other Creatures that sleep in the Winter, was exceeding fat: And certain it is, (as it is commonly believed) that Sleep doth nourish much, both for that the Spirits do less spend the nourishment in Sleep, than when living Creatures are awake: And because (that which is to the present purpose) it helpeth to thrust out the nourishment into the parts. Therefore in aged-men, and weak Bodies, and such as abound not with Choler, a short sleep after dinner doth help to nourish; for in such Bodies there is no fear of an over-hasty digestion, which is the inconvenience of *Post-meridian Sleeps.* Sleep also in the morning, after the taking of somewhat of easie digestion; as Milk from the Cow, nourishing Broth, or the like, doth further nourishment: But this would be done sitting upright, that the Milk or Broth may pass the more speedily to the bottom of the Stomack.

The fourth Means is to provide, that the parts themselves may draw to them the nourishment strongly. There is an excellent observation of *Aristotle*, that a great reason why Plants (some of them) are of greater age than Living Creatures is, for that they yearly put forth new Leaves and Boughs; whereas Living Creatures put forth (after their period of growth) nothing that is young, but Hair and Nails, which are Excrements, and no Parts. And it is most certain, that whatsoever is young, doth draw nourishment better, than that which is old; and then (that which is the mystery of that observation) young Boughs and Leaves, calling the Sap up to them, the same nourisheth the Body in the passage. And this we see notably proved also, in that the oft cutting or polling of *Hedges*, *Trees*, and *Herbs*, doth conduce much to their lasting. Transfer therefore this observation to the helping of nourishment in Living Creatures: The Noblest and Principal Use whereof is, for the Prolongation of Life; Restauration of some degree of Youth, and Inteneration of the Parts: For certain it is, that there are in Living Creatures Parts that nourish and repair easily, and parts that

nourish

nourish and repair hardly; and you must refresh, and renew thofe that are eafie to nourifh, that the other may be re'refhed, and (as it were) drink in nourifhment in the paffage. Now we fee that *Draught Oxen* put into good Pafture, recover the Flefh of young Beef; and Men after long emaciating Diets, wax plump and fat, and almoft new: So that you may furely conclude, that the frequent and wife ufe of thofe emaciating Diets, and of Purgings; and perhaps of fome kinde of Bleeding, is a principal means of prolongation of life, and reftoring fome degree of Youth: For as we have often faid, *Death* cometh upon Living Creatures like the Torment of *Mezentius*,

Mortua quinetiam jungebat corpora vivis,
Componens Manibufque Manus, atque oribus ora.

For the parts in Mans body eafily repairable (as Spirits, Blood, and Flefh) die in the embracement of the parts hardly repairable as Bones, Nerves, and Membranes) and likewife fome Entrails (which they reckon amongft the Spermatical Parts) are hard to repair: Though that divifion of Spermatical and Menftrual Parts, be but a conceit. And this fame obfervation alfo may be drawn to the prefent purpofe of nourifhing emaciated Bodies: And therefore *Gentle Frication* draweth forth the nourifhment, by making the parts a little hungry and heating them, whereby they call forth nourifhment the better. This *Frication* I wifh to be done in the morning. It is alfo beft done by the Hand, or a piece of Scarlet-Wool, wet a little with Oyl of Almonds, mingled with a fmall quantity of Bay-Salt, or Saffron: We fee that the very Currying of Horfes doth make them fat, and in good liking.

59. The fifth means is, to further the very act of *Affimilation of Nourifhment*; which is done by fome outward *emollients*, that make the parts more apt to Affimilate. For which I have compounded an ointment of excellent odor, which I call *Roman* ointment, *vide* the Receit. The ufe of it would be between fleeps; for in the latter fleep, the parts affimulate chiefly.

60.
Experiment Solitary, touching *Filum Medicinale*.

THere be many *Medicines*, which by themfelves would do no cure, but perhaps hurt, but being applied in a certain order, one after another, do great cures. I have tried (my felf) a Remedy for the *Gout*, which hath feldom failed, but driven it away in Twenty four hours fpace: It is firft to apply a *Pultaß*, of which, *vide* the Receit, and then a Bath or Fomentation, of which, *vide* the Receit, and then a Plaifter, *vide* the Receit. The *Pultaß* relaxed the Pores, and maketh the humor apt to exhale. The Fomentation calleth forth the Humor by Vapors; but yet in regard of the way made by the *Pultaß*, draweth gently; and therefore draweth the Humors out, and doth not draw more to it: For it is a Gentle Fomentation, and hath withal a mixture (though very little) of fome ftupefactive. The Plaifter is a moderate Aftringent Plaifter, which repelleth new humor from falling. The *Pultaß* alone would make the part more foft and weak, and apter to take the defluxion and impreffion of the Humor. The Fomentation alone, if it were too weak, without way made by the *Pultaß*, would draw forth little; if too ftrong, it would draw to the part, as well as draw from it. The Plaifter alone would pen the Humor already contained in the part, and fo exafperate it, as well as forbid new Humor; therefore they muft be all taken in order, as is faid: The *Pultaß* is to be laid to for two or three hours; the Fomentation for a quarter of an hour, or fomewhat better, being ufed hot, and feven or eight times repeated; the Plaifter to continue on ftill, till the part be well confirmed.

There

THere is a secret way of *Cure*, unpractiſed by *Aſſuetude* of that which in itſelf hurteth. *Poyſons* have been made by ſome Familiar, as hath been ſaid. *Ordinary Keepers* of the ſick of the *Plague*, are ſeldom infected. Enduring of Tortures, by cuſtom hath been made more eaſie : The brooking of enormous quantity of Meats, and ſo of Wine, or ſtrong drink, hath been by cuſtom made to be without Surfeit or Drunkenneſs. And generally Diſeaſes that are Chronical, as *Coughs*, *Phthiſicks*, ſome kinde of *Palſies*, *Lunacies*, &c. are moſt dangerous at the firſt : Therefore a wiſe *Phyſitian* will conſider, whether a Diſeaſe be incurable, or whether the juſt cure of it be not full of peril ; and if he finde it to be ſuch, let him reſort to *Palliation*, and alleviate the Symptom without buſying himſelf too much with the perfect cure : And many times (if the Patient be indeed patient) that courſe will exceed all expectation. Likewiſe the Patient himſelf may ſtrive, by little and little to overcome the Symptom in the Exacerbation, and ſo by time turn ſuffering into Nature.

DIvers Diſeaſes, eſpecially Chronical, (ſuch as *Quartan Agues*) are ſometimes cured by *Surfeit* and *Exceſſes* ; as exceſs of Meat, exceſs of Drink, extraordinary Faſting, extraordinary ſtirring, or Laſſitude, and the like. The cauſe is, for that Diſeaſes of continuance, get an adventitious ſtrength from Cuſtom, beſides their material cauſe from the Humors : So that the breaking of the Cuſtom doth leave them onely to their firſt cauſe ; which, if it be any thing weak, will fall off. Beſides, ſuch Exceſſes do excite and ſpur *Nature*, which thereupon riſeth more forcibly againſt the Diſeaſe.

THere is in the Body of Man, a great conſent in the Motion of the ſeveral parts : We ſee it is Childrens ſport, to prove whether they can rub upon their Breſt with one hand, and pat upon their Forehead with another ; and ſtraight ways they ſhall ſometimes rub with both hands, or pat with both hands. We ſee, that when the Spirits that come to the Noſtrils, expel a bad ſent, the Stomack is ready to expel by vomit. We finde that in *Conſumptions of the Lungs*, when *Nature* cannot expel by Cough, Men fall into *Fluxes* of the Belly, and then they die. So in *Peſtilent Diſeaſes*, if they cannot be expelled by *Sweat*, they fall likewiſe into *Looſneſs*, and that is commonly Mortal. Therefore *Phyſitians* ſhould ingeniouſly contrive, how by Motions that are in their power, they may excite inward Motions that are not in their power, by conſent ; as by the ſtench of Feathers, or the like, they cure the riſing of the *Mother*.

HIppocrates Aphoriſm, in *Morbu Minus*, is a good profound *Aphoriſm*. It importeth, that Diſeaſes contrary to the *Complexion*, *Age*, *Sex*, Seaſon of the year, Diet, &c. are more dangerous than thoſe that are concurrent. A Man would think it ſhould be otherwiſe ; For that when the Accident of Sickneſs, and the Natural diſpoſition, do ſecond the one the other ; the Diſeaſe ſhould be more forcible. And (ſo no doubt) it is, if you ſuppoſe like quantity of Matter. But that which maketh good the *Aphoriſm*, is, becauſe ſuch Diſeaſes do ſhew a greater collection of Matter, by that they are able to overcome thoſe Natural inclinations to the contrary. And therefore in Diſeaſes of that kinde, let the *Phyſitian* apply himſelf more to *Purgation*, than to *Alteration* ; becauſe the offence is in the quantity, and the qualities are rectified of themſelves.

 Phyſitians

PHyſitians do wiſely preſcribe, that there be Preparatives uſed before Juſt Purgations; for certain it is, that *Purgers* do many times great hurt, if the Body be not accommodated, both before and after the Purging. The hurt that they do, for want of Preparation before Purging, is by the ſticking of the Humors, and their not coming fair away; which cauſeth in the Body great perturbations, and ill accidents, during the Purging; and alſo the diminiſhing and dulling of the working of the Medicine it ſelf, that it purgeth not ſufficiently: Therefore the work of *Preparation* is double, to make the Humors fluide and mature, and to make the paſſages more open; For thoſe both help to make the Humors paſs readily: And for the former of theſe, *Syrups* are moſt profitable; and for the latter, *Apozums* or *Preparing Broths*; *Clyſters* alſo help left the *Medicine* ſtop in the Guts, and work gripingly. But it is true, that Bodies abounding with Humors, and fat Bodies, and open Weather, are *Preparatives* in themſelves; becauſe they make the Humors more fluid: But let a *Phyſician* beware how he purge after hard Froſty Weather, and in a lean Body, without *Preparation*. For the hurt that they may do after *Purging*, it is cauſed by the lodging of ſome Humors in ill places; for it is certain, that there be Humors which ſomewhere placed in the Body, are quiet, and do little hurt; in other places (eſpecially Paſſages) do much miſchief. Therefore it is good after Purging, to uſe *Apozums* and *Broths*, not ſo much opening as thoſe uſed before Purging, but Abſturſive and Mundifying Clyſters alſo are good to conclude with, to draw away the relicks of the Humors that may have deſcended to the lower region of the Body.

BLood is ſtanched divers ways: Firſt, by Aſtringents and Repercuſſive *Medicines*. Secondly, by drawing of the Spirits and Blood inwards, which is done by cold; as *Iron* or a *Stone* laid to the Neck doth ſtanch the Bleeding of the Noſe; alſo it hath been tried, that the *Teſticles* being put into ſharp Vinegar, hath made a ſudden receſs of the Spirits, and ſtanched Blood. Thirdly, by the Receſs of the Blood by Sympathy; ſo it hath been tried, that the part that bleedeth, being thruſt into the body of a Capon, Sheep, new ript and bleeding, hath ſtanched Blood; the Blood, as it ſeemeth, ſucking and drawing up, by ſimilitude of ſubſtance, the Blood it meeteth with, and ſo it ſelf going back. Fourthly, by Cuſtom and Time; ſo the Prince of *Aurange*, in his firſt hurt by the Spaniſh Boy, could finde no means to ſtanch the Blood, either by *Medicine* or *Ligament*, but was fain to have the Orifice of the Wound ſtopped by Mens Thumbs, ſucceeding one another for the ſpace at the leaſt of two days; and at the laſt the Blood by cuſtom onely retired. There is a fifth way alſo in uſe, to let Blood in an adverſe part for a Revulſion.

IT helpeth, both in *Medicine* and *Aliment*, to change and not to continue the ſame *Medicine* and *Aliment* ſtill. The cauſe is, for that Nature by continual uſe of any thing, groweth to a ſatiety and dulneſs, either of Appetite or Working. And we ſee that Aſſuetude of things hurtful, doth make them leeſe their force to hurt; As *Poyſon*, which with uſe ſome have brought themſelves to brook. And therefore it is no marvel, though things helpful by cuſtom, leeſe their force to help, I count intermiſſion almoſt the ſame thing with change; for that, that hath been intermitted, is after a ſort new.

It

IT is found by Experience, that in Diets of *Guiacum*, *Sarza*, and the like, (especially, if they be strict) the *Patient* is more troubled in the beginning than after continuance ; which hath made some of the more delicate sort of Patients, give them over in the midst; Supposing, that if those Diets trouble them so much at first; they shall not be able to endure them to the end. But the cause is, for that all those Diets, to dry up *Humors*, *Rheums*, and the like ; and they cannot dry up until they have first attenuated : And while the *Humor* is attenuated, it is more fluid, than it was before, and troubleth the Body a great deal more, until it be dryed up, and consumed. And therefore *Patients* must expect a due time, and not check at them at the first.

THe producing of *Cold* is a thing very worthy the Inquisition, both for use and disclosure of causes. For *Heat* and *Cold* are *Natures* two hands, whereby she chiefly worketh ; and *Heat* we have in readiness, in respect of the *Fire* : But for *Cold*, we must stay till it cometh, or seek it in deep Caves, or high Mountains ; and when all is done, we cannot obtain it in any great degree : For Furnaces of Fire are far hotter than a Summers Sun, but Vaults or Hills are not much colder than a Winters Frost.

The first means of producing *Cold*, is that which *Nature* presenteth us withal ; namely, the expiring of *Cold* out of the inward parts of the Earth in *Winter*, when the Sun hath no power to overcome it ; the Earth being (as hath been noted by some (*Primum Frigidum.*) This hath been asserted, as well by Ancient as by Modern *Philosophers* : It was the tenet of *Parmenides* it was the opinion of the Author of the Discourse in *Plutarch*, (for I take it, that Book was not *Plutarchs* own) *De primo Frigido*. It was the opinion of *Telesius*, who hath renewed the Philosophy of *Parmenides*, and is the best of the *Novelists*.

The second cause of *Cold* is, the contact of cold Bodies ; for Cold is Active and Transitive into Bodies adjacent, as well as Heat ; which is seen in those things that are touched with Snow or cold Water. And therefore, whosoever will be an *Enquirer* into *Nature*, let him resort to a Conservatory of Snow and Ice ; such as they use of delicacy, to cool Wine in Summer : Which is a poor and contemptible use, in respect of other uses that may be made of such Conservatories.

The third cause is the Primary Nature of all Tangible Bodies ; for it is well to be noted, That all things whatsoever (Tangible are of themselves) Cold ; except they have an accessory heat by Fire, Life, or Motion : For even the Spirit of Wine, or Chymical Oyls, which are so hot in operation, are to the first touch, Cold ; and Air it self compressed, and condensed a little by blowing, is Cold.

The fourth cause is, the Density of the Body ; for all dense Bodies are colder than most other Bodies, as *Mettals*, *Stone*, *Glass*, and they are longer in heating than softer Bodies. And it is certain, that *Earth*, *Dense*, *Tangable*, hold all of the Nature of Cold : The cause is, for that all *Matters Tangible* being Cold, it must needs follow, that where the Matter is most congregate the Cold is the greater.

The fifth cause of *Cold*, or rather of increase and vehemency of *Cold*, is A quick Spirit inclosed in a cold Body ; as will appear to any that shall attentively consider of Nature in many instances. We see *Nitre* (which hath a quick Spirit) is Cold, more cold to the Tongue than a Stone ; so Water

is

is colder than Oyl, becaufe it hath a quicker Spirit; for all Oyl, though it hath the tangible parts better digefted than Water, yet hath it a duller Spirit: So *Snow* is colder than Water, becaufe it hath more Spirit within it : So we fee that *Salt* put to *Ice* (as in the producing of the *Artificial Ice*) encreafeth the activity of cold : So fome *Infects* which have Spirit of Life, as *Snakes* and *Silkworms*, are to the touch, Cold. So *Quick-filver* is the coldeft of Metals, becaufe it is fulleft of Spirit.

74.   The fixth caufe of Cold is, the chaffing and driving away of Spirits, fuch as have fome degree of Heat ; for the banifhing of the Heat muft nee 's leave any Body cold. This we fee in the operation of *Opium*, and *Stupefactives* upon the Spirits of Living Creatures; and it were not amifs to try *Opium* by laying it upon the top of a *Weather-Glaf*, to fee whether it will contract the Air; but I doubt it will not fucceed : For befides that, the vertue of *Opium* will hardly penetrate thorow fuch a body as Glafs, I conceive that *Opium*, and the like, make the Spirits flie rather by Malignity, than by Cold.

75.   Seventhly, the fame effect muft follow upon the exhaling or drawing out of the warm Spirits, that doth upon the flight of the Spirits. There is an opinion, that the Moon is Magnetical of Heat, as the Sun is of Cold and Moifture : It were not amifs therefore to try it with warm waters ; the one expofed to the Beams of the Moon, the other with fome skreen betwixt the Beams of the Moon and the Water : As we ufe to the Sun for fhade, and to fee whether the former will cool fooner. And it were alfo good to enquire, what other means there may be, to draw forth the Exile heat which is in the Air; for that may be a fecret of great power to produce cold Weather.

Experiments in Confort, touching the *Verfion* and *Tranfmutation* of the *Air* in to *Water*.

  WE have formerly fet down the Means of turning Air into Water, in the *Experiment* 27. But becaufe it is *Magnale Natura*, and tendeth to the fubduing of a very great effect, and is alfo of manifold ufe: We will adde fome inftances in Confort that give light thereunto.

76.   It is reported by fome of the Ancients, that Sailers have ufed every night, to hang Fleeces of Wool on the fides of their *Ships*, the Wool towards the Water ; and that they have crufhed frefh water out of them, in the Morning, for their ufe. And thus much we have tried, that a quantity of Wool tied loofe together, being let down into a deep Well ; and hanging in the middle, fome three Fathom from the Water for a night, in the Winter time, increafed in weight, (as I now remember) to a fifth Part.

77.   It is reported by one of the Ancients, that in *Lydia*, near *Pergamus*, there were certain Workmen in time of Wars, fled into Caves ; and the Mouth of the Caves being ftopped by the Enemies, they were famifhed. But long time after, the dead Bodies were found, and fome Veffels which they had carried with them, and the Veffels full of Water; and that Water thicker, and more towards Ice, than common Water; which is a notable inftance of *Condenfation* and *Induration* by *Burial under Earth* (in Caves) for long time ; and of *Verfion* alfo (as it fhould feem) of the Air into Water; if any of thofe Veffels were empty. Try therefore a fmall Bladder hung in *Snow*, and the like in *Nitre*, and the like in Quick-filver : And if you finde the Bladders faln or fhrunk, you may be fure the Air is condenfed by the Cold of thofe Bodies, as it would be in a Cave under Earth.

It

It is reported of very good credit, that in the *East-Indies* if you set a Tub of Water open in a Room where *Cloves* are kept, it will be drawn dry in Twenty four hours, though it stand at some distant from the *Cloves.* In the Countrey, they use many times in deceit, when their Wooll is new shorn, to set some Pails of Water by in the same Room, to encrease the weight of the Wooll : But it may be, that the Heat of the Wool remaining from the Body of the Sheep, or the heat gathered by the lying close of the Wool, helpeth to draw the watry vapor; but that is nothing to the Version.

It is reported also credibly, that Wool new shorn, being laid casually upon a Vessel of *Verjuice,* after some time hath drunk up a great part of the *Verjuice,* though the Vessel were whole without any flaw, and had not the Bung-hole open.   In this instance there is (upon the by) to be noted, the *Percolation* or *Suing* of the *Verjuice* thorow the Wood ; for *Verjuice* of it self would never have passed through the Wood : So, as it seemeth, it must be first in a kinde of vapor before it pass.

It is especially to be noted, that the cause that doth facilitate the Version of Air into Water, when the Air is not in gross, but subtilly mingled with tangible Bodies, is, (as hath been partly touched before) for that tangible Bodies have an antipathy with Air; and if they finde any Liquid Body that is more dense near them, they will draw it ; and after they have drawn it, they will condense it more, and in effect incorporate it : For we see that a Spunge, or Wooll, or Sugar, or a Woollen-cloth, being put but in part, in Water or Wine, will draw the Liquor higher, and beyond the place, where the Water or Wine cometh. We see also, that *Wood, Lute-strings,* and the like, do swell in moist seasons ; as appeareth by the breaking of the strings, the hard turning of the Pegs, and the hard drawing forth of Boxes, and opening of Wainscot doors, which is a kinde of infusion ; and is much like to an infusion in Water, which will make Wood to swell ; as we see in the filling of the Chops of Bowls by laying them in Water.   But for that part of these *Experiments,* which concerneth *Attraction* we will reserve into the proper Title of *Attraction.*

There is also a Version of Air into Water, seeing in the sweating of *Marbles,* and other *Stones ;* and of Wainscot before, and in moist weather. This must be, either by some moisture the Body yieldeth, or else by the moist Air thickned against the hard Body. But it is plain, that it is the latter ; for that we see Wood painted with Oyl-colour, will sooner gather drops in a moist night, than Wood alone ; which is caused by the smoothness and closeness, which letteth in no part of the vapor, and so turneth it back and thickneth it into Dew.   We see also, that breathing upon a Glass, or smooth Body, giveth a Dew ; and in Frosty mornings (such as we call *Rime Frosts*) you shall finde drops of Dew upon the inside of Glass-windows : And the Frost it-self upon the ground, is but a Version or Condensation of the moist vapors of the night, into a watry substance : Dews likewise, and Rain, are but the returns of moist vapors condensed ; the Dew, by the cold onely of the Sun departure, which is the gentler cold; Rains, by the cold of that which they call the *Middle Region* of the Air, which is the more violent Cold.

It is very probable (as hath been touched) that that which will turn Water into Ice, will likewise turn Air some degree nearer unto Water. Therefore try the *Experiment* of the Artificial turning Water into Ice (whereof we shall speak in another place) with Air in place of Water, and

the

the Ice about it. And although it be a greater alteration to turn Air into Water, than Water into Ice; yet there is this hope, that by continuing the Air longer time, the effect will follow; for that artificial conversion of Water into Ice, is the work of a few hours; and this of Air may be tried by a moneths space, or the like.

INduration or *Lapidification* of Substances more soft, is likewise another degree of Condensation, and is a great alteration in Nature. The effecting and accelerating thereof, is very worthy to be enquired it is effected by three means.

The first is by Cold, whose property is to condense, and constipate, as hath been said.

The second is by Heat, which is not proper but by consequence; for the heat doth attenuate, and by attenuation doth send forth the Spirit, and moister part of a Body; and upon that, the more gross of the tangible parts do contract and serve themselves together; both to avoid *Vacuum* (as they call it) and also to munite themselves against the force of the Fire, which they have suffered.

And the third is by Assimilation, when a hard Body assimilateth a soft, being contiguous to it.

The examples of *Induration* taking them promiscuously, are many: As the Generation of *Stones* within the Earth, which at the first are but Rude Earth or Clay; and so of *Minerals*, which come (no doubt) at first of Juyces Concrete, which afterward indurate: And so of *Porcellane*, which is an Artificial Cement, buried in the Earth a long time; and so the making of *Brick* and *Tile*; also the making of *Glass*, of a certain *Sand* and *Brake-Roots*, and some other matters; also the *Exudations* of *Rock Diamonds* and *Chrystal*, which harden with time; also the *Induration* of *Bead-Amber*, which at first is a soft substance, as appeareth by the *Flies* and *Spiders*, which are found in it, and many more. But we will speak of them distinctly.

83.
    For *Indurations* by *Cold*, there be few Trials of it; for we have no strong or intense cold here on the surface of the Earth, so near the Beams of the Sun and the Heavens, the likeliest tryal is by Snow and Ice; for as Snow and Ice, especially being holpen, and their cold activated by Nitre or Salt, will turn Water into Ice, and that in a few hours: So it may be it will turn Wood or stiff Clay into Stone in longer time. Put therefore into a Conserving Pit of Snow and Ice, (adding some quantity of Salt and Nitre) a piece of Wood, or a piece of tough Clay, and let it lie a moneth or more.

84.
    Another tryal is by *Metalline Waters*, which have virtual Cold in them. Put therefore Wood or Clay into *Smiths* water, or other *Metalline water*, and try whether it will not harden in some reasonable time. But I understand it of *Metalline waters*, that come by washing or quenching, and not of Strong Waters that come by dissolution; for they are too Corrosive to consolidate.

85.
    It is already found, that there are some Natural Spring-waters that will inlapidate Wood; so as you shall see one piece of Wood, whereof the part above the Water shall continue Wood; and the part under the Water, shall be turned into a kinde of Gravelly Stone. It is likely those Waters are of some Metalline Mixture; but there would be more particular inquiry made of them. It is certain, that an Egg was found, having lain many years in the

bottom of a Moar, where the Earth had somewhat overgrown it : And this Egg was come to the hardness of a Stone, and had the colours of the White and Yolk perfect ; and the Shell shining in small Grains, like Sugar or Alablaster.

Another Experience there is of *Induration by Cold*, which is already found, which is, That *Metals* themselves are hardned by often heating, and quenching in Cold-water : For Cold ever worketh most potently upon Heat precedent.

86.

For *Induration by Heat*, it must be considered, That Heat, by the exhaling of the moister parts, doth either harden the Body; as in Bricks, Tiles, &c. Or if the Heat be more fierce, maketh the grosser part of it self, run and melt; as in the making of ordinary Glass, and in the Vitrification of Earth, (as we see in the inner parts of Furnaces) and in the Vitrification of Brick, and of Metals. And in the former of these , which is the hardning by Baking, without Melting , the Heat hath these degrees : First, It Indurateth, and then maketh Fragile ; and lastly, It doth Incincrate and Calcinate.

87.

But if you desire to make an *Induration with Toughness*, and less *Fragility*, a middle way would be taken , which is that which *Aristotle* hath well noted, but would be throughly verified. It is, to decoct Bodies in Water for two or three days ; but they must be such Bodies, into which the Water will not enter ; as Stone and Metal. For if they be Bodies, into which the Water will enter, then long seething will rather soften than indurate them, as hath been tried in Eggs, &c. Therefore , softer Bodies must be put into Bottles, and the Bottles hung into Water seething, with the Mouths open above the Water, that no Water may get in : For by this Means, the Virtual Heat of the Water will enter ; and such a Heat, as will not make the Body adust or fragile : But the Substance of the Water will be shut out. This Experiment we made, and it sorted thus , It was tryed with a piece of Free-stone, and with Pewter, put into the Water at large ; the Free-stone we found received in some Water ; for it was softer and easier to scrape, than a piece of the same stone kept dry. But the Pewter, into which no Water could enter, became more white, and liker to Silver, and less flexible by much. There were also put into an Earthen Bottle, placed as before, a good pellet of Clay, a piece of Cheese, a piece of Chalk, and a piece of Freestone. The Clay came forth almost of the hardness of Stone : The Cheese likewise very hard, and not well to be cut : The Chalk and the Free stone much harder then they were. The colour of the Clay inclined not a whit to the colour of Brick, but rather to white, as in ordinary drying by the Sun. Note, that all the former tryals were made by a boyling upon a good hot fire, renewing the Water as it consumed, with other hot Water ; but the boyling was but for Twelve hours onely : And it is like, that the Experiment would have been more effectual, if the boyling had been for two or three days, as we prescribed before.

88.

As touching *Assimilation* (for there is a degree of *Assimilation*, even in Inanimate Bodies) we see examples of it in some Stones, in Clay grounds, lying near to the top of the Earth where Pebble is ; in which you may manifestly see divers Pebbles gathered together, and a crust of Cement or Stone between them, as hard as the Pebbles themselves. And it were good to make a tryal of purpose, by taking Clay, and putting in it divers Pebble-stones, thick set, to see whether in continuance of time, it will not be harder than other Clay of the same lump, in which no Pebbles are set. We see also in Ruins

89.

of

of old Walls, especially towards the bottom, the Morter will become as hard as the Brick : We see also, that the Wood on the sides of Vessels of Wine, gathereth a crust of *Tartar* harder than the Wood it self ; and Scales likewise grow to the Teeth, harder than the Teeth themselves.

90.

    Most of all, *Induration by Assimilation* appeareth in the bodies of Trees, and Living Creatures : For no nourishment that the Tree receiveth, or that the Living Creature receiveth, is so hard as Wood, Bone, or Horn, &c. but is indurated after by Assimilation.

91.
Experiment
Solitary,
touching the
Version of Wa-
ter into Air.

THe Eye of the Understanding, is like the Eye of the Sense : For as you may see great objects through small Crannies, or Levels ; so you may see great Axioms of Nature, through small and contemptible instances. The speedy depredation of Air upon watry moisture, and version of the same into Air, appeareth in nothing more visible than in the sudden discharge, or vanishing of a little Cloud of Breath, or Vapor, from Glass or the Blade of a Sword, or any such polished Body ; such as doth not at all detain or imbibe the moisture : For the mistiness scattereth and breaketh up suddenly. But the like Cloud, if it were oily or fatty, will not discharge ; not because it sticketh faster, but because Air preyeth upon Water, and Flame, and Fire, upon Oyl ; and therefore, to take out a spot of Grease, they use a Coal upon brown Paper, because fire worketh upon Grease or Oyl, as Air doth upon Water. And we see Paper oiled, or Wood oiled, or the like, last long moist ; but wet with Water, dry or putrifie sooner. The cause is, for that Air meddleth little with the moisture of oyl.

92.
Experiment
Solitary,
touching the
Force of Vni-
on.

THere is an admirable demonstration in the same trifling instance of the little Cloud upon Glass, or Gems, or Blades of Swords of the force of Union, even in the least quantities, and weakest Bodies, how much it conduceth to preservation of the present form, and the resisting of a new. For mark well the discharge of that Cloud, and you shall see it ever break up, first in the skirts, and last in the midst. We see likewise, that much Water draweth forth the Juyce of the Body infused, but little Water is imbibed by the Body : And this is a principal cause, why, in operation upon Bodies, for their Version or Alteration, the tryal in great quantities doth not answer the tryal in small, and so deceiveth many ; for that (I say) the greater Body resisteth more any alteration of Form, and requireth far greater strength in the Active Body that should subdue it.

93.
Experiment
Solitary,
touching the
Producing of
Feathers and
Hairs of di-
vers Colours.

WE have spoken before in the Fifth Instance, of the cause of *Orient Colours* in *Birds* ; which is by the fineness of the Strainer, we will now endeavor to reduce the same Axiom to a Work. For this Writing of our *Sylva Sylvarum*, is (to speak properly) not *Natural History*, but a high kinde of *Natural Magick*. For it is not a discription onely of Nature, but a breaking of Nature, into great and strange Works. Try therefore the anointing over of Pigeons, or other Birds, when they are but in their Down, or of Whelps, cutting their Hair as short as may be, or of some other Beast ; with some oyntment, that is not hurtful to the flesh, and that will harden and stick very close, and see whether it will not alter the colours of the Feathers, or Hair. It is received, that the pulling off the first Feathers of Birds clean, will make the new come forth White : And it is certain, that White is a penurious colour, and where moisture is scant. So Blew Violets, and other Flowers, if they be starved, turn pale and white.

Birds,

Birds, and Horfes, by age or fcars, turn white ; and the hoar Hairs of Men, come by the fame reafon. And therefore in Birds, it is very likely, that the Feathers that come firft, will be many times of divers colours, according to the nature of the Birds ; for that the skin is more porous, but when the skin is more fhut and clofe, the Feathers will come white. This is a good Experiment, not onely for the producing of Birds and Beafts of ftrange colours, but alfo, for the difclofure of the nature of colours themfelves; which of them require a finer porofity, and which a groffer.

IT is a work of providence that hath been truly obferved by fome; that the Yolk of the Egg conduceth little to the Generation of the Bird, but onely to the nourifhment of the fame : For if a Chicken be opened when it is new hatched, you fhall finde much of the Yolk remaining. And it is needful, that Birds that are fhaped without the Females Womb, have in the Egg, as well matter of nourifhment, as matter of generation for the Body. For after the Egg is laid, and fevered from the body of the Hen, it hath no more nourifhment from the Hen, but onely a quickning heat when fhe fitteth. But Beafts and Men need not the matter of nourifhment within themfelves; becaufe they are fhaped within the Womb of the Female, and are nourifhed continually from her body.

94.
Experiment Solitary, touching the Nourifhment of Living Creatures before they be brought forth.

IT is an inveterate and received opinion, That *Cantharides* applied to any part of the Body, touch the Bladder, and exulcerate it, if they ftay on long. It is likewife received, that a kinde of *Stone*, which they bring out of the *Weft-Indies*, hath a peculiar force to move Gravel, and to diffolve the *Stone* ; infomuch, as laid but to the Wreft, it hath fo forcibly fent down Gravel, as Men have been glad to remove it, it was fo violent.

95.
Experiments in Confort, touching Sympathy and Antipathy for Medicinal ufe.

It is received and confirmed by daily experience, that the Soals of the Feet, have great affinity with the Head, and the Mouth of the Stomack: As we fee, Going wetfhod, to thofe that ufe it not, affecteth beth ; Applications of hot Powders to the Feet, attenuate firft, and after dry the Rheume. And therefore a Phyfician that would be myftical, prefcribeth for the cure of the Rheume, That a Man fhould walk continually upon a Camomil-Alley; meaning, that he fhould put Camomil within his Socks. Likewife, Pigeons bleeding, applied to the Soals of the Feet, eafe the Head; and So-poriferous Medicines applied unto them, provoke fleep.

96.

It feemeth, that as the Feet have a fympathy with the Head ; fo the Wrefts and Hands have a fympathy with the Heart. We fee the affects and Paffions of the Heart, and Spirits, are notably difclofed by the Pulfe : And it is often tryed, that Juyces of *Stock-gilly-flowers*, *Rofe-campion*, *Garlick*, and other things, applied to the Wrefts, and renewed, have cured long Agues. And I conceive, that wafhing with certain Liquors the Palms of the Hands, doth much good : And they do well in Heats of Agues to hold in the Hands, Eggs of Alablafter, and Balls of Cryftal.

Of thefe things we fhall fpeak more, when we handle the Title of Sympathy *and* Antipathy, *in the proper place.*

97.

THe knowledge of Man (hitherto) hath been determined by the view or fight; fo that whatfoever is invifible, either in refpect of the finenefs of the Body it felf, or the fmallnefs of the Parts, or of the fubtilty of the Motion,

98.
Experiment Solitary, touching the Secret Proceffes of Nature.

Motion, is little inquired. And yet these be the things
principally, and without which, you cannot make an
Indications of the proceedings of Nature. The Spiri
that are in all Tangible Bodies, are scarce known: So
them for *Vacuum*, whereas they are the most active
times they take them for Air, from which they diff
much as Wine from Water, and as Wood from I
they will have them to be Natural Heat, or a Portior
Fire, whereas some of them are crude and cold: And
have them to be the Vertues and Qualities of the Ta
they see, whereas they are things by themselves: An
come to Plants and Living Creatures, they call then
superficial speculations they have ; like Prospectives
ward, when they are but Paintings. Neither is this a
but infinitely material in Nature : For Spirits are no
tural Body, rarified to a Proportion, and included i
of Bodies, as in an Integument : And they be no le
the other, then the Dense or Tangible Parts: And the
Bodies whatsoever, more or less, and they are never (al
from them, and their Motions, principally proceed
Concoction, Maturation, Putrefaction, Vivification, and most
ture. For, as we have figured them in our *Sapientiá Ve*
Proserpina, you shall in the Infernal Regiment hear h
but most of *Proserpina :* For Tangible Parts in Bodi
and the Spirits do (in effect) all. As for the differenc
in Bodies, the industry of the *Chymists* hath given som
by their separations, the *Oily, Crude, Pure, Impure, Fiu*
and the like. And the *Physitians* are content to acknow
Drugs have divers parts ; as that *Opium* hath a stupefac
ing part ; the one moving Sleep, the other a Sweat
Ruburb hath Purging parts, and Astringing parts, &c.
quisition is weakly and negligently handled. And for th
ences of the Minute parts, and the posture of them
also hath great effects) they are not at all touched : A
the Minute Parts of Bodies, which do so great effects
observed at all ; because they are invisible, and incur
yet they are to be deprehended by experience. As
when they charged him to hold, that the World wa
Moats, as were seen in the Sun. *Atomus* (saith he) n
perientia esse convincitur : Atomum enim nemo nunquam v
the tumult in the parts of solid Bodies, when they ar
is the cause of all flights of Bodies thorow the Air, and
Motions , (as hath been partly touched before, an
handled in due place,) is not seen at all, but neverthe
not, or inquire it not attentively and diligently, you f
discern, and muchless to produce, a number of N
Again, as to the Motions Corporal, within the Ei
whereby the effects (which were mentioned before)
rits and the Tangible parts (which are *Arefaction,*
Maturation, &c.) they are not at all handled ; But th
names of *Vertues,* and *Natures,* and *Actions,* and *Passions,*
words.

IT is certain, that of all *Powers in Nature*, Heat is the chief; both in the Frame of *Nature*, and in the Works of *Art*. Certain it is likewise, that the effects of Heat, are most advanced, when it worketh upon a Body without loss or dissipation of the matter, for that ever betrayed the account. And therefore it is true, that the power of Heat is best perceived in Distillations, which are performed in close Vessels and Receptacles. But yet there is a higher degree; For howsoever Distillations do keep the Body in Cells and Cloysters, without going abroad, yet they give space unto Bodies to turn into Vapor, to return into Liquor, and to separate one part from another. So as *Nature* doth expatiate, although it hath not full liberty; whereby the true and ultime operations of Heat, are not attained: But if Bodies may be altered by Heat, and yet no such Reciprocation of Rarefaction, and of Condensation, and of Separation, admitted; then it is like that this *Proteus* of Matter, being held by the Sleeves, will turn and change into many Metamorphoses. Take therefore a square Vessel of Iron, in form of a Cube, and let it have good thick and strong sides; put it into a Cube of Wood, that may fill it as close as may be, and let it have a cover of Iron as strong (at least) as the sides, and let it be well Luted, after the manner of the *Chymists*; then place the Vessel within burning *Coals* kept quick kindled, for some few hours space; then take the Vessel from the Fire, and take off the Cover, and see what is become of the Wood, I conceive, that since all Inflamation and Evaporation are utterly prohibited, and the Body still turned upon it self, that one of these two Effects will follow, Either that the Body of the Wood will be turned into a kinde of *Amalgama*, (as the *Chymists* call it,) or, that the finer part will be turned into Air, and the grosser stick as it were baked, and incrustate upon the sides of the Vessel, being become of a denser matter, than the Wood it self, crude. And for another tryal, take also Water, and put it in the like Vessel, stopped as before; but use a gentler Heat, and remove the Vessel sometimes from the fire; and again, after some small time, when it is cold, renew the heating of it, and repeat this alteration some few times; and if you can once bring to pass, that the Water which is one of the simplest of Bodies, be changed in Colour, Odor, or Taste, after the manner of Compound Bodies, you may be sure that there is a great work wrought in Nature, and a notable entrance made in strange changes of Bodies, and productions; and also a way made to do that by Fire, in small time, which the *Sun* and *Age* do in long time. But if the admirable effects of this *Distillation* in close, (for so we call it) which is like the Wombs and Matrices of Living Creatures, where nothing expireth nor separateth: We will speak fully, in the due place. Not that we aim at the making of *Paracelsus* Pigmeys, or any such prodigious follies; but that we know the effects of Heat will be such, as will scarce fall under the conceit of Man, if the force of it be altogether kept in.

THere is nothing more certain in *Nature*, than that it is impossible for any Body to be utterly annihilated; but that as it was the work of the Omnipotency of *God*, to make *Somewhat* of *Nothing*: So it requireth the like omnipotency, to turn *Somewhat* into *Nothing*. And therefore it is well said by an obscure Writer of the Sect of the *Chymists*, That there is no such way to effect the strange *Transmutations of Bodies*, as to endeavor and urge by all means, the reducing of them to *Nothing*. And herein is contained alfo a great fecret of *Prefervation of Bodies* from change ; for if you can prohibit, that they neither turn into *Air*, becaufe no *air* cometh to them, nor go into the *Bodies Adjacent*, becaufe they are utterly Heterogeneal, nor make a round and circulation within themfelves ; they will never change, though they be in their Nature never fo perifhable or mutable. We fee how *Flies* and *Spiders*, and the like, get a *Sepulchre* in *Amber*, more durable than the *Monument* and *Embalming* of the *Body* of any *King*. And I conceive the like will be of Bodies put into *Quick-filver*. But then they muft be but thin, as a leaf or a peece of *Paper* or *Parchment* ; for if they have a greater craffitude, they will alter in their own Body, though they fpend not. But of this, we fhall fpeak more when we handle the Title of *Confervation of Bodies*.

NATURAL
HISTORY.

Century II.

Ufick in the Practice, hath been well purfued, and in good Variety ; but in the Theory, and efpecially in the yielding of the Caufes of the Practick, very weakly ; being reduced into certain Myftical fubtilties, and not much truth. We fhall therefore, after our manner, joyn the *Contemplative* and *Active Part* together.

All Sounds are either *Mufical Sounds*, which we call *Tones*; whereunto there may be an *Harmony*, which *Sounds* are ever equal : As Singing, the Sounds of Stringed, and Wind-Inftruments, the Ringing of Bells, &c. or Immufical Sounds, which are ever unequal : Such as are the Voice in Speaking, all Whifperings, all Voices of Beafts and Birds (except they be Singing Birds ;) all Percuffions, of Stones, Wood, Parchment, Skins, (as in Drums) and infinite others.

101.

The Sounds that produce Tones, are ever from fuch *Bodies* as are in their Parts and Pores equal ; as well as the Sounds themfelves are equal: And fuch are the Percuffions of Metal, as in *Bells*; of *Glaß*, as in the fillipping of a *Drinking Glaß*; of *Air*, as in *Mens Voices* whileft they fing, in *Pipes, Whiftles, Organs, Stringed Inftruments, &c.* And of Water, as in the *Nightingals Pipes of Regals,* or *Organs,* and other *Hydraulicks,* which the Ancients had; and *Nero* did fo much efteem, but are now loft. And if any Man think, that the *String* of the *Bow,* and the *String* of the *Vial,* are neither of them equal Bodies, and yet produce Tones; he is in an error. For the Sound is not created between the *Bow* or *Plectrum,* and the *String*; but between the *String* and the *Air*; no more than it is between the Finger or Quill, and the String in other Inftruments. So there are (in effect) but three *Percuffions* that

102.

                                                        create

create Tones; Percussion of Metals (comprehending *Glass*, and the like) Percussions of Air, and Percussions of Water.

103.   The *Diapason* or *Eight* in *Musick*, is the sweetest Concord; inomuch, as it is in effect an *Unison*; as we see in *Lutes* that are strung in the base strings with two strings, one an *Eighth* above another, which make but as one found; and every Eighth Note in Ascent, (as from Eight to Fifteen, from Fifteen to Twenty two, and so *in infinitum*) are but *Scales of Diapason*. The cause is dark, and hath not been rendred by any, and therefore would be better contemplated. It seemeth that Air (which is the subject of Sounds) in Sounds that are not Tones (which are all unequal as hath been said) admitteth much variety; as we see in the Voices of Living Creatures, and likewise in the Voices of several Men; for we are capable to discern several Men by their Voices) and in the Conjugation of Letters, whence *Articulate Sounds* proceed; which of all others, are most various. But in the Sounds which we call Tones (that are ever equal) the Air is not able to cast it self into any such variety; but is forced to recur into one and the same Posture or Figure, onely differing in greatness and smallness. So we see Figures may be made of Lines, crooked and straight, in infinite variety, where there is inequality; but Circles or Squares, or Triangles Equilateral, (which are all Figures of equal Lines) can differ but in greater or lesser.

104.   It is to be noted (the rather, lest any Man should think that there is any thing in this number of Eight, to create the *Diapason*) that this computation of Eight, is a thing rather received than any true computation. For a true computation ought ever to be, by distribution into equal Portions. Now there be intervenient in the rise of Eight (in Tones) two Beemols or Half-Notes; so as if you divide the Tones equally, the Eighth is but Seven whole and equal Notes: And if you subdivide that into Half-Notes, (as it is in the stops of a *Lute*) it maketh the number of Thirteen.

105.   Yet this is true, That in the ordinary Rises and Falls of the Voice of Man (not measuring the Tone by whole Notes and Half Notes, which is the equal Measure) there fall out to be two Beemols (as hath been said) between the *Unison* and the *Diapason*; and this varying is natural. For if a Man would endeavor to raise or fall his Voice still by Half-Notes, like the stops of a Lute, or by whole Notes alone, without Halfs as far as an Eighth; he will not be able to frame his Voice unto it, which sheweth that after every three whole Notes, *Nature* requireth, for all Harmonical use, one Half-Note to be interposed.

106.   It is to be considered, That whatsoever vertue is in *Numbers*, for conducing to concent of Notes, is rather to be ascribed to the *Ante-number*, than to the *Entire-number*; as namely, that the Sound returneth after Six, or after Twelve: So that the Seventh or the Thirteenth is not the Matter, but the Sixth, or the Twelfth; and the Seventh and the Thirteenth, are but the Limits and Boundaries of the Return.

107.   The Concords in Musick which are *Perfect*, or *Semiperfect*, between the *Unison* and the *Diapason*, are the Fifth, which is the most *Perfect*; the Third next, and the Sixth which is more harsh: And as the *Ancients* esteemed, and so do my self, and some other yet, the Fourth which they call *Diatesseron*; as for the Tenth, Twelfth, Thirteenth, and so *in infinitum*, they be but Recurrences of the former; *viz.* of the Third, the Fifth, and the Sixth, being an Eighth respectively from them.

For

For *Discords*, the Second and the Seventh, are of all others, the most odious in *Harmony* to the Sense; whereof, the one is next above the *Unison*, the other next under the *Diapason*; which may shew, that *Harmony* requireth a competent distance of Notes.

In *Harmony*, if there be not a *Discord* to the *Base*, it doth not disturb the *Harmony*, though there be a *Discord* to the higher parts; so the *Discord* be not of the Two that are odious: And therefore the ordinary Concent of Four parts consisteth of an Eighth, a Fifth, and a Third to the *Base*; but that Fifth is a Fourth to the Trebble, and the Third is a Sixth. And the cause is, for that the Base striking more Air, doth overcome and drown the Trebble (unless the Discord be very odious) and so hideth a small imperfection For we see, that in one of the lower strings of a Lute, there soundeth not the sound of the Trebble, nor any mixt sound, but onely the sound of the *Base*.

We have no *Musick* of *Quarter-Notes*, and it may be they are not capable of *Harmony*; for we see the *Half-Notes* themselves do but interpose sometimes. Nevertheless, we have some *Slides* or *Relishes* of the Voice or Strings, as it were, continued without Notes, from one Tone to another, rising or falling, which are delightful.

The causes of that which is *Pleasing* or ingrate to the *Hearing*, may receive light by that which is *Pleasing* or ingrate to the *Sight*. There be two things pleasing to the sight (leaving *Pictures* and *Shapes* aside, which are but Secondary Objects, and please or displease but in Memory;) these two are Colours and Order. The pleasing of Colour symbolizeth with the *Pleasing* of any *Single Tone* to the Ear; but the pleasing of Order doth symbolize with *Harmony*. And therefore we see in *Garden-knots*, and the *Frets of Houses*, and all equal and well answering *Figures*, (as *Globes*, *Pyramides*, *Cones*, *Cylinders*, &c.) how they please; whereas unequal Figures are but Deformities. And both these pleasures, that of the Eye, and that of the Ear, are but the effects of equality, good proportion, or correspondence: So that (out of question) Equality and Correspondence are the causes of *Harmony*. But to finde the Proportions of that Correspondence, is more abstruse; whereof, notwithstanding we shall speak somewhat (when we handle *Tones*, in the general enquiry of Sounds.

Tones are not so apt altogether to procure *Sleep*, as some other sounds: As the Wind, the Purling of Water, Humming of Bees, a sweet Voice of one that readeth, &c. The cause whereof is, for that *Tones*, because they are equal and slide not, do more strike and erect the Sense, than the other. And overmuch attention hindereth sleep.

There be in *Musick* certain *Figures* or *Tropes*, almost agreeing with the *Figures* of *Rhetorick*, and with the *Affections* of the *Minde*, and other *Senses*. First, The *Division* and *Quavering*, which please so much in *Musick*, have an agreement with the Glittering of Light; As the *Moon-Beams* playing upon a Wave. Again, the *Falling* from a *Discord* to a *Concord*, which maketh great sweetness in *Musick*, hath an agreement with the *affections*, which are reintegrated to the better, after some dislikes; it agreeth also with the taste, which is soon glutted with that which is sweet alone. The sliding from the Close or Cadence, hath an agreement with the *Figure* in *Rhetorick*, which they call *Prater Expectatum*; for there is a pleasure, even in being deceived. The Reports and Fuges have an agreement with the *Figures* in *Rhetorick* of Repetition and Traduction. The *Tripla's* and *Changing of times*, have an agreement with the

108.

109.

110.

111.

112.

113.

the changes of Motions ; as when Galliard time, and Meafure time, are in
the Medly of one Dance.

114.   It hath been anciently held, and obferved, That the *Senfe of Hearing*, and
the *Kindes of Mufick*, have moft operation upon *Manners* ; as to incourage
Men, and make them warlike ; to make them foft and effeminate ; to make
them grave ; to make them light ; to make them gentle and inclined to
pity, &c.   The caufe is, for that the *Senfe of Hearing* ftriketh the Spirits
more immediately, than the other *Senfes*, and more incorporeally than
the *Smelling :* For the *Sight*, *Tafte*, and *Feeling*, have their Organs, not of fo
prefent and immediate accefs to the Spirits, as the Hearing hath.   And
as for the Smelling (which indeed worketh alfo immediately upon the Spirits, and is forcible while the objeck remaineth) it is with a communication of the Breath or Vapor of the objeck oderate : But Harmony entring
eafily, and mingling not at all, and coming with a manifeft motion ; doth
by cuftom of often affecking the Spirits, and putting them into one kinde
of pofture, alter not a little the nature of the Spirits, even when the objeck is removed.   And therefore we fee, that Tunes and Airs, even in their
own nature, have in themfelves fome affinity with the Affeckions : As
there be Merry Tunes, Doleful Tunes, Solemn Tunes ; Tunes inclining
Mens mindes to Pity, Warlike Tunes, &c.   So as it is no marvel, if they
alter the Spirits, confidering that Tunes have a predifpofition to the Motion of the Spirits in themfelves.   But yet it hath been noted, that though
this variety of Tunes, doth difpofe the Spirits to variety of Paffions, conform unto them ; yet generally, *Mufick* feedeth that difpofition of the Spirits which it findeth.   We fee alfo, that feveral Airs and Tunes, do pleafe
feveral Nations, and Perfons according to the fympathy they have with their
Spirits.

Experiments
in Confort,
touching
Sounds ; and
firft touching
the *Nullity,*
and *Entity of
Sounds.*

PErfpective hath been with fome diligence inquired ; and fo hath the Nature of Sounds, in fome fort, as far as concerneth *Mufick*, but the Nature of Sounds in general, hath been fuperficially obferved.   It is one of
the fubtilleft pieces of Nature.   And befides, I practife, as I do advife:
Which is after long inquiry of things, immerfe in matter, to enterpofe fome
fubjeck which is immateriate or lefs materiate ; fuch as this of Sounds : To
the end, that the intelleck may be rectified, and become not partial.

115.   It is firft to be confidered, what great motions there are in Nature
which pafs without found or noife.   The Heavens turn about in a moft rapide
motion, without noife to us perceived, though in fome dreams they have
been faid to make an excellent Mufick.   So the motions of the Comets, and
Fiery Meteors as *Stella Cadens*, &c.) yield no noife.   And if it be thought, that
it is the greatnefs of diftance from us, whereby the found cannot, be heard ;
we fee that Lightnings and Corufcations, which are near at hand, yield no
found neither ; and yet in all thefe, there is a percuffion and divifion of the
Air.   The Winds in the Upper Region (which move the Clouds above
(which we call the Rack) and are not perceived below) pafs without noife.
The lower Winds in a Plain, except they be ftrong, make no noife ; but a-
mongft Trees, the noife of fuch Winds will be perceived.   And the Winds
(generally) when they make a noife, do ever make it unequally, rifing and falling, and fometimes (when they are vehement) trembling at the height of
their blaft.   Rain or Hail falling, though vehemently, yieldeth no noife, in
paffing through the Air, till it fall upon the Ground, Water, Houfes, or the
like.   Water in a River (though a fwift ftream, is not heard in the Channel,
                                                                                but

but runneth in filence, if it be of any depth ; but the very Stream upon Shal-
lows, or Gravel, or Pebble, will be heard. And Waters, when they bear upon the Snore, or are ftraitned, (as in the falls of Bridges) or are dafhed againft
themfelves by Winds, give a roaring noife. Any peece of Timber, or hard
Body, being thruft forwards by another Body continguous, without knocking giveth no noife. And fo *Bodies* in weighing, one upon another, though
the upper Body prefs the lower Body down, make no noife. So the motion
of the Minute parts of any folid Body, (which is the principal caufe of violent
Motion, though unobferved) paffeth without found : For that found, that is
heard fometimes, is produced onely by the breaking of the Air, and not by
the impulfion of the parts. So it is manifeft, that where the anterior Body
giveth way as faft as the pofterior cometh on, it maketh no noife, be the
motion never fo great or fwift.

*Air open and at large, maketh no noife, except it be fharply percuffed ;
as in the found of a ftring, where Air is purcuffed by a hard and ftiff Body, and
with a fharp loofe : For if the ftring be not ftrained, it maketh no noife ; but
where the Air is pent and ftrained, there breath or other blowing (which
carry but a gentle percuffion) fuffice to create found ; as in Pipes and Wind
Inftruments. But then you muft note, that in *Recorders* which go with a
gentle breath, the Concave of the Pipe (were it not for the Fipple that ftrait-
neth the Air much more then the fimple Concave) would yield no found.
For, as for other Wind-Inftruments, they require a forcible breath, as *Trumpets, Cornets, Hunters, Horns, &c.* Which appeareth by the blown Cheeks o
him that windeth them. *Organs* alfo are blown with a ftrong wind by the
Bellows. And note again, that fome kinde of Wind-Inftruments are blown
at a fmall hole in the fide, which ftraineth the breath at the firft entrance;
the rather, in refpect of their traverfe, and ftop above the hole which performeth the Fipples part ; as it is feen in *Flutes* and *Fifes,* which will not give
found by a blaft at the end, as *Recorders* do, &c. Likewife in all Whiftling,
you contract the Mouth ; and to make it more fharp, Men fometimes ufe their
finger.

But in open Air, if you throw a Stone or a Dart, they give no found :
No more do Bullets, except they happen to be a little hollowed in the cafting ; which hollownefs penneth the Air : Nor yet Arrows, except they be
ruffled in their Feathers, which likewife penneth the Air As for fmall Whiftles or Shepherds Oaten Pipes, they give a found, becaufe of their extream
flendernefs, whereby the Air is more pent than in a wider Pipe. Again, the
voices of Men and Living Creatures, pafs through the Throat, which penneth the breath. As for the *Jews-Harp,* it is a fharp percuffion, and befides hath
the vantage of penning the Air in the Mouth.

Solid Bodies, if they be very foftly percuffed, give no found ; as when a
Man treadeth very foftly upon Boards. So Chefts or Doors in fair weather,
when they open eafily, give no found. And Cart-wheels fqueek not when
they are liquored.

The *Flame of Tapers* or *Candles,* though it be a fwift motion and breaketh
the Air, yet paffeth without found. Air in Ovens, though (no doubt) it doth
(as it were) boil, and dilate it felf, and is repercuffed, yet it is without noife.

Flame percuffed by Air, giveth a noife ; As in blowing of the Fire by Bellows, greater than if the Bellows fhould blow upon the Air it felf. And fo
likewife: Flame percuffing the Air ftrongly (as when Flame fuddenly taketh
and openeth) giveth a noife : So great Flames, whiles the one impelleth the
other, give a bellowing found.

There

115.

117.

118.

119.

120.   There is a conceit runneth abroad, that there should be a White Powder, which will discharge a piece without noise, which is a dangerous experiment, if it should be true : For it may cause secret Murthers, but it seemeth to me unpossible ; for if the Air pent, be driven forth and strike the Air open, it will certainly make a noise. As for the White Powder, (if any such thing be that may extinguish or dead the noise) it is like to be a mixture of Petre and Sulphure, without Coal. For Petre alone will not take Fire. And if any Man think, that the sound may be extinguished or deaded, by discharging the pent Air, before it cometh to the Mouth of the Peece, and to the open Air, that is not probable ; for it will make more divided sounds : As if you should make a Cross-barrel hollow, thorow the Barrel of a Peece, it may be it would give several sounds, both at the Nose and the sides. But I conceive, that if it were possible to bring to pass, that there should be no Air pent at the Mouth of the Peece, the Bullet might flie with small or no noise. For first it is certain, there is no noise in the Percussion of the Flame upon the Bullet. Next the Bullet, in piercing thorow the Air, maketh no noise, as hath been said ; and then, if there be no pent Air, that striketh upon open Air, there is no cause of noise, and yet the flying of the Bullet will not be staid. For that motion (as hath been oft said) is in the parts of the Bullet, and not in the Air. So as tryal must be made by taking some small Concave of *Minal*, no more than you mean to fill with Powder, and laying the Bullet in the Mouth of it half out in the open Air.

121.   I heard it affirmed by a Man that was a great dealer in Secrets, but he was but vain ; That there was a *Conspiracy* (which himself hindred) to have killed Queen *Mary*, Sister to Queen *Elizabeth*, by a *Burning-Glass*, when she walked in St. *James* Park, from the Leads of the House. But thus much, no doubt, is true, That if *Burning-Glasses* could be brought to a great strength, (as they talk generally of *Burning-Glasses*, that are able to burn a Navy) the Percussion of the Air alone, by such a *Burning-Glass*, would make no noise ; no more than is found in *Corruscations*, and *Lightnings* without *Thunders*.

122.   I suppose that *Impression* of the *Air* with *Sounds*, asketh a time to be conveighed to the Sense, as well as the *Impression* of *Species visible*, or else they will not be heard. And therefore, as the Bullet moveth so swift, that it is invisible, so the same swiftness of motion maketh it inaudible ; for we see that the apprehension of the Eye, is quicker then that of the Ear.

123.   All *Eruptions of Air*, though small and slight, give an entity of sound, which we call *Crackling, Puffing, Spiting, &c.* As in Bay-salt, and Bay-leaves cast into the fire ; so in *Chesnuts*, when they leap forth of the Ashes, so in green wood laid upon the fire, especially Roots ; so in Candles that spit flame, if they be wet ; so in Rasping, Sneezing, &c. So in a Rose leaf gathered together into the fashion of a Purse, and broken upon the Forehead, or Back of the Hand, as Children use.

124.
Experiments in Consort, touching *Production*, *Conservation*, *and Delation of Sounds ; and the office of the Air therein.*

THE cause given of Sound, that it should be an *Elision of the Air* (whereby, if they mean any thing, they mean Cutting or Dividing, or else an Attenuating of the Air) is but a term of Ignorance ; and the motion is but a catch of the Wit upon a few Instances, as the manner is in the *Philosophy* received. And it is common with Men, that if they have gotten a pretty expression by a word of *Art*, that expression goeth currant, though it be empty of matter. This conceit of *Elision*, appeareth most manifestly to be false, in that the Sound of a Bell string, or the like, continueth melting, sometime after the Percussion ; but ceaseth straight-ways, if the Bell or String be touched and stayed; whereas, if it were the *Elision* of the *Air*, that made the Sound, it could not be that the touch of the Bell or String, should extinguish so suddenly that motion, caused by the *Elision* of the *Air*. This appeareth yet more manifestly, by Chiming with a Hammer upon the out-side of a Bell; for the Sound will be according to the inward Concave of the Bell : Whereas the *Elision* or *Attenuation* of the *Air* cannot be, but onely between the Hammer, and the outside of the Bell. So again, if it were an *Elision*, a broad Hammer, and a Bodkin, struck upon Metal, would give a diverse Tone, as well as a diverse Loudness : But they do not so ; for though the Sound of the one be louder, and of the other softer, yet the Tone is the same. Besides, in Eccho's (whereof some are as loud as the Original Voice) there is no new *Elision*, but a Repercussion onely. But that, which convinceth it most of all, is, That Sounds are generated, where there is no Air at all. But these, and the like conceits, when Men have cleared their Understanding, by the light of Experience, will scatter and break up like a Mist.

It is certain, that Sounds is not produced at the first; but with some Local Motion of the Air or Flame, or some other *Medium*; nor yet without some resistance, either in the Air, or the Body percussed. For if there be a meer yielding or cession, it produceth no Sound, as hath been said. And therein Sounds differ from Light or Colours which pass through the Air, or other Bodies, without any Local Motion of the Air, either at the first, or after. But you must attentively distinguish between the Local Motion of the Air (which is but *Vehiculum causæ, A Carrier of the Sounds*,) and the Sounds themselves conveighed in the Air. For as to the former, we see manifestly, that no Sound is produced (no not by Air it self against other Air, as in Organs, &c.) but with a perceptible Blast of the Air, and with some re-sistance of the Air strucken. For, even all Speech, (which is one of the gentlest Motions of Air,) is with expulsion of a little Breath. And all Pipes have a blast, as well as a Sound. We see also manifestly, that Sounds are car-ried with Wind : And therefore Sounds will be hard further with the Wind, than against the Wind ; and likewise, do rise and fall with the intension or remission of the Wind : But for the Impression of the Sound, it is quite an-other thing. and is utterly without Local Motion of the Air, perceptible ; and in that resembleth the species visible : For after a Man hath lured, or a Bell is rung, we cannot discern any Perceptible Motion (at all) in the Air, as long as the sound goeth, but onely at the first. Neither doth the Wind (as far as it carrieth a Voice) with the Motion thereof, confound any of the deli-cate, and Articulate Figurations of the Air, in variety of Words. And if a Man speak a good loudness against the flame of a Candle, it will not make it tremble much ; though most, when those Letters are pronounced, which contract the mouth, as F, S, V, and some others. But gentle breathing, or blowing without speaking, will move the Candle far more. And it is the more probable, that Sound is without any Local Motion of the Air, because as it differeth from the sight, in that it needeth a Local Motion of the Air at first : So it paralleleth in so many other things with the sight, and radiation of things invisible, which (without all question) induce no Local Motion in the Air, as hath been said.

Nevertheless it is true, that upon the noise of Thunder, and great Ord-nance, Glass Windows will shake, and Fishes are thought to be strayed with the

the Motion, caufed by noife upon the Water. But thefe effects are from
the local motion of the Air, which is a concomitant of the Sourd (as hath
been faid) and not from the Sound.

127.   It hath been anciently reported, and is ftill received, that extream ap-
plaufes, and fhouting of people, affembled in great multitudes, have fo rarified, and broken the Air, that Birds flying over, have faln down, the Air being not able to fupport them. And it is believed by fome, that great Ringing of Bells in populous Cities, hath chafed away Thunder; and alfo diffipated peftilent Air: All which may be alfo from the concuffion of the Air,
and not from the Sound.

128.   A very great found near hand, hath ftrucken many deaf; and at the
inftant they have found, as it were, the breaking of a Skin of Parchment in
their Ear : And my felf, ftanding near one that lured loud and fhrill, had
fuddenly an offence, as if fomewhat had broken, or been diflocated in my
Ear, and immediately after a loud Ringing; (not an ordinary Singing, or
Hiffing, but far louder, and differing ; fo as I feared fome Deafnefs. But
after fome half quarter of an hour, it vanifhed. This effect may be truly
referred unto the Sound ; for (as is commonly received) an overpotent
Object doth deftroy the Senfe ; and Spiritual Species, (both Vifible and
Audible,) will work upon the fenfories, though they move not any other
Body.

129.   In *Delation of Sounds*, the enclofure of them preferveth them, and
caufeth them to be heard further. And we finde in Rowls of Parchment, or
Truncks, the Mouth being laid to the one end of the Rowl of Parchment,
or Trunck, and the Ear to the other, the Sound is heard much further then
in the open Air. The caufe is, for that the Sound fpendeth, and is diffipated
in the open Air ; but in fuch Concaves, it is conferved and contracted. So
alfo in a Piece of Ordnance, if you fpeak in the Touch-hole, and another
lay his Ear to the Mouth of the Piece, the Sound paffeth, and is far better
heard than in the open Air.

130.   It is further to be confidered, how it proveth and worketh when the
Sound is not enclofed, all the length of his way, but paffeth partly through
open Air ; as where you fpeak fome diftance from a Trunck, or where the
Ear is fome diftance from the Trunck, at the other end ; or where both
Mouth and Ear are diftant from the Trunck. And it is tryed, that in a long
Trunck of fome Eight or ten foot, the found is holpen, though both the
Mouth, and the Ear be a handful or more, from the ends of the Trunck; and
fomewhat more holpen, when the Ear of the Hearer is near, than when the
Mouth of the Speaker. And it is certain, that the Voice is better heard in a
Chamber from abroad, than abroad from within the Chamber.

131.   As the *Enclofure* that is round about and entire, preferveth the Sound ; fo
doth a Semi-concave, though in a lefs degree. And therefore, if you divide
a Trunck, or a Cane into two, and one fpeak at the one end, and you lay
your Ear at the other, it will carry the Voice further, than in the Air at large.
Nay further, if it be not a full Semi-concave; but if you do the like upon the
Maft of a Ship, or a long Pole, or a Piece of Ordnance (though one fpeak
upon Surface of the Ordnance, and not at any of the Bores) the Voice will
be heard further then in the Air at large.

132.   It would be tryed, how, and with what proportion of difadvantage,
the Voice will be carried in an Horn, which is a Line Arched; or in a
Trumpet, which is a Line Retorted ; or in fome Pipe that were Sinuous.

It

It is certain, (howſoever it croſs the received opinion) that Sounds may be created without Air, though Air be the moſt favorable different of Sounds. Take a Veſſel of Water, and knap a pair of Tongs ſome depth within the Water, and you ſhall hear the Sound of the Tongs well, and not much diminiſhed, and yet there is no Air at all preſent.

Take one Veſſel of Silver, and another of Wood, and fill each of them full of water, and then knap the Tongs together as before, about an handful from the bottom, and you ſhall finde the Sound much more reſounding from the Veſſel of Silver, than from that of Wood; and yet if there be no Water in the Veſſel, ſo that you knap the Tongs in the Air, you ſhall finde no difference between the Silver, and the Wooden Veſſel, whereby beſide the main point of creating ſound without Air, you may collect two things; the one, that the ſound communicateth with the bottom of the Veſſel; the other, that ſuch a communication paſſeth far better thorow Water than Air.

Strike any hard Bodies together in the midſt of a flame, and you ſhall hear the ſound with little difference, from the ſound in the Air.

The *Pneumatical part*, which is in all *Tangible Bodies*, and hath ſome affinity with the Air, performeth in ſome degree, the parts of the Air; as when you knock upon an empty Barrel, the ſound is (in part) created by the Air on the outſide, and (in part) by the Air in the inſide; for the ſound will be greater or leſſer, as the Barrel is more empty, or more full; but yet the ſound participateth alſo with the Spirit in the Wood, thorow which it paſſeth from the outſide to the inſide; and ſo it cometh to paſs in the chiming of Bells on the outſide, where alſo the ſound paſſeth to the inſide; and a number of other like inſtances, whereof we ſhall ſpeak more when we handle the *Communication of Sounds*.

It were extream groſneſs to think (as we have partly touched before) that the ſound in Strings is made, or produced between the Hand and the String, or the Quill and the String, or the Bow and the String: For thoſe are but *Vehicula motus.* paſſages to the Creation of the ſound, the ſound being produced between the String and the Air; and that not by any impulſion of the Air, from the fi ſt Motion of the String; but by the return or reſult of the String, which was ſtrained by the touch to his former place; which Motion of Reſult is quick and ſharp, whereas the firſt Motion is ſoft and dull. So the Bow tortureth the String continually, and thereby holdeth it in a continual Trepidation.

TAke a Trunk, and let one whiſtle at the one end, and hold your ear at the other and you ſhall finde the ſound ſtrike ſo ſharp, as you can ſcarce endure it. The cauſe is, for that ſound diffuſeth it ſelf in round, and ſo ſpendeth it ſelf: But if the ſound, which would ſcatter in open Air, be made to go all into a *Canale*; it muſt needs give greater force to the ſound. And ſo you may note, that incloſures do not onely preſerve ſound, but alſo encreaſe and ſharpen it.

A *Hunters Horn*, being greater at one end, than at the other, doth encreaſe the ſound more, than if the Horn were all of an equal bore. The cauſe is, for that the Air and Sound, being firſt contracted at the leſſer end, and afterwards having more room to ſpred at the greater end, do dilate themſelves, and in coming out, ſtrike more Air, whereby the ſound is the greater, and baſer. And even Hunters Horns, which are ſometimes

madeftraight, and not oblick, are ever greater at the lower end. It would
be tryed alfo in Pipes, being made far larger at the lower end, or being
made with a Belly towards the lower end, and then iffuing into a ftraight concave again.

140.   There is in S*r.* *Jamefes* Fields, a Conduit of Brick, unto which joyneth
a low Vault; and at the end of that, a round Houfe of Stone; and in the
Brick Conduit there is a Window, and in the round Houfe a Slit or Rift of
fome little breadth; if you cry out in the Rift, it will make a fearful roaring
at the Window. The caufe is the fame with the former: For that all Concaves that proceed from more narrow to more broad, do amplifie the Sound
at the coming out.

141.   *Hawks Bells* that have holes in the fides, give a greater ring, than if the
Pellet did ftrike upon Brafs in the open Air. The caufe is the fame with
the firft inftance of the Trunck: Namely, for that the Sound, enclofed
with the fides of the Bell, cometh forth at the holes unfpent and more
ftrong.

142.   In *Drums*, the clofenefs round about, that preferveth the Sound
from difperfing, maketh the noife come forth at the Drum-hole, far
more loud and ftrong, than if you fhould ftrike upon the like skin, extended in the open Air. The caufe is the fame with the two precedent.

143.   *Sounds* are better heard, and further off in an Evening, or in the Night,
than at the Noon or in the Day. The caufe is, for that in the Day, when the
Air is more thin (no doubt) the Sound pierceth better; but when the Air is
more thick (as in the Night) the Sound fpendeth and fpredeth abroad lefs;
and fo it is a degree of Enclofure. As for the night, it is true alfo, that the
general filence helpeth.

144.   There be two kindes of *Reflections of Sounds*; the one at Diftance, which
is the Eccho, wherein the original is heard diftinctly, and the Reflexion
alfo diftinctly; of which, we fhall fpeak hereafter. The other in Concurrence; when the Sound reflecting (the Reflexion being near at hand) returneth immediately upon the original, and fo iterateth it not, but am-
plifieth it. Therefore we fee, that Mufick upon the Water foundeth
more; and fo likewife, Mufick is better in Chambers Wainfcotted than
Hanged.

145.   The Strings of a *Lute*, or *Viol*, or *Virginals*, do give a far greater Sound,
by reafon of the Knot, and Board, and Concave underneath, than if there
were nothing but onely the Flat of a Board, without that Hollow and Knot,
to let in the upper Air into the lower. The caufe is, the Communication of
the upper Air with the lower, and penning of both from expence or difperfing.

146.   An *Irifh Harp* hath open Air on both fides of the Strings; and it hath
the Concave or Belly, not along the Strings, but at the end of the Strings.
It maketh a more refounding Sound, than a *Bandora*, *Orpharion*, or *Cittern*,
which have likewife Wire-ftrings. I judge the caufe to be, for that open Air
on both fides helpeth, fo that there be a Concave; which is therefore beft
placed at the end.

147.   In a *Virginal*, when the Lid is down, it maketh a more exile Sound than
when the Lid is open. The caufe is, for that all fhutting in of Air, where
there is no competent Vent, dampeth the Sound; which maintaineth likewife the former inftance: For the Belly of the Lute, or Viol, doth pen the
Air fomewhat.

There

There is a Church at *Glocester*, (and as I have heard, the like is in some other places) where if you speak against a Wall softly, another shall hear your voice better a good way off, than near hand. Inquire more particularly of the fame of that place. I suppose there is some Vault, or Hollow, or Isle, behinde the Wall, and some passage to it, towards the further end of that Wall against which you speak : So as the voice of him that speaketh slideth along the Wall, and then entreth at some passage, and communicateth with the Air of the Hollow ; for it is preserved somewhat by the plain Wall; but that is too weak to give a Sound audible, till it hath communicated with the back Air.   148.

Strike upon a Bow-string, and lay the Horn of the Bow near your Ear, and it will increase the Sound, and make a degree of a Tone. The cause is for that the sensory, by reason of the close holding is percussed, before the Air disperseth. The like is, if you hold the Horn betwixt your Teeth. But that is a plain *Dilation* of the *Sound*, from the Teeth to the *Instrument of Hearing* ; for there is a great entercourse between those two parts, as appeareth by this, that a harsh grating Tune setteth the Teeth on edge. The like falleth out, if the Horn of the Bow be put upon the Temples ; but that is but the slide of the Sound from thence to the ear.   149.

If you take a Rod of Iron or Brass, and hold the one end to your ear and strike upon the other, it maketh a far greater Sound, than the like stroke upon the Rod, not made so contiguous to the Ear. By which, and by some other instances that have been partly touched, it should appear ; that Sounds do not onely slide upon the surface of a smooth Body, but do also communicate with the Spirits that are in the Pores of the Body.   150.

I remember in *Trinity-Colledge* in *Cambridge*, there was an upper Chamber, which being thought weak in the Roof of it, was supported by a Pillar of Iron, of the bigness of ones arm, in the midst of the Chamber, which, if you had struck, it would make a little flat noise in the Room where it was struck; but it would make a great bomb in the Chamber beneath.   151.

The sound which is made by Buckets in a Well, when they touch upon the Water, or when they strike upon the side of the Well, or when two Buckets dash the one against the other. These Sounds are deeper and fuller, than if the like Percussion were made in the open Air. The cause is the penning and enclosure of the Air in the Concave of the Well.   152.

Barrels placed in a Room under the Floor of a Chamber, make all noises in the same Chamber more full and resounding.   153.

So that there be five ways (in general) of *Majoration of Sounds*, *Enclosure Simple*, *Enclosure in the Dilatation*, *Communication*, *Reflexion*, *Concurrent*, and *Approach to the Sensory*.

For Exility of the Voice, or other Sounds: It is certain, that the Voice doth pass thorow solid and hard Bodies, if they be not too thick ; and thorow Water, which is likewise a very close Body, and such an one as letteth not in Air. But then the Voice or other Sound is reduced, by such passage to a great weakness or exility. If therefore you stop the Holes of a *Hawks Bell*, it will make no ring, but a flat noise or rattle. And so doth the *Ætites* or *Eagles Stone*, which hath a little stone within it.   154.

And as for Water, it is a certain Tryal: Let a man go into a Bath, and take a Pail and turn the bottom upward, and carry the mouth of it (even) down to the level of the Water, and so press it down under the Water some handful and an half, still keeping it even, that it may not tilt on either side, and so the Air get out: Then let him that is in the Bath, dive   155.

with his head so far under Water, as he may put his head into the Pail, and there will come as much Air bubbling forth, as will make room for his head. Then let him speak, and any that shall stand without, shall hear his voice plainly, but yet made extream sharp and exile, like the voice of Puppets: But yet the Articulate Sounds of the words will not be confounded. Note, that it may be much more handsomly done, if the Pail be put over the Mans head above Water, and then he cowre down, and the Pail be pressed down with him. Note, that a man must kneel or sit, that he may be lower than the Water. A man would think, that the *Sicilian* Poet had knowledge of this Experiment; for he saith, that *Hercules's* Page *Hylas* went with a Water-pot, to fill it at a pleasant Fountain that was near the shore, and that the Nymphs of the Fountain fell in love with the Boy, and pulled him under the Water, keeping him alive; and that *Hercules* missing his Page, called him by his name aloud, that all the shore rang of it; and that *Hylas* from within the Water answered his Master; but (that which is to the present purpose) with so small and exile a voice, as *Hercules* thought he had been three miles off, when the Fountain (indeed) was fast by.

156.   In *Lutes* and Instruments of Strings, if you stop a string high, whereby it hath less scope to tremble, the Sound is more Trebble, but yet more dead.

157.   Take two Sawcers, and strike the edge of the one against the bottom of the other, within a Pail of Water, and you shall finde that as you put the Sawcers lower and lower, the Sound groweth more flat, even while part of the Sawcer is above the Water; but that flatness of Sound is joyned with a harshness of Sound, which, no doubt, is caused by the inequality of the Sound, which cometh from the part of the Sawcer under the Water, and from the part above. But when the Sawcer is wholly under the Water, the sound becometh more clear, but far more low, and as if the sound came from a far off.

158.   A soft body dampeth the sound, much more than a hard; and if a Bell hath cloth or silk wrapped about it, it deadeth the sound more than if it were Wood. And therefore in *Clericals*, the Keyes are lined, and in Colledges they use to line the Table-men.

159.   Tryal was made in a *Recorder* after these several manners. The bottom of it was set against the Palm of the Hand, stopped with Wax round about, set against a Damask Cushion, thrust into Sand, into Ashes, into Water, (half an inch under the Water) close to the bottom of a Silver Basin, and still the Tone remained: But the bottom of it was set against a Woollen Carpet, a Lining of Plush, a Lock of Wool, (though loosly put in;) against Snow, and the sound of it was quite deaded, and but breath.

160.   Iron hot produceth not so full a sound, as when it is cold; for while it is hot, it appeareth to be more soft, and less resounding. So likewise warm Water, when it falleth maketh not so full a sound as cold; and I conceive it is softer, and nearer the nature of Oyl; for it is more slippery, as may be perceived, in that it scowreth better.

161.   Let there be a *Recorder* made with two Fipples at each end one; the Trunck of it of the length of two Recorders, and the holes answerable towards each end, and let two play the same Lesson upon it, at an Unison; and let it be noted, whether the sound be confounded, or amplified, or dulled. So likewise let a Cross be made of two Truncks (thorowout)

hollow,

hollow ; and let two speak or sing, the one long ways the other traverse. And let two hear at the opposite ends ; and note, whether the Sound be confounded, amplified, or dulled.　Which two instances will also give light to the mixture of Sounds, whereof we shall speak hereafter.

A *Bellows*, blown into the hole of a Drum, and the Drum then strucken, maketh the Sound a little flatter, but no other apparent alteration. The cause is manifest ; partly for that it hindreth the issue of the Sound ; and partly for that it maketh the Air being blown together, less moveable.

162.

THe Loudness and Softness of Sounds, is a thing distinct from the Magnitude and Exility of Sounds ; for a *Base-string*, though softly strucken, giveth the greater Sound ; but a *Trebble-string*, if hard strucken, will be heard much further off.　And the cause is, for that the *Base-string* striketh more Air ; and the *Trebble* less Air, but with a sharper percussion.

It is therefore the strength of the Percussion, that is a principal cause of the loudness or softness of Sounds : As in knocking, harder or softer ; Winding of a Horn, stronger or weaker ; Ringing of an Hand bell, harder or softer. &c.　And the strength of this Percussion consisteth, as much or more, in the hardness of the Body percussed, as in the force of the Body percussing :　For if you strike against a Cloth, it will give a less sound ; if against Wood, a greater ; if against a Metal, yet a greater ; and in Metals, if you strike against Gold, (which is the more pliant) it giveth the flatter sound ; if against Silver or Brass, the more ringing sound.　As for Air, where it is strongly pent, it matcheth a hard Body.　And therefore we see in discharging of a piece, what a great noise it maketh.　We see also, that the Charge with Bullet, or with Paper wet, and hard stopped ; or with Powder alone rammed in hard, maketh no great difference in the loudness of the report.

The sharpness or quickness of the Percussion, is a great cause of the loudness, as well as the strength :　As in a Whip or Wand, if you strike the Air with it, the sharper and quicker you strike it, the louder sound it giveth.　And in playing upon the Lute or Virginals, the quick stroke or touch is a great life to the Sound.　The cause is, for that the quick striking cutteth the Air speedily, whereas the soft striking, doth rather beat than cut.

165.

THe *Communication of Sounds* (as in Bellies of *Lutes*, empty Vessels, &c.) hath been touched obiter, in the *Majoration of Sounds :*　But it is fit also to make a little of it apart.

The Experiment, for greatest Demonstration of Communication of Sounds, is the Chiming of Bells ; where, if you strike with a Hammar upon the upper part, and then upon the midst, and then upon the lower, you shall finde the sound to be more Trebble, and more Base, according unto the Concave on the inside, though the Percussion be onely on the outside.

166.

When the Sound is created between the Blast of the Mouth, and the Air of the Pipe, it hath nevertheless some communication with the matter of the sides of the Pipe, and the spirits in them contained :　For in a Pipe or Trumpet of Wood and Brass, the sound will be diverse ; so if the Pipe be covered

167

with Cloth or Silk, it will give a diverfe Sound from that it would do of it felf ; fo if the Pipe be a little wet on the infide, it will make a differi.g Sound, from the fame Pipe dry.

168.

That Sound made within Water, doth communicate better with a hard Body thorow Water, than made in Air, it doth with Air. *Vide Experimentum,* 134.

WE have fpoken before (in the Inquifition touching *Mufick*) of *Mufical Sounds*, whereunto there may be a Concord or Difcord in two Parts ; which *Sounds* we call *Tones*, and likewife of *Immufical Sounds* ; and have given the caufe, that the Tone proceedeth of Equality, and the other of Inequality. And we have alfo expreffed there, what are the Equal Bodies that give Tones, and what are the Unequal that give none. But now we fhall fpeak of fuch Inequality of Sounds, as proceedeth not from the Nature of the Bodies themfelves, but is accidental, Either from the Roughnefs or Obliquity of the Paffage, or from the Doubling of the Percutient, or from the Trepidation of the Motion.

169.

A Bell if it have a Rift in it, whereby the found hath not a clear paffage, giveth a hoarfe and jarring found ; fo the Voice of Man, when by cold taken, the Wefil groweth rugged, and (as we call it) furred, becometh hoarfe. And in thefe two inftances, the Sounds are ingrate, becaufe they are meerly unequal ; but if they be unequal in equality, then the Sound is Grateful, but Purling.

170.

All *Inftruments* that have either Returns, as Trumpets ; or Flexions, as Cornets; or are drawn up, and put from, as Sackbuts, have a Purling Sound ; But the Recorder or Flute that have none of thefe Inequalities, give a clear Sound. Neverthelefs, the Recorder itfelf or Pipe, moiftened a little in the infide, foundeth more folemnly, and with a little Purling or Hiffing. Again, a Wreathed String, fuch as are in the Bafe Strings of Bandoraes, giveth alfo a Purling Sound.

171.

Lut a Lute-ftring, if it be meerly unequal in his parts, giveth a harfh and untuneable Sound, which ftrings we call falfe, being bigger in one place, than in another ; and therefore Wire-ftrings are never falfe. We fee alfo, that when we try a falfe Lute-ftring, we ufe to extend it hard between the Fingers, and to fillip it ; and if it giveth a double fpecies, it is true ; but if it giveth a trebble or more, it is falfe.

172.

Waters, in the noife they make as they run, reprefent to the Ear a trembling noife ; and in Regals (where they have a Pipe, they call the *Nightingale-Pipe*, which containeth Water) the Sound hath a continual trembling. And Children have alfo little things they call Cocks, which have water in them ; and when they blow, or whiftle in them, they yield a trembling noife ; which Trembling of Water, hath an affinity with the Letter L. All which Inequalities of Trepidation, are rather pleafant, than otherwife.

173.

All Bafe Notes, or very Trebble Notes, give an Afper Sound ; for that the Bafe ftriketh more Air, than it can well ftrike equally ; and the Trebble cutteth the Air fo fharp, as it returneth too fwift, to make the Sound equal ; and therefore a Mean or Tenor is the fweeteft part.

174.

We know nothing, that can at pleafure make a *Mufical* or *Immufical Sound*, by voluntary Motion, but the Voice of Man and Birds. The caufe is (no doubt) in the Wefil or Wind-Pipe, (which we call *Afperia Arteria*,)

which

which being well extended, gathered equality; as a Bladder that is wrinckled, if it be extended, becometh smooth. The extension is always, more in Tones, than in Speech; therefore the inward voice or whisper, can never give a Tone. And in singing, there is (manifestly) a greater working and labor of the Throat, than in speaking; as appeareth in the thrusting out, or drawing in of the Chin, when we sing.

175.   The *Humming of Bees* is an unequal buzzing, and is conceived by some of the Ancients, not to come forth at their Mouth, but to be an inward Sound; but (it may be) it is neither, but from the motion of their Wings; for it is not heard, but when they stir.

176.   All Metals quenched in Water, give a sibillation or hissing sound (which hath an affinity with the Letter Z.) notwithstanding the Sound be created between the Water or Vapor, and the Air. Seething also, if there be but small store of Water in a Vessel, giveth a hissing sound; but boyling in a full Vessel, giveth a bubbling sound, drawing somewhat near to the Cocks used by Children.

177.   Tryal would be made, whether the *Inequality*, or interchange of the *Medium*, will not produce an Inequality of Sound; as if three Bells were made one within another, and Air betwixt each; and then the outermost Bell were chimed with a Hammer, how the Sound would differ from a simple Bell. So likewise take a Plate of Brass, and a Plank of Wood, and joyn them close together, and knock upon one of them, and see if they do not give an unequal Sound. So make two or three Partitions of Wood in a Hogshead, with holes or knots in them; and mark the difference of their sound, from the sound of an Hogshead, without such partitions.

178.   I T is evident, that the Percussion of the greater quantity of Air, causeth the baser Sound; and the less quantity, the more trebble Sound. The Percussion of the greater quantity of Air, is produced by the greatness of the Body percussing; by the Latitude of the Concave, by which the Sound passeth, and by the Longitude of the same Concave. Therefore we see, that a Base-string is greater than a Trebble; a Base-pipe hath a greater bore than a Trebble: And in Pipes, and the like, the lower the Note holes be, and the further off from the Mouth of the Pipe, the more Base sound they yield; and the nearer the Mouth, the more Trebble. Nay more, if you strike an entire Body, as an Andiron of Brass, at the top it maketh a more Trebble sound, and at the bottom a Baser.

Experiments in Consort, touching the more Trebble, and the more Base Tones or Musical Sounds.

179.   It is also evident, that the sharper or quicker Percussion of Air, causeth the more Trebble sound; and the slower or heavier, the more Base sound. So we see in Strings, the more they are wound up and strained (and thereby give a more quick start back) the more Trebble is the sound; and the slacker they are, or less wound up, the Baser is the sound. And therefore a bigger String more strained, and a lesser String less strained, may fall into the same Tone.

180.   *Children, Women, Eunuchs,* have more small and shrill Voices than Men. The reason is, not for that Men have greater heat, which may make the voice stronger, (for the strength of a Voice or Sound, doth make a difference in the loudness or softness, but not in the Tone) but from the dilatation of the Organ, which (it is true) is likewise caused by heat; but the cause of changing the voice at the years of puberty, is most obscure. It seemeth to be for that, when much of the moisture of the Body, which did before irregate

the

the Parts, is drawn down to the Spermatical Vessels, it leaveth the Body more hot than it was; whence cometh the dilatation of the Pipes: For we see plainly all effects of Heat do then come on; as Pilosity, more roughness of the skin, hardness of the flesh, &c.

181.   The industry of the *Musitian*, hath produced two other means of *Straining*, or *Intension of Strings*, besides their *Winding up*. The one is the *Stopping* of the *String* with the *Finger*; as in the Necks of Lutes, Viols, &c. The other is the *Shortness* of the *String*; as in Harps, Virginals, &c. Both these have one and the same reason, for they cause the *String* to give a quicker start.

182.   In the straining of a String, the further it is strained, the less superstraining goeth to a Note: For it requireth good winding of a String, before it will make any Note at all. And in the stops of Lutes, &c. the higher they go, the less distance is between the Frets.

183.   If you fill a *Drinking Glass* with Water, (especially one sharp below, and wide above) and fillip upon the Brim, or outside; and after, empty part of the Water, and so more and more, and still try the Tone by filliping; you shall finde the Tone fall, and be more Base as the Glass is more empty.

THe just and measured Proportion of the Air percussed, towards the Baseness or Trebbleness of Tones, is one of the greatest secrets in the Contemplation of Sounds. For it discovereth the true Coincidence of Tones into Diapasons, which is the return of the same Sound. And so of the Concords and Discords, between the Unison and Diapason; which we have touched before in the *Experiments of Musick*, but think fit to resume it here as a principal part of our Inquiry, touching the *Nature of Sounds*. It may be found out in the Proportion of the Winding of Strings, in the Proportion of the Distance of Frets, and in the Proportion of the Concave of Pipes, &c. But most commodiously in the last of these.

184.   Try therefore the Winding of a String once about, as soon as it is brought to that extension as will give a Tone, and then of twice about, and thrice about, &c. And mark the scale or difference of the Rice of the Tone, whereby you shall discover in one, two effects; both the proportion of the Sound towards the Dimension of the Winding, and the proportion likewise of the Sound towards the String, as it is more or less strained. But note that to measure this, the way will be to take the length in a right line of the String, upon any Winding about of the Peg.

185.   As for the Stops, you are to take the number of Frets, and principally the length of the Line, from the first stop of the String, unto such a stop as shall produce a *Diapason* to the former stop, upon the same String.

186.   But it will best (as it is said) appear in the *Bores of Wind-Instruments*; and therefore cause some half dozen Pipes to be made in length, and all things else a like, with a single double, and so one to a sextuple Bore; and so mark what fall of Tone every one giveth. But still in these three last instances you must diligently observe, what length of String, or distance of Stop, or concave of Air, maketh what rise of Sound. As in the last of these (which, as we said, is that which giveth the aptest demonstration) you must set down what increase of Concave goeth to the making of a Note higher, and what of two Notes, and what of three Notes, and so up to the Diapason: For then the great secret of Numbers and Proportions will appear. It is not

unlikely,

unlikely, that thofe that make Recorders, &c. know this already; for
that they make them in Sets. And likewife Bell-Founders in fitting the
tune of their Bells: So that enquiry may fave tryal. Surely, it hath been
obferved by one of the Ancients, that an empty Barrel knocked upon wi h
the finger, giveth a Diapafon to the Sound of the like Barrel full: But how
that fhould be, I do not well underftand, for that the knocking of a Barrel
full or empty, doth fcarce give any Tone.

    There is required fome fenfible difference in the Proportion of creat-
ing a Note towards the Sound it felf, which is the Paffive; and that it
be not too near, but at a diftance: For in a Recorder, the three upper-
moft holes yield one Tone, which is a Note lower than the Tone of the
firft three. And the like (no doubt) is required in the winding or ftopping
of Strings.   *187.*

THere is another difference of Sounds, which we will call *Exterior* and
Interior. It is not Soft nor Loud; nor it is not Bafe, nor Trebble; nor
t is not *Mufical*, nor *Immufical*. Though it be true, that there can be no
Tone in an *Interior Sound*; but on the other fide, in an *Exterior Sound*, there
may be both *Mufical* and *Immufical*. We fhall therefore enumerate them,
rather than precifely diftinguifh them; though to make fome adumbration
of (that we mean) the Interior, is rather an Impulfion or Contufion of
the Air, than an *Elyfion* or *Section* of the fame; fo as the Percuffion of the
one towards the other, differeth as a Blow differeth from a Cut.

    In Speech of Man, the Whifpering, (which they call *Sufurrus* in La-
tin,) whether it be louder or fofter, is an Interior Sound; but the Speaking out, is an Exterior Sound: And therefore you can never make a Tone,
nor fing in Whifpering; but in Speech you may. So Breathing, or Blowing by the Mouth, Bellows, or Wind (though loud) is an Interior Sound;
but the blowing thorow a Pipe, or Concave (though foft) is an Exterior.
So likewife, the greateft Winds, if they have no coarctation, or blow not
hollow, give any Interior Sound; the whiftling or hollow Wind, yieldeth
a finging, or Exterior Sound; the former being pent by fome other
Body, the latter being pent in by his own Denfity: And therefore we fee,
That when the Wind bloweth hollow, it is a fign of Rain; the flame, as it
moveth within it felf, or is blown by a Bellows, giveth a murmur or Interior
Sound.   *188.*

    There is no hard Body, but ftruck againft another hard Body, will yield
an Exterior Sound, greater or leffer; infomuch, as if the Percuffion be over-
foft, it may induce a nullity of found, but never an Interior Sound; as when
one treadeth fo foftly, that he is not heard.   *189.*

    Where the Air is the Percutient, pent or not pent, againft a hard Body,
it never giveth an Exterior Sound; as if you blow ftrongly with a Bellows
againft a Wall.   *190.*

    Sounds (both Exterior and Interior) may be made as well by Suction, as
by emiffion of the Breath; as in Whiftling, or Breathing.   *191.*

IT is evident, and it is one of the ftrangeft fecrets in Sounds; that the
whole Sound is not in the whole Air onely, but the whole Sound is
alfo in every fmall part of the Air. So that all the curious diverfity of Arti-
                                     culate

culate founds of the voice of Man or Birds, will enter into a fmall crany, inconfufed.

193.   The unequal agitation of the *Winds*, and the like, though they be material to the carriage of the Sounds, further or lefs way ; yet they do not confound the Articulation of them at all, within that diftance that they can be heard, though it may be, they make them to be heard lefs way, than in a ftill, as hath been partly touched.

194.   Over-great diftance confoundeth the Articulation of Sounds, as we fee, that you may hear the found of a Preachers voice, or the like, when you cannot diftinguifh what he faith. And one Articulate found will confound another, as when many fpeak at once.

195.   In the Experiment of fpeaking under VVater, when the voice is reduced to fuch an extream exhility, yet the Articulate founds (which are the words) are not confounded, as hath been faid.

196.   I conceive that an extream fmall, or an extream great found, cannot be Articulate, but that the Articulation requireth a mediocrity of found : For that the extream fmall found confoundeth the Articulation by contracting, and the great found by difperfing ; and although (as was formerly faid) a Sound Articulate, already created, will be contracted into a fmall crany ; yet the firft Articulation requireth more dimenfion.

197.   It hath been obferved, that in a Room, or in a Chappel, Vaulted below, and Vaulted likewife in the Roof, a Preacher cannot be heard fo well, as in the like places not fo Vaulted. The caufe is, for that the fubfequent words come on, before the precedent words vanifh ; and therefore the Articulate Sounds are more confufed, though the grofs of the Sound be greater.

198.   The motions of the *Tongue*, *Lips*, *Throat*, *Palate*, &c. which go to the making of the feveral *Alphabetical Letters* are worthy inquiry, and pertinent to the prefent Inquifition of Sounds : But becaufe they are fubtil and long to defcribe, we will refer them over, and place them amongft the *Experiments of Speech*. The *Hebrews* have been diligent in it, and have affigned which Letters are *Labial*, which *Dental*, which *Guttural*, &c. As for the *Latins* and *Grecians*, they have diftinguifhed between *Semi-vowels* and *Mutes* ; and in *Mutes*, between *Muta Tenues*, *Media* and *Afpirata*, not amifs, but yet not diligently enough. For the fpecial ftrokes and motions that create thofe Sounds, they have little enquired ; as that the Letters, B. P. F. M. are not expreffed, but with the contracting, or fhutting of the Mouth ; that the Letters N. and B. cannot be pronounced, but that the Letter N. will turn into M. as *Hecatonba* will be *Hecatomba*. That M. and T. cannot be pronounced together, but P. will come between ; as *Emtus*, is pronounced *Emptus*, and a number of the like : So that if you enquire to the full, you will finde, that to the making of the whole Alphabet, there will be fewer fimple Motions required, than there are Letters.

199.   The Lungs are the moft fpongy part of the Body, and therefore ableft to contract and dilate it felf ; and where it contracteth it felf, it expelleth the Air, which thorow the *Artire*, *Throat*, and *Mouth*, maketh the Voice : But yet *Articulation* is not made, but with the help of the *Tongue*, *Pallate*, and the reft of thofe they call *Inftruments of Voice*.

There

There is found a Similitude between the Sound that is made by *Inanimate Bodies*, or by *Animate Bodies*, that have no Voice Articulate, and divers Letters of Articulate Voices ; and commonly Men have given such names to those Sounds as do allude unto the Articulate Letters. As *Trembling of Water* hath resemblance with the Letter L. *Quenching of Hot Metals* with the Letter Z. *Snarling of Dogs* with the Letter R. The *Noise of Scritch-Owls* with the Letters Sh. *Voice of Cats* with the Dipthong Eu. *Voice of Chucko s* with the Dipthong Ou. *Sounds of Strings* with the Letters Ng. So that if a Man (for curiosity or strangeness sake) would make a Puppet, or other dead Body, to pronounce a word : Let him consider on the one part, the Motion of the *Instruments of Voice* ; and on the other part, the like Sounds made in *Inanimate Bodies* ; and what Conformity there is, that causeth the Similitude of *Sounds* ; and by that he may minister light to that effect.

TURAL STORY.

Century III.

L *Sounds* (whatsoever) move round, that is to say, On all sides, Upwards, Downwards, Forewards, and Backwards : This appeareth in all Instances.

Sounds do not require to be conveighed to the *Sense* in a right Line, as *Visibles* do, but may be archied, though it be true they move strongest in a right Line ; which neverthelels is not caused by the rightnels of the Line, but by the shortnels of the distance. *Linea recta brevissima* see if a Wall be between, and you speak on the one other ; which is not because the sound passeth thorow over the Wall.

topped and repercussed, it cometh about on the other : So, if in a Coach, one side of the Boot be down, and Begger beg on the close side, you would think that he . So likewise, if a Bell or Clock, be (for example) a Chamber, and the Window of that Chamber be that is in the Chamber, will think the sound came from

hey spred round, so that (there is an orb, or spherical t they move strongest, and go furthest in the Fore-Local Impulsion of the Air. And therefore in Preach-he Preachers voice better before the Pulpit than be-les, though it stand open. So a *Harquebuz* or *Ordnance* forwards, from the mouth of the Piece, than back-

ed, that Sounds do move better downwards, than up-aced high above the people : And when the *Ancient*

F   *Generals*

201.
Experiments in Consort, touching the Motions of Sounds, in what Lines they are Circular, Oblick, Straight, Vpwards, Downwards, Forwards, Backwards.

202.

203.

204.

205.

Generals spake to their Armies, they had ever a Mount of Turff caſt up, where upon they ſtood. But this may be imputed to the ſtops and obſtacles which the voice meeteth with, when one ſpeaketh upon the level. But there ſeemeth to be more in it ; for it may be, that Spiritual Species, both of things viſible, and Sounds, do move better downwards than upwards. It is a ſtrange thing, that to Men ſtanding below on the ground, thoſe that be on the top of *Pauls,* ſeem much leſs than they are, and cannot be known : But to Men above thoſe below, ſeem nothing ſo much leſſened, and may be known ; yet it is true, That all things to them above, ſeem alſo ſomewhat contracted and better collected into figure ; as Knots in Gardens ſhew beſt from an upper Window or Tarras.

206.　　But to make an exact tryal of it, let a Man ſtand in a Chamber, not much above the Ground, and ſpeak out at the Window thorow a Trunck, to one ſtanding on the Ground as ſoftly as he can, the other laying his Ear cloſe to the Trunck : Then *Via verſa,* let the other ſpeak below keeping the ſame proportion of ſoftneſs; and let him in the Chamber lay his Ear to the Trunck. And this may be the apteſt means to make a Judgment, whether Sounds deſcend or aſcend better.

207.
Experiments
in Conſort,
touching the
Laſting and
Periſhing of
Sounds ; and
touching the
time they re-
quire to the
*Generation or
Delation.*

AFter that *Sound* is created (which is in a moment) we finde it continueth ſome ſmall time, melting by little and little. In this there is a wonderful error amongſt Men, who take this to be a continuance of the firſt Sound ; whereas (in truth) it is a Renovation, and not a Continuance : For the Body percuſſed, hath by reaſon of the Percuſſion, a Tripidation wrought in the minute parts, and ſo reneweth the Percuſſion of the Air. This appeareth manifeſtly, becauſe that the Melting ſound of a Bell, or of a ſtring ſtrucken, which is thought to be a Continuance, ceaſeth as ſoon as the Bell or ſtring are touched. As in a Virginal, as ſoon as ever the Jack falleth, and toucheth the ſtring, the ſound ceaſeth ; and in a Bell, after you have chimed upon it, if you touch the Bell, the ſound ceaſeth. And in this you muſt diſtinguiſh, that there are two Trepidations, The one Manifeſt and Local ; as of the Bell, when it is Penſile ; the other Secret, of the Minute parts, ſuch as is deſcribed in the ninth Inſtance. But it is true, that the Local helpeth the Secret greatly. We ſee likewiſe, that in Pipes, and other Wind Inſtruments, the ſound laſteth no longer than the breath bloweth. It is true, that in Organs there is a confuſed murmur for a while, after you have played, but that is but while the Bellows are in falling.

208.　　It is certain, that in the noiſe of great Ordnance, where many are ſhot off together, the ſound will be carried (at the leaſt) twenty miles upon the Land, and much further upon the Water, but then it will come to the Ear ; not in the inſtant of the ſhooting off, but it will come an hour, or more later : This muſt needs be a Continuance of the firſt Sound ; for there is no Trepidation which ſhould renew it. And the touching of the Ordnance would not extinguiſh the ſound the ſooner : So that in great Sounds, the Continuance is more than Momentany.

209.　　To try exactly the time wherein Sound is delated, Let a Man ſtand in a Steeple, and have with him a Taper, and let ſome Veil be put before the Taper, and let another Man ſtand in the Field a mile off ; then let him in the Steeple ſtrike the Bell, and in the ſame inſtant withdraw the Veil, and ſo let him in the Field tell by his Pulſe, what diſtance of time there is between the Light ſeen, and the Sound heard : For it is certain, That the Delation of

Light

Light is in an inftant. This may be tried in far greater diftances, allowing greater Lights and Sounds.

It is generally known and obferved, that Light and the object of Sight, move fwifter than Sound ; for we fee the flafh of a piece is feen fooner, than the noife is heard. And in hewing Wood, if one fome diftance off, he fhall fee the Arm lifted up for a fecond ftroke, before he hear the noife of the firft ; and the greater the diftance, the greater is the prevention: As we fee in *Thunder*, which is far off, where the *Lightning* precedeth the crack a good fpace.

Colours, when they reprefent themfelves to the Eye, fade not nor melt not by degrees, but appear ftill in the fame ftrength ; but Sounds melt, and vanifh, by little and little. The caufe is, for that Colours participate nothing with the motion of the Air, but Sounds do. And it is a plain argument that Sound participateth of fome Local Motion of the Air, (as a caufe *Sine quâ non*) in that it perifheth fo fuddenly : For in every Section, or Impulfion of the Air, the Air doth fuddenly reftore and reunite it felf, which the Water alfo doth, but nothing fo fwiftly.

IN the Tryals of the Paffage, or not Paffage of Sounds, you muft take heed you miftake not the paffing by the fides of a Body, for the paffing thorow a Body; and therefore you muft make the Intercepting Body very clofe ; for Sound will pafs thorow a fmall chinck.

Where Sound paffeth thorow a hard, or clofe Body (as thorow Water, thorow a Wall, thorow Metal, as in Hawks Bells ftopped, &c.) the hard or clofe Body, muft be but thin and fmall ; for elfe it deadeth and extinguifheth the Sound utterly. And therefore, in the Experiment of Speaking in Air under Water, the voice muft not be very deep within the Water, for then the Sound pierceth not. So if you fpeak on the further fide of a clofe Wall, if the Wall be very thick, you fhall not be heard ; and if there were an Hogshead empty, whereof the fides were fome two foot thick, and the Bunghole ftopped. I conceive, the refounding found by the Communication of the outward Air with the Air within, would be little or none, but onely you fhall hear the noife of the outward knock, as if the Veffel were full.

It is certain, that in the paffage of Sounds thorow hard Bodies, the Spirit or Pneumatical part of the hard Body it felf doth co-operate ; but much better, when the fides of that hard Body are ftruck, than when the percuffion is onely within, without touch of the fides. Take therefore a *Hawks-Bell*, the holes ftopped up, and hang it by a thred within a Bottle-Glafs, and ftop the Mouth of the Glafs very clofe with Wax, and then fhake the Glafs, and fee whether the Bell give any found at all, or how weak? But note, that you muft inftead of Thred take a Wire, or elfe let the Glafs have a great Belly, left when you fhake the Bell, it dafh upon the fides of the Glafs.

It is plain that a very long and down right arch for the Sound to pafs, will extinguifh the Sound quite, fo that that Sound, which would be heard over a Wall, will not be heard over a Church ; nor that Sound, which will be heard, if you ftand fome diftance from the VVall, will be heard if you ftand clofe under the VVall.

So tan d Foraminous Bodies in the firft creation of the Sound, will dead it ; for the ftriking againft Cloth or Fur, will make little found, as hath been faid : But in the paffage of the found, they will admit it better than harder Bodies, as we fee, that Curtains and Hangings will not ftay the found much ; but Glafs windows, if they be very clofe, will check a found more, than the like thicknefs of Cloth. VVe fee alfo in the rumbling of the Belly, how eafily the Sound paffeth thorow the Guts and Skin.

210.

211.

Experiments in Confort, touching the Paffage and Interception of Sounds.
212.

213.

214.

215.

F 2

It

216. It is worthy the inquiry, whether great Sounds (as of Ordnance or Bells) become not more Weak and Exile, when they pass thorow small Cranies. For the Subtilties of Articulate Sounds, (it may be) may pass thorow small Cranies, not confused ; but the magnitude of the Sound (perhaps) not so well.

217.
Experiments in Consort, touching the Medium of Sounds.
THe *Mediums* of Sounds, are Air, soft and porous Bodies ; also Water, and hard Bodies refuse not altogether to be *Mediums of Sounds*. But all of them are dull and unapt differents, except the Air.

218 In Air, the thinner or drier Air, carrieth not the Sound so well, as the more dense ; as appeareth in Night Sounds, and Evening Sounds, and Sounds in moist Weather, and Southern Winds. The reason is already mentioned in the Title of *Majoration of Sounds* ; being, for that thin Air is better pierced, but thick Air preserveth the Sound better from waste : Let further Tryal be made by hollowing in Mists, and gentle Showers ; for (it may be) that will somewhat dead the Sound.

219. How far forth Flame may be a *Medium of Sounds*, (especially of such Sounds as are created by Air, and not betwixt hard Bodies) let it be tried in speaking, where a Bonefire is between ; but then you must allow for some disturbance, the noise that the Flame it self maketh.

220. Whether any other Liquors being made *Mediums*, cause a diversity of Sound from Water, it may be tryed : As by the knapping of the Tongs, or striking the bottom of a Vessel filled either with Milk or with Oyl ; which though they be more light, yet are they more unequal Bodies than Air.

Of the Natures *of the* Mediums, *we have now spoken* ; *as for the* Disposition *of the said* Mediums, *it doth consist in the Penning, or not Penning of the* Air ; *of which, we have spoken before in the Title of* Delation of Sounds. *It consisteth also in the* Figure *of the* Concave, *through which it passeth. Of which, we will speak next.*

Experiments in Consort, what the Figures of the Pipes or Concaves, or the Bodies differents, conduce to the Sounds.
HOw the *Figures of Pipes* or *Concaves*, through which *Sounds* pass , or of other *Bodies* different ; conduce to the variety and alteration of the *Sounds*, either in respect of the greater quantity , or less quantity of Air, which the *Concaves* receive ; or in respect of the carrying of Sounds longer or shorter way ; or in respect of many other Circumstances, they have been touched, as falling into other Titles. But those *Figures* which we now are to speak of, we intend to be, as they concern the Lines, through which Sound passeth : As *Straight, Crooked, Angular, Circular, &c.*

221. The Figure of a Bell partaketh of the *Pyramis*, but yet coming off, and dilating more suddenly. The *Figure of a Hunters Horn*, and *Cornet*, is oblick, yet they have likewise straight Horns : which if they be of the same bore with the oblick, differ little in Sound, save that the straight require somewhat a stronger blast. The *Figure of Recorders*, and *Flutes*, and *Pipes*, are straight ; but the *Recorder* hath a less bore, and a greater, above and below. The *Trumpet* hath the *Figure* of the *Letter S*. which maketh that Purling Sound. &c. Generally, the straight Line hath the cleanest and roundest Sound, and the crooked the more Hoarse, and Jarring.

222. Of a Sinuous Pipe that may have some four Flexions, tryal would be made. Likewise of a Pipe made like a Cross, open in the midst ; and so
likewise

likewife of an *Angular Pipe* ; and fee what will be the effect of thefe feveral Sounds. And fo again of a *Circular Pipe* : As if you take a Pipe perfect round, and make a hole whereinto you fhall blow, and another hole not far from that ; but with a traverfe or ftop between them : So that your breath may go the Round of the Circle, and come forth at the fecond hole. You may try likewife Percuffions of folid Bodies of feveral Figures : As *Globes, Flats, Cubes, Croffes, Triangles, &c.* And their Combinations ; as *Flat* againft *Flat*, and *Convex* againft *Convex*, and *Convex* againft *Flat, &c.* And mark well the diverfities of the Sounds. Try alfo the difference in found of feveral Craffitudes of hard Bodies percuffed, and take knowledge of the diverfities of the founds. I my felf have tried, That a *Bell of Gold* yieldeth an excellent found, not inferior to that of *Silver* or *Brafs*, but rather better. Yet we fee that a piece of money of *Gold*, foundeth far more flat than a piece of money of *Silver*.

223. The Harp hath the concave, not along the ftrings, but acrofs the ftrings ; and no *Inftrument* hath the found fo melting and prolonged, as the *Irifh Harp*. So as I fuppofe, that if a *Virginal* were made with a double Concave ; the one all the length as the *Virginal* hath, the other at the end of the *ftrings*, as the *Harp* hath : it muft needs make the found perfecter, and not fo fhallow, and jarring. You may try it without any Sound-board along, but onely Harp wife, at one end of the ftrings ; or laftly, with a double concave, at each end of the ftrings one.

224. THere is an apparent diverfity between the *Species Vifible* and *Audible*, in this. That the *Vifible* doth not mingle in the *Medium*, but the *Audible* doth. For if we look abroad, we fee Heaven, a number of Stars, Trees, Hills, Men, Beafts, at once ; and the Species of the one, doth not confound the other : But if fo many Sounds come from feveral parts, one of them would utterly confound the other. So we fee, That Voices or Conforts of *Mufick* do make a harmony by mixture, which Colours do not. It is true neverthelefs, that a great light drowneth a fmaller, that it cannot be feen ; as the Sun that of a Gloworm, as well as a great found drowneth a leffer. And I fuppofe likewife, that if there were two Lanthorns of Glafs, the one a Crimfin, and the other an Azure, and a Candle within either of them, thofe coloured lights, would mingle and caft upon a White Paper, a Purple colour. And even in colours, they yield a faint and weak mixture ; for White Walls make rooms more lightfome, than Black, &c. But the caufe of the Confufion in Sounds, and the Inconfufion in Species Vifible, is, For that the Sight worketh in right Lines, and maketh feveral Cones ; and fo there can be no Coincidence in the Eye, or Vifual Point : But Sounds that move in oblick and arcuate Lines, muft needs encounter, and difturb the one the other.

Experiments in Confort, touching the *Mixture of Sounds*.

225. The fweeteft and beft Harmony is, when every Part or Inftrument is not heard by it felf, but a conflation of them all, which requireth to ftand fome diftance off. Even as it is in the mixture of perfumes, or the taking of the fmells of feveral Flowers in the Air.

226. The difpofition of the Air, in other qualities, except it be joyned with Sound, hath no great operation upon Sounds : For whether the Air be lightfome or dark, hot or cold, quiet or ftirring, (except it be with noife) fweet fmelling, or ftinking, or the like ; it importeth not much. Some petty alteration or difference it may make.

227. But Sounds do difturb and alter the one the other: Sometimes the one drowning the other, and making it not heard; fometimes the one jarting and difcording with the other, and making a confufion: fometimes the one mingling and compounding with the other, and making an harmony.

228. Two Voices of like loudnefs, will not be heard twice as far, as one of them alone; and two Candles of like light, will not make things feem twice as far off, as one. The caufe is profound, but it feemeth, that the Impreffions from the objects of the Senfes, do mingle refpectively, every one with his kinde; but not in proportion, as is before demonftrated: And the reafon may be, becaufe the firft impreffion, which is from Privative to Active, (as from Silence to Noife, or from Darknefs to Light,) is a greater degree, than from lefs noife, to more noife, or from lefs light, to more light. And the reafon of that again may be, For that the Air, after it hath received a charge, doth not receive a furcharge, or greater charge, with like appetite, as it doth the firft charge. As for the increafe of Vertue generally, what proportion it beareth to the increafe of the Matter, it is a large Field, and to be handled by it felf.

229.
Experiments in Confort, touching Meloration of Sounds.

 ALL Reflexions Concurrent, do make Sounds greater; but if the Body that createth, either the original Sound, or the Reflexion, be clean and fmooth, it maketh them fweeter. Tryal may be made of a *Lute* or *Vial*, with the Belly of polifhed Brafs inftead of Wood. We fee, that even in the open Air, the *Wire-ftring* is fweeter than the *ftring of Guts*. And we fee, that for *Reflexion*, *Water* excelleth; as in *Mufick* near the Water, or in *Eccho's*.

230. It hath been tryed, that a *Pipe*, a little moiftned on the infide, but yet fo as there be no drops left, maketh a more folemn found, than if the Pipe were dry; but yet with a fweet degree of *Sibilation* or *Purling*, as we touched it before in the Title of *Equality*. The caufe is, for that all things porous, being fuperficially wet, and (as it were) between dry and wet, become a little more even and fmooth; but the Purling (which muft needs proceed of Inequality) I take to be bred between the fmoothnefs of the inward Surface of the Pipe which is wet, and the reft of the Wood of the Pipe, unto which the wet cometh not, but it remaineth dry.

231. In Frofty weather, *Mufick* within doors foundeth better; which may be, by reafon not of the difpofition of the Air, but of the Wood or String of the Inftrument, which is made more crifp, and fo more porous and hollow; and we fee that *Old Lutes* found better than *New*, for the fame reafon: And fo do *Lute-ftrings* that have been kept long.

232. Sound is likewife meliorated by the mingling of open Air with pent Air: Therefore tryal may be made of a *Lute* or *Vial* with a double Belly, making another Belly with a knot over the ftring; yet fo, as there be room enough for the ftrings, and room enough to play below that Belly. Tryal may be alfo made of an *Irifh Harp*, with a concave on both fides, whereas it ufeth to have it but on one fide. The doubt may be, left it fhould make too much refounding, whereby one Note would overtake another.

233. If you fing in the hole of a *Drum*, it maketh the finging more fweet. And fo I conceive it would, if it were a Song in Parts fung into feveral *Drums*; and for handfomnefs and ftrangenefs fake, it would not be amifs to have a Curtain between the place where the *Drums* are, and the hearers.

234. When a found is created in the *Wind-Inftrument*, between the Breath and Air, yet if the found be communicate with a more equal Body of the Pipe,

it meliorateth the found. For (no dobut) there would be a differing found in a Trumpet or Pipe of Wood, and again, in a Trumpet or Pipe of Brass, It were good to try *Recorders* and *Hunters Horns* of *Brass*, what the found would be.

Sounds are meliorated by the Intension of the Sense, where the common Sense is collected most to the particular Sense of Hearing, and the Sight suspended: And therefore Sounds are sweeter, as well as greater, in the Night than in the Day ; and I suppose, they are sweeter to blinde men, than to others : And it is manifest, that between sleeping and waking, (when all the Senses are bound and suspended) *Musick* is far sweeter than when one is fully waking.   235

IT is a thing strange in Nature, when it is attentively considered, How Children and some Birds learn to imitate Speech. They take no mark at all of the Motion of the Mouth of him that speaketh, for Birds are as well taught in the dark, as by light. The sounds of Speech are very curious and exquisite ; so one would think it were a Lesson hard to learn. It is true, that it is done with time, and by little and little, and with many essays and proffers : But all this dischargeth not the wonder. It would make a Man think (though this, which we shall say, may seem exceeding strange) that there is some transmission of Spirits , and that the Spirit of the Teacher put in motion, should work with the Spirits of the Learner, a predisposition to offer to imitate, and so to perfect the imitation by degrees. But touching Operations by Transmissions of Spirits (which is one of the highest secrets in Nature) we shall speak in due place, chiefly when we come to inquire of Imagination. But as for Imitation, it is certain, That there is in Men, and other Creatures, a predisposition to imitate. We see how ready Apes and Monkies are to imitate all motions of Man : And in the catching of Dottrels, we see how the foolish Bird playeth the Ape in gestures : And no Man (in effect) doth accompany with others , but he learneth (ere he is aware) some Gesture, or Voice, or Fashion of the other.   236. Experiments in Consort, touching the *Imitation of Sounds*.

In Imitation of *Sounds*, that Man should be the Teacher, is no part of the matter : For Birds will learn one of another, and there is no reward by feeding, or the like, given them for the imitation : And besides, you shall have Parrets that will not onely imitate Voices, but Laughing, Knocking, Squeaking of a Door upon the Hinges, or of a Cart-wheel, and (in effect) any other noise they hear.   237.

No Beast can imitate the Speech of Man, but Birds onely : For the Ape it self, that is so ready to imitate otherwise, attaineth not any degree of imitation of Speech. It is true, that I have known a Dog, that if one howled in his ear, he would fall a howling a great while. What should be the aptness of Birds, in comparison of Beasts, to imitate the Speech of Man, may be further inquired. We see that Beasts have those parts, which they count the *Instruments of Speech*, (as *Lips*, *Teeth*, &c.) liker unto Man than Birds. As for the *Neck*, by which the *Throat* passeth , we see many Beasts have it for the length, as much as Birds. What better gorge or attire Birds have, may be further inquired. The Birds that are known to be speakers, are *Parrets*, *Pyes*, *Jays*, *Daws*, and *Ravens* : Of which, *Parrets* have an adunck Bill, but the rest not.   238.

But I conceive, that the aptness of Birds is not so much in the conformity of the Organs of Speech, as in their Attention. For Speech must come by Hearing and Learning ; and Birds give more heed, and mark Sounds more   239.

more than Beasts ; because naturally they are more delighted with them, and practise them more, as appeareth in their Singing. We see also, that those that teach Birds to sing, do keep them waking, to increase their attention. We see also, that Cock-Birds, amongst Singing-Birds, are ever the better singers, which may be, because they are more lively, and listen more.

240.   *Labor* and *Intention* to imitate *Voices*, doth conduce much to *Imitation* : And therefore we see, that there be certain *Pantomimi*, that will represent the Voices of *Players* of *Interludes*, so to life, as if you see them not, you would think they were those *Players* themselves, and so the Voices of other men that they hear.

241.   There have been some that could counterfeit the distance of Voices, (which is a secondary object of Hearing) in such sort ; as when they stand fast by you, you would think the Speech came from afar off, in a fearful manner. How this is done, may be further enquired ; but I see no great use of it, but for Imposture, in counterfeiting ghosts or spirits.

THere be three kindes of *Reflexions of Sounds* ; a *Reflexion Concurrent*, a *Reflexion Iterant*, which we call *Eccho*, and a *Super-reflexion*, or an *Eccho* of an *Eccho*, whereof the first hath been handled in the Title of *Magnitude of Sounds*. The latter two we will now speak of.

242.   The *Reflexion of Species Visible* by *Mirrors*, you may command, because passing it Right Lines, they may be guided to any point : But the *Reflexion of Sounds*, is hard to master ; because the sound filling great spaces in arched Lines, cannot be so guided. And therefore, we see there hath not been practised any means to make Artificial Eccho's. And no Eccho already known, returneth in a very narrow room.

243.   The Natural Eccho's are made upon Walls, Woods, Rocks, Hills, and Banks : As for Waters being near, they make a Concurrent Eccho ; but being further off, (as upon a large River) they make an Interant Eccho : For there is no difference between the Concurrent Eccho, and the Iterant, but the quickness or slowness of the return. But there is no doubt, but Water doth help the Delation of Eccho, as well as it helpeth the Delation of Original Sounds.

244.   It is certain (as hath been formerly touched,) that if you speak thorow a Trunck, stopped at the further end, you shall finde a blast return upon your mouth, but no sound at all. The cause is, for that the closeness, which preserveth the original, is not able to preserve the reflected sound ; besides that, Eccho's are seldom created, but by loud Sounds. And therefore there is less hope of Artificial Eccho's in Air, pent in a narrow concave. Nevertheless it hath been tryed, that one leaning over a Well of Twenty five fathom deep, and speaking, though but softly, (yet not so soft as a whisper) the Water returned a good audible Eccho. It would be tryed, whether speaking in Caves, where there is no issue, save where you speak, will not yield Eccho's as Wells do.

245.   The Eccho cometh as the Original Sound doth in a round orb of Air : It were good to try the creating of the Eccho, where the Body repercussing maketh an Angle : As against the Return of a Wall, &c. Also we see that in *Mirrors*, there is the like Angle of Incidence, from the Object to the Glass, and from the Glass to the Eye. And if you strike a Ball side-long, not full upon the Surface, the rebound will be as much the contrary way ; whether

ther there be any such refilience in Eccho's (that is; Whether a Man shall hear better, if he stand aside the Body repercussing, than if he stand where he speaketh, or any where in a right Line between) may be tried; Tryal likewife would be made, by standing nearer the place of repercussing, than he that speaketh; and again, by standing further off, than he that speaketh, and fo knowledge would be taken, whether Eccho's, as well as Original Sounds, be not strongest near hand.

There be many places, where you shall hear a number of Eccho's one after another; and it is, when there is variety of *Hills* or *Woods*, fome nearer, fome further off: So that the return from the further, being last created, will be likewife last heard.   246.

As the Voice goeth round, as well towards the back, as towards the front of him that speaketh; fo likewife doth the Eccho, for you have many Back-eccho's to the place where you stand.   247.

To make an Eccho that will report three, or four, or five words dinstinctly, it is requisite, that the Body repercussing be a good distance off: For if it be near, and yet not fo near, as to make a Concurrent Eccho, it choppeth with you upon the fudden. It is requisite likewife, that the Air be not much pent: For Air, at great distance, pent, worketh the fame effect with Air at large, in a fmall distance. And therefore in the Tryal of Speaking in the Well, though the Well was deep, the Voice came back suddenly, and would bear the report but of two words.   248.

From Eccho's upon Eccho's, there is a rare instance thereof in a place, which I will now exactly defcribe. It is fome Three or four Miles from *Paris*, near a Town called *Pont-Carenton*; and fome Bird-bolt shot or more from the River of *Sean*. The Room is a Chappel, or fmall Church; the Walls all standing, both at the fides, and at the ends; two rows of Pillars after the manner of Ifles of Churches, also standing; the Roof all open, not fo much as any Embowment near any of the Walls left. There was against every Pillar, a stack of Billers above a Mans height, which the Watermen, that bring Wood down the *Sean*, in Stacks, and not in Boats, laid there (as it feemeth) for their eafe. Speaking at the one end, I did hear it return the Voice Thirteen feveral times; and I have heard of others, that it would return Sixteen times; for I was there about three of the Clock in the Afternoon; and it is best, (as all other Eccho's are) in the Evening. It is manifest, that it is not Eccho's from feveral places, but a tossing of the Voice, as a Ball too and fro; like to Reflexions in Looking-Glasses; where if you place one Glafs before, and another behinde, you shall fee the Glafs behinde with the Image, within the Glafs before; and again, the Glafs before in that: And divers fuch Super-Reflexions, till the *Species speciei* at last die: For it is every return weaker, and more shady. In like manner, the Voice in that Chappel, createth *Speciem speciei*, and maketh fucceeding Super-Reflexions; for it melteth by degrees, and every Reflexion is weaker than the former: So that, if you fpeak three words, it will (perhaps) fome three times report you the whole three words; and then the two latter words for fometimes, and then the last word alone for fometimes, still fading and growing weaker. And whereas in Eccho's of one return, it is much to hear Four or five words. In this Eccho of fo many Returns, upon the matter, you hear above Twenty words for three.   249.

The

250. The like Eccho upon Eccho, but onely with two reports, hath been obferved to be, if you ftand between a Houfe and a Hill, and lure towards the Hill ; for the Houfe will give a Back Eccho : One taking it from the other, and the latter the weaker.

251. There are certain *Letters*, that an Eccho will hardly exprefs : As S for one, efpecially being principal in a word. I remember well, that when I went to the Eccho at *Pont-Carenton*, there was an old *Parifian* that took it to be the Work of Spirits, and of good Spirits. For (faid he) call *Satan*, and the Eccho will not deliver back the *Devils* name : But will fay, *Vat'en*, which is as much in *French*, as *Apage*, or *Avoid*. And thereby I did hap to finde, that an Eccho would not return S, being but a Hiffing and an Interior Sound.

252. Eccho's are fome more fudden, and chap again as foon as the Voice is delivered, as hath been partly faid ; others are more deliberate, that is, give more fpace between the Voice and the Eccho, which is caufed by the Local nearnefs or diftance : Some will report a longer train of words, and fome a fhorter : Some more loud (full as loud as the Original, and fometimes more loud) and fome weaker and fainter.

253. Where Eccho's come from feveral parts, at the fame diftance they muft needs make (as it were) a Quire of Eccho's, and fo make the Report greater, and even a continued Eccho ; which you fhall finde in fome Hills that ftand encompaffed, Theatre-like.

254. It doth not yet appear, that there is *Refraction in Sounds*, as well as in *Species Vifible*. For I do not think, that if a Sound fhould pafs through divers *Mediums*, as *Air, Cloth, Wood*, it would deliver the Sound in a differing place, from that unto which it is deferred ; which is the proper effect of Refraction. But *Majoration*, which is alfo the Work of *Refraction*, appeareth plainly in Sounds, (as hath been handled at full) but it is not by diverfity of *Mediums.*

Experiments in Confort, touching the Confent and Diffent between *Vifibles* and *Audibles.*

WE have *Obiter*, for Demonftrations fake, ufed in divers *Inftances*, the *Examples* of the *Sight*, and *Things Vifible*, to illuftrate the *Nature of Sounds*. But we think good now to profecute that Comparifon more fully.

Confent of Vifibles and Audibles.

255. **B**Oth of them fpred themfelves in Round, and fill a whole Flore or Orb unto certain Limits ; and are carried a great way, and do languifh and leffen by degrees, according to the Diftance of the Objects from the Senfories.

256. Both of them have the whole Species in every fmall portion of the *Air* or *Medium*, fo as the Species do pafs through fmall Cranies, without confufion : As we fee ordinarily in Levels, as to the Eye ; and in Cranies, or Chinks, as to the Sound.

257. Both of them are of a fudden and eafie Generation and Delation, and likewife perifh fwiftly and fuddenly ; as if you remove the Light, or touch the Bodies that give the Sound.

Both

Both of them do receive and carry exquifite, and accurate differences; as of Colours, Figures, Motions, Diftances, in *Vifibles*; and of Articulate Voices, Tones, Songs, and Quaverings, in *Audibles*. 258

Both of them in their Vertue and Working, do not appear to emit any Corporal Subftance into their *Mediums*, or the Orb of their Vertue; neither again to rife or ftir any evident Local Motion in their *Mediums* as they pals, but onely to carry certain Spiritual Species. The perfect knowledge of the caufe whereof, being hitherto fcarcely attained, we fhall fearch and handle in due place. 259.

Both of them feem not to generate or produce any other effect in Nature, but fuch as appertaineth to their proper Objects and Senfes, and are otherwife barren. 260.

But both of them in their own proper action, do work three manifeft effects. The firft, in that the ftronger pieces drowneth the leffer: As the light of the Sun, the light of a Gloworm, the report of an Ordnance, the Voice. The fecond, in that an Object of furcharge or excefs, deftroyeth the Senfe: As the light of the Sun the eye, a violent found (near the Ear) the Hearing. The third, in that both of them will be reverberate: As in Mirrors, and in Eccho's. 261.

Neither of them doth deftroy or hinder the Species of the other, although they encounter in the fame *Medium*: As Light or Colour hinder not found, nor *è contrà*. 262.

Both of them affect the Senfe in Living Creatures, and yield Objects of Pleafure and Diflike; yet neverthelefs, the Objects of them do alfo (if it be well obferved) affect and work upon dead things; namely fuch, as have fome conformity with the Organs of the two Senfes: As *Vifibles* work upon a *Looking-glafs*, which is like the Pupil of the Eye; and *Audibles* upon the places of *Eccho*, which refemble, in fome fort, the cavern and ftructure of the Ear. 263.

Both of them do diverfly work, as they have their *Medium* diverfly difpofed. So a *Trembling Medium* (as fmoak) maketh the object feem to tremble; and *Rifing* or *Falling Medium* (as Winds) maketh the Sounds to rife or fall. 264.

To both, the *Medium*, which is the moft propitious and conducible, is Air; For Glafs or Water, &c. are not compairable. 265.

In both of them, where the object is fine and accurate, it conduceth much to have the Senfe intentive, and erect; infomuch, as you contract your eye, when you would fee fharply, and erect your ear, when you would hear attentively; which in Beafts that have ears moveable, is moft manifeft. 266.

The Beams of Light, when they are multiplied and conglomerate, generate heat; which is a different action, from the action of Sight: And the Multiplication and Conglomeration of Sounds, doth generate an extream Rarefaction of the Air; which is an action materiate, differing from the action of Sound. If it be true (which is anciently reported) that Birds, with great fhouts, have faln down. 267.

Diffent

Diſſent of Viſibles and Audibles.

268.   THe *Species of Viſibles,* ſeem to be *Emiſſion's of Beams* from the *Object* ſeen, almoſt like Odors, ſave that they are more incorporeal; but the *Species of Audibles,* ſeem to participate more with *Local Motion,* like *Percuſſions* or *Impreſſions* made upon the *Air.* So that whereas all Bodies do ſeem to work in two manners, Either by the *Communication* of their *Natures,* or by the *Impreſſions* and *Signatures* of their *Motions.* The Diffuſion of *Species Viſible,* ſeemeth to participate more of the former *Operation,* and the *Species Audible* of the latter.

269.   The Species of Audibles ſeem to be carried more manifeſtly thorow the Air, than the Species of Viſibles: For (I conceive) that a contrary ſtrong Wind will not much hinder the ſight of Viſibles, as it will do the hearing of Sounds.

270.   There is one difference above all others, between Viſibles and Audibles, that is the moſt remarkable; as that whereupon many ſmaller differences do depend; Namely, that Viſibles (except Lights) are carried in Right Lines, and Audibles in Arcuate Lines. Hence it cometh to paſs, that Viſibles do not intermingle and confound one another, as hath been ſaid before, but Sounds do. Hence it cometh, that the ſolidity of Bodies doth not much hinder the ſight, ſo that the Bodies be clear, and the Pores in a Right Line, as in Glaſs, Cryſtal, Diamonds, Water, &c. But a thin Scarf or Handkerchief, though they be Bodies nothing ſo ſolid, hinder the ſight: Whereas (contrariwiſe) theſe Porous Bodies, do not much hinder the Hearing, but ſolid Bodies do almoſt ſtop it, or at leaſt attenuate it: Hence alſo it cometh, that to the Reflexion of Viſibles, ſmall Glaſſes ſuffice, but to the Reverberation of Audibles, are required greater ſpaces, as hath likewiſe been ſaid before.

271.   Viſibles are ſeen further off, than Sounds are heard; allowing neverthelefs the rate of their bigneſs: For otherwiſe, a great Sound will be heard further off, than a ſmall Body ſeen.

272.   Viſibles require (generally) ſome diſtance between the object, and the Eye to be better ſeen; whereas in Audibles, the nearer the approach of the Sound is to the Senſe the better; but in this, there may be a double error. The one, becauſe to Seeing there is required Light, and any thing that toucheth the Pupil of the Eye (all over) excludeth the Light. For I have heard of a perſon very credible, (who himſelf was cured of a Cataract in one of his Eyes) that while the Silver-needle did work upon the ſight of his Eye, to remove the Film of the Cataract, he never ſaw any thing more clear or perfect, than that white Needle: Which (no doubt) was, becauſe the Needle was leſſer than the Pupil of the Eye, and ſo took not the light from it. The other error may be, For that the object of Sight doth ſtrike upon the Pupil of the Eye, directly without any interception; whereas the Cave of the Ear doth hold off the Sound a little from the Organ: And ſo neverthelefs there is ſome diſtance required in both.

273.   Viſibles are ſwifter carried to the Senſe, than Audibles; as appeareth in Thunder and Lightning; Flame, and Report of a Piece; Motion of the Air, in hewing of Wood. All which have been ſet down heretofore, but are proper for this Title.

I con-

I conceive alſo, that the *Species of Audibles*, do hang longer in the Air than thoſe of *Viſibles :* For although even thoſe of Viſibles do hang ſome time, as we ſee in *Rings* turned, that ſhew like ſpheres. In *Lute-ſtrings* fillipped, a *Fire-brand* carried a long, which leaveth a train of light behinde it, and in the Twilight, and the like : Yet I conceive that *Sounds*, ſtay longer becauſe they are carried up and down with the Wind ; and becauſe of the diſtance of the time in *Ordnance* diſcharged, and heard twenty miles off   274.

In *Viſibles* there are not found Objects ſo odious and ingrate to the *Senſe*, as in *Audibles*. For foul *Sights* do rather diſpleaſe, in that they excite the memory of foul things, than in the immediate Objects. And therefore in *Pictures*, thoſe foul Sights do not much offend ; but in *Audibles*, the grating of a Saw when it is ſharpned, doth offend ſo much, as it ſetteth the Teeth on edge ; and any of the harſh *Diſcords in Muſicks*, the Ear doth ſtraightways refuſe.   275.

In *Viſibles*, after great light, if you come ſuddenly into the dark, or contrariwiſe out of the dark into a glaring Light. The eye is dazled for a time, and the *Sight* confuſed ; but whether any ſuch effect be after great *Sounds*, or after a deeper ſilence may be better enquired. It is an old Tradition, that thoſe that dwell near the Cataracts of *Nilus*, are ſtrucken deaf : But we finde no ſuch effect in Cannoniers, nor Millers, nor thoſe that dwell upon Bridges.   276.

It ſeemeth, that the *Impreſſion of Colour* is ſo weak, as it worketh not, but by a Cone of direct Beams, or right Lines, whereof the Baſis is in the Object and the Vertical point in the Eye : So as there is a corradiation and conjunction of Beams ; and thoſe Beams ſo ſent forth, yet are not of any force to beget the like borrowed or ſecond Beams, except it be by *Reflexion*, whereof we ſpeak not. For the Beams paſs and give little tincture to that Air which is adjacent ; which if they did, we ſhould ſee Colours out of a right line. But as this in Colours, ſo otherwiſe it is in the *Body of Light.* For when there is a skreen between the Candle and the Eye, yet the light paſſeth to the Paper whereon one writeth, ſo that the light is ſeen where the body of the flame is not ſeen ; and where any Colour (if it were placed where the body of the flame is) would not be ſeen. I judge that *Sound* is of this latter nature : For when two are placed on both ſides of a Wall, and the voice is heard, I judge it is not onely the *original ſound*, which paſſeth in an *Arched line* ; but the *ſound*, which paſſeth above the Wall in a *Right line*, begetteth the like Motion round about it, as the firſt did, though more weak.   277.

ALl *Concords and Diſcords of Muſick* (no doubt) *Sympathies* and *Antipathies of Sounds*, and ſo (likewiſe) in that *Muſick*, which we call *Broken Muſick*, or *Conſort Muſick* ; ſome *Conſorts of Inſtruments* are ſweeter than others, (a thing not ſufficiently yet obſerved ;) as the *Iriſh-Harp* and *Baſe-Vial* agree well ; the *Recorder* and *Stringed Muſick* agree well ; *Organs* and the *Voice* agree well, &c. But the *Virginals* and the *Lute*, or the *Welſh-Harp* and *Iriſh-Harp*, or the *Voice* and *Pipes* alone, agree not ſo well ; but for the *Melioration* of *Muſick*, there is yet much left (in this Point of *Exquiſite Conſorts*) to try and enquire.

278.
Experiments in Conſort, touching the *Sympathy* or *Antipathy* of *Sounds*, one with another.

There is a common obſervation, That if a *Lute* or *Vial* be laid upon the back with a ſmall ſtraw upon one ſide of the *ſtrings*, and another *Lute* or *Vial* be laid by it ; and in the other *Lute* or *Vial* the *Vniſon* to that *ſtring* be ſtrucken, it will make the *ſtring* move ; which will appear both to the Eye, and by the ſtraws falling off. The like will be if the *Diapaſon* or *Eight* to that *ſtring* be ſtrucken, either in the ſame *Lute* or *Vial*, or in others lying by : But in none of theſe there is any report of Sound that can be diſcerned, but onely Motion.   279.

　It

230

It was deviſed, That a Vial ſhould have a Lay of Wire-ſtrings below, as cloſe to the Belly as a *Lute*, and then the Strings of Guts mounted upon a Bridge, as in ordinary *Vials* ; to the end, that by this means, the upper Strings ſtrucken, ſhould make the lower reſound by Sympathy, and ſo make the Muſick the better ; which, if it be to purpoſe, than Sympathy worketh as well by report of Sound, as by Motion. But this device, I conceive, to be of no uſe, becauſe the upper Strings which are ſtopped in great variety, cannot maintain a *Diapaſon* or a *Vniſon* with the lower, which are never ſtopped. But if it ſhould be of uſe at all, it muſt be in Inſtruments which have no ſtops, as *Virginals* and *Harps* ; wherein tryal may be made of two rows of Strings, diſtant the one from the other.

281.

The Experiment of Sympathy may be transferred (perhaps) from Inſtruments of Strings, to other Inſtruments of Sound. As to try, if there were in one Steeple two Bells of Uniſon, whether the ſtriking of the one would move the other, more than if it were another accord : And ſo in *Pipes*, if they be of equal bore and ſound,) whether a little Straw or Feather would move in the one *Pipe*, when the other is blown at an *Vniſon*.

282.

It ſeemeth both in *Ear* and *Eye*, the Inſtrument of *Senſe* hath a Sympathy or Similitude with that which giveth the Reflexion (as hath been touched before.) For as the ſight of the Eye is like a Chryſtal, or Glaſs, or Water ; ſo is the Ear a ſinuous Cave with a hard Bone, to ſtop and reverberate the Sound: Which is like to the places that report Eccho's.

283.
**Experiments
in Conſort,
touching the
Hindring or
Helping of the
Hearing.**

Hen a Man yawneth, he cannot hear ſo well. The cauſe is, for that the Membrane of the Ear is extended; and ſo rather caſteth off the Sound, than draweth it to.

284.

We hear better when we hold our Breath, than contrary, inſomuch, as in all liſtening to attain a Sound a far off, Men hold their Breath. The cauſe is, for that in all Expiration, the motion is outwards, and therefore rather driveth away the voice than draweth it: And beſides, we ſee that in all labor to do things with any ſtrength, we hold the Breath ; and liſtening after any Sound that is heard with difficulty, is a kinde of labor.

285.

Let it be tryed, for the help of the Hearing, (and I conceive it likely to ſucceed) to make an Inſtrument like a Tunnel ; the narrow part whereof may be of the bigneſs of the hold of the Ear ; and the broader end much larger ; like a Bell at the skirts, and the length half a foot or more. And let the narrow end of it be ſet cloſe to the Ear. And mark whether any Sound abroad in the open Air, will not be heard diſtinctly, from further diſtance, than without that Inſtrument ; being (as it were) an *Ear ſpectacle*. And I have heard there is in *Spain*, an Inſtrument in uſe to be ſet to the Ear, that helpeth ſomewhat thoſe that are Thick of Hearing.

286.

If the Mouth be ſhut cloſe, nevertheleſs there is yielded by the Roof of the Mouth, a Murmur ; ſuch as is uſed by Dumb men : But if the Noſtrils be likewiſe ſtopped, no ſuch Murmur can be made, except it be in the bottom of the Pallate towards the Throat. Whereby it appeareth manifeſtly, that a Sound in the Mouth , except ſuch as aforeſaid, if the Mouth be ſtopped, paſſeth from the Pallate through the Noſtrils.

287.
**Experiments
in Conſort,
touching the
Spiritual and
Fine Nature
of Sounds.**

He *Repercuſſion of Sounds*, (which we call Eccho) is a great Argument of the *Spiritual Eſſence* of *Sounds*. For if it were Corporeal, the Repercuſſing ſhould be created in the ſame manner, and by like Inſtruments, with

the

the original Sound : But we fee what a number of exquifite Inftruments muft concur in fpeaking of words, whereof there is no fuch matter in the returning of them, but onely a plain ftop, and repercuffion.

The exquifite Differences of Articulate Sounds, carried along in the Air, fhew that they cannot be Signatures or Impreffions in the Air, as hath been well refuted by the Ancients. For it is true, that Seals make excellent Impreffions ; and fo it may be thought of Sounds in their firft generation : But then the Delation and Continuance of them , without any new fealing, fhew apparently they cannot be Impreffions.

All Sounds are fuddenly made, and do fuddenly perifh ; but neither that, nor the exquifite Differences of them, is matter of fo great admiration : For the Quaverings, and Warblings of Lutes, and Pipes are as fwift ; and the Tongue (which is no very fine Inftrument) doth in fpeech, make no fewer motions, than there be letters in all the words which are uttered. But that Sounds fhould not onely be fo fpeedily generated, but carried fo far every way, in fuch a momentany time, deferveth more admiration. As for example, If a man ftand in the middle of a Field, and fpeak aloud, he fhall be heard a Furlong in round , and that fhall be in articulate Sounds, and thofe fhall be entire in every little portion of the Air ; and this fhall be done in the fpace of lefs than a minute.

The fudden Generation and Perifhing of Sounds, muft be one of thefe two ways : Either, that the Air fuffereth fome force by Sound, and then re-ftoreth it, as Water doth ; which being divided, maketh many circles, till it reftore it felf to the Natural confiftence ; or otherwife, that the Air doth willingly imbibe the Sound as grateful, but cannot maintain it ; for that the Air hath (as it fhould feem) a fecret and hidden Appetite of receiving the Sound at the firft ; but then other grof, and more materiate qualities of the Air ftraight ways fuffocate it, like unto Flame which is generated with alacrity, but ftraight quenched by the enmity of the Air, or other Ambient Bodies.

There be thefe differences (in general) by which *Sounds* are divided:

    1. *Mufical, Immufical.*
    2. *Trebble, Bafe.*
    3. *Flat, Sharp.*
    4. *Soft, Loud.*
    5. *Exterior, Interior.*
    6. *Clean, Harfh,* or *Purling.*
    7. *Articulate, Inarticulate.*

We have labored (as may appear) in this *Inquifition of Sounds* diligently ; both becaufe *Sound* is one of the moft hidden portions of *Nature*, (as we faid in the beginning) and becaufe it is a *Vertue* which may be called *Incorporeal* and *Immateriate*, whereof there be in *Nature* but few. Be-fides, we were willing (now in thefe our firft *Centuries*) to make a pattern or prefident of an *Exact Inquifition* ; and we fhall do the like hereafter in fome other fubjects which require it. For we defire that Men fhould learn and perceive how fevere a thing the true *Inquifition of Nature* is ; and fhould accuftom themfelves by the light of particulars, to enlarge their mindes to the amplitude of the World ; and not to reduce the World to the narrownefs of their Mindes.

     Metals

<table>
<tr><td valign="top">

291.
Experiment
Solitary,
touching the
Orient Colours
in Dissolution
of Metals.

</td><td>

METals give orient and fine Colours in Dissolution; as Gold giveth an excellent Yellow, Quick-silver an excellent Green, Tin giveth an excellent Azure. Likewise in their Putrefactions, or Rusts; as Vermilion, Verdegrease, Bise, Cirrus, &c. And likewise in their Vitrifications. The cause is, for that by their strength of Body, they are able to endure the Fire, or Strong-waters, and to be put into an equal posture, and again, to retain part of their principal Spirit: Which two things (equal posture, and quick Spirits) are required chiefly, to make Colours lightsome.

</td></tr>
<tr><td valign="top">

292.
Experiment
Solitary,
touching
Prolongation
of Life.

</td><td>

IT conduceth unto long Life, and to the more placide Motion of the Spirits, which thereby do less prey and consume the Juyce of the Body: either that *Mens actions be free and voluntary*, that nothing be done *invitâ minerva*, but *secundum genium*; or, on the other side, that the *Actions of Men be full of Regulation, and commands within themselves:* For then the victory and performing of the command, giveth a good disposition to the Spirits, especially if there be a proceeding from degree to degree, for then the sense of victory is the greater. An example of the former of these, is in a Countrey life; and of the latter, in *Monks* and *Philosophers*, and such as do continually enjoyn themselves.

</td></tr>
<tr><td valign="top">

293.
Experiment
Solitary,
touching
Appetite of
Union in
Bodies.

</td><td>

IT is certain, that in all Bodies, there is an *Appetite of Union*, and Evitation of Solution of Continuity: And of this Appetite there be many degrees, but the most remarkable, and fit to be distinguished, are three. The first in Liquors, the second in hard Bodies, and the third in Bodies cleaving or tenacious. In Liquors this Appetite is weak; we see in Liquors, the Threding of them in Stillicides (as hath been said) the falling of them in round drops (which is the form of Union) and the staying of them for a little time in Bubbles and Froth. In the second degree or kinde, this Appetite is strong; as in Iron, in Stone, in Wood, &c. In the third, this Appetite is in a *Medium* between the other two: For such Bodies do partly follow the touch of another Body, and partly stick and continue to themselves; and therefore they rope and draw themselves in threds, as we see in *Pitch, Glew, Birdlime, &c.* But note, that all solid Bodies are cleaving more or less: and that they love better the touch of somewhat that is tangible, than of Air. For Water in small quantity cleaveth to any thing that is solid, and so would Metal too, if the weight drew it not off. And therefore Gold Foliate, or any Metal Foliate, cleaveth: But those Bodies which are noted to be clammy, and cleaving, are such as have a more indifferent Appetite (at once) to follow another Body, and to hold to themselves. And therefore they are commonly *Bodies* ill mixed, and which take more pleasure in a *Foreign Body*, that in preserving there own consistence, and which have little predominance in *Drought* or *Moisture*.

</td></tr>
<tr><td valign="top">

294.
Experiment
Solitary,
touching the
like Operations
of Heat and
Time.

</td><td>

TIme and *Heat* are fellows in many effects. *Heat* drieth *Bodies* that do easily expire; as Parchment, Leaves, Roots, Clay, &c. And so doth *Time* or *Age* arefie; as in the same *Bodies, &c. Heat* dissolveth and melteth *Bodies* that keep in their *Spirits*, as in divers *Liquefactions*; and so doth Time, in some *Bodies* of a softer consistence: As is manifest in Honey, which by *Age* waxeth more liquid, and the like in Sugar; and so in old Oyl, which is ever more clear and more hot in medicinable use. *Heat* causeth the Spirits to search some issue out of the *Body*, as in the *Volatility*

</td></tr>
</table>

of Metals ; and so doth Time, as in the Rust of Metals. But generally Heat doth that in small time, which Age doth in long.

SOme things which pass the Fire, are softest at first, and by Time grow hard, as the Crum of Bread. Some are harder when they come from the Fire, and afterwards give again, and grow soft as the Crust of Bread, Bisket, Sweet-Meats, Salt, &c. The cause is, for that in those things which wax hard with Time, the work of the Fire is a kinde of melting ; and in those that wax soft with Time, (contrariwise) the work of the Fire is a kinde of Baking ; and whatsoever the Fire baketh, Time doth in some degree dissolve.

295.
Experiment Solitary, touching the Differing Operations of Fire, and Time.

MOtions pass from one Man to another, not so much by exciting Imagination as by Invitation, especially if there be an Aptness or Inclination before. Therefore Gaping, or Yawning, and Stretching, do pass from Man to Man ; for that that causeth Gaping or Stretching is, when the Spirits are a little Heavy, by any Vapor, or the like. For then they strive (as it were) to wring out, and expel that which loadeth them. So Men drowzy and desirous to sleep ; or before the fit of an Ague, do use to yawn and stretch, and do likewise yield a Voice or Sound, which is an Interjection of Expulsion : So that if another be apt and prepared to do the like, he followeth by the sight of another. So the Laughing of another maketh to laugh.

296.
Experiment Solitary, touching Motions by imitation.

THere be some known Diseases that are Infectious, and others that are not. Those that are infectious, are first, Such as are chiefly in the Spirits, and not so much in the Humors, and therefore pass easily from Body to Body; such are Pestilences Lippitudes, and such like. Secondly, such as taint the breath, which we see passeth manifestly from Man to Man, and not invisible as the affects of the Spirits do ; such are Consumptions of the Lungs, &c. Thirdly, Such as come forth to the skin, and therefore taint the Air, or the Body adjacent ; especially, if they consist in an unctuous substance, not apt to dissipate; such are Scabs, and Leprosie. Fourthly, such as are meerly in the Humors, and not in the Spirits, Breath, or Exhalations : And therefore they never infect, but by touch onely ; and such a touch also, as cometh within the *Epidermis,* as the venome of the *French Pox,* and the biting of a *Mad-Dog.*

297.
Experiment Solitary, touching Infectious diseases.

MOst Powders grow more close and coherent by mixture of Water, than by mixture of Oyl, though Oyl be the thicker Body; as *Meal, &c.* The reason is the Congruity of Bodies, which if it be more, maketh a perfecter imbibition, and incorporation ; which in most Powders is more between them and Water, than between them and Oyl: But Painters colours ground, and ashes, do better incorporate with Oyl.

298.
Experiment Solitary, touching the Incorporation of Powders and Liquors.

MUch Motion and Exercise is good for some Bodies, and sitting and less motion, for others. If the Body be hot, and void of superfluous Moistures, too much Motion hurteth ; and it is an error in *Physitians,* to call too much upon Exercise. Likewise, Men ought to beware, that they use not Exercise, and a spare diet, both ; but if much Exercise, then a plentiful diet ; and if sparing diet, then little Exercise. The Benefits that come of Exercise are. First, that it sendeth nourishment into the parts more forcibly.

299.
Experiment Solitary, touching Exercise of the Body.

Secondly, That it helpeth to excern by Sweat, and so maketh the parts affimilate the more perfectly. Thirdly, that it maketh the substance of the Body more solid and compact; and so less apt to be consumed and depredated by the Spirits. The Evils that come of Exercise, are, First, That it maketh the Spirits more hot and predatory. Secondly, That it doth abforbe likewise, and attenuate too much the moisture of the Body. Thirdly, That it maketh too great Concussion, (especially, if it be violent) of the inward parts, which delight more in rest. But generally Exercise, if it be much, is no friend to prolongation of life; which is one cause, Why Women live longer then Men, because they stir less.

SOme Food we may use long, and much, without glutting; as Bread, Flesh that is not Fat, or Rank, &c. Some other (though pleasant) glutteth sooner, as Sweet-Meats, Fat-Meats, &c. The cause is, for that Appetite consisteth in the emptiness of the Mouth, of the Stomach, or possessing it with somewhat that is astringent; and therefore, cold and dry: But things that are sweet and fat, are more filling, and do swim and hang more about the Mouth of the Stomach, and go not down so speedily; and again turn sooner to Choler, which is hot, and ever abateth the appetite. We see also, that another cause of Satiety, is an Over-custom; and of Appetite, is Novelty. And therefore Meats, if the same be continually taken, induce Loathing. To give the reason of the distaste of Satiety, and of the pleasure in Novelty, and to distinguish not onely in Meats and Drinks, but also in Motions, Loves, Company, Delight, Studies, what they be that Custom maketh more grateful; and what more tedious, were a large Field. But for Meats, the cause is Attraction, which is quicker, and more excited towards that which is new, than towards that whereof there remaineth a relish by former use. And (generally) it is a rule, That whatsoever is somewhat ingrate at first, is made grateful by **Custom**; but whatsoever is too pleasing at first, groweth quickly to Satiate.

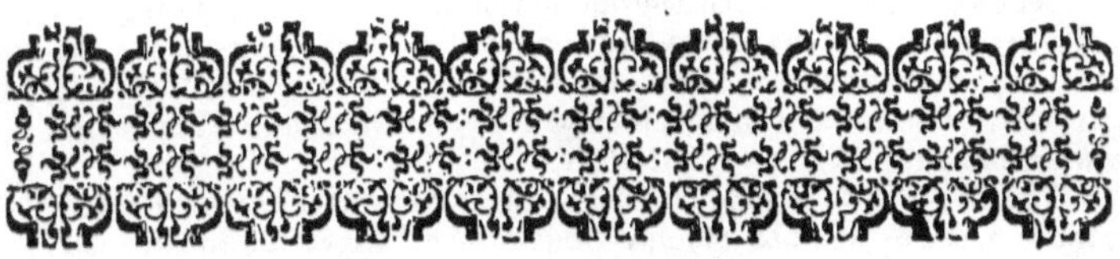

NATURAL HISTORY.

Century IV.

Cceleration of Time, in *Works of Nature*, may well be esteemed *Inter Magualia Natura*. And even in *Divine Miracles Accelerating of the Time*, is next to the Creating of the Matter. We will now therefore proceed to the enquiry of it ; and for *Acceleration of Germination*, we will refer it over unto the place, where we shall handle the *Subject of Plants*, generally ; and will now begin with other *Accelerations*.

Experiments in Consort, touching the *Clarification of Liquors*, and *the Accelerating thereof*.

Liquors are (many of them) at the first, thick and troubled ; As *Must*, *Wort*, *Juyce of Fruits*, *or Herbs* expressed, &c. And by *Time*, they settle and clarifie. But to make them clear, before the *Time*, is a great work ; for it is a *Spur to Nature*, and putteth her out of her pace : And besides, it is of good use for making Drinks, and Sauces , Potable, and Serviceable, speedily. But to know the Means of Accelerating Clarification, we must first know the causes of Clarification. The first cause is, by the Separation of the grosser parts of the Liquor, from the finer. The second, by the equal distribution of the Spirits of the Liquor, with the tangible parts ; for that ever representeth Bodies clear and untroubled. The third, by the refining the Spirit it self, which thereby giveth to the Liquor more splendor, and more lustre.

301.

First, For Separation : It is wrought by weight ; as in the ordinary residence or settlement of Liquors. By Heat, by Motion, by Precipitation, or Sublimation, (that is, a calling of the several parts, either up or down, which is a kinde of Attraction,) by Adhesion ; as when a Body, more viscous, is mingled and agitated with the Liquor ; which viscous Body (afterwards severed)

302.

vered) draweth with it the groſſer parts of the Liquor: And laſtly, by Percolation or Paſſage.

303.   Secondly, For the even Diſtribution of the Spirits, it is wrought by
gentle heat, and by Agitation of Motion ; (for of Time we ſpeak not, becauſe it is that we would anticipate and repreſent :) And it is wrought alſo,
by mixture of ſome other Body, which hath a vertue to open the Liquor, and
to make the Spirits the better paſs thorow.

304.   Thirdly, For the refining of the Spirit, it is wrought likewiſe by Heat,
by motion, and by mixture of ſome Body which hath vertue to attenuate.
So therefore (having ſhewed the cauſes) for the accelerating of Clarification
in general, and the enducing of it ; take theſe Inſtances and Tryals.

305.   It is in common practice, to draw Wine or Beer, from the Lees, (which
we call *Racking*) whereby it will clarifie much the ſooner : For the Lees,
though they keep the drink in heart , and make it laſting ; yet withal
they caſt up ſome ſpiſſitude : and this Inſtance is to be referred to Separation.

306.   On the otherſide, it were good to try, what, the adding to the Liquor,
more Lees than his own, will work ; for though the Lees do make the Liquor
turbide, yet they refine the Spirits. Take therefore a Veſſel of new Beer, and
take another Veſſel of new Beer, and rack the one Veſſel from the Lees, and
pour the Lees of the racked Veſſel into the unracked Veſſel, and ſee the effect.
This Inſtance is referred to the Refining of the Spirits.

307.   Take new Beer, and put in ſome quantity of ſtale Beer into it, and ſee
whether it will not accelerate the Clarification, by opening the Body of the
Beer, and cutting the groſſer parts, whereby they may fall down into Lees.
And this Inſtance again is referred to *Separation.*

308.   The longer *Molt* or *Herbs,* or the like, are infuſed in *Liquor,* the more
thick and troubled the *Liquor* is ; but the longer they be decocted in the *Liquor,*
the clearer it is. The reaſon is plain, becauſe in Infuſion, the longer it is, the
greater is the part of the groſs Body that goeth into the Liquor : But in Decoction, though more goeth forth, yet it either purgeth at the top, or ſettleth
at the bottom.   And therefore the moſt exact way to clarifie is, firſt, to Infuſe, and then to take off the Liquor and decoct it ; as they do in Beer, which
hath Molt firſt infuſed in the Liquor, and is afterwards boiled with the Hop.
This alſo is referred to *Separation.*

309.   Take hot Embers, and put them about a Bottle filled with new Beer, almoſt to the very neck ; let the Bottle be well ſtopped, leſt it flie out : And
continue it, renewing the Embers every day by the ſpace of ten days, and then
compare it with another Bottle of the ſame Beer ſet by.   Take alſo Lime,
both quenched and unquenched, and ſet the Bottles in them *ut ſuprà.*   This
Inſtance is referred, both to the even Diſtribution, and alſo to the Refining
of the *Spirits by Heat.*

310.   Take Bottles and ſwing them, or carry them in a Wheel-Barrow upon
rough Ground, twice in a day : But then you may not fill the Bottles full,
but leave ſome Air ; for if the Liquor come cloſe to the ſtopple, it cannot
play nor flower : And when you have ſhaken them well either way, pour
the Drink in another Bottle, ſtopped cloſe after the uſual manner ; for if it
ſtay with much Air in it, the Drink will pall, neither will it ſettle ſo perfectly in all the parts. Let it ſtand ſome Twenty four hours, then take it, and
put it again into a Bottle with Air, *ut ſuprà* ; and thence into a Bottle ſtopped,
ut ſuprà ; and ſo repeat the ſame operation for ſeven days. Note, that in the
emptying of one Bottle into another, you muſt do it ſwiftly, leſt the Drink
                                                                              pall.

pall. It were good also to try it in a Bottle with a little air below the Neck without emptying. This Instance is referred to the even *Distribution* and *Refining* of the *Spirits* by *Motion.*

As for Percolation, inward, and outward (which belongeth to *Separation,*) Tryal would be made of Clarifying by Adhesion, with Milk put into new Beer, and stirred with it: For it may be, that the grosser part of the Beer will cleave to the *Milk;* the doubt is, whether the Milk will sever well again, which is soon tried. And it is usual in clarifying *Ippocrasse* to put in Milk, which after severeth and carrieth with it the grosser parts of the *Ippocrass,* as hath been said elsewhere. Also for the better Clarification by Percolation ; when they Tun new Beer, they use to let it pass through a Strainer, and it is like the finer the Strainer is, the clearer it will be.

311.

THe *Accelerating of Maturation,* we will now enquire of, and of *Maturation* it self. It is of three natures, the *Maturation of Fruits,* the *Maturation of Drinks,* and the *Maturation of Imposthumes and Vlcers.* This last we refer to another place, where we shall handle *Experiments Medicinal.* There be also other Maturations, as of Metals; &c. whereof we speak as occasion serveth. But we will begin with that of Drinks, because it hath such affinity with the Clarification of Liquors.

For the Maturation of Drinks, it is wrought by the Congregation of the Spirits together, whereby they digest more perfectly the grosser parts ; and it is effected, partly by the same means that Clarification is (whereof we spake before:) But then note, that an extream Clarification doth spred the Spirits so smooth, as they become dull, and the drink dead, which ought to have a little flowring. And therefore all your clear *Amber drink* is flat.

312.

We see the degrees of Maturation of Drinks, in Must, in Wine, as it is drunk, and in Vinegar. Whereof Must hath not the Spirits well congregated, Wine hath them well united, so as they make the parts somewhat more Oyly, Vinegar hath them congregated, but more Jejune, and in smaller quantity; the greatest and finest Spirit and part being exhaled: For we see Vinegar is made by setting the Vessel of Wine against the hot Sun. And therefore Vinegar will not burn, for that much of the finer part is exhaled.

313.

The refreshing and quickning of Drink palled or dead, is by enforcing the motion of the Spirit. So we see that open weather relaxeth the Spirit, and maketh it more lively in Motion. We see also Bottelling of Beer or Ale, while it is new and full of Spirit, (so that it spirteth when the stopple is taken forth) maketh the Drink more quick and windy. A Pan of Coals in the Cellar, doth likewise good, and maketh the Drink work again. New Drink put to Drink that is dead, provoketh it to work again : Nay, which is more (as some affirm) a Brewing of new Beer, set by old Beer, maketh it work again : It were good also to enforce the Spirits by some mixtures, that may excite and quicken them, as by the putting into the Bottles, Nitre, Chalk, Lime, &c. We see Cream is matured, and made to rise more speedily by putting in cold Water ; which, as it seemeth, getteth down the Whey.

314.

It is tryed, that the burying of Bottles of Drink well stopped, either in dry Earth, a good depth, or in the bottom of a Well within Water; and best

315.

of

of all, the hanging of them in a deep Well ſomewhat above the Water, for ſome fortnights ſpace, is an excellent means of making Drink freſh and quick: For the cold doth not cauſe any exhaling of the Spirits at all, as heat doth, though it rarifieth the reſt that remain: But cold maketh the Spirits vigorous, and irritateth them, whereby they incorporate the parts of the Liquor perfectly.

316. As for the *Maturation of Fruits*, it is wrought by the calling forth of the Spirits of the Body outward, and ſo ſpreading them more ſmoothly; and likewiſe by digeſting, in ſome degree, the groſſer parts: And this is effected by Heat, Motion, Attraction, and by a Rudiment of Putrefaction: For the Inception of Putrefaction hath in it a *Maturation*.

317. There were taken Apples, and laid in Straw, in Hay, in Flower, in Chalk, in Lime, covered over with Onions, covered over with Crabs, cloſed up in Wax, ſhut in a Box, &c. There was alſo an Apple hanged up in ſmoak. Of all which the Experiment ſorted in this manner.

318. After a moneths ſpace, the Apple, encloſed in Wax, was as Green and freſh as at the firſt putting in, and the Kernels continued White. The cauſe is, for that all excluſion of open Air, (which is ever predatory) maintaineth the Body in his firſt freſhneſs and moiſture; but the inconvenience is, that it taſteth a little of the Wax, which, I ſuppoſe, in a Pomegranate, or ſome ſuch thick coated fruit, it would not do.

319. The Apple hanged in the ſmoak, turned like an old Mellow-Apple wrinkled, dry, ſoft, ſweet, yellow within. The cauſe is, for that ſuch a degree of heat, which doth neither melt nor ſcorch (for we ſee that in a greater heat, a roaſt Apple ſoftneth and melteth, and Pigs feet made of quarters of Wardens, ſcortch and have a skin of coal) doth Mellow, and not adure: The ſmoak alſo maketh the Apple (as it were) ſprinkled with Soot, which helpeth to mature. We ſee, that in drying of Pears and Prunes, in the Oven, and removing of them often as they begin to ſweat, there is a like operation: but that is with a far more intenſe degree of heat.

320. The Apples covered in the Lime and Aſhes, were well matured as appeared both in their yellowneſs and ſweetneſs. The cauſe is, for that that Degree of Heat, which is in Lime and Aſhes, (being a ſmoothering heat) is of all the reſt moſt proper; for it doth neither Liquefie nor Arefie, and that is true Maturation. Note, that the taſte of thoſe Apples was good, and therefore it is the Experiment fitteſt for uſe.

321. The Apples covered with Crabs and Onions, were likewiſe well matured. The cauſe is not any heat, but for that the Crabs and the Onions draw forth the Spirits of the Apple, and ſpred them equally thorow out the Body; which taketh away hardneſs. So we ſee one Apple ripeneth againſt another. And therefore in making of Cider, they turn the Apples firſt upon a heap; ſo one Cluſter of Grapes, that toucheth another whileſt it groweth, ripeneth faſter. *Botrus contra Botrum citius matureſcit.*

322. The Apples in Hay and the Straw, ripened apparently, though not ſo much as the other, but the Apple in the Straw, more. The cauſe is, for that the Hay and Straw have a very low degree of Heat, but yet cloſe and ſmoothering, and which dryeth not.

323. The Apple in the cloſe Box was ripened alſo. The cauſe is, for that all Air kept cloſe, hath a degree of warmth; as we ſee in Wool, Fur, Pluſh, &c.

Note.

Note, That all thefe were compared with another Apple of the fame kinde that lay of it felf; and in comparifon of that, were more fweet, and more yellow, and fo appeared to be more ripe

Take an Apple, or Pear, or other like Fruit, and roul it upon a Table hard: We fee in common experience, that the rouling doth foften and fweeten the Fruit prefently, which is nothing but the fmooth diftribution of the Spirits into the parts; for the unequal diftribution of the Spirits maketh the harrifhnefs : But this hard rouling is between Concoction, and a fimple Maturation; therefore, if you fhould roul them but gently perhaps twice a day, and continue it fome feven days, it is like they would Mature more finely, and like unto the *Natural Maturation.*

Take an Apple, and cut out a piece of the top and cover it, to fee whether that *Solution of Continuity* will not haften a Maturation. We fee that where a *Wafp,* or a *Fly,* or a *Worm,* hath bitten in a *Grape* or any *Fruit,* it will fweeten haftily.

Take an Apple, *&c.* and prick it with a Pin full of Holes, not deep, and fmear it a little with Sack, or Cinnamon Water, or Spirit of Wine, every day for ten days, to fee if the *Virtual Heat* of the Wine, or Strong-Waters, will not Mature it.

In thefe Tryals alfo as was ufed in the firft, fet another of the fame Fruits by, to compare them, and try them by their Yellownefs, and by their Sweetnefs.

THe World hath been much abufed by the opinion of Making of Gold. The Work it felf, I judge to be poffible; but the Means (hitherto propounded) to effect it, are in the Practice, full of Error and Impofture; and in the Theory, full of unfound Imaginations. For to fay, that *Nature* hath an invention to make all Metals Gold; and that, if fhe were delivered from Impediments, fhe would perform her own work; and that, if the Crudities, Impurities, and Leprofies of Metals were cured, they would become Gold; and that a little quantity of the Medicine in the Work of Projection, will turn a Sea of the bafer Metal into Gold by multiplying. All thefe are but dreams, and fo are many other Grounds of *Alchymy.* And to help the matter, the *Alchymifts* call in likewife many vanities, out of *Aftrology, Natural Magick,* Superftitious Interpretations of Scriptures, Auricular Traditions, Feigned Teftimonies of Ancient Authors, and the like. It is true, on the other fide, they have brought to light not a few profitable Experiments, and thereby made the World fome amends: But we, when we fhall come to handle the *Verfion* and *Tranfmutation of Bodies,* and the Experiments concerning *Metals* and *Minerals;* will lay open the true Ways and Paffages of *Nature,* which may lead to this great effect. And we commend the wit of the *Chinefes,* who defpair of making of Gold, but are mad upon the making of Silver. For certain it is, That it is more difficult to make Gold, (which is the moft ponderous and materiate amongft Metals) of other Metals, lefs ponderous and lefs materiate, than (*Vice verfa*) to make Silver of Lead, or Quick-filver; both which are more ponderous than Silver: So that they need rather a further degree of *Fixation,* than any *Condenfation:* In the mean time, by occafion of handling the *Axioms* touching *Maturation,* we will direct a tryal touching the *Maturing of Metals,* and thereby turning fome of them into Gold; for we conceive indeed, That a perfect good *Concoction,* or *Digeftion,* or *Maturation* of fome *Metals* will produce Gold. And here we call to minde, that we knew a *Dutchman* that had wrought himfelf into the belief of a

great

324.

325.

326.

Experiment Solitary, touching the Making of Gold.

great person, by undertaking, that he could make Gold : Whose discourse was, That Gold might be made, but that the *Alchymists* over-fired the work : For (he said) the making of Gold did require a very temperate Heat, as being in *Nature* a subterrany work, where little Heat cometh ; but yet more to the making of Gold, than of any other Metal : And therefore, that he would do it with a great Lamp , that should carry a temperate and equal Heat, and that it was the work of many Moneths.   The device of the Lamp was folly, but the overfiring now used, and the equal Heat to be required, and the making it a work of some good time, are no ill discourses.

We resort therefore to our *Axioms* of *Maturation*, in effect touched before.

The first is, That there be used a Temperate Heat ; for they are ever Temperate Heats that Disgests, and Mature; wherein we mean Temperate, according to the Nature of the Subject : For that may be Temperate to Fruits and Liquors, which will not work at all upon Metals.

The second is, That the Spirit of the Metal be quickned, and the Tangible Parts opened : For without those two operations, the Spirit of the Metal, wrought upon, will not be able to disgest the Parts.

The third is, That the Spirits do spred themselves even, and move not subsultorily, for that will make the parts close and pliant. And this requireth a Heat that doth not rise and fall, but continue as equal as may be.

The fourth is, That no part of the Spirit be emitted but detained: For if there be Emission of Spirit , the Body of the Metal will be hard and churlish. And this will be performed, partly by the temper of the Fire, and partly by the closeness of the Vessel.

. The fifth is, That there be choice made of the likeliest and best prepared Metal for the Version ; for that will facilitate the Work.

The sixth is, That you give time enough for the Work, not to prolong hopes (as the *Alchymists* do, but indeed to give *Nature* a convenient space to work in.

These principles most certain and true, we will now derive a direction of Tryal out of them, which may (perhaps) by further Meditation be improved.

327.   Let there be a small Furnace made of a Temperate Heat ; let the heat be such as may keep the Metal perpetually molten, and no more ; for that above all, importeth to the Work : For the Material, take Silver, which is the Metal, that in Nature, symbolizeth most with Gold ; put in also, with the Silver a tenth part of Quick-silver, and a twelfth part of Nitre by weight : Both these to quicken and open the Body of the Metal; and so let the Work be continued by the space of Six Moneths, at the least.   I wish also, That there be as sometimes an Injection of some Oyled Substance ; such as they use in the recovering of Gold, which by vexing with Separations hath been made churlish : And this is, to lay the parts more close and smooth, which is the main work.   For Gold (as we see) is the closest (and therefore the heaviest) of Metals; and is likewise the most flexible and tensible. Note, That to think to make Gold of Quick-silver because it is the heaviest, is a thing not to be hoped ; for Quick-silver will not endure the mannage of the Fire : Next to Silver, I think Copper were fittest to be the Material.

                                                                Gold

GOld hath thefe Natures: Greatnefs of VVeight, Clofenefs of Parts, Fixation, Pliantnefs or Softnefs, Immunity from Ruft, Colour or Tincture of Yellow. Therefore the fure way (though moft about) to make Gold, is to know the caufes of the feveral Natures before rehearfed, and the Axioms concerning the fame. For if a Man can make a Metal that hath all thefe Properties, let Men difpute, whether it be Gold, or no ?

328.
Experiment Solitary, touching the *Nature of Gold.*

THe Enducing and Accelerating of Putrefaction, is a fubject of a very Univerfal Enquiry. For Corruption is a Reciprocal to Generation; and they two are as Natures to Terms or Boundaries; and the Guides to Life and Death. Putrefaction is the VVork of the Spirits of Bodies, which ever are unquiet to get forth and congregate with the Air, and to enjoy the Sun-Beams. The getting forth, or fpreding of the Spirits, (which is a degree of getting forth) have five differing operations. If the Spirits be detained within the Body, and move more violently, there followeth Colliquation; as in Metals, &c. If more mildely, there followeth Digeftion or Maturation; as in Drinks and Fruits. If the Spirits be not meerly detained, but Protrude a little, and that Motion be confufed, and inordinate, there followeth Putrefaction; which ever diffolveth the Confiftence of the Body into much inequality; as in Flefh, Rotten Fruits, Shining VVood, &c. and alfo in the Ruft of Metals. But if that Motion be in a certain order, there followeth Vivification and Figuration; as both in Living Creatures bred of Putrefaction, and in Living Creatures perfect. But if the Spirits iffue out of the Body, there followeth Deficcation, Induration, Confumption, &c. As in Brick, evaporation of Bodies Liquid, &c.

Experiments in Confort, touching the *Enducing and Accelerating of Putrefaction.*

The Means to enduce and accelerate Putrefaction, are, Firft, By adding fome crude or watry moifture; as in VVetting of any Flefh, Fruit, Wood, with Water, &c. For contrariwife, Unctuous and Oyly Subftances preferve.

329.

The fecond is, By Invitation or Excitation; as when a rotten Apple lieth clofe to another Apple that is found; or when Dung (which is a fubftance already putrified) is added to other Bodies. And this is alfo notably feen in Church-yards, where they bury much; where the Earth will confume the Corps, in far fhorter time than other Earth will.

330.

The third is, By Clofenefs and Stopping, which detaineth the Spirits in Prifon, more then they would, and thereby irritateth them to feek iffue; as in Corn and Cloaths which wax mufty; and therefore open Air (which they call *Aer perflabilis*) doth preferve: And this doth appear more evidently in Agues, which come (moft of them) of obftructions and penning the Humors, which thereupon Putrifie.

331.

The fourth is, By Solution of Continuity; as we fee an Apple will rot fooner, if it be cut or pierced, and fo will Wood, &c. And fo the Flefh of Creatures alive, where they have received any wound.

332.

The fifth is, Either by the Exhaling, or by the driving back of the principal Spirits, which preferve the confiftence of the Body; fo that when their Government is diffolved every part returneth to his Nature, or Homogeny. And this appeareth in Urine and Blood, when they cool and thereby break. It appeareth alfo in the Gangreen or Mortification of Flefh, either by Opiates, or by Intenfe Colds. I conceive alfo, the fame effect

333.

's in Peſtilences, for that the malignity of the infecting vapor, daunteth the principal Spirits, and maketh them flie, and leave their Regiment; and then the Humors, Fleſh, and Secondary Spirits, do diſſolve and break, as in an Anarchy.

334.   The ſixth is, VVhen a Forreign Spirit, ſtronger and more eager than the Spirit of the Body, entreth the Body, as in the ſtinging of Serpents. And this is the cauſe (generally) that upon all Poyſons followeth Swelling; and we ſee Swelling followeth alſo, when the Spirits of the Body it ſelf congregate too much; as upon blows and bruiſes, or when they are pent in too much, as in Swelling upon Cold. And we ſee alſo, that the Spirits coming of Putrefaction of Humors in Agues, &c. which may be counted as Foreign Spirits, though they be bred within the Body, do extinguiſh and ſuffocate the Natural ſpirits and heat.

335.   The ſeventh is, By ſuch a weak degree of heat, as ſetteth the Spirits in a little Motion, but is not able either to digeſt the parts, or to iſſue the Spirits, as is ſeen in Fleſh kept in a room that is not cool; whereas in a cool and wet Larder it will keep longer. And we ſee, that Vivification (whereof Putrefaction is the Baſtard Brother) is effected by ſuch ſoft heats; as the hatching of Eggs, the heat of the VVomb, &c.

336.   The eighth is, By the releaſing of the Spirits, which before were cloſe kept by the ſolidneſs of their coveriture, and thereby their appetite of iſſuing checked; as in the artificial ruſts induced by Strong waters in Iron, Lead, &c. And therefore wetting haſtneth Ruſt or Putrefaction of any thing, becauſe it ſoftneth the Cruſt, for the Spirits to come forth.

337   The ninth is, By the enterchange of heat and cold, or wet and dry; as we ſee in the Mouldring of Earth in Froſts, and Sun; and in the more haſty rotting of VVood, that is ſometimes wet, ſometimes dry.

338.   The tenth is, By time, and the work, and procedure of the Spirits themſelves, which cannot keep their ſtation; eſpecially, if they be left to themſelves, and there be not Agitation or Local Motion. As we ſee in Corn not ſtirred, and Mens Bodies not exerciſed.

339.   All Moulds are Inceptions of Putrefaction; as the Moulds of Pyes and Fleſh the Moulds of Orenges and Lemmons, which Moulds afterwards turn into VVorms, or more odious Putrefactions: And therefore (commonly) prove to be of ill odor. And if the Body be liquid, and not apt to putrifie totally, it will caſt up a Mother in the top, as the Mothers of Diſtilled waters.

340.   Moſs is a kinde of Mold of the Earth and Trees: But it may be better ſorted as a Rudiment of Germination, to which we refer it.

Experiments in Conſort, touching *Prohibiting and Preventing Putrefaction.*

IT is an Enquiry of excellent uſe to enquire of the Means of Preventing or Staying of Putrefaction; for therein conſiſteth the Means of Conſervation of Bodies: For Bodies have two kindes of Diſſolutions, the one by Conſumption and Diſiccation, the other by Putrefaction. But as for the Putrefactions of the Bodies of Men and Living Creatures (as in Agues, VVorms, Conſumptions of the Lungs, Impoſthums, and Ulcers, both inwards and outwards) they are a great part of Phyſick and Surgery: And therefore we will reſerve the Enquiry of them to the proper place, where we ſhall handle Medicinal Experiments of all ſorts. Of the reſt, we will now enter into an Enquiry, wherein much light may be taken from that which hath been ſaid of the Means to enduce or accelerate Putrefaction: For the removing that which cauſed Putrefaction, doth prevent and avoid Putrefaction.

The

The firſt Means of prohibiting or checking Putrefaction is cold; for ſo we ſee that Meat and Drink will laſt longer, unputrified, or unſowred, in Winter, than in Summer : And we ſee that Flowers, and Fruits; put in conſervatories of Snow, keep freſh.   And this worketh by the Detention of the Spirits, and conſtipation of the Tangible parts.   341.

The ſecond is Aſtriction : For Aſtriction prohibiteth Diſſolution; as we ſee (generally) in Medicines, whereof ſuch as are Aſtringents do inhibit Putre- faction : And by the ſame reaſon of Aſtringency, ſome ſmall quantity of Oyl of Vitriol, will keep freſh water long from putrifying.   And this Aſtriction is in a ſubſtance that hath a virtual cold, and it worketh (partly) by the ſame means that cold doth.   342.

The third is; The excluding of the Air; and again, the expoſing to the Air : For theſe contraries, (as it cometh often to paſs) work the ſame effect, according to the nature of the Subject-matter.   So we ſee, that Beer or Wine in Bottles cloſe ſtopped, laſt long; that the Garners under Ground keep Corn longer, than thoſe above Ground ; and that Fruit cloſed in Wax, keepeth freſh : And likewiſe, Bodies put in Honey, and Flower, keep more freſh : And Liquors, Drinks, and Juyces, with a little Oyl caſt on the top, keep freſh.   Contrariwiſe, we ſee that Cloath and Ap- parel, not aired, do breed Moaths and Mould; and the Diverſity is, that in Bodies that need Detention of Spirits, the Excluſion of the Air doth good ; as in Drinks, and Corn: But in Bodies that need Emiſſion of Spirits, to diſcharge ſome of the ſuperfluous moiſture, it doth hurt, for they require airing.   343.

The fourth is Motion, and Stirring; for Putrefaction asketh Reſt: For the ſubtil Motion which Putrefaction requireth, is diſturbed by any Agi- tation, and all Local Motion keepeth Bodies integral, and their parts together : As we ſee, that turning over of Corn in a Garner; or Let- ting it run like an Hour-Glaſs, from an upper Room into a lower, doth keep it ſweet : And running Waters putrifie not ; and in Mens Bodies, exerciſe hindreth Putrefaction; and contrarywiſe Reſt, and want of Mo- tion or ſtoppings (whereby the running of Humors, or the Motion of Perſpiration, is ſtayed) further Putrefaction; as we partly touched a little before.   344.

The fifth is, The Breathing forth of the Adventitious Moiſture in Bodies, for as wetting doth haſten Putrefaction ; ſo convenient drying (whereby the more Radical Moiſture is onely kept in) putteth back Putre- faction: So we ſee that Herbs and Flowers, if they be dried in the ſhade, or dried in the hot Sun, for a ſmall time keep beſt.   For the Emiſſion of the looſe and adventitious Moiſture, doth betray the Radical Moiſture, and car- ryeth it out for company.   345.

The ſixth is, The ſtrengthning of the Spirits of Bodies ; for as a great heat keepeth Bodies from Putrefaction ; but a tepide heat enclineth them to Putrefaction : So a ſtrong Spirit likewiſe preſerveth, and a weak or faint Spirit diſpoſeth to corruption.   So we finde, that Salt-water corrupteth not ſo ſoon as freſh; and ſalting of Oyſters, and powdring of Meat, keepeth them from Putrefaction.   It would be tryed alſo, whether Chalk, put in- to Water, or Drink, doth not preſerve it from Putrifying, or ſpeedy Sour- ing.   So we ſee that Strong-Beer will laſt longer than ſmall, and all things, that are hot and aromatical, do help to preſerve Liquors, or Powders, &c. which they do, as well by ſtrengthning the Spirits, as by ſoaking out the looſe Moiſture.   346.

H 2

The

347. The seventh is, *Separation of the cruder parts,* and thereby making the Body more equal ; for all unperfect mixture is apt to putrifie, and Watry substances are more apt to putrifie, than oily. So, we see distilled Waters will last longer than raw Waters , and things that have passed the Fire, do last longer than those that have not passed the Fire ; as dried Pears, &c.

348. The eighth is, The *drawing forth continually of that part, where the Putre-faction beginneth :* Which is (commonly) *the looje and watry moisture* ; not onely for the reason before given, that it provoketh the radical moisture to come forth with it ; but because being detained in the Body, the Putrefaction taking hold of it, infecteth the rest : As we see in the Embalming of Dead Bodies. And the same reason is, of preserving Herbs, or Fruits, or Flowers, in Bran or Meal.

349. The ninth is, The *commixture of any thing that is more oyly or sweet :* For such Bodies are least apt to putrifie, the Air working little upon them, and they not putrifying preserve the rest. And therefore we see Syrrups and Oyntments will last longer than Juyces.

350. The tenth is, The *commixture of somewhat that is dry ;* for Putrefaction beginneth first from the Spirits, and then from the moisture ; and that that is dry, is unapt to putrifie. And therefore smoak preserveth flesh ; as we see in Bacon, and Neats-Tongues, and *Martlemas-Beef, &c.*

351. The opinion of some of the Ancients, That blown Airs do preserve Bodies longer than other Airs , seemeth to me probable ; for that the blown Airs, being over-charged and compressed , will hardly receive the exhaling of any thing, but rather repulse it. It was tryed in a blown Bladder, whereinto flesh was put, and likewise a Flower, and it sorted not : For dry Bladders will not blow, and new Bladders rather further Putrefaction. The way were therefore, to blow strongly with a pair of Bellows, into a Hogshead, putting into the Hogshead (before) that which you would have preserved ; and in the instant that you withdraw the Bellows, stop the hole close.

352.
Experiment
Solitary,
touching
Wood Shining
in the Dark.

THe Experiment of Wood that shineth in the dark, we have diligently driven and pursued : The rather, for that of all things that give light here below, it is the most durable, and hath least apparent motion. Fire and Flame are in continual expence ; Sugar shining onely while it is in scraping ; and Salt-water while it is in dashing ; Gloworms have their shining while they live, or a little after ; onely Scales of Fishes (putrified) seem to be of the same nature with shining Wood. And it is true, that all Putrefaction hath with it an inward motion, as well as Fire or Light. The tryal sorted thus.

1. The shining is in some pieces more bright, in some more dim ; but the most bright of all doth not attain to the light of a Gloworm. 2. The Woods that have been tryed to shine, are chiefly Sallow and Willow ; also, the Ash and Hasle, it may be, it holdeth in others. 3. Both Roots, and Bodies do shine, but the Roots better. 4. The colour of the shining part, by day-light, is in some pieces white, in some pieces inclining to red ; which in the Country they call the White and Red Carret. 5. The part that shineth, is (for the most part) somewhat soft, and moist to feel to ; but some was found to be firm and hard ; so as it might be figured into a Cross, or into Beads, &c. But you must not look to have an Image, or the like, in any thing that is Lightsom ; for even a Face in Iron red hot, will

will not be seen, the light confounding the small differences of lightsome and darksome, which shew the figure. 6. There was the shining part pared off, till you came to that, that did not shine; but within two days the part contiguous began also to shine, being laid abroad in the Dew; so as it seemeth the putrefaction spredeth. 7. There was other dead Wood of like kinde that was laid abroad, which shined not at the first; but after a nights lying abroad, begin to shine. 8. There was other Wood that did first shine, and being laid dry in the House, within five or six days lost the shining; and laid abroad again, recovered the shining. 9. Shining Woods being laid in a dry room, within a seven night lost their shining; but being laid in a Cellar, or dark room, kept the shining. 10. The boring of holes in that kinde of Wood, and then laying it abroad, seemeth to conduce to make it shine; the cause is, for that all solution of continuity, doth help on putrefaction, as was touched before. 11. No Wood hath been yet tryed to shine that was cut down alive, but such as was rooted both in Stock and Root while it grew. 12. Part of the Wood that shined, was steeped in Oyl and retained the shining a fortnight. 13. The like succeeded in some steeped in Water, and much better. 14. How long the shining will continue, if the Wood be laid abroad every night, and taken in and sprinkled with Water in the day, is not yet tryed. 16. Tryal was made of laying it abroad in frosty weather, which hurt it not. 16. There was a great piece of a Root, which did shine, and the shining part was cut off, till no more shined; yet after two nights, though it were kept in a dry Room, it got a shining.

THe bringing forth of Living Creatures may be accelerated in two respects: The one, if the Embryon ripeneth and perfecteth sooner; the other, if there be some cause from the Mothers Body of Expulsion or putting it down: Whereof the former is good, and argueth strength; the latter is ill, and cometh by accident or disease. And therefore the Ancient observation is true, that the *Childe born in the Seventh Moneth,* doth commonly well; but *Born in the Eighth Moneth,* doth (for the most part) die. But the cause assigned is fabulous, which is, That in the Eighth Moneth should be the return of the reign of the Planet *Saturn,* which (as they say) is a Planet malign; whereas in the Seventh is the reign of the *Moon,* which is a Planet propitious. But the true cause is, for that where there is so great a prevention of the ordinary time, it is the lustines of the Childe; but when it is less, it is some indisposition of the Mother.

353.
Experiment Solitary, touching the *Acceleration of Birth.*

TO Accelerate Growth or Stature, it must proceed; Either from the Plenty of the Nourishment, or from the Nature of the Nourishment, or from the Quickning and Exciting of the Natural heat. For the first, Excess of Nourishment, is hurtful; for it maketh the Childe corpulent, and growing in breadth, rather than in height. And you may take an Experiment from Plants, which if they spred much, are seldom tall. As for the Nature of the Nourishment; First, it may not be too dry, and therefore Children in Dairy Countreys do wax more tall, than where they feed more upon Bread and Flesh. There is also a received tale, that boyling of Daisie-Roots in Milk (which it is certain are great dryers) will make Dogs little. But so much is true, That an over-dry Nourishment in Childhood putteth back Stature. Secondly, The Nourishment must be of an opening

354.
Experiment Solitary, touching the *Acceleration of Growth and Stature.*

Nature; for that attenuateth the Juyce, and furthereth the Motion of the Spirits upwards. Neither is it without cause, that *Xenophon* in the Nouriture of the *Persian Children*, doth so much commend their feeding upon *Cardamon*, which (he saith) made them grow better, and be of a more active habit. *Cardamon* is in Latin, *Nasturtium*, and with us *Water-cresses*; which, it is certain, is an Herb, that whilst it is young, is friendly to Life. As for the quickning of Natural Heat, it must be done chiefly with exercise; and therefore (no doubt) much going to School, where they sit so much, hindereth the growth of Children; whereas Countrey-People, that go not to School, are commonly of better stature. And again, Men must beware how they give Children any thing that is cold in operation; even long sucking doth hinder both Wit and Stature. This hath been tryed, that a Whelp that hath been fed with *Nitre* in *Milk*, hath become very little, but extream lively: For the Spirit of Nitre is cold. And though it be an excellent Medicine in strength of years for Prolongation of Life; yet it is in Children and young Creatures an enemy to growth; and all for the same reason. For Heat is requisite to Growth. But after a Man is come to his middle age, Heat consumeth the Spirits; which the coldness of the Spirit of Nitre doth help to condence and correct.

THere be two great Families of Things, you may term them by several names, *Sulphureous* and *Mercureal*, which are the *Chymists* words: (For as for their *Salt*, which is their third Principle, it is a Compound of the other two,) *Inflamable*, and *Not Inflamable*; *Mature* and *Crude*, *Oily* and *Watry*: For we see that in *Subterranies* there are, as the Fathers of their Tribes, Brimstone and Mercury; In Vegetables and Living Creatures, there is Water and Oyl; in the Inferior order of Pneumaticals, there is Air and Flame; and in the Superior, there is the Body of the Star, and the Pure Skey. And these Pairs, though they be unlike in the Primitive Differences of Matter, yet they seem to have many consents; for Mercury and Sulphure are principal materials of Metals; Water and Oyl are principal materials of Vegetables and Animals, and seem to differ but in Maturation or Concoction. Flame (in Vulgar Opinion) is but Air incensed, and they both have quickness of Motion, and facility of Cession, much alike: And the Interstellar Skey, (though the opinion be vain, that the Star is the Denser Part of his Orb,) hath notwithstanding so much affinity with the Star, that there is a rotation of that, as well as of the Star. Therefore, it is one of the greatest *Magnalia Natura*, to turn Water or Watry Juyce into Oyl or Oyly Juyce: Greater in Nature, than to turn Silver or Quick-silver into Gold.

355. The Instances we have wherein Crude and Watry Substance, turneth into Fat and Oyly, are of four kindes. First, In the Mixture of Earth and Water, which mingled by the help of the Sun, gathered a Nitrous Fatness, more than either of them have severally; As we see, in that they put forth Plants, which need both Juyces.

356. The second is in the Assimilation of Nourishment, made in the Bodies of Plants, and Living Creatures; whereof Plants turn the Juyce of meer Water and Earth, into a great deal of Oyly matter: Living Creatures, though much of their Fat, and Flesh, are out of Oyly Aliments, (as Meat, and Bread,) yet they assimilate also in a measure their Drink of Water,

                   &c.

&c. But thefe two ways of Verfion of Water into Oyl, (namely, by Mixture and by Affimilation) are by many Paffages, and Percolations, and by continuance of foft Heats, and by circuits of Time.

The third is in the Inception of Putrefaction ; as in Water corrupted, and the Mothers of Waters diftilled, both which have a kinde of Fatnefs or Oyl.   *357.*

The fourth is in the Dulcoration of fome Metals ; as *Saccharum Saturni, &c.*   *358.*

The Intenfion of Verfion of Water into a more Oyly fubftance is by Digeftion : For Oyl is almoft nothing elfe but Water digefted and this Digeftion is principally by Heat ; which Heat muft be either outward or inward. Again, It may be by Provocation or Excitation, which is caufed by the mingling of Bodies already Oyly or Digefted, for they will fomewhat communicate their Nature with the reft. Digeftion alfo is ftrongly effected by direct Affimilation of Bodies Crude into Bodies digefted ; as in Plants and Living Creatures, whofe nourifhment is far more Crude than their Bodies. But this Digeftion is by a great compafs as hath been faid. As for the more full handling of thefe two principles, whereof this is but a tafte; (the enquiry of which, is one of the profoundeft enquiries of Nature,) we leave it to the title of Verfion of Bodies ; and likewife to the title of the Firft Congregations of Matter, which like a General Affembly of Eftates, doth give Law to all Bodies.   *359.*

A *Chamelion* is a Creature about the bignefs of an ordinary *Lizard*, his Head unproportionably big, his eyes great ; he moveth his Head without the writhing of his Neck (which is inflexible) as a *Hog* doth : His Back crooked, his Skin fpotted with little Tumors, lefs eminent nearer the Belly, his Tail flender and long ; on each Foot he hath five Fingers ; three on the outfide, and two on the infide ; his Tongue of a marvellous length, in refpect of his Body, and hollow at the end, which he will lanch out to prey upon *Flies*. Of colour Green, and of a dusky Yallow, brighter and whiter towards the Belly, yet fpotted with Blew, White, and Red. If he be laid upon Green, the Green predominateth ; if upon Yellow, the Yellow ; not fo, if he be laid upon Blew, or Red, or White, onely the Green fpots receive a more orient luftre ; laid upon Black, he looketh all Black, though not without a mixture of Green. He feedeth not onely upon Air, (though that be his principal fuftenance,) for fometimes he taketh *Flies*, as was faid ; yet fome that have kept *Chamelions* a whole year together, could never perceive that ever they fed upon any thing elfe but Air, and might obferve their Bellies to fwell after they had exhaufted the Air, and clofed their Jaws, which they open commonly againft the Rayes of the Sun. They have a foolifh Tradition in Magick, that if a *Chamelion* be burnt upon the top of an Houfe, it will raife a Tempeft, fuppofing (according to their vain Dreams of Sympathies) becaufe he nourifheth with Air, his Body fhould have great vertue to make impreffion upon the Air.   *360.*
Experiment Solitary, touching Chamelions.

I T is reported by one of the Ancients, that in part of *Media*, there are eruptions of Flames out of Plains, and that thofe Flames are clear, and caft not forth fuch fmoak, and afhes, and pumice, as Mountain Flames do. The reafon (no doubt) is, becaufe the Flame is not pent, as it is in Mountains, and Earthquakes which caft Flame. There be alfo fome blinde Fires,   *361.*
Experiment Solitary, touching Subterrany Fires.
under

under Stone, which flame not out, but Oyl being poured upon them, they flame out. The cause whereof is, for that it seemeth the Fire is so choaked, as not able to remove the Stone, it is heat rather than flame, which nevertheless is sufficient to enflame the Oyl.

362.
Experiment Solitary, touching *Nitre.*

IT is reported, that in some Lakes the Water is so Nitrous, as if foul Cloaths be put into it, it scoureth them of it self : And if they stay any whit long they moulder away. And the scouring Vertue of Nitre is the more to be noted, because it is a Body cold ; and we see warm Water scoureth better than cold. But the cause is, for that it hath a subtil Spirit, which severeth and divideth any thing that is foul, and viscous, and sticketh upon a Body.

363.
Experiment Solitary, touching *Congealing of Air.*

TAke a Bladder, the greatest you can get ; full it full of Wind, and tye it about the Neck with a Silk thred waxed ; and upon that likewise Wax very close ; so that when the Neck of the Bladder drieth, no Air may possibly get in nor out. Then bury it three or four foot under the Earth, in a Vault, or in a Conservatory of Snow, the Snow being made hollow about the Bladder ; and after some fortnights distance, see whether the Bladder be shrunk : For if it be, then it is plain, that the coldness of the Earth or Snow, hath condensed the Air, and brought it a degree nearer to Water : Which is an Experiment of great consequence.

364.
Experiment Solitary, touching *Congealing of Water into Chryftal.*

IT is a report of some good credit, that in deep Caves there are Pensile Chryftal, and degrees of Chryftal that drop from above, and in some other (though more rarely) that rise from below. Which though it be chiefly the work of cold, yet it may be, that Water that passeth thorow the Earth, gathereth a Nature more clammy, and fitter to congeal, and become solid than Water of it self. Therefore tryal would be made to lay a heap of Earth in great Frosts, upon a hollow Vessel, putting a Canvase between, that it falleth not in ; and pour Water upon it, in such quantity as will be sure to soak thorow, and see whether it will not make an harder Ice in the bottom of the Vessel, and less apt to dissolve than ordinarily. I suppose also, that if you make the Earth narrower at the bottom than at the top, in fashion of Sugar Loaf reversed, it will help the Experiment. For it will make the Ice, where it issueth, less in bulk ; and evermore smallness of quantity is a help to Version.

365.
Experiment Solitary, touching *Preserving of Rose Leaves, both in Colour and Smell.*

TAke Damask Roses and pull them, then dry them upon the top of an House, upon a Lead or Tarras in the hot Sun, in a clear day, between the hours (onely) of Twelve and two or thereabouts. Then put them into a sweet dry Earthen Bottle or a Glass with narrow mouths, stuffing them close together, but without bruising : Stop the Bottle or Glass close, and these Roses will retain, not onely their smell perfect, but their colour fresh for a year at least. Note, that nothing doth so much destroy any Plant, or other Body, either by *Putrefaction*, or *Arefaction*, as the *Adventitious Moisture*, which hangeth loose in the Body, if it be not drawn out. For it betrayeth and colleth forth the Innate and Radicall Moisture along with it when it self goeth forth. And therefore in *Living Creatures*, moderate sweat doth preserve the Juyce of the Body. Note, that these Roses when you take them from the drying, have little

or

or no smell; so that the smell is a second smell that issueth out of the Flower afterwards.

THe continuance of Flame, according unto the diversity of the Body enflamed, and other circumstances, is worthy the enquiry; chiefly, for that though Flame be (almost) of a momentany lasting, yet it receiveth the More, and the Less: We will first therefore speak (at large) of Bodies enflamed, wholly, and immediately, without any Wick to help the Inflammation. A spoonful of Spirit of Wine, a little heated was taken, and it burnt as long as came to 116 Pulses. The same quantity of Spirit of Wine, mixed with the sixth part of a spoonful of Nitre, burnt but to the space of 94 Pulses. Mixed with the like quantity of Bay-Salt 83 Pulses. Mixed with the like quantity of Gun-powder, which dissolved into a Black-water 110 Pulses. A Cube or Pellet of Yellow Wax, was taken, as much as half the Spirit of Wine, and set in the midst, and it burnt onely to the space of 87 Pulses. Mixed with the sixth part of a spoonful of Milk, it burnt to the space of 100 Pulses; and the Milk was crudled. Mixed with the sixth part of a spoonful of Water, it burnt to the space of 86 Pulses; with an equal quantity of Water, onely to the space of four Pulses. A small Pebble was laid in the midst, and the Spirit of Wine burnt to the space of 94 Pulses. A piece of Wood of the bigness of an Arrow, and about a Fingers length, was set up in the midst, and the Spirit of Wine burnt to the space of 94 Pulses. So that the Spirit of Wine Simple, endureth the longest, and the Spirit of Wine with the Bay-salt, and the equal quantity of Water, were the shortest.

Consider well, whether the more speedy going forth of the Flame, be caused by the greater vigor of the Flame in burning; or by the resistance of the Body mixed, and the aversion thereof to take Flame: Which will appear by the quantity of the Spirit of Wine, that remaineth after the going out of the Flame. And it seemeth clearly to be the latter, for that the mixture of things least apt to burn, is the speediest in going out, and note by the way, that Spirit of Wine burned, till it go out of it self, will burn no more, and tasteth nothing so hot in the mouth as it did; no nor yet sour, (as if it were a degree towards Vinegar) which burnt Wine doth, but flat and dead.

Note, that in the Experiment of Wax aforesaid, the Wax dissolved in the burning, and yet did not incorporate it self with the Spirit of Wine, to produce one Flame; but wheresoever the Wax floated, the Flame forsook it; till at last it spred all over and put the Flame quite out.

The Experiments of the Mixtures of the Spirit of Wine enflamed, are things of discovery, and not of use: But now we will speak of the continuance of Flames, such as are used for Candles, Lamps, or Tapers, consisting of Inflamable Matters, and of a Wick that provoketh Inflamation. And this importeth not onely discovery, but also use and profit: for it is a great saving in all such Lights, if they can be made as fair and bright as others, and yet last longer. Wax pure made into a Candle, and Wax mixed severally into Candle-stuff with the particulars that follow, (*Viz. Water, Aqua-vitæ, Milk, Bay-salt, Oyl, Butter, Nitre, Brimstone, Saw-dust,*) every of these bearing a sixth part to the Wax; and every of these Candles mixed, being of the same weight and wick, with the Wax pure; proved thus in the burning, and lasting. The swiftest in consuming was that with Saw-dust, which first burned fair till some part of the Candle was consumed;

and

and the duſt gathered about the ſnaſte ; but then it made the ſnaſte big, and long, and to burn duskiſhly, and the Candle waſted in half the time of the Wax pure. The next in ſwiftneſs, were the Oyl and Butter, which conſumed by a fifth part ſwifter than the pure Wax. Then followed in ſwiftneſs the clear Wax it ſelf ; then the Bay-ſalt, which laſted about an eight part longer than the clear Wax ; then followed the *Aqua-vitæ*, which laſted about a fifth part longer than the clear Wax ; then follow the Milk and Water, with little difference from the *Aqua-vitæ*, but the Water ſloweſt. And in theſe four laſt, the VVick would ſpit forth little ſparks : For the Nitre, it would not hold lighted above ſome twelve Pulſes : But all the while it would ſpit out portions of Flame, which afterwards would go out into a vapor. For the Brimſtone, it would hold lighted much about the ſame with the Nitre ; but then after a little while, it would harden and cake about the ſnaſte : So that the mixture of Bay-ſalt with VVax, will win an eighth part of the time of laſting, and the VVater a fifth.

370.   After the ſeveral materials were tryed, Tryal was likewiſe made of ſeveral VVicks ; as of ordinary Cotten, Sowing Thred, *Ruſh*, *Silk*, *Straw*, and *Wood*. The Silk, Straw, and Wood; would flame a little, till they came to the Wax, and then go out; of the other three, the Thred conſumed faſter than the Cotten, by a ſixth part of time ; the Cotten next ; then the Ruſh conſumed ſlower than the Cotton, by at leaſt a third part of time. For the bigneſs of the Flame, the Cotton, and Thred, caſt a Flame much alike, and the Ruſh much leſs and dimmer. *Quære*, whether VVood and VVicks both, as in Torches conſume faſter, than the VVicks Simple?

371.   VVe have ſpoken of the ſeveral Materials, and the ſeveral VVicks ; but to the laſting of the Flame, it importeth alſo, not onely, what the material is, but in the ſame material, whether it be hard, ſoft, old, new, &c. Good Houſwives to make their Candles burn the longer, uſe to lay them (one by one) in Bran or Flower, which make them harder, and ſo they conſume the ſlower. Inſomuch, as by this means they will out-laſt other Candles of the ſame ſtuff, almoſt half in half. For Bran and Flower have a vertue to harden, ſo that both age, and lying in the Bran doth help to the laſting. And we ſee that VVax Candles laſt longer then Tallow-Candles, becauſe VVax is more firm and hard.

372.   The laſting of Flame alſo dependeth upon the eaſie drawing of the Nouriſhment; as we ſee in the Court of *England*, there is a ſervice which they call *All-Night*; which is (as it were) a great Cake of Wax, with the Wick in the midſt; whereby it cometh to paſs, that the Wick fetcheth the Nouriſhment further off. We ſee alſo, that Lamps laſt longer, becauſe the Veſſel is far broader than the breadth of a Taper or Candle.

373.   Take a Turreted Lamp of Tin made in the form of a Square ; the height of the Turret, being thrice as much as the length of the lower part, whereupon the Lamp ſtandeth ; make onely one hole in it, at the end of the return, furtheſt from the Turret. Reverſe it, and fill it full of Oyl, by that hole ; and then ſet it upright again, and put a Wick in at the hole, and lighten it : You ſhall finde that it will burn ſlow, and a long time : Which is cauſed (as was ſaid laſt before) for that the Flame fetcheth the Nouriſhment a far off. You ſhall finde alſo, that as the Oyl waſteth and deſcendeth, ſo the top of the Turret, by little and little filleth with Air ; which is cauſed by the Rarefaction of the Oyl by the heat. It were worthy the obſervation to make a hole, in the top of the Turret, and to try, when

the

the Oyl is almoſt conſumed ; whether the Air made of the Oyl, if you put to it a flame of a Candle, in the letting of it forth, will enflame. It were good alſo to have the Lamp made, not of Tin, but of Glaſs ; that you may ſee how the Vapor or Air gathereth by degrees in the top.

A fourth point, that importeth the laſting of the Flame, is the cloſe-neſs of the Air, wherein the Flame burneth. We ſee, that if Wind blow-eth upon a Candle, it waſteth apace ; we ſee alſo, it laſteth longer in a Lan-thorn, than at large. And there are Traditions of Lamps and Candles, that have burnt a very long time in Caves and Tombs.

A fifth point, that importeth the laſting of the Flame, is the Nature of the Air where the Flame burneth; whether it be hot or cold, moiſt or dry. The Air, if it be very cold, irritateth the Flame, and maketh it burn more fiercely, (as Fire ſcorcheth in Froſty weather) and ſo furthereth the Conſumption. The Air once heated, (I conceive) maketh the Flame burn more mildly, and ſo helpeth the continuance. The Air, if it be dry, is in-different; the Air, if it be moiſt, doth in a degree quench the Flame, (as we ſee Lights will go out in the Damps of Mines ;) and howſoever maketh it burn more dully, and ſo helpeth the continuance.

BUrials in Earth ſerve for Preſervation, and for Condenſation, and for Induration of Bodies. And if you intend Condenſation or Induration, you may bury the Bodies ſo, as Earth may touch them ; as if you would make Artificial Porcellane, &c. And the like you may do for Conſerva-tion, if the Bodies be hard and ſolid, as Clay, Wood, &c. But if you intend Preſervation of Bodies, more ſoft and tender, then you muſt do one of theſe two : Either you muſt put them in caſes, whereby they may not touch the Earth ; or elſe you muſt Vault the Earth, whereby it may hang over them, and not touch them : For if the Earth touch them, it will do more hurt by the moiſture, cauſing them to putrifie, than good by the virtual cold, to conſerve them, except the Earth be very dry and ſandy.

An *Orenge, Lemmon,* and *Apple,* wrapt in a Linning Cloth, being buried for a fortnights ſpace four foot deep within the Earth, though it were in a moiſt place, and a rainy time ; yet came forth no ways mouldy or rotten, but were become a little harder than they were, otherwiſe freſh in their colour, but their Juyce ſomewhat flatted. But with the Burial of a fortnight more, they become putrified.

A Bottle of Beer buried in like manner as before, became more lively, better taſted, and clearer than it was : And a Bottle of Wine, in like manner. A Bottle of Vinegar ſo buried, came forth more lively and more odoriferous, ſmelling almoſt like a Violet. And after the whole Moneths Burial, all the three came forth as freſh and lively, if not better than before.

It were a profitable Experiment, to preſerve Orenges, Lemmons, and Pomgranates, till Summer ; for then their price will be mightily encreaſed. This may be done, if you put them in a Pot or Veſſel well covered that the moiſture of the Earth come not at them ; or elſe by put-ting them in a Conſervatory of Snow. And generally, whoſoever will make Experiments of Cold, let him be provided of three things, a Conſervatory of Snow, a good large Vault, twenty foot at leaſt under the Ground, and a deep Well.

There

374.

375.

376.
Experiments in Conſort, touching Burials or In-fuſions of di-vers Bodies in Earth.

377.

378.

379.

380.

There hath been a Tradition, that Pearl, and Coral, Surchois-Stone, that have loſt their Colours, may be recovered by burying in the Earth; which is a thing of great profit, if it would ſort : But upon tryal of ſix weeks Burial, there followed no effect. It were good ro try it in a deep Well, or in a Conſervatory of Snow, where the cold may be more conſtringent ; and ſo make the Body more united, and thereby more reſplendent.

381.

Experiment Solitary, touching the *Affects in Mens Bodies from ſeveral Winds.*

MEns *Bodies* are heavier and leſs diſpoſed to Motion when Southern Winds blow, then when Northern. The cauſe is, for that when the Southern Winds blow, the Humors do (in ſome degree) melt, and wax fluide, and ſo flow into the parts ; as it is ſeen in Wood, and other Bodies, which when the Southern Winds blow, do ſwell. Beſides, the Motion and Activity of the Body conſiſteth chiefly in the ſinews, which, when the Southern Wind bloweth, are more relax.

382.

Experiment Solitary, touching *Winter and Summers Sickneſſes.*

IT is commonly ſeen, that more are ſick in the Summer, and more dye in the Winter ; except it be in Peſtilent Diſeaſes, which commonly reign in Summer or Autumn. The reaſon is, becauſe Diſeaſes are bred (indeed) chiefly by Heat ; but then they are cured moſt by Sweat and Purge, which in the Summer cometh on, or is provoked more eaſily : As for Peſtilent Diſeaſes, the Reaſon why moſt dye of them in Summer, is becauſe they are bred moſt in the Summer ; for otherwiſe, thoſe that are touched are in moſt danger in the Winter.

383.

Experiment Solitary, touching *Peſtilential Seaſons.*

THe general opinion is, That Years hot and moiſt, are moſt Peſtilent ; upon the ſuperficial Ground, that Heat and Moiſture cauſe Putrefaction. In *England* it is found not true; for, many times, there have been great Plagues in dry years. VVhereof the cauſe may be, for that drought in the Bodies of Iſlanders, habituate to moiſt Airs, doth exaſperate the Humors, and maketh them more apt to Putrifie or Enflame; beſides, it tainteth the VVaters (commonly) and maketh them leſs wholſome. And again in *Barbary*, the Plagues break up in the Summer-Moneths, when the VVeather is hot and dry.

384.

Experiment Solitary, touching *An Error received about Epidemical Diſeaſes.*

MAny Diſeaſes, (both Epidemical and others) break forth at particular times. And the cauſe is falſly imputed to the conſtitution of the Air, at that time, when they break forth or reign; whereas it proceedeth (indeed) from a Precedent Sequence, and Series of the Seaſons of the Year : And therefore *Hippocrates*, in his Prognoſticks, doth make good obſervations of the Diſeaſes, that enſue upon the Nature of the precedent four Seaſons of the Year.

385.

Experiment Solitary, touching the *Alteration or Preſervation of Liquors in Wells, or deep Vaults.*

TRyal hath been made with Earthen Bottles, well ſtopped, hanged in a VVell of Twenty Fathom deep, at the leaſt ; and ſome of the Bottles have been let down into the VVater, ſome others have hanged above, within about a Fathom of the VVater ; and the Liquors ſo tryed have been, Beer, (not new, but ready for drinking) and VVine, and Milk. The proof hath been, that both the Beer, and the VVine, (as well within VVater, as above) have not been palled or deaded at all ; but as good, or ſomewhat better than Bottles of the ſame Drinks and ſtaleneſs, kept in a Celler. But thoſe which did hang above VVater, were apparently the beſt ; and that Beer did

flower

flower a little ; Whereas that under Water did not, though it were fresh.
The Milk foured, and began to putrifie. Nevertheless it is true, that there is a
Village near *Blois*, where in deep Caves they do thicken Milk, in such fort,
that it becometh very pleasant ; which was some cause of this tryal of hanging Milk in the Well : But our proof was naught, neither do I know, whether that Milk in those Caves be first boyled.   It were good therefore to try
it with Milk fodden, and with Cream ; for that Milk of it self, is such a Compound Body of Cream, Cruds, and Whey, as it is easily turned and diffolved.
It were good also to try the Beer, when it is in Wort, that it may be seen,
whether the hanging in the Well, will accelerate the ripening and clarifying
of it.

Ivers, we see, do Stut. The cause may be (in most) the Refrigeration of
the Tongue, whereby it is less apt to move ; and therefore we see,
that Naturals do generally Stut : And we see, that in those that Stut , if they
drink Wine moderately, they Stut less, because it heateth : And so we see,
that they that Stut, do Stut more in the first offer to speak, than in continuance;
because the Tongue is, by motion, somewhat heated.   In some also, it may
be (though rarely) the dryness of the Tongue , which likewise maketh it
less apt to move as well as cold; for it is an affect that cometh to some wise
and great Men, as it did unto *Moses*, who was *Lingua Præpedita* : And many
Stutters (we finde) are very Cholerick Men, Choler enducing a dryness in
the Tongue.

386.
Experiment
Solitary,
touching
Stutting.

Mells, and other Odors, are sweeter in the Air, at some distance, than near
the Nose ; as hath been partly touched heretofore. The cause is double,
first, The finer mixture, or incorporation of the Smell. For we see, that in
Sounds likewise, they are sweetest, when we cannot hear every part by it self.
The other reason is, For that all sweet Smells have joyned with them some
Earthy or Crude Odors ; and at some distance the Sweet, which is the more
spiritual, is perceived ; and the Earthy reacheth not so far.

387.
Experiments
in Consort,
touching the
Smells.

Sweet Smells are most forcible in dry Substances, when they are broken ;
and so likewise in *Orenges* or *Lemmons*, the nipping off their Rinde, giveth out
their smell more : And generally, when Bodies are moved or stirred, though
not broken, they smell more, as a Sweet-Bag waved. The cause is double;
the one, for that there is a greater emiffion of the Spirit, when way is made :
And this holdeth in the Breaking, Nipping, or Crushing ; it holdeth also,
(in some degree) in the Moving. But in this last, there is a concurrence of
the second cause, which is the Impulsion of the Air, that bringeth the sent
faster upon us.

388.

The daintiest smells of Flowers, are out of those Plants whose Leaves
smell not ; as *Violets, Rofes, Wall-flowers, Gilly-flowers, Pincks, Wood-bine, Vine-
flowers, Apple-blooms, Limetree-blooms, Bean-blooms, &c.* The cause is, for that
where there is heat and strength enough in the Plant to make the Leaves
odorate, there the smell of the Flower is rather evanide and weaker, than
that of the Leaves ; as it is in *Rofemary-flowers, Lavender-flowers,* and *Sweet-Brier
Rofes* : But where there is less heat, there the Spirit of the Plant is digested
and refined, and severed from the grosser Juyce in the Efflorescence, and not
before.

389.

I

Most

390.

Moſt Odors ſmell beſt, broken, or cruſht, as hath been ſaid ; but Flowers preſſed or beaten, do loſe the freſhneſs and ſweetneſs of their Odor. The cauſe is, for that when they are cruſhed, the groſſer and more earthy Spirit cometh out with the Finer, and troubleth it ; whereas in ſtronger Odors there are no ſuch degrees of the iſſue of the ſmell.

391.
Experiments in Conſort, touching the Goodneſs and Choice of Water.

IT is a thing of very good uſe, to diſcover the goodneſs of Waters. The taſte to thoſe that drink Water onely doth ſomewhat : But other Experiments are more ſure. Firſt, try Waters by weight, wherein you may finde ſome difference, though not much : And the lighter, you may account the better.

392.

Secondly, Try them by boiling upon an equal fire ; and that which conſumeth away faſteſt, you may account the beſt.

393.

Thirdly, Try them in ſeveral Bottles or open Veſſels, matches in every thing elſe, and ſee which of them laſt longeſt without ſtench or corruption ; and that which holdeth unputrified longeſt, you may likewiſe account the beſt.

394.

Fourthly, Try them by making Drinks, ſtronger or ſmaller, with the ſame quantity of Malt ; and you may conclude, that that Water, which maketh the ſtronger Drink, is the more concocted and nouriſhing ; though perhaps it be not ſo good for Medicinal uſe. And ſuch VVater (commonly) is the VVater of large and navigable Rivers ; and likewiſe in large and clean Ponds of ſtanding VVater : For upon both them, the Sun hath more power than upon Fountains, or ſmall Rivers. And I conceive, that Chalk-water is next them the beſt, for going furtheſt in Drink. For that alſo helpeth concoction, ſo it be out of a deep VVell ; for then it cureth the rawneſs of the VVater ; but Chalky-water towards the top of the Earth, is too fretting, as it appeareth in Laundry of Cloaths, which wear out apace, if you uſe ſuch VVaters.

395.

Fifthly, The Houſwives do finde a difference in Waters, for the bearing or not bearing of Soap ; and it is likely, that the more fat water will bear Soap beſt, for the hungry water doth kill the unctuous nature of the Soap.

396.

Sixthly, You may make a judgment of Waters according to the place, whence they ſpring or come. The Rain-water is by the Phyſitians eſteemed the fineſt and the beſt ; but yet it is ſaid to putrifie ſooneſt, which is likely, becauſe of the fineneſs of the Spirit ; and in Conſervatories of Rain-water, (ſuch as they have in *Venice, &c*) they are found not ſo choice Waters ; (the worſe perhaps) becauſe they are covered aloft, and kept from the Sun. Snow-water is held unwholeſome, inſomuch, as the people that dwell at the Foot of the Snow Mountains, or otherwiſe upon the aſcent, (eſpecially the VVomen) by drinking of Snow-water, have great bags hanging under their Throats. VVell VVater, except it be upon Chalk, or a very plentiful Spring maketh Meat red, which is an ill ſign. Springs on the tops of high Hills are the beſt ; for both they ſeem to have a Lightneſs and Appetite of Mounting ; and beſides, they are moſt pure and unmingled : And again are more percolated through a great ſpace of Earth. For VVaters in Valleys, joyn in effect under ground with all VVaters of the ſame Level ; whereas Springs on the tops of Hills, paſs through a great deal of pure Earth with leſs mixture of other VVaters.

396.

Seventhly, Judgment may be made of *Waters* by the Soyl whereupon the VVater runneth, as Pebble is the cleaneſt and beſt taſted ; and next to that

Clay.

Clay-water; and thirdly, Water upon Chalk; Fourthly, that upon Sand; and worst of all, upon Mud. Neither may you trust *Waters* that taste sweet, for they are commonly found in Rising-grounds of great Cities, which must needs take in a great deal of filth.

IN *Peru*, and divers parts of the *West-Indies*, though under the Line, the Heats are not so intolerable. as they be in *Barbary*, and the Skirts of the *Torrid Zone.* The causes are, first, the great Brizes which the motion of the Air in great Circles (such as are under the Girdle of the World) produceth, which do refrigerate; and therefore in those parts, Noon is nothing so hot when the Brizes are great, as about nine or ten of the clock in the Forenoon. Another cause is, for that the length of the Night, and the Dews thereof, do compence the Heat of the day. A third cause is, the stay of the Sun; not in respect of day and night (for that we spake of before) but in respect of the Season: For under the Line, the Sun crosseth the Line, and maketh two Summers and two Winters; but in the skirts of the *Torrid Zone*, it doubleth and goeth back again, and so maketh one long Summer.

THe heat of the Sun maketh Men black in some Countreys, as in *Æthiopia* and *Guinny, &c* Fire doth it not as we see in Glass-Men, that are continually about the Fire. The reason may be, because Fire doth lick up the Spirits and Blood of the Body, so as they exhale; so that it ever maketh Men look Pale and Sallow; but the Sun which is a gentler heat, doth but draw the Blood to the outward parts, and rather concocteth it, then soaketh it: And therefore, we see that all *Æthiopes* are fleshly, plump, and have great Lips. All which betoken moisture retained, and not drawn out. We see also, that the *Negroes* are bred in Coun'reys that have plenty of Water, by Rivers or otherwise: For *Mero*, which was the *Metropolis* of *Æthiopia*, was upon a great Lake; and *Congo*, where the *Negroes* are, is full of Rivers. And the confines of the River *Niger*, where the *Negroes* also are, are well watered; and the Region about *Capo Verde* is likewise moist, insomuch, as it is pestilent through moisture: But the Countreys of the *Abyssenes*, and *Barbary*, and *Peru*, where they are Tawney. and Olivaster, and Pale, are generally more sandy and dry. As for the *Æthiopes*, as they are plump and fleshly, so (it may be) they are Sanguine and Ruddy coloured, if their Black Skin would suffer it to be seen.

SOme Creatures do move a good while after their head is off, as Birds. Some a very little time, as Men and all Beasts. Some move, though cut in several pieces, as Snakes, Eels, Worms, Flies, &c. First, therefore it is certain, that the immediate cause of Death, is the resolution or extinguishment of the Spirits; and that the destruction or corruption of the Organs, is but the mediate cause. But some Organs are so peremptorily necessary, that the extinguishment of the Spirits doth speedily follow; but yet so, as there is an Interim of a small time. It is reported by one of the Ancients, of credit, That a Sacrificed Beast hath lowed after the Heart hath been severed; and it is a report also of credit, That the Head of a Pig hath been opened, and the Brain put into the Palm of a Mans Hand, trembling, without breaking any part of it, or severing it from the Marrow of the Back-bone: during which time, the Pig hath been, in all appearance, stark dead, and without motion: And after a small time the Brain hath been replaced,

398.
Experiment Solitary, touching the Temperate Heat under the Æquinoctial.

399.
Experiment Solitary, touching the Coloration of Black and Tawny Mors.

400.
Experiment Solitary, touching Motion after the Instant of Death.

and the Skull of the Pig cloſed, and the Pig hath a little after gone about. And certain it is, that an Eye upon Revenge, hath been thruſt forth, ſo as it hanged a pretty diſtance by the Viſual Nerve; and during that time, the Eye hath been without any power of Sight; and yet after (being replaced) recovered Sight. Now the *Spirits* are chiefly in the Head, and Cells of the Brain, which in Men and Beaſts are large; and therefore, when the Head is off, they move little or nothing: But Birds have ſmall Heads, and therefore the *Spirits* are a little more diſperſed in the Sinews, whereby Motion remaineth in them a little longer; inſomuch, as it is extant in ſtory, that an Emperor of *Rome*, to ſhew the certainty of his hand, did ſhoot a great Forked Arrow at an *Eſtrich*, as ſhe ran ſwiftly upon the Stage, and ſtroke off her Head; and yet ſhe continued the race a little way with her Head off. As for Worms, and Flies, and Eels, the *Spirits* are diffuſed almoſt all over; and therefore they move in their ſeveral pieces.

NATURAL HISTORY.

Century V.

E will now enquire of *Plants* or *Vegetables*; and we shall do it with diligence. They are the principal part of the *Third days Work*; they are the first *Producat*, which is the word of *Animation*, for the other words are but the words of Essence; and they are of excellent and general use, For *Food*, *Medicine*, and a number of *Medicinal Arts*.

Experiments in Consort, touching the *Acceleration of Germination*.

There were sown in a Bed, *Turnip seed, Raddish-seed, Wheat, Cucumber-seed,* and *Pease*. The Bed we call a Hot-bed, and the manner of it is this. There was taken *Horse-dung*, old, and well rotted; this was laid upon a Bank half a foot high, and supported round about with Planks; and upon the top was cast sifted Earth, some two fingers deep; and then the Seed sprinkled upon it, having been steeped all night in Water mixed with Cow-dung. The *Turnip-seed*, and the *Wheat*, came up half an inch above ground, within two days after, without any watering; the rest the third day. The Experiment was made in *October*, and (it may be) in the Spring, the Accelerating would have been the speedier. This is a noble Experiment; for, without this help, they would have been four times as long in coming up. But there doth not occur to me, at this present, any use thereof, for profit, except it should be for Sowing of *Pease*, which have their price very much increased by the early coming. It may be tryed also with Cherries, Strawberries, and other Fruit which are dearest, when they come early.

401.

There was Wheat steeped in Water mixed with Cow dung, other in Water mixed with Horse-dung, other in Water mixed with Pigeon-dung,

402.

I 3 other

other in Urine of Man, other in Water mixed with Chalk powder'd, other in Water mixed with Soot, other in Water mixed with Ashes, other in Water mixed with Bay-Salt, other in Claret Wine, other in Malmsey, other in Spirit of Wine. The proportion of the mixture was, a fourth part of the ingredients to the Water, save that there was not of the Salt above an eight part. The Urine, and Winds, and Spirit of Wine, were simple without mixture of Water; the time of steeping was twelve hours; the time of the year *October*. There was also other Wheat sown unsteeped, but watred twice a day with warm Water; there was also other Wheat sown simple, to compare it with the rest. The event was, that those that were in the mixture of Dung, and Urine, Soot, Chalk, Ashes, and Salt, came up within six days; and those that afterwards proved the highest, thickest, and most lusty, were, first the Urine, and then the Dungs; next the Chalk, next the Soot, next the Ashes, next the Salt, next the Wheat simple of it self unsteeped and unwatered, next the watered twice a day with warm Water next the Claret Wine. So that these three last were slower than the ordinary Wheat of it self; and this Culture did rather retard than advance. As for those that were steeped in Malmsey, and Spirit of Wine, they came not up at all. This is a rich Experiment for profit ; for the most of the steepings are cheap things, and the goodness of the crop is a great matter of gain ; if the goodness of the crop answer the earliness of the coming up, as it is like it will, both being from the vigor of the Seed ; which also partly appeared in the former Experiment, as hath been said. This Experiment would be tryed in other Grains, Seeds, and Kernels; for it may be some steeping will agree best with some Seeds. It would be also tryed with Roots steeped as before, but for longer time ; it would be tryed also in several seasons of the Year, especially in the Spring.

403.   *Strawberries* watered now and then (as once in three days) with Water, wherein hath been steeped Sheeps-dung, or Pigeons-dung, will prevent and come early. And it is like the same effect would follow in other *Berries, Herbs, Flowers, Grains, or Trees*; and therefore it is an Experiment, though vulgar in *Strawberries*, yet not brought into use generally : For it is usual to help the Ground with Muck, and likewise to recomfort it sometimes with Muck put to the Roots, but to water it with Muck-water, which is like to be more forcible, is not practised.

404.   *Dung*, or *Chalk*, or *Blood*, applied in substance (seasonably) to the Roots of Trees, doth set them forwards. But to do it unto *Herbs*, without mixture of Water or Earth, it may be these helps are too hot.

405.   The former means of helping Germination, are either by the goodness and strength of the Nourishment, or by the comforting and exciting the Spirits in the Plant, to draw the Nourishment better. And of this latter kinde concerning the comforting of the Spirits of the Plant, are also the experiments that follow ; though they be not applications to the Root or Seed. The planting of Trees warm upon a Wall, against the South or South-East Sun, doth hasten their coming on and ripening; and the South-East is found to be better than the South-West, though the South-West be the hotter Coast. But the cause is chiefly, for that the heat of the morning succeedeth the cold of the night ; and partly, because (many times) the South-West Sun is too parching. So likewise planting of them upon the Back of a Chimney where a fire is kept, doth hasten their coming on, and ripening : Nay more, the drawing of the Boughs into the inside of a room, where a Fire is continually kept, worketh the same effect ; which

hath

hath been tryed with Grapes; infomuch, as they will come a Moneth earlier, then the Grapes abroad.

Befides the two Means of Accelerating Germination, formerly defcribed; that is to fay, the mending of the Nourifhment; comforting of the Spirit of the Plant; there is a third, which is the making way for the eafie coming to the Nourifhment, and drawing it. And therefore gentle digging and loofning of the Earth about the Roots of Trees, and the removing Herbs and Flowers into new Earth, once in two years (which is the fame thing, for the new Earth is ever loofer) doth greatly further the profpering and earlinefs of Plants.   406.

But the moft admirable Acceleration by facilitating the Nourifhment, is that of Water. For a Standard of a *Damask Rofe* with the Root on, was fet in a Chamber, where no Fire was, upright in an Earthen Pan, full of fair Water, without any mixture, half a foot under the Water, the Standard being more than two foot high above the Water. Within, in the fpace of ten days, the Standard did put forth a fair green Leaf, and fome other little Buds, which ftood at a ftay without any fhew of decay or withering, more then feven days. But afterwards that Leaf faded, but the young Buds did fprout on, which afterward opened into fair Leaves, in the fpace of three Moneths, and continued fo a while after, till upon removal we left the tryal. But note, that the Leaves were fomewhat paler, and light-coloured then the Leaves ufe to be abroad. Note, that the firft Buds were in the end of *October*, and it is likely, that if it had been in the Spring time, it would have put forth with greater ftrength, and (it may) be to have grown on to bear Flowers. By this means, you may have (as it feemeth) Rofes fet in the midft of a Pool, being fupported with fome ftay; which is matter of rarenefs and pleafure, though of fmall ufe. This is the more ftrange, for that the like Rofe Standard was put at the fame time, into Water mixed with Horfe-dung, the Horfe-dung about the fourth part to the Water, and in four Moneths fpace (while it was obferved) put not forth any Leaf, though divers Buds at the firft, as the other.   407.

A *Dutch Flower* that had a *Bulbous Root*, was likewife put at the fame time all under Water, fome two or three fingers deep; and within feven days fprouted, and continued long after further growing. There were alfo put in, a *Beet-root*, a *Borrage-root*, and a *Raddish-root*, which had all their Leaves cut almoft clofe to the Roots; and within fix weeks had fair Leaves, and fo continued till the end of *November*.   408.

Note, that if Roots, or Peafe, or Flowers may be accelerated in their coming and ripening, there is a double profit; the one in the high price that thofe things bear when they come early; the other in the fwiftnefs of their returns: For in fome Grounds which are ftrong, you fhall have a Raddifh, &c. come in a moneth, that in other Grounds will not come in two, and fo make double returns.   409.

Wheat alfo was put into the Water, and came not forth at all; fo as it feemeth there muft be fome ftrength and bulk in the Body, put into the Water, as it is in Roots; for Grains, or Seeds, the cold of the Water will mortifie. But cafually fome Wheat lay under the Pan, which was fomewhat moiftened by the fuing of the Pan, which in fix weeks (as aforefaid) looked mouldy to the eye, but it was fprouted forth half a fingers length.   410.

It feemeth by thefe Inftances of Water, that for nourifhment the Water is almoft all in all, and that the Earth doth but keep the Plant upright, and fave it from over-heat, and over-cold; and therefore is a comfortable Experiment for good Drinkers. It proveth alfo that our former opinion, that   411.

Drink

Drink incorporate with Fleſh or Roots (as in *Capon-Beer, &c.*) will nouriſh more eaſily than Meat and Drink taken ſeverally.

412. The Houſing of Plants (I conceive) will both Accelerate Germination, and bring forth Flowers and Plants in the colder Seaſons: And as we Houſe-hot Countrey Plants, as *Lemmons, Orenges, Myrtles*, to ſave them; ſo we may Houſe our own Country Plants to forward them, and make them come in the cold Seaſons, in ſuch ſort, that you may have *Violets, Strawberries, Peaſe*, all Winter: So that you ſow or remove them at fit times. This Experiment is to be referred unto the comforting of the *Spirit* of the Plant by warmth as well as Houſing their Boughs, &c. So then the means to Accelerate Germination, are in particular eight, in general three.

413.

Experiments in Conſort, touching the Putting back or Retardation of Germination.

TO make *Roſes* or other *Flowers* come late, it is an Experiment of Pleaſure. For the Ancients eſteemed much of *Roſa Sera*, and indeed the *November Roſe* is the ſweeteſt, having been leſs exhaled by the Sun. The Means are theſe, Firſt, The cutting off their tops immediately after they have done bearing, and then they will come again the ſame year about *November*; but they will not come juſt on the tops where they were cut, but out of thoſe Shoots which were (as it were) Water-boughs. The cauſe is, for that the Sap, which otherwiſe would have fed the top, (though after bearing) will, by the diſcharge of that, divert unto the Side-ſprouts, and they will come to bear, but later.

414. The ſecond is the *Pulling of the Buds of the Roſe*, when they are newly knotted, for then the ſide Branches will bear. The cauſe is the ſame with the former: For *cutting off the Tops, and pulling off the Buds*, work the ſame effect, in Retenſion of the Sap for a time, and Diverſion of it to the Sprouts that were not ſo forward.

415. The third is the cutting off ſome few of the Top-boughs in the Spring time but ſuffering the lower Boughs to grow on. The cauſe is, for that the Boughs do help to draw up the Sap more ſtrongly; and we ſee that in Pouling of Trees, many do uſe to leave a Bough or two on the top to help to draw up the Sap. And it is reported alſo, That if you graft upon the Bough of a Tree, and cut off ſome of the old Boughs, the new Cions will periſh.

416. The fourth is by laying the Roots bare about *Chriſtmas* ſome days. The cauſe is plain, for that it doth arreſt the Sap from going upwards for a time; which arreſt, is afterwards releaſed by the covering of the Root again with Earth, and then the Sap getteth up, but later.

417. The fifth is the removing of the Tree ſome Moneth before it Buddeth. The cauſe is, for that ſome time will be required after the Remove, for the Reſetling, before it can draw the Juyce; and that time being loſt, the bloſſom muſt needs come forth later.

418. The ſixth is the Grafting of Roſes in *May*, which commonly Gardiners do not till *July*, and then they bear not till the next year; but if you graft them in *May*, they will bear the ſame year, but late.

419. The ſeventh is the Girding of the Body of the Tree about with ſome Packthred; for that alſo in a degree reſtraineth the Sap, and maketh it come up more late, and more ſlowly.

420. The eighth is the Planting of them in a Shade or in a Hedge. The cauſe is, partly the keeping out of the Sun, which haſtneth the Sap to riſe, and partly the robbing of them of Nouriſhment by the ſtuff in the Hedge;

theſe

thefe means may be practifed upon other, both Trees, and Flowers, *Mutatis mutandis.*

Men have entertained a conceit that fheweth prettily, namely, That if you graft a Late-coming-Fruit, upon a Stock of a Fruit-tree that cometh early, the Graft will bear Fruit early, as a Peach upon a Cherry: And contrariwife, if an Early-coming-Fruit upon a Stock of a Fruit-tree that cometh late, the Graft will bear Fruit late; as a Cherry upon a Peach. But thefe are but imaginations, and untrue. The caufe is, for that the Cions over-ruleth the Stock quite, and the Stock is but Paffive onely, and giveth Aliment, but no Motion to the Graft.

421.

WE will fpeak now, how to make *Fruits, Flowers,* and *Roots* larger, in more plenty and fweeter than they ufe to be; and how to make the *Trees* themfelves more tall, more fpred, and more hafty and fudden, than they ufe to be. Wherein there is no doubt, but the former *Experiments* of *Acceleration* will ferve much to thefe purpofes. And again, that thefe *Experiments* which we fhall now fet down, do ferve alfo for *Acceleration,* becaufe both Effects proceeds from the encreafe of Vigor in the Tree; but yet to avoid confufion. And becaufe fome of the Means are more proper for the one effect, and fome for the other. We will handle them apart.

Experiments in Confort, touching the Melioration of Fruit Trees, and Plants.

It is an affured Experience, That an heap of Flint or Stone, laid about the bottom of a wilde Tree, (as in Oak, Elm, Afh, &c.) upon the firft planting, doth make it profper double as much as without it. The caufe is, for that it retaineth the moifture which falleth at any time upon the Tree, and fuffereth it not to be exhaled by the Sun. Again, it keepeth the Tree warm from cold Blafts and Frofts, as it were in an Houfe. It may be alfo, there is fomewhat in the keeping of it fteady at the firft. *Quere,* if laying of Straw fome height about the Body of a Tree, will not make the Tree forwards: For though the Root giveth the Sap, yet it is the Body that draweth it. But you muft note, that if you lay Stones about the Stalk of Lettuce, or other Plants that are more foft, it will over-moiften the Roots, fo as the *Worms* will eat them.

422.

A Tree at the firft fetting, fhould not be fhaken, untill it hath taken Root fully; And therefore fome have put too little Forks about the bottom of their Trees, to keep them upright; but after a years rooting, then fhaking doth the Tree good by loofning of the Earth, and (perhaps) by exercifing (as it were) and ftirring the Sap of the Tree.

423

Generally, the cutting away of Boughs and Suckers at the Root and Body, doth make Trees grow high; and contrariwife, the Poling and Cutting of the top, maketh them grow, fpred, and bufhy; as we fee in Pollords, &c.

424.

It is reported, That to make hafty growing Coppice wood, the way is, to take Willow, Sallow, Popler, Alder, of fome feven years growth; and to fet them, not upright, but a-flope, a reafonable depth under the Ground; and then inftead of one Root they will put forth many, and fo carry more fhoots upon a Stem.

425.

When you would have many new Roots of Fruit-Trees, take a low Tree, and bow it, and lay all his Branches a flat upon the ground, and caft Earth upon them, and every twig will take Root. And this is a very profitable Experiment for coftly Trees; (for the Boughs will make Stocks without charge) fuch as are *Apricots, Peaches, Almonds, Cornelians, Mulberries, Figs, &c.*

426.

&c. The like is continually practised with Vines, Roses, Musk-Roses, &c.

427.   From *May* to *July* you may take off the Bark of any Bough, being of the bignels of Three or four Inches, and cover the bare place, somewhat above and below with Loam, well tempered with Horse-dung, binding it fast down. Then cut off the Bough about *Alhollantide* in the bare place, and set it in Ground, and it will grow to be a fair Tree in one year. The cause may be, for that the Bearing from the Bark, keepeth the Sap from delcending towards Winter, and so holdeth it in the Bough; and it may be also, that Loam and Horse-dung applied to the bare place, do moiften it and cherish it, and make it more apt to put forth the Root. Note, that this may be a general means for keeping up the Sap of Trees in their Boughs, which may ferve to other effects.

428.   It hath been practifed in Trees that shew fair and bear not, to bore a hole thorow the Heart of the Tree, and thereupon it will bear. Which may be, for that the Tree before hath too much Repletion, and was oppreffed with his own Sap; for Repletion is an enemy to Generation.

429.   It hath been practifed in Trees that do not bear, to cleave two or three of the chief Roots, and to put into the Cleft a small Pebble which may keep it open, and then it will bear. The cause may be, for that a Root of a Tree may be (as it were) hide-bound, no lefs then the Body of the Tree; but it will not keep open without somewhat put into it.

430.   It is usually practifed to set Trees that require much Sun, upon Walls against the South; as *Apricots*, *Peaches*, *Plumbs*, *Vines*, *Figs*, and the like. It hath a double commodity; the one, the heat of the Wall by reflexion; the other, the taking away of the shade: For when a Tree groweth round, the upper Boughs over shaddow the lower, but when it is spred upon a Wall, the Sun cometh alike upon the upper and lower Branches.

431.   It hath also been practifed (by some) to pull some Leaves from the Trees so spred, that the Sun may come upon the Bough and Fruit the better. There hath been practifed also a curiofity, to set a Tree upon the North fide of a Wall, and at a little height, to draw him through the Wall, and spred him upon the South fide; conceiving, that the Root and lower part of the Stock should enjoy the frefhnefs of the shade, and the upper Boughs and Fruit, the comfort of the Sun; but it forted not. The cause is, for that the Root requireth some comfort from the Sun, though under Earth, as well as the Body; and the lower part of the Body more than the upper, as we fee in compafing a Tree below with ftraw.

432.   The lownefs of the Bough, where the Fruit cometh, maketh the Fruit greater, and to ripen better; for you shall ever fee in *Apricotes*, *Peaches*, or *Melo-Cotones* upon a Wall, the greateft Fruits towards the bottom. And in *France* the Grapes that make the Wine, grow upon the low Vines, bound to small Stakes; and the raifed Vines in Arbors, make but Verjuyce. It is true, that in *Italy*, and other Countreys where they have hotter Sun, they raife them upon Elms and Trees: But I conceive, that if the French manner of Planting low, were brought in ufe, their Wines would be ftronger and sweeter: But it is more chargeable in refpect of the Props. It were good to try whether a Tree grafted somewhat near the ground, and the lower Boughs onely maintained, and the higher continually proyned off, would not make a larger Fruit.

433.   To have Fruit in greater Plenty, the way is to graft, not onely upon young Stocks, but upon divers Boughs of an old Tree; for they will bear

great

great numbers of Fruit; whereas if you graft but upon one Stock, the Tree can bear but few.

434. The digging yearly about the Roots of Trees, which is a great means, both to the Acceleration and Melioration of Fruits, is practised in nothing but in Vines; which, if it were transferred unto other Trees and Shrubs, (as Roses, &c.) I conceive, would advance them likewise.

435. It hath been known, that a Fruit-tree hath been blown up (almost) by the Roots, and set up again, and the next year bare exceedingly. The cause of this was nothing but the loosening of the Earth, which comforteth any Tree, and is fit to be practised more than it is in Fruit-trees: For Trees cannot be so fitly removed into new Grounds, as Flowers and Herbs may.

436. To revive an old Tree, the digging of it about the Roots, and applying new Mould to the Roots, is the way. We see also that Draught-Oxen put into fresh Pasture, gather new and tender flesh; and in all things, better nourishment than hath been used, doth help to renew, especially, if it be not onely better but changed, and differing from the former.

437. If an Herb be cut off from the Roots in the beginning of Winter, and then the Earth be trodden and beaten down hard with the Foot and Spade, the Roots will become of very great magnitude in Summer. The reason is, for that the moisture being forbidden to come up in the Plant, stayeth longer in the Root, and so dilateth it. And Gardiners use to tread down any loose Ground after they have sown Onions, or Turnips, &c.

438. If *Panicum* be laid below, and about the bottom of a Root, it will cause the Root to grow to an excessive bigness. The cause is, for that being it self of a spungy substance, it draweth the moisture of the Earth to it, and so feedeth the Root. This is of greatest use for *Onions*, *Turnips*, *Parsnips*, and *Carrets*.

439. The shifting of Ground is a means to better the Tree and Fruit; but with this Caution, That all things do prosper best, when they are advanced to the better. Your Nursery of Stocks ought to be in a more barren Ground, than the Ground is whereunto you remove them. So all *Grafiers* prefer their Cattle from meaner Pastures to better. We see also, that hardness in youth lengthneth life, because it leaveth a cherishing to the better of the Body in Age: Nay, in exercises it is good to begin with the hardest, as Dancing in thick Shooes, &c.

440. It hath been observed, that hacking of Trees in their Bark, both down-right, and a cross, so as you make them rather in slices, than in continued Hacks, doth great good to Trees, and especially delivereth them from being Hide-bound, and killeth their Moss.

441. Shade to some Plants conduceth to make them large and prosperous more than Sun; as in Strawberries, and Bays, &c. Therefore amongst Straw-berries, sow here and there some Borrage-Seed; and you shall finde the Straw-berries under those Leaves, far more large than their fellows. And Bays you must plant to the North, or defend them from the Sun by a Hedg Row; and when you sow the Berries, weed not the Borders for the first half year; for the Weed giveth them Shade.

442. To increase the Crops of Plants, there would be considered, not onely the increasing the Lust of the Earth, or of the Plant, but the saving also of that which is spilt. So they have lately made a tryal to set VVheat; which nevertheless hath been left off, because of the trouble and pains; yet so much is true, that there is much saved by the Setting, in comparison of

that

that which is Sown; both by keeping it from being picked up by Birds, and by avoiding the shallow lying of it, whereby much that is sown, taketh no Root.

443. It is prescribed by some of the Ancients, that you take small Trees, upon which Figs or other Fruit grow, being yet unripe, and cover the Trees in the middle of Autumn with Dung until the Spring, and then take them up in a warm day, and replant them in good Ground; and by that means, the former years Tree will be ripe, as by a new Birth, when other Trees of the same kinde do but blossom. But this seemeth to have no great probability.

444. It is reported, That if you take Nitre; and mingle it with VVater, to the thickness of Honey, and therewith anoint the Bud, after the Vine is cut, it will sprout forth within eight days. The cause is like to be (if the Experiment be true) the opening of the Bud, and of the parts contiguous, by the Spirit of the Nitre; for Nitre is (as it were) the life of Vegetables.

445. Take *Seed* or *Kernels* of *Apples*, *Pears*, *Orenges*; or a *Peach*, or a *Plumb-Stone* &c. And put them into a *Squill*, (which is like a great *Onion*) and they will come up much earlier than in the Earth it self. This I conceive to be as a kinde of Grafting in the Root; for as the Stock of a Graft yieldeth better prepared nourishment to the Graft, than the Crude Earth, so the Squill doth the like to the Seed; and, I suppose, the same would be done, by putting Kernels into a Turnip, or the like, save that the Squill is more vigorous and hot. It may be tryed also, with putting Onion-Seed into an Onion-Head, which thereby (perhaps) will bring forth a larger and earlier Onion.

446. The pricking of a Fruit in several places, when it is almost at his bigness, and before it ripeneth, hath been practised with success, to ripen the Fruit more suddenly. We see the example of the biting of Wasps or Worms upon Fruit (whereby it manifestly) ripeneth the sooner.

447. It is reported, That *Alga Marina (Sea-weed)* put under the Roots of Colworts, and (perhaps) of other Plants, will further their growth. The vertue (no doubt) hath relation to Salt, which is a great help to Fertility.

448. It hath been practised to cut off the Stalks of Cucumbers, immediately after their bearing close by the Earth; and then to cast a pretty quantity of Earth upon the Plant that remaineth, and they will bear the next year Fruit long before the ordinary time. The cause may be, for that the Sap goeth down the sooner, and is not spent in the Stalk or Leaf, which remaineth after the Fruit. Where note, that the Dying in the Winter, of the Roots or Plants that are Annual, seemeth to be partly caused by the over-expence of the Sap into Stalk and Leaves; which being prevented, they will super annuate, if they stand warm.

449. The pulling off many of the Blossoms from a Fruit-tree, doth make the Fruit fairer. The cause is manifest, for that the Sap hath the less to nourish. And it is a common experience, That if you do not pull off some Blossoms, the first time a Tree bloometh, it will blossom it self to death.

450. It were good to try what would be the effect, if all the Blossoms were pulled from a Fruit-tree, or the Acorns and Chesnut-buds, &c. from a wilde Tree, for two years together. I suppose, that the Tree will either put forth the third year bigger, and more plentiful Fruit; or else, the same years, larger Leaves, because of the Sap stored up.

It

It hath been generally received, that a Plant watred, with warm Water, will come up sooner and better, than with cold Water, or with Showers. But the Experiment of watering Wheat with warm Water (as hath been said) succeeded not; which may be, because the tryal was too late in the Year, *viz.* in the end of *October*. For the Cold then coming upon the Seed, after it was made more tender by the warm Water, might check it.

451.

There is no doubt, but that Grafting (for the most part) doth meliorate the Fruit. The cause is manifest, for that the nourishment is better prepared in the Stock, than in the Crude Earth: But yet note well, that there be some Trees that are said to come up more happily from the Kernel, than from the Graft; as the *Peach*, and *Melocotone*. The cause, I suppose to be, for that those Plants require a nourishment of great moisture; and though the nourishment of the Stock be finer, and better prepared, yet it is not so moist and plentiful, as the nourishment of the Earth. And indeed we see those Fruits are very cold Fruits in their Nature.

452.

It hath been received, that a smaller Pear grafted upon a Stock that beareth a greater Pear, will become great. But I think it is as true, as that of the Prime-Fruit upon the late Stock, and *è Controverso*, which we rejected before; for the Cions will govern. Nevertheless, it is probable enough, that if you can get a Cions to grow upon a Stock of another kinde, that is much moister than his own Stock, it may make the Fruit greater, because it will yield more plentiful nourishment, though it is like it will make the Fruit baser. But generally the grafting is upon a dryer Stock; as the Apple upon a Crab, the Pear upon a Thorn, &c. Yet it is reported, that in the *Low-Countreys* they will graft an Apple-Cions upon the Stock of a Colewort, and it will bear a great flaggy Apple; the Kernel of which, if it be set, will be a Colewort, and not an Apple. It were good to try, whether an Apple-Cions will prosper, if it be grafted upon a Sallow or upon a Poplar, or upon an Alder, or upon an Elm, or upon an Horse-Plum, which are the moistest of Trees. I have heard that it hath been tryed upon an Elm, and succeeded.

453.

It is manifest by experience, That Flowers removed, wax greater, because the nourishment is more easily come by in the loose Earth. It may be, that oft regrafting of the same Cions, may likewise make Fruit greater; as if you take a Cions, and graft it upon a Stock the first year; and then cut it off, and graft it upon another Stock the second year, and so for a third, or fourth year, and then let it rest, it will yield afterward, when it beareth, the greater Fruit.

454.

Of Grafting, *there are many Experiments worth the noting, but those we reserve to a proper place.*

It maketh Figs better, if a Fig-tree, when it beginneth to put forth Leaves, have his top cut off. The cause is plain, for that the Sap hath the less to feed, and the less way to mount: But it may be the Fig will come somewhat later, as was formerly touched. The same may be tried likewise in other Trees.

455.

It is reported, That Mulberries will be fairer, and the Tree more fruitful, if you bore the Trunk of the Tree thorow in several places, and thrust into the places bored, Wedges of some hot Trees; as *Turpentine, Mastick-tree, Guaiacum, Juniper, &c.* The cause may be, for that Adventive heat doth chear up the Native Juyce of the Tree.

456.

It is reported, That Trees will grow greater and bear better Fruit, if you put Salt, or Lees of Wine, or Blood to the Root. The cause may be the encreasing

457.

K

creafing the Luft or Spirit of the Root : Thefe things being more forcible
than ordinary compofts.

458.   It is reported by one of the Ancients, that Artichoaks will be lefs prick-
ly, and more tender, if the Seeds have their tops dulled or grated off upon
a Stone.

459.   *Herbs* will be tenderer, and fairer, if you take them out of Beds when
they are newly come up, and remove them into Pots with better Earth. The
remove from Bed to Bed was fpoken of before ; but that was in feveral
years, this is upon the fudden. The caufe is the fame with other removes,
formerly mentioned.

460.   *Cole-worts* are reported by one of the Ancients, to profper exceedingly,
and to be better tafted, if they be fometimes watred with Salt-water, and
much more with Water mixed with Nitre ; the Spirit of which is lefs Adu-
rent than Salt.

461.   It is reported, That *Cucumbers* will prove more tender and dainty, if
their Seeds be fteeped (little) in Milk ; the caufe may be, for that the Seed
being mollified with the Milk, will be too weak to draw the groffer Juyce of
the Earth, but onely the finer. The fame Experiment may be made in Artichoaks, and other Seeds ; when you would take away, either their Flafhi-
nefs or Bitternefs. They fpeak alfo, that the like effect followeth of fteeping in Water mixed with Honey ; but that feemeth to me not fo probable,
becaufe Honey hath too quick a Spirit.

462.   It is reported, That *Cucumbers* will be lefs Watry, and more Melon-
like, if in the Pit where you fet them, you fill it (half way up) with Chaff, or
fmall Sticks, and then power Earth upon them ; for *Cucumbers*, as it feemeth,
do extreamly affect moifture, and over-drink themfelves ; which this Chaff,
or Chips forbiddeth. Nay it is further reported, That if when a Cucumber
is grown, you fet a Pot of water about five or fix inches diftance from it,
it will in Four and twenty hours fhoot fo much out as to touch the Pot ;
which if it be true, it is an Experiment of an higher nature than belongeth
to this Title : For it difcovereth Perception in Plants to move towards that
which fhould help and comfort them, though it be at a diftance. The ancient
Tradition of the Vine is far more ftrange : It is, that if you fet a ftake, or
prop, fome diftance from it, it will grow that way, which is far ftranger (as
is faid) than the other : For that Water may work by a Sympathy of Attraction : But this of the Stake feemeth to be a reafonable difcourfe.

463.   It hath been touched before, that Terebration of Trees doth make them
profper better. But it is found alfo, that it maketh the Fruit fweeter, and
better. The caufe is, for that notwithftanding the Terebration, they may
receive Aliment fufficient, and yet no more than they can well turn, and
difgeft ; and withal do fweat out the courfeft and unprofitableft Juyce, even
as it is in Living Creatures ; which, by moderate feeding, and exercife, and
fweat, attain the foundeft habit of Body.

464.   As Terebration doth meliorate Fruit, fo, upon the like reafon, doth
Letting of Plants Blood ; as Pricking Vines, or other Trees, after they be of
fome growth, and thereby letting forth Gum or Tears, though this be not to
continue, as it is in Terebration, but at fome Seafons. And it is reported,
that by this artifice, *Bitter Almonds* have been turned into fweet.

465.   The Ancients for the Dulcorating of Fruit, do commend Swines dung
above all other Dung, which may be, becaufe of the moifture of that Beaft,
whereby the Excrement hath lefs Acrimony ; for we fee Swines and Pigs
Flefh is the moifteft of flefhes.

It

It is observed by some, that all Herbs wax sweeter, both in smell and taste, if after they be grown up some reasonable time, they be cut, and so you take the latter Sprout. The cause may be, for that the longer the Juyce stayeth in the Root and Stalk, the better it concocteth. For one of the chief causes, why Grains, Seeds, and Fruits, are more nourishing than Leaves, is the length of time, in which they grow to Maturation. It were not amiss to keep back the Sap of Herbs, or the like, by some fit means till the end of Summer, whereby (it may be) they will be more nourishing.

466

As Grafting doth generally advance and Meliorate Fruits, above that which they would be, if they where set of Kernels or Stones, in regard the nourishment is better concocted. So (no doubt) even in Grafting, for the same cause the choice of the Stock doth much; always provided, that it be somewhat inferior to the Cions. For otherwise it dulleth it. They commend much the Grafting of Pears, or Apples, upon a Quince.

467.

Besides the Means of Melioration of Fruits before-mentioned, it is set down as tryed, that a mixture of Bran and Swines Dung or Chaff and Swines-Dung (especially laid up together for a moneth to rot) is a very great nourisher and comforter to a Fruit-tree.

468.

It is delivered, that Onions wax greater if they be taken out of the Earth, and laid a drying twenty days, and then set again; and yet more, if the outermost Pill be taken off all over.

469.

It is delivered by some, that if one take the Bough of a low Fruit-tree, newly budded, and draw it gently, without hurting it, into an Earthen pot perforate at the bottom to let in the Plant, and then cover the Pot with Earth, it will yield a very large Fruit within the Ground. Which Experiment is nothing but potting of Plants, without removing and leaving the Fruit in the Earth. The like (they say) will be effected by an empty Pot without Earth in it, put over a Fruit, being propped up with a stake as it hangeth upon the Tree, and the better, if some few Pertusions be made in the Pot. VVherein, besides the defending of the Fruit from extremity of Sun or VVeather, some give a reason, that the Fruit loving and coveting the open Air and Sun, is invited by the Pertusions to spred and approach as near the open Air as it can, and so inlargeth in Magnitude.

470.

All Trees in high and Sandy Grounds, are to be set deep; and in VVatry Grounds more shallow. And in all Trees when they be removed (especially Fruit-trees) care ought to be taken, that the sides of the Trees be coasted, (North and South, &c.) as they stood before. The same is said also of Stone out of the Quarry, to make it more durable, though that seemeth to have less reason; because the Stone lyeth not so near the Sun, as the Tree groweth.

471.

Timber Trees in a Coppice-wood, do grow better than in an open Field; both, because they offer not to spred so much, but shoot up still in height, and chiefly, because they are defended from too much Sun and Wind, which do check the growth of all Fruit; and so (no doubt) Fruit-trees, or Vines, set upon a Wall, against the Sun, between Elbows and Butrisses of Stone, ripen more than upon a plain Wall.

472.

It is said, that if *Potado Roots* be set in a Pot filled with Earth, and then the Pot with Earth be set likewise within the Ground, some two or three inches, the Roots will grow greater than ordinary. The cause may be, for that having Earth enough within the Pot to nourish them; and then being stopped by the bottom of the Pot from putting strings downward, they must needs grow greater in breadth and thickness. And it may be

473.

K 2

that

that all Seeds, Roots, potted, and so set into the Earth, will prosper the better.

474.   The cutting off the Leaves of Raddish, or other Roots, in the beginning of Winter before they wither; and covering again the Root, something high with Earth, will preserve the Root all Winter, and make it bigger in the Spring following, as hath been partly touched before. So that there is a double use of this cutting off the Leaves: For in Plants, where the Root is the Esculent, as Raddish, and Parsnips, it will make the Root the greater; and so it will do to the Heads of Onions, and where the Fruit is the Esculent, by strengthning the Root, it will make the Fruit also the greater.

475.   It is an Experiment of great pleasure to make the Leaves of shaddy Trees, larger than ordinary. It hath been tryed (for certain) that a Cions of a Weech Elm, grafted upon the stock of an ordinary Elm will put forth Leaves, almost as broad as the brim of ones Hat. And it is very likely, that as in Fruit-Trees, the Graft maketh a greater Fruit; so in Trees that bear no Fruit, it will make the greater Leaves. It would be tryed therefore in Trees of that kinde chiefly; as *Birch*, *Ash*, *Willow*, and especially the *Shining Willow*, which they call *Swallow-Tail*, because of the pleasure of the Leaf.

476.   The Barrenness of Trees by accident (besides the weakness of the Soil Seed, or Root, and the injury of the Weather) coming either of their overgrowing with Moss, or their being hide bound, or their planting too deep, or by issuing of the Sap too much into the Leaves: For all these three are remedies mentioned before.

WE see that in Living Creatures that have Male and Female, there is copulation of several kindes, and so Compound Creatures; as the *Mule*, that is generated betwixt the *Horse* and *Ass*; and some other Compounds which we call Monsters, though more rare: And it is held, that that *Proverb*, *Africa semper aliquid Monstri parit*, cometh, for that the Fountains of Waters there being rare, divers sorts of Beasts come from several parts to drink, and so being refreshed fall to couple, and many times with several kindes. The compounding or mixture of Kindes in Plants is not found out; which, nevertheless, if it be possible is more at command than that of Living Creatures, for that their lust requireth a voluntary motion; wherefore it were one of the most notable Experiments touching Plants, to finde it out, for so you may have great variety of new Fruits, and flowers yet unknown. Grafting doth it not, that mendeth the Fruit, or doubleth the Flowers, &c. But it hath not the power to make a new Kind. For the Cions ever over-ruleth the Stock.

477.   It hath been set down by one of the Ancient, That if you take two Twigs of several Fruit Trees, and flat them on the sides, and then binde them close together, and set them in the ground, they will come up in one Stock; but yet they will put forth in their several Fruits without any commixture in the Fruit. Wherein note (by the way) that Unity of Continuance, is easier to procure, than Unity of Species. It is reported also, That Vines of Red and White Grapes, being set in the Ground, and the upper parts being flatted, and bound close together, will put forth Grapes of the several colours, upon the same Branch; and Grape-stones of several colours within the same Grape: But the more, after a year or two, the unity (as it seemeth) growing more perfect. And this will likewise help, if from

the

the firſt uniting, they be often watred ; for all moiſture helpeth to Union.
And it is preſcribed alſo to binde the Bud, as ſoon as it cometh forth, as well
as the Stock, at the leaſt for a time.

They report, that divers Seeds put into a Clout, and laid in Earth well
dunged, will put up *Plants* contiguous ; which (afterwards) being bound in,
their Shoots will incorporate. The like is ſaid of *Kernels* put into a *Bottle*,
with a narrow mouth, filled with Earth.

It is reported, that young Trees of ſeveral kindes ſet contiguous without any binding, and very often watred in a fruitful ground, with the very
luxury of the Trees, will incorporate and grow together. Which ſeemeth
to me the likelieſt means that hath been propounded ; for that the binding
doth hinder the natural ſwelling of the Tree, which, while it is in motion,
doth better unite.

478.

479.

THere are many ancient and received Traditions and Obſervations,
touching the *Sympathy* and *Antipathy* of *Plants* ; for that ſome will
thrive beſt growing near others, which they impute to *Sympathy* ; and ſome
worſe which they impute to *Antipathy*. But theſe are idle and ignorant conceits, and forſake the true indication of the cauſes ; as the moſt part of *Experiments*, that concern *Sympathies* and *Antipathies* do. For as to *Plants*, neither
is there any ſuch ſecret Friendſhip, or Hatred, as they imagine. And
if we ſhould be content to call it *Sympathy* and *Antipathy*, it is utterly miſtaken ;
for their *Sympathy* is an *Antipathy*, and their *Antipathy* is a *Sympathy* : For it is
thus, whereſoever one *Plant* draweth ſuch a particular Juyce out of the
Earth, as it qualifieth the Earth, ſo as that Juyce which remaineth is fit for
the other *Plant*, there the Neighborhood doth good, becauſe the nouriſhments are contrary, or ſeveral : But where two *Plants* draw (much) the
ſame Juyce, there the Neighborhood hurteth ; for the one deceiveth the
other.

Experiments
in Conſort,
touching the
Sympathy and
Antipathy of
Plants.

Firſt, therefore, all *Plants* that do draw much nouriſhment from the
Earth, and ſo ſoak the Earth, and exhauſt it, hurt all things that grow by
them ; as great Trees, (eſpecially *Aſhes*) and ſuch Trees, as ſpred their
Roots near the top of the ground. So the *Colewort* is not an enemy (though
that were anciently received) to the *Vine* onely ; but it is an enemy to any
other *Plant* ; becauſe it draweth ſtrongly the fatteſt Juyce of the Earth.
And if it be true, that the *Vine*, when it creepeth near the *Colewort*, will turn
away : This may be, becauſe there it findeth worſe nouriſhment ; for
though the Root be where it was, yet (I doubt) the Plant will bend as it
nouriſheth.

480.

Where *Plants* are of ſeveral Natures, and draw ſeveral Juyces out of
the Earth, there (as hath been ſaid) the one ſet by the other helpeth : As it
is ſet down by divers of the Ancients, that *Rew* doth proſper much, and becometh ſtronger, if it be ſet by a *Fig-Tree* : Which (we conceive) is cauſed
not by reaſon of Friendſhip, but by Extraction of contrary Juyces ; the
one drawing Juyce fit to reſult ſweet, the other bitter. So they have ſet down
likewiſe, that a *Roſe* ſet by *Garlick* is ſweeter ; which likewiſe may be, becauſe
the more Fetide Juyce of the Earth goeth into the *Garlick*, and the more
oderate into the *Roſe*.

481.

This we ſee manifeſtly, That there be certain *Corn-Flowers* which come
ſeldom or never in other places, unleſs they be ſet, but onely amongſt

482.

K 3

Corn: As the blew Bottle a kinde of yellow Mary-Gold, Wilde Poppey, and Fumitory. Neither can this be by reafon of the culture of the Ground, by Ploughing or Furrowing, as fome Herbs and Flowers will grow but in Ditches new caft, for if the ground lye fallow and unfown, they will not come: So as it fhould feem to be the Corn that qualifieth the Earth, and prepareth it for their growth.

483.   This obfervation if it holdeth (as it is very probable) is of great ufe, for the meliorating of tafte in Fruits, and Efculent Herbs, and of the fent of Flowers. For I do not doubt, but if the Fig-tree do make the Rew more ftrong and bitter, (as the Ancients have noted) good ftore of Rew planted about the Fig-tree, will make the Fig more fweet. Now the taftes that do moft offend in Fruits, and Herbs, and Roots, are bitter, harfh, four, and watrifh, or flafhy. It were good therefore to make the Tryals following.

484.   Take Wormwood or Rew, and fet it near Lettuce, or Coleflory, or Artichoak; and fee whether the Lettuce, or the Coleflory, &c. become not the fweeter.

485.   Take a Service-tree, or a Cornelian-tree, or an Elder-tree, which we know have Fruits of harfh and binding Juyce, and fet them near a Vine or Fig-tree, and fee whether the Grapes or Figs will not be the fweeter.

486.   Take Cucumbers or Pumpions, and fet them (here and there) amongft Musk-Melons, and fee whether the Melons will not be more winy, and better tafted. Set Cucumbers (likewife) amongft Raddifh, and fee whether the Raddifh will not be made the more biting.

487.   Take Sorrel and fet it amongft Rafps, and fee whether the Rafps will not be the fweeter.

488.   Take Common Bryar, and fet it amongft Violets or Wall-flowers, and fee whether it will not make the Violets or Wall-flowers fweeter, and lefs earthy in their fmell. So fet Lettuce or Cucumbers, amongft Rofemary or Bays, and fee whether the Rofemary or Bays, will not be the more oderate or aromatical.

489.   Contrariwife, you muft take heed how you fet Herbs together that draw much the like Juyce. And therefore I think Rofemary will leefe in fweetnefs, if it be fet with Lavender or Bays, or the like. But yet, if you will correct the ftrength of an Herb, you fhall do well to fet other like Herbs by him, to take him down; and if you would fet Tanfey by Angelica, it may be the Angelica would be the weaker and fitter for mixture in perfume. And if you fhould fet Rew by Common Wormwood, it may be, the Wormwood would turn to be liker *Roman* Wormwood.

490.   This Axiom is of large extent; and therefore would be fevered, and refined by Tryal. Neither muft you expect to have a grofs difference by this kinde of Culture, but onely further Perfection.

491.   Tryal would be alfo made in Herbs, Poyfonous, and Purgative, whofe ill quality (perhaps) may be difcharged or attempted, by fetting ftronger Poyfons or Purgatives by them.

492.   It is reported, That the Shrub called *Our Ladies Seal*, (which is a kinde of Briony) and Coleworts, fet near together, one or both will die. The caufe is, for that they be both great Depredators of the Earth, and one of them ftarveth the other. The like is faid of Reed, and a Brake, both which are fucculent; and therefore the one deceiveth the other. And the like of Hemlock and Rew, both which draw ftrong Juyces;

493.   Some of the Ancients, and likewife divers of the Modern Writers, that have labored in Natural Magick, have noted a Sympathy between the Sun,

Moon,

Moon, and some principal Stars, and certain Herbs, and Plants. And so they have denominated some Herbs Solar, and some Lunar, and such like toys put into great words. It is manifest, that there are some Flowers that have respect to the Sun in two kindes; the one by opening and shutting, and the other by bowing and inclining the Head. For Marygolds, Tulippas, Pimpernel, and indeed most flowers do open or spred their Leaves abroad, when the Sun shineth serene and fair: And again, (in some part) close them, or gather them inward, either toward night, or when the Sky is overcast. Of this, there needeth no such solemn Reason to be assigned, as to say, That they rejoyce at the presence of the Sun, and mourn at the absence thereof. For it is nothing else, but a little loading of the Leaves, and swelling them at the bottom, with the moisture of the Air; whereas the dry Air doth extend them. And they make it a piece of the wonder, That Garden Claver will hide the Stalk, when the Sun sheweth bright, which is nothing but a full expansion of the Leaves; for the bowing and inclining the Head, it is found in the great Flower of the Sun, in Marygolds, Wartwort, Mallow flowers, and others. The cause is somewhat more obscure than the former: But I take it to be no other, but that the part, against which the Sun beateth, waxeth more faint and flaccide in the Stalk, and thereby less able to support the Flower.

What a little Moisture will do in Vegetables, even though they be dead, and severed from the Earth, appeareth well in the Experiment of *Juglers.* They take the Beard of an Oat, which (if you mark it well) is wreathed at the bottom, and one smooth entire straw at the top. They take onely the part that is wreathed, and cut off the other, leaving the Beard half the bredth of a finger in length. Then they make a little Cross of a Quill longways, of that part of the Quill which hath the Pith; and Cross-ways of that piece of the Quill without Pith, the whole Cross being the bredth of a finger high: Then they prick the bottom where the Pith is, and thereinto they put the *Oaten-Beard*, leaving half of it sticking forth of the Quill: Then they take a little white Box of Wood to deceive men, as if somewhat in the Box did work the feat; in which, with a Pin, they make a little hole, enough to take Beard, but not to let the Cross sink down, but to stick: Then likewise, by way of Imposture, they make a question: As, who is the fairest Woman in the company? or who hath a Glove or Card? and cause another to name divers persons; and upon every naming, they stick the Cross in the Box, having first put it towards their Mouth, as if they charmed it, and the Cross stirreth not: But when they come to the person that they would take, as they hold the Cross to their Mouth, they touch the Beard with the tip of their Tongue, and wet it, and so stick the Cross in the Box, and then you shall see it turn finely and softly, three or four turns, which is caused by the untwining of the Beard by the moisture. You may see it more evidently if you stick the Cross between your fingers, instead of the Box: And therefore you may see, that this Motion, which is effected by so little wet, is stronger than the closing or bending of the Head of a Marygold.

It is reported by some, That the Herb called *Rosa-Solis* (whereof they make *Strong-waters*) will at the Noon-day, when the Sun shineth hot and bright, have a great Dew upon it. And therefore, that the right name is *Ros Solis*; which they impute to a delight and sympathy that it hath with the Sun. Men favor wonders. It were good first to be sure, That the Dew that is found upon it, be not the Dew of the Morning preserved,

when

when the Dew of other *Herbs* is breathed away: For it hath a fmooth and thick Leaf that doth not difcharge the Dew fo foon as other *Herbs,* that are more Spungy and Porous. And it may be *Purflane,* or fome other Herb doth the like, and is not marked. But if it be fo, that it hath more Dew at Noon than in the Morning, then fure it feemeth to be an exudation of the *Herb* it felf. As Plums fweat when they are fet into the Oven : For you will not (I hope) think, that it is like *Gideons* Fleece of Wooll, that the Dew fhould fall upon that, and no where elfe.

496.

It is certain, that the *Hony-dews* are found more upon *Oak Leaves,* than upon *Afh,* or *Beech,* or the like: But whether any caufe be from the Leaf it felf, to concoct the Dew; or whether it be onely, that the Leaf is clofe and fmooth (and therefore drinketh not in the Dew, but preferveth it) may be doubted. It would be well inquired, whether *Manna* the *Drug,* doth fall but upon certain *Herbs* or *Leaves* onely. *Flowers* that have deep *Sockets,* do gather in the bottom, a kinde of *Honey* ; as *Honey-Suckles* (both the *Woodbine,* and the *Trifoil*) *Lillies,* and the like. And in them certainly the *Flower* beareth part with the *Dew.*

497.

The Experience is, That the Froth, which they call *Woodfare,* (being like a kinde of Spittle; is found but upon certain Herbs, and thofe hot ones ; as *Lavender, Lavender-cotton, Sage, Hyffope, &c.* Of the caufe of this enquire further, for it feemeth a fecret. There falleth alfo *Mildew* upon *Corn,* and fmutteth it : But it may be, that the fame falleth alfo upon other Herbs, and is not obferved.

498.

It were good, Tryal were made, whether the great confent between Plants and Water, which is a principal nourifhment of them, will make an Attraction or Diftance, and not at touch onely. Therefore take a Veffel, and in the middle of it make a falfe bottom of courfe Canvas ; fill it with Earth above the Canvas, and let not the Earth be watred, then fow fome good Seeds in that Earth : But under the Canvas, fome half a foot in the bottom of the Veffel, lay a great Spunge, thorowly wet in Water, and let it lie fome ten days ; and fee whether the Seeds will fprout, and the Earth become more moift, and the Spunge more dry. The Experiment formerly mentioned of the Cucumber, creeping to the Pot of Water, is far ftranger than this.

499.
Experiments
in Confort,
touching the
*Making herbs
and fruits
Medicinable.*

THe altering of the Sent, Colour, or Tafte of Fruit, by Infufing, Mixing, or Letting into the Bark, or Root of the Tree, Herb, or Flower, any Coloured, Aromatical, or Medicinal Subftance, are but fancies. The caufe is, for that thofe things have paffed their period, and nourifh not; and all alteration of Vegetables, in thofe qualities, muft be by fomewhat that is apt to go into the nourifhment of the Plant. But this is true, that where Kine feed upon Wilde Garlick, their Milk tafted plainly of the Garlick. And the Flefh of Muttons is better tafted where the Sheep feed upon Wilde Thyme, and other wholfome Herbs. *Galen* alfo fpeaketh of the curing of the *Scirrus* of the *Liver,* by Milk of a Cow, that feedeth upon certain Herbs ; and *Honey* in *Spain* fmelleth (apparently) of the *Rofemary,* or *Orenge,* from whence the Bee gather it: And there is an old Tradition of a Maiden that was fed with *Napellus,* (which is counted the ftrongeft poyfon of all Vegetables) which with ufe, did not hurt the Maid, but poyfoned fome that had carnal company with her. So it is obferved by fome, that there is a vertuous *Bezoar,* and another without vertue, which appear to the fhew alike ; but the vertuous is taken from the Beaft, that feedeth upon the Mountains, where

there

there are Theriacel Herbs ; and that without vertue, from those that fed in the Valleys, where no such Herbs are.   Thus far I am of opinion, that as steeped Wines and Beers are very Medici al, and likewise Bread tempered with divers powders ; so of *Meat* also, (as *Flesh, Fish, Milk,* and *Eggs*) that they may be made of great use for Medicine and Diet, if the *Beast, Fowl,* or *Fish,* be fed with a special kinde of food, fit for the disease. It were a dangerous thing also for secret empoysonments.   But whether it may be applied unto Plants, and Herbs, I doubt more, because the nourishment of them is a more common Juyce ; which is hardly capable of any special quality until the Plant do assimilate it.

But left our incredulity may prejudice any profitable operations in this kinde (especially since many of the Ancients have set them down) we think good briefly to propound the four Means, which they have devised of making Plants Medicinable. The first is by slitting of the Root, and infusing into it the Medicine, as *Hellebore, Opium, Scammony, Triacle. &c.* and then binding it up again. This seemeth to me the least probable, because the Root draweth immediately from the Earth, and so the nourishment is the more common and less qualified ; and besides, it is a long time in going up, ere it come to the Fruit. The second way is, to perforate the Body of the Tree, and there to infuse the Medicine, it hath the less way, and the less time to go up.   The third is, the steeping of the Seed or Kernel in some Liquor wherein the Medicine is infused ; which I have little opinion of, because the Seed (I doubt) will not draw the parts of the matter which have the propriety ; but it will be far the more likely, if you mingle the Medicine with Dung, for that the Seed, naturally drawing the moisture of the Dung, may call in withal some of the propriety. The fourth is, the Watering of the Plant oft, with an infusion of the Medicine.   This, in one respect may have more force than the rest, because the Medication is oft renewed, whereas the rest are applied, but at one time ; and therefore the vertue may the sooner vanish. But still I doubt, that the Root is somewhat too stubborn to receive those fine Impressions ; and besides (as I have said before) they have a great Hill to go up.   I judge therefore the likeliest way to be the perforation of the Body of the Tree, in several places, one above the other, and the filling of the Holes with Dung mingled with the Medicine. And the Watring of those Lumps of Dung, with Squirts of an Infusion of the Medicine in dunged Water, once in three or four days.

500.

NATURAL HISTORY.

Century V I.

Ur Experiments we take care to be (as we have often said,) either *Experimenta Fructifera*, or *Lucifera*; either of Use, or of Discovery: For we hate Impostures, and despise Curiosities. Yet because we must apply our selves somewhat to others, we will set down some Curiosities touching Plants.

It is a Curiosity to have several Fruits upon one Tree; and the more, when some of them come early, and some come late: So that you may have, upon the same Tree, ripe Fruits all Summer. This is easily done by Grafting of several Cions upon several Boughs of a Stock, in a good ground, plentifully fed. So you may have all kindes of Cherries, and all kindes of Plumbs, and Peaches, and Apricots upon one Tree: But, I conceive the Diversity of Fruits must be such, as will graft upon the same Stock: And therefore, I doubt, whether you can have Apples, or Pears, or Orenges, upon the same Stock, upon which you graft Plumbs.

501.

It is a Curiosity to have Fruits of divers Shapes and Figures. This is easily performed by Moulding them, when the Fruit is young, with Moulds of Earth or Wood. So you may have Cucumbers, &c. as long as a Cane, or as round as a Sphere, or formed like a Cross. You may have also Apples in the form of Pears or Lemmons. You may have also Fruit in more accurate Figures; as we said of Men, Beasts, or Birds, according as you make the Moulds, wherein you must understand, that you make the Mould big enough to contain the whole Fruit, when it is grown to the greatest; for else you will choak the spreding of the Fruit, which otherwise would spred it self, and fill the Concave, and so be turned into the shape desired; as it is in Mould-works of Liquid things. Some doubt may be conceived,

502.

ceived, that the keeping of the Sun from the Fruit, may hurt it : But there isordinary experience of Fruit that groweth covered. *Quare* also, whether some small holes may not be made in the Wood, to let in the Sun. And note, that it were beft to make the Moulds partible, glued, or cemented together, that you may open them when you take out the Fruit.

503.   It is a curiofity to have *Infcriptions* or *Engravings*, in Fruit or Trees. This is eafily performed, by writing with a *Needle*, or *Bodkin*, or *Knife*, or the like, when the Fruit or Trees are young ; for as they grow, fo the Letters will grow more large, and graphical.

> ———— *Tenerifque meos incidere Amores*
> *Arboribus, crefcent illa, crefcetis Amores.*

504.   You may have Trees apparelled with Flowers or Herbs by boring holes in the Bodies of them, and putting into them Earth holpen with Muck, and fetting Seeds or Slips, of *Violets, Strawberries, Wilde Time, Camomil,* and fuch like in the Earth, wherein they do but grow in the Tree, as they do in Pots, though (perhaps) with fome feeding from the Trees. As it would be tryed alfo with Shoots of *Vines,* and Roots of *Red-Rofes* ; for it may be, they being of a more Ligneous Nature, will incorporate with the Tree it felf.

505.   It is an ordinary curiofity to form Trees and Shrubs (as *Rofemary, Juni-per,* and the like) into fundry fhapes ; which is done by moulding them within, and cutting them without. But they are but lame things, being too fmall to keep Figure ; great Caftles made of Trees upon Frames of Timber, with Turrets and Arches, were anciently matters of magnifi-cence.

506.   Amongft curiofities, I fhall place Colouration, though it be fomewhat better ; for Beauty in Flowers is their pre-eminence. It is obferved by fome, that *Gilly-Flowers, Sweet-Williams, Violets,* that are coloured, if they be neg-lected, and neither Watered, nor new Moulded, nor Tranfplanted, will turn White. And it is probable, that the White, with much culture, may turn coloured ; for this is certain, That the white colour cometh of fcarcity of Nourifhment; except in Flowers that are onely white, and admit no other colours.

507·   It is good therefore to fee what Natures do accompany what colours ; for by that you fhall have light, how to induce colours, by producing thofe Natures. Whites are more inodorate (for the moft part) than Flowers of the fame kinde coloured ; as is found in fingle White Violets, White Rofes, White Gilly-Flowers, White Stock-Gilly-Flowers, &c. We finde al-fo, that Bloffoms of Trees that are White, are commonly inodorate ; as Cherries, Pears, Plums, whereas thofe of Apples, Crabs, Almonds, and Peaches, are blufhy, and fmell fweet. The caufe is, for that the fubftance that maketh the Flower, is of the thinneft and fineft of the Plant ; which alfo maketh Flowers to be of fo dainty Colours. And if it be too fparing and thin, it attaineth no ftrength of odor, except it be in fuch Plants as are very fucculent; whereby they need rather to be fcanted in their nourifh-ment, than replenifhed, to have them fweet. As we fee in White Satyrion, which is of a dainty fmell; and in Bean-flowers, &c. And again, if the Plant be of Nature to put forth White Flowers onely, and thofe not thin or dry, they are commonly of rank and fulfome fmell ; as May-Flowers and White Lillies.

508.   Contrariwife, in Berries, the White is commonly more delicate and fweet in tafte, than the Coloured ; as we fee in white Grapes, in white Rafpes, in white Strawberries, in white Currans, &c. The caufe is for that the

the coloured are more juyced, and courser juyced; and therefore not so well and equally concocted, but the white are better proportioned to the digestion of the *Plant*.

But in *Fruits*, the white commonly is meaner, as in *Pear-Plumbs*, *Damosins*, &c. and the choicest Plumbs are black; the *Mulberry*, (which though they call it a *Berry*, is a Fruit) is better the Black, than the White. The *Harvest* White-Plumb, is a base Plumb, and the *Perdoccio* and White Date-Plumb, are no very good Plumbs. The cause is, for that they are all over-watry: Whereas an higher Concoction is required for sweetness, or pleasure of taste; and therefore all your dainty Plumbs, are a little dry, and come from the Stone; as the *Muskle-Plumb*, the *Damosin-Plumb*, the *Peach*, the *Apricot*, &c. Yet some *Fruits* which grow not to be Black, are of the Nature of Berries; sweetest such as are paler, as the *Cœur-Cherry*, which inclineth more to White, is sweeter than the Red; but the *Egriot* is more sowre.

Take *Gilliflowers Seed*, of one kinde of *Gilliflowers* (as of the *Clove-Gilliflower* which is the most common) and sow it, and there will come up Gilliflowers, some of one colour, and some of another, casually, as the Seed meeteth with nourishment in the Earth: So that the Gardiners finde, that they may have two or three Roots amongst an hundred that are rare, and of great price, as *Purple Carnation* of several stripes. The cause is (no doubt) that in Earth, though it be contiguous, and in one Bed there are very several Juyces; and as the Seed doth casually meet with them, so it cometh forth. And it is noted especially, that those which do come up Purple, do always come up single; the Juyce, as it seemeth, not being able to suffice a succulent colour, and a double Leaf. This *Experiment* of several colours, coming up from one Seed, would be tryed also in *Larks-foot*, *Monk-hood*, *Poppy*, and *Hollioak*.

Few Fruits are coloured Red within; the *Queen-Apple* is, and another Apple, called the *Rose-Apple*; *Mulberries* likewise, and *Grapes*, though most toward the skin. There is a *Peach* also, that hath a circle of Red towards the stone; and the *Egriot-Cherry* is somewhat Red within: But no *Pear*, nor *Warden*, nor *Plumb*, nor *Apricot*, although they have (many times) Red sides, are coloured Red within. The cause may be enquired.

The general colour of *Plants* is Green, which is a colour that no *Flower* is of. There is a greenish *Prime-Rose*, but it is pale, and scarce a green; the Leaves of some Trees turn a little Murrey or Reddish, and they be commonly young Leaves that do so; as it is in *Oaks* and *Vines*. And *Haste-Leaves* rot into a Yellow; and some *Hollies* had part of their Leaves Yellow, that are (to all seeming) as fresh and shining as the Green. I suppose also, that Yellow is a less succulent colour than Green, and a degree nearer White. For it hath been noted, that those Yellow Leaves of *Holly*, stand ever toward the North or North-East. Some *Roots* are Yellow, as *Carrets*; and some *Plants*, Blood-red, Stalk and Leaf, and all; as *Amaranthus*. Some *Herbs* incline to Purple and Red; as a kinde of *Sage* doth; and a kinde of *Mint*, and *Rosa Solis*, &c. And some have White Leaves, as another kinde of *Sage*, and another kinde of *Mint*: But *Azure* and a fair *Purple* are never found in Leaves. This sheweth, that *Flowers* are made of a refined Juyce of the Earth, and so are Fruits; but Leaves of a more course and common.

It is a curiosity also to make *Flowers* double, which is effected by often removing them into new Earth; as on the contrary part, double *Flowers*,

509.

510.

511.

512.

513.

by neglecting, and not removing, prove single. And the way to do it speedily, is to sow or set Seeds, or Slips of Flowers; and as soon as they come up, to remove them into new ground that is good : Enquire also, whether inoculating of Flowers, (as Stock-Gilliflowers, Roses, Musk-Roses, &c.) doth not make them double. There is a Cherry-Tree that hath double Blossoms, but that Tree beareth no Fruit; and, it may be, that the same means which applied to the Tree, doth extreamly accelerate the Sap to rise and break forth, would make the Tree spend it self in Flowers, and those to become double, which were a great pleasure to see, especially In Apple-trees, Peach-trees, and Almond-trees, that have Blossoms Blush coloured.

514. The making of Fruits without Core or Stone, is likewise a curiosity, and somewhat better; because whatsoever maketh them so, is like to make them more tender and delicate. If a Cions or Shoot fit to be set in the Ground, have the Pith finely taken forth (and not altogether, but some of it left, the better to save the life) it will bear a Fruit with little or no Core or Stone. And the like is said to be of dividing a quick Tree down to the Ground, and taking out the Pith, and then binding it up again.

515. It is reported also, that a Citron grafted upon a Quince will have small or no Seeds ; and it is very probable, that any sowre Fruit grafted upon a Stock that beareth a sweeter Fruit, may both make the Fruit sweeter, and more void of the harsh matter of Kernels or Seeds.

516. It is reported, that not onely the taking out of the Pith, but the stopping of the Juyce of the Pith from rising in the midst, and turning it to rise on the outside, will make the Fruit without Core or Stone; as if you should bore a Tree clean thorow, and put a wedge in. It is true, there is some affinity between the Pith and the Kernel, because they are both of a harsh substance, and both placed in the midst.

517. It is reported, that Trees watered perpetually with warm Water, will make a Fruit with little or no Core or Stone. And the rule is general, That whatsoever will make a wilde Tree, a Garden Tree, will make a Garden Tree to have less Core or Stone.

518.

Experiments
in Consort,
touching the
Degenerating
of Plants, and
of the Trans-
mutation of
them, one into
another.

THe Rule is certain, That Plants for want of Culture, degenerate to be baser in the same kinde ; and sometimes so far, as to change into another kinde. 1. The standing long, and not being removed, maketh them degenerate. 2. Drought, unless the Earth of it self be moist, doth the like. 3. So doth removing into worse Earth, or forbearing to compost the Earth ; as we see, that Water-Mint turneth into Field-Mint, and the Colewort into Rape by neglect, &c.

519. Whatsoever Fruit useth to be set upon a Root, or a Slip, if it be sown, will degenerate; Grapes sown, Figs, Almonds, Pomegranate Kernels sown, make the Fruits degenerate, and become wilde. And again, most of those Fruits that use to be grafted, if they be set of Kernels, or Stones degenerate. It is true, that Peaches (as hath been touched before) do better upon Stones set, than upon grafting : And the rule of Exception should seem to be this, That whatsoever Plant requireth much moisture, prospereth better upon the Stone or Kernel, than upon the Graft. For the Stock, though it giveth a finer nourishment, yet it giveth a scanter, than the Earth at large.

520. Seeds, if they be very old, and yet have strength enough to bring forth a Plant, make the Plant degenerate. And therefore skilful Gardiners make tryal of the Seeds, before they buy them, whether they be good or no, by putting

them

them in Water gently boiled; and if they be good, they will sprout within half an hour.

It is strange which is reported, That *Basil* too much exposed to the Sun, doth turn into *Wilde Time* : Although those two Herbs seem to have small Affinity; but Basil is almost the onely hot Herb that hath fat and succulent Leaves; which Oylines if it be drawn forth by the Sun, it is like it will make a very great change. 521.

There is an old Tradition, that *Boughs of Oak* put into the Earth, will put forth *Wilde Vines*; which if it be true, (no doubt) it is not the *Oak* that turneth into a *Vine*, but the *Oak-bough* putrifying, qualifieth the Earth to put forth a *Vine* of it self. 522.

It is not impossible, and I have heard it verified, that upon cutting down of an old Timber-Tree, the Stub hath put out sometimes a Tree of another kinde; as that Beech hath put forth Birch : Which if it be true, the cause may be, for that the old Stub is too scant of Juyce to put forth the former Tree; and therefore putteth forth a Tree of smaller kinde, that needeth less Nourishment. 523.

There is an opinion in the Countrey, That if the same Ground be oft sown with the Grain that grew upon it, it will, in the end, grow to be of a baser kinde. 524.

It is certain, that in Sterile Years, Corn sown will grow to another kinde. 525.

Grandia sæpe quibus mandavimus Hordea Sulcis,
Infœlix Lolium, & steriles dominatur Avena.

And generally it is a Rule, that Plants that are brought forth by Culture, as Corn, will sooner change into other Species, than those that come of themselves : For that Culture giveth but an Adventitious Nature, which is more easily put off.

This work of the *Transmutation* of *Plants*, one into another, is *inter Magnalia Naturæ*: For the *Transmutation of Species* is, in the vulgar Philosophy, pronounced impossible : And certainly, it is a thing of difficulty, and requireth deep search into Nature : But seeing there appear some manifest instances of it, the opinion of impossibility is to be rejected, and the means thereof to be found out. We see that in *Living Creatures*, that come of Putrefaction, there is much Transmutation of one into another. As Caterpillers turn into Flies, &c. And it should seem probable, that whatsoever Creature having life, is generated without Seed, that Creature will change out of one Species into another; for it is the Seed, and the Nature of it, which locketh and boundeth in the Creature, that it doth not expatiate. So as we may well conclude, that seeing the Earth of it self, doth put forth Plants without Seed; therefore Plants may well have a Transmigration of Species. Wherefore wanting Instances, which do occur, we shall give Directions of the most likely tryals : And generally, we would not have those that read this work of *Sylva Sylvarum*, account it strange, or think that it is an overhaste, that we have set down particulars untried : For contrariwise; in our own estimation, we account such particulars more worthy than those that are already tryed and known. For these latter must be taken as you finde them, but the other do level point blank at the inventing of causes, and Axioms.

L 2

526.　Firſt, therefore you muſt make account, that if you will have one Plant change into another, you muſt have the Nouriſhment over-rule the Seed: And therefore you are to practiſe it by Nouriſhments as contrary as may be, to the Nature of the Herb; ſo neverthelels as the Herb may grow, and like-wiſe with Seeds that are of the weakeſt ſort, and have leaſt vigor. You ſhall do well therefore to take Marſh Herbs, and plant them upon tops of Hills and Champaigns; and ſuch Plants as require much moiſture, upon Sandy and very dry grounds. As for example, Marſh-Mallows, and Sedge upon Hills, Cucumber and Lettuce Seeds, and Coleworts upon a Sandy Plat; ſo contrariwiſe plant Buſhes, Heath, Ling, and Brakes upon a Wet or Marſh Ground. This I conceive alſo, that all Eſculent and Garden Herbs, ſet upon the tops of Hills, will prove more *Medicinal*, though leſs Eſculent, than they were before. And it may be likewiſe, ſome Wilde Herbs you may make Salet Herbs. This is the firſt Rule for Tranſmutation of Plants.

527.　The ſecond Rule ſhould be to bury ſome few Seeds of the Herb you would change amongſt other Seeds; and then you ſhall ſee whether the Juyce of thoſe other Seeds do not ſo qualifie the Earth, as it will alter the Seed whereupon you work. As for example, Put Parſly-ſeed amongſt Onion-ſeed, or Lettuce-ſeed amongſt Parſly-ſeed, or Baſil-ſeed amongſt Thyme-ſeed, and ſee the change of taſte or otherwiſe. But you ſhall do well to put the Seed you would change into a little Linnen Cloth, that it mingle not with the Foreign Seed.

528.　The third Rule ſhall be the making of ſome medly, or mixture of Earth, with ſome other Plants bruiſed, or ſhaved, either in Leaf or Root: As for ex-ample make Earth, with a mixture of Colewort Leaves ſtamped, and ſet in it Artichoaks, or Parſnips: So take Earth made with *Majoram*, or *Origannum*, or *Wilde Thyme*, bruiſed, or ſtamped, and ſet in it *Fennel-ſeed*, &c. In which operation, the Proces of Nature ſtill will be, (as I conceive,) not that the Herb you work upon, ſhould draw the Juyce of the Foreign Herb: (for that opinion we have formerly rejected) but there will be a new confection of mould, which perhaps will alter the Seed, and yet not to the kinde of the former Herb.

529.　The fourth Rule ſhall be to mark what Herbs ſome Earths do put forth of themſelves, and to take that Earth, and to Pot it, or to Veſſel it; and into that, ſet the Seed you would change: As for Example, take from under Walls, or the like; where Nettles put forth in abundance, the Earth which you ſhall there finde, without any String or Root of the Nettles; and pot that Earth, and ſet in it Stock-Gilly-flowers, or Wall-flowers, &c. Or ſow in the Seeds of them, and ſee what the event will be; or take Earth, that you have prepared to put forth *Muſhrooms* of it ſelf, (whereof you ſhall finde ſome inſtances following,) and ſow it in Purſlane-ſeed, or Lettuce-ſeed; for in theſe Experiments, it is likely enough, that the Earth being accuſtomed to ſend forth one kinde of Nouriſhment, will alter the new Seed.

530.　The fifth Rule ſhall be, to make the Herb grow contrary to his nature, as to make Ground Herbs riſe in height: As for example, Carry Camomile, or Wilde Thyme, or the Green Strawberry, upon ſticks, as you do Hops upon Poles, and ſee what the event will be.

531.　The ſixth Rule ſhall be to make Plants grow out of the Sun, or open Air; for that is a great mutation in Nature, and may induce a change in the Seed: As barrel up Earth, and ſow ſome Seed in it, and put in the bottom of a Pond, or put it in ſome great hollow Tree; try alſo the ſowing
of

of Seeds in the bottoms of Caves ; and Pots with Seeds sown, hanged up in Wells, some distance from the Water, and see what the event will be.

IT is certain, that *Timber-Trees* in *Coppice Woods*, grow more upright, and more free from under Boughs, than those that stand in the Fields. The cause whereof is, for that *Plants* have a natural motion to get to the Sun : and besides, they are not glutted with too much nourishment ; for that the Coppice shareth with them, and Repletion ever hindreth stature. Lastly, they are kept warm, and that ever in Plants helpeth mounting.

532.
Experiments in Consort, touching the Procerity, and Lowness, and Artificial Dwarfing of Trees.

Trees that are of themselves full of Heat, (which heat appeareth by their inflamable Gums) as Firrs, and Pines, mount of themselves in height without Side-boughs, till they come towards the top. The cause is partly heat, and partly tenuity of Juyce ; both which send the Sap upwards. As for Juniper, it is but a Shrub, and groweth not big enough in Body to maintain a tall Tree.

533.

It is reported, that a good strong Canvas, spred over a Tree grafted low, soon after it putteth forth, will dwarf it, and make it spred. The cause is plain ; for that all things that grow, will grow as they finde room.

534.

Trees are generally set of *Roots* or *Kernels* ; but if you set them of *Slips,* (as of some *Trees* you may, by name the *Mulberry*) some of the *Slips* will take ; and those that take, (as is reported) will be *Dwarf-trees* The cause is, for that a *Slip* draweth nourishment more weakly, than either a *Root* or *Kernel.*

535.

All *Plants* that put forth their Sap hastily, have their Bodies not proportionable to their length, and therefore they are Winders and Creepers ; as *Ivy, Briony, Hops, Woodbine :* Whereas Dwarfing requireth a slow putting forth, and less vigor of mounting.

536.

THe Scripture saith, That *Solomon* wrote a Natural History, from the *Cedar* of *Libanus,* to the *Moss* growing upon the Wall ; for so the best *Translations* have it. And it is true, that *Moss* is but the *Rudiment* of a *Plant,* and (as it were) the *Mould* of *Earth* or *Bark.*

Experiments in Consort, touching the Rudiments of Plants, and of the Excrescences of Plants, or Super-Plants.
537.

Moss groweth chiefly upon Ridges of Houses, tiled or thatched, and upon the Crests of Walls, and that Moss is of a lightsome and pleasant Green. The growing upon Slopes is caused for that Moss, as on the one side it cometh of Moisture and Water, so on the other side the Water must but slide, and not stand or pool. And the growing upon Tiles, or Walls, &c. is caused, for that those dried Earths, having not moisture sufficient to put forth a *Plant,* do practice Germination by putting forth Moss ; though when by age, or otherwise, they grow to relent and resolve, they sometimes put forth Plants, as Wall flowers. And almost all Moss hath here and there little Stalks, besides the low Thrum.

Moss groweth upon Alleys, especially such as lye cold, and upon the North ; as in divers Tarrasses. And again, if they be much trodden ; or if they were at the first gravelled : For wheresoever Plants are kept down, the Earth putteth forth Moss.

538.

539. Old Ground, that hath been long unbroken up, gathereth Moss; and therefore Husbandmen use to cure their Pasture-Grounds, when they grow to Moss, by Tilling them for a year, or two: Which also dependeth upon the same cause: for that the more sparing and starving Juyce of the Earth, insufficient for Plants, doth breed Moss.

540. Old Trees are more Mossie, (far) than young; for that the Sap is not so frank as to rise all to the Boughs, but tireth by the way, and putteth out *Moss.*

541. *Fountains* have *Moss* growing upon the Ground about them;
  Muscosi Fontes————
The cause is, for that the *Fountains* drain the Water from the Ground adjacent, and leave but sufficient moisture to breed *Moss*; and besides, the coldness of the Water conduceth to the same.

542. The *Moss* of *Trees*, is a kinde of Hair; for it is the Juyce of the Tree, that is excerned, and doth not assimilate, and upon great Trees the Moss gathereth a figure, like a Leaf.

543. The moisture sort of Trees yield little Moss, as we see in *Asps, Poplars, Willows, Beeches, &c.* Which is partly caused for the reason that hath been given of the frank putting up of the Sap into the Boughs; and partly, for that the Barks of those Trees are more close and smooth, than those of Oaks, and Ashes, whereby the Moss can the hardlier issue out.

544. In Clay Grounds, all Fruit Trees grow full of Moss, both upon Body and Boughs; which is caused, partly by the coldness of the Ground, whereby the Plants nourish less; and partly by the roughness of the Earth, whereby the Sap is shut in, and cannot get up, to spred so frankly as it should do.

545. We have said heretofore, that if Trees be hide-bound, they wax less fruitful and gather Moss; and that they are holpen by hacking, &c. And therefore by the reason of contraries, if Trees be bound in with Cords or some outward Bands, they will put forth more Moss: Which (I think) hapneth to Trees that stand bleak, and upon the cold Winds. It would also be tried, whether, if you cover a Tree, somewhat thick upon the top, after his powling, it will not gather more Moss. I think also, the Watring of Trees with cold Fountain Water will make them grow full of Moss.

546. There is a Moss the *Perfumers* have, which cometh out of Apple-Trees, that hath an excellent sent. *Quære,* particularly for the manner of the growth, and the nature of it. And for this Experiments sake, being a thing of price, I have set down the last Experiments, how to multiply and call on Mosses.

  Next unto Moss, I will speak of *Mushromes*, which are likewise an unperfect Plant. The Mushromes have two strange properties; the one, that they yield so delicious a Meat; the other, that they come up so hastily, as in a night, and yet they are unsown. And therefore such as are Upstarts in State, they call in reproach, *Mushromes.* It must needs be therefore, that they be made of much moisture; and that moisture fat, gross, and yet somewhat concocted. And (indeed) we finde, that *Mushromes* cause the accident, which we call *Incubus,* or the *Mare* in the Stomach. And therefore the Surfeit of them may suffocate and empoyson. And this sheweth, that they are windy; and that windiness is gross, and swelling, not sharp or griping. And upon the same reason *Mushromes* are a venereous Meat.

It

It is reported, that the Bark of white or Red Poplar, (which are of the moifteft of Trees) cut fmall, and caft into Furrows well dunged, will caufe the ground to put forth *Mushromes*, at all feafons of the year fit to be eaten, fome add to the mixture Leaven of Bread, refolved in Water.

547.

It is reported, that if a Hilly-field, where the ftubble is ftanding, be fet on fire, in the fhowry feafon, it will put forth great ftore of *Mushromes*.

548.

It is reported, that *Harts-Horn* fhaken, or in fmall pieces, mixed with Dung, and watred, putteth up *Mushromes*. And we know that *Harts-Horn* is of a fat and clammy fubftance : And it may be *Ox-Horn* would do the like.

549.

It hath been reported, though it be fcarce credible, that Ivy hath grown out of a *Stags-Horn*; which they fuppofe did rather come from a confrication of the Horn upon the Ivy, than from the Horn it felf. There is not known any fubftance, but Earth, and the Procedeurs of Earth, (as *Tile-Stone, &c.*) that yieldeth any Mofs, or Herby fubftance. There may be tryal made of fome Seeds, as that Fennel-Seed, Muftard-Seed, and Rape-Seed, put into fome little holes made in the Horns of Stags, or Oxen, to fee if they will grow.

550.

There is alfo another unperfect Plant, that (in fhew) is like a great Mufhrome : And it is fometimes as broad as ones Hat, which they call a *Toads-ftool*; but it is not Efculent, and it groweth (commonly) by a dead Stub of a Tree, and likewife about the Roots of rotten Trees; and therefore feemeth to take his Juyce from Wood putrified. Which fheweth by the way, that Wood putrified yieldeth a frank moifture.

551.

There is a Cake that groweth upon the fide of a dead Tree, that hath gotten no name, but it is large and of a Chefnut colour, and hard and pithy; whereby it fhould feem, that even dead Trees forget not their putting forth, no more than the Carcaffes of Mens Bodies that put forth Hair and Nails for a time.

552.

There is a Cod or Bag that groweth commonly in the Fields; that at firft is hard like a Tennis-Ball, and white; and after growth of a Mufhrome colour, and full of light duft upon the breaking; and is thought to be dangerous for the eyes, if the Powder get into them, and to be good for Kibes. Belike it hath a Corrofive, and fretting Nature.

553.

There is an Herb called *Jews-Ear*, that groweth upon the Roots, and lower parts of the Bodies of Trees, efpecially of Elders, and fometimes Afhes. It hath a ftrange propriety; for in warm Water, it fwelleth, and openeth extreamly. It is not green, but of a dusky brown colour. And it is ufed for fquinancies, and inflamations in the Throat, whereby it feemeth to have a mollifying, and lenifying vertue.

554.

There is a kinde of Spongy excrefcence, which groweth chiefly upon the Roots of the Lafer-Tree, and fometimes upon Cedar, and other Trees. It is very white, and light, and fryable; which we call *Agarick*. It is famous in Phyfick for the purging of tough Flegm. And it is alfo an excellent opener for the Liver, but offenfive to the Stomach; and in tafte it is, at the firft fweet and after bitter.

555.

We finde no Super-Plant, that is a formed Plant, but *Miffeltoe*. They have an idle Tradition, that there is a Bird called a *Miffel-Bird*, that feedeth upon a Seed, which many times fhe cannot digeft, and fo expelleth it whole with her Excrement ; which falling upon a Bough of a Tree, that hath fome rift, putteth forth *Miffeltoe*. But this is a Fable ; for it is not probable, that Birds fhould feed upon that they cannot digeft. But allow that,

556.

that, yet it cannot be for other Reasons : For first, it is found but upon certain Trees; and those Trees bear no such Fruit, as may allure that Bird to fit and feed upon them. It may be, that Bird feedeth upon the Misseltoe-Berries, and so is often found there; which may have given occasion to the tale. But that which maketh an end of the question is, that Misseltoe hath been found to put forth under the Boughs, and not (onely) above the Boughs; so it cannot be any thing that falleth upon the Bough. Misseltoe groweth chiefly upon Crab-trees, Apples-trees, sometimes upon Hasles, and rarely upon Oaks; the Misseltoe whereof is counted very Medicinal. It is ever green, Winter and Summer, and beareth a white glistering Berry; and it is a Plant, utterly differing from the Plant, upon which it groweth. Two things therefore may be certainly set down : First, that Superfœtation must be by abundance of Sap, in the Bough that putteth it forth. Secondly, that that Sap must be such as the Tree doth excern, and cannot assimilate, for else it would go into a Bough; and besides, it seemeth to be more fat and unctuous, than the ordinary Sap of the Tree; both by the Berry which is clammy, and by that it continueth green Winter and Summer, which the Tree doth not.

557.   This *Experiment of Misseltoe* may give light to other practices; therefore tryal would be made, by ripping of the Bough of a Crab-tree in the Bark, and watering of the Wound every day, with warm water dunged, to see if it would bring forth Misseltoe, or any such like thing. But it were yet more likely, to try it with some other watering or anointing, that were not so natural to the Tree as Water is; as Oyl, or Barm of Drink, &c. So they be such things as kill not the Bough.

558.   It were good to try, what *Plants* would put forth, if they be forbidden to put forth their natural Boughs : Powl therefore a Tree, and cover it, some thickness with Clay on the top, and see what it will put forth. I suppose it will put forth Roots; for so will a Cions, being turned down into Clay. Therefore in this Experiment also, the Tree would be closed with somewhat that is not so natural to the Plant as Clay is; try it with Leather, or Cloth, or Painting, so it be not hurtful to the Tree. And it is certain, that a Brake hath been known to grow out of a Pollard.

559.   A Man may count the Prickes of Trees to be a kinde of Excrescence, for they will never be Boughs, nor bear Leaves. The Plants that have Prickles, are Thorns, Black and White; Bryer, Rose, Lemmon-trees, Crab-trees, Goosberry, Berberry; these have it in the Bough. The Plants that have Prickles in the Leaf are, Holly, Juniper, Whin-bush, Thistle; Nettles also have a small venemous Prickle; so hath Borrage, but harmless. The cause must be, hasty putting forth, want of moisture, and the closeness of the Bark : For the haste of the Spirit to put forth, and the want of nourishment to put forth a Bough, and the closeness of the Bark, cause Prickles in Boughs; and therefore they are ever like a *Pyramis,* for that the moisture spendeth after a little putting forth. And for Prickles in Leaves, they come also of putting forth more Juyce into the Leaf, that can spred in the Leaf smooth; and therefore the Leaves otherwise are rough, as Burrage and Nettles are. As for the Leaves of Holly, they are smooth, but never plain, but as it were with folds for the same cause.

560.   There be also *Plants,* that though they have no Prickles, yet they have a kinde of Downey or Velvet Rine upon their Leaves; as *Rose-Campion, Stock-Gilliflowers, Colts-foot;* which Down or Nap cometh of a subtile Spirit, in a soft or fat substance. For it is certain, that both *Stock-Gilliflowers,* and *Rose-Campions,*

Campions, ftamped, have been applied (with fuccefs) to the Wrefts of thofe that have had *Tertian* or *Quartan Agues* ; and the *Vapor* or *Colts-foot* have a fanative vertue towards the Lungs, and the Leaf alfo is healing in *Surgery.*

Another kinde of Excrefcence is an Exudation of Plants, joyned with Putrefaction, as we fee in Oak-Apples, which are found chiefly upon the Leaves of Oaks, and the like upon Willows : And Countrey people have a kinde of Prediction, that if the Oak-Apple, broken, be full of Worms, it is a fign of a peftilent year ; which is a likely thing, becaufe they grow of corruption.   561.

There is alfo upon *Sweet*, or other *Bryer*, a fine Tuft, or Brufh of Mofs of divers colours ; which if you cut, you fhall ever finde full of little white Worms.   562.

ITis certain, that *Earth* taken out of the Foundations of *Vaults* and *Houfes* and bottoms of *Wells*, and then put into Pots, will put forth fundry kinde of *Herbs* : But fome time is required for the Germination ; for if it be taken but from a Fathom deep, it will put forth the firft year, if much deeper, not till after a year or two.

563.
Experiments in Confort, touching the Producing of perfect Plants without Seeds.

The nature of the *Plants* growing out of the *Earth* fo taken up, doth follow the nature of the Mould it felf, as if the Mould be foft and fine, it putteth forth foft *Herbs* ; as *Grafs*, *Plantine*, and the like : If the *Earth* be harder and courfer, it putteth forth *Herbs* more rough, as *Thiftles*, *Firs*, &c.   564.

It is common Experience, that where *Alleys* are clofe gravelled, the Earth putteth forth the firft year *Knot Grafs*, and after *Spire Grafs*. The caufe is, for that the hard Gravel or Pebble at the firft laying, will not fuffer the *Grafs* to come forth upright, but turneth it to finde his way where it can ; but after that the Earth is fomewhat loofened at the top, the ordinary Grafs cometh up.   565.

It is reported, that Earth being taken out of fhady and watry Woods, fome depth, and potted, will put forth Herbs of a fat and juycy fubftance; as *Penny-wort*, *Purflane*, *Houfleek*, *Penny-Royal*, &c.   566.

The Water alfo doth fend forth Plants that have no Roots fixed in the bottom ; but they are lefs perfect Plants being almoft but Leaves, and thofe fmall ones: Such is that we call *Duck-weed*, which hath a Leaf no bigger then a Thyme Leaf, but of a frefher Green, and putteth forth a little ftring into the Water, far from the bottom. As for the Water-Lilly, it hath a Root in the Ground; and fo have a number of other Herbs that grow in Ponds.   567.

It is reported by fome of the *Ancients*, and fome *Modern Teftimony* likewife, that there be fome Plants, that grow upon the top of the Sea; being fuppofed to grow of fome concretion of Slime from the Water, where the *Sun* heateth hot, and where the *Sea* ftirreth little. As for the *Alga Marina*, (Sea-weed) and *Eringium* (*Sea-Thiftle*) both the Roots ; but have *Sea-weed* under the Water, the *Sea Thiftle* but upon the Shore.   568.

The *Ancients* have noted, that there are fome Herbs that grow out of *Snow*, laid up clofe together, and putrified: and that they are all bitter, and they name one efpecially, *Flomus*, which we call *Moth-Mullein*. It is certain, that Worms are found in *Snow* commonly, like Earth-worms ; and therefore it is not unlike, that it may likewife put forth Plants.   569.

The

570.   The Ancients have affirmed, that there are some Herbs that grow out of Stone, which may be, for that it is certain, that Toads have been found in the middle of a Freestone. We see also, that Flints lying above ground gather Moss; and Wall-flowers, and some other Flowers grow upon Walls. But whether upon the main Brick or Stone, or whether out of the Lime, or Chinks, is not well observed. For Elders and Ashes have been seen to grow out of Steeples; but they manifestly grow out of Clefts, insomuch as, when they grow big, they will disjoyn the Stone. And besides, it is doubtful, whether the Mortar it self putteth it forth, or whether some Seeds be not let fall by Birds. There be likewise Rock-Herbs, but I suppose those are, where there is some Mould or Earth. It hath likewise been found, that great Trees, growing upon Quarries, have put down their Root into the Stone.

571.   In some Mines in *Germany*, as is reported, there grow in the bottom Vegetables; and the Workfolks use to say, They have *Magical Vertue,* and will not suffer men together them.

572.   The Sea-sands seldom bear Plants. Whereof the cause is yielded by some of the Ancients, for that the Sun exhaleth the Moisture, before it can incorporate with the Earth, and yield a Nourishment for the Plant. And it is affirmed also, that Sand hath (always) his Root in Clay ; and that there be no Veins of Sand, any great depth within the Earth.

573.   It is certain, that some Plants put forth for a time of their own store, without any Nourishment from Earth, Water, Stone, &c. Of which, *vide the Experiment* 29.

574.
*Experiments
in Consort,
touching
Foreign Plants*

    IT is reported, That Earth that was brought out of the *Indies,* and other remote Countreys for Ballast for Ships, cast upon some Grounds in *Italy,* did put forth Foreign Herbs, to us in *Europe* not known ; and, that which is more, that of their Roots, Barks, and Seeds, contused together, and mingled with other Earth, and well watred with warm Water, there came forth Herbs much like the other.

575.   Plants, brought out of hot Countreys, will endeavor to put forth at the same time, that they do usually do in their own climate ; and therefore to preserve them, there is no more required than to keep them from the injury of putting back by Cold. It is reported also, that Grain out of the hotter Countreys translated into the Colder, will be more foreward than the ordinary Grain of the cold Countrey. It is likely, that this will prove better in Grains, than in Trees ; for that Grains are but Annual, and so the vertue of the Seed is not worn out, whereas in a Tree, it is embased by the Ground, to which it is removed.

576.   Many Plants, which grow in the hotter Countreys, being set in the colder, will nevertheless, even in those cold Countreys, being sown of Seeds late in the Spring come up and abide most part of the Summer ; as we finde it in Orenge, and Lemmon Seeds, &c. The Seeds whereof, sown in the end of *April,* will bring forth excellent Sallets, mingled with other Herbs. And I doubt not, but the Seeds of Clove-Trees, and Pepper-Seeds, &c. If they could come hither Green enough to be sown, would do the like.

There

THere be some *Flowers*, *Blossoms*, *Grains*, and *Fruits*, which come more early, and others which come more late in the year. The Flowers that come early with us, are, *Prime-Roses*, *Violets*, *Anemonies*, *Water-Daffa-dillies*, *Crocus Vernus*, and some early *Tulippa's*. And they are all cold Plants, which therefore (as it should seem) have a quicker Perception of the heat of the Sun increasing, than the hot Herbs have, as a cold hand will sooner finde a little warmth, than a hot. And those that come next after, are Wall-Flowers, Cowslips, Hyacinths, Rosemary-flowers, &c. And after them Pinks, Roses, Flowerdeluces, &c. And the latest are, Gilly-flowers, Holly-Oaks, Larks-Foot, &c. The earliest Blossoms are, the Blossoms of Peaches, Almonds, Cornelians, Mezerions, &c. And they are of such Trees, as have much moisture, either Watery, or Oyly. And therefore *Crocus Vernus* also, being an Herb that hath an Oyly Juyce, putteth forth early. For those also finde the Sun sooner than the dryer Trees. The Grains are, first Rye and Wheat, then Oats and Barley, then Pease and Beans; for though Green Pease and Beans be eaten sooner, yet the dry ones that are used for Horse-meat, are ripe last; and it seemeth, that the fatter Grain cometh first. The earliest Fruits are, Strawberries, Cherries, Gooseberries, Corrans; and after them early Apples, early Pears, Apricots, Rasps; and after them, Damosins, and most kinde of Plumbs, Peaches, &c. And the latest are, Apples, Wardens, Grapes, Nuts, Quinces, Almonds, Sloes, Brier-berries, Heps, Medlars, Services, Cornelians, &c.

577.
Experiments in Consort, touching the Seasons in which Plants come forth.

It is to be noted, That (commonly) Trees that ripen latest, blossom soonest; as Peaches, Cornelians, Sloes, Almonds, &c. And it seemeth to be a work of providence that they blossom so soon, for otherwise they could not have the Sun long enough to ripen.

578.

There be Fruits (but rarely) that come twice a year; as some Pears, Strawberries, &c. And it seemeth, they are such as abound with nourishment, whereby after one period, before the Sun waxeth too weak, they can endure another. The *Violet* also, amongst Flowers, cometh twice a year, especially the double White; and that also is a Plant full of moisture. *Roses* come twice, but it is not without cutting, as hath been formerly said.

579.

In *Muscovia*, though the Corn come not up till late Spring, yet their Harvest is as early as ours. The cause is, for that the strength of the Ground is kept in with the Snow; and we see with us, that if it be a long Winter, it is commonly a more plentiful year: And after those kinde of Winters likewise, the Flowers and Corn which are earlier and later, do come commonly at once, and at the same time; which troubleth the Husbandman many times: For you shall have Red-Roses and Damask-Roses come together, and likewise the Harvest of Wheat and Barley. But this hapneth ever, for that the earlier stayeth the later, and not that the later cometh sooner.

580.

There be divers Fruit Trees, in the hot Countreys, which have Blossoms, and young fruit, and ripe fruit, almost all the year, succeeding one another. And it is said, the Orenge hath the like with us, for a great part of Summer, and so also hath the Fig. And no doubt, the Natural Motion of Plants is to have so: But that either they want Juyce to spend, or they meet with the cold of the Winter. And therefore this Circle of ripening cannot be, but in succulent Plants, and hot Countreys.

581.

Some

582. Some Herbs are but *Annual*, and die *Root* and all once a year ; as *Borrage, Lettuce, Cucumbers, Musk-Melons, Basil, Tobacco, Mustard-seed,* and all kindes of Corn ; some continue many years, as *Hyssope, Germander, Lavender, Fennel, &c.* The cause of the Dying is double ; the first is, the tendernes and weaknes of the Seed, which maketh the period in a small time, as it is in *Borrage, Lettuce, Cucumbers, Corn, &c.* And therefore none of these are hot. The other cause is, for that some Herbs can worse endure cold, as *Basil, Tobacco, Mustard seed* ; and these have (all) much heat.

583.
Experiments in Consort, touching the Lasting of Herbs and Trees.

THe lasting of *Plants*, is most in those that are largest of Body, as *Oaks, Elm, Chesnut,* the *Loat-tree, &c.* And this holdeth in Trees, but in Herbs it is often contrary ; for Borrage, Coleworts, Pompions, which are Herbs of the largest size, are of small durance ; whereas *Hyssope, Winter-Savory, Germander, Time, Sage,* will last long. The cause is, for that Trees last according to the strength, and quantity of their Sap and Juyce, being well munited by their Bark, against the injuries of the Air : But Herbs draw a weak Juyce, and have a soft Stalk ; and therefore those amongst them which last longest, are Herbs of strong smell, and with a sticky stalk.

584. Trees that bear Mast and Nuts, are commonly more lasting than those that bear Fruits, especially the moister Fruits ; as Oaks, Beeches, Chesnuts, Walnuts, Almonds, Pine trees, &c. last longer than Apples, Pears, Plumbs, &c. The cause is, the fatnes, and oylines of the Sap ; which ever wasteth less, than the more Watry.

585. Trees that bring forth their Leaves late in the year, and cast them likewise late, are more lasting than those that sprout their Leaves early, or shed them betimes. The cause is, for that the late coming forth, sheweth a moisture more fixed ; and the other loose, and more easily resolved. And the same cause is, that wilde Trees last longer than Garden-trees ; and in the same kinde, those whose Fruit is acide more than those whose Fruit is sweet.

586. Nothing procureth the lasting of Trees, Bushes, and Herbs, so much as often cutting ; for every cutting causeth a renovation of the Juyce of the Plant ; that it neither goeth so far, nor riseth so faintly, as when the Plant is not cut : Insomuch, as *Annual Plants*, if you cut them seasonably, and will spare the use of them, and suffer them to come up still young, will last more years than one, as hath been partly touched ; such as is Lettuce, Purslane, Cucumber, and the like. And for great Trees, we see almost all overgrown Trees in Church-yards, or near ancient Building, and the like, are Pollards or Dottards, and not Trees at their full height.

587. Some *Experiment* would be made, how by Art to make Plants more lasting than their ordinary period ; as to make a Stalk of Wheat, &c. last a whole year. You must ever presuppose, that you handle it so, as the Winter killeth it not ; for we speak onely of prolonging the Natural Period. I conceive, that the Rule will hold, That whatsoever maketh the Herb come later, than at his time will make it last longer time : It were good to try it in a Stalk of Wheat, &c. set in the shade, and encompassed with a case of Wood, not touching the Straw, to keep out open Air.

588. As for the Preservation of Fruits, as well upon the Tree or Stalk, as gathered, we shall handle it under the Title of *Conservation of Bodies.*

The

THe Particular Figures of *Plants* we leave to their descriptions, but some few things in general, we will observe. Trees and Herbs, in the growing forth of their Boughs and Branches, are not figured, and keep no order. The cause is, for that the Sap, being restrained in the Rinde and Bark, breaketh not forth at all, (as in the Bodies of Trees, and Stalks of Herbs,) till they begin to branch, and then, when they make an eruption, they break forth casually, where they finde best way in the Bark or Rinde. It is true, that some Trees are more scattered in their Boughs: as *Sallow trees, Warden-trees, Quince-trees, Medlar-trees, Lemmon trees, &c.* Some are more in the form of a *Pyramis*, and come almost to tod; as the *Pear-trees* (which the Criticks will have to borrow his name of πῦρ Fire) *Orenge-trees, Fir-trees, Service trees, Lime-trees, &c.* And some are more spred and broad, as *Beeches, Horn-beam, &c.* The rest are more indifferent. The cause of scattering the Boughs is, the hasty breaking forth of the Sap; and therefore those Trees rise not in a Body of any height, but Branch near the Ground. The cause of the *Pyramis* is, the keeping in of the Sap, long before it branch, and the spending of it, when it beginneth to branch, by equal degrees: The spreding is caused, by the carrying up of the Sap plentifully, without expence, and then putting it forth speedily, and at once.

There be divers Herbs, but no Trees, that may be said to have some kinde of order, in the putting forth of their Leaves: For they have Joynts, or Knuckles, as it were stops in their Germination; as have *Gilliflowers, Pinks, Fennel, Corn, Reeds,* and *Canes.* The cause whereof is, for that the Sap ascendeth unequally, and doth (as it were) tire and stop by the way. And it seemeth, they have some closenels and hardness in their Stalk, which hindereth the Sap from going up, until it hath gathered into a knot, and so is more urged to put forth. And therefore, they are most of them hollow, when the Stalk is dry; as *Fennel Stalks, Stubble,* and *Canes.*

Flowers have (all) exquisite *Figures*, and the Flower numbers are (chiefly) five and four; as in *Prime-Roses, Bryer-Roses, single Musk-Roses, single Pinks,* and *Gilliflowers, &c.* which have five Leaves; *Lillies, Flower-de-luces, Borage, Bugloß &c.* which have four Leaves. But some put forth Leaves not numbred, but they are ever small ones; as *Marigolds, Trifole, &c.* We see also, that the Sockets, and Supporters of Flowers, are Figured; as in the five Brethren of the *Rose, Sockets* of *Gilliflowers, &c.* Leaves also are all figured, some round, some long, none square, and many jagged on the sides; which Leaves of *Flowers* seldom are. For, I account, the jagging of *Pinks,* and *Gilliflowers,* to be like the inequality of *Oak-leaves,* of *Vine-leaves,* or the like; but they seldom or never have any small Purls.

OF *Plants* some few put forth their Blossoms before their Leaves; as *Almonds, Peaches, Cornelians, Black-Thorn, &c.* But most put forth some Leaves before their Blossoms; as *Apples, Pears, Plumbs, Cherry, White-Thorn, &c.* The cause is for that those that put forth their Blossoms first, have either an acute and sharp spirit; (and therefore commonly they all put forth early in the *Spring,* and ripen very late, as most of the particulars before mentioned) or else an oyly Juyce, which is apter to put out Flowers than Leaves.

Of *Plants* some are Green all Winter, others cast their Leaves. There are Green all Winter, *Holly, Ivy, Box, Firr, Eugh, Cypreß, Juniper, Bays, Rosemary, &c.* The cause of the holding Green, is the close and compact sub-

stance

588
Experiments in Consort, touching the several Figures of Plants.

589.

590.

591.
Experiments in Consort, touching Some principal differences in Plants.

592.

stance of their Leaves, and the Pedicles of them. And the cause of that again, is, either the rough and viscous Juyce of the Plant, or the strength and heat thereof. Of the first sort, is *Holly*; which is of so viscous a Juyce, as they make Birdlime of the Bark of it. The Stalk of *Ivy* is tough, and not fragile, as we see it in other small Twigs dry. *Firr* yieldeth Pitch. *Box* is a fast and heavy Wood, as we see it in Bowls. *Eugh* is a strong and tough Wood, as we see it in Bows. Of the second sort, is *Juniper*, which is a Wood odorate, and maketh a hot Fire. *Bays* is likewise a hot and aromatical Wood, and so is *Rosemary* for a Shrub. As for the Leaves, their density appeareth in that, either they are smooth and shining, as in *Bays, Holly, Ivy, Box, &c.* or in that they are hard and spiry, as in the rest. And tryal would be made of Grafting of *Rosemary*, and *Bays*, and *Box*, upon a *Holly* Stock, because they are Plants that come all Winter. It were good to try it also with Grafts of other Trees, either Fruit trees, or Wild-trees, to see whether they will not yield their Fruit, or bear their Leaves later, and longer in the Winter; because the Sap of the *Holly* putteth forth most in the Winter. It may be also a Mezerion-tree grafted upon a *Holly*, will prove both an earlier, and a greater Tree.

593.   There be some Plants that bear no Flower, and yet bear Fruit; there be some that bear Flowers, and no Fruit; there be some that bear neither Flowers nor Fruit. Most of the great Timber-trees, (as Oaks, Beeches, &c.) bear no apparent Flowers; some few (likewise) of the Fruit-trees, as Mulberry, Walnuts, &c. And some Shrubs, (as Juniper, Holly, &c.) bear no Flowers. Divers Herbs also bear Seeds, (which is as the Fruit,) and yet bear no Flowers, as Purslane, &c. Those that bear Flowers, and no Fruit, are few, as the double Cherry, the Sallow, &c. But for the Cherry, it is doubtful, whether it be not by Art or Culture; for if it be by Art, then tryal would be made, whether Apples and other Fruits Blossoms may not be doubled. There are some few, that bear neither Fruit, nor Flower; as the Elm, the Poplars, Box, Braks, &c.

594.   There be some Plants that shoot still upwards, and can support them-selves, as the greatest part of Trees and Plants: There be some other, that creep along the Ground, or wind about other Trees, or props, and cannot support themselves; as Vines, Ivy, Bryar, Briony, Wood-bines, Hops, Climatis, Camomil, &c. The cause is, (as hath been partly touched) for that all Plants, (naturally) move upwards; but if the Sap put up too fast, it maketh a slender Stalk, which will not support the weight; and therefore these latter sort are all swift and hasty comers.

THe first and most ordinary help is *Stercoration*. The *Sheeps-dung* is one of the best; and next, the *Dung* of *Kine*; and thirdly, that of *Horses*; which is held to be somewhat too hot, unless it be mingled; that of *Pigeons* for a Garden, as a small quantity of Ground, excelleth. The ordering of Dung is, if the Ground be Arable, to spred it immediately before the Plough-ing and Sowing, and so to Plough it in: For if you spred it long before, the Sun will draw out much of the fatness of the Dung: If the Ground be Grazing Ground, to spred it somewhat late towards Winter, that the Sun may have the less power to dry it up. As for special *Composts* for *Gardens* (as a *Hot Bed, &c.*) we have handled them before.

596.   The Second kinde of Compost is, the spreding of divers kindes of Earth; as *Marl, Chalk, Sea Sand, Earth upon Earth, Pond-Earth*, and the mixtures of them. *Marl* is thought to be the best, as having most fatness. And not
heating

heating the Ground too much. The next is *Sea-sand*, which (no doubt) obtained a special vertue by the *Salt*; for *Salt* is the first rudiment of life. Chalk over-heateth the Ground a little ; and therefore is best upon cold Clay Grounds, or moist Grounds : But I heard a great *Husband* say, that it was a common error to think that Chalk helpeth Airable Grounds, but helpeth not Grazing Grounds, whereas (indeed) it helpeth Grass as well as Corn. But that which breedeth the error is, because after the chalking of the Ground, they wear it out with many Crops, without rest ; and then (indeed) afterwards it will bear little Grass; because the Ground is tired out. It were good to try the laying of Chalk upon Airable Grounds, a little while before Ploughing, and to Plough it in, as they do the Dung ; but then it must be Friable first, by Rain or Lying : As for *Earth* it compasseth it self ; for I knew a great *Garden*, that had a *Field* (in a manner) poured upon it, and it did bear Fruit excellently the first year of the Planting ; for the Surface of the *Earth* is ever the fruitfullest: And *Earth* so prepared hath a double Surface. But it is true, as I conceive, that such *Earth* as hath *Salt-Peter* bred in it, if you can procure it without too much charge, doth excel. The way to hasten the breeding of *Salt-Peter*, is to forbid the *Sun*, and the growth of Vegetables. And therefore, if you make a large Hovel, thatched, over some quantity of Ground ; nay, if you do but planck the Ground over, it will breed *Salt-Peter*. As for *Pond-earth* or *River-earth*, it is a very good compost, especially, if the *Pond* have been long uncleansed, and so the Water be not too hungry; and I judge it will be yet better, if there be some mixture, of Chalk.

The third help of Ground is, by some other Substances that have vertue to make Ground Fertile, though they be not meerly *Earth*, wherein Ashes excel ; insomuch as the *Countreys* about *Ætna* and *Vesuvius* have a kinde of amends made them, for the mischief the eruptions (many times) do, by the exceeding fruitfulness of the soyl, caused by the Ashes scattered about. Soot also, though thin, spred in a *Field* or *Garden*, is tryed to be a very good compost. For *Salt* it is too costly ; but it is tryed, that mingled with Seed-corn, and sown together, it doth good: And I am of opinion, that Chalk in *Powder*, mingled with Seed-corn, would do good; perhaps as much as Chalking the Ground all over. As for the steeping of the Seeds in several mixtures with Water, to give them vigor, or watring Grounds with Compost-water, we have spoken of them before.

The fourth help of Ground is, the suffering of Vegetables to die into the Ground, and so to fatten it ; as the Stubble of Corn, especially Pease. *Brakes* cast upon the Ground in the beginning of Winter, will make it very fruitful. It were good (also) to try whether Leaves of Trees swept together, with some Chalk and Dung mixed, to give them more heart, would not make a good Compost : For there is nothing lost, so much as Leaves of Trees, and as they lie scattered, and without mixture, they rather make the Ground sour, than otherwise.

The fifth help of Ground is, Heat and Warmth. It hath been anciently practised to burn *Heath*, and *Ling* and *Sedge*, with the vantage of the Wind, upon the Ground. We see, that Warmth of Walls and Inclosures, mendeth Ground ; we see also, that lying open to the *South*, mendeth Ground ; we see again that the Foldings of Sheep help Gound as well by their warmth, as by their compost: And it may be doubted, whether the covering of the Ground with *Brakes*, in the beginning of the Winter (whereof we spake in the last *Experiment*) helpeth it not, by reason of the Warmth. Nay, some very good

 Husbands

Husbands do suspect, that the gathering up of Flints in Flinty Ground, and laying them on heaps (which is much used) is no good Husbandry for that they would keep the Ground warm.

600. The sixth help of Ground is, by Watring and Irrigation, which is in two manners; The one by Letting in, and Shutting out Waters, at seasonable times; for Water, at some seasons, and with reasonable stay, doth good; but at some other seasons, and with too long stay, doth hurt. And this serveth onely for Meadows, which are along some River. The other way is to bring Water from some hanging Grounds, where there are Springs into the lower Grounds, carrying it in some long Furrows; and from those Furrows, drawing it traverse to spred the Water: And this maketh an excellent improvement, both for Corn and Grass. It is the richer, if those hanging Grounds, be fruitful, because it washeth off some of the fatness of the Earth; but howsoever it profiteth much. Generally where there are great overflows in Fens, or the like, the drowning of them in the Winter, maketh the Summer following more fruitful: The cause may be for, that it keepeth the Ground warm, and nourisheth it. But the Fen-men hold, that the Sewers must be kept so, as the Water may not stay too long in the Spring, till the Weeds and Sedge be grown up; for then the Ground will be like a Wood which keepeth out the Sun, and so continueth the wet; whereby it will never graze (to purpose) that year. Thus much for Irrigation; but for Avoidances, and Drainings of Water, where there is too much, and the helps of Ground in that kinde, we shall speak of them in another place.

NATURAL

NATURAL HISTORY.

Century *VII*.

He differences between *Animate* and *Inanimate Bodies*, we shall handle fully under the Title of *Life*, and *Living Spirits*, and *Powers*. We shall therefore make but a brief mention of them in this place. The main differences are two. All Bodies have Spirits, and Pneumatical parts within them; but the main differences between *Animate* and *Inanimate* are two. The first is, that the Spirits of things animate, are all contined with themselves, and are branched in Veins, and secret Sanales, as Blood is: And in Living Creatures, the Spirits have not onely Branches, but certain Sells or Seats, where the principal Spirits do reside, and whereunto the rest do resort: But the Spirits in things Inanimate are shut in, and cut off by the Tangible parts; and are not pervious one to another, as Air is in Snow. The second main difference is, that the Spirits of Animate Bodies are all in some degree (more or less) kindled and inflamed, and have a fine commixture of Flame, and an Ærial substance: But Inanimate Bodies have their Spirits no whit inflamed or kindled. And this difference consisteth not in the Heat or Coolness of Spirits; for *Cloves* and other Spices, *Naptha* and *Petroleum*, have exceeding hot Spirits (hotter a great deal than *Oyl*, *Wax*, or *Tallow*, &c.) but not inflamed. And when any of those weak and temperate Bodies come to be inflamed, than they gather a much greater heat, than others have uninflamed, besides their light and motion, &c.

The differences which are secondary, and proceed from these two radical differences are, first, *Plants* are all figurate and determinate, which inanimate Bodies are not; for look how far the Spirit is able to spred and continue it self, so far goeth the shape or figure, and then is determined. Secondly, *Plants* do nourish, inanimate Bodies do not; they have an Accretion, but no Alimentation. Thirdly, *Plants* have a period of life, which inanimate Bodies have not. Fourthly, they have a succession and propagation of their kinde, which is not in Bodies inanimate.

601.
Experiments in Consort, touching the *Affinities and Differences, between Plants and Inanimate Bodies.*

602.

M 3

The

603.   The differences between *Plants* and *Metals*, or *Fossils* besides those four beforementioned, (for *Metals* I hold inanimate) are these: First, *Metals* are more durable than *Plants*: Secondly, they are more solid and hard: Thirdly, they are wholly subterrany; whereas *Plants* are part above *Earth*, and part under *Earth*.

604.   There be very few *Creatures* that participate of the Nature of *Plants*, and *Metals* both; *Coral* is one of the nearest of both kindes, another is *Vitriol*, for that is aptest to sprout with moisture.

605.   Another special Affinity is between *Plants* and *Mould*, or *Putrefaction*: For all Putrefaction, (if it dissolve not in Arefaction) will in the end issue into *Plants* or *Living Creatures* bred of Putrefaction. I account *Moss*, and *Mushromes*, and *Agarick*, and other of those kindes, to be but *Moulds* of the Ground, Walls, and Trees, and the like. As for *Flesh*, and *Fish*, and *Plants* themselves, and a number of other things, after a *Mouldiness*, or *Rottenness*, or *Corrupting*, they will fall to breed *Worms*. These Putrefactions, which have *Affinity* with *Plants*, have this difference from them; that they have no succession or propagation, though they nourish, and have a period of Life, and have likewise some Figure.

606.   I left once, by chance, a *Citron* cut in a close room, for three Summer-moneths, that I was absent; and at my return, there were grown forth out of the Pith cut, *Tufts of Hairs*, an inch long, with little black Heads as if they would have been some *Herb*.

607.

Experiments in Consort, touching the Affinities and Differences of Plants, and Living Creatures: And the Confines and Participles of them.

THe Affinities and Differences between *Plants* and *Living Creatures*, are these that follow. They have both of them, *Spirits* continued and branched, and also inflamed. But first in *Living Creatures* the *Spirits* have a *Cell* or *Seat*, which *Plants* have not, as was also formerly said. And secondly, the *Spirits* of *Living Creatures* hold more of *Flame*, than the *Spirits* of *Plants* do; and these two are the Radical differences. For the Secondary differences, they are as follow. First, Plants are all fixed to the Earth; whereas all Living Creatures are severed, and of themselves. Secondly, Living Creatures have Local Motion, Plants have not. Thirdly, Living Creatures nourish from their upper parts by the Mouth chiefly; Plants nourish from below, namely from the Roots. Fourthly, Plants have their Seed and Seminal parts uppermost, Living Creatures have them lowermost; and therefore it was said, not Elegantly alone, but Philosophically: *Homo est Planta inversa*, *Man is like a Plant turned upwards*; For the Root in Plants, is as the Head in Living Creatures. Fifthly, *Living Creatures* have a more exact Figure than Plants. Sixthly, Living Creatures have more diversity of Organs within their Bodies and (as it were) inward Figures than Plants have. Seventhly, Living Creatures have Sense, which Plants have not. Eightly, Living Creatures have Voluntary Motion, which Plants have not.

608.   For the difference of *Sexes* in *Plants*, they are oftentimes by name distinguished; as *Male-Piony*, *Female-Piony*; *Male Rosemary*, *Female-Rosemary*; *He-Holly*, *She-Holly*, &c. But Generation by Copulation (certainly) extendeth not to Plants. The nearest approach of it, is between the He-Palm, and the She-Palm, which (as they report) if they grow near, incline the one to the other; insomuch as, (that which is more strange) they doubt not to report, that to keep the Trees upright from bending, they tye Ropes or Lines from the one to the other, that the contact might be enjoyned by the contact of a middle Body. But this may be feigned, or at least amplified. Nevertheless, I am

am apt enough to think, that this same *Binarium* of a stronger and a weaker, like unto *Masculine* and *Feminine*, doth hold in all Living Bodies. It is confounded sometimes; as in some Creatures of Putrefaction, wherein no marks of distinction appear; and it is doubled sometimes, as in Hermaphrodites: but generally there is a degree of strength in most Species.

609. The Participles or Confiners between Plants and Living Creatures, are such chiefly as are fixed, and have not Local Motion of remove; though they have a Motion in their parts, such as are Oysters, Cockles, and such like. There is a fabulous Narration, That in the *Northern Countreys* there should be an Herb that groweth in the likeness of a *Lamb*, and feedeth upon the Grass, in such sort, as it will bear the Grass round about. But, I suppose, that the Figure maketh the Fable; for so we see there be Bee-flowers, &c. And as for the Grass, it seemeth the Plant, having a great stalk and top, doth prey upon the Grass a good way about, by drawing the Juyce of the *Earth* from it.

610.
Experiments
Promiscuous
touching
Plants.

THe *Indian Fig* boweth his Roots down so low in one year, as of it self It taketh Root again; and so multiplieth from Root to Root, making of one Tree a kinde of Wood. The cause is, the plenty of the Sap, and the softness of the stalk, which maketh the Bough, being over-loaden, and not stiffly upheld, weigh down. It hath Leaves as broad as a little Target, but the Fruit no bigger than Beans. The cause is, for that the continual shade increaseth the Leaves, and abateth the Fruit; which nevertheless is of a pleasant taste. And that (no doubt) is caused, by the suppleness and gentleness of the Juyce of that Plant, being that which maketh the Boughs also so flexible.

611. It is reported by one of the *Ancients*, that there is a certain *Indian Tree*, having few, but very great Leaves, three cubits long, and two broad; and that the Fruit being of good taste, groweth out of the Bark. It may be, there be Plants that pour out the Sap so fast, as they have no leisure, either to divide into many Leaves, or to put forth Stalks to the Fruit. With us Trees generally have small Leaves in comparison. The *Fig* hath the greatest, and next it the *Pine*, *Mulberry*, and *Sycamore*, and the least are those of the *Willow*, *Birch*, and *Thorn*. But there be found Herbs with far greater Leaves than any Tree; as the *Bur*, *Gourd*, *Cucumber*, and *Colewort*. The cause is, (like to that of the *Indian Fig*) the hasty and plentiful putting forth of the Sap.

612. There be three things in use for sweetness, *Sugar*, *Honey*, *Manna*. For *Sugar*, to the *Ancients* it was scarce known, and little used. It is found in Canes; *Quære*, whether to the first *Knuckle*, or further up? and whether the very Bark of the Cane it self do yield Sugar, or no? For *Honey*, the *Bee* maketh it, or gathereth it; but I have heard from one, that was industrious in Husbandry, that the labor of the *Bee* is about the Wax, and that he hath known in the beginning of *May*, Honey-Combs empty of *Honey*, and within a fortnight, when the sweet Dews fall, filled like a Cellar. It is reported by some of the *Ancients*, that there is a Tree called *Occhus*, in the Valleys of *Hyrcania*, that distilleth Honey in the Mornings. It is not unlike, that the Sap and Tears of some Trees may be sweet. It may be also, that some sweet Juyces, fit for many uses, may be concocted out of Fruits, to the thickness of Honey, or perhaps of Sugar; the likeliest are Raisins of the Sun, Figs, and Corrans: The Means may be enquired.

613. The *Ancients* report of a Tree, by the *Persian Sea*, upon the Shore-sands, which

which is nourished with the Salt-water; and when the Tide ebbeth, you shall see the Roots, as it were, bare without Bark (being, as it seemeth, corroded by the Salt) and grasping the Sands like a Crab, which nevertheless beareth a Fruit. It were good to try some hard Trees, as a Service-Tree or Fir-Tree, by setting them within the Sands.

614.   There be of Plants which they use for Garments, these that follow, *Hemp, Flax, Cotton, Nettles,* (whereof they make *Nettle Cloth*) *Sericum,* which is a growing Silk; they make also *Cables* of the *Bark* of *Lime-Trees.* It is the *Stalk* that maketh the *Filaceous* matter commonly, and sometimes the *Down* that groweth above.

615.   They have in some Countreys, a Plant of a *Rosie-colour,* which shutteth in the Night, openeth in the Morning, and openeth wide at Noon; which the Inhabitants of those Countreys say, is a Plant that sleepeth. There be Sleepers enough then; for almost all Flowers do the like.

616.   Some Plants there are, but rare, that have a Mossie or Downy Root, and likewise that have a number of Threds like Beards, as *Mandrakes;* whereof *Witches* and *Impostors* make an ugly Image, giving it the form of a face at the top of the Root, and leave those strings to make a broad Beard down to the foot. Also there is a kinde of *Nard in Crete* (being a kinde of *Thu)* that hath a Root hairy, like a Rough-footed Doves foot. So as you may see, there are of Roots, *Bulbous Roots, Fibrous Roots,* and *Hirsute Roots.* And, I take it, in the *Bulbous,* the Sap hastneth most to the Air and Sun: In the *Fibrous,* the Sap delighteth more in the Earth, and therefore putteth downward: and the *Hirsute* is a middle between both, that besides the putting forth upwards and downwards, putteth forth in round.

617.   There are some *Tears* of *Trees* which are kembed from the *Beards* of *Goats;* for when the *Goats* bite and crop them, especially in the Mornings, the Dew being on, the Tear cometh forth, and hangeth upon their Beards: Of this sort is some kinde of *Ladanum.*

618.   The irrigation of the Plane-tree by Wine, is reported by the *Ancients,* to make it fruitful. It would be tryed likewise with Roots; for upon Seeds it worketh no great effect.

619.   The way to carry Foreign Roots a long way, is to vessel them close in Earthen vessels; but if the Vessels be not very great, you must make some holes in the bottom, to give some refreshment to the Roots; which otherwise (as it seemeth) will decay, and suffocate.

620.   The ancient *Cinnamon,* was, of all other Plants, while it grew, the dryest; and those things which are known to comfort other Plants, did make that more steril; for in showers it prospered worst: It grew also amongst Bushes of other kindes, where commonly Plants do not thrive, neither did it love the Sun. There might be one cause of all those effects, namely, the sparing nourishment, which that Plant required. *Quære,* how far *Cassia,* which is now the substitute of *Cinnamon,* doth participate of these things.

621.   It is reported by one of the *Ancients,* that *Cassia,* when it is gathered, is put into the Skins of Beasts newly fleyed; and that the Skins corrupting, and breeding Worms, the Worms do devour the Pith and Marrow of it, and so make it hollow, but meddle not with the Bark, because to them it is bitter.

622.   There were in ancient time, *Vines* of far greater Bodies, then we know any; for there have been Cups made of them, and an Image of *Jupiter.* But it is like they were wilde Vines; for the Vines that they use for Wine, are so

often

often cut; and so much digged and dressed, that their Sap spendeth into the Grapes, and so the Stalk cannot increase much in bulk. The Wood of Vines is very durable, without rotting. And that which is strange, though no Tree hath the Twigs, while they are green, so brittle, yet the Wood dried is extream tough, and was used by the Captains of Armies amorgst the *Romans* for their Cudgels.

623. It is reported, That in some places, Vines are suffered to grow like Herbs spreding upon the Ground, and that the Grapes of those Vines are very great. It were good to make tryal, whether Plants that use to be born up by props, will put forth greater Leaves, and greater Fruits if they be laid along the Ground ; as *Hops, Ivy, Woodbine, &c.*

624. *Quinces* or *Apples &c.* if you will keep them long, drown them in *Honey*; but because *Honey* (perhaps) will give them a taste over-lushious, it were good to make tryal in Powder of Sugar, or in Syrrup of Wine onely boiled to height. Both these would likewise be tried in Orenges, Lemmons, and Pomegranates ; for the Powder of Sugar, and Syrrup of Wine, will serve for times more than once.

625. The *Conservation of Fruit* would be also tried in Vessels, filled with fine Sand, or with Powder of Chalk , or in Meal and Flower, or in Dust of Oak-wood, or in Mill.

626. Such Fruits as you appoint for long keeping, you must gather before they be full ripe, and in a fair and dry day, towards Noon ; and when the Wind bloweth not South, and when the Moon is under the Earth, and in decrease.

627. Take Grapes, and hang them in an empty Vessel, well stopped ; and set the Vessel not in a Cellar, but in some dry place, and it is said, they will last long. But it is reported by some, they will keep better in a Vessel half full of Wine, so that the Grapes touch not the Wine.

628. It is reported, that the preserving of the Stalk, helpeth to preserve the Grape ; especially, if the Stalk be put into the Pith of Elder, the Elder not touching the Fruit.

629. It is reported by some of the *Ancients*, that Fruit put into Bottles, and the Bottles let down into Wells under water, will keep long.

630. Of Herbs and Plants, some are good to eat Raw ; as Lettuce, Endive, Purslane, Tarragon, Cresses, Cucumbers, Musk-Melons, Radish,&c. Others onely after they are boiled, or have passed the Fire ; as Parsley, Clary, Sage, Parsnips, Turnips, Asparagus, Artichoaks, (though they also being young are eaten raw.) But a number of Herbs are not esculent at all ; as Wormwood, Grass, Green-Corn, Centory, Hyssope, Lavender, Balm, &c. The causes are, for that the Herbs that are not esculent, do want the two tastes, in which nourishment resteth ; which are fat and sweet, and have (contrariwise) bitter and over-strong tastes, or a juyce so crude, as cannot be ripened to the degree of Nourishment, Herbs, and Plants, that are Esculent raw, have fatness, or sweetness (as all Esculent Fruits) such are Onions, Lettuce, &c. But then it must be such a fatness (for as for sweet things, they are in effect always esculent) as is not over-gross, as loading of the Stomack ; for Parsnips and Leeks have fatness ; but it is too gross and heavy without boiling. It must be also in a substance somewhat tender ; for we see Wheat, Barley, Artichoaks, are no good Nourishment, till they have passed the Fire ; but the Fire doth ripen, and maketh them soft and tender, and so they become esculent. As for Raddish, and Tarragon, and the like, they are for Condiments, and not for Nourishment ; and even some of those Herbs, which are

not

not efculent, are notwithstanding poculent; as *Hops, Broom, &c. Quare,* what Herbs are good for Drink, befides the two aforenamed; for that it may (perhaps) eafe the charge of Brewing, if they make Beer to require lefs Malt, or make it laft longer.

631. Parts fit for the nourifhment of *Man* in *Plants*, are *Seeds, Roots,* and *Fruits*; but chiefly *Seeds* and *Roots*. For *Leaves*, they give no nourifhment at all, or very little; no more do *Flowers*, or *Bloffoms*, or *Stalks*. The reafon is, for that *Roots*, and *Seeds*, and *Fruits*, (in as much as all *Plants* confift of an Oyly, and Watry fubftance commixed) have more of the Oyly fubftance, and *Leaves, Flowers, &c.* of the Watry. And fecondly, they are more conco&ed, for the *Root*, which continueth ever in the *Earth*, is ftill concoéted by the *Earth*; and *Fruits* and *Grains* (we fee) are half a year, or more in concoéting; whereas *Leaves* are out, and perfe& in a Moneth.

632. *Plants* (for the moft part) are more ftrong, both in tafte and fmell in the *Seed*, than in the *Leaf* and *Root*. The caufe is, for that in *Plants* that are not of a fierce and eager fpirit, the vertue is increafed by Conco&ion and Maturation, which is ever moft in the *Seed*; but in *Plants* that are of a fierce and eager fpirit, they are ftronger whileft the fpirit is inclofed in the *Root*; and the fpirits do but weaken and diffipate, when they come to the *Air* and *Sun*: as we fee in *Onions, Garlick, Dragon &c.* Nay, there be *Plants* that have their *Roots* very hot and aromatical, and their *Seeds* rather infipide as *Ginger*. The caufe is (as was touched before) for that the heat of thofe *Plants* is very diffipable; which under the *Earth* is contained and held in, but when it cometh to the Air, it exhaleth.

633. The Juyces of *Fruits*, are either Watry or Oyly. I reckon amongft the Watry, all the *Fruits*, out of which, Drink is exprelfed; as the *Grape*, the *Apple*, the *Peer*, the *Cherry*, the *Pomegranate, &c.* And there are fome others, which though they be not in ufe for Drink, yet they appear to be of the fame nature; as *Plums, Services, Mulberries, Rafps, Orenges, Lemmons, &c.* And for thofe Juyces that are fo flefhy, as they cannot make Drink by Expreffion, yet perhaps) they may make Drink by mixture of Water.

Poculaque admiftis imitantur vitea Sorbis.

And it may be *Heps* and *Brier-Berries* would do the like. Thofe that have Oyly Juyces, are *Olives, Almonds, Nuts* of all forts, *Pine-Apples, &c.* and their Juyces are all inflamable. And you muft obferve alfo, that fome of the Watry Juyces, after they have gathered fpirit, will burn and enflame, as *Wine*. There is a third kinde of *Fruit* that is fweet, without either fharpnefs or oylinefs; fuch as is the *Fig* and the *Date*.

634. It hath been noted, that moft Trees, and efpecially thofe that bear *Maft*, are fruitful but once in two years. The caufe, no doubt, is the expence of Sap; for many *Orchard Trees* well cultured, will bear divers years together.

635. There is no Tree, which befides the Natural Fruit, doth bear fo many Baftard Fruits as the *Oak* doth; for befides the *Acorn*, it beareth *Galls, Oak-Apples*, and certain *Oak-Nuts*, which are inflamable; and certain *Oak-Berries* flicking clofe to the Body of the Tree without Stalk. It beareth alfo *Miffeltoe*, though rarely. The caufe of all thefe may be, the clofenefs, and folidnefs of the Wood, and Pithe of the *Oak*; which maketh feveral Juyces finde feveral Eruptions. And therefore, if you will devife to make any *Super-Plants*, you muft ever give the Sap plentiful rifing, and hard iffue.

There

There are two Excrescences which grow upon Trees, both of them
in the nature of *Mushromes*; the one the *Romans* called *Boletus*, which groweth upon the Roots of Oaks, and was one of the dainties of their Table:
The other is *Medicinal*, that is called *Agarick* (whereof we have spoken
before) which groweth upon the tops of Oaks; though it be affirmed
by some, that it groweth also at the Roots. I do conceive, that many Excrescences of Trees grow chiefly, where the Tree is dead or faded; for
that the Natural Sap of the Tree, corrupteth into some Prenatural substance.

The greater part of Trees bear most, and best on the lower Boughs;
as *Oaks*, *Figs*, *Walnuts*, *Pears*, &c. But some bear best on the top Boughs, as
Crabs, &c. Those that bear best below, are such, as shade doth more good to
than hurt: For generally all Fruits bear best lowest, because the Sap itreth,
not having but a short way. And therefore in Fruits spred upon Walls, the
lowest are the greatest, as was formely said: So it is, the shade that hindreth
the lower Boughs, except it be in such Trees as delight in shade, or at least
bear it well. And therefore they are either strong Trees, as the Oak, or else
they have large Leaves, as the Walnut and Fig, or else they grow in *Pyramis*
as the Pear. But if they require very much Sun, they bear best on the top;
as it is Crabs, Apples, Plumbs, &c.

There be Trees that bear best when they begin to be old; as Almonds,
Pears, Vines, and all Trees that give Mast. The cause is, for that all Trees that
bear Mast have an oyly Fruit; and young Trees have a more watry Juyce, and
less concocted; and of the same kinde also is the Almond. The Pear likewise
though it be not oyly, yet it requireth much Sap, and well concocted; for
we see it is a heavy Fruit and solid, much more than Apples, Plumbs, &c. As
for the Vine, it is noted that it beareth more Grapes when it is young; but
Grapes that make better Wine when it is old, for that the Juyce is the better
concocted: And we see, that Wine is inflamable, so as it hath a kinde of oyli-
ness. But the most part of Trees, amongst which are Apples, Plumbs, &c.
bear best when they are young.

There be Plants that have a Milk in them when they are cut; as Figs,
Old Lettuce, Sow-thistles, Spurge, &c. The cause may be an Inception of
Putrefaction: For those Milks have all an Acrimony, though one would think
they should be Lenitive. For if you write upon Paper with the Milk of the
Fig, the Letters will not be seen, until you hold the Paper before the fire,
and then they wax brown; which sheweth, that it is a sharp or fretting
Juyce. Lettuce is thought poysonous, when it is so old as to have Milk:
Spurge is a kinde of poyson in it self; and as for Sow-thistles, though Coneys
eat them, yet Sheep and Cattel will not touch them; and besides, the Milk
of them, rubbed upon Warts, in short time weareth them away: Which
sheweth the Milk of them to be Corrowsive. We see also, that Wheat and
other Corn sown, if you take them forth of the Ground, before they sprout,
are full of Milk; and the beginning of Germination is ever a kinde of Putrefaction of the Seed. *Euphorbium* also hath a Milk, though not very white,
which is of a great Acrimony. And *Saladine* hath a yellow Milk, which hath
likewise much Acrimony, for it cleanseth the Eyes; it is good also for
Cataracts.

Mushromes are reported to grow, as well upon the Bodies of Trees, as
upon their Roots, or upon the Earth, and especially upon the Oak. The
cause is, for that strong Trees are towards such Excrescences in the nature
of Earth, and therefore put forth *Moss*, *Mushromes*, and the like.

636.
637.
638.
639.
640.

The

641.   There is hardly found a *Plant* that yieldeth a red Juyce in the Blade or Ear, except it be the Tree that beareth *Sanguis Draconis;* which groweth chiefly in the Island *Soquotra:* The Herb *Aramanthus* (indeed) is red all over; and *Brasil* is red in the Wood, and so is *Red Sanders.* The Tree of *Sanguis Draconis* groweth in the form of a Sugar-Loaf; it is like the Sap of that *Plant* concocteth in the Body of the Tree. For we see, that Grapes and Pomegranates are red in the Juyce, but are Green in the Tear. And this maketh the Tree of *Sanguis Draconis* lesser towards the top, because the Juyce hasteneth not up; and besides, it is very Astringent, and therefore of slow motion.

642.   It is reported, that Sweet Moss, besides that upon the Apple-trees, groweth likewise (sometimes) upon Poplars, and yet (generally) the Poplar is a smooth Tree of Bark, and hath little Moss. The Moss of the Larix-tree burneth also sweet, and sparkleth in the burning. *Quære,* of the Mosses of Odorate Trees; as *Cedar, Cypress, Lignum, Aloes, &c.*

643.   The *Death,* that is most without pain, hath been noted to be upon the taking of the Potion of *Hemlock;* which in Humanity was the form of execution of capital offenders in *Athens.* The Poyson of the *Aspe,* that *Cleopatra* used, hath some affinity with it. The cause is, for that the torments of Death are chiefly raised by the strife of the Spirits; and these Vapors quench the Spirits by degrees; like to the death of an extream old Man. I conceive it is less painful then *Opium,* because *Opium* hath parts of heat mixed.

644.   There be *Fruits* that are sweet before they ripen, as *Mirabolanes;* so *Fennel-seeds* are sweet before they ripen, and after grow spicy; and some never ripen to be sweet; as *Tamarinds, Barberries, Crabs, Sloes, &c.* The cause is, for that the former kinde have much and subtile heat, which causeth early sweetness; the latter have a cold and acide Juyce, which no heat of the Sun can sweeten. But as for the *Mirabolane,* it hath parts of contrary natures, for it is sweet and astringent.

645.   There be few Herbs that have a Salt taste; and contrariwise, all Blood of Living Creatures hath a saltness; the cause may be, for that Salt, though it be the Rudiment of Life, yet in Plants the original taste remaineth not; for you shall have them bitter, sowre, sweet, biting, but seldom salt: But in Living Creatures, all those high tastes may happen to be (sometimes) in the humors, but are seldom in the flesh, or substance; because it is of a more oyly Nature, which is not very susceptible of those tastes; and the saltness it self of Blood, is but a light and secret saltness: And even among Plants, some do participate of saltness, as *Alga Marina, Samphire, Scurvy Grass, &c.* And they report there is in some of the *Indian Seas,* a Swiming Plant, which they call *Salgazus,* spreding over the Sea, in sort, as one would think it were a Meadow. It is certain, that out of the Ashes of all Plants, they extract a Salt which they use in Medicines.

646.   It is reported by one of the *Ancients,* that there is an Herb, growing in the Water, called *Lincostis,* which is full of Prickles: This Herb putteth forth another small Herb out of the Leaf, which is imputed to some moisture, that is gathered between the Prickles, which putrified by the Sun, germinateth. But I remember also, I have seen, for a great rarity, one Rose grow out of another, like Honey-Suckles, that they call Top and Top-gallants.

647.   *Barley* (as appeareth in the *Malting*) being steeped in Water three days, and afterwards the Water drained from it, and the Barley turned upon a dry Floar, will sprout half an inch long, at least: And if it be let alone, and

not

not turned, much more, until the heart be out. What will do the same; try it also with Pease and Beans. This Experiment is not like that of the Orpin and *Semper-vive*; for there it is of the old store, for no Water is added, but here it is nourished from the Water. The Experiment would be further driven; for it appeareth already, by that which hath been said, that Earth is not necessary to the first sprouting of Plants, and we see, that Rose-Buds set in Water, will blow: Therefore try whether the Sprouts of such Grains may not be raised to a further degree, as to an Herb or Flower, with Water onely, or some small commixture of Earth: For if they will; it should seem by the Experiments before, both of the Malt, and of the Roses, that they will come far faster on in Water then in Earth; for the nourishment is easilier drawn out of Water then out of Earth. It may give some light also that Drink infused with Flesh, as that with the Capon, &c. will nourish faster and easilier, then Meat and Drink together. Try the same Experiment with Roots, as well as with Grains. As for example, take a Turnip and steep it a while, and then dry it, and see whether it will sprout.

648. *Malt* in the Drenching will swell, and that in such a manner, as after the putting forth in sprouts, and the drying upon the Kiln, there will be gained, at least, a Bushel in eight, and yet the sprouts are rubbed off, and there will be a Bushel of Dust besides the Malt; which I suppose to be, not onely by the loose and open laying of the Parts, but by some addition of substance drawn from the Water, in which it was steeped.

649. *Malt* gathereth a sweetness to the taste, which appeareth yet more in the Wort. The Dulcoration of things is worthy to be tryed to the full; for that Dulcoration importeth a degree to nourishment. And the making of things inalimental to become alimental, may be an Experiment of great profit for making new victual.

650. Most Seeds in the growing, leave their Husk or Rind about the Root; but the Onion will carry it up, that it will be like a cap upon the top of the young Onion. The cause may be, for that the Skin or Husk is not easie to break; as we see by the pilling of Onions, what a holding substance the Skin is.

651. *Plants* that have curled Leaves, do all abound with moisture, which cometh so fast on, as they cannot spred themselves plain, but must needs gather together. The weakest kinde of curling is roughness, as in Clary and Bur. The second is, curling on the sides; as in Lettuce and young Cabbage. And the third is, folding into an Head, as in Cabbage full grown, and Cabbage Lettuce.

652. It is reported, that Firr and Pine, especially if they be old and putrefied, though they shine not as some rotten Woods do, yet in the sudden breaking they will sparkle like hard Sugar.

653. The Roots of Trees do (some of them) put downwards deep into the Ground; as the *Oak, Pine, Firr, &c.* Some spred more towards the Surface of the Earth; as the *Ash, Cypress-tree, Olive, &c.* The cause of this latter may be, for that such Trees as love the Sun, do not willingly descend far into the Earth; and therefore they are (commonly) Trees that shoot up much; for in their Body their desire of approach to the Sun maketh them spred the less. And the same reason, under Ground, to avoid recess from the Sun, maketh them spred the more. And we see it cometh to pass in some Trees which have been planted too deep in the Ground, that for love of approach to the Sun, they forsake their first Root, and put out another more towards the top of the Earth. And we see also, that

the

the Olive is full of Oily Juyce, and Aſh maketh the beſt Fire, and Cypreſs is an hot Tree. As for the Oak, which is of the former ſort, it loveth the Earth, and therefore groweth ſlowly. And for the Pine, and Firr likewiſe, they have ſo much heat in themſelves, as they need leſs the heat of the Sun. There be Herbs alſo, that have the ſame difference; as the Herb they call *Morſus Diaboli*, which putteth the Root down ſo low, as you cannot pull it up without breaking; which gave occaſion to the name and fable, for that it was ſaid it was ſo wholeſome a Root, *That the Devil when it was gathered, bit it for envy.* And ſome of the *Ancients* do report, that there was a goodly Firr (which they deſired to remove whole) that had a Root under ground eight cubits deep, and ſo the Root came up broken.

654.   It hath been obſerved, that a Branch of a Tree being unbarked ſome ſpace at the bottom, and ſo ſet into the Ground, hath grown even of ſuch Trees, as if the Branch were ſet with the Bark on, they would not grow; yet contratiwiſe we ſee, that a Tree pared round in the Body above Ground will die. The cauſe may be, for that the unbarkt part draweth the nouriſhment beſt, but the Bark continueth it onely.

655.   *Grapes* will continue freſh and moiſt all Winter long, if you hang them cluſter by cluſter in the Roof of a warm Room, eſpecially, if when you gather the cluſter, you take off with the cluſter ſome of the ſtock.

656.   The Reed or Cane is a watry Plant, and groweth not but in the Water. It hath theſe properties, That it is hollow, that it is knuckled, both Stalk and Root, that being dry it is more hard and fragile then other Wood, that it putteth forth no Boughs, though many Stalks out of one Root. It differeth much in greatneſs, the ſmalleſt being fit for thatching of Houſes, and ſtopping the chinks of Ships better then Glew or Pitch. The ſecond bigneſs is uſed for Angle-rods and Staves, and in *China* for beating of offenders upon the Thighs. The differing kindes of them are, the common Reed, the *Caſſia Fiſtula*, and the *Sugar-Reed*. Of all Plants it boweth the eaſieſt, and riſeth again. It ſeemeth, that amongſt Plants which are nouriſhed with mixture of Earth and Water, it draweth moſt nouriſhment from Water; which maketh it the ſmootheſt of all others in Bark, and the holloweſt in Body.

657.   The Sap of *Trees*, when they are let Blood, is of differing Natures. Some more watry and clear, as that of Vines, of Beeches, of Pears; ſome thick, as Apples; ſome Gummy, as Cherries; ſome frothy, as Elms; ſome milky, as Figs. In Mulberries, the Sap ſeemeth to be (almoſt) towards the Bark onely; for if you cut the *Tree* a little into the Bark with a Stone, it will come forth, if you pierce it deeper with a tool, it will be dry. The *Trees* which have the moiſteſt Juyces in their Fruit, have commonly the moiſteſt Sap in their Body; for the Vines and Pears are very moiſt, Apples ſomewhat more ſpongy: the Milk of the Fig hath the quality of the Rennet, to gather Cheeſe, and ſo have certain ſour Herbs wherewith they make Cheeſe in Lent.

658.   The *Timber* and *Wood* are in ſome *Trees* more clean, in ſome more knotty; and it is a good tryal, to try it by ſpeaking at one end, and laying the Ear at the other: For if it be knotty, the voice will not paſs well. Some have the Veins more varied and Chamloted; as *Oak*, whereof Wainſcot is made; *Maple*, whereof *Trenchers* are made: Some more ſmooth, as *Firr* and *Walnut*; ſome do more eaſily breed Worms and Spiders; ſome more hardly, as it is ſaid of *Iriſh Trees*. Beſides, there be a number of

differences

differences that concern their ufe : As Oak, Cedar, and Cheffnut, are the beft builders. Some are beft for Plough-timber, as Afh; fome for Peers, that are fometimes wet and fometimes dry, as Elm; fome for Planchers, as Deal; fome for Tables, Cupboards and Desks, as Walnuts; fome for Ship-timber, as Oaks that grow in moift Grounds, for that maketh the Timber tough, and not apt to rift with Ordnance, wherein Englifh and Irifh Timber are thought to excel) fome for Mafts of Ships, as Firr and Pine, becaufe of their length, ftraightnefs, and lightnefs; fome for Pale, as Oak; fome for Fuel, as Afh: And fo of the reft.

659. The coming of Trees and Plants in certain Regions, and not in others, is fometimes cafual; for many have been tranflated, and have profpered well; as _Damask Rofes_, that have not been known in _England_ above an hundred years, and now are fo common. But the liking of Plants in certain Soyls more then in others, is meerly Natural; as the Firr and Pine love the Mountains; the Poplar, Willow, Sallow, and Alder, love Rivers and moift places; the Afh loveth Coppices, but is beft in Standards alone; Juniper loveth Chalk, and fo do moft Fruit-trees; Sampire groweth but upon Rocks; Reeds and Ofiers grow where they are wafhed with Winter; the Vine loveth fides of Hills turning upon the South-Eaft Sun, &c.

660. The putting forth of certain Herbs, difcovereth of what nature the Ground where they put forth is; as wilde Thyme fheweth good Feeding Ground for Cattel; Bettony and Strawberries fhew Grounds fit for Wood; Camomile fheweth mellow Grounds fit for Wheat; Muftard-feed growing after the Plough, fheweth a good ftrong Ground alfo for Wheat; Burnet fheweth good Meadow, and the like.

661. There are found in divers Countreys, fome other Plants that grow out of Trees and Plants; befides Miffeltoe: As in _Syria_ there is an Herb called _Caffyus_, that groweth out of tall Trees, and windeth it felf about the fame Tree where it groweth, and fometimes about Thorns. There is a kinde of Polypode that groweth out of Trees, though it windeth not. So likewife an Herb called _Faunos_ upon the Wilde Olive; and an Herb called _Hippophafton_ upon the Fullers Thorn, which, they fay, is good for the Falling-ficknefs.

662. It hath been obferved by fome of the _Ancients_, that howfoever cold and Eafterly winds are thought to be great enemies to Fruit, yet neverthelefs South-winds are alfo found to do hurt, efpecially in the Bloffoming time, and the more, if fhowers follow. It feemeth they call forth the moifture too faft. The Weft winds are the beft. It hath been obferved alfo, that green and open Winters do hurt Trees, infomuch, as if two or three fuch Winters come together, Almond-Trees, and fome other Trees will die: The caufe is the fame with the former, becaufe the Luft of the Earth overfpendeth it felf; howfoever fome other of the _Ancients_ have commended warm Winters.

663. _Snows_ lying long caufe a fruitful year. For firft, they keep in the ftrength of the Earth: Secondly, they water the Earth better then Rain; for in Snow the Earth doth (as it were) fuck the Water as out of the Teat: Thirdly, the moifture of Snow is the fineft moifture, for it is the Froth of the Cloudy Waters.

664. _Showers_, if they come a little before the ripening of Fruits, do good to all fucculent and moift Fruits, as _Vines, Olives, Pomejranates_; yet it is rather for plenty then for goodnefs, for the beft Wines are in the dryeft Vintages.

Small showers are likewise good for Corn, so as parching heats come not upon them. Generally, Night-showers are better then Day showers; for that the Sun followeth not so fast upon them : And we see, even in watering by the Hand, it is best in Summer time to water in the Evening.

665. The differences of *Earths*, and the tryals of them, are worthy to be diligently enquired. The Earth that with showers doth easily soften, is commended; and yet some Earth of that kinde will be very dry and hard before the showers. The Earth that casteth up from the Plough a great clod, is not so good as that which casteth up a smaller clod. The Earth that putteth forth Moss easily, and may be called *Mouldy*, is not good. The Earth that smelleth well upon the Digging, or Ploughing, is commended; as containing the Juyce of Vegetables almost already prepared. It is thought by some, that the ends of low Rain-bows fall more upon one kinde of Earth then upon another : As it may well be, for that Earth is most roscide; and therefore it is commended for a sign of a good Earth. The poorness of the Herbs (it is plain) sheweth the poorness of the Earth, and especially, if they be in colour more dark : But if the Herbs shew withered or blasted at the top, it sheweth the Earth to be very cold; and so doth the Mossiness of Trees. The Earth whereof the Grass is soon parched with the Sun and toasted, is commonly forced Earth, and barren in his own nature. The tender, chessom, and mellow Earth is the best; being meer Mould, between the two extreams of Clay and Sand, especially, if it be not Loamy and Binding. The Earth that after Rain will scarce be Ploughed, is commonly fruitful; for it is cleaving, and full of Juyce.

666. It is strange, which is observed by some of the *Ancients*, that Dust helpeth the fruitfulness of Trees, and of Vines by name; insomuch, as they cast Dust upon them of purpose. It should seem that that powdring, when a shower cometh, maketh a kinde of soyling to the Tree, being Earth and Water finely laid on. And they note, that Countreys where the Fields and Ways are dusty, bear the best Vines.

667. It is commended by the *Ancients* for an excellent help to Trees, to lay the Stalks and Leaves of *Lupines* about the Roots, or to Plough them into the Ground, where you will sow Corn. The burning also of the cuttings of Vines, and casting them upon Land, doth much good. And it was generally received of old, that dunging of Grounds when the West-wind bloweth, and in the decrease of the Moon, doth greatly help; the Earth (as it seemeth) being then more thirsty, and open to receive the Dung.

668. The Graffing of Vines upon Vines (as I take it) is not now in use. The *Ancients* had it, and that three ways; the first was *Insition*, which is the ordinary manner of Graffing : The second was *Terebration*, through the middle of the Stock, and putting in the Cions there : And the third was Paring of two Vines that grow together to the Marrow, and binding them close.

669. The Diseases and ill Accidents of Corn, are worthy to be enquired, and would be more worthy to be enquired, if it were in Mens power to help them; whereas many of them are not to be remedied. The Mildew is one of the greatest, which (out of question) cometh by closeness of Air; and therefore in Hills, or large Champain Grounds, it seldom cometh, such as is with us *York*'s Woald. This cannot be remedied, otherwise then that in Countreys of small enclosure the Grounds be turned into larger Fields : Which I have known to do good in some Farms.

Another

Another Difeafe is the putting forth of Wilde Oats, whereinto Corn often-times (efpecially Barley) doth degenerate. It hapneth chiefly from the weaknefs of the Grain that is fown ; for if it be either too old or mouldy, it will bring forth wilde Oats. Another difeafe is the fatiety of the Ground ; for if you fow one Ground ftill with the fame Corn (I mean not the fame Corn that grew upon the fame Ground, but the fame kinde of Grain, as Wheat, Barley, &c.) it will profper but poorly ; therefore be fides the refting of the Ground, you muft vary the Seed. Another ill Accident is from the Winds, which hurt at two times ; at the flowring by fhaking off the Flowers, and at the full ripening by fhaking out the Corn. Another ill Accident is Drought at the fpindling of the Corn, which with us is rare, but in hotter Countreys common, infomuch as the word *Calamitas* was firft derived from *Calamus*, when the Corn could not get out of the ftalk. Another ill Accident is Over-wet at fowing time, which with us breedeth much Dearth, infomuch as the Corn never cometh up ; and (many times) they are forced to re-fow Summer-Corn, where they fowed Winter-Corn. Another ill Accident is bitter Frofts, continued without Snow, efpecially in the beginning of the Winter, after the Seed is new fown. Another Difeafe is Worms, which fometimes breed in the Root, and happen upon hot Suns and fhowers immediately after the fowing ; and another Worm breedeth in the Ear it felf, efpecially when hot Suns break often out of Clouds. Another Difeafe is Weeds ; and they are fuch, as either choak and over-fhadow the Corn, and bear it down, or ftarve the Corn, and deceive it of nourifh-ment. Another Difeafe is, over-ranknefs of the Corn, which they ufe to remedy by Mowing it after it is come up, or putting Sheep into it. Another ill Accident is, laying of Corn with great Rains near or in Harveft. Another ill Accident is, if the Seed happen to have touched Oyl, or any thing that is fat ; for thofe fubftances have an antipathy with nourifhment of Water.

670. The remedies of the Difeafes of Corn have been obferved as followeth. The Steeping of the Grain before Sowing, a little time in Wine, is thought a prefervative ; the Mingling of Seed-Corn with Afhes, is thought to be good ; the Sowing at the wane of the Moon, is thought to make the Corn found. It hath not been practifed, but it is thought to be of ufe to make fome Miffel-lane in Corn ; as if you fow a few Beans with Wheat, your Wheat will be the better. It hath been obferved, that the fowing of Corn with Houfleek doth good. Though Grain that toucheth Oyl or Fat receiveth hurt, yet the fteeping of it in the Dregs of Oyl, when it beginneth to putrefie, (which they call *Amurca*) is thought to affure it againft Worms. It is reported alfo, that if Corn be moved, it will make the Grain longer, but emptier, and having more of the Husk.

671. It hath been noted, that Seed of a year old is the beft, and of two or three years is worfe ; and that which is more old is quite barren, though (no doubt) fome Seed and Grain laft better then others. The Corn which in the Vanning lieth loweft is the beft ; and the Corn which broken or bitten, retaineth a little yellownefs , is better then that which is very white.

672. It hath been obferved, that of all Roots of Herbs, the Root of Sorrel goeth the furtheft into the Earth, infomuch as it hath been known to go three cubits deep ; and that it is the Root that continueth fit (longeft) to be fet again, of any Root that groweth. It is a cold and acide Herb, that (as it feem-eth) loveth the Earth, and is not much drawn by the Sun.

673.   It hath been obſerved, that ſome Herbs like beſt being watered with Salt-water; as *Radiſh, Beet, Rue, Penny royal.* This tryal would be extended to ſome other Herbs; eſpecially ſuch as are ſtrong, as *Tarragon, Muſtard-ſeed, Rocket,* and the like.

674.   It is ſtrange, that it is generally received, how ſome poyſonous Beaſts affect odorate and wholſome Herbs; as, that the *Snake* loveth Fennel, that the *Toad* will be much under Sage, that *Frogs* will be in Cinquefoil. It may be it is rather the Shade, or other Coverture, that they take liking in, then the virtue of the Herb.

675.   It were a matter of great profit, (ſave that I doubt it is too conjectural to venture upon) if one could diſcern what Corn, Herbs, or Fruits, are like to be in Plenty or Scarcity, by ſome Signs and Prognoſticks in the beginning of the year: For as for thoſe that are like to be in *Plenty,* they may be bargained for upon the Ground; as the old relation was of *Thales,* who to ſhew how eaſie it was for a Philoſopher to be rich, when he foreſaw a great plenty of Olives, made a Monopoly of them. And for *Scarcity,* Men may make profit in keeping better the old ſtore. Long continuance of Snow is believed to make a fruitful year of Corn; an early Winter, or a very late Winter, a barren year of Corn; an open and ſerene Winter, an ill year of Fruit. Theſe we have partly touched before; but other Prognoſticks of like nature are diligently to be enquired.

676.   There ſeem to be in ſome Plants ſingularities, wherein they differ from all other. The Olive hath the oyly part onely on the outſide, whereas all other Fruits have it in the Nut or Kernel. The Firr hath (in effect) no Stone, Nut, nor Kernel; except you will count the little Grains, Kernels. The Pomegranate and Pine-Apple have onely, amongſt Fruits, Grains, diſtinct in ſeveral Cells. No Herbs have curled Leaves, but Cabbage and Cabbage-Lettuce. None have double Leaves, one belonging to the Stalk, another to the Fruit or Seed, but the Artichoak. No Flower hath that kinde of ſpred that the Wood-bine hath. This may be a large Field of Contemplation; for it ſheweth, that in the Frame of Nature there is, in the producing of ſome Species, a compoſition of Matter, which hapneth oft, and may be much diverſified; in others, ſuch as hapneth rarely, and admitteth little variety. For ſo it is likewiſe in Beaſts; Dogs have a reſemblance with Wolves and Foxes, Horſes with Aſſes, Kine with Buſles, Hares with Coneys, &c. And ſo in Birds; Kites and Keſtrels have a reſemblance with Hawks; Common Doves with Ring-Doves and Turtles; Black-Birds with Thruſhes and Maviſſes; Crows with Ravens, Daws, and Choughs, &c. But Elephants and Swine amongſt Beaſts, and the Bird of Paradiſe, and the Peacock amongſt Birds, and ſome few others, have ſcarce any other Species that have affinity with them.

We leave the Deſcription of *Plants* and their Virtues to *Herbals,* and other like Books of *Natural Hiſtory,* wherein Mens diligence hath been great, even to Curioſity. For our *Experiments* are onely ſuch, as do ever aſcend a degree to the deriving of Cauſes, and extracting of Axioms, which we are not ignorant, but that ſome, both of the *Ancient* and *Modern Writers* have alſo labored; but their Cauſes and Axioms are ſo full of Imagination, and ſo infected with the old received *Theories,* as they are meer Inquinations of Experience, and concoct it not.

It

IT hath been obferved by fome of the *Ancients*, that Skins, efpecially of *Rams* newly pulled off, aed applied to the Wounds of Stripes, do keep them from fwelling and exulcerating, and likewife heal them, ard clofe them up; and that the Whites of Eggs do the fame. The caufe is, a temperate Conglutination; for both Bodies are clammy and vifcous, and do bridle the Deflux of Humors to the hurts, without penning them in too much.

YOu may turn (almoft) all Flefh into a fatty fubftance, if you take Flefh and cut it into pieces, and put the pieces into a Glafs covered with Parchment, and fo let the Glafs ftand fix or feven hours in boyling Water. It may be an experiment of profit, for making of Fat or Greafe for many ufes: But then it muft be of fuch Flefh as is not edible; as *Horfes, Dogs, Bears, Foxes, Badgers, &c.*

IT is reported by one of the *Ancients*, that new Wine put into Veffels well ftopped, and the Veffels let down into the Sea, will accelerate very much the making of them ripe and potable; the fame would be tryed in Wort.

BEafts are more Hairy then Men; and Savage Men more then Civil; and the Plumage of Birds exceedeth the Pilofity of Beafts. The caufe of the fmoothnefs in Men, is not any abundance of Heat and Moifture, though that indeed caufeth Pilofity; but there is requifite to Pilofity, not fo much Heat and Moifture, as Excrementitious Heat and Moifture; (for whatfoever affimilateth goeth not into the Hair) and Excrementitious Moifture aboundeth moft in Beafts, and Men that are more favage. Much the fame Reafon is there of the Plumage of Birds; for Birds affimilate lefs, and excern more then Beafts, for their Excrements are ever aliquid, and their Flefh (generally) more dry; befide, they have not Inftruments for Urine, and fo all the Excrementitious Moifture goeth into the Feathers: And therefore it is no marvel though Birds be commonly better Meat then Beafts, becaufe their flefh doth affimilate more finely, and fe-cerneth more fubtilly. Again, the Head of Man hath Hair upon the firft Birth, which no other part of the Body hath. The caufe may be want of Perfpiration; for much of the matter of Hair, in the other parts of the Body goeth forth by infenfible Perfpiration. And befides, the Skull being of a more folid fubftance, nourifheth and affimilateth lefs, and excerneth more; and fo likewife doth the Chin. We fee alfo that Hair cometh not upon the Palms of the Hands, nor Soals of the Feet, which are parts more perfpirable. And Children likewife are not Hairy, for that their Skins are more perfpirable.

BIrds are of fwifter motion then Beafts; for the flight of many Birds is fwifter then the race of any Beafts. The caufe is, for that the Spirits in Birds are in greater proportion, in comparifon of the bulk of their Body, then in Beafts. For as for the reafon that fome give, that they are partly carried, whereas Beafts go, that is nothing; for by that reafon, fwimming fhould be fwifter then running: And that kinde of carriage alfo, is not without labor of the Wing.

The

677.
Experiment
Solitary,
touching
Healing of
Wounds.

678.
Experiment
Solitary,
touching
Fat diffufed in
Flefh.

679.
Experiment
Solitary,
touching
Ripening of
Drink before
the time.

680.
Experiment
Solitary,
touching
Pilofity and
Plumage.

681.
Experiment
Solitary,
touching the
Quicknefs of
Motion in
Birds.

681.
Experiment
Solitary,
touching the
*Different
clearnefs of the
Sea.*

THe *Sea* is clearer when the North-wind bloweth, then when the South-wind. The caufe is, for that *Salt-water* hath a little Oylinefs in the Surface thereof, as appeareth in very hot days : And again, for that the Southern-wind relaxeth the Water fomewhat ; as no Water boyling, is fo clear as cold Water.

683.
Experiment
Solitary,
touching the
*Different
Heats of Fire
and Boiling
Water.*

FIre burneth *Wood,* making it firft Luminous, then black and brittle, and laftly, broken and incinerate ; fcalding Water doth none of thefe. The caufe is, for that by Fire the Spirit of the Body is firft refined, and then emitted ; whereof the refining or attenuation caufeth the light, and the emiffion ; firft the fragility, and after the diffolution into Afhes, neither doth any other Body enter. But in Water, the Spirit of the Body is not refined fo much ; and befides, part of the Water entreth, which doth increafe the Spirit, and in a degree extinguifh it ; therefore we fee that hot Water will quench Fire. And again, we fee that in Bodies wherein the Water doth not much enter, but onely the heat paffeth, hot Water worketh the effects of Fire : As in Eggs boiled and roafted, (into which the Water entreth not at all) there is fcarce difference to be difcerned ; but in Fruit and Flefh, whereinto the Water entreth in fome part, there is much more difference.

684.
Experiment
Solitary,
touching the
*Qualification
of Heat by
Moifture.*

THe bottom of a Veffel of boyling Water (as hath been obferved) is not very much heated, fo as men may put their hand under the Veffel, and remove it. The canfe is, for that the moifture of Water, as it quencheth Coals where it entreth, fo it doth allay heat where it toucheth. And therefore note well, that moifture, although it doth not pafs through Bodies without Communication of fome fubftance (as heat and cold do) yet it worketh manifeft effects ; not by entrance of the Body, but by qualifying of the heat and cold, as we fee in this inftance. And we fee likewife, that the water of things diftilled in water, (which they call the *Bath*) differeth not much from the water of things diftilled by Fire. We fee alfo, that Pewter-Difhes with Water in them will not melt eafily, but without it they will. Nay, we fee more, that Butter or Oyl, which in themfelves are inflamable, yet by the virtue of their moifture will do the like.

685.
Experiment
Solitary,
touching
Yawning.

IT hath been noted by the *Ancients,* that it is dangerous to pick ones Ear whileft he Yawneth. The caufe is, for that in Yawning, the inner Parchment of the Ear is extended by the drawing in of the Spirit and Breath ; for in Yawning and Sighing both, the Spirit is firft ftrongly drawn in, and then ftrongly expelled.

686.
Experiment
Solitary,
touching the
Hiccough.

IT hath been obferved by the *Ancients,* that Sneezing doth ceafe the Hiccough. The caufe is, for that the Motion of the Hiccough is a lifting up of the Stomach ; which Sneezing doth fomewhat deprefs, and divert the motion another way. For firft, we fee that the Hiccough cometh of fulnefs of Meat, (efpecially in Children) which caufeth an extenfion of the Stomach : We fee alfo, it is caufed by acide Meats or Drinks, which is by the pricking of the Stomach. And this motion is ceafed, either by Diverfion, or by Detention of the Spirits : Diverfion, as in Sneezing ; Detention, as we fee holding of the Breath doth help fomewhat to ceafe the Hiccough, and putting a Man into an earneft ftudy doth the like, as is commonly ufed : And Vinegar put to the Noftrils or Gargarized doth it alfo ; for that it is Aftringent, and inhibiteth the motion of the Spirit.

Looking

LOoking againſt the Sun doth induce Sneezing. The cauſe is, not the heating of the Noſtrils; for then the holding up of the Noſtrils againſt the Sun, though one wink, would do it, but the drawing down of the moiſture of the Brain: For it will make the Eyes run with water, and the drawing of moiſture to the Eyes, doth draw it to the Noſtrils by Motion of Conſent, and ſo followeth Sneezing. As contrariwiſe, the Tickling of the Noſtrils within doth draw the moiſture to the Noſtrils, and to the Eyes by conſent, for they alſo will water. But yet it hath been obſerved, that if one be about to ſneeze, the rubbing of the Eyes till they run with water, will prevent it. Whereof the cauſe is, for that the humor which was deſcending to the Noſtrils, is diverted to the Eyes.

THe Teeth are more by cold drink, or the like, affected, then the other parts. The cauſe is double; the one, for that the reſiſtance of Bone to cold, is greater then of Fleſh; for that the Fleſh ſhrinketh, but the Bone reſiſteth, whereby the Cold becometh more eager. The other is, for that the Teeth are parts without Blood, whereas Blood helpeth to qualiſe the cold. And therefore we ſee, that the Sinews are much affected with Cold, for that they are parts without Blood. So the Bones in ſharp Colds wax brittle; and therefore it hath been ſeen, that all contuſions of Bones in hard weather, are more difficult to cure.

IT hath been noted, that the Tongue receiveth more eaſily tokens of Diſeaſes then the other parts; as of heats within, which appear moſt in the blackneſs of the Tongue. Again, Pied Cattel are ſpotted in their Tongues, &c. The cauſe is (no doubt) the tenderneſs of the part, which thereby receiveth more eaſily all alterations then any other parts of the Fleſh.

WHen the Mouth is out of taſte, it maketh things taſte ſometimes ſalt, chiefly bitter, and ſometimes loathſome, but never ſweet. The cauſe is, the corrupting of the moiſture about the Tongue, which many times turneth bitter, and ſalt, and loathſome, but ſweet never; for the reſt are degrees of corruption.

IT was obſerved in the *Great Plague* of the laſt year, that there were ſeen in divers Ditches, and low Grounds about *London*, many Toads that had Tails two or three inches long at the leaſt, whereas Toads (uſually) have no Tails at all; which argueth a great diſpoſition to putrefaction in the Soil and Air. It is reported likewiſe, that Roots (ſuch as *Carrots* and *Parſnips*) are more ſweet and luſcious in infectious years then in other years.

WIſe *Phyſicians* ſhould with all diligence inquire what Simples Nature yieldeth, that have extream ſubtile parts without any Mordication or Acrimony; for they undermine that which is hard, they open that which is ſtopped and ſhut, and they expel that which is offenſive gently, without too much perturbation. Of this kinde are *Elder-flowers*, which therefore are proper for the Stone; of this kinde is the *Dwarf-pine*, which is proper for the Jaundies; of this kinde is *Harts-horn*, which is proper for Agues and Infections; of this kinde is *Piony*, which is proper for Stoppings in the Head; of this kinde is *Fumitory* which is proper for the Spleen;
and

and a number of others. Generally, divers Creatures bred of Putrefaction, though they be somewhat loathsome to take, are of this kinde ; as *Earth-worms, Timber-sows, Snails, &c.* And I conceive, that the *Trochises* of *Vipers* (which are so much magnified) and the flesh of Snakes some ways condited and corrected (which of late are grown into some credit) are of the same nature. So the parts of Beasts putrefied (as *Castoreum* and *Musk*, which have extream subtil parts) are to be placed amongst them. We see also, that putrefaction of Plants (as *Agarick* and *Jews-Ear*) are of greatest vertue. The cause is, for that putrefaction is the subtilest of all motions in the parts of Bodies. And since we cannot take down the lives of Living Creatures (which some of the *Paracelsians* say, if they could be taken down, would make us Immortal,) the next is, for subtilty of operation to take Bodies putrefied, such as may be safely taken.

693.
Experiments
in Consort,
touching
Venus.

IT hath been observed by the *Ancients*, that much use of *Venus* doth dim the sight, and yet *Eunuchs*, which are unable to generate, are (neverthelefs) also dim-sighted. The cause of dimness of sight in the former, is the expence of Spirits ; in the latter, the over-moisture of the Brain ; for the over-moisture of the Brain doth thicken the Spirits visual, and obstructeth their passages, as we see by the decay in the sight in Age, where also the diminution of the Spirits concurreth as another cause. We see also, that blindness cometh by Rheums and Cataracts Now in *Eunuchs* there are all the notes of moisture ; as the swelling of their Thighs, the loosness of their Belly, the smoothness of their skin, &c.

694.

The pleasure in the Act of *Venus*, is the greatest of the pleasures of the Senses ; the matching of it with Itch is improper, though that also be pleasing to the touch, but the causes are profound. First, all the Organs of the Senses qualifie the motions of the Spirits, and make so many several species of motions, and pleasures or displeasures thereupon, as there be diversities of Organs. The Instruments of *Sight, Hearing, Taste,* and *Smell,* are of several frame, and so are the parts for Generation ; therefore *Scaliger* doth well to make the pleasure of Generation a *sixth Sense.* And if there were any other differing Organs, and qualified Perforations for the Spirits to pass, there would be more then the *Five Senses* : Neither do we well know, whether some Beasts and Birds have not *Senses* that we know not, and the very Sent of Dogs is almost a sense by it self. Secondly, the Pleasures of the Touch are greater and deeper then those of the other *Senses,* as we see in *Warming* upon *Cold,* or *Refrigeration* upon *Heat* : For as the Pains of the Touch are greater then the offences of other Senses, so likewise are the Pleasures. It is true, that the affecting of the Spirits immediately, and (as it were) without an Organ, is of the greatest pleasure ; which is but in two things, *Sweet smells* and *Wine,* and the like *Sweet vapors.* For Smells, we see their great and sudden effect in fetching Men again when they swown ; for Drink, it is certain, that the pleasure of Drunkenness is next the pleasure of *Venus* ; and great Joyes (likewise) make the Spirits move and touch themselves ; and the pleasure of *Venus* is somewhat of the same kinde.

695.

It hath been always observed, that Men are more inclined to *Venus* in the Winter, and Women in the Summer. The cause is, for that the Spirits in a Body more hot and dry, (as the Spirits of Men are) by the Summer are more exhaled and dissipated, and in the Winter more condensed and kept entire ; but in Bodies that are cold and moist, (as Womens are) the Summer
doth

doth cherish the Spirits, and calleth them forth, the Winter doth dull them. Furthermore, the Abstinence or Intermission of the use of *Venus*, in moist and well habituate Bodies, breedeth a number of Diseases; and especially dangerous imposthumations. The reason is evident, for that it is a principal evacuation, especially of the Spirits; for of the Spirits, there is scarce any evacuation, but in *Venus* and exercise. And therefore the omission of either of them breedeth all diseases of Repletion.

Experiments in Consort, touching the Insecta.

THe nature of Vivification is very worthy the enquiry; and as the Nature of things is commonly better perceived in small then in great, and in unperfect then in perfect, and in parts then in whole; so the Nature of Vivification is best enquired in Creatures bred of Putrefaction. The contemplation whereof hath many excellent Fruits. First, in disclosing the original of Vivification. Secondly, in disclosing the original of Figuration. Thirdly, in disclosing many things in the nature of perfect Creatures, which in them lie more hidden. And fourthly, in traducing by way of operation, some observations in the *Insecta*, to work effects upon perfect Creatures. Note, that the word *Insecta* agreeth not with the matter, but we ever use it for brevities sake, intending by it Creatures bred of Putrefaction.

The *Insecta* are found to breed out of several matters: Some breed of Mud or Dung; as the *Earth-worms, Eels, Snakes, &c.* For they are both Putrefactions: For Water in Mud do putrefie, as not able to preserve it self; and for Dung, all Excrements are the refuse and putrefactions of nourishment. Some breed in Wood, both growing and cut down. *Quare*, in what Woods most, and at what seasons. We see that the Worms with many feet, which round themselves into Balls; are bred chiefly under Logs of *Timber*, but not in the *Timber*, and they are said to be found also (many times) in Gardens where no Logs are. But it seemeth their Generation requireth a coverture both from Sun, and Rain or Dew, as the *Timber* is; and therefore they are not venemous, but (contrariwise) are held by the Physitians to clarifie the Blood. It is observed, that *Cimices* are found in the holes of Bed-sides. Some breed in the Hair of Living Creatures; as *Lice* and *Tikes*, which are bred by the sweat close kept, and somewhat airified by the Hair. The Excrements of Living Creatures do not onely breed *Insecta* when they are excerned, but also while they are in the Body; as in Worms, whereto Children are most subject, and are chiefly in the Guts. And it hath been lately observed by Physitians, that in many *Pestilent Diseases* there are Worms found in the upper parts of the Body, where Excrements are not, but onely humors putrefied. *Fleas* breed principally of Straw or Mats, where there hath been a little moisture, or the Chamber and Bed-straw kept close, and not aired. It is received, that they are killed by strewing Wormwood in the Rooms. And it is truly observed, that bitter things are apt rather to kill then engender Putrefaction, and they be things that are fat or sweet that are aptest to putrefie. There is a Worm that breedeth in Meal of the shape of a large white Maggot, which is given as a great dainty to Nightingales. The Moth breedeth upon Cloth, and other Lanifices, especially if they be laid up dankish and wet. It delighteth to be about the flame of a Candle. There is a Worm called a *Wevil*, bred under Ground, and that feedeth upon Roots, as Parsnips, Carrots, &c. Some breed in Waters, especially shaded, but they must be by standing Waters; as the Water-Spider that hath six Legs. The Fly called the *Gad flie* breedeth of somewhat that swimeth upon the top of the Water, and

696.

is

is most about Ponds. There is a Worm that breedeth of the Dregs of Wine decayed, which afterwards (as is observed by some of the *Ancients*) turneth into a *Gnat*. It hath been observed by the *Ancients*, that there is a Worm that breedeth in old Snow, and is of colour reddish, and dull of motion, and dieth soon after it cometh out of Snow; which should shew that Snow hath in it a secret warmth, for else it could hardly vivifie. And the reason of the dying of the Worm may be the sudden exhaling of that little Spirit, as soon as it cometh out of the cold, which had shut it in. For as Butter-flies quicken with heat, which were benummed with cold; so Spirits may exhale with heat, which were preserved in cold. It is affirmed, both by the *Ancient* and *Modern* observation, that in Furnaces of Copper and Brass, where Chalcites is (which is Vitriol) often cast in to mend the working, there riseth suddenly a Fly which sometimes moveth, as if it took hold on the Walls of the Furnace; sometimes is seen moving in the fire below, and dieth presently as soon as it is out of the Furnace. Which is a noble instance, and worthy to be weighed; for it sheweth that as well violent heat of fire, as the gentle heat of Living Creatures will vivifie, if it have matter proportionable. Now the great axiom of Vivification is, that there must be heat to dilate the Spirit of the Body, an Active Spirit to be dilated, matter viscous or tenacious to hold in the Spirit, and that matter to be put forth and figured. Now a Spirit dilated by so ardent a fire as that of the Furnace, as soon as ever it cooleth never so little, congealeth presently. And (no doubt) this action is furthered by the Chalcites, which hath a Spirit that will put forth and germinate, as we see in Chymical Tryals. Briefly, most things putrefied bring forth *Insecta* of several names, but we will not take upon us now to enumerate them all.

697. The *Insecta* have been noted by the Ancients to feed little: But this hath not been diligently observed; for Grashoppers eat up the Green of whole Countreys, and Silk-worms devour Leaves swiftly, and Ants make great provision. It is true, that Creatures that sleep and rest much, eat little, as Dormice and Bats, &c. they are all without Blood; which may be, for that the Juyce of their Bodies is almost all one; not Blood, and Flesh, and Skin, and Bone, as in perfect Creatures: The integral parts have extream variety, but the similar parts little. It is true, that they have (some of them) Diaphragms, and an Intestine; and they have all Skins, which in most of the *Insecta*, are cast often. They are not (generally) of long life; yet Bees have been known to live seven years; and Snakes are thought, the rather for the casting of their spoil, to live till they be old; and Eels, which many times breed of putrefaction, will live and grow very long; and those that enterchange from Worms to Flies in the Summer, and from Flies to Worms in the Winter, have been kept in Boxes four years at the least; yet there are certain Flies that are called *Ephemera* that live but a day. The cause is, the exility of the Spirit, or perhaps the absence of the Sun; for that if they were brought in, or kept close, they might live longer. Many of the *Insecta* (as Butter-flies and other Flies) revive easily, when they seem dead, being brought to the Sun or Fire. The cause whereof is, the diffusion of the Vital Spirit, and the easie dilating of it by a little heat. They stir a good while after their heads are off, or that they be cut in pieces; which is caused also, for that their Vital Spirits are more diffused throughout all their parts, and less confined to Organs then in perfect Creatures.

698. The *Insecta* have voluntary Motion, and therefore imagination. And whereas some of the *Ancients* have said, that their Motion is indeterminate, and their imagination indefinite, it is negligently observed; for Ants go right forwards.

forwards to their Hills: and *Bees* do (admirably) know the way from a *Floury* Heath, two or three miles off to their Hives. It may be *Gnats* and *Flies* have their Imagination more mutable and giddy, as small *Birds* likewife have. It is faid by fome of the Ancients, that they have onely the *Senfe of Feeling,* which is manifeftly untrue; for if they go forth right to a place, they muft needs have *Sight:* Befides, they delight more in one Flower or Herb, then in another, and therefore have tafte. And *Bees* are called with found upon Brafs, and therefore they have hearing. Which fheweth likewife, that though their Spirits be diffufed, yet there is a Seat of their Senfes in their Head.

Other obfervations concerning the Infecta, *together with the Enumeration of them, we refer to that place where we mean to handle the Title of* Animals *in general.*

A Man leapeth better with weights in his hands, then without. The caufe is, for that the weight (if it be proportionable) ftrengthneth the Sinews, by contracting them; for otherwife, where no contraction is needful, weight hindreth. As we fee in *Horfe Races,* Men are curions to forefee that there be not the leaft weight upon the one Horfe more then upon the other. In Leaping with Weights, the Arms are firft caft backwards, and then forwards, with fo much the greater force; for the hands go backward before they take their raife, *Quere,* if the contrary motion of the Spirits, immediately before the Motion we intend, doth not caufe the Spirits as it were to break forth with more force; as Breath alfo drawn, and kept in, cometh forth more forcibly: And in cafting of any thing, the Arms, to make a greater fwing, are firft caft backward.

699.
Experiment Solitary, touching Leaping.

OF *Mufical Tones* and unequal *Sounds,* we have fpoken before, but touch the pleafure and difpleafure of the Senfes not fo fully. Harfh *Sounds,* as of a *Saw* when it is fharpned, Grinding of one Stone againft another, fqueaking or fcrieching noifes, make a fhivering or horror in the Body, and fet the Teeth on edge. The caufe is, for that the objects of the Ear do affect the Spirits (immediately) moft with pleafure and offence. We fee there is no colour that affecteth the Eye much with difpleafure. There be fights that are horrible, becaufe they excite the memory of things that are odious or fearful; but the fame things painted, do little affect. As for *Smells, Taftes,* and *Touches,* they be things that do affect by a Participation or Impulfion of the body of the Object. So it is *Sound* alone that doth immediately and incorporeally affect moft. This is moft manifeft in *Mufick,* and *Concords,* and *Difcords* in *Mufick:* For all *Sounds,* whether they be fharp or flat, if they be fweet, have a roundnefs and equality; and if they be harfh, are unequal: For a *Difcord* it felf, is but a harfhnefs of divers founds meeting. It is true, that inequality, not ftaid upon, but pafling, is rather an increafe of fweetnefs; as in the Purling of a Wreathed String, and in the raucity of a *Trumpet,* and in the *Nightingale-Pipe* of a *Regal,* and in a *Difcord* ftraight falling upon a *Concord:* But if you ftay upon it, it is offenfive. And therefore there be thefe three degrees of pleafing and difpleafing in Sounds; *Sweet founds, Difcords,* and *Harfh founds,* which we call by divers names, as *Scrieching,* or *Grating,* fuch as we now fpeak of. As for the fetting of the Teeth on edge, we plainly fee what an intercourfe there is between the Teeth, and the Organ of the Hearing, by the taking of the end of a Bow between the Teeth, and ftriking upon the String.

700.
Experiment Solitary, touching the *Pleafures and Difpleafures of the Senfes, efpecially of Hearing.*

NATURAL HISTORY.

Century *VIII*.

Here be *Minerals* and *Fossiles* in great variety, but of *Veins* of *Earth Medicinal* but few. The chief are, *Terra Lemnia*, *Terra Sigillata communis*, and *Bolus Arminus*; whereof *Terra Lemnia* is the chief. The Vertues of them are for Curing of *Wounds*, Stanching of *Blood*, Stopping of *Fluxes* and *Rheums*, and Arresting the Spreding of *Poyson*, *Infection*, and *Putrefaction*: And they have of all other *Simples* the perfectest and purest quality of *Drying*, with little or no mixture of any other quality. Yet it is true, that the *Bole Arminick* is the most cold of them, and that *Terra Lemnia* is the most hot; for which cause the Island *Lemnos* where it is digged, was in the old *Fabulous Ages* consecrated to *Vulcan*.

ABout the Bottom of the *Sereights* are gathered great quantities of *Spunges*, which are gathered from the sides of *Rocks*, being as it were a large, but tough *Moss*. It is the more to be noted, because that there be but few Substances, Plant-like, that grow deep within the Sea for they are gathered sometime Fifteen fathom deep: And when they are laid on Shore, they seem to be of great Bulk; but crushed together, will be transported in a very small room.

IT seemeth that *Fish* that are used to the Salt-water, do nevertheless delight more in fresh. We see that *Salmons* and *Smelts* love to get into Rivers, though it be against the Stream. At the Haven of *Constantinople* you shall have great quantities of *Fish* that come from the *Euxine Sea*, that when they come into the Fresh-water, do inebriate and turn up their Bellies, so as you may take them with your hand. I doubt there hath not been sufficient Ex-

periment

periment made of putting *Sea fish* into Fresh-water, Po
a thing of great use and pleasure ; for so you may ha
good distance from the Sea : And besides, it may be
pleasanter, and may fall to breed. And it is said, th
which are put into Pits, where the Sea goeth and cor
there is a Fresh-water coming also to them when the
by that means fatter, and more grown.

704.
Experiment
Solitary,
touching
*Attraction by
Similitude of
Substance.*

THe *Turkish Bow* giveth a very forcible Shoot, inf
known, that the *Arrow* hath pierced a Steel Tar;
of two Inches thick : But that which is more stran;
headed with Wood, hath been known to pierce throug
eight Inches thick. And it is certain, that we had in u
fight, short *Arrows*, which they called *Sprights*, with
save Wood sharpned ; which were discharged out of
pierce through the sides of Ships, where a Bullet we
this dependeth upon one of the greatest secrets in all N
Similitude of *Substance* will cause Attraction, where the
from the Motion of Gravity : For if that were taken aw
Lead, and *Gold* would draw *Gold,* and *Iron* would drav
of the *Load-stone.* But this same Motion of Weight
a meer Motion of Matter, and hath no affinity with
doth kill the other Motion, except it self be killed by :
in these instances of Arrows, for then the Motion of
tude of Substance beginneth to shew it self. But we f
of *Nature* fully in due place.

705.
Experiment
Solitary,
touching
*Certain drinks
in Turkey.*

THey have in *Turky,* and the *East,* certain *Confect
Servers,* which are like to *Candid Conserves,* and a
Lemmons, or *Sugar* and *Citrons,* or *Sugar* and *Violets,* and
and some mixture of *Amber* for the more delicate perf
dissolve in Water, and thereof make their Drink, beca
Wine by their Law. But I do much marvel, that no I n
or *German,* doth set up Brewing in *Constantinople,* consid
quantity of Barley. For as for the general sort of Mer
cause of Drinking Water ; for that it is no small savir
ones drink : But the better sort might well be at the col
the less at it, because I see *France, Italy,* or *Spain,* have no
or Ale ; which (perhaps) if they did, would better b
their Complexions. It is likely it would be matter of
should begin it in *Turkey.*

706.
Experiments
in Consort,
touching
Sweat.

IN *Bathing* in hot water, sweat (nevertheless) comet!
der the Water. The cause is, first, for that sweat is
tion. And that kinde of Colliquation is not made c
Heat, or an over-moist Heat. For over-moisture doth!
the Heat ; as we see, that even hot water quencheth Fire
shutteth the Pores. And therefore Men will sooner!
the Sun or Fire, then if they stood naked : And E
with hot water, do provoke in Bed a Sweat more dain
hot. Secondly, Hot water doth cause Evaporation f
it spendeth the matter in those parts under the Water,

Sweat. Again, Sweat cometh more plentifully, if the Heat be increased by degrees, then if it be greatest at first. or equal. The cause is, for that the Pores are better opened by a gentle Heat, then by a more violent; and by their opening the Sweat, issueth more abundantly. And therefore *Physicians* may do well, when they provoke Sweat in Bed by Bottles, with a Decoction of *Sudorifick Herbs* in *Hot Water*, to make two degrees of Heat in the Bottles, and to lay in the Bed the less-heated first, and after half an hour the more-heated.

707. *Sweat* is salt in taste. The cause is, for that that part of the Nourishment which is fresh and sweet, turneth into Blood and Flesh; and the Sweat is onely that part which is separate and excerned. Blood also raw, hath some saltness more then Flesh; because the Assimilation into Flesh, is not without a little and subtile excretion from the Blood.

708. *Sweat* cometh forth more out of the upper parts of the Body then the lower. The reason is, because those parts are more replenished with Spirits, and the Spirits are they that put forth Sweat; besides, they are less fleshy, and Sweat issueth (chiefly) out of the parts that are less fleshy and more dry, as the Forehead and Brest.

709. Men sweat more in sleep then waking, and yet sleep doth rather stay other Fluxions, then cause them; as *Rheums, Loosness* of the *Body, &c.* The cause is, for that in *Sleep* the Heat and Spirits do naturally move inwards, and there rest. But when they are collected once within, the Heat becometh more violent and irritate, and thereby expelleth *Sweat.*

710. *Cold Sweats* are (many times) Mortal and near *Death*, and always ill and suspected; as in great *Fears, Hypochondriacal Passions. &c.* The cause is, for that *Cold Sweats* come by a relaxation or forsaking of the *Spirits*, whereby the Moisture of the Body, which Heat did keep firm in the parts, severeth and issueth out.

711. In those *Diseases* which cannot be discharged by *Sweat, Sweat* is ill, and rather to be stayed; as in *Diseases* of the *Lungs*, and *Fluxes* of the *Belly*; but in those *Diseases* which are expelled by *Sweat*, it easeth and lightneth; as in *Agues, Pestilences, &c.* The cause is, for that *Sweat* in the latter sort is partly Critical, and sendeth forth the *Matter* that offendeth: But in the former, it either proceedeth from the Labor of the *Spirits*, which sheweth them oppressed; or from Motion of *Consent*, when *Nature* not able to expel the *Disease* where it is seated, moveth to an Expulsion indifferent over all the *Body.*

712. Experiment Solitary, touching the Gloworm.

THe Nature of the *Gloworm* is hitherto not well observed. Thus much we see, that they breed chiefly in the hottest Moneths of *Summer*; and that they breed not in *Champaign*, but in *Bushes* and *Hedges.* Whereby it may be conceived, that the *Spirit* of them is very fine, and not to be refined but by *Summer heats.* And again, that by reason of the fineness, it doth easily exhale. In *Italy*, and the Hotter Countreys, there is a Flie they call *Lucciole*, that shineth as the *Gloworm* doth, and it may be is the *Flying-Gloworm*: but that Flie is chiefly upon *Fens* and *Marishes.* But yet the two former observations hold, for they are not seen but in the heat of *Summer*; and *Sedge*, or other Green of the *Fens* give as good shade as Bushes. It may be the *Gloworms* of the Cold Countreys ripen not so far as to be winged.

713. Experiments in Consort, touching the Impressions which the Passions of the Mind make upon the Body.

THe Passions of the *Mind* work upon the Body the impressions following. *Fear*, causeth *Paleness, Trembling*, the *Standing* of the *Hair* upright,

right, Starting, and Serieching. The Paleness is caused, for that the Blood runneth inward to succor the Heart. The Trembling is caused, for that through the flight of the Spirits inward, the outward parts are destituted, and not sustained. Standing upright of the Hair is caused, for that by shutting of the Pores of the Skin, the Hair that lyeth asloap must needs rise. Starting is both an apprehension of the thing feared, (and in that kinde it is a motion of shrinking ;) and likewise an Inquisition in the beginning what the matter should be, (and in that kinde it is a motion of Erection ;) and therefore when a Man would listen suddenly to any thing, he starteth ; for the Starting is an Erection of the Spirits to attend. Serieching is an appetite of expelling that which suddenly striketh the Spirits. For it must be noted, that many Motions, though they be unprofitable to expel that which hurteth, yet they are Offers of Nature, and cause Motions by Consent ; as in Groaning, or Crying upon Pain.

714. Grief and Pain, cause Sighing, Sobbing, Groaning, Screaming, and Roaring, Tears, Distorting of the Face, Grinding of the Teeth, Sweating. Sighing is caused by the drawing in of a greater quantity of Breath to refresh the Heart that laboreth ; like a great draught when one is thirsty. Sobbing is the same thing stronger. Groaning, and Screaming, and Roaring, are caused by an appetite of Expulsion, as hath been said ; for when the Spirits cannot expel the thing that hurteth in their strife to do it, by Motion of Consent they expel the Voice. And this is when the Spirits yield, and give over to resist ; for if one do constantly resist Pain, he will not groan. Tears are caused by a Contraction of the Spirits of the Brain ; which Contraction by consequence astringeth the Moisture of the Brain, and thereby sendeth Tears into the Eyes. And this Contraction or Compression causeth also Wringing of the Hands ; for Wringing is a Gesture of Expression of Moisture. The Distorting of the Face is caused by a Contention, first, to bear and resist, and then to expel ; which maketh the Parts knit first, and afterwards open. Grinding of the Teeth is caused (likewise) by a Gathering and Serring of the Spirits together to resist ; which maketh the Teeth also to set hard one against another. Sweating is also a Compound Motion by the Labor of the Spirits, first to resist, and then to expel.

715. Joy causeth a Chearfulness and Vigor in the Eyes, Singing, Leaping, Dancing, and sometimes Tears. All these are the effects of the Dilatation and coming forth of the Spirits into the outward parts, which maketh them more lively and stirring. We know it hath been seen, that Excessive sudden Joy hath caused present Death, while the Spirits did spred so much as they could not retire again. As for Tears, they are the effects of Compression of the Moisture of the Brain, upon Dilatation of the Spirits. For Compression of the Spirits worketh an Expression of the Moisture of the Brain by consent, as hath been said in Grief : But then in Joy it worketh it diversly, *viz.* By Propulsion of the Moisture, when the Spirits dilate, and occupy more room.

716. Anger causeth Paleness in some, and the going and coming of the colour in others ; also Trembling in some, Swelling, Foaming at the Mouth, Stamping, Bending of the Fist. Paleness, and Going, and Coming of the Colour, are caused by the Burning of the Spirits about the Heart ; which to refresh themselves, call in more Spirits from the outward parts. And if the Paleness be alone, without sending forth the colour again, it is commonly joyned with some fear : But in many there is no Paleness at all, but contrariwise Redness about the Cheeks and Gils ; which is by the sending forth of the
Spirits,

Spirits, in an appetite to Revenge. Trembling in Anger is likewise by a calling in of the Spirits, and is commonly when Anger is joyned with Fear. Swelling is caused both by a Dilatation of the Spirits by over-heating, and by a Liquefaction or Boiling of the Humors thereupon. Foaming at the Mouth is from the same cause, being an Ebullition. Stamping and Bending of the Fist are caused by an Imagination of the Act of Revenge.

Light Displeasure or Dislike causeth shaking of the Head, Frowning, and Knitting of the Brows. These effects arise from the same cause that Trembling and Horror do; namely, from the Retiring of the Spirits, but in a less degree. For the Shaking of the Head, is but a slow and definite Trembling; and is a Gesture of slight refusal: And we see also, that a dislike causeth often that Gesture of the Hand, which we use when we refuse a thing, or warn it away. The Frowning and Knitting of the Brows, is a Gathering or Serring of the Spirits, to resist in some measure. And we see also, this Knitting of the Brows will follow upon earnest Studying, or Cogitation of any thing, though it be without dislike.   717.

Shame causeth Blushing, and casting down of the Eyes. Blushing is the Resort of Blood to the Face, which in the Passion of Shame, is the part that laboreth most. And although the Blushing will be seen in the whole Brest, if it be naked, yet that is but in passage to the Face. As for the casting down of the Eyes, it proceedeth of the Reverence a Man beareth to other Men, whereby, when he is ashamed, he cannot endure to look firmly upon others: And we see, that Blushing and the Casting down of the Eyes both, are more when we come before many; *Ore Pompeii quid mollius? Nunquam non coram pluribus erubuit;* and likewise, when we come before *Great* or *Reverend Persons.*   718.

Pity causeth sometimes Tears, and a Flexion or Cast of the Eye aside. Tears come from the cause, that they do in Grief: For Pity is but Grief in anothers behalf. The Cast of the Eye, is a Gesture of Aversion or Lothness to behold the object of Pity.   719.

Wonder causeth Astonishment, or an Immovable Posture of the Body, Casting up of the Eyes to Heaven, and Lifting up of the Hands. For Astonishment, it is caused by the Fixing of the Minde upon one object of Cogitation, whereby it doth not spatiate and transcur as it useth: For in Wonder the Spirits flie not, as in Fear; but onely settle, and are made less apt to move. As for the Casting up of the Eyes, and Lifting up of the Hands, it is a kinde of Appeal to the Deity, which is the Author, by Power and Providence of strange Wonders.   720.

Laughing causeth a Dilatation of the Mouth and Lips; a continued Expulsion of the Breath, with the loud Noise, which maketh the Interjection of Laughing; Shaking of the Brest and Sides; Running of the Eyes with Water, if it be violent and continued. Wherein first it is to be understood, that Laughing is scarce (properly) a Passion, but hath his Source from the Intellect; for in Laughing, there ever precedeth a conceit of somewhat ridiculous. And therefore it is proper to Man. Secondly, that the cause of Laughing, is but a light touch of the Spirits, and not so deep an Impression as in other Passions. And therefore (that which hath no Affinity with the Passions of the Minde) it is moved, and that in great vehemency, onely by Tickling some parts of the Body. And we see, that Men even in a grieved state of Minde, yet cannot sometimes forbear Laughing. Thirdly, it is ever joyned with some degree of Delight: And therefore Exhilaration hath some Affinity with Joy, though it be much Lighter Motion. *Res severa est verum Gaudium.*   721.

Fourthly,

Fourthly, That the object of it is *Deformity, Absurdity, Shrewd turns*, and the like. Now to speak of the causes of the effects before-mentioned, whereunto these general Notes give some light. For the Dilatation of the *Mouth* and *Lips*, continued Expulsion of the *Breath* and *Voice*, and Shaking of the *Brests* and *Sides*, they proceed (all) from the Dilatation of the *Spirits*, especially being sudden. So likewise the *Running* of the *Eyes* with Water, (as hath been formerly touched, where we spake of the *Tears* of *Joy* and *Grief*) is an effect of Dilatation of the *Spirits*. And for *Suddenneß*, it is a great part of the *Matter:* For we see that any *Shrewd turn* that lighteth upon another, or any *Deformity, &c.* moveth *Laughter* in the instant, which after a little time it doth not. So we cannot *Laugh* at any thing after it is stale, but whilest it is new. And even in *Tickling*, if you tickle the sides, and give warning, or give a hard or continued touch, it doth not move *Laughter* so much.

722.   *Lust* causeth a *Flagrancy* in the *Eys*, and *Priapism*. The cause of both these is, for that in *Lust* the *Sight* and the *Touch*, are the things desired; and therefore the *Spirits* resort to those parts which are most affected. And note well in general, (for that great use may be made of the observation) that (evermore) the *Spirits* in all *Passions* resort most to the parts that labor most, or are most affected. As in the last, which hath been mentioned, they resort to the *Eyes* and *Venereous parts*; in *Fear* and *Anger* to the *Heart*; in *Shame* to the *Face*; and in *Light dislikes* to the *Head*.

723.
Experiments in Consort, touching Drunkenneß. IT hath been observed by the *Ancients*, and is yet believed, That the *Sperm* of *Drunken-men* is unfruitful. The cause is, for that it is over-moistned, and wanteth Spissitude. And we have a merry saying, *That they that go drunk to Bed, get Daughters.*

724.   *Drunken-men* are taken with a plain Defect or Destitution in *Voluntary Motion*; they reel, they tremble, they cannot stand, nor speak strongly. The cause is, for that the Spirits of the Wine oppress the Spirits Animal, and occupate part of the place where they are, and so make them weak to move; and therefore *Drunken-men* are apt to fall asleep. And *Opiates* and *Stupefactives* (as *Poppy, Henbane, Hemlock, &c.*) induce a kinde of *Drunkenneß* by the grosness of their *Vapor*, as Wine doth by the quantity of the *Vapor*. Besides, they rob the Spirits Animal of their *Matter* whereby they are nourished; for the Spirits of the Wine, prey upon it as well as they, and so they make the Spirits less supple and apt to move.

725.   *Drunken-men* imagine every thing turneth round; they imagine also, that things come upon them; they see not well things afar off; those things that they see near hand, they see out of their place; and (sometimes) they see things double. The cause of the imagination that things turn round is, for that the Spirits themselves turn, being compressed by the Vapor of the Wine; (for any Liquid Body upon Compression turneth, as we see in Water:) And it is all one to the sight, whether the *Visual Spirits* move, or the Object moveth, or the *Medium* moveth; and we see, that long turning round breedeth the same imagination. The cause of the imagination that things come upon them is, for that the *Spirits Visual* themselves draw back, which maketh the Object seem to come on; and besides, when they see things turn round and move, Fear maketh them think they come upon them. The cause that they cannot see things afar off, is the weakness of the Spirits; for in every *Megrim* or *Vertigo*, there is an Obtenebration joyned with a semblance of Turning round, which we see also in the lighter sort of *Swoonings.*
The

The caufe of feeing things out of their place, is the refraction of the Spirits vifual; for the vapor is as an unequal *Medium*, and it is as the fight of things out of place in Water. The caufe of feeing things double, is the fwift and unquiet motion of the Spirits (being opprefled) to and fro; for (as was faid before) the motion of the Spirits vifual, and the motion of the object make the fame appearances; and for the fwift motion of the object, we fee that if you fillip a *Lute* ftring, it fheweth double or trebble.

726.

Men are fooner Drunk with fmall draughts then with great: And again, Wine fugared, inebriateth lefs then Wine pure: The caufe of the former is, for that the Wine defcendeth not fo faft to the Bottom of the Stomack, but maketh longer ftay in the upper part of the Stomack; and fendeth Vapors fafter to the Head, and therefore inebriateth fooner. And for the fame reafon, Sops in Wine (quantity for quantity) inebriate more then Wine of it felf: The caufe of the latter is, for that the Sugar doth infpiffate the Spirits of the Wine, and maketh them not fo eafie to refolve into Vapor. Nay further, it is thought to be fome remedy againft inebriating, if Wine fugared be taken after Wine pure. And the fame effect is wrought, either by Oyl or Milk taken upon much Drinking.

727.
Experiment Solitary, touching the *Help or hurt of Wine, though Made rarely ufed.*

THe ufe of Wine in dry and confumed Bodies is hurtful; in moift and full Bodies it is good. The caufe is, for that the Spirits of the Wine do prey upon the Dew or radical moifture (as they term it) of the Body, and fo deceive the Animal Spirits: But where there is moifture enough, or fuperfluous, there Wine helpeth to digeft and deficcate the moifture.

728.
Experiment Solitary, touching Catterpillers.

THe *Caterpiller* is one of the moft general of Worms, and breedeth of Dew and Leaves; for we fee infinite number of *Catterpillers* which breed upon Trees and Hedges, by which the Leaves of the Trees or Hedges are in great part confumed; as well by their breeding out of the Leaf, as by their feeding upon the Leaf. They breed in the Spring chiefly, becaufe then there is both Dew and Leaf. And they breed commonly when the Eaft Winds have much blown: The caufe whereof is, the drynefs of that Wind; for to all Vivification upon Putrefaction, it is requifite the matter be not too moift: And therefore we fee they have *Cobwebs* about them, which is a fign of a flimy drynefs; as we fee upon the Ground, whereupon by Dew and Sun *Cobwebs* breed all over. We fee alfo the Green *Catterpiller* breedeth in the inward parts of *Rofes*, efpecially not blown where the Dew fticketh: But efpecially *Catterpillers*, both the greateft and the moft, breed upon *Cabbages*, which have a fat Leaf, and apt to putrifie. The *Catterpiller* toward the end of Summer waxeth volatile, and turneth to a *Butterflie*, or perhaps fome other Flie. There is a *Catterpiller* that hath a Fur or Down upon him, and feemeth to have affinity with the *Silk-worm*.

729.
Experiment Solitary, touching the *Flies Cantharides.*

THe *Flies Cantharides*, are bred of a *Worm* or *Catterpiller*, but peculiar to certain Fruit-trees; as are the Fig-tree, the Pine-tree, and the Wilde Bryar; all which bear fweet Fruit, and Fruit that hath a kinde of fecret biting or fharpnefs. For the Fig hath a Milk in it that is fweet and corrofive; the Pine-Apple hath a Kernel that is ftrong and abfterfive; the Fruit of the Bryar is faid to make Children, or thofe that eat them, fcabbed. And therefore no marvel though Cantharides have fuch a Corrofive and Cauterizing quality; for there is not one other of the *Infects*, but is bred of a duller matter. The Body of the Cantharides is bright coloured; and it may be, be, that the delicate coloured Dragon Flies may have likewise some Corrosive quality.

730.
Experiments
in Consort,
touching
Lassitude.

Lassitude is remedied by Bathing or Anointing with Oyl and warm Water. The cause is, for that all *Lassitude* is a kinde of Contusion and Compression of the Parts; and Bathing and Anointing give a Relaxion or Emollition: And the mixture of Oyl and Water is better then either of them alone, because Water entreth better into the Pores, and Oyl after entry softneth better. It is found also, that the taking of *Tobacco* doth help and discharge *Lassitude*. The reason whereof is partly, because by chearing or comforting of the Spirits, it openeth the Parts compressed or contused: And chiefly, because it refresheth the Spirits by the Opiate Vertue thereof, and so dischargeth Weariness, as Sleep likewise doth.

731.

In going up a Hill the *Knees* will be most weary; in going down a Hill, the *Thighs*. The cause is, for that in the Lift of the Feet, when a man goeth up the Hill, the weight of the Body beareth most upon the *Knees*; and in going down the Hill, upon the Thighs.

732.
Experiment
Solitary,
touching the
Casting of the
Skin and Shell
in some Creatures.

The casting of the *Skin*, is by the Ancients compared to the breaking of the *Secundine* or *Call*, but not rightly; for that were to make every casting of the Skin a new Birth: And besides, the *Secundine* is but a general Cover, not shaped according to the Parts; but the Skin is shaped according to the Parts. The Creatures that cast their Skin are, the *Snake*, the *Viper*, the *Grashopper*, the *Lizard*, the *Silk-worm*, &c. Those that cast their Shell are, the *Lobster*, the *Crab*, the *Cra-fish*, the *Hodmandod* or *Dodman*, the *Tortoise*, &c. The old Skins are found, but the old Shells never: So as it is like they scale off, and crumble away by degrees. And they are known by the extream tenderness and softness of the new Shell; and somewhat by the freshness of the colour of it. The cause of the casting and Skin and Shell should seem to be the great quantity of matter in those Creatures, that is fit to make Skin or Shell: And again, the loosness of the Skin or Shell, that sticketh not close to the Flesh. For it is certain, that it is the new Skin or Shell that putteth off the old. So we see that in *Deer*, it is the young Horn that putteth off the old. And in Birds, the young Feathers put off the old; and so Birds that have much matter for their Beak, cast their Beaks, the new Beak putting off the old.

733.
Experiments
in Consort,
touching the
Postures of the
Body.

Lying not Erect but Hollow, which is in the making of the Bed, or with the *Legs* gathered up, which is in the posture of the Body, is the more wholesome. The reason is, the better comforting of the Stomack, which is by that less pensile; and we see, that in weak Stomacks, the laying up of the Legs high, and the Knees almost to the Mouth, helpeth and comforteth. We see also, that *Gally-slaves*, notwithstanding their misery otherwise, are commonly fat and fleshy; and the reason is, because the Stomack is supported somewhat in sitting, and is pensile in standing or going. And therefore for Prolongation of Life, it is good to chuse those Exercises where the Limbs move more then the Stomack and Belly; as in Rowing and in Sawing, being set.

734.

Megrims and *Giddiness* are rather when we *Rise*, after long sitting, then while we sit. The cause is, for that the Vapors which were gathered by sitting, by the sudden Motion flie more up into the Head.

735.

Leaning upon any Part maketh it Num, and, as we call it, *Asleep*.

The

The caufe is, for that the Compreffion of the Parts fuffereth not the Spirits to have free accefs ; and therefore, when we come out of it, we feel a ftinging or pricking, which is the re-entrance of the Spirits.

IT hath been noted, That thofe Years are peftilential and unwholfome, when there are great numbers of Frogs, Flies, Locufts, &c. The caufe is plain ; for that thofe Creatures being ingendred of Putrefaction, when they abound, fhew a general difpofition of the Year, and conftitution of the Air to Difeafes of Putrefaction. And the fame Prognoftick (as hath been faid before) holdeth, if you finde Worms in Oak-Apples. For the Conftitution of the Air appeareth more fubtilly in any of thefe things, then to the fenfe of Man.

736.
Experiment
Solitary,
touching
Peftilential
Years.

IT is an obfervation amongft Country people, that Years of ftore of *Haws* and *Heps,* do commonly portend cold Winters ; and they afcribe it to *Gods* Providence, that (as the *Scripture* faith) reacheth even to the falling of a Sparrow; and much more is like to reach to the Prefervation of Birds in fuch Seafons. The Natural caufe alfo may be the want of Heat, and abundance of Moifture in the Summer precedent, which putteth forth thofe Fruits, and muft needs leave great quantity of cold Vapors not diffipate, which caufeth the cold of the Winter following.

737.
Experiment
Solitary,
touching the
Prognofticks of
Hard Winters.

THey have in *Turkey* a Drink called *Coffee,* made of a Berry of the fame name, as black as Soot, and of a ftrong fent, but not aromatical, which they take, beaten into powder, in Water as hot as they can drink it: And they take it, and fit at it in their *Coffee-Houfes,* which are like our Taverns. This Drink comforteth the Brain and Heart, and helpeth Digeftion. Certainly this Berry *Coffee,* the Root and Leaf *Betel,* the Leaf *Tobacco,* and the Teare of *Poppy,* (*Opium*) of which, the *Turks* are great takers (fuppofing it expelleth all fear ; do all condence the Spirits, and make them ftrong and aleger. But it feemeth they are taken after feveral manners ; for *Coffee* and *Opium* are taken down, *Tobacco* but in Smoak, and *Betel* is but champed in the Mouth with a little Lime. It is like, there are more of them, if they were well found out, and well corrected. *Quare,* of *Henbane-feed,* of *Mandrake,* of *Saffron,* Root and Flower, of *Folium Indum,* of *Ambergreece,* of the *Affyrian Amomum,* if it may be had ; and of the *Scarlet Powder* which they call *Kermez ;* and (generally) of all fuch things as do inebriate and provoke fleep. Note, that *Tobacco* is not taken in Root or Seed, which are more forcible ever then Leaves.

738.
Experiment
Solitary,
touching
Medicines that
Condence and
Relieve the
Spirits.

THe *Turks* have a black Powder made of a Mineral called *Alcohole,* which with a fine long Pencil they lay under their Eye-lids, which doth colour them black, whereby the White of the Eye is fet off more white. With the fame Powder they colour alfo the Hairs of their Eye-lids, and of their Eye-brows, which they draw into embowed Arches. You fhall finde that *Xenophon* maketh mention, that the *Medes* ufed to paint their Eyes. The *Turks* ufe with the fame Tincture to colour the Hair of their Heads and Beards black: And divers with us that are grown Gray, and yet would appear young, finde means to make their Hair black, by combing it (as they fay) with a Leaden Comb, or the like. As for the *Chinefes,* who are of an ill Complexion, (being *Olivafter*) they paint their Cheeks Scarlet, efpecially their *King* and *Grandees.* Generally, *Barbarous People* that go naked, do not onely paint

739.
Experiment
Solitary,
touching
Paintings of
the Body.

them-

themselves, but they pounce and rase their skin, that the Painting may not be taken forth, and make it into Works : So do the *West-Indians* ; and so did the ancient *Picts* and *Britons.* So that it seemeth Men would have the colours of *Birds Feathers,* if they could tell how, or at least they will have gay Skins in stead of gay Cloaths.

740.
Experiment Solitary, touching the Use of Bathing and Anointing.

IT is strange that the use of *Bathing* as a part of *Diet* is left. With the *Romans* and the *Grecians* it was as usual as Eating or Sleeping ; and so is it amongst the *Turks* at this day ; whereas, with us it remaineth but as a part of Physick. I am of opinion, that the use of it as it was with the *Romans,* was hurtful to health ; for that it made the Body soft and easie to waste. For the *Turks* it is more proper, because their drinking Water, and feeding upon Rice, and other Food of small nourishment, maketh their Bodies so solid and hard, as you need not fear that *Bathing* should make them frothy. Besides, the *Turks* are great sitters, and seldom walk ; whereby they sweat less, and need *Bathing* more. But yet certain it is, that *Bathing,* and especially *Anointing,* may be so used, as it may be a great help to Health, and Prolongation of Life. But hereof we shall speak in due place, when we come to handle *Experiments Medicinal.*

741.
Experiment Solitary, touching Chamoletting of Paper.

THe *Turks* have a pretty Art of *Chamoletting* of *Paper,* which is not with us in use. They take divers Oyled Colours, and put them severally (in drops) upon Water, and stir the Water lightly, and then wet their Paper (being of some thickness) with it ; and the Paper will be waved and veined like *Chamolet* or *Marble.*

742.
Experiment Solitary, touching Cuttle-Ink.

IT is somewhat strange, that the Blood of all Birds, and Beasts, and Fishes, should be of a Red colour, and onely the Blood of the Cuttle should be as black as Ink. A man would think that the cause should be the high Concoction of that Blood ; for we see in ordinary Puddings, that the Boyling turneth the Blood to be black ; and the Cuttle is accounted a delicate Meat, and is much in request.

743.
Experiment Solitary, touching Encrease of Weight in Earth.

IT is reported of credit, That if you take *Earth* from Land adjoyning to the River of *Nile,* and preserve it in that manner, that it neither come to be wet nor wasted, and weigh it daily, it will not alter weight until the Seventeenth of *June,* which is the day when the River beginneth to rise, and then it will grow more and more ponderous till the River cometh to his height. Which if it be true, it cannot be caused but by the Air, which then beginneth to condense ; and so turneth within that small Mould into a degree of Moisture, which produceth weight. So it hath been observed, that *Tobacco* cut and weighed, and then dryed by the Fire, loseth weight ; and after being laid in the open Air, recovereth weight again. And it should seem, that as soon as ever the River beginneth to increase, the whole Body of the Air thereabouts suffereth a change : For (that which is more strange) it is credibly affirmed, that upon that very day, when the River first riseth, great Plagues in *Cairo* use suddenly to break up.

744.
Experiments in Consort, touching Sleep.

THose that are very cold, and especially in their *Feet,* cannot get to *Sleep.* The cause may be, for that in Sleep is required a free respiration, which cold doth shut in and hinder : For we see, that in great Colds, one can scarce

draw

draw his Breath. Another caufe may be, for that Cold calleth the Spirits to fuccor; and therefore they cannot fo well clofe, and go together in the Head, which is ever requifite to Sleep   And for the fame caufe, Pain and noife hinder fleep, and darknefs (contrariwife) furthereth fleep.

Some noifes (whereof we fpake in the 112 *Experiment*) help Sleep; as the blowing of the Wind, the trickling of Water, humming of Bees, foft finging, reading, &c. The caufe is, for that they move in the Spirits a gentle attention; and whatfoever moveth attention, without too much labor, ftilleth the natural and difcurfive motions of the Spirits.   745.

Sleep nourifheth, or at leaft preferveth, Bodies a long time, without other nourifhment.   Beafts that fleep in Winter, (as it is noted of wilde Bears) during their fleep wax very fat, though they eat nothing.   Bats have been found in Ovens, and other hollow clofe places, matted one upon another; and therefore it is likely that they fleep in the VVinter time, and eat nothing.   *Quære* whether Bees do not fleep all VVinter, and fpare their Honey.   Butter-flies, and other Flies, do not onely fleep, but lie as dead all VVinter; and yet with a little heat of Sun or Fire revive again. A Dormoufe, both VVinter and Summer will fleep fome days together, and eat nothing.   746.

TO reftore Teeth in Age, were *Magnale Naturæ*, it may be thought of; but howfoever, the nature of the Teeth deferveth to be enquired of, as well as the other parts of Living Creatures Bodies.   Experiments in Confort, touching Teeth and hard Subftances in the Bodies of Living Creatures.

There be five parts in the *Bodies* of *Living Creatures* that are of hard fubftances; the *Skull*, the *Teeth*, the *Bones*, the *Horns*, and the *Nails*. The greateft quantity of hard fubftance continued, is towards the Head; for there is the Skull of one entire Bone, there are the Teeth, there are Maxillary Bones, there is the hard Bone that is the Inftrument of Hearing, and thence iffue the Horns. So that the building of Living Creatures Bodies is like the building of a Timber-houfe, where the VValls and other parts have Columns and Beams; but the Roof is in the better fort of Houfes, all Tile, or Lead, or Stone. As for *Birds*, they have three other hard fubftances proper to them; the *Bill*, which is of the like matter with the Teeth, for no Birds have Teeth; the Shell of the Egg, and their Quills; for as for their Spur, it is but a Nail. But no *Living Creatures* that have Shells very hard (as *Oyfters*, *Cockles*, *Mufcles*, *Shalops*, *Crabs*, *Lobfters*, *Craw-fifh*, *Shrimps*, and efpecially the *Tortoife*) have *Bones* within them, but onely little *Grifles*.   747.

Bones, after full growth, continue at a ftay, and fo doth the *Skull*. Horns, in fome Creatures, are caft and renewed: Teeth ftand at a ftay, except their wearing. As for *Nails*, they grow continually, and *Bills* and *Beaks* will overgrow, and fometimes be caft, as in *Eagles* and *Parrots*.   748.

Moft of the hard fubftances flie to the extreams of the Body; as Skull, Horns, Teeth, Nails, and Beaks; onely the Bones are more inward, and clad with Flefh. As for the Entrails; they are all without Bones, fave that a Bone is fometimes found in the *Heart* of a *Stag*, and it may be in fome other Creatures.   749.

The *Skull* hath *Brains*, as a kinde of *Marrow* within it. The *Back-bone* hath one kinde of *Marrow*, which hath an affinity with the Brain; and other Bones of the Body have another. The *Jaw-bones* have no *Marrow* fevered, but a little *Pulp* of *Marrow* diffufed. Teeth likewife are thought to have a kinde of *Marrow* diffufed, which caufeth the Senfe and Pain: But it   750 is rather Sinew ; for Marrow hath no Sense, no more then Blood. Horn is alike throughout, and so is the Nail.

751.   None other of the hard substances have Sense, but the Teeth ; and the Teeth have Sense, not onely of Pain, but of Cold.

But we will leave the *Enquiries* of other *Hard Substances* unto their several places, and now enquire onely of the *Teeth.*

752.   The *Teeth* are in Men of three kindes, *Sharp*, as the *Fore-teeth* ; *Broad*, as the *Back-teeth*, which we call the *Molar-teeth*, or *Grinders* ; and *Pointed-teeth*, or *Canine*, which are between both. But there have been some Men that have had their *Teeth* undivided, as of one whole *Bone*, with some little mark in the place of the Division, as *Pyrrhus* had. Some Creatures have over-long or out-growing *Teeth*, which we call *Fangs* or *Tusks* ; as *Boars*, *Pikes*, *Salmons*, and *Dogs*, though less. Some *Living Creatures* have *Teeth* against *Teeth*, as *Men* and *Horses* : and some have *Teeth*, especially their *Master-teeth* indented one within another like *Saws*, as *Lions* ; and so again have *Dogs*. Some *Fishes* have divers Rows of *Teeth* in the *Roofs* of their *Mouths* ; as *Pikes*, *Salmons*, *Trouts*, &c. and many more in Salt-waters. *Snakes* and other *Serpents* have venemous *Teeth*, which are sometimes mistaken for their *Sting.*

753.   No Beast that hath *Horns* hath upper-teeth ; and no Beast that hath Teeth above, wanteth them below. But yet if they be of the same kinde, it followeth not, that if the hard matter goeth not into upper-teeth, it will go into *Horns* ; nor yet *è converso*, for *Does* that have no *Horns*, have no upper-teeth.

754.   *Horses* have, at three years old, a Tooth put forth which they call the *Colts-tooth* ; and at four years old, there cometh the *Mark-tooth*, which hath a hole so big as you may lay a Pease within it ; and that weareth shorter and shorter every year, till that at eight years old the Tooth is smooth , and the hole gone ; and then they say, That *the Mark is out of the Horses Mouth.*

755.   The Teeth of Men breed first ; when the Childe is about a year and half old, and then they cast them, and new come about seven years old. But divers have Backward-teeth come forth at twenty, yea, some at thirty, and forty. *Quære* of the manner of the coming of them forth. They tell a tale of the old Countess of *Desmond*, who lived till she was Sevenscore years old, that she did Dentire twice or thrice, casting her old Teeth, and others coming in their place.

756.   Teeth are much hurt by Sweet-meats, and by Painting with *Mercury*, and by things over-hot, and by things over-cold, and by Rheums. And the pain of the Teeth, is one of the sharpest of pains.

757.   Concerning Teeth, these things are to be considered. 1. The preserving of them. 2. The keeping of them white. 3. The drawing of them with least pain. 4. The staying and easing of the Tooth-ach. 5. The binding in of Artificial Teeth, where Teeth have been strucken out. 6. And last of all, that great one, of restoring Teeth in Age. The instances that give any likelihood of restoring Teeth in Age, are, The late coming of Teeth in some, and the renewing of the Beaks in Birds, which are commaterial with Teeth. *Quære* therefore more particularly how that cometh. And again, the renewing of Horns. But yet that hath not been known to have been provoked by Art ; therefore let tryal be made, whether Horns may be procured to grow in Beasts that are not horned, and how ; and whether they may be procured to come larger then usual, as to make an Ox or a Deer

have

have a greater Head of Horns; and whether the Head of a Deer, that by age is more fpitted, may be brought again to be more branched. For thefe tryals and the like will fhew, Whether by art fuch hard matter can be called and provoked. It may be tryed alfo, whether Birds may not have fomething done to them when they are young, whereby they may be made to have greater or longer Bills, or greater and longer Talons : And whether Children may not have fome Wafh, or fomething to make their Teeth better and ftronger. *Coral* is in ufe as an help to the Teeth of Children.

SOme Living Creatures generate but at certain feafons of the year; as *Deer, Sheep, Wilde Coneys, &c.* and moft forts of *Birds* and *Fifhes :* Others at any time of the year, as *Men* ; and all Domeftick Creatures , as *Horfes, Hogs, Dogs, Cats, &c.* The caufe of Generation at all feafons, feemeth to be Fulnefs; for Generation is from Redundance. This Fulnefs arifeth from two caufes, Either from the Nature of the Creature, if it be Hot, and Moift, and Sanguine, or from Plenty of Food. For the firft, *Men, Horfes, Dogs, &c.* which breed at all feafons, are full of Heat and Moifture; *Doves* are the fulleft of Heat and Moifture amongft *Birds,* and therefore breed often, the *Tame Dove* almoft continually. But *Deer* are a Melancholick dry Creature, as appeareth by their fcarfulnefs, and the hardnefs of their Flefh. *Sheep* are a cold Creature, as appeareth by their mildnefs, and for that they feldom drink. Moft forts of *Birds* are of a dry fubftance in comparifon of *Beafts ; Fifhes* are cold. For the fecond caufe, Fulnefs of Food, *Men, Kine, Swine, Dogs, &c.* feed full. And we fee, that thofe Creatures which, being Wilde, generate feldom, being tame, generate often; which is from warmth and fulnefs of food. We finde that the time of going to *Rut* of *Deer* is in *September,* for that they need the whole Summers Feed and Grafs to make them fit for Generation ; and if Rain come early about the middle of *September,* they go to Rut fomewhat the fooner; if Drought, fomewhat the later. So Sheep, in refpect of their fmall heat, generate about the fame time, or fomewhat before. But for the moft part, Creatures that generate at certain feafons generate in the Spring; as Birds and Fifhes : For that the end of the Winter, and the heat and comfort of the Spring prepareth them. There is alfo another reafon why fome Creatures generate at certain feafons, and that is the Relation of their time of Bearing to the time of Generation ; for no Creature goeth to generate whileft the Female is full, nor whileft fhe is bufie in fitting, or rearing her young; and therefore it is found by experience, that if you take the Eggs or Young-ones out of the Nefts of Birds, they will fall to generate again three or four times one after another.

Of Living Creatures, fome are longer time in the Womb, and fome fhorter. Women go commonly nine Moneths, the Cow and the Ewe about fix Moneths, Does go about nine Moneths, Mares eleven Moneths, Bitches nine Weeks ; Elephants are faid to go two years, for the received Tradition of ten years is fabulous. For Birds there is double enquiry; the diftance between the treading or coupling, and the laying of the Egg ; and again, between the Egg laid, and the difclofing or hatching. And amongft Birds there is lefs diverfity of time then amongft other Creatures, yet fome there is; for the Hen fitteth but three weeks, the Turky-hen, Goofe and Duck, a moneth. *Quare* of others. The caufe of the great difference of times amongft Living Creatures is, either from the nature of the Kind,

758.
Experiments in Confort, touching the *Generation and Bearing of Living Creatures in the Womb.*

759.

or from the conſtitution of the Womb. For the former, thoſe that are longer in coming to their maturity or growth, are longer in the Womb, as is chiefly ſeen in Men; and ſo Elephants, which are long in the Womb, are long time in coming to their full growth. But in moſt other Kinds, the conſtitution of the Womb (that is, the hardneſs or dryneſs thereof) is concurrent with the former cauſe. For the Colt hath about four years of growth, and ſo the Fawn, and ſo the Calf; but Whelps, which come to their growth (commonly) within three quarters of a year, are but nine weeks in the Womb. As for Birds, as there is leſs diverſity amongſt them in the time of their bringing forth, ſo there is leſs diverſity in the time of their growth, moſt of them coming to their growth within a twelve-moneth.

760. Some Creatures bring forth many young ones at a Burthen; as Bitches, Hares, Coneys, &c. ſome (ordinarily) but one; as Women, Lioneſſes, &c. This may be cauſed, either by the quantity of Sperm required to the producing one of that Kind; which if leſs be required, may admit greater number; if more, fewer: Or by the Partitions and Cells of the Womb, which may ſever the Sperm.

761.
*Experiments
in Conſort,
touching
Species viſible.*

THere is no doubt but Light by Refraction will ſhew greater, as well as things coloured; for like as a ſhilling in the bottom of the Water will ſhew greater, ſo will a Candle in a Lanthorn in the bottom of the Water. I have heard of a practice, that Gloworms in Glaſſes were put in the Water to make the Fiſh come. But I am not yet informed, whether when a *Diver* diveth, having his eyes open, and ſwimmeth upon his back, whether (I ſay) he ſeeth things in the Air, greater or leſs. For it is manifeſt, that when the eye ſtandeth in the finer *medium,* and the object is in the groſſer, things ſhew greater; but contrariwiſe, when the eye is placed in the groſſer *medium,* and the object in the finer, how it worketh I know not.

762. It would be well boulted out, whether great Refractions may not be made upon Reflexions, as well as upon direct beams. For example, we ſee, that take an empty Baſon, put an *Angel* of *Gold,* or what you will into it; then go ſo far from the Baſon till you cannot ſee the Angel, becauſe it is not in a right Line; then fill the Baſon with Water, and you ſhall ſee it out of his place, becauſe of the Reflexion. To proceed therefore, put a Looking-glaſs into a Baſon of Water; I ſuppoſe you ſhall not ſee the Image in a right Line, or at equal Angles, but aſide. I know not whether this *Experiment* may not be extended ſo, as you might ſee the Image, and not the Glaſs; which for beauty and ſtrangeneſs were a fine proof, for then you ſhall ſee the Image like a Spirit in the Air. As for example, if there be a Ciſtern or Pool of Water, you ſhall place over againſt it a picture of the Devil, or what you will, ſo as you do not ſee the Water, then put a Looking glaſs in the Water: Now if you can ſee the Devils picture aſide, not ſeeing the Water, it will look like a Devil indeed. They have an old tale in *Oxford,* That Fryer *Bacon* walked between two Steeples; which was thought to be done by Glaſſes, when he walked upon the Ground.

763.
*Experiments
in Conſort,
touching the
Imiſſion and
Percuſſion.*

A Weighty Body put into Motion, is more eaſily impelled then at firſt when it reſteth. The cauſe is, partly becauſe Motion doth diſcuſs the Torpour of ſolid Bodies, which beſide their Motion of Gravity, have in them a Natural Appetite not to move at all; and partly, becauſe a Body that reſteth doth get, by the reſiſtance of the Body upon which it reſteth, a ſtronger
compreſſion

compreſſion of parts then it hath of it ſelf, and therefore needeth more force to be put in motion. For if a weighty Body be penſile, and hang but by a thred, the percuſſion will make an impulſion very near as eaſily as if it were already in motion.

A Body over-great or over-ſmall, will not be thrown ſo far as a Body of a middle ſize; ſo that (it ſeemeth) there muſt be a commenſuration or proportion between the Body moved, and the force, to make it move well. The cauſe is, becauſe to the Impulſion there is requiſite the force of the Body that moveth, and the reſiſtance of the Body that is moved; and if the Body be too great, it yieldeth too little; and if it be too ſmall, it reſiſteth too little.

It is common experience, that no weight will preſs or cut ſo ſtrong being laid upon a Body, as falling or ſtrucken from above. It may be the Air hath ſome part in furthering the percuſſion: But the chief cauſe I take to be, for that the parts of the Body moved, have by impulſion, or by the motion of gravity continued, a compreſſion in them as well downwards, as they have when they are thrown or ſhot through the Air forwards. I conceive alſo, that the quick looſe of that motion preventeth the reſiſtance of the Body below; and priority of the force (always) is of great efficacy, as appeareth in infinite inſtances.

Tickling is moſt in the *Soles* of the *Feet*, and under the *Arm-holes*, and on the *Sides*. The cauſe is, the thinneſs of the Skin in thoſe parts, joyned with the rareneſs of being touched there; for all *Tickling* is a light motion of the Spirits, which the thinneſs of the Skin, and ſuddenneſs and rareneſs of touch do further: For we ſee a Feather or a Ruſh drawn along the Lip or Cheek, doth tickle; whereas a thing more obtuſe, or a touch more hard, doth not. And for ſuddenneſs, we ſee no man can tickle himſelf: We ſee alſo, that the Palm of the Hand, though it hath as thin a Skin as the other parts mentioned, yet is not ticklſh, becauſe it is accuſtomed to be touched. *Tickling* alſo cauſeth *Laughter*. The cauſe may be the emiſſion of the Spirits, and ſo of the Breath, by a flight from *Titillation*; for upon *Tickling*, we ſee there is ever a ſtarting or ſhrinking away of the part to avoid it; and we ſee alſo, that if you tickle the Noſtrils with a Feather or Straw; it procureth *Sneezing*, which is a ſudden emiſſion of the Spirits, that do likewiſe expel the moiſture. And *Tickling* is ever painful, and not well endured.

IT is ſtrange, that the River of *Nilus* overflowing, as it doth the Countrey of *Egypt*, there ſhould be nevertheleſs little or no Rain in that Countrey. The cauſe muſt be, either in the Nature of the Water, or in the Nature of the Air, or of both. In the Water, it may be aſcribed either unto the long race of the Water; for ſwift-running Waters vapor not ſo much as ſtanding Waters, or elſe to the concoction of the Water; for Waters well concocted, vapor not ſo much as Waters raw, no more then Waters upon the fire do vapor ſo much, after ſome time of boyling, as at the firſt. And it is true, that the Water of *Nilus* is ſweeter then other Waters in taſte; and it is excellent good for the *Stone*, and Hypochondriacal Melancholy, which ſheweth it is lenifying; and it runneth through a Countrey of a hot Climate, and flat, without ſhade either of Woods or Hills, whereby the Sun muſt needs have great power to concoct it. As for the Air (from whence I conceive this want of Showers cometh chiefly) the cauſe muſt be,

for

for that the Air is of it self thin and thirsty, and as soon as ever it getteth any moisture from the Water, it imbibeth, and dissipateth it in the whole Body of the Air, and suffereth it not to remain in Vapor, whereby it might breed Rain.

768.
Experiment Solitary, touching *Clarification.*

IT hath been touched in the Title of Percolations, (namely, such as are inwards) that the Whites of Eggs and Milk do clarifie; and it is certain, that in *Egypt* they prepare and clarifie the Water of *Nile*, by putting it into great Jars of Stone, and stirring it about with a few stamped Almonds, wherewith they also besmear the Mouth of the Vessel; and so draw it off, after it hath rested some time. It were good to try this Clarifying with Almonds in new Beer or Must, to hasten and perfect the Clarifying.

769.
Experiment Solitary, touching *Plants without Leaves.*

THere be scarce to be found any Vegetables that have Branches and no Leaves, except you allow Coral for one. But there is also in the Desarts of *S. Macario* in *Egypt*, a Plant which is long, Leafless, brown of colour, and branched like Coral, save that it closeth at the top. This being set in Water within House, spredeth and displayeth strangely; and the people thereabout have a superstitious belief, that in the Labor of Women it helpeth to the easie Deliverance.

770.
Experiment Solitary, touching the *Materials of Glass.*

THe *Crystalline Venice-Glass* is reported to be a mixture, in equal portions, of Stones brought from *Pavia*, by the River *Ticinum*, and the Ashes of a Weed called by the *Arabs*, *Kali*, which is gathered in a Desart between *Alexandria* and *Rosetta*; and is by the *Egyptians* used first for Fuel, and then they crush the Ashes into lumps like a Stone, and so sell them to the *Venetians* for their Glass-works.

771.
Experiment Solitary, touching *Prohibition of Putrefaction, and the long Conservation of Bodies.*

IT is strange, and well to be noted, how long Carcasses have continued uncorrupt, and in their former Dimensions; as appeareth in the *Mummies* of *Egypt*, having lasted, as is conceived (some of them) three thousand years. It is true, they finde means to draw forth the Brains, and to take forth the Entrails, which are the parts aptest to corrupt. But that is nothing to the wonder; for we see what a soft and corruptible substance the Flesh of all the other parts of the Body is. But it should seem, that according to our observation and axiom, in our hundredth *Experiment*, *Putrefaction*, which we conceive to be so natural a Period of Bodies, is but an accident, and that Matter maketh not that haste to Corruption that is conceived; and therefore Bodies in shining Amber, in Quick-silver, in Balms, (whereof we now speak) in Wax, in Honey, in Gums, and (it may be) in Conservatories of Snow, &c. are preserved very long. It need not go for repetition, if we resume again that which we said in the aforesaid *Experiments* concerning *Annihilation*, namely, That if you provide against three causes of *Putrefaction*, *Bodies* will not corrupt. The first is, that the Air be excluded; for that undermineth the Body, and conspireth with the Spirit of the Body to dissolve it. The second is, that the Body adjacent and ambient be not Commaterial, but meerly Heterogeneal towards the Body that is to be preserved; for if nothing can be received by the one, nothing can issue from the other; such are Quick-silver and White Amber to Herbs and Flies, and such Bodies. The third is, that the Body to be preserved, be not of that gross that it may corrupt within it self, although no part of it issue into the Body adjacent; and therefore it must be rather thin
and

and small in ea of Bulk. There is a fourth Remedy also, which is, That if the Body to be preserved, be of bulk, as a Corps is, then the Body that inclofeth it must have a virtue to draw forth and dry the moisture of the inward Body; for else the Putrefaction will play within, though nothing issue forth. I remember _Livy_ doth relate, that there were found at a time two Coffins of Lead in a Tomb, whereof the one contained the Body of King _Numa_, it being some Four hundred years after his death; and the other, his Books of Sacred Rites and Ceremonies, and the Discipline of the Pontiffs: And that in the Coffin that had the Body, there was nothing (at all) to be seen but a little light Cinders about the sides; but in the Coffin that had the Books, they were found as fresh as if they had been but newly written, being written in Parchment, and covered over with Watch-candles of Wax three or four fold. By this it seemeth, that the _Romans_ in _Numa's_ time were not so good Embalmers as the _Egyptians_ were; which was the cause that the Body was utterly consumed. But I finde In _Plutarch_ and others, that when _Augustus Cæsar_ visited the Sepulchre of _Alexander_ the Great in _Alexandria_, he found the Body to keep his Dimension; but withal, that notwithstanding all the Embalming (which no doubt was of the best) the Body was so tender, as _Cæsar_ touching but the Nose of it, defaced it. Which maketh me finde it very strange, that the _Egyptian Mummies_ should be reported to be as hard as Stone-pitch: For I finde no difference but one, which indeed may be very material; namely, that the ancient _Egyptian Mummies_ were shrowded in a number of folds of Linnen, besmeared with Gums, in manner of Sear-cloth; which it doth not appear, was practised upon the Body of _Alexander_.

NEar the Castle of _Catie_, and by the Wells _Assan_, in the Land of _Idumæa_, a great part of the way, you would think the Sea were near hand, though it be a good distance of: And it is nothing, but the shining of the _Nitre_ upon the _Sea-sands_; such abundance of _Nitre_ the Shores there do put forth.

772.
Experiment Solitary, touching the _Abundance of Nitre in certain Sea-shores._

THe _Dead-Sea_, which vomiteth up _Bitumen_, is of that Crassitude, as Living Bodies, bound hand and foot, and cast into it, have been borne up and not sunk: Which sheweth, that all sinking into Water, is but an overweight of the Body put into the Water, in respect of the Water; so that you may make Water so strong and heavy of _Quick-silver_, (perhaps) or the like, as may bear up Iron; of which I see no use, but Imposture. We see also, that all Metals, except Gold, for the same reason swim upon Quick-silver.

773.
Experiment Solitary, touching _Bodies that are borne up by Water._

IT is reported, that at the Foot of a Hill near the _Mare mortuum_, there is a Black Stone (whereof _Pilgrims_ make Fires) which burneth like a Coal, and diminisheth not, but onely waxeth brighter and whiter. That it should do so, is not strange; for we see Iron red hot burneth and consumeth not. But the strangeness is, that it should continue any time so; for Iron, as soon as it is out of the Fire, deadeth straight-ways. Certainly, it were a thing of great use and profit, if you could finde out Fuel that would burn hot, and yet last long: Neither am I altogether incredulous, but there may be such Candles as (they say) are made of _Salamanders_ Wool, being a kinde of Mineral which whiteneth also in the burning, and consumeth not. The Question is this, Flame must be made of somewhat; and commonly it

774.
Experiment Solitary, touching _Fuel that consumeth little or nothing._

is

is made of some tangible Body which hath weight ; but it is not impossible, perhaps, that it should be made of Spirit or Vapor in a Body, (which Spirit or Vapor hath no weight) such as is the matter of *Ignis fatuus.* But then you will say, that that Vapor also can last but a short time. To that it may be answered, That by the help of Oyl and Wax, and other Candle-stuff, the flame may continue, and the wick not burnt.

<table>
<tr><td>

775.
Experiment
Solitary,
Oeconomical
touching cheap
Fewel.

</td><td>

SEa-coal last longer then *Char-coal* ; and *Char-coal* of *Roots*, being coaled into great pieces, last longer then ordinary *Char coal.* *Turf,* and *'Peat,* and *Cow-sheards* are cheap Fewels, and last long. *Small coal* or *Char-coal* poured upon *Char-coal* make them last longer. *Sedge* is a cheap Fewel to Brew or Bake with, the rather, because it is good for nothing else. Tryal would be made of some mixture of *Sea-coal* with *Earth,* or *Chalk* ; for if that mixture be, as the *Sea-coal-men* use it privily, to make the Bulk of the *Coal* greater, it is deceit ; but if it be used purposely, and be made known, it is saving.

</td></tr>
</table>

<table>
<tr><td>

776.
Experiment
Solitary,
touching the
Gathering of
Wind for
Freshneß.

</td><td>

IT is at this day in use in *Gaza,* to couch *Pot-sherds* or *Vessels* of *Earth* in their *Walls,* to gather the Wind from the top, and to pass it down in Spouts into Rooms. It is a device for freshness in great Heats. And it is said, there are some Rooms in *Italy* and *Spain* for freshness, and gathering the Winds and Air in the Heats of Summer ; but they be but Pennings of the Winds, and enlarging them again, and making them reverberate, and go round in Circles, rather then this device of Spouts in the Wall.

</td></tr>
</table>

<table>
<tr><td>

777.
Experiment
Solitary,
touching the
Tryals of
Airs.

</td><td>

THere would be used much diligence in the choice of some Bodies and Places (as it were) for the tasting of Air, to discover the wholesomeness or unwholesomeness as well of Seasons, as of the Seats of Dwellings. It is certain, that there be some Houses wherein Confitures and Pies, will gather Mould more then in others ; and I am perswaded, that a piece of raw Flesh or Fish, will sooner corrupt in some Airs then in others. They be noble *Experiments* that can make this discovery ; for they serve for a Natural Divination of Seasons, better then the Astronomers can by their Figures ; and again, they teach men where to chuse their dwelling for their better health.

</td></tr>
</table>

<table>
<tr><td>

778.
Experiment
Solitary,
touching
Increasing of
Milk in
Milk-Beasts.

</td><td>

THere is a kinde of *Stone* about *Bethlehem* which they grinde to powder, and put into Water, whereof Cattel drink, which maketh them give more Milk. Surely, there would be some better Tryals made of Mixtures of Water in Ponds for Cattel, to make them more Milch, or to fatten them, or to keep them from *Murrain.* It may be, *Chalk* and *Nitre* are of the best.

</td></tr>
</table>

<table>
<tr><td>

779.
Experiment
Solitary,
touching
Sand of the
Nature of
Glaß.

</td><td>

IT is reported, that in the Valley near the Mountain *Carmel* in *Judea,* there is a Sand, which of all other, hath most affinity with Glass, insomuch, as other Minerals laid in it, turn to a glassie substance without the fire ; and again, Glass put into it, turneth into the Mother-sand. The thing is very strange, if it be true ; and it is likeliest to be caused by some natural Furnace of Heat in the Earth, and yet they do not speak of any Eruption of Flames It were good to try in Glass-works, whether the crude Materials of Glass mingled with Glass, already made and remoulten, do not facilitate the making of Glass with less heat.

</td></tr>
</table>

In

IN the Sea, upon the *South-West* of *Sicily*, much Coral is found. It is a Submarine Plant, it hath no leaves, it brancheth onely when it is under Water; it is soft, and green of colour; but being brought into the Air, it becometh hard, and shining red, as we see. It is said also to have a white Berry, but we finde it not brought over with the Coral: Belike it is cast away as nothing worth. Iiquire better of it, for the discovery of the Nature of the Plant.

780.
Experiment Solitary, touching the Growth of Coral.

THe *Manna* of *Calabria* is the best, and in most plenty. They gather it from the Leaf of the *Mulberry-tree*; but not of such *Mulberry-trees* as grow in the Valleys: And *Manna* falleth upon the Leaves by night, as other Dews do. It should seem, that before those Dews come upon Trees in the Valleys, they dissipate and cannot hold out. It should seem also, the Mulberry-leaf it self hath some coagulating virtue, which inspissateth the Dew, for that it is not found upon other Trees: And we see by the Silk-worm, which feedeth upon that Leaf, what a dainty smooth Juice it hath; and the Leaves also (especially of the Black Mulberry) are somewhat bristly, which may help to preserve the Dew. Certainly, it were not amiss to observe a little better the Dews that fall upon Trees or Herbs growing on *Mountains*; for it may be, many Dews fall that spend before they come to the Valleys. And I suppose, that he that would gather the best *May* Dew for Medicine, should gather it from the Hills.

781.
Experiment Solitary, touching the Gathering of Manna.

IT is said, they have a manner to prepare their *Greek Wines*, to keep them from Fuming and Inebriating, by adding some *Sulphur* or *Allum*; whereof the one is Unctuous, and the other is Astringent. And certain it is, that those two Natures do repress the Fumes. This *Experiment* would be transferred unto other Wine and Strong-Beer, by putting in some like Substances while they work; which may make them both to Fume less, and to inflame less.

782.
Experiment Solitary, touching the Correcting of Wine.

IT is conceived by some, (not improbably) that the reason why Wild-fires (whereof the principal ingredient is *Bitumen*) do not quench with Water, is, for that the first concretion of *Bitumen*, is a mixture of a fiery and watry substance; so is not *Sulphur*. This appeareth, for that in the place near *Puteoli*, which they call the *Court of Vulcan*, you shall hear under the Earth a horrible thundring of Fire and Water conflicting together; and there break forth also Spouts of boiling Water. Now that place yieldeth great quantities of *Bitumen*; whereas *Ætna*, and *Vesuvius*, and the like, which consist upon *Sulphur*, shoot forth Smoak, and Ashes, and Pumice, but no Water. It is reported also, that *Bitumen* mingled with Lime, and put under Water, will make, as it were, an artificial Rock, the substance becometh so hard.

783.
Experiment Solitary, touching the Materials of Wildfire.

THere is a Cement compounded of Flower, Whites of Eggs, and Stone powdred, that becometh hard as Marble, wherewith *Piscina Mirabilis*, near *Cumis*, is said to have the Walls plaistered. And it is certain, and tried, that the Powder of Load-stone and Flint, by the addition of Whites of Eggs and Gum-dragon, made into Paste, will in a few days harden to the hardness of a Stone.

784.
Experiment Solitary, touching Plaister growing as hard as Marble.

It

IT hath been noted by the *Ancients*, that in full or impure Bodies, Ulcers or Hurts in the Legs are hard to cure, and in the Head more easie. The cause is, for that Ulcers or Hurts in the Legs require Desiccation, which by the defluxion of Humors to the lower parts is hindred, whereas Hurts and Ulcers in the Head require it not; but, contrariwise, Dryness maketh them more apt to Consolidate. And in Modern observation, the like difference hath been found between French-men and English men; whereof the ones Constitution is more dry, and the others more moist: And therefore a Hurt of the Head is harder to cure in a French-man, and of the Leg in an English-man.

IT hath been noted by the *Ancients*, that *Southern Winds* blowing much without Rain, do cause a *Feverous Disposition* of the *Year*; but with Rain, not. The cause is, for that *Southern Winds* do of themselves qualifie the Air to be apt to cause *Fevers*; but when Showers are joyned, they do refrigerate in part, and check the soultry Heat of the Southern Wind. Therefore this holdeth not in the Sea-coasts, because the vapor of the Sea without Showers doth refresh.

IT hath been noted by the *Ancients*, that Wounds which are made with Brass, heal more easily then Wounds made with Iron. The cause is, for that Brass hath in it self a Sanative virtue, and so in the very instant helpeth somewhat; but Iron is Corrosive, and not Sanative. And therefore it were good that the Instruments which are used by Chirurgions about Wounds were rather of Brass then Iron.

IN the cold Countreys, when Mens Noses and Ears are mortified, and (as it were) Gangrened with cold, if they come to a Fire, they rot off presently. The cause is, for that the few Spirits that remain in those parts are suddenly drawn forth, and so Putrefaction is made compleat. But Snow put upon them helpeth, for that it preserveth those Spirits that remain till they can revive; and besides, Snow hath in it a secret warmth; as the *Monk* proved out of the Text, *Qui dat Nivem sicut Lanam, Gelu sicut Cineres spargit*; whereby he did infer, that Snow did warm like Wool, and Frost did fret like Ashes. Warm Water also doth good, because by little and little it openeth the pores, without any sudden working upon the Spirits. This *Experiment* may be transferred unto the cure of *Gangrenes*, either coming of themselves, or induced by too much applying of *Opiates*; wherein you must beware of dry Heat, and resort to things that are Refrigerant, with an inward warmth and virtue of cherishing.

WEigh Iron and *Aqua-fortis* severally, then dissolve the Iron in the *Aqua-fortis*, and weigh the Dissolution; and you shall finde it to bear as good weight as the Bodies did severally, notwithstanding a good deal of waste by a thick vapor that issueth during the working; which sheweth, that the opening of a Body doth increase the weight. This was tryed once or twice, but I know not whether there were any Error in the Tryal.

TAke of *Aqua-fortis* two Ounces, of *Quick-silver* two Drachms, (for that charge the *Aqua-fortis* will bear) the Dissolution will not bear a Flint as big as a *Nutmeg*; yet (no doubt) the increasing of the weight of

Water

Water will increase his power of bearing; as we see Broyn, when it is salt enough, will bear an Egg. And I remember well a Physitian, that used to give some Mineral Baths for the Gout &c. And the Body when it was put into the Bath, could not get down so easily as in ordinary Water. But it seemeth, the weight of the Quickfilver, more then the weight of a Stone, doth not compense the weight of a Stone, more then the weight of the *Aqua-fortis.*

LEt there be a Body of unequal weight, (as of Wood and Lead, or Bone and Lead;) if you throw it from you with the light end forward, it will turn, and the weightier end will recover to be forwards, unless the Body be over-long. The cause is, for that the more Dense Body hath a more violent pressure of the parts from the first impulsion; which is the cause (though heretofore not found out, as hath been often said) of all Violent Motions: And when the hinder part moveth swifter (for that it less endureth pressure of parts) then the forward part can make way for it, it must needs be that the Body turn over; for (turned) it can more easily draw forward the lighter part. *Galilæus* noteth it well, That if an open Trough, wherein Water is, be driven faster then the Water can follow, the Water gathereth upon an heap towards the hinder end, where the motion began; which he supposeth (holding confidently the motion of the Earth) to be the cause of the Ebbing and Flowing of the Ocean, because the Earth over-runneth the Water. Which Theory though it be false, yet the first *Experiment* is true; as for the inequality of the pressure of parts, it appeareth manifestly in this, That if you take a body of Stone or Iron, and another of Wood, of the same magnitude and shape, and throw them with equal force, you cannot possibly throw the Wood so far as the Stone or Iron.

IT is certain (as it hath been formerly in part touched) that Water may be the *Medium* of Sounds. If you dash a Stone against a Stone in the bottom of the Water, it makes a Sound; so a long Pole struck upon Gravel, in the bottom of the Water, maketh a Sound. Nay, if you should think that the Sound cometh up by the Pole, and not by the Water, you shall finde that an Anchor let down by a Rope maketh a Sound; and yet the Rope is no solid Body, whereby the Sound can ascend.

ALl objects of the Senses which are very offensive, do cause the Spirits to retire; and upon their flight, the parts are (in some degree) destitute, and so there is induced in them a trepidation and horror. For Sounds, we see, that the grating of a Saw, or any very harsh noise, will set the Teeth on edge, and make all the Body shiver. For Tastes, we see, that in the taking of a Potion, or Pills, the Head and the Neck shake. For odious smells, the like effect followeth, which is less perceived, because there is a remedy at hand, by stopping of the Nose. But in Horses, that can use no such help, we see the smell of a Carrion, especially of a dead Horse, maketh them flie away, and take on almost, as if they were mad. For Feeling, if you come out of the Sun suddenly into a shade, there followeth a chilness or shivering in all the Body. And even in Sight, which hath (in effect) no odious object, coming into sudden darkness, induceth an offer to shiver.

THere is in the City of *Ticinum* in *Italy,* a Church that hath Windows onely from above; it is in Length an hundred Feet, in Bredth twenty Feet, and in Height near fifty, having a Door in the midst. It reporteth, the

791.
Experiment Solitary, touching the *Flying of unequal Bodies in the Air.*

792.
Experiment Solitary, touching *Water, that it may be the Medium of Sounds.*

793.
Experiment Solitary, of the *Flight of the Spirits upon odious Objects.*

794.
Experiment Solitary, touching the *Super-Reflexion of Echoes.*

the voice twelve or thirteen times. If you ſtand by the cloſe end-wall over againſt the Door, the Echo fadeth and dieth by little and little, as the Echo at *Pont-Charenton* doth, and the voice ſoundeth as if it came from above the Door ; and if you ſtand at the lower end, or on either ſide of the Door, the Echo holdeth ; but if you ſtand in the Door, or in the midſt juſt over againſt the Door, not. Note, that all Echoes ſound better againſt old Walls then new, becauſe they are more dry and hollow.

795.
Experiment Solitary, touching the force of Imagination, Imitating that of the Senſe.

THoſe effects which are wrought by the percuſſion of the Senſe, and by things in Fact, are produced likewiſe in ſome degree by the Imagination : Therefore if a man ſee another eat ſour or acide things, which ſet the Teeth on edge, this object tainteth the Imagination ; ſo that he that ſeeth the thing done by another, hath his own Teeth alſo ſet on edge. So if a man ſee another turn ſwiftly and long, or if he look upon Wheels that turn, himſelf waxeth Turn-ſick. So if a man be upon a high place, without Rails, or good hold, except he be uſed to it, he is ready to fall ; for imagining a fall, it putteth his ſpirits into the very action of a fall. So many upon the ſeeing of others Bleed, or Strangled, or Tortured, themſelves are ready to faint, as if they bled, or were in ſtrife.

796.
Experiment Solitary, touching Preſervation of Bodies.

TAke a *Stock-Gilliflower*, and tie it gently upon a ſtick, and put them both both into a Stoop-glaſs full of Quick-ſilver, ſo that the Flower be covered ; then lay a little weight upon the top of the Glaſs, that may keep the ſtick down ; and look upon them after four or five days, and you ſhall finde the Flower freſh, and the Stalk harder and leſs flexible then it was. If you compare it with another Flower, gathered at the ſame time, it will be the more manifeſt. This ſheweth, that *Bodies* do preſerve excellently in *Quick-ſilver* ; and not preſerve onely, but by the coldneſs of the *Quick-ſilver,* indurate. For the freſhneſs of the Flower may be meerly Conſervation, (which is the more to be obſerved, becauſe the *Quick-ſilver* preſſeth the *Flower*) but the ſtifneſs of the Stalk cannot be without Induration from the cold (as it ſeemeth) of the *Quick ſilver.*

797.
Experiment Solitary, touching the Growth or Multiplying of Metals.

IT is reported by ſome of the *Ancients,* That in *Cyprus* there is a kinde of Iron, that being cut into little pieces, and put into the ground, if it be well watered, will encreaſe into greater pieces. This is certain, and known of old, that Lead will multiply and encreaſe ; as hath been ſeen in old *Statues* of Stone, which have been put in *Cellars,* the Feet of them being bound with *Leaden bands* ; where (after a time) there appeared, that the Lead did ſwell, inſomuch, as it hanged upon the Stone like Warts.

798.
Experiment Solitary, touching the Drowning of the more Baſe Metal, in the more Precious.

I Call that drowning of Metals, when the baſer Metal is ſo incorporate with the more rich, as it can by no means be ſeparated again ; which is a kinde of Verſion, though falſe ; as if *Silver* ſhould be inſeparably incorporated with *Gold,* or *Copper* and *Lead* with *Silver.* The *Ancient Electrum* had in it a fifth of *Silver* to the *Gold,* and made a Compound Metal, as fit for moſt uſes as *Gold,* and more reſplendent, and more qualified in ſome other properties ; but then that was eaſily ſeparated. This to do privily, or to make the Compound paſs for the rich Metal ſimple, is an adulteration or counterfeiting ; but if it be done avowedly and without diſguiſing, it may be a great ſaving of the richer Metal. I remember to have heard of a man ſkilful in Metals, that a fifteenth part of *Silver* incorporate with
Gold

Gold is the onely Substance which hath nothing in it Volatile, and yet melteth without much difficult.. The Melting sheweth, that it is not jejune or scarce in Spirit. So that the fixing of it is not want of Spirit to flie out, but the equal spreding of the Tangible parts, and the close coacervation of them; whereby they have the less appetite, and no means (at all) to issue forth. It were good therefore to try whether Glass Re-molten, do lose any weight; for the parts in Glass are evenly spred, but they are not so close as in Gold; as we see by the easie admission of Light Heat, and Cold, and by the smalness of the weight. There be other Bodies fixed, which have little or no Spirit, so as there is nothing to flie out; as we see in the Stuff, whereof Coppels are made, which they put into Furnaces, upon which Fire worketh not. So that there are three causes of Fixation; the *Even-spreding* both of the *Spirits* and *Tangible parts*; the *Closeness* of the *Tangible parts*; and the *Jejuneness* or *Extream Comminution* of *Spirits*: Of which three, the two first may be joyned with a *Nature Liquefiable*, the last not:

.799.
Experiment Solitary, touching *Fixation of Bodies*.

IT is a profound *Contemplation in Nature*, to consider of the Emptiness (as we may call it) or Insatisfaction of several Bodies, and of their appetite to take in others. Air taketh in Lights, and Sounds, and Smells, and Vapors: And it is most manifest, that it doth it with a kinde of Thirst, as not satisfied with his own former Consistence; for else it would never receive them in so suddenly and easily. *Water* and all *Liquors* do hastily receive dry and more Terrestrial Bodies proportionable; and Dry Bodies, on the other side, drink in Waters and Liquors: So that (as it was well said by one of the *Ancients*, of Earthy and Watry Substances) one is a Glue to another. *Parchments*, *Skins*, *Cloth*, *&c.* drink in Liquors; though themselves be entire Bodies, and not comminuted, as *Sand* and *Ashes*, nor apparently porous. *Metals* themselves do receive in readily *Strong-waters*, and *Strong-waters* likewise do readily pierce into *Metals* and *Stones*; and that *Strong-water* will touch upon *Gold*, that will not touch upon *Silver*, and *è converso*. And *Gold*, which seemeth by the weight to be the closest and most solid Body, doth greedily drink in *Quick-silver*. And it seemeth, that this Reception of other Bodies is not violent; for it is (many times) reciprocal, and, as it were, with consent. Of the cause of this, and to what Axiom it may be referred, consider attentively; for as for the pretty assertion, That *Matter* is like a *Common Strumpet* that desireth all *Forms*, it is but a Wandring Notion. Onely *Flame* doth not content it self to take in any other Body; but either to overcome, and turn another Body into it self, as by victory, or it self to die and go out:

800.
Experiment Solitary, touching the *Restless Nature of Things in themselves and their Desire to Change*.

NATURAL
HISTORY.

Century IX.

T is certain, That all *Bodies* whatſoever, though they have no Senſe, yet they have Perception: For when one *Body* is applied to another, there is a kinde of Electi-on, to embrace that which is agreeable, and to exclude or expel that which is ingrate: And whether the *Body* be alterant or altered, evermore a Perception precedeth Operation; for elſe all *Bodies* would be alike one to an-other. And ſometimes this Perception in ſome kinde of *Bodies* is far more ſubtil then the Senſe; ſo that the Senſe is but a dull thing in compariſon of it. We ſee a *Weather-glaſſ* will finde the leaſt difference of the Weather in Heat or Cold, when Men finde it not. And this Perception alſo is ſometimes at diſtance, as well as upon the touch; as when the *Load-ſtone* draweth Iron, or Flame fireth *Naphtha* of *Babylon* a great diſtance off. It is therefore a ſubject of a very *Noble Enquiry*, to enquire of the more *ſubtil Perceptions*; for it is another Key to open *Nature*, as well as the *Senſe*, and ſometimes better: And beſides, it is a principal means of *Natural Divination*; for that which in theſe Perceptions appeareth early, in the great effects cometh long after. It is true alſo, that it ſerveth to diſcover that which is hid, as well as to foretel that which is to come, as it is in many *ſubtil Tryals*: As to try whether *Seeds* be old or new, the *Senſe* cannot inform; but if you boil them in Water, the new Seeds will ſprout ſooner. And ſo of Water, the taſte will not diſcover the beſt Water; but the ſpeedy conſuming of it, and many other means which we have heretofore ſet down, will diſcover it. So in all *Phyſiognomy*, the *Lineaments* of the *Body* will diſcover thoſe Natural Inclinations of the Minde, which Diſſimulation will conceal, or Diſcipline will ſuppreſs. We ſhall therefore now handle onely thoſe two *Perceptions* which pertain to *Natural Divination* and *Diſcovery*, leaving the handling of

Q 2

Perception

Perception in other things to be difpofed elfwhere.   Now it is true, that *Divination* is attained by other *means* ;   as if you know the caufes, if you know the *Concomitants*, you may judge of the effect to follow ;   and the like may be faid of *Difcovery*.   But we tye our felves here to that *Divination* and *Difcovery* chiefly, which is caufed by an early or fubtil *Perception*.

The aptnefs or propenfion of Air or Water to corrupt or putrefie, (no doubt) is to be found before it break forth into manifeft effects of Dif-eafes, Blafting, or the like.   We will therefore fet down fome Prognofticks of Peftilential and unwholfome years.

801. The Wind blowing much from the South without Rain, and Worms in the Oak-Apple, have been fpoken of before.   Alfo the plenty of Frogs, Grafhoppers, Flies, and the like Creatures bred of Putrefaction, doth portend Peftilential years.

802. Great and early Heats in the Spring, (and namely in *May*) without Winds, portend the fame.   And generally fo do years with little Wind or Thunder.

803. Great Droughts in Summer, lafting till towards the end of *Auguft*, and fome gentle fhowers upon them, and then fome dry weather again, do portend a Peftilent Summer the year following :   For about the end of *Auguft*, all the fweetnefs of the Earth which goeth into *Plants* or *Trees* is exhaled ;   (and much more if the *Auguft* be dry) fo that nothing then can breath forth of the Earth but a grofs vapor, which is apt to corrupt the Air ;   and that vapor by the firft fhowers, if they be gentle, is releafed, and cometh forth abundantly.   Therefore they that come abroad foon after thofe fhowers are commonly taken with ficknefs. And in *Africk* no Body will ftir out of doors after the firft fhowers.   But if the firft fhowers come vehemently, then they rather wafh and fill the Earth, then give it leave to breath forth prefently.   But if dry weather come again, then it fixeth and continueth the corruption of the Air upon the firft fhowers begun, and maketh it of ill influence even to the next Summer, ex-cept a very Frofty Winter difcharge it, which feldom fucceedeth fuch Droughts.

804. The leffer Infections of the *Small-Pox*, *Purple Feavers*, *Agues* in the Sum-mer precedent, and hovering all Winter, do portend a great *Peftilence* in the Summer following :   For Putrefaction doth not rife to its height at once.

805. It were good to lay a piece of raw Flefh or Fifh in the open Air ; and if it putrefie quickly, it is a fign of a difpofition in the Air to Pu-trefaction.   And becaufe you cannot be informed, whether the Putrefacti-on be quick or late, except you compare this Experiment with the like Experiment in another year ;   it were not amifs in the fame year, and at the fame time, to lay one piece of Flefh or Fifh in the open Air, and another of the fame kinde and bignefs within doors :   For I judge, that if a general difpofition be in the Air to putrefie, the Flefh or Fifh will fooner putrefie abroad, where the Air hath more power then in the Houfe, where it hath lefs, being many ways corrected.   And this Experi-ment would be made about the end of *March* ;   for that feafon is likeft to difcover what the Winter hath done, and what the Summer following will do upon the Air.   And becaufe the Air (no doubt) receiveth great tincture and infufion from the Earth, it were good to try that expofing of Flefh

or

or Fish both upon a Stake of Wood, some height above the Earth, and upon the flat of the Earth.

Take *May Dew*, and see whether it putrefie quickly, or no; for that likewise may disclose the quality of the Air, and vapor of the Earth, more or less corrupted. **806.**

A dry *March*, and a dry *May*, portend a wholesome Summer, if there be a showring *April* between; but otherwise it is a sign of a *Pestilential year*. **807.**

As the discovery of the disposition of the Air is good for the *Prognosticks* of wholesome and unwholesome years; so it is of much more use for the choice of places to dwell in; at the least for Lodges and Retiring-places for Health, (for Mansion-Houses respect provisions as well as health) wherein the *Experiments* above mentioned may serve. **808.**

But for the choice of Places or Seats, it is good to make tryal, not onely of aptness of Air to corrupt, but also of the moisture and dryness of the Air, and the temper of it in heat or cold; for that may concern health diversly. We see that there be some Houses wherein *Sweet Meats* will relent, and *Baked Meats* will mould, more then in others; and *Wainscot* will also sweat more, so that they will almost run with Water: All which (no doubt) are caused chiefly by the moistness of the Air in those Seats. But because it is better to know it before a Man buildeth his House, then to finde it after, take the *Experiments* following. **809.**

Lay Wool, or a Sponge, or Bread in the place you would try, comparing it with some other places, and see whether it doth not moisten, and make the Wool or Sponge, &c. more ponderous then the other: And if it do, you may judge of that place, as situate in a gross and moist Air. **810.**

Because it is certain that in some places, either by the Nature of the Earth, or by the situation of Woods and Hills, the Air is more unequal then in others; and inequality of Air is ever an enemy to health: It were good to take two Weather-Glasses, matches in all things, and to set them for the same hours of one day in several places where no shade is nor enclosures; and to mark when you set them, how far the Water cometh; and to compare them when you come again, how the Water standeth then. And if you finde them unequal, you may be sure, that the place where the Water is lowest is in the warmer Air, and the other in the Colder. And the greater the inequality is of the ascent or descent of the Water, the greater is the inequality of the temper of the Air. **811.**

The *Predictions* likewise of cold and long Winters, and hot and dry Summers, are good to be known, as well for the discovery of the causes, as for divers Provisions. That of *Plenty of Haws*, and *Heps*, and *Bryar-Berries*, hath been spoken of before. If *Wainscot* or *Stone*, that have used to sweat, be more dry in the beginning of Winter, or the drops of the Eavs of Houses come more slowly down then they use, it portendeth a hard and frosty Winter. The cause is, for that it sheweth an inclination of the Air to dry Weather, which in Winter is ever joyned with Frost. **812.**

Generally a moist and a cool Summer, portendeth a hard Winter. The cause is, for that the vapors of the Earth are not dissipated in the Summer by the Sun; and so they rebound upon the Winter. **813.**

A hot and dry Summer and Autumn, and especially if the heat and drought extend far into *September*, portendeth an open beginning of Winter, and colds to succeed toward the latter part of the Winter, and the beginning of the Spring. For till then the former heat and drought bear the sway, and the vapors are not sufficiently multiplied. **814.**

815.   An open and warm Winter portendeth a hot and dry Summer: For the Vapors disperse into the Winter showers; whereas Cold and Frost keepeth them in, and transporteth them into the late Spring and Summer following.

816.   *Birds* that use to change Countreys at certain Seasons, if they come earlier, do shew the temperature of Weather according to that Countrey whence they came: As the Winter-Birds, (namely, *Woodcocks, Feldefares &c.*) if they come earlier, and out of the *Northern Countreys,* with us shew cold Winters. And if it be in the same Countrey, then they shew a temperature of Season, like unto that Season in which they come; as *Swallows Bats, Cuckoes, &c.* that come towards Summer, if they come early, shew a hot Summer to follow.

817.   The *Prognosticks* more immediate of Weather to follow soon after, are more certain then those of Seasons: The Resounding of the Sea upon the Shore, and the Murmur of Winds in the Woods, without apparent Wind, shew Wind to follow. For such Winds, breathing chiefly out of the Earth, are not at the first perceived, except they be pent by Water or Wood. And therefore a Murmur out of Caves likewise portendeth as much.

818.   The Upper Regions of the Air, perceive the Collection of the matter of Tempest and Winds before the Air here below. And therefore the obscuring of the smaller Stars, is a sign of Tempests following. And of this kinde you shall finde a number of instances in our *Inquisition de Ventis.*

819.   Great Mountains have a Perception of the disposition of the Air to Tempests sooner, then the Valleys or Plains below. And therefore they say in *Wales, When certain Hills have their Night-caps on, they mean mischief.* The cause is, for that Tempests which are for the most part bred above in the Middle Region, (as they call it) are soonest perceived to collect in the places next it.

820.   The Air and Fire have subtil Perceptions of Wind rising before Men finde it. We see the trembling of a Candle will discover a Wind, that otherwise we do not feel; and the Flexious burning of Flames doth shew the Air beginneth to be unquiet; and so do Coals of fire, by casting off the ashes more then they use. The cause is, for that no Wind at the first, till it hath struck and driven the Air, is apparent to the Sense; but flame is easier to move then Air. And for the Ashes, it is no marvel though Wind unperceived shake them off; for we usually try which way the Wind bloweth, by casting up Grass or Chaff, or such light things into the Air.

821.   When Wind expireth from under the Sea, as it causeth some resoundings of the Water, (whereof we spake before) so it causeth some light motions of Bubbles, and white Circles of Froth. The cause is, for that the Wind cannot be perceived by the Sense, until there be an Eruption of a great quantity from under the Water, and so it getteth into a Body, whereas in the first putting up, it cometh in little portions.

822.   We spake of the Ashes that Coals cast off, and of Grass and Chaff carried by the Wind; so any light thing that moveth when we find no Wind, sheweth a Wind at hand: As when Feathers or Down of Thistles flie to and fro in the Air.

For *Prognosticks* of Weather from *Living Creatures*, it is to be noted, That Creatures that live in the open Air (*sub dio*) must needs have a quicker impression from the Air, then Men that live most within doors; and especially Birds who live in the Air freest and clearest, and are aptest by their voice to tell tales what they finde, and likewise by the motion of their flight to express the same.

Water-

VVater-fowls (at *Sea-Gulls*, *Moor-Hens*, &c.) when they flock and flie together from the Sea towards the Shores ; and contrariwise Land Birds, (as *Crows Swallows*, &c. when they flie from the Land to the VVaters, and beat the VVaters with their VVings, do foreshew Rain and VVind. The cause is, Pleasure that both kindes take in the moistness and density of the Air, and so desire to be in motion, and upon the VVing, whither-soever they would otherwise go : For it is no marvel that VVater-fowl do joy most in that Air which is likest VVaters ; and Land Birds also (many of them) delight in Bathing and moist Air. For the same reason also, many Birds do prune their Feathers, and Geese do gaggle, and Crows seem to call upon Rain. All which is but the comfort they seem to receive in the relenting of the Air.

The *Heron* when she soareth high, (so as sometimes she is seen to pass over a Cloud) sheweth VVinds : But *Kites* flying aloft, shew fair and dry weather. The cause may be, for that they both mount most into the Air of that temper wherein they delight. And the *Heron*, being a VVater-fowl, taketh pleasure in the Air that is condensed ; and besides, being but heavy of VVing, needeth the help of the grosser Air. But the *Kite* affecteth not so much the grossness of the Air, as the cold and freshness thereof; for being a *Bird of Prey*, and therefore hot, she delighteth in the fresh Air, and (many times) flieth against the VVind ; as *Trouts* and *Salmons* swim against the stream. And yet it is true also, that all Birds finde an ease in the depth of the Air, as Swimmers do in a deep VVater. And therefore when they are also, they can uphold themselves with their VVings spred, scarce moving them.

Fishes when they play towards the top of the VVater, do commonly foretel Rain. The cause is, for that a Fish hating the dry, will not approach the Air till it groweth moist ; and when it is dry will flee it, and swim lower.

Beasts do take comfort (generally) in a moist Air, and it maketh them eat their Meat better ; and therefore *Sheep* will get up betimes in the morning to feed against Rain ; and Cattle, and Deer, and Coneys will feed hard before Rain ; and a *Heifer* will put up his Nose, and snuff in the Air against Rain.

The *Trifoil* against Rain, swelleth in the Stalk, and so standeth more upright ; for by wet, Stalks do erect, and Leaves bow down. There is a small Red Flower in the Stubble-fields, which Countrey people call the *VVincopipe* ; which, if it open in the Morning, you may be sure of a fair day to follow.

Even in *Men*, *Aches*, and *Hurts*, and *Corns*, do engrieve either towards Rain, or towards Frost ; for the one maketh the Humors more to abound, and the other maketh them sharper. So we see both extreams bring the *Gout*.

Worms, *Vermine*, &c. do foreshew (likewise) Rain ; for *Earth-worms* will come forth, and *Moles* will cast up more, and *Fleas* bite more against Rain.

Solid Bodies likewise foreshew Rain : As Stones and Wainscot when they sweat, and Boxes and Pegs of Wood when they draw and wind hard ; though the former be but from an outward cause, for that the Stone or Wainscot turneth and beateth back the Air against it self ; but the latter is an inward swelling of the Body of the VVood it self.

823.
824.
825.
826.
827.
828.
829.
830.

Appetite

APpetite is moved chiefly by things that are cold and dry. The cause is, for that Cold is a kinde of indigence of Nature, and calleth upon supply, and so is Dryness: And therefore all sour things (as *Vinegar, Juyce of Lemmons, Oyl of Vitriol, &c.*) provoke Appetite. And the Disease which they call *Appetitus Caninus,* consisteth in the Matter of an Acide and Glassie Phlegm in the Mouth of the Stomack. *Appetite* is also moved by sour things, for that sour things induce a contraction in the *Nerves,* placed in the Mouth of the Stomack, which is a great cause of Appetite. As for the cause why Onions, and Salt, and Pepper in Baked Meats move Appetite, it is by Vellication of those Nerves; for Motion whetteth. As for *Wormwood, Olives, Capers,* and others of that kinde, which participate of Bitterness, they move Appetite by Abstersion. So as there be four principal causes of Appetite; the Refrigeration of the Stomack joyned with some Dryness, Contraction, Vellication, and Abstersion; besides Hunger, which is an emptiness; and yet over-fasting doth (many times) cause the Appetite to cease; for that want of Meat maketh the Stomack draw Humors, and such Humors as are light and Cholerick, which quench Appetite most.

IT hath been observed by the *Ancients,* that where a *Rainbow* seemeth to hang over, or to touch, there breatheth forth a sweet smell. The cause is, for that this happeneth but in certain matters which have in themselves some Sweetness, which the gentle Dew of the *Rainbow* doth draw forth; and the like do soft Showers, for they also make the Ground sweet: But none are so delicate as the Dew of the *Rainbow* where it falleth. It may be also, that the Water it self hath some Sweetness; for the *Rainbow* consisteth of a Glomeration of small drops, which cannot possibly fall but from the Air that is very low, and therefore may hold the very Sweetness of the Herbs and Flowers as a Distilled Water: For Rain and other Dew that fall from high cannot preserve the smell, being dissipated in the drawing up; neither do we know, whether some Water it self may not have some degree of Sweetness. It is true, that we finde it sensibly in no Pool, River, nor Fountain; but good Earth newly turned up, hath a freshness and good sent; which Water, if it be not too equal, (for equal objects never move the Sense) may also have. Certain it is, that *Bayfalt,* which is but a kinde of Water congealed, will sometimes smell like *Violets.*

TO sweet Smells, heat is requisite to concoct the Matter, and some Moysture to spred the Breath of them: For heat, we see that Woods and Spices are more odorate in the Hot Countreys, then in the Cold. For Moisture, we see that things too much dryed lose their Sweetness; and Flowers growing smell better in a Morning or Evening, then at Noon. Some sweet smells are destroyed by approach to the Fire; as *Violets, Wall-flowers, Gilliflowers, Pinks,* and generally all Flowers that have cool and delicate Spirits. Some continue both on the fire, and from the fire, as *Rose-water, &c.* Some do scarce come forth, or at least not so pleasantly, as by means of the fire; as *Juniper, Sweet Gums, &c.* and all smells that are enclosed in a fast Body; but (generally) those smells are the most grateful where the degree of heat is small, or where the strength of the smell is allayed; for these things do rather wo the Sense, then satiate it. And therefore the smell of *Violets* and *Roses* exceedeth in sweetness that of Spices; and Gums, and the strongest sort of smells, are best in a weft afar off.

It

IT is certain, that no smell issueth but with emission of some corporeal substance; not as it is in Light, and Colours, and Sounds: For we see plainly that smell doth spred nothing that distance that the other do. It is true, that some Woods of *Orenges*, and *Heaths* of *Rosemary*, will smell a great way into the Sea, perhaps twenty Miles; but what is that, since a peal of Ordnance will do as much, which moveth in a small compass, whereas those Woods and Heaths are of vast spaces? Besides, we see that smells do adhere to hard Bodies; as in perfuming of *Gloves, &c.* which sheweth them corporeal; and do last a great while, which Sounds and Light do not.

THe *Excrements* of most Creatures smell ill, chiefly to the same Creature that voideth them: For we see, besides that of Man, that Pigeons and Horses thrive best, if their Houses and Stables be kept sweet, and so of Cage-Birds; and the Cat burieth that which she voideth. And it holdeth chiefly in those Beasts which feed upon Flesh. *Dogs* (almost) onely of Beasts delight in fetide odors; which sheweth there is somewhat in their sense of smell differing from the smells of other Beasts. But the cause why *Excrements* smell ill is manifest, for that the Body it self rejecteth them, much more the Spirits: And we see, that those *Excrements* that are of the first digestion smell the worst, as the *Excrements* from the *Belly*; those that are from the second digestion, less ill, as *Vrine*; and those that are from the third, yet less; for Sweat is not so bad as the other two, especially of some persons that are full of heat. Likewise most Putrefactions are of an odious smell, for they smell either sertile or mouldy. The cause may be, for that Putrefaction doth bring forth such a consistence as is most contrary to the consistence of the Body whilest it is sound, for it is a meer dissolution of that form. Besides, there is another reason, which is profound: And it is, That the objects that please any of the senses, have (all) some equality, and (as it were) order in their composition, but where those are wanting the object is ever ingrate. So mixture of many disagreeing colours is never unpleasant to the Eye: Mixture of discordant Sounds is unpleasant to the Ear; mixture or hotch-potch of many tastes is unpleasant to the taste; harshness and ruggedness of Bodies is unpleasant to the touch. Now it is certain, that all Putrefaction, being a dissolution of the first form, is a meer confusion, and unformed mixture of the part. Nevertheless, it is strange, and seemeth to cross the former observation, that some Putrefactions and Excrements do yield excellent Odors; as *Civit* and *Musk*, and, as some think, *Amber-greece*, for divers take it (though unprobably) to come from the Sperm of Fish; and the Moss we spake of from *Apple-trees* is little better then an Excretion. The reason may be, for that there passeth in the Excrements, and remaineth in the Putrefactions, some good spirits, especially where they proceed from Creatures that are very hot. But it may be also joyned with a further cause, which is more subtil; and it is, that the Senses love not to be over-pleased, but to have a commixture of somewhat that is in it self ingrate. Certainly, we see how Discords in Musick, falling upon Concords, make the sweetest strains: And we see again what strange tastes delight the taste; as *Red-herrings*, *Caviare*, *Parmesan*, *&c.* And it may be the same holdeth in smells. For those kinde of smells that we have mentioned are all strong, and do pull and vellicate the Sense. And we finde also, that places where men Urine commonly have some smell of Violets. And Urine, if one hath eaten Nutmeg, hath so too.

The

834.
Experiment Solitary, touching the *Corporeal Substance of Smells.*

835.
Experiment Solitary, touching *Fetide and Fragrant Odors.*

The ſlothful, general, and indefinite Contemplations and Notions of the *Elements,* and their Conjugations of the Influences of *Heaven,* of *Hot, Cold, Moiſture, Drought, Qualities Active, Paſive* and the like, have ſwallowed up the true *Paſſages,* and *Proceſſes,* and *Affects,* and *Conſiſtencies of Matter,* and *Natural Bodies.* Therefore they are to be ſet aſide, being but notional, and ill limited ; and definite axioms are to be drawn out of meaſured inſtances, and ſo aſſent to be made to the more general axioms by Scale. And of theſe kindes of *Proceſſes* of *Nature,* and *Characters* of *Matter,* we will now ſet down ſome inſtances.

<table><tr><td valign="top">

836.
Experiment
Solitary,
touching the
Cauſes of Pu-
trefaction.

</td><td>

ALl Putrefactions come chiefly from the inward Spirits of the Body, and partly alſo from the *Ambient Body,* be it Air, Liquor, or whatſoever elſe. And this laſt, by two means; either by ingreſs of the ſubſtance of the Ambient Body into the Body putrefied, or by excitation and ſolicitation of the Body putrefied, and the parts thereof, by the Body Ambient. As for the received opinion, that Putrefaction is cauſed either by Cold, or Peregrine and Preternatural Heat, it is but nugation : For Cold in things inanimate, is the greateſt enemy that is to Putrefaction, though it extinguiſheth Vivification, which ever conſiſteth in Spirits attenuate, which the Cold doth congeal and coagulate. And as for the *Peregrine head,* it is thus far true. That if the proportion of the *Adventive heat,* be greatly predominant to the *Natural heat,* and *Spirits of the Body,* it tendeth to diſſolution, or notable alteration. But this is wrought by t miſſion, or Suppreſſion, or Suffocation of the Native Spirits, and alſo by the Diſordination and Diſcompoſure of the Tangible parts, and other paſſages of Nature, and not by a conflict of Heats.

</td></tr><tr><td valign="top">

837.
Experiment
Solitary,
touching
Bodies unper-
fectly mixt.

</td><td>

IN verſions or main Alterations of Bodies, there is a *Medium* between the Body, as it is at firſt, and the Body reſulting ; which *Medium* is *Corpus imperfectè Miſtum,* and is tranſitory, and not durable; as *Miſts Smoaks Vapors, Chylus* in the *Stomack, Living Creatures* in the firſt *Vivification* ; and the middle action which produceth ſuch *Imperfect Bodies,* is fitly called (by ſome of the *Ancients*) *Inquination* or *Inconcoction,* which is a kinde of *Putrefaction* ; for the parts are in confuſion till they ſettle one way or other.

</td></tr><tr><td valign="top">

838.
Experiment
Solitary,
touching
Concoction and
Crudity.

</td><td>

THe word *Concoction* or *Digeſtion,* is chiefly taken into uſe from Living Creatures, and their Organs, and from thence extended to Liquors and Fruits,&c. Therefore they ſpeak of Meat concocted, Urine and Excrements concocted; and the Four Digeſtions (in the Stomack, in the Liver, in the Arteries and Nerves, and in the ſeveral parts of the Body) are likewiſe called *Concoctions,* and they are all made to be the works of *Heat.* All which notions are but ignorant catches of a few things, which are moſt obvious to Mens obſervations. The conſtanteſt notion of *Concoction* is, that it ſhould ſignifie the degrees of alteration of one Body into another, from *Crudity* to *Perfect Concoction,* which is the ultimity of that action or proceſs. And while the Body to be converted and altered is too ſtrong for the efficient that ſhould convert or alter it, (whereby it reſiſteth, and holdeth faſt in ſome degree the firſt Form or Conſiſtence) it is (all that while) Crude and Inconcoct, and the Proceſs is to be called *Crudity* and *Inconcoction.* It is true, that Concoction is in great part the work of *Heat;* but not the work of *Heat* alone : For all things that further the *Converſion* or *Alteration* (as *Reſt,* Mixture of a Body already concocted, &c.) are alſo means to *Concoction.* And there

</td></tr></table>

there are of Concoction two Periods; the one Assimilation, or absolute Conversion and Subaction; the other Maturation: Whereof, the former is most conspicuous in the Bodies of *Living Creatures,* in which there is an *Absolute Conversion* and *Assimilation* of the *Nourishment* into the Body, and likewise in the Bodies of Plants; and again. in Metals, where there is a full Transmutation. The other (which is Maturation) is seen in Liquors and Fruits; wherein there is not desired, nor pretended, an utter Conversion, but onely an Alteration to that Form which is most sought for Mans use; as in Clarifying of Drinks, Ripening of Fruits, &c. But note, that there be two kindes of *Absolute Conversions.* The one is, when a Body is converted into another Body which was before; as when Nourishment is turned into Flesh: That is it which we call *Assimilation.* The other is, when the *Conversion* is into a Body meerly new, and which was not before; as if *Silver* should be turned to *Gold,* or *Iron* to *Copper.* And this *Conversion* is better called, by distinction sake, *Transmutation.*

THere are also divers other great alterations of Matter and Bodies, besides those that tend to *Concoction* and *Maturation;* for whatsoever doth so alter a Body, as it returneth not again to that it was, may be called *Alteratio Major:* As when Meat is Boiled, or Rosted, or Fried, &c. or when Bread and Meat are Baked; or when Cheese is made of Curds, or Butter of Cream, or Coals of Wood, or Bricks of Earth; and a number of others. But to apply *Notions Philosophical* to *Plebeian Terms;* or to say, where the *Notions* cannot fitly be reconciled, that there wanteth a *Term* or *Nomenclature* for it, (as the *Ancients* used) they be but shifts of *Ignorance:* For *Knowledge* will be ever a Wandring and Indigested thing, if it be but a commixture of a few *Notions* that are at hand, and occur, and not excited from sufficient number of instances, and those well collated.

The *Consistencies of Bodies* are very divers: *Dense, Rare, Tangible, Pneumatical; Volatile, Fixed; Determinate,* not *Determinate; Hard, Soft; Cleaving,* not *Cleaving; Congelable,* not *Congelable; Liquefiable,* not *Liquefiable; Fragile, Tough; Flexible, Inflexible; Tractile,* or to be drawn forth in length, *Intractile; Porous, Solide; Equal* and *Smooth, Vnequal; Venous* and *Fibrous,* and with *Grains, Entire,* and divers others. All which to refer to *Heat* and *Cold,* and *Moisture* and *Drought,* is a Compendious and Inutile *Speculation.* But of these see principally our *Abecedarium Naturæ,* and otherwise *sparsum* in this our *Sylva Sylvarum.* Nevertheless, in some good part, we shall handle divers of them now presently.

L*iquefiable* and *not Liquefiable* proceed from these causes. *Liquefaction* is ever caused by the Detention of the Spirits, which play within the Body, and open it. Therefore such Bodies as are more Turgid of Spirit, or that have their Spirits more streightly imprisoned, or again, that hold them better pleased and content, are *Liquefiable:* For these three *Dispositions of Bodies* do arrest the Emission of the Spirits. An example of the first two Properties is in Metals, and of the last in Grease, Pitch, Sulphur, Butter, Wax, &c. The Disposition not to Liquefie, proceedeth from the easie Emission of the Spirits, whereby the grosser parts contract; and therefore Bodies *jejune* of Spirits, or which part with their Spirits more willingly, are not *Liquefiable;* as Wood, Clay, Freestone, &c. But yet even many of those Bodies that will not melt, or will hardly melt, will notwithstanding soften; as Iron in the
Forge,

Forge, and a Stick bathed in hot Ashes, which thereby becometh more Flexible. Moreover, there are some Bodies which do *Liquefie* or dissolve by *Fire* ; as *Metals, Wax, &c.* and other Bodies which dissolve in Water, as *Salt, Sugar, &c.* The cause of the former proceedeth from the Dilatation of the Spirits by Heat : The cause of the latter proceedeth from the opening of the Tangible Parts, which desire to receive the Liquor. Again, there are some Bodies that dissolve with both; as *Gum, &c.* And those be such Bodies as on the one side have good store of Spirit, and on the other side have the Tangible parts indigent of Moisture; for the former helpeth to the dilating of the Spirits by the Fire, and the latter stimulateth the parts to receive the Liquor.

841.
Experiment Solitary, touching the Bodies Fragile and Tough.

OF Bodies some are Fragile, and some are Tough and not Fragile ; and in the breaking, some Fragile Bodies break but where the force is, some shatter and flie in many pieces. Of Fragility, the cause is an impotency to be extended ; and therefore Stone is more Fragile then Metal; and so Fictile Earth is more Fragile then Crude Earth, and Dry Wood then Green. And the cause of this unaptness to Extension, is the small quantity of Spirits (for it is the Spirit that furthereth the Extension or Dilatation of Bodies ;) and it is ever concomitant with Porosity, and with Driness in the Tangible parts. Contrariwise, Tough Bodies have more Spirits , and fewer Pores, and Moister Tangible parts : Therefore we see, that Parchment or Leather will stretch , Paper will not ; Woollen-Cloth will tenter, Linnen scarcely.

842.
Experiment Solitary, touching the Two kindes of Pneumaticals in Bodies.

ALL solid Bodies consist of Parts of two several *Natures* ; *Pneumatical,* and *Tangible* : And it is well to be noted, that the *Pneumatical Substance* is in some Bodies, the Native Spirit of the Body ; and in some other, plain Air that is gotten in; as in Bodies desiccate, by Heat, or Age : For in them, when the Native Spirit goeth forth, and the Moisture with it, the Air with time getteth into the Pores. And those Bodies are ever the more Fragile ; for the Native Spirit is more Yielding and Extensive (especially to follow the Parts) than Air. The Native Spirits also admit great diversity ; as Hot, Cold, Active, Dull, &c. Whence proceed most of the Vertues, and Qualities (as we call them) of Bodies : But the Air intermixt, is without Vertues, and maketh things insipid, and without any extimulation.

843.
Experiment Solitary, touching Concretion and Dissolution of Bodies.

THe *Concretion of Bodies* is (commonly) solved by the contrary; as Ice, which is congealed by Cold, is dissolved by Heat ; Salt and Sugar, which are excocted by Heat, are dissolved by Cold and Moisture. The cause is, for that these operations are rather returns to their former Nature, than alterations ; so that the contrary cureth. As for Oyl, it doth neither easily congeal with Cold, nor thicken with Heat. The cause of both Effects, though they be produced by contrary efficients, seemeth to be the same ; and that is, because the Spirit of the Oyl, by either means, exhaleth little : For the Cold keepeth it in, and the Heat (except it be vehement) doth not call it forth. As for Cold, though it take hold of the Tangible Parts, yet as to the Spirits, it doth rather make them swell, than congeal them : As when Ice is congealed in a Cup, the Ice will swell instead of contracting, and sometimes rift.

Of

OF Bodies, some (we see) are hard, and some soft: The hardness is caused (chiefly) by the Jejuneness of the Spirits; and their imparity with the Tangible parts: Both which, if they be in a greater degree, maketh them not onely hard, but fragile, and less enduring of pressures as *Steel, Stone. Glass, Dry Wood, &c.* Softness cometh (contrariwise) by the greater quantity of Spirits, (which ever helpeth to induce yielding and cession;) and by the more equal spreding of the Tangible parts, which thereby are more sliding, and following; as in *Gold, Lead, Wax, &c.* But note, that soft Bodies (as we use the word) are of two kindes; the one, that easily giveth place to another Body, but altereth not Bulk by rising in other places; and therefore we see that Wax, if you put any thing into it, doth not rise in Bulk, but onely giveth place: For you may not think, that in Printing of Wax, the Wax riseth up at all; but onely the depressed part giveth place, and the other remaineth as it was. The other that altereth Bulk in the Cession, as Water, or other Liquors, if you put a Stone, or any thing into them, they give place (indeed) easily, but then they rise all over; which is a false Cession, for it is in place, and not in Body.

ALl *Bodies Ductile,* and *Tensile,* (as Metals) that will be drawn into Wires; Wool, and Tow that will be drawn into Yarn or Thred; have in them the Appetite of Not discontinuing, strong; which maketh them follow the force that pulleth them out; and yet so, as not discontinue or forsake their own Body. Viscous Bodies (likewise) as *Pitch, Wax, Birdlime, Cheese* toasted, will draw forth and roap. But the difference between Bodies fibrous, and Bodies viscous, is plain; For all **Wooll**, and **Tow**, and **Cotton**, and **Silk** (especially raw Silk) have, besides their desire of continuance, in regard of the tenuity of their Thred, a greediness of Moisture, and by Moisture to joyn and incorporate with other Thred, especially, if there be a little Wreathing, as appeareth by the twisting of Thred, and the practice of Twirling about of Spindles. And we see also, that Gold and Silver Thred cannot be made without Twisting.

THe differences of impressible, and not impressible; figurable, and not figurable; mouldable, and not mouldable; scissible, and not scissible; and many other Passions of Matter, are Plebeian Notions, applied unto the Instruments and Uses which Men ordinarily practise; but they are all but the effects of some of these causes following, which we will enumerate without applying them, because that would be too long. The first is the Cession, or not Cession of Bodies, into a smaller space, or room, keeping the outward Bulk, and not flying up. The second is, the stronger or weaker Appetite, in Bodies, to continuity, and to flie discontinuity. The third is, the disposition of Bodies, to contract, or not contract; and again, to extend, or not extend. The fourth is, the small quantity, or great quantity of the Pneumatical in Bodies. The fifth is, the nature of the Pneumatical, whether it be Native Spirit of the Body, or common Air. The sixth is, the Nature of the Native Spirits in the Body, whether they be Active, and Eager, or Dull, and Gentle. The seventh is, the emission or detension of the Spirits in Bodies. The eighth is, the dilatation or contraction of the Spirits in Bodies, while they are detained. The nineth is, the collocation of the Spirits in Bodies, whether the collocation be equal or unequal; and again, whether the Spirits be coacervate or diffused. The tenth is, the density or rarity of the Tangible parts.

R   The

the eleventh is the Equality or Inequality of the Tangible parts ; the twelfth is the Difgeftion or Crudity of the Tangible parts ; the thirteenth is the Nature of the Matter, whether Sulphureous, or Mercurial, or Watry, or Oily, Dry, and Terreftrial; or Moift and Liquid ; which Natures of Sulphureous and Mercurial, feem to be Natures Radical and Principal ; the fourteenth is the placing of the Tangible parts, in Length or Tranfverfe (as it is in the Warp, and the Woof of Textiles;) more inward or more outward, &c. The fifteenth is the Porofity or Imporofity betwixt the Tangible parts, and the greatnefs or fmallnefs of the Pores ; the fixteenth is the Collocation and pofture of the Pores. There may be more caufes, but thefe do occur for the prefent.

<table><tr><td>847.
Experiment
Solitary,
touching
Induration by
Sympathy.</td><td>TAke Lead and melt it, and in the midft of it, when it beginneth to congeal, make a little dint or hole, and put Quick-filver wrapped in a piece of Linnen into that hole, and the Quick-filver will fix, and run no more, and endure the Hammer. This is a noble inftance of Induration, by confent of one Body with another, and Motion of Excitation to imitate ; for to afcribe it onely to the vapor of the Lead, is lefs probable. Quære, whether the fixing may be in fuch a degree, as it will be figured like other Metals ? For if fo, you may make Works of it for fome purpofes, fo they come not near the Fire.</td></tr></table>

T Ake Lead and melt it, and in the midft of it, when it beginneth to congeal, make a little dint or hole, and put Quick-filver wrapped in a piece of Linnen into that hole, and the Quick-filver will fix, and run no more, and endure the Hammer. This is a noble inftance of Induration, by confent of one Body with another, and Motion of Excitation to imitate ; for to afcribe it onely to the vapor of the Lead, is lefs probable. *Quære,* whether the fixing may be in fuch a degree, as it will be figured like other Metals ? For if fo, you may make Works of it for fome purpofes, fo they come not near the Fire.

848.
Experiment
Solitary,
touching
*Honey and
Sugar.*

S Ugar hath put down the ufe of Honey, infomuch, as we have loft thofe obfervations and preparations of Honey, which the *Ancients* had, when it was more in price. Firft, it feemeth, that there was in old time Tree-honey, as well as Bee-honey, which was the Year or Blood iffuing from the Tree ; infomuch, as one of the *Ancients* relateth, that in *Tribefond,* there was Honey iffuing from the Box-trees, which made Men mad. Again, in ancient time, there was a kinde of Honey, which either of the own Nature, or by Art, would grow as hard as Sugar, and was not fo lufhious as ours ; they had alfo a Wine of Honey, which they made thus. They crufhed the Honey into a great quantity of Water, and then ftrained the liquor, after they boiled it in a Copper to the half ; then they poured it into Earthen Veffels for a fmall time, and after turned it into Veffels of Wood, and kept it for many years. They have alfo, at this day in *Ruffia,* and thofe Northern Countreys, *Mead Simple,* which (well made and feafoned) is a good wholefom Drink, and very clear. They ufe alfo in *Wales,* a Compound Drink of *Mead,* with Herbs and Spices. But mean while it were good, in recompence of that we have loft in Honey, there were brought in ufe a *Sugar-Mead* (for fo we may call it) though without any mixture at all of Honey ; and to brew it, and keep it ftale, as they ufe *Mead* ; for certainly, though it would not be fo abfterfive, and opening, and folutive a Drink as *Mead* ; yet it will be more grateful to the Stomack, and more lenitive, and fit to be ufed in fharp Difeafes: For we fee, that the ufe of Sugar in Beer and Ale, hath good effects in fuch cafes.

849.
Experiment
Solitary,
touching the
*Finer forts of
Bafe Metals.*

I T is reported by the *Ancients,* that there is a kinde of *Steel,* in fome places, which would polifh almoft as white and bright as Silver. And that there was in *India* a kinde of Brafs, which (being polifhed) could fcarce be difcerned from Gold. This was in the Natural Ure, but I am doubtful, whether Men have fufficiently refined Metals, which we count Bafe : As, whether Iron, Brafs, and Tin, be refined to the height ? But when they

come

come to such a fineness, as serveth the ordinary use, they try no
further.

THere have been found certain *Cements* under *Earth*, that are very soft,
and yet taken forth in othe Sun, harden as hard as Marble: There are
also ordinary Quarries in *Sommerset-shire*, which in the Quarry cut soft to
any bigness, and in the Building prove firm, and hard.

*L*Iving *Creatures* (generally) do change their Hair with Age, turning to
be Gray and White; as is seen in *Men*, though some earlier, some
later; in *Horses*, that are Dappled and turn White; in *Old Squirrels*, that turn
Grisly, and many others. So do some *Birds*; as *Cygnets* from Gray turn
White; *Hawks* from Brown turn more White: And some *Birds* there be,
that upon their Moulting, do turn Colour; as *Robin-Redbreast*, after their
Moulting grow to be Red again by degrees; so do *Gold-Finches* upon the
Head. The cause is, for that Moisture doth (chiefly) colour Hair and Feathers; and Dryness turneth them Gray and White; now Hair in Age waxeth Dryer, so do Feathers. As for Feathers, after Moulting, they are young
Feathers, and so all one as the Feathers of young Birds. So the Beard is
younger than the Hair of the Head, and doth (for the most part) wax hoary
later. Out of this ground, a Man may devise the Means of altering the colour of *Birds*, and the Retardation of Hoary-Hairs. But of this see the *Fifth
Experiment*.

*T*He difference between *Male* and *Female*, in some *Creatures*, is not to be
discerned, otherwise than in the parts of Generation; as in *Horses* and
Mares, *Dogs* and *Bitches*, *Doves* he and she, and others. But some differ in
magnitude, and that diversly: For in most the *Male* is the greater, as in *Man*,
Pheasants, *Peacocks*, *Turkies*, and the like; and in some few, as in *Hawks*, the
Female. Some differ in the Hair and Feathers, both in the quantity, crispation,
and colours of them; as *He-Lions* are Hirsute, and have great Mains; the
She's are smooth like *Cats*. *Bulls* are more crisp upon the Forehead than *Cows*;
the *Peacock*, and *Phesant-cock*, and *Goldfinch-cock*, have glorious and fine colours;
the *Hens* have not. Generally, the he's in *Birds* have the fairest Feathers. Some
differ in divers features; as *Bucks* have Horns, *Does* none; *Rams* have more
wreathed Horns than *Ewes*; *Cocks* have great Combs and Spurs, *Hens* little
or none; *Boars* have great Fangs, *Sows* much less; the *Turkey-cock* hath great
and swelling Gills the *Hen* hath less; *Men* have generally deeper and stronger
voices than *Women*. Some differ in faculty, as the *Cock* amongst *Singing Birds*,
are the best singers. The chief cause of all these (no doubt) is, for that the
Males have more strength of heat than the *Females*: which appeareth manifestly in this, that all young Creatures *Males* are like *Females*, and so are *Eunuchs*, and *Gelt Creatures* of all kindes, liker *Females*. Now heat causeth greatness of growth, generally, where there is moisture enough to work upon:
But if there be found in any *Creature* (which is seen rarely) an over-great
heat in proportion to the moisture, in them the *Female* is the greater; as
in *Hawks* and *Sparrows*. And if the heat be ballanced with the moisture,
then there is no difference to be seen between *Male* and *Female*; as in the
instances of *Horses* and *Dogs*. We see also, that the Horns of *Oxen* and *Cows*,
for the most part, are larger than the *Bulls*, which is caus'd by abundance
of moisture, which in the Horns of the *Bull* faileth. Again, Heat causeth
Pilosity, and Crispation; and so likewise Beards in *Men*. It also expelleth

the margin notes:

850.
Experiment
Solitary,
touching
Cements and
Quarries.

851.
Experiment
Solitary,
touching the
Altering of
the Colour of
Hairs and
Feathers.

852.
Experiment
Solitary,
touching the
Differences of
Living Crea-
tures Male
and Female.

finer moisture, which want of heat cannot expel ; and that is the cause of the beauty and variety of Feathers : Again, Heat doth put forth many Excrescences, and much solid matter, which want of Heat cannot do. And this is the cause of Horns, and of the greatness of them ; and of the greatness of the Combs, and Spurs of Cocks, Gills of Turkey-Cocks, and Fangs of Boars. Heat also dilateth the Pipes and Organs which causeth the deepness of the Voice. Again, Heat refineth the Spirits, and that causeth the Cock-singing Bird to excel the Hen.

853.
Experiment
Solitary,
touching the
*Comparative
Magnitude of
Living Creatures.*

THere be Fishes greater than any Beasts ; as the *Whale* is far greater than the *Elephant*. And Beasts are (generally) greater than Birds. For Fishes, the cause may be, that because they live not in the Air, they have not their moisture drawn, and soaked by the Air, and Sun-Beams. Also they rest always, in a manner, and are supported by the Water ; whereas Motion and Labor do consume. As for the greatness of Beasts, more than of Birds, it is caused, for that Beasts stay longer time in the Womb than Birds, and there nourish, and grow ; whereas in Birds, after the Egg laid, there is no further growth, or nourishment from the Female ; for the sitting doth vivifie, and not nourish.

854.
Experiment
Solitary,
touching
*Excussation of
Fruits,*

WE have partly touched before the Means of producing Fruits, without Coars, or Stones. And this we add further, that the cause must be abundance of moisture ; for that the Coar, and Stone, are made of a dry Sap : And we see, that it is possible to make a Tree put forth onely in Blossom without Fruit ; as in *Cherries* with double Flowers, much more in Fruit without Stones, or Coars. It is reported, that a Cions of an Apple, grafted upon a Colewort-stalk, sendeth forth a great Apple without a Coar. It is not unlikely, that if the inward Pith of a Tree were taken out, so that the Juyce came onely by the Bark, it would work the effect. For it hath been observed, that in Pollards, if the Water get in on the top, and they become hollow, they put forth the more. We add also, that it is delivered for certain by some, that if the Cions be grafted, the small ends downwards, it will make Fruit have little, or no Coars, and Stones.

855.
Experiment
Solitary,
touching the
*Melioration of
Tobacco.*

TObacco is a thing of great price, if it be in request. For an Acre of it will be worth (as is affirmed) Two hundred pounds by the year towards charge. The charge of making the Ground, and otherwise, is great, but nothing to the profit. But the *English Tobacco* hath small credit, as being too dull and earthy : Nay, the *Virginian Tobacco*, though that be in a hotter climate, can get no credit for the same cause. So that a tryal to make *Tobacco* more Aromatical, and better concocted here in *England*, were a thing of great profit. Some have gone about to do it, by drenching the *English Tobacco*, in a Decoction or Infusion of *Indian Tobacco*. But those are but sophistications and toyes ; for nothing that is once perfect, and hath run his race, can receive much amendment ; you must ever resort to the beginnings of things for Melioration. The way of Maturation of *Tobacco* must (as in other Plants) be from the Heat, either of the Earth, or of the Sun. We see some leading of this in Musk-Melons, which are sown upon a hot Bed, dunged below, upon a Bank turned upon the South Sun, to give Heat by Reflection ; laid upon Tiles, which increaseth the Heat ; and covered with Straw, to keep them from Cold ; they remove them also, which addeth some Life : And by these helps they become as good in

England, as in *Italy*, or *Provence*. These and the like means may be tried in *Tobacco*. Enquire also of the steeping of Roots, in some such Liquor, as may give them Vigor to put forth strong.

HEat of the Sun, for the Maturition of Fruits; yea, and the heat of Vivification of Living Creatures, are both represented and supplied by the heat of Fire; and likewise, the heats of the Sun, and life, are represented one by the other. *Trees*, set upon the Backs of Chimneys, do ripen Fruit sooner. *Vines*, that have been drawn in at the Window of a Kitchin, have sent forth Grapes, ripe a moneth (at least) before others. *Stoves*, at the Back of Walls, bring forth *Oreuges* here with us. *Eggs*, as is reported by some, have been hatched in the warmth of an *Oven*. It is reported by the *Ancients*, that the *Estrich* layeth her Eggs under Sand, where the heat of the Sun discloseth them.

BArley in the Boyling swelleth not much; *Wheat* swelleth more, *Rize* extreamly; insomuch, as a quarter of a Pint (unboiled) will arise to a Pint boiled. The cause (no doubt) is, for that the more close and compact the Body is, the more it will dilate. Now *Barley* is the most hollow, *Wheat* more solid than that, and *Rize* most solid of all. It may be also, that some Bodies have a kinde of Lentor, and more depertible nature than others; as we see it evident in colouration; for a small quantity of *Saffron*, will tinct more, than a very great quantity of *Bresil*, or *Wine*.

FRuit groweth sweet by Rowling or Pressing them gently with the Hand; as *Rowling Pears*, *Damasins*, &c. By *Rottenness*; as *Medlars*, *Services*, *Sloes*, *Heps*, &c. By *Time*; as *Apples*, *Wardens*, *Pomegranates*, &c. By certain special *Maturations*; as by laying them in *Hay*, *Straw*, &c. And by *Fire*; as in *Roasting*, *Stewing*, *Baking*, &c. The cause of the sweetness by Rowling, and Pressing is, Emollition, which they properly enduce; as in beating of *Stock-fish*, *Flesh*, &c. By *Rottenness* is, for that the Spirits of the Fruit, by Putrefaction, gather heat, and thereby disgest the harder part: For in all Putrefactions there is a degree of heat. By *Time* and *Keeping* is, because the Spirits of the Body, do ever feed upon the tangible parts, and attenuate them. By several Maturations is, by some degree of heat. And by Fire is, because it is the proper work of Heat to refine, and to incorporate; and all sourness consisteth in some grosness of the Body: And all incorporation doth make the mixture of the Body, more equal, in all the parts, which ever enduceth a milder taste.

OF *Fleshes*, some are edible; some, except it be in Famine, not. As those that are not edible, the cause is, for that they have (commonly) too much bitterness of taste; and therefore those Creatures, which are fierce and cholerick, are not edible; as *Lions*, *Wolves*, *Squirrels*, *Dogs*, *Foxes*, *Horses*, &c. As for *Kine*, *Sheep*, *Goats*, *Deer*, *Swine*, *Conneys*, *Hares*, &c. We see they are milde, and fearful. Yet it is true, that *Horses* which are Beasts of courage, have been and are eaten by some Nations; as the *Scythians* were called *Hippophagi*; and the *Chineses* eat *Horf-flesh* at this day; and some Gluttons have used to have Colts-flesh baked. In *Birds*, such as are *Carnivora*, and Birds of Prey, are commonly no good Meat; but the reason is, rather the Cholerick Nature of those Birds, than their Feeding upon Flesh; for *Puits*, *Gulls*, *Shorelers*, *Ducks*, do feed upon Flesh, and yet are

good

Side notes:

856 Experiment Solitary, touching Several Heats working the same Effects.

857. Experiment Solitary, touching Swelling and Dilatation in Boyling.

858. Experiment Solitary, touching the Dulcoration of Fruits.

859. Experiment Solitary, touching Flesh Edible, and not Edible.

good Meat. And we fee, that thofe Birds which are of Prey, or feed upon Flefh, are good Meat, when they are very Young; as *Hawks*, *Rooks*, out of the Neft, *Owls*. Mans flefh is not eaten. The Reafons are three.

Firft, Becaufe Men in Humanity do abhor it.

Secondly, Becaufe no Living Creature, that dieth of it felf, is good to eat; and therefore the *Cannibals* (themfelves) eat no Mans flefh, of thofe that die of themfelves, but of fuch as are flain.

The third is, Becaufe there muft be generally) fome difparity between the Nourifhment, and the Body nourifhed; and they muft not be overnear, or like: Yet we fee, that in great weaknefſes and Confumptions, Men have been fuftained with Womans Milk. And *Picinus* fondly (as I conceive) advifeth, for the Prolongation of Life, that a Vein be opened in the Arm of fome wholfome young man, and the blood to be fucked. It is faid, that Witches do greedily eat Mans flefh, which if it be true, befides a devillifh Appetite in them, it is likely to proceed; for that Mans flefh may fend up high and pleafing Vapors, which may ftir the Imagination, and Witches felicity is chiefly in Imagination, as hath been faid.

860.
Experiment Solitary, touching the *Salamander*.

THere is an ancient received Tradition of the *Salamander*, that it liveth in the Fire, and hath force alfo to extinguifh the fire. It muft have two things, if it be true, to this operation. The one, a very clofe skin, whereby flame, which in the midft is not fo hot, cannot enter: For we fee, that if the Palm of the Hand be anointed thick with White of Eggs, and then *Aquavita* be poured upon it, and enflamed, yet one may endure the flame a pretty while. The other is fome extream cold and quenching vertue, in the Body of that Creature which choaketh the fire. We fee that Milk quencheth Wildfire better than VVater, becaufe it entreth better.

861.
Experiment Solitary, touching the Contrary operations of Time, upon Fruits and Liquors.

TIme doth change Fruit (as *Apples*, *Pears*, *Pomegranates*, &c.) from more four to more fweet; but contrariwife, Liquors (even thofe that are of the Juyce of Fruit) from more fweet to more four; as, *Wort*, *Muft*, *New Verjuyce*, &c. The caufe is, the Congregation of the Spirits together; for in both kindes, the Spirit is attenuated by Time; but in the firft kinde, it is more diffufed, and more maftered by the groffer parts, which the Spirits do but digeft: But in Drinks the Spirits do reign, and finding lefs oppofition of the parts, become themfelves more ftrong, which caufeth alfo more ftrength in the Liquor; fuch, as if the Spirits be of the hotter fort, the Liquor becometh apt to burn; but in time, it caufeth likewife, when the higher Spirits are evaporated more fournefs.

862.
Experiment Solitary, touching Blows and Bruifes.

IT hath been obferved by the *Ancients*, that Plates of Metal, and efpecially of Brafs, applied prefently to a blow, will keep it down from fwelling. The caufe is Repercuſſion, without Humectation, or entrance of any Body: For the Plate hath onely a virtual cold, which doth not fearch into the hurt; whereas all Plaifters and Oynments do enter. Surely, the caufe that blows and bruifes induce fwellings is, for that the Spirits reforting to fuccor the part that laboreth, draw alfo the humors with them: For we fee, that it is not the repulfe, and the return of the humor in the part ftrucken that caufeth it; for that Gouts, and Toothachs caufe fwelling, where there is no Percuffion at all.

The

THe nature of the *Orris* Root, is almost singular, for there be few odo-riferous Roots; and in those that are in any degree sweet, it is but the same sweetness with the Wood or Leaf: But the *Orris* is not sweet in the Leaf, neither is the flower any thing so sweet as the Root. The Root seem-eth to have a tender dainty heat, which when it cometh above ground to the Sun, and the Air, vanisheth: For it is a great Mollifier, and hath a smell like a Violet.

IT hath been observed by the *Antients* that a great Vessel full, drawn into Bottles; and then the Liquor put again into the Vessel, will not fill the Vessel again, so full as it was, but that it may take in more Liquor; and that this holdeth more in Wine, than in Water. The cause may be trivial, name-ly, by the expence of the Liquor, in regard some may stick to the sides of the Bottles: But there may be a cause more subtil, which is, that the Liquor in the Vessel, is not so much compressed, as in the Bottle; because in the Vessel, the Liquor meeteth with Liquor chiefly; but in the Bottles, a small quantity of Liquor meeteth with the sides of the Bottles, which compress it so, that it doth not open again.

WAter being contiguous with Air cooleth it, but moisteneth it not, except it Vapor. The cause is, for that Heat and Cold have a Virtual Transition, without Communication of substance, but moisture not; and to all madefaction there is required an imbibition: But where the Bodies are of such several Levity, and Gravity, as they mingle not, they can follow no imbibition. And therefore, Oyl likewise, lieth at the top of the Water, without commixture: And a drop of Water running swiftly over a Straw or smooth Body, wetteth not.

STarlight Nights, yea, and bright *Moonshine Nights*, are colder than *Cloudy Nights*. The cause is, the driness and Fineness of the Air, which thereby becometh more piercing and sharp; and therefore great Continents are colder than Islands. And as for the *Moon*, though it self inclineth the Air to moisture, yet when it shineth bright, it argueth the Air is dry. Also close Air is warmer than open Air, which (it may be) is, for that the true cause of cold, is an expiration from the Globe of the Earth, which in open places is stronger. And again, Air it self, if it be not altered by that expiration, is not without some secret degree of heat; as it is not likewise without some secret degree of Light: For otherwise Cats, and Owls, could not see in the Night; but that Air hath a little Light, proportionable to the Visual Spirits of those Creatures.

THe Eyes do move one and the same way; for when one Eye moveth to the Nostril, the other moveth from the Nostril. The cause is Motion of Consent, which in the Spirits and Parts Spiritual, is strong. But yet use will induce the contrary; for some can squint when they will. And the common Tradition is, that if Children be set upon a Table with a Candle behinde them, both Eyes will move outwards, as affecting to see the Light, and so induce Squinting.

We see more exquisitely with one Eye shut, than with both open. The cause is, for that the Spirits Visual unite themselves more, and so become
stronger.

863.
Experiment
Solitary,
touching the
Orris Root.

864
Experiment
Solitary,
touching the
*Compression of
Liquors.*

865.
Experiment
Solitary,
touching the
*Working of
Water upon
Air contigu-
ous.*

866.
Experiment
Solitary,
touching the
*Nature of
Air.*

867.
Experiments
in Consort,
touching the
*Eyes and
Sight.*

868.

stronger. For you may see, by looking in a Glass, that when you shut one Eye, the Pupil of the other Eye, that is open, dilateth.

869. The Eyes, if the sight meet not in one Angle, see things double. The cause is, for that seeing two things, and seeing one thing twice, worketh the same effect: And therefore a little Pellet, held between two Fingers, laid a cross, seemeth double.

870. Pore-blind Men, see best in the dimmer light; and likewise have their sight stronger near hand, than those that are not Poreblind, and can read and write smaller Letters. The cause is, for that the Spirits Visual, in those that are Poreblind, are thinner and rarer, than in others; and therefore the greater light disperseth them. For the same cause they need contracting; but being contracted, are more strong than the Visual Spirits of ordinary eyes are; as when we see thorow a Level; the sight is the stronger: And so is it, when you gather the Eye-lids somewhat close: And it is commonly seen in those that are Poreblind, that they do much gather the eye-lids together. But old Men, when they would see to read, put the Paper somewhat a far off. The cause is, for that old Mens Spirits Visual, contrary to those of Pore-blind Men unite not, but when the object is at some good distance from their Eyes.

871. Men see better when their Eyes are over-against the Sun or a Candle, if they put their Hand a little before their Eye. The Reason is, for that the Glaring of the Sun, or the Candle, doth weaken the Eye; whereas the Light circumfused is enough for the Perception. For we see, that an over-light maketh the Eyes dazel, insomuch as perpetual looking against the Sun, would cause Blindness. Again, if Men come out of a great light, into a dark room; and contrariwise, if they come out of a dark room into a light room, they seem to have a Mist before their Eyes, and see worse than they shall do after they have staid a little while, either in the light, or in the dark. The cause is, for that the Spirits Visual, are upon a sudden change disturbed, and put out of order; and till they be recollected, do not perform their Function well. For when they are much dilated by light, they cannot contract suddenly; and when they are much contracted by darkness, they cannot dilate suddenly. And excess of both these, (that is, of the Dilatation, and Contraction of the Spirits Visual) if it be long, destroyeth the Eye. For as long looking against the Sun, or Fire, hurteth the Eye by Dilatation, so curious painting in small Volumes, and reading of small Letters, do hurt the Eye by contraction.

872. It hath been observed, that in Anger the Eyes wax red; and in Blushing, not the Eyes, but the Ears, and the parts behind them. The cause is, for that in Anger, the Spirits ascend and wax eager; which is most easily seen in the Eyes, because they are translucide, though withal it maketh both the Cheeks, and the Gils red; but in Blushing, it is true, the Spirits ascend likewise to succor, both the Eyes and the Face, which are the parts that labor: But when they are repulsed by the Eyes, for that the Eyes, in shame do put back the Spirits that ascend to them, as unwilling to look abroad: For no Man, in that passion, doth look strongly, but dejectedly; and that repulsion from the Eyes, diverteth the Spirits and heat more to the Ears, and the parts by them.

873. The objects of the Sight, may cause a great pleasure and delight in the Spirits, but no pain or great offence; except it be by Memory, as hath been said. The Glimpses and Beams of Diamonds that strike the Eye, *Indian Feathers,* that have glorious colours, the coming into a fair Garden, the coming

into

into a fair Room richly furnished; a beautiful perſon, and the like, do delight and exhilarate the Spirits much. The reaſon, why it holdeth not in the offence is, for that the Sight is moſt ſpiritual of the Senſes, whereby it hath no object groſs enough to offend it. But the cauſe (chiefly) is, for that there be no active objects to offend the Eye. For Harmonical Sounds, and Diſcordant Sounds, are both Active and Poſitive; ſo are ſweet ſmells, and ſtinks; ſo are bitter, and ſweets, in taſtes; ſo are over-hot, and over-cold, in touch; but blackneſs, and darkneſs, are indeed but privatives; and therefore have little or no Activity. Somewhat they do contriſtate, but very little.

W**Ater** of the *Sea*, or otherwiſe, looketh blacker when it is moved; and whiter when it reſteth. The cauſe is, for that by means of the Motion, the Beams of Light paſs not ſtraight, and therefore muſt be darkned; whereas when it reſteth, the Beams do paſs ſtraight. Beſides, ſplendor hath a degree of whiteneſs, eſpecially, if there be a little repercuſſion; for a Looking-Glaſs with the Steel behinde, looketh whiter than Glaſs ſimple. This *Experiment* deſerveth to be driven further, in trying by what means Motion may hinder Sight.

S**Hell-fiſh** have been by ſome of the *Ancients*, compared and ſorted with the *Inſects*; but I ſee no reaſon why they ſhould, for they have Male, and Female, as other Fiſh have; neither are they bred of Putrefaction, eſpecially ſuch as do move. Neverthelẽſs it is certain, that Oyſters, and Cockles, and Muſſels, which move not, have not diſcriminate Sex. *Quære*, in what time, and how they are bred? It ſeemeth, that Shells of Oyſters are bred where none were before; and it is tryed, that the great Horſe-Muſle, with the fine ſhell, that breedeth in Ponds, hath bred within thirty years: But then, which is ſtrange, it hath been tryed, that they do not onely gape and ſhut as the Oyſters do, but remove from one place to another.

T**He** *Senſes* are alike ſtrong, both on the right ſide, and on the left; but the Limbs on the right ſide are ſtronger. The cauſe may be, for that the Brain, which is the Inſtrument of Senſe, is alike on both ſides; but Motion, and habilities of moving, are ſomewhat holpen from the Liver, which lieth on the right ſide. It may be alſo, for that the Senſes are put in exerciſe, indifferently on both ſides from the time of our Birth; but the Limbs are uſed moſt on the right ſide, whereby cuſtom helpeth: For we ſee, that ſome are left-handed, which are ſuch as have uſed the left-hand moſt.

F**Rictions** make the parts more fleſhy, and full: As we ſee both in Men, and in the Currying of Horſes, &c. The cauſe is, for that they draw greater quantity of Spirits and Blood to the parts; and again, becauſe they draw the Aliment more forcibly from within; and again, becauſe they relax the Pores, and ſo make better paſſage for the Spirits, Blood, and Aliment: Laſtly, becauſe they diſſipate, and diſgeſt any Inutile, or Excrementitious moiſture, which lieth in the Fleſh; all which help Aſſimilation. *Frictions* alſo do, more fill and impinguate the Body, than Exerciſe. The cauſe is, for that in *Frictions*, the inward parts are at reſt; which in exerciſe are beaten (many times) too much: And for the ſame reaſon (as we have noted heretofore) Galliſlaves are fat and fleſhy, becauſe they ſtir the Limbs more, and the inward parts leſs.

All

873.
Experiment
Solitary,
touching
Globes ap-
pearing Flat
at distance.

ALl *Globes* a far off, appear flat. The cause is, for that distance, being a secundary object of light, is not otherwise discerned, than by more or less light; which disparity, when it cannot be discerned, all seemeth one: As it is (generally) in objects not distinctly discerned; for so Letters, if they be so far off, as they cannot be discerned, shew but as duskish Paper; and all Engravings and Embossings (a far off) appear p'ain.

879.
Experiment
Solitary,
touching
Shadows.

THe uttermost parts of *Shadows*, seem ever to tremble. The cause is, for that the little Moats which we see in the Sun, do ever stir, though there be no Wind; and therefore those moving, in the meeting of the Light and the Shadow, from the Light to the Shadow, and from the Shadow to the Light, do shew the shadow to move, because the *Medium* moveth.

880.
Experiment
Solitary,
touching the
Rowling and
Breaking of
the Seas.

SHallow and *Narrow Seas*, break more than deep and large. The cause is, for that the Impulsion being the same in both; where there is a greater quantity of Water, and likewise space enough, there the Water rouleth, and moveth, both more slowly, and with a sloper rise and fall: But where there is less Water, and less space, and the Water dasheth more against the bottom; there it moveth more swiftly, and more in Precipice: For in the breaking of the Waves, there is ever a Precipice.

881.
Experiment
Solitary,
touching the
Dulcoration of
Salt water.

IT hath been observed by the *Ancients*, that *Salt-water* boiled, or boiled and cooled again, is more potable, than of it self raw; and yet the taste of *Salt*, in Distillations by *Fire*, riseth not: For the Distilled Water will be fresh. The cause may be, for that the Salt part of the Water, doth partly rise into a kinde of Scum on the top, and partly goeth into a Sediment in the bottom; and so is rather a separation, than an evaporation. But it is too gross to rise into a vapor; and so is a bitter taste likewise: For simple distilled Waters of *Wormwood*, and the like, are not bitter.

882.
Experiment
Solitary,
touching the
Return of
Saltness in
Pits upon the
Sea-shore.

IT hath been set down before, that *Pits* upon the *Sea-shores* turn into fresh Water, by Percolation of the Salt through the Sand: But it is further noted, by some of the *Ancients*, that in some places of *Africk*, after a time, the Water in such Pits will become brakish again. The cause is, for that after a time, the very Sands, thorow which the *Salt-Water* passeth, become Salt; and so the Strainer it self is tincted with Salt. The remedy therefore is to dig still new Pits, when the old wax brackish; as if you would change your Strainer.

883.
Experiment
Solitary,
touching
Attraction by
Similitude of
Substance.

IT hath been observed by the *Ancients*, that *Salt-water* will dissolve *Salt* put into it, in less time, than Fresh Water will dissolve it. The cause may be, for that the Salt in the precedent Water, doth by similitude of Substance, draw the Salt new put in, unto it; whereby it diffuseth in the Liquor more speedily. This is a noble *Experiment*, if it be true; for it sheweth means of more quick and easie Infusions, and it is likewise a good instance of Attraction by Similitude of Substance. Try it with Sugar put into Water, formerly sugred, and into other Water unsugred.

884.
Experiment
Solitary,
touching
Attraction.

PUt *Sugar* into *Wine*, part of it above, part under the *Wine*; and you shall finde (that which may seem strange) that the *Sugar* above the *Wine*, will soften and dissolve sooner than that within the Wine. The cause is, for that
the

the Wine entreth that part of the Sugar which is under the Wine, by fimple Infufion or Spreding; but that part above the Wine is likewife forced
by Sucking: For all Spongy Bodies expel the Air, and draw in Liquor, if
it be contiguous; as we fee it alfo in Sponges, put part above the Water. It
is worthy the inquiry, to fee how you may make more accurate Infufions,
by help of Attraction.

W Ater in Wells is warmer in Winter than in Summer; and fo Air in
Caves. The caufe is, for that in the higher parts, under the Earth,
there is a degree of fome heat (as appeareth in fulphureous Veins, &c.)
which fhut clofe in (as in Winter) is the more; but if it perfpire (as it doth
in Summer) it is the lefs.

885.
Experiment
Solitary,
touching
Heat upon
Earth.

I T is reported, that amongft the *Leucadians*, in ancient time, upon a fuper-
ftition, they did ufe to precipitate a Man from a high Cliff into the Sea;
tying about him with ftrings, at fome diftance, many great Fowls; and fixing unto his Body divers Feathers fpred, to break the fall. Certainly many
Birds of good Wing (as *Kites*, and the like) would bear up a good weight
as they flie; and fpreding of Feathers thin and clofe, and in great bredth,
will likewife bear up a great weight, being even laid without tilting upon
the fides. The further extenfion of this Experiment for Flying, may be
thought upon.

886.
Experiment
Solitary,
touching
*Flying in the
Air.*

T Here is in fome places (namely, in *Cephalonia*) a little Shrub, which
they call *Holy Oak*, or *Dwarf Oak*. Upon the Leaves whereof there
rifeth a Tumor, like a Blifter; which they gather, and rub out of it, a certain red duft, that converteth (after a while) into Worms, which they kil
with Wine, (as is reported) when they begin to quicken: With this Duft
they Die Scarlet.

887.
Experiment
Solitary,
touching the
*Dye of Scar-
let.*

I N *Zant*, it is very ordinary, to make Men impotent, to accompany with
their Wives. The like is practifed in *Gafcony*, where it is called *Nover l'*
Eguillete. It is practifed alvvays upon the Wedding day. And in *Zant*, the
Mothers themfelves do it by vvay of prevention, becaufe thereby they hinder
other Charms, and can undo their ovvn. It is a thing the *Civil Law* taketh
knovvledge of, and therefore is of no light regard.

888.
Experiment
Solitary,
touching
Maleficiating.

I T is a common Experiment, but the caufe is miftaken. Take a Pot, (or
better a Glafs, becaufe therein you may fee the Motion) and fet a Candle
lighted in the Bottom of a Bafon of Water; and turn the Mouth of the Pot
or Glafs over the Candle, and it vvill make the Water rife. They afcribe it
to the dravving of heat, vvhich is not true: For it appeareth plainly to be
but a Motion of *Nexe*, vvhich they call *Ne detur vacuum*, and it proceedeth
thus; The Flame of the Candle as foon, as it is covered, being fuffocated
by the clofe Air, leffeneth by little and little: During vvhich time, there is
fome little afcent of Water, but not much; for the Flame occupying lefs
and lefs room, as it leffenet, the Water fucceedet. But upon the inftant
of the Candles going out, there is a fudden rife of a great deal of Water; for
that that the Body of the Flame filleth no more place, and fo the Air and
Water fucceed. It vvorketh the fame effect, if inftead of Water, you put
Flovver, or Sand, into the Bafon: Which fhevveth, that it is not the Flames
dravving the Liquor, as Nourifhment, as it is fuppofed; for all Bodies are
alike

889.
Experiment
Solitary,
touching the
*Rife of Water
by Means of
Flame.*

alike unto it, as it is ever in motion of *Nexe*; infomuch, as I have feen the
Glafs, being held by the hand, hath lifted up the Bafon, and all : The motion
of *Nexe* did fo clafp the bottom of the Bafon. That *Experiment*, when the
Bafon was lifted up, was made with Oyl, and not with Water. Neverthelefs
this this is true, that at the very firft fetting of the Mouth of the Glafs, upon
the bottom of the Bafon, it draweth up the Water a little, and then ftandeth
at a ftay, almoft till the Candles going out, as was faid. This may fhew fome
Attraction at firft; but of this we will fpeak more, when we handle Attracti-
ons by Heat.

Experiments
in Confort,
touching the
Influences of
the Moon.

OF the Power of the *Celeftial Bodies*, and what more fecret influences
they have, befides the two manifeft influences of Heat and Light, we
fhall fpeak, when we handle *Experiments* touching the *Celeftial Bodies* : Mean
while, we will give fome Directions for more certain Tryals of the Vertue
and Influences of the Moon, which is our neareft Neighbor.

The Influences of the Moon (moft obferved) are four ; the drawing
forth of Heat; the Inducing of Putrefaction; the increafe of Moifture ; the
exciting of the Motions of Spirits.

890.

For the drawing forth of Heat, we have formerly prefcribed to take
Water warm, and to fet part of it againft the Moon-beams, and part of it
with a Skreen between ; and to fee whether that which ftandeth expofed to
the Beams will not cool fooner. But becaufe this is but a fmall interpofition,
(though in the Sun we fee a fmall fhade doth much) it were good to try it
when the Moon fhineth, and when the Moon fhineth not at all; and with
Water warm in a Glafs-bottle as well as in a Difh, and with Cinders, and
with Iron red-hot, &c.

891.

For the inducing of Putrefaction, it were good to try it with Flefh or
Fifh expofed to the Moon-beams, and again expofed to the Air when the
Moon fhineth nor, for the like time, to fee whether will corrupt fooner;
and try it alfo with Capon, or fome other fowl laid abroad, to fee whether it
will mortifie and become tender fooner. Try it alfo with dead Flies or dead
Worms, having a little Water caft upon them, to fee whether will putrefie
fooner. Try it alfo with an Apple or Orenge, having holes made in their
tops, to fee whether will rot or mould fooner. Try it alfo with *Holland*
Cheefe, having Wine put into it, whether it will breed Mites fooner or
greater.

892.

For the increafe of Moifture, the opinion received is, that Seeds will
grow fooneft, and Hair, and Nails, and Hedges, and Herbs, cut, &c. will
grow fooneft, if they be fet or cut in the increafe of the Moon: Alfo, that
Brains in Rabits, Wood-cocks, Calves, &c. are fulleft in the Full of the
Moon ; and fo of Marrow in the Bones, and fo of Oyfters and Cockles ;
which of all the reft are the eafieft tried, if you have them in Pits.

893.

Take fome Seeds or Roots (as Onions, &c.) and fet fome of them immediately after the Change, and others of the fame kinde immediately after
the Full : Let them be as like as can be, the Earth alfo the fame as near as
may be, and therefore beft in Pots : Let the Pots alfo ftand where no Rain
or Sun may come to them, left the difference of the Weather confound the
Experiment. And then fee in what time the Seeds fet, in the increafe of the
Moon, come to a certain height, and how they differ from thofe that are fet
in the decreafe of the Moon.

It

It is like, that the Brain of Man waxeth moister and fuller upon the Full of the Moon; and therefore it were good for those that have moist Brains, and are great Drinkers, to take fume of *Lignum Aloes, Rosemary, Frankincense, &c.* about the Full of the Moon. It is like also, that the Humors in Mens Bodies increase and decrease, as the Moon doth; and therefore it were good to purge some day or two after the Full, for that then the Humors will not replenish so soon again.

As for the exciting of the motion of the Spirits, you must note, that the growth of Hedges, Herbs, Hair, &c. is caused from the Moon, by exciting of the Spirits; as well as by increase of the moisture. But for Spirits in particular, the great instance is in *Lunacies*.

There may be other secret effects of the influence of the Moon, which are not yet brought into observation. It may be, that if it so fall out, that the Wind be North or North-East, in the Full of the Moon, it increaseth Cold; and if South or South-West, it disposeth the Air for a good while to warmth and rain; which would be observed.

It may be that Children and young Cattel that are brought forth in the Full of the Moon, are stronger and larger then those that are brought forth in the Wane; and those also which are begotten in the Full of the Moon: So that it might be good Husbandry, to put Rams and Bulls to their Females somewhat before the Full of the Moon. It may be also, that the Eggs laid in the Full of the Moon, breed the better Bird; and a number of the like effects, which may be brought into observation. *Quare* also, whether great Thunders and Earth-quakes be not most in the Full of the Moon.

THe turning of Wine to Vinegar, is a kinde of Putrefaction; and in making of Vinegar, they use to set Vessels of Wine over against the Noon Sun, which calleth out the more Oily Spirits, and leaveth the Liquor more sour and hard. We see also, that Burnt-Wine is more hard and astringent then Wine unburnt. It is said, that *Cider* in Navigations under the Line ripeneth, when *Wine* or *Beer* soureth. It were good to set a Rundlet of *Verjuice* over against the Sun in Summer; as they do Vinegar, to see whether it will ripen and sweeten.

THere be divers Creatures that sleep all Winter; as the *Bear*, the *Hedg-hog*, the *Bat*, the *Bee, &c.* These all wax fat when they sleep, and egest not. The cause of their fattening, during their sleeping-time, may be the want of assimilating; for whatsoever assimilateth not to Flesh, turneth either to sweat or fat. These Creatures, for part of their sleeping time, have been observed not to stir at all; and for the other part, to stir, but not to remove, and they get warm and close places to sleep in. When the *Flemmings* wintred in *Nova Zembla*, the *Bears* about the middle of *November* went to sleep; and then the *Foxes* began to come forth, which durst not before. It is noted by some of the *Ancients*, that the She Bear-breedeth, and lieth in with her young during that time of Rest, and that a Bear big with young, hath seldom been seen.

SOme *Living Creatures* are procreated by Copulation between Male and Female, some by Putrefaction; and of those which come by Putrefaction, many do (nevertheless) afterwards procreate by Copulation. For the cause of both Generations: First, it is most certain, that the cause of all Vivi-

S

fication,

fication is a gentle and proportionable heat, working upon a glutinous and yielding substance ; for the heat doth bring forth Spirit in that substance, and the substance being gluttinous, produceth two effects ; the one, That the Spirit is detained, and cannot break forth ; the other, That the matter being gentle and yielding, is driven forwards by the motion of the Spirits, after some swelling into shape and members. Therefore all Sperm, all Menstruous substance, all matter whereof Creatures are produced by Putrefaction, have evermore a Closeness, Lentor, and Sequacity. It seemeth therefore that the Generation by Sperm onely, and by Putrefaction, have two different causes. The first is, for that Creatures which have a definite and exact shape (as those have which are procreated by Copulation) cannot be produced by a weak and casual heat ; nor out of matter, which is not exactly prepared according to the Species, The second is, for that there is a greater time required for Maturation of perfect Creatures ; for if the time required in Vivification be of any length, then the Spirit will exhale before the Creature be mature ; except it be inclosed in a place where it may have continuance of the heat, access of some nourishment to maintain it, and closeness that may keep it from exhaling ; and such places, or the Wombs and Matrices of the Females : And therefore all Creatures made of Putrefaction, are of more uncertain shape, and are made in shorter time, and need not so perfect an enclosure, though some closeness be commonly required. As for the Heathen opinion, which was, That upon great mutations of the World, perfect Creatures were first ingendred of Concretion, as well as Frogs, and Worms, and Flies, and such like, are now ; we know it to be vain : But if any such thing should be admitted, discoursing according to sense, it cannot be, except you admit of a *Chaos* first, and commixture of Heaven and Earth ; for the Frame of the World once in order, cannot effect it by any excess or casualty.

NATURAL HISTORY.

Century X.

THe Philofophy of *Pythagoras* (which was full of Super-ftition) did firft plant a Monftrous Imagination, which afterwards was, by the School of *Plato*, and others, watred and nourifhed. It was, That *the World was one entire perfeft Living Creature* ; infomuch, as *Apollonius* of *Tyana*, a *Pythagorean* Prophet, affirmed, That the Ebb-ing and Flowing of the Sea was the Refpiration of the World, drawing in Water as Breath, and putting it forth again. They went on, and inferred, That if the World were a Living Creature, it had a Soul and Spirit ; which alfo they held, calling it *Spiritus Mundi*, the Spirit or Soul of the World; by which, they did not intend *God*, (for they did admit of a *Deity* befides) but onely the Soul, or Effential Form of the Univerfe. This *Foundation* being laid, they might build upon it what they would ; for in a *Living Creature*, though never fo great (as for example, in a great Whale) the Senfe and the Affects of any one part of the Body inftantly make a Tranfcurfion throughout the whole Body : So that by this they did infinuate, that no diftance of place, nor want or indifpofition of Matter, could hinder Magical Operations ; but that (for example) we might here in *Europe* have Senfe and Feeling of that which was done in *China*; and likewife, we might work any effect without and againft Matter : And this not holden by the co-operation of Angels or Spirits but onely by the Unity and Harmony of Nature. There were fome alfo that ftaid not here, but went further, and held, That if the Spirit of Man (whom they call the *Microcofm*) do give a fit touch to the Spirit of the World, by ftrong Imaginations and Beliefs, it might command Nature ; for *Paracelfus*, and fome darkfome *Authors* of Magick, do afcribe to Imagination exalted the Power of Miracle-working Faith. With thefe vaft and bottomlefs Follies Men have been (in part) entertained.

But

But we, that hold firm to the Works of God, and to the Senſe, which is Gods Lamp, (*Lux ipſa Dei Spiraculum Hominis*) will enquire with all Sobriety and Severity, whether there be to be found in the Foot-ſteps of Nature any ſuch Tranſmiſſion and Influx of Immateriate Virtues ; and what the force of Imagination is, either upon the Body Imaginant, or upon another Body : Wherein it will be like that labor of *Hercules* in purging the Stable of *Augeas*, to ſeparate from Superſtitious and Magical Arts and Obſervations, any thing that is clean and pure Natural, and not to be either contemned or condemned. And although we ſhall have occaſion to ſpeak of this in more places then one, yet we will now make ſome entrance thereinto.

901.
Experiments in Conſort Monitory, touching Tranſmiſſion of Spirits, and the Force of Imagination.

MEn are to be admoniſhed, that they do not withdraw credit from the Operations by Tranſmiſſion of Spirits and Force of Imagination, becauſe the effects fail ſometimes. For as in Infection and Contagion from Body to Body, (as the Plague, and the like) it is moſt certain, that the Infection is received (many times) by the Body Paſſive, but yet is by the ſtrength and good diſpoſition thereof repulſed, and wrought out, before it be formed into a Diſeaſe ; ſo much more in Impreſſions from Minde to Minde, or from Spirit to Spirit, the Impreſſion taketh, but is encountred and overcome by the Minde and Spirit, which is Paſſive, before it work any manifeſt effect : And therefore they work moſt upon weak Mindes and Spirits ; as thoſe of Women, Sick Perſons, Superſtitious and fearful Perſons, Children, and young Creatures.

            Neſcio quis teneros oculus mihi faſcinat Agnos :

The *Poet* ſpeaketh not of Sheep, but of Lambs. As for the weakneſs of the Power of them upon Kings and Magiſtrates, it may be aſcribed (beſides the main, which is the Protection of God over thoſe that execute his place) to the weakneſs of the Imagination of the Imaginant ; for it is hard for a Witch or a Sorcerer to put on a belief, that they can hurt ſuch perſons.

902.

     Men are to be admoniſhed on the other ſide, that they do not eaſily give place and credit to theſe operations, becauſe they ſucceed many times: For the cauſe of this ſucceſs is (oft) to be truly aſcribed unto the force of Affection and Imagination upon the Body Agent, and then by a ſecondary means it may work upon a diverſe Body. As for example, If a man carry a *Planets Seal* or a *Ring*, or ſome part of a *Beaſt*, believing ſtrongly that it will help him to obtain his *Love*, or to keep him from danger of hurt in *Fight*, or to prevail in a *Sute*, *&c.* it may make him more active and induſtrious ; and again, more confident and perſiſting, then otherwiſe he would be. Now the great effects that may come of Induſtry and Perſeverance (eſpecially in civil buſineſs) who knoweth not ? For we ſee audacity doth almoſt binde and mate the weaker ſort of Mindes ; and the ſtate of Humane Actions is ſo variable, that to try things oft, and never to give over, doth wonders : Therefore it were a meer fallacy and miſtaking to aſcribe that to the Force of Imagination upon another Body, which is but the Force of Imagination upon the proper Body ; for there is no doubt but that Imagination and vehement Affection work greatly upon the Body of the Imaginant, as we ſhall ſhew in due place.

903.

     Men are to be admoniſhed, that as they are not to miſtake the cauſes of theſe Operations, ſo much leſs they are to miſtake the Fact or Effect, and raſhly to take that for done which is not done. And therefore, as divers wiſe Judges have preſcribed and cautioned, Men may not too raſhly

believe

believe the Confession of Witches, nor yet the evidence against them: For the Witches themselves are Imaginative, and believe oft-times they do that which they do not ; and people are credulous in that point; and ready to impute Accidents and Natural operations to Witchcraft. It is worthy the observing, that both in ancient and late times, (as in the *Thessalian* Witches, and the meetings of Witches that have been recorded by so many late Confessions) the great wonders which they tell of carrying in the Air, transforming themselves into other Bodies, &c. are still reported to be wrought, not by Incantation or Ceremonies, but by Ointments and Anointing themselves all over. This may justly move a Man to think, that these Fables are the effects of Imagination ; for it is certain, that Ointments do all (if they be laid on any thing thick) by stopping of the Pores, shut in the Vapor, and send them to the head extreamly. And for the particular Ingredients of those Magical Ointments, it is like they are opiate and soporiferous. For Anointing of the Forehead, Neck, Feet, Back-bone, we know is used for procuring dead sleeps. And if any Man say, that this effect would be better done by inward potions ; answer may be made, that the Medicines which go to the Ointments are so strong, that if they were used inwards, they would kill those that use them ; and therefore they work potently, though outwards.

We will divide the several kindes of the operations by transmission of Spirits and Imagination, which will give no small light to the *Experiments* that follow. All operations by transmission of Spirits and Imagination have this, that they work at distance, and not at touch ; and they are these being distinguished.

The first is, The Transmission or Emission of the thinner and more airy parts of Bodies, as in Odors and Infections; and this is, of all the rest, the most corporeal. But you must remember withal, that there be a number of those Emissions, both unwholesome and wholesome, that give no smell at all : For the Plague many times when it is taken giveth no-sent at all, and there be many good and healthful Airs, as they appear by Habitation, and other proofs, that differ not in Smell from other Airs. And under this head you may place all Imbibitions of Air, where the substance is material, odor-like, whereof some nevertheless are strange, and very suddenly diffused ; as the alteration which the Air receiveth in *Egypt* almost immediately upon the rising of the River of *Nilus*, whereof we have spoken.

The second is, the Transmission or Emission of those things that we call Spiritual Species, as Visibles and Sounds; the one whereof we have handled, and the other we shall handle in due place. These move swiftly and at great distance, but then they require a *Medium* well disposed, and their Transmission is easily stopped.

The third is, the Emissions which cause Attraction of certain Bodies at distance; wherein though the Loadstone be commonly placed in the first rank. yet we think good to except it, and refer it to another Head : But the drawing of *Amber*, and *Jet*, and other *Electrick Bodies*, and the Attraction in *Gold* of the *Spirit* of *Quick-silver* at distance, and the Attraction of Heat at distance, and that of fire to *Naphtha*, and that of some Herbs to Water, though at distance, and divers others, we shall handle ; but yet not under this present title, but under the title of Attraction in general.

904.

905.

906.

S 3   The

907. The fourth is, the Emission of Spirits, and Immateriate Powers and Virtues, in those things which work by the universal configuration and Sympathy of the World; not by Forms, or Celestial Influxes, (as is vainly taught and received) but by the Primitive Nature of Matter, and the seeds of things. Of this kinde is (as we yet suppose) the working of the Loadstone, which is by consent with the Globe of the Earth; of this kinde is the motion of Gravity, which is by consent of dense Bodies with the Globe of the Earth: Of this kinde is some disposition of Bodies to Rotation, and particularly from East to West; of which kinde, we conceive the Main Float and Refloat of the Sea is, which is by consent of the Universe, as part of the *Diurnal Motion.* These *Immateriate Virtues* have this property differing from others, that the diversity of the *Medium* hindreth them not, but they pass through all *Mediums*, yet at determinate distances. And of these we shall speak, as they are incident to several Titles.

908. The fifth is, the Emission of Spirits; and this is the principal in our intention to handle now in this place, namely, the operation of the Spirits of the minde of Man upon other Spirits; and this is of a double nature; the operation of the Affections, if they be vehement; and the operation of the Imagination, if it be strong. But these two are so coupled, as we shall handle them together; for when an envious or amorous aspect doth infect the Spirits of another, there is joyned both Affection and Imagination.

909. The sixth is, the influxes of the *Heavenly Bodies*, besides those two manifest ones of Heat and Light. But these we will handle, where we handle the *Celestial Bodies* and *Motions.*

910. The seventh is, the operations of *Sympathy*, which the Writers of *Natural Magick* have brought into an *Art or Precept*; and it is this, That if you desire to super-induce any Virtue or Disposition upon a Person, you should take the *Living Creature*, in which that Virtue is most eminent and in perfection; of that Creature you must take the parts wherein that Virtue chiefly is collocate. Again, you must take the parts in the time, and act when that Virtue is most in exercise, and then you must apply it to that part of Man, wherein that Virtue chiefly consisteth. As if you would super-induce *Courage* and *Fortitude*, take a *Lion*, or a *Cock*; and take the *Heart*, *Tooth*, or *Paw* of the *Lion*; or the *Heart*, or *Spur* of the *Cock*: Take those parts immediately after the *Lion* or the *Cock* have been in fight, and let them be worn upon a Mans heart or wrist. Of these and such like *Sympathies* we shall speak under this present Title.

911. The eighth and last is, an Emission of Immateriate Virtues, such as we are a little doubtful to propound it is so prodigious, but that it is so constantly avouched by many: And we have set it down as a Law to our selves, to examine things to the bottom; and not to receive upon credit, or reject upon improbabilities, until there hath passed a due examination. This is the *Sympathy* of *Individuals*; for as there is a *Sympathy of Species*, so (it may be) there is a *Sympathy* of *Individuals*; that is, that in things, or the parts of things that have been once contiguous or entire, there should remain a transmission of Virtue from the one to the other, as between the Weapon and the Wound. Whereupon is blazed abroad the operation of *Vnguentum Teli*, and so of a piece of Lard, or stick of Elder, &c. That if part of it be consumed or putrefied, it will work upon the other parts severed. Now we will pursue the instances themselves.

The

THe *Plague* is many times taken without manifest sense, as hath been
said; and they report, that where it is found it hath a sent of the smell
of a Mellow Apple, and (as some say) of May-flowers: And it is also received, that smells of Flowers that are Mellow and Lushious, are ill for the
Plague; as *White Lilies, Cowslips,* and *Hyacinths.*

912.
Experiments in Consort, touching Emission of Spirits in Vapor or Exhalation Odor-like

The *Plague* is not easily received by such as continually are about them
that have the *Plague,* as *Keepers* of the Sick, and Physicians; nor again by
such as take *Antidotes,* either inward (as *Mithridate, Juniper-berries, Rue, Leaf,*
and *Seed, &c.*) or outward (as *Angelica, Zedoary,* and the like in the Mouth;
Tar, Galbanum, and the like in Perfume:) Nor again, by old people, and such
as are of a dry and cold complexion. On the other side, the *Plague* taketh
soonest hold of those that come out of a fresh Air, and of those that are fasting, and of Children; and it is likewise noted to go in a Blood more then
to a stranger.

913.

The most pernicious Infection, next the *Plague,* is the smell of the Goal,
when Prisoners have been long, and close, and nastily kept; whereof we
have had in our time, experience twice or thrice, when both the *Judges* that
sat upon the Goal, and numbers of those that attended the business, or were
present, sickned upon it, and died. Therefore it were good wisdom, that in
such cases the Goal were aired before they be brought forth.

914.

Out of question, if such foul smells be made by Art, and by the Hand,
they consist chiefly of Mans flesh, or sweat, putrefied; for they are not those
stinks which the Nostrils straight abhor and expel, that are most pernicious,
but such Airs as have some similitude with Mans body, and so insinuate themselves, and betray the Spirits. There may be great danger in using such Compositions in great Meetings of People within Houses; as in *Churches,* at *Ar-
raignments,* at *Plays* and *Solemnities,* and the like: For poysoning of Air is no
less dangerous, then poysoning of Water, which hath been used by the *Turks*
in the Wars, and was used by *Emanuel Comnenus* towards the Christians, when
they passed through his Countrey to the *Holy Land.* And these empoysonments of Air are the more dangerous in Meetings of People, because the
much breath of People doth further the reception of the Infection. And
therefore when any such thing is feared, it were good those publick places
were perfumed before the *Assemblies.*

915.

The empoysonment of particular persons by Odors, hath been reported
to be in perfumed Gloves, or the like. And it is like they mingle the poyson
that is deadly with some smells that are sweet, which also maketh it
the sooner received. *Plagues* also have been raised by Anointings of the
Chinks of Doors, and the like; not so much by the touch, as for that it is
common for men, when they finde any thing wet upon their fingers, to
put them to their Nose; which men therefore should take heed how they
do. The best is, that these Compositions of Infectious Airs cannot be made
without dangers of death to them that make them; but then again, they
may have some *Antidotes* to save themselves; so that men ought not to be
secure of it.

916.

There have been in divers Countreys great *Plagues* by the putrefaction of
great swarms of *Grashoppers* and *Locusts,* when they have been dead and cast
upon heaps.

917.

It hapneth oft in *Mines,* that there are Damps which kill either by
Suffocation, or by the poysonous nature of the *Minerals*; and those that
deal

918.

deal much in Refining, or other works about Metals and Minerals, have their Brains hurt and ſtupefied by the Metalline Vapors. Amongſt which, it is noted, that the Spirits of Quick-ſilver ever flie to the Skull, Teeth, or Bones; inſomuch, as *Gilders* uſe to have a piece of Gold in their Mouth to draw the Spirits of Quick-ſilver; which Gold afterwards they finde to be whitned. There are alſo certain Lakes and Pits, ſuch as that of *Avernus*, that poyſon Birds (as is ſaid) which flie over them, or Men that ſtay too long about them.

919.   The Vapor of Char-coal or Sea-coal in a cloſe room, hath killed many; and it is the more dangerous, becauſe it cometh without any ill ſmell, but ſtealeth on by little and little, inducing onely faintneſs, without any manifeſt ſtrangling. When the *Dutchmen* wintred at *Nova Zembla*, and that they could gather no more ſticks, they fell to make fire of ſome Sea-coal they had, wherewith (at firſt) they were much refreſhed; but a little after they had ſat about the fire, there grew a general ſilence and lothneſs to ſpeak amongſt them; and immediately after, one of the weakeſt of the Company fell down in a ſwoon: Whereupon, they doubting what it was, opened their door to let in Air, and ſo ſaved themſelves. The effect (no doubt) is wrought by the inſpiſſation of the Air, and ſo of the Breath and Spirits. The like enſueth in Rooms newly Plaiſtred, if a fire be made in them; whereof no leſs Man then the Emperor *Jovinianus* died.

920   *Vide the Experiment* 803. Touching the *Infectious Nature* of the Air upon the firſt Showers after long Drought.

921.   It hath come to paſs, that ſome *Apothecaries*, upon ſtamping of *Coloquintida*, have been put into a great Scouring by the Vapor onely.

922.   It hath been a practice to burn a *Pepper* they call *Guinny-Pepper*, which hath ſuch a ſtrong Spirit, that it provoketh a continual *Sneezing* in thoſe that are in the Room.

923.   It is an Ancient Tradition, that *Blear Eyes* infect *Sound Eyes*; and that a *Menſtruous Woman* looking in a Glaſs doth ruſt it: Nay, they have an opinion, which ſeemeth fabulous, That *Menſtruous Women* going over a *Field* or *Garden*, do *Corn* and *Herbs* good by killing the Worms.

924.   The Tradition is no leſs ancient, that the *Baſilisk* killeth by aſpect; and that the *Woolf*, if he ſeeth a *Man* firſt, by aſpect ſtriketh a *Man* hoarſe.

925.   *Perfumes* convenient do dry and ſtrengthen the Brain, and ſtay Rheums and Defluxions; as we finde in Fume of *Roſemary* dried, and *Lignum Aloes*, and *Calamus* taken at the Mouth and Noſtrils. And no doubt, there be other Perfumes that do moiſten and refreſh, and are fit to be uſed in Burning Agues, Conſumptions, and too much wakefulneſs; ſuch as are *Roſe-water*, *Vinegar*, *Lemmon-pills*, *Violets*, the Leaves of *Vines* ſprinkled with a little *Roſe-water*, &c.

926.   They do uſe in ſudden Faintings and Swoonings, to put a Handkerchief with Roſe-water, or a little Vinegar to the Noſe, which gathereth together again the Spirits, which are upon point to reſolve and fall away.

927.   *Tobacco* comforteth the Spirits, and diſchargeth wearineſs; which it worketh, partly by opening, but chiefly by the opiate virtue, which condenſeth the Spirits. It were good therefore to try the taking of Fumes by Pipes (as they do in *Tobacco*) of other things, as well to dry and comfort, as for other intentions. I wiſh tryal be made of the drying Fume of *Roſemary* and *Lignum Aloes*, before mentioned in Pipe; and ſo of *Nutmegs* and *Folium Indum*, &c.

                                                      The

The following of the Plough hath been approved for refreshing the Spirits, and procuring Appetite; but to do it in the Ploughing for Wheat or Rye is not so good, because the Earth hath spent her sweet breath in Vegetables put forth in Summer. It is better therefore to do it when you sow Barley. But because Ploughing is tied to Seasons, it is best to take the Air of the Earth new turned up by digging with the Spade, or standing by him that diggeth. *Gentlewomen* may do themselves much good by kneeling upon a Cushion, and Weeding. And these things you may practise in the best Seasons; which is ever the early Spring, before the Earth putteth forth the Vegetables, and in the sweetest Earth you can chuse. It would be done also when the Dew is a little off the Ground, lest the Vapor be too moist. I knew a great Man that lived long, who had a clean Clod of Earth brought to him every morning as he late in his Bed; and he would hold his head over it a good pretty while. I commend also sometimes in digging of new Earth, to pour in some Malmsey or Greek Wine, that the Vapor of the Earth and Wine together may comfort the Spirits the more; provided always it be not taken for a Heathen Sacrifice or Libation to the Earth.

They have in *Physick* use of *Pomanders*, and knots of Powders for drying of Rheums, comforting of the Heart, provoking of Sleep, &c. for though those things be not so strong as Perfumes, yet you may have them continually in your hand, whereas Perfumes you can take but at times; and besides, there be divers things that breath better of themselves then when they come to the Fire; as *Nigella Romana*, the Seed of *Melanthium, Amomum, &c.*

There be two things which (inwardly used) do cool and condense the Spirits; and I wish the same to be tried outwardly in Vapors. The one is *Nitre;* which I would have dissolved in Malmsey, or Greek Wine, and so the smell of the Wine taken; or, if you would have it more forcible, pour of it upon a Fire-pan well heated, as they do *Rose-water* and *Vinegar.* The other is, the distilled Water of Wilde Poppey; which I wish to be mingled at half with *Rose-water*, and so taken with some mixture of a few *Cloves* in a Perfuming-pan. The like would be done with the distilled Water of Saffron-Flowers.

Smells of *Musk*, and *Amber*, and *Civit*, are thought to further Venereous Appetite; which they may do by the refreshing and calling forth of the Spirits.

Incense and Niderous smells (such as were of *Sacrifices*) were thought to intoxicate the Brain, and to dispose men to devotion; which they may do by a kinde of sadness and contristation of the Spirits, and partly also by Heating and Exalting them. We see that amongst the Jews, the principal perfume of the Sanctuary was forbidden all common uses.

There be some Perfumes prescribed by the Writers of *Natural Magick*, which procure pleasant Dreams; and some others (as they say) that procure Prophetical Dreams, as the Seeds of *Flax, Fleawort, &c.*

It is certain, that Odors do in a small degree, nourish, especially the Odor of Wine; and we see Men an hungred do love to smell hot Bread. It is related, that *Democritus* when he lay a dying, heard a Woman in the House complain, that she should be kept from being at a Feast and Solemnity (which she much desired to see) because there would be a Corps in the House: Whereupon he caused Loaves of new Bread to be sent for, and opened them, and poured a little Wine into them, and so kept himself alive with the

the Odor of them till the Feast was past. I knew a Gentleman that would fast (sometimes) three or four, yea, five days, without Meat, Bread, or Drink; but the same Man used to have continually a great Wisp of Herbs that he smelled on, and amongst those Herbs some esculent Herbs of strong sent, as *Onions, Garlick, Leeks,* and the like.

935.　They do use for the Accident of the *Mother* to burn Feathers, and other things of ill Odor; and by those ill smells the rising of the Mother is put down.

936.　There be Airs which the Physicians advise their Patients to remove unto in *Consumptions,* or upon recovery of long sicknesses, which (commonly) are plain Champaigns, but Grasing, and not over-grown with Heath, or the like; or else Timber-shades, as in Forests, and the like. It is noted also, that Groves of Bays do forbid Pestilent Airs; which was accounted a great cause of the wholesome Air of *Antiochia.* There be also some Soyls that put forth Odorate Herbs of themselves, as *VVilde Thyme, VVilde Marjoram, Penny-royal, Camomile;* and in which, the *Bryar-Roses* smell almost like *Musk-Roses;* which (no doubt) are signs that do discover an excellent Air.

937.　It were good for men to think of having healthful Air in their Houses; which will never be, if the Rooms be low-roofed, or full of Windows and Doors; for the one maketh the Air close, and not fresh; and the other, maketh it exceeding unequal, which is a great enemy to health. The Windows also should not be high up to the Roof (which is in use for Beauty and Magnificence) but low. Also Stone-walls are not wholesome; but Timber is more wholesome, and especially Brick; nay, it hath been used by some with great success, to make their Walls thick, and to put a Lay of Chalk between the Bricks to take away all dampishness.

938.
Experiment
Solitary,
touching the
Emissions of
Spiritual Species, which
affect the
Senses.

THese Emissions (as we said before) are handled, and ought to be handled by themselves, under their proper Titles; that is, Visibles, and Audibles, each apart: In this place, it shall suffice to give some general Observations common to both. First, they seem to be Incorporeal. Secondly, they work swiftly. Thirdly, they work at large distances. Fourthly, in curious varieties. Fifthly, they are not effective of any thing, nor leave any work behinde them, but are energies meerly; for their working upon mirrors and places of Echo doth not alter any thing in those Bodies; but it is the same Action with the Original, onely repercussed. And as for the shaking of Windows, or rarifying the Air by great noises, and the Heat caused by Burning-Glasses, they are rather Concomitants of the Audible and Visible Species, then the effects of them. Sixthly, they seem to be of so tender and weak a Nature, as they affect onely such a Rare and Attenuate Substance as is the Spirit of Living Creatures.

939.
Experiments
in Consort,
touching
Emission of
Immateriate
Virtues from
the Mindes
and Spirits of
Men, either by
Affections or
by Imaginations, or by other
Impressions.

IT is mentioned in some Stories, that where Children have been exposed or taken away young from their Parents, and that afterward they have approached to their Parents presence, the Parents (though they have not known them) have had a secret Joy, or other Alteration thereupon.

940.　There was an *Egyptian Soothsayer* that made *Antonius* believe, that his *genius* (which otherwise was brave and confident) was, in the presence of *Octavianus Cæsar,* poor and cowardly; and therefore, he advised him to absent himself (as much as he could) and remove far from him. The *Soothsayer* was thought to be suborned by *Cleopatra,* to make him live in *Egypt,* and other
remote

remote places from *Rome*. Howſoever, the conceit of a predominant or maſtering Spirit of one Man over another is ancient, and received ſtill, even in vulgar opinion.

There are conceits, that ſome Men that are of an ill and melancholly nature, do incline the company into which they come, to be ſad and ill diſpoſed; and contrariwiſe, that others that are of a jovial nature do diſpoſe the company to be merry and chearful : And again, that ſome Men are lucky to be kept company with, and employed, and others unlucky. Certainly it is agreeable to reaſon, that there are at the leaſt ſome light effluxions from Spirit to Spirit when Men are in preſence one with another, as well as from Body to Body.

It hath been obſerved, that old Men have loved young company, and been converſant continually with them, have been of long life ; their Spirits (as it ſeemeth) being recreated by ſuch company. Such were the Ancient Sophiſts and Rhetoricians, which ever had young Auditors and Diſciples ; as *Gorgias, Protagoras, Iſocrates, &c.* who lived till they were an hundred years old ; and ſo likewiſe did many of the *Grammarians* and *School-maſters* : Such as was *Orbilius, &c.*

Audacity and confidence doth, in civil buſineſſes, ſo great effect, as a Man may (reaſonably) doubt, that beſides the very daring, and earneſtneſs, and perſiſting, and importunity, there ſhould be ſome ſecret binding and ſtooping of other Mens ſpirits to ſuch perſons.

The Affections (no doubt) do make the Spirits more powerful and active, and eſpecially thoſe Affections which draw the Spirits into the Eyes ; which are two, Love and Envy, which is called *Oculus Malus*. As for Love, the *Platoniſts* (ſome of them) go ſo far, as to hold, That the Spirit of the Lover doth paſs into the Spirits of the perſon loved, which cauſeth the deſire of return into the Body whence it was emitted, whereupon followeth that appetite of contract and conjunction which is in Lovers. And this is obſerved likewiſe, that the Aſpects that procure Love, are not gazings, but ſudden glances and dartings of the Eye. As for Envy, that emitteth ſome malign and poiſonous Spirits, which take hold of the Spirit of another ; and is likewiſe of greateſt force, when the Caſt of the Eye is oblique. It hath been noted alſo, That it is moſt dangerous, where the envious Eye is caſt upon perſons in glory, and triumph, and joy. The reaſon whereof is, for that at ſuch times the Spirits come forth moſt into the outward parts, and ſo meet the percuſſion of the envious eye more at hand ; and therefore it hath been noted, That after great triumphs, Men have been ill diſpoſed for ſome days following. We ſee the opinion of Faſcination is ancient for both effects, of procuring Love, and ſickneſs cauſed by Envy ; and Faſcination is ever by the Eye. But yet if there be any ſuch infection from Spirit to Spirit, there is no doubt, but that it worketh by preſence, and not by the Eye alone, yet moſt forcibly by the Eye.

Fear and Shame are likewiſe infective : For we ſee that the ſtarting of one, will make another ready to ſtart, and when one man is out of countenance in a company, others do likewiſe bluſh in his behalf.

Now we will ſpeak of the *Force of Imagination* upon other *Bodies*, and of the means to exalt and ſtrengthen it. Imagination, in this place, I underſtand to be the repreſentation of an Individual Thought. Imagination is of three kindes ; the firſt, joyned with *Belief* of that which is to come; the ſecond, joyned with *Memory* of that which is paſt; and the third is, of *Things preſent*, or as if they were preſent : For I comprehend in this, Imaginations feigned,

941.

942.

943.

944.

945.

feigned, and at pleasure : As if one should imagine such a Man to be in the Vestments of a *Pope*, or to have Wings. I single out for this time that which is with *Faith* or *Belief* of that which is to come. The Inquisition of this Subject in our way (which is by Induction) is wonderful hard, for the things that are reported are full of Fables ; and new *Experiments* can hardly be made but with extream Caution, for the Reason which we will after declare.

The *Power of Imagination* is in three kindes. The first, upon the Body of the imaginant, including likewise the Childe in the Mothers Womb. The second is, the power of it upon dead bodies, as Plants, Wood, Stone, Metal, &c. The third is, the power of it upon the Spirits of Men and Living Creatures. And with this last we will onely meddle.

The *Probleme* therefore is, Whether a Man constantly and strongly believing that such a thing shall be, (as that such an one will love him, or that such an one will grant him his request, or that such an one shall recover a sickness, or the like) it doth help any thing to the effecting of the thing it self. And here again we must warily distinguish ; for it is not meant (as hath been partly said before) that it should help by making a man more stout, or more industrious ; (in which kinde, constant belief doth much) but meerly by a secret operation, or binding, or changing the Spirit of another. And in this it is hard (as we began to say) to make any new experiment ; for I cannot command my self to believe what I will, and so no tryal can be made. Nay it is worse, for whatsoever a Man imagineth doubtingly, or with fear, must needs do hurt, if Imagination have any power at all ; for a Man representeth that oftner that he feareth, then the contrary.

The help therefore is, for a Man to work by another, in whom he may create belief, and not by himself, until himself have found by experience, that Imagination doth prevail ; for then experience worketh in himself Belief, if the Belief that such a thing shall be joyned with a Belief, that his Imagination may procure it.

946.

For example, I related one time to a Man that was curious and vain enough in these things, *That I saw a kinde of Jugler that had a Pair of Cards, and vvould tell a man vvhat Card he thought.* This pretended *Learned Man* told me, it was a mistaking in me. *For* (said he) *it vvas not the knovvledge of the Mans thought (for that is proper to God) but it vvas the inforcing of a thought upon him, and binding his Imagination by a stronger, that he could think no other Card.* And thereupon he asked me a Question or two, which I thought he did but cunningly, knowing before what used to be the feats of the *Jugler. Sir,* (said he) *do you remember vvhether he told the Card the Man thought himself, or bad another to tell it ?* I answered, (as was true) *That he bad another tell it.* Whereunto he said, *So I thought : For* (said he) *himself could not have put on so strong an Imagination, but by telling the other the Card (vvho believed, that the Jugler vvas some strange man, and could do strange things) that other man caught a strong Imagination.* I hearkned unto him, thinking for a vanity he spake prettily. Then he asked me another Question : Saith he, *Do you remember vvhether he bad the Man think the Card first, and aftervvards told the other Man in his Ear what he should think ; or else, that he did whisper first in the Mans Ear that should tell the Card, telling, That such a Man should think such a Card, and after bad the Man think a Card ?* I told him, (as was true) *That he did first whisper the Man in the Ear, that such a Man should think such a Card.* Upon this, the *Learned Man* did much exult and please himself. saying, *Lo, you may see that my opinion is right : For if the Man had thought first, his thought had been fixed ; but the other imagining first, bound his thought.* Which though it did somewhat sink with me, yet I

made

made it lighter then I thought, and said, *I thought it was confederacy between the Jugler, and the two Servants*; though (indeed) I had no reason so to think. for they were both my Fathers servants, and he had never plaid in the House before. The *Jugler* also did cause a Garter to be held up; and took upon him to know that such an one should point in such a place of the Garter, as it should be near so many Inches to the longer end, and so many to the shorter; and still he did it by first telling the imaginer, and after bidding the actor think.

Having told this Relation, not for the weight thereof, but because it doth handsomly open the nature of the Question, I return to that I said, That *Experiments of Imagination* must be practised by others, and not by a Mans self. For there be three means to fortifie Belief; the first is Experience, the second is Reason, and the third is Authority. And that of these which is far the most potent, is Authority: For Belief upon Reason or Experience will stagger.

For Authority, it is of two kindes: Belief in an Art, and Belief in a Man. And for things of Belief in an Art, a Man may exercise them by himself; but for Belief in a Man, it must be by another. Therefore if a Man believe in Astrology, and finde a figure prosperous; or believe in Natural Magick, and that a Ring with such a Stone, or such a piece of a Living Creature carried, will do good, it may help his Imagination; but the Belief in a Man is far the more active. But howsoever all Authority must be out of a Mans self, turned (as was said) either upon an Art, or upon a Man; and where Authority is from one Man to another, there the second must be Ignorant, and not learned, or full of thoughts: And such are (for the most part) all Witches and superstitious persons; whose beliefs, tied to their Teachers and Traditions, are no whit controlled either by Reason or Experience: And upon the same reason, in Magick they use (for the most part) Boys and young People; whose spirits easiliest take Belief and Imagination.

Now to fortifie Imagination, there be three ways: The Authority whence the Belief is derived; Means to quicken and corroborate the Imagination; and Means to repeat it and refresh it.

947.

For the Authority we have already spoken. As for the second, namely, the Means to quicken and corroborate the Imagination, we see what hath been used in Magick, (if there be in those practices any thing that is purely Natural) as Vestments, Characters, Words, Seals, some parts of Plants, or Living Creatures, Stones, choice of the Hour, Gestures and Motions; also Incenses and Odors; choice of Society, which increaseth Imagination, Diets and Preparations for some time before. And for Words; there have been ever used, either barbarous words of no sense, lest they should disturb the Imagination; or words of similitude, that may second and feed the Imagination: And this was ever as well in Heathen Charms, as in Charms of later times. There are used also Scripture words, for that the Belief that Religious Texts and Words have power, may strengthen the Imagination. And for the same reason Hebrew words (which amongst us is counted the holy Tongue, and the words more mystical) are often used.

948.

For the refreshing of the Imagination (which was the third Means of Exalting it) we see the practices of Magick; as in Images of Wax, and the like, that should melt by little and little, or some other things buried in Muck, that should putrefie by little and little, or the like: For so oft as the Imaginant doth think of those things, so oft doth he represent to his Imagination the effect of that he desireth.

949.

T

If

950.

If there be any power in Imagination, it is less credible that it should be so incorporeal and immateriate a Virtue, as to work at great distances, or through all *Mediums*, or upon all Bodies; but that the distance must be competent, the *Medium* not adverse, and the Body apt and proportionate. Therefore if there be any operation upon Bodies in absence by Nature, it is like to be conveyed from Man to Man, as *Fame* is: As if a *Witch* by Imagination should hurt any afar off, it cannot be naturally, but by working upon the Spirit of some that cometh to the *Witch*, and from that party upon the Imagination of another, and so upon another, till it come to one that hath resort to the party intended; and so by him, to the party intended himself. And although they speak, that it sufficeth to take a Point, or a piece of the Garment, or the Name of the party, or the like; yet there is less credit to be given to those things, except it be by working of evil spirits.

The *Experiments* which may certainly demonstrate the power of Imagination upon other Bodies, are few or none; for the *Experiments* of *Witchcraft* are no clear proofs, for that they may be by a tacite operation of malign Spirits; we shall therefore be forced in this Inquiry, to resort to new *Experiments*, wherein we can give onely Directions of Tryals, and not any *Positive Experiments*. And if any man think that we ought to have staid till we had made *Experiment* of some of them our selves, (as we do commonly in other Titles) the truth is, that these Effects of Imagination upon other Bodies, have so little credit with us, as we shall try them at leisure: But in the mean time we will lead others the way.

951.

When you work by the Imagination of another, it is necessary that he by whom you work have a precedent opinion of you that you can do strange things, or that you are a Man of Art, as they call it; for else the simple affirmation to another, that this or that shall be, can work but a weak impression in his Imagination.

952.

It were good, because you cannot discern fully of the strength of Imagination in one Man, more then another, that you did use the Imagination of more then one, that so you may light upon a strong one. As if a Physician should tell three or four of his Patients servants that their Master shall surely recover.

953.

The Imagination of one that you shall use (such is the variety of Mens mindes) cannot be always alike constant and strong; and if the success follow not speedily, it will faint and lose strength. To remedy this, you must pretend to him whose Imagination you use several degrees of Means by which to operate: As to prescribe him, that every three days, if he finde not the success apparent, he do use another Root, or part of a Beast, or Ring, &c. as being of more force; and if that fail, another; and if that, another, till seven times. Also you must prescribe a good large time for the effect you promise; as if you should tell a servant of a sick man, that his Master shall recover, but it will be fourteen days ere he findeth it apparently, &c. All this to entertain the Imagination, that it waver less.

954.

It is certain, that potions or things taken into the Body, Incenses and Perfumes taken at the Nostrils, and oyntments of some parts, do (naturally) work upon the Imagination of him that taketh them. And therefore it must needs greatly cooperate with the Imagination of him whom you use, if you prescribe him, before he do use the Receit for the Work which he desireth, that he do take such a Pill, or a spoonful of Liquor, or burn such an Incense, or anoint his Temples, or the Soles of his Feet, with such an Oyntment or Oyl: And you must chuse for the Composition of such Pill, Perfume, or

Oynt-

Oyntment, such Ingredients as do make the Spirits a little more grofs or muddy, whereby the Imagination will fix the better.

The Body Paffive, and to be wrought upon, (I mean not of the Imaginant) is better wrought upon (as hath been partly touched) at fome times then at others; As if you fhould prefcribe a fervant about a fick perfon, (whom you have poffeffed that his Mafter fhall recover) when his Mafter is faft afleep; to ufe fuch a Root, or fuch a Root. For Imagination is like to work better upon fleeping men, then men awake; as we fhall fhew when we handle Dreams.

We finde in the *Art of Memory*, that *Images vifible* work better then other conceits; As if you would remember the word *Philofophy*, you fhall more furely do it by imagining that fuch a Man (for Men are beft places) is reading upon *Ariftotles* Phyficks, then if you fhould imagine him to fay, *I will go ftudy Philofophy*. And therefore this obfervation would be tranflated to the fubject we now fpeak of; for the more luftrous the Imagination is, it filleth and fixeth the better. And therefore I conceive, that you fhall in that *Experiment* (whereof we fpake before) of binding of thoughts, lefs fail, if you tell one that fuch an one fhall name one of twenty men, then if it were one of twenty Cards. The *Experiment* of binding of thoughts would be diverfified and tried to the full: And you are to note, whether it hit for the moft part, though not always.

It is good to confider upon what things Imagination hath moft force: And the rule (as I conceive) is, that it hath moft force upon things that have the lighteft and eafieft motions; and therefore above all upon the Spirits of Men, and in them upon fuch affections as move lighteft: As upon procuring of Love, binding of Luft, which is ever with Imagination upon Men in fear, or Men in irrefolution, and the like: Whatfoever is of this kinde would be throughly enquired. Tryals likewife would be made upon Plants, and that diligently: As if you fhould tell a man that fuch a Tree would die this year, and will him at thefe and thefe times to go unto it, to fee how it thriveth. As for inanimate things, it is true, that the motions of fhuffling of Cards, or cafting of Dice, are very light motions; and there is a folly very ufeful, That Gamefters imagine, that fome that ftand by them, bring them ill luck. There would be tryal alfo made, of holding a Ring by a thred in a Glafs, and telling him that holdeth it before, that it fhall ftrike fo many times againft the fide of the Glafs, and no more; or of holding a Key between two Mens fingers without a charm; and to tell thofe that hold it, that at fuch a name it fhall go off their fingers. For thefe two are extream light motions. And howfoever, I have no opinion of thefe things, yet fo much I conceive to be true, That ftrong Imagination hath more force upon things living, or that have been living, then things meerly inanimate; and more force likewife upon light and fubtil motions, then upon motions vehement or ponderous.

It is an ufual obfervation, That if the Body of one murthered be brought before the Murtherer, the wounds will bleed afrefh. Some do affirm, That the dead Body, upon the prefence of the Murtherer hath opened the eyes; and that there have been fuch like motions as well where the party murthered hath been ftrangled or drowned, as where they have been killed by wounds. It may be that this participateth of a miracle, by *Gods* juft judgment, who ufually brings murthers to light. But if it be Natural, it muft be referred to Imagination.

The tying of the point upon the day of Marriage, to make Men impotent

tent towards their *Wives*, which (as we have formerly touched) is so frequent in *Zant* and *Gascony*, if it be Natural, must be referred to the Imagination of him that tieth the Point. I conceive it to have the less affinity with *Witchcraft*, because not peculiar persons onely, (such as *Witches* are) but any Body may do it.

950.
Experiments
in Consort
touching the
Secret Virtue
of Sympathy
and Anti-
*pathy.*THere be many things that work upon the *Spirits of Men* by *Secret Sympathy* and *Antipathy.* The virtues of *Precious Stones* worn, have been anciently and generally received, and curiously assigned to work several effects. So much is true, that *Stones* have in them fine *Spirits*, as appeareth by their splendor: And therefore they may work by consent upon the *Spirits* of *Men*, to comfort and exhilarate them. Those that are the best for that effect, are the *Diamond*, the *Emerald*, the *Jacynth Oriental*, and the *Gold-stone*, which is the *yellow Topaz*. As for their particular Proprieties, there is no credit to be given to them. But it is manifest, that Light above all things, excelleth in comforting the *Spirits* of *Men*; and it is very probable, that Light varied doth the same effect with more novelty. And this is one of the causes why *Precious Stones* comfort. And therefore it were good to have *Tincted Lanthorns*, or *Tincted Skreens* of *Glass* coloured into *Green*, *Blue*, *Carnation*, *Crimson*, *Purple*, *&c.* and to use them with Candles in the night. So likewise to have round *Glasses*, not onely of *Glass* coloured through, but with Colours laid between *Crystals*, with handles to hold in ones hand. *Prisms* are also comfortable things. They have of *Paris-work*, *Looking-Glasses*, bordered with broad Borders of small *Crystal*, and great counterfeit *Precious Stones* of all Colours, that are most glorious and pleasant to behold, especially in the night. The *Pictures* of *Indian Feathers* are likewise comfortable and pleasant to behold. So also fair and clear *Pools* do greatly comfort the *Eyes Spirits*; especially when the *Sun* is not glaring but overcast, or when the *Moon* shineth.

961. There be divers sorts of *Bracelets* fit to comfort the *Spirits*; and they be of three Intentions; *Refrigerant*, *Corroborant*, and *Aperient*. For *Refrigerant* I wish them to be of *Pearl*, or of *Coral*, as is used. And it hath been noted that *Coral*, if the party that weareth it be ill disposed, will wax pale; which I believe to be true, because otherwise distemper of heat will make *Coral* lose colour. I commend also *Beads* or little *Plates* of *Lapis Lazuli*, and *Beads* of *Nitre*, either alone, or with some *Cordial mixture.*

962. For *Corroboration* and *Comfortation*, take such *Bodies* as are of Astringent quality without manifest cold. I commend *Bead-Amber*, which is full of Astriction, but yet is unctuous, and not cold, and is conceived to impinguate those that wear such *Beads*. I commend also *Beads* of *Harts-Horn* and *Ivory*, which are of the like nature; also *Orenge-Beads*, also *Beads* of *Lignum Aloes*, macerated first in *Rose-water* and dried.

963. For opening, I commend Beads, or pieces of the Roots of *Cardum Benedictus*; also of the *Roots* of *Peony* the *Male*, and of *Orras*, and of *Calamus Aromaticus*, and of *Rew*.

964. The Cramp (no doubt) cometh of contraction of Sinews; which is manifest, in that it cometh either by cold or driness, as after *Consumptions* and long *Agues*; for Cold and Driness do (both of them) contract and corrugate. We see also, that chafing a little above the place in pain, easeth the Cramp; which is wrought by the Dilatation of the contracted Sinews by heat. There are in use for the prevention of the Cramp, two things: The one, *Rings* of *Sea-Horse Teeth* worn upon the *Fingers*; the other, *Bands*
of

of *Green Perwinckle* (the *Herb*) tied about the Calf of the Leg, or the Thigh, &c. where the Cramp useth to come. I do finde this the more strange, because neither of these have any Relaxing Virtue, but rather the contrary. I judge therefore that their working is rather upon the Spirits within the *Nerves* to make them strive less, then upon the Bodily substance of the *Nerves*.

965. I would have tryal made of two other kindes of Bracelets for comforting the Heart and Spirits. The one of the *Trochisch* of *Vipers* made into little pieces of Beads; for since they do great good inwards (especially for *Pestilent Agues*) it is like they will be effectual outwards, where they may be applied in greater quantity. There would be *Trochischs* likewise made of *Snakes*, whose flesh dried is thought to have a very opening and Cordial Virtue. The other is of Beads made of the Scarlet Powder, which they call *Kermes*, which is the principal Ingredient in their *Cordial-Confection Alkermes*. The Beads would be made up with *Amber-Griece*, and some *Pomander*.

966. It hath been long received, and confirmed by divers tryals, that the Root of the *Male-Peony* dried, tied to the Neck, doth help the *Falling-sickness*; and likewise the *Incubus*, which we call the *Mare*. The cause of both these *Diseases*, and especially of the *Epilepsie* from the Stomack, is the grossness of the Vapors which rise and enter into the Cells of the Brain: And therefore the working is by extream and subtil Attenuation, which that Simple hath. I judge the like to be in *Castoreum*, *Musk*, *Ren-Seed*, *Agnus Castus Seed*. &c.

967. There is a Stone which they call the *Blood-Stone*, which worn, is thought to be good for them that bleed at the Nose; which (no doubt) is by astriction and cooling of the Spirits. *Quere*, if the Stone taken out of the *Toads* Head, be not of the like virtue, for the *Toad* loveth Shade and Coolness.

968. Light may be taken from the *Experiment* of the *Horse-tooth Ring*, and the *Garland* of *Perwinckle*, how that those things which asswage the strife of the Spirits, do help diseases, contrary to the Intention desired; for in the curing of the Cramp, the Intention is to relax the Sinews; but the contraction of the Spirits, that they strive less, is the best help: So to procure easie Travails of Women, the Intention is to bring down the Childe; but the help is, to stay the coming down too fast; whereunto they say the *Toad-stone* likewise helpeth. So in *Pestilent Fevers*, the Intention is to expel the Infection by Sweat and Evaporation; but the best means to do it, is by *Nitre, Diascordium*, and other cool things, which do for a time arrest the Expulsion, till Nature can do it more quietly. For as one saith prettily, *In the quenching of the flame of a Pestilent Ague, Nature is like People that come to quench the Fire of an House; which are so busie, as one of them letteth another.* Surely it is an excellent Axiome, and of manifold use, that whatsoever appeaseth the contention of Spirits furthereth their action.

969. The Writers of *Natural Magick* commend the wearing of the spoil of a Snake, for preserving of Health. I doubt it is but a conceit; for that the Snake is thought to renew her youth by casting her spoil. They might as well take the Beak of an Eagle, or a piece of a Harts-horn, because those renew.

970. It hath been anciently received, (for *Pericles* the *Athenian* used it) and it is yet in use, to wear little Bladders of Quick-silver, or Tablets of Arsenick, as preservatives against the Plague: Not, as they conceive, for any comfort they yield to the Spirits; but for that being poysons themselves, they draw the venome to them from the Spirits.

971.   *Vide the Experiments* 95, 96, and 97. touching the several *Sympathies* and *Antipathies* for *Medicinal* use.

972.   It is said, that the Guts or Skin of a Woolf being applied to the Belly do cure the Colick. It is true, that the Woolf is a Beast of great Edacity and Digestion; and so it may be the parts of him comfort the Bowels.

973.   We see *Scare-crows* are set up to keep Birds from Corn and Fruit. It is reported by some, that the Head of a Woolf, whole, dried and hanged up in a *Dove-house*, will scare away Vermin, such as are *Weasils*, *Pole-cats*, and the like. It may be the Head of a Dog will do as much; for those Vermin with us, know Dogs better then Wolves.

974.   The Brains of some Creatures, (when their Heads are rosted) taken in Wine, are said to strengthen the Memory; as the Brains of Hares, Brains of Hens, Brains of Deer, &c. And it seemeth to be incident to the Brains of those Creatures that are fearful.

975.   The Oyntment that Witches use, is reported to be made of the Fat of Children digged out of their Graves; of the Juices of Smallage, Woolf-bane, and Cinquefoil, mingled with the Meal of Fine Wheat. But I suppose, that the Soporiferous Medicines are likest to do it; which are Henbane, Hemlock, Mandrake, Moonshade, Tobacco, Opium, Saffron, Poplar leaves, &c.

976.   It is reported by some, that the affections of Beasts when they are in strength, do add some virtue unto inanimate things: As that the Skin of a Sheep devoured by a Woolf moveth itching; that a stone bitten by a Dog in anger, being thrown at him, drunk in Powder provoketh Choler.

977.   It hath been observed, that the diet of Women with Childe, doth work much upon the Infant. As if the Mother eat Quinces much, and Coriander-feed (the nature of both which, is to repress and stay vapors that ascend to the Brain) it will make the Childe ingenious: And on the contrary side, if the Mother eat (much) Onions or Beans, or such vaporous food, or drink Wine or strong drink immoderately, or fast much, or be given to much musing, (all which send or draw vapors to the Head) it indangereth the Childe to become Lunatick, or of imperfect memory: And I make the same judgment of Tobacco often taken by the Mother.

978.   The Writers of *Natural Magick* report, that the Heart of an Ape worn near the Heart, comforteth the Heart, and increaseth audacity. It is true, that the Ape is a merry and bold Beast. And that the same Heart likewise of an Ape applied to the Neck or Head, helpeth the Wit, and is good for the Falling sickness. The Ape also is a witty Beast, and hath a dry Brain; which may be some cause of attenuation of Vapors in the Head. Yet it is said to move Dreams also. It may be the Heart of a Man would do more, but that it is more against Mens mindes to use it; except it be in such as wear the Reliques of Saints.

979.   The Flesh of a Hedghog dressed and eaten, is said to be a great dryer. It is true, that the Juice of a Hedghog must needs be harsh and dry, because it putteth forth so many Prickles: For Plants also that are full of Prickles are generally dry; as Bryars, Thorns, Barberries. And therefore the ashes of a Hedghog are said to be a great desiccative of Fistula's.

980.   Mummy hath great force in stanching of Blood; which as it may be ascribed to the mixture of Balms that are Glutenous, so it may also partake of a secret propriety, in that the Blood draweth Mans flesh. And it is approved, that the Moss which groweth upon the Scull of a Dead Man unburied will stanch Blood potently. And so do the dregs or powder of Blood, severed from the Water and dried.

It

It hath been practised to make *White Swallows*, by anointing of the Eggs with Oyl. Which effect may be produced by the stopping of the Pores of the Shell, and making the Juice that putteth forth the Feathers afterwards more penurious, And it may be, the anointing of the Eggs will be as effectual as the anointing of the Body. Of which, *Vide the Experiment* 93.

981.

It is reported, that the White of an Egg or Blood mingled with Salt-water, doth gather the saltness, and maketh the water sweeter. This may be by Adhesion; as in the *Sixth Experiment* of *Clarification*. It may be also, that Blood, and the White of an Egg, (which is the matter of a Living Creature) have some Sympathy with Salt; for all Life, hath a Sympathy with Salt. We see that Salt laid to a cut finger, healeth it; so, as it seemeth, Salt draweth Blood, as well as Blood draweth Salt.

982.

It hath been anciently received, that the Sea-Hare hath an antipathy with the Lungs, (if it cometh near the Body) and erodeth them. Whereof the cause is conceived to be a quality it hath of heating the Breath and Spirits; as *Cantharides* have upon the watry parts of the Body, as Urine and Hydropical Water. And it is a good rule, That whatsoever hath an operation upon certain kindes of Matters, that in Mans Body worketh most upon those parts wherein that kinde of matter aboundeth.

983.

Generally that which is Dead, or Corrupted, or Excerned, hath antipathy with the same thing when it is alive, and when it is sound, and with those parts which do excern: As a Carcass of Man is most infectious and odious to Man, a Carrion of an Horse to an Horse, &c. Purulent matter of Wounds and Ulcers, Carbuncles, Pox, Scabs, Leprosie, to sound Flesh; and the Excrements of every Species to that Creature that excerneth them. But the Excrements are less pernicious then the corruptions.

984.

It is a common experience, That Dogs know the Dog-killer; when as in times of Infection some pety fellow is sent out to kill the Dogs; and that though they have never seen him before, yet they will all come forth, and bark, and flie at him.

985.

The *Relations* touching the Force of Imagination, and the Secret Instincts of Nature, are so uncertain, as they require a great deal of Examination ere we conclude upon them. I would have it first throughly inquired, whether there be any secret passages of Sympathy between Persons of near Blood; as *Parents, Children, Brothers, Sisters, Nurse-children, Husbands, Wives,* &c. There be many reports in *History*, that upon the death of Persons of such nearness, Men have had an inward feeling of it. I my self remember, that being in *Paris*, and my Father dying in *London*, two or three days before my Fathers death, I had a dream, which I told to divers *English Gentlemen*, that my Fathers House in the Countrey was Plaistered all over with Black Mortar. There is an opinion abroad, (whether idle, or no I cannot say) That loving and kinde Husbands have a sense of their Wives breeding Childe by some accident in their own Body.

986.

Next to those that are near in Blood, there may be the like passage and instincts of Nature between great Friends and Enemies. And sometimes the revealing is unto another person, and not to the party himself. I remember *Philippus Comineus* (a grave Writer) reporteth, That the Archbishop of *Vienna* (a Reverend Prelat) said (one day) after Mass to King *Lewis* the Eleventh of *France, Sir, Your Mortal Enemy is dead*; what time, *Charles Duke* of *Burgundy* was slain at the Battel of *Granson* against the *Switzers*. Some tryal also would be made, whether Pact or Agreement do any thing; as if two Friends should agree, That such a day in every Week, they being in far distant places, should

987.

ſhould pray one for another, or ſhould put on a *Ring* or *Tablet* one for another fake; whether, if one of them ſhould break their Vow and Promiſe, the other ſhould have any feeling of it in abſence.

988.   If there be any force in Imaginations and Affections of ſingular Perſons, it is probable the force is much more in the Joynt-Imaginations and Affections of Multitudes ; as if a victory ſhould be won or loſt in remote parts, Whether is there not ſome ſenſe thereof in the people whom it concerneth, becauſe of the great joy or grief that many men are poſſeſſed with at once ? *Pius Quintus,* at the very time when that memorable victory was won by the *Chriſtians* againſt the *Turks,* at the Naval Battel of *Lepanto,* being then hearing of Cauſes in the Conſiſtory, brake off ſuddenly, and ſaid to thoſe about him, *It is now more then time we ſhould give thanks to God for the great Victory he hath granted us againſt the Turks.* It is true, that Victory had a Sympathy with his Spirit, for it was meerly his work to conclude the League : t may be that *Revelation* was *Divine.* But what ſhall we ſay then to a number of Examples amongſt the *Grecians* and *Romans,* where the People being in Theatres at Plays, have had news of Victories and Overthrows ſome few days, before any Meſſenger could come ?

It is true, that that may hold in theſe things which is the general Root of Superſtition; namely, that men obſerve when things hit, and not when they miſs, and commit to Memory the one, and forget and paſs over the other. But touching *Divination* and the miſgiving of Mindes, we ſhall ſpeak more when we handle in general the *Nature of Mindes,* and *Souls,* and *Spirits.*

989.   We having given formerly ſome *Rules of Imagination,* and touching the fortifying of the ſame ; we have ſet down alſo ſome few Inſtances and Directions of the force of Imagination upon *Beaſts, Birds, &c.* upon *Plants,* and upon *Inanimate Bodies :* Wherein you muſt ſtill obſerve, that your Tryals be upon Subtil and Light Motions, and not the contrary; for you will ſooner by Imagination bind a Bird from Singing then from Eating or Flying; and I leave it to every man to chuſe *Experiments* which himſelf thinketh moſt commodious, giving now but a few Examples of every of the three kindes.

990.   Uſe ſome Imaginant (obſerving the *Rules* formerly preſcribed) for binding of a Bird from ſinging, and the like of a Dog from barking. Try alſo the Imagination of ſome, whom you ſhall accommodate with things to fortifie it in Cock-Fights, to make one Cock more hardy, and the other more cowardly. It would be tried alſo in flying of Hawks, or in courſing of a Deer or Hart with Grey-hounds, or in Horſe-races, and the like comparative Motions; for you may ſooner by Imagination, quicken or ſlack a motion, then raiſe or ceaſe it; as it is eaſier to make a Dog go ſlower, then to make him ſtand ſtill, that he may not run.

991.   In *Plants* alſo you may try the force of Imagination upon the lighter ſort of Motions; as upon the ſudden fading or lively coming up of Herbs; or upon their bending one way or other, or upon their cloſing and opening, &c.

992.   For Inanimate things, you may try the force of Imagination upon ſtaying the working of Beer, when the Barm is put in ; or upon the coming of Butter or Cheeſe, after the Churning, or the Rennet be put in.

993.   It is an ancient *Tradition,* every where alleaged, for example of ſecret Proprieties and Influxes, That the *Torpedo Marina,* if it be touched with a long ſtick, doth ſtupefie the hand of him that toucheth it. It is one degree of
working

working at diftance, to work by the continuance of a fit *Medium* ; as Sound will be conveyed to the Ear by ftriking upon a Bow-ftring, if the Horn of the Bow be held to the Ear.

The Writers of *Natural Magick* do attribute much to the Virtues that come from the parts of Living Creatures, fo as they be taken from them, the Creatures remaining ftill alive; as if the Creature ftill living did infufe fome immateriate Virtue and Vigor into the part fevered. So much may be true, that any part taken from a Living Creature newly flain, may be of greater force, then if it were taken from the like Creature dying of it felf; becaufe it is fuller of Spirit.

Tryal would be made of the like parts of Individuals in Plants and Living Creatures ; as to cut off a Stock of a Tree, and to lay that which you cut off to putrefie, to fee whether it will decay the reft of the Stock; or if you fhould cut off part of the Tail, or Leg of a Dog, or a Cat, and lay it to putrefie, to fee whether it will fefter, or keep from healing, the part which remaineth.

It is received, that it helpeth to continue love, If one wear a Ring or a Bracelet of the Hair of the party beloved. But that may be by the exciting of the Imagination; and perhaps a Glove, or other like Favor, may as well do it.

The Sympathy of Individuals that have been entire; or have touched, is of all others, the moft incredible ; yet according unto our faithful manner of Examination of Nature, we will make fome little mention of it. The taking away of Warts, by rubbing them with fomewhat that afterwards is put to wafte and confume, is a common Experiment ; and I do apprehend it the rather, becaufe of mine own experience. I had from my Childhood a Wart upon one of my Fingers ; afterwards, when I was about fixteen years old, being then at *Paris*, there grew upon both my hands a number of Warts (at leaft an hundred) in a moneths fpace. The *Englifh Ambaffadors Lady*, who was a Woman far from Superftition, told me one day fhe would help me away with my Warts. Whereupon fhe got a piece of Lard with the skin on, and rubbed the Warts all over with the fat fide, and amongft the reft that Wart which I had from my Childhood ; then fhe nailed the piece of Lard, with the fat towards the Sun, upon a poft of her Chamber-window, which was to the South. The fuccefs was, that within five weeks fpace all the Warts went quite away, and that Wart which I had fo long endured, for company. But at the reft I did little marvel, becaufe they came in a fhort time, and might go away in a fhort time again ; but the going of that which had ftaid fo long doth yet ftick with me. They fay the like is done by rubbing of Warts with a green Elder-ftick, and then burying the ftick to rot in muck. It would be tried with Corns and Wens, and fuch other Excrefcences: I would have it alfo tried with fome parts of Living Creatures that are neareft the nature of Excrefcences ; as the Combs of Cocks, the Spurs of Cocks, the Horns of Beafts, &c. and I would have it tried both ways; both by rubbing thofe parts with Lard or Elder as before ; and by cutting off fome piece of thofe parts, and laying it to confume, to fee whether it will work any effect towards the Confumption of that part which was once joyned with it.

It is conftantly received and avouched, that the anointing of the Weapon that maketh the Wound, will heal the Wound it felf. In this Experiment, upon the relation of men of credit, (though my felf, as yet, am not fully inclined to believe it) you fhall note the Points following. Firft, the Oyntment wherewith this is done, is made of divers Ingredients ; whereof the

ftrangeft

994.

995.

996.

997.

998.

ſtrangeſt and hardeſt to come by, are the Moſs upon the Skull of a dead Man unburied, and the Fats of a Boar, and a Bear killed in the act of generation. Theſe two laſt I could eaſily ſuſpect to be preſcribed as a ſtartling hole, that if the *Experiment* proved not, it might be pretended, that the Beaſts were not killed in the due time ; for as for the Moſs, it is certain there is great quantity of it in *Ireland*, upon ſlain Bodies laid on heaps unburied. The other Ingredients are the Blood-ſtone in Powder, and ſome other things which ſeem to have a virtue to ſtanch blood, as alſo the Moſs hath. And the deſcription of the whole Oyntment is to be found in the *Chymical Diſpenſatory* of *Crollius*. Secondly, The ſame kinde of Oynment applied to the hurt it ſelf, worketh not the effect, but onely applied to the weapon. Thirdly, (which I like well) they do not obſerve the confecting of the Oyntment under any certain Conſtellation ; which commonly is the excuſe of Magical Medicines when they fail, that they were not made under a fit figure of Heaven. Fourthly, it may be applied to the Weapon, though the party hurt be at great diſtance. Fifthly, it ſeemeth the Imagination of the party to be cured is not needful to concur, for it may be done without the knowledge of the party wounded : And thus much hath been tried, that the Oyntment (for *Experiments* ſake) hath been wiped off the Weapon without the knowledge of the party hurt, and preſently the party hurt hath been in great rage of pain, till the weapon was reanointed. Sixthly, It is affirmed, That if you cannot get the weapon, yet if you put an Inſtrument of Iron or Wood, reſembling the weapon into the Wound, whereby it bleedeth, the anointing of that Inſtrument will ſerve and work the effect. This I doubt ſhould be a device to keep this ſtrange form of Cure in requeſt and uſe, becauſe many times you cannot come by the Weapon it ſelf. Seventhly, the Wound muſt be at firſt waſhed clean with White-wine, or the parties own Water, and then bound up cloſe in fine Linnen, and no more dreſſing renewed till it be whole. Eighthly, the Sword it ſelf muſt be wrapped up cloſe as far as the Oyntment goeth, that it take no wind. Ninthly, the Oyntment, if you wipe it off from the Sword and keep it, wil ſerve again, and rather increaſe in vertue then diminiſh. Tenthly, it will cure in far ſhorter time, then Oyntments of Wounds commonly do. Laſtly, it will cure a Beaſt as well as a Man ; which I like beſt of all the reſt, becauſe it ſubjecteth the matter to an eaſie tryal.

999.
Experiment
Solitary,
touching
Secret Proprieties.

I Would have Men know, that though I reprehend the eaſie paſſing over of the cauſes of things, by aſcribing them to ſecret and hidden virtues and proprieties (for this hath arreſted and laid aſleep all true Inquiry and Indications ;) yet I do not underſtand, but that in the practical part of knowledge much will be left to Experience and Probation, whereunto Indication cannot ſo fully reach ; and this is not onely in *Specie*, but in *Individuo*. So in Phyſick, if you will cure the *Jaundies*, it is not enough to ſay, that the Medicine muſt not be cooling, for that will hinder the opening which the diſeaſe requireth ; that it muſt not be hot, for that will exaſperate Choler ; that it muſt go to the Gall, for there is the obſtruction which cauſeth the diſeaſe, &c. But you muſt receive from Experience, that Powder of *Chamæpytis*, or the like, drunk in Beer, is good for the *Jaundies*. So again, a wiſe Phyſician doth not continue ſtill the ſame Medicine to a Patient, but he will vary, if the firſt Medicine doth not apparently ſucceed ; for of thoſe Remedies that are good for the *Jaundies*, *Stone*, *Agues*, &c. that will do good in one Body, which will not do good in another, according to the correſpondence the Medicine hath to the Individual Body.

The

THe delight which Men have in *Popularity, Fame, Honor, Submißion,* and *Subjection* of other *Mens Mindes, Wills,* or *Affections* (although these things may be desired for other ends) seemeth to be a thing in it self, without contemplation of consequence, grateful, and agreeable to the Nature of Man. This thing (surely) is not without some signification, as if all Spirits and Souls of Men came forth out of one *Divine Limbus* ; else, why be Men so much affected with that which others think or say ? The best temper of Mindes, desireth good Name and true Honor ; the lighter, Popularity and Applause ; the more depraved, Subjection and Tyranny ; as is seen in great Conquerors and Troublers of the World, and yet more in Arch-Hereticks, for the introducing of new Doctrines, is likewise an affectation of Tyranny over the Understandings and Beliefs of Men.

A

A TABLE

Of the chief Matters contained in the

CENTURIES.

F.

 cause

Y.

Z.

His Lordships usual Receipt for the Gout (to which, the Sixtieth Experiment hath reference) was this.

To be taken in this order.

1. *The Poultice.*

℞. Of Manchet, about three Ounces, the Crum onely, thin cut; let it be boiled in Milk till it grow to a Pulp; add in the end, a Dram and a half of the Powder of Red Roses.
Of Saffron ten Grains.
Of Oyl of Roses an Ounce.
    Let it be spred upon a Linnen Cloth, and applied luke-warm, and continued for three hours space.

2. *The Bath or Fomentation.*

℞. Of Sage-Leaves, half an handful.
Of the Root of Hemlock sliced, six Drams.
Of Briony Roots, half an Ounce.
Of the Leaves of Red Roses, two Pugils.
    Let them be boiled in a Pottle of Water wherein Steel hath been quenched, till the Liquor come to a Quart; after the straining, put in half an handful of Bay-Salt.
    Let it be used with Scarlet-Cloth, or Scarlet-Wool, dipped in the Liquor hot, and so renewed seven times; all in the space of a quarter of an hour or little more.

3. *The Plaister.*

℞. *Emplastrum Diacalcitheos*, as much as is sufficient for the part you mean to cover; let it be dissolved with Oyl of Roses in such a consistence as will stick, and spred upon a piece of Holland, and applied.

F I N I S.

ARTICLES

OF

ENQUIRY,

TOUCHING

METALS & MINERALS.

Written by the Right Honorable,

FRANCIS BACON,

BARON of *VERULAM*,

Viscount St. *Alban*.

Thought fit to be added, to this WORK

OF HIS

NATURAL HISTORY.

Nevvly put forth in the Year, 1661.
By the former Publisher.

LONDON,
Printed for *VVilliam Lee* at the Turks-head
in *Fleetstreet*. 1669.

ARTICLES

OF

ENQUIRY,

TOUCHING

METALS & MINERALS.

He first Letter of the Alphabet is, the Compounding, Incorporating, or Union, of Metals or Minerals.

With what Metals, Gold will incorporate, by Simple Colliquefactions, and with what not ? And in what quantity it will incorporate ? and what kinde of Body the Compound makes ?

Gold with Silver, which was the ancient *Electrum.*
Gold with Quick-silver.
Gold with Lead.
Gold with Copper.
Gold with Brass.
Gold with Iron.
Gold with Tin.

So likewise of Silver.

Silver with Quick-silver.
Silver with Lead.
Silver with Copper.
Silver with Brass.
Siver with Iron.
Silver with Tin.

So likewife of Quick-filver.
 Quick-filver with Lead.
 Quick-filver with Copper.
 Quick-filver with Brafs.
 Quick-filver with Iron.
 Quick-filver with Tin.

So of Lead.
 Lead with Copper.
 Lead with Brafs.
 Lead with Iron.
 Lead with Tin.

So of Copper.
 Copper with Brafs.
 Copper with Iron.
 Copper with Tin.

So of Brafs.
 Brafs with Iron.
 Brafs with Tin.

So of Iron.
 Iron with Tin.

What are the Compound Metals, which are common, and known ? And what are the Proportions of their mixtures ? As
Lattin of Brafs, and the Calaminar-ftone.
Bell-metal of, &c.
The counterfeit Plate, which they call Alchumy.
The Decompofites of three Metals, or more, are too long to enquire, except there be fome Compofitions of them already obferved.
It is alfo to be obferved, Whether any two Metals which will not mingle of themfelves, will mingle with the help of another ; and what ?
What Compounds will be made of Metal, with Stone, and other Foffiles ? As Lattin is made with Brafs, and the Calaminar-ftone. As all the Mettals with Vitriol : All with Iron poudered. All with Flint, &c.

*Some few of thefe would be enquired of, to difclofe the Nature
of the reft.*

WHether Metals, or other Foffiles, will incorporate with Molten Glafs ? And what Body it makes ?
The quantity in the mixture would we well confidered : For fome fmall quantity, perhaps, would incorporate ; as in the Allays of Gold, and Silver Coyn.
Upon the Compound Body, three things are chiefly to be obferved. The Colour, the Fragility or Pliantnefs, the Volatility or Faxation, compared with the Simple Bodies.
For prefent ufe or profit, this is the Rule. Confider the price of the two Simple Bodies ; confider again the Dignity of the one above the
other

other, in use. Then see, if you can make a compound that will save more in the price, then it will lose in the dignity of the use. As for example, Consider the price of Brass Ordnance; consider again the price of Iron Ordnance; and consider, wherein the Brass Ordnance doth excel the Iron Ordnance in use. Then if you can make a Compound of Brass and Iron Ordnance, that will be near as good in use, and much cheaper in price, there is profit both to the private and to the Commonwealth.

So of Gold and Silver, the price is double of Twelve. The dignity of Gold above Silver is not much; the splendor is alike, and more pleasing to some eye, As in Cloth of Silver, Silver Lace, silvered Rapiers, &c. The main dignity is, that Gold bears the Fire, which Silver doth not; but that is an excellency in Nature, but it is nothing at all in use. For any dignity in use, I know none, but that Silvering will sully and canker more then Gilding; which, if it may be corrected, with a little mixture of Gold, there is profit: And I do somewhat marvel, that the later ages have lost the ancient *Electrum*, which was a mixture of Silver with Gold; whereof, I conceive, there may be much use both in Coyn, Plate, and Gilding.

It is to be noted, that there is in the Version of Metals, impossibility, or at least great difficulty; as in making of Gold, Silver, Copper : On the other side, in the adulterating or counterfeiting of Metals there is deceit and villainy; but it should seem there is a middle way, and that is, by new compounds, if the ways of incorporating were well known.

What Incorporation or Imbibition, Metals will receive from Vegetables, without being dissolved might be inquired. As when the Armorers make their Steel more tough and plyant, by the aspersion of Water, or Juyce of Herbs : When Gold being grown somewhat churlish by recovering, is made more plyant by throwing in shreds of Tanned Leather, or by Leather oyled.

Note, that in these, and the like shews of Imbibition, it were good to try by the weight, whether the weight be increased, or no? For if it be not, it is to be doubted, that there is no Imbibition of Substance; but onely, that the Application of the other Body, doth dispose and invite the Metal to another posture of parts then of it self, it would have taken.

After the Incorporation of Metals, by simple Colliquefaction, for the better discovery of the Nature : And Consents and Dissents of Metals by incorporating of their Dissolutions, it would be enquired.

What Metals being dissolved by Strong-waters, will incorporate well together, and what not? which is to be inquired particularly, as it was in Colliquefactions.

There is to be observed in those Dissolutions, which will not incorporate what the effects are : As the Ebullition, the Precipitation to the bottom, the Ejaculation towards the top, the Suspension in the midst, and the like.

Note, that the Dissents of the Menstrua, or Strong-waters, may hinder the Incorporation, as well as the Dissents of the Metals themselves: Therefore where the Menstrua are the same, and yet the Incorporation followeth not, you may conclude, the Dissent is in the Metals, but where the Menstrua are several, not so certain.

THe Second Letter of the Crofs Row, is the Separation of Metals, and Minerals. Separation is of three forts; the firft is, The feparating of the pure Metal from the Ure or Drofs, which we call Refining. The fecond is, The drawing one Metal or Mineral out of another, which we may call Extracting. The third, The feparating of any Metal into his Original or Elements, or call them what you will) which work we call Precipitation.

For Refining, we are to enquire of it according to the feveral Metals; As Gold, Silver, &c. Incidently, we are to enquire of the firft Stone, or Ure, or Spar, or Marcafite of Metals feverally; and what kinde of Bodies they are; and of the degrees of Richnefs.

Alfo, we are to enquire of the Means of feparating, whether by Fire, parting Waters, or otherwife.

Alfo, for the manner of Refining, you are to fee how you can multiply the Heat, or haften the Opening; and to fave charge, in the Refining.

The means of this is in three manners; that is to fay, In the Blaft of the Fire: In the manner of the Furnace to multiply Heat, by Union and Reflexion: And by fome Additament or Medicines, which will help the Bodies to open them the fooner:

Note, the quickning of the Blaft, and the multiplying of the Heat in the Furnace, may be the fame for all Metals; but the Additaments muft be feveral according to the natures of the Metals.

Note again, That if you think the multiplying of the Additament in the fame Proportion that you multiply the Ure, the work will follow, you may be deceived: For quantity in the Paffive will add more refiftance, then the fame quantity in the Active will add force.

For Extracting, you are to enquire what Metals contain others, and likewife what not? As Lead Silver, Copper Silver, &c.

Note, although the charge of Extraction fhould exceed the worth, yet that is not the matter; For, at leaft, it will difcover Nature and Poffibility, the other may be thought on afterwards.

We are likewife to enquire, what the differences are of thofe Metals, which contain more or lefs, other Metals; and how that agrees with the poornefs or richnefs of the Metals, or Ure, in themfelves: As the Lead, that contains moft Silver, is accounted to be more brittle; and yet otherwife poorer in it felf.

For Principiation, I cannot affirm, whether there be any fuch thing, or no. And, I think, the Chymifts make too much ado about it. But howfoever it be, whether Solution or Extraction, or a kinde of Converfion by the Fire, it is diligently to be enquired, What Salts, Sulphur, Vitriol, Mercury, or the like Simple Bodies are to be found in the feveral Metals; and in what quantity.

The

THe third Letter of the Crofs-Row, is the variation of Metals into feveral Shapes, Bodies, or Natures ; the particulars whereof follow.

Tincture.
Turning to Ruft.
Calcination.
Sublimation.
Precipitation.
Amalgamatizing, or turning into a foft Body.
Vitrification.
Opening or Diffolving into Liquor.
Sprouting, or Branching, or Arborefcence.
Induration and Mollification.
Making tough or brittle.
Volatility and Fixation.
Tranfmutation or Verfion.

For Tincture, it is to be enquired how Metals may be tincted, through and through; and with what, and into what colours: As Tincting-Silver yellow, Tincting-Copper white, and Tincting red, green, blew, efpecially with keeping the luftre.

  Item, Tincture of Glafs.
  Item, Tincture of Marble, Flint, or other Stone.

For turning to Ruft, two things are chiefly to be enquired: By what Corrofives it is done, and into what colours it turns: As Lead into white, which they call *Serus* ; Iron into yellow, which they call *Crocus Martis:* Quick-filver into Vermilion, Brafs into green, which they call *Verdegraß,* &c.

For Calcination, to enquire how every Metal is calcined? And into what kinde of Body? And what is the exquifiteft way of Calcination?

For Sublimation, to enquire the manner of Subliming; and what Metals endure Subliming; and what Body the Sublimate makes?

For Precipitation likewife, By what ftrong Waters every Metal will precipitate? or with what Additaments? and in what time? and into what Body?

So for Amalgama, what Metals will endure it? What are the means to do it? And what is the manner of the Body?

For Vitrification likewife, what Metals will endure it? what are the means to do it? into what colour it turns? and further, where the whole
                Metal

Metal is turned into Glafs? and when the Metal doth but hang in the Glaf-
fie part? alfo what weight the vitrified Body bears, compared with the
crude Body? Alfo becaufe Vitrification is accounted, a kinde of death of
Metals, what Vitrification will admit, of turning back again, and what
not?

For Diffolution into Liquor, we are to enquire, what is the proper
Menftruum to diffolve any Metal? And in the Negative, what will touch
upon the one, and not upon the other? And what feveral *Menftrua* will
diffolve any Metal? And which moft exactly? *Item*, the procefs or motion
of the Diffolution? The manner of Rifing, Boiling, Vaporing? More
violent or more gentle? Caufing much heat, or lefs? *Item*, the quantity or charge the Strong-Water will bear, and then give over? *Item*,
the colour into which the Liquor will turn? Above all, it is to be enquired,
whether there be any *Menftruum*, to diffolve any Metal that is not fretting and
corroding; but openeth the Body by fympathy, and not by mordacity or
violent penetration?

For Sprouting or Branching, though it be a thing but tranfitory, and
a kinde of toy or pleafure; yet there is a more ferious ufe of it: For that it
difcovers the delicate motions of fpirits, when they put forth, and cannot
get forth, like unto that which is in vegetables.

For Induration or Mollification, it is to be enquired, what will make
Metals harder and harder, and what will make them fofter and fofter? And
this Enquiry tendeth to two ends;

Firft, for Ufe; As to make Iron foft by the Fire, makes it malleable.

Secondly, Becaufe Induration is a degree towards Fixation; and
Mollification towards Volatility: And therefore the Inquiry of them, will
give light towards the other.

For tough and brittle, they are much of the fame kinde with the
two former, but yet worthy of an Inquiry apart: Efpecially to joyn
Hardnefs to Toughnefs; as making Glafs malleable, &c. And
making Blades, ftrong to refift, and pierce, and yet not eafie to
break.

For Volatility and Fixation, it is a principal Branch to be enquired. The utmoft degree of Fixation is, That whereupon no Fire
will work, nor Strong-water joyned with Fire, if there be any fuch
Fixation poffible: The next is, when Fire fimply will not work without Strong-waters: The next is, when it will endure Fire not blown,
or fuch a ftrength of Fire: The next is, when it will not endure Fire,
but yet is malleable: The next is, when it is not malleable, but yet it
is not fluent, but ftupified. So of Volatility, the utmoft degree is,
when it will flee away without returning: The next is, when it will
flee up, but with eafie return: The next, when it will flee upwards,
over the Helm, by a kinde of Exufflation, without Vaporing:
                                                              The

The next is, when it will melt, though not rise ; And the next, when it will soften, though not melt. Of all these, diligent inquiry is to be made, in several *Metals* ; especially of the more extream degrees.

For Transmutation or Version, if it be real and true, it is the furtheft point of Art ; and would be well distinguished from Extraction, from Restitution, and from Adulteration. I hear much of turning Iron into Copper ; I hear also of the growth of Lead in weight, which cannot be without a Conversion of some Body into Lead : But whatsoever is of this kinde, and well approved, is diligently to be inquired, and set down.

THe fourth Letter of the Cross Row, is Restitution. First therefore, it is to be enquired in the Negative ; what Bodies will never return, either by reason of their extream fixing, as in some Vitrifications, or by extream Volatility.

It is also to be enquired of the two Means of Reduction ; and first by the Fire, which is but by Congregation of Homogeneal parts.

The second is, by drawing them down, by some Body, that hath consent with them : As Iron draweth down Copper in Water ; Gold draweth Quick-silver in vapor ; whatsoever is of this kinde, is very diligently to be enquired.

Also it is to be enquired, what Time or Age will reduce without the help of Fire or Body ?

Also it is to be enquired, what gives Impediment to Union or Restitution, which is sometimes called Mortification ; as when Quick-silver is mortified with Turpentine, Spittle, or Butter.

Lastly, it is to be enquired how the Metal restored, differeth in any thing from the Metal raw or crude ? As whether it becometh not more churlish, altered in colour, or the like ?

C　　　　　　　　THE

THE
BOOK-SELLER
UNTO THE
READER.

I Received some Moneths since, these Articles of Enquiry, touching Metals and Minerals, from the hands of the Reverend Dr. Rawley, who hath published several of the Lord Verulams Works since his Death (he having been his Lordships Chaplain) and who hath been careful to Correct at the Press this little Piece (an Addition to the Natural History) according to the Original Copy, remaining amongst his Lordships Manuscripts: Amongst which there is nothing more of that subject to be found, so as no more Additions can be expected:

W. Lee.

FINIS.

HISTORY

Natural and Experimental

OF

LIFE & DEATH:

OR,

Of the Prolongation of LIFE.

Written in Latin by the Right Honorable
FRANCIS Lord *Verulam*,
Viscount St. *Albans*.

LONDON,
Printed for *William Lee* at the Turks-head
in *Fleetstreet*. 1669.

LONDON
Printed for W. ... .

TO THE READER.

I Am to give Advertisement, that there came forth of late a *Translation* of this *Book* by an unknown *Person*, who though he wished well to the propagating of his *Lordships Works*, yet he was altogether unacquainted with his *Lordships* stile and manner of Expressions, and so published a *Translation* lame and defective in the whole. Whereupon I thought fit to recommend the same to be translated anew by a more diligent and zealous Pen, which hath since travelled in it; and though it still comes short of that lively and incomparable Spirit and Expression, which lived and died with the *Author*, yet I dare avouch it to be much more warrantable and agreeable then the former. It is true, this *Book* was not intended to have been published in *English*; but seeing it hath been already made free of that *Language*, whatsoever benefit or delight may redound from it, I commend the same to the *Courteous* and *Judicious Reader*.

W. R.

To

To the present Age and Posterity, Greeting.

ALthough *I had ranked the* History of Life *and* Death *as the last amongst my* Six Monethly Designations; *yet I have thought fit, in respect of the prime use thereof, (in which the least loß of time ought to be esteemed precious) to invert that order, and to send it forth in the second place. For I have hope, and wish, that it may conduce to a common good; and that the* Nobler *sort of* Physicians *will advance their thoughts, and not employ their times wholly in the sordidneß of* Cures, *neither be honored for* Necessity *onely, but that they will become* Coadjutors *and* Instruments *of the Divine Omnipotence and Clemency in Prolonging and Renewing the* Life of Man; *especially seeing I prescribe it to be done by safe, and convenient, and civil ways, though hitherto unaßayed. For though we* Christians *do continually aspire and pant after the* Land of Promise; *yet it will be a token of* Gods *favor towards us, in our journeyings through this* Worlds Wilderneß, *to have our* Shoes *and* Garments *(I mean those of our frail* Bodies*) little worn or impaired.*

FR. ST. ALBANS.

THE

THE HISTORY

OF

Life and Death.

The Preface.

IT is an ancient faying and complaint, That *Life* is fhort and *Art* long; wherefore it behoveth us, who make it our chiefeft aim to perfect *Arts*, to take upon us the confideration of *Prolonging Mans Life*, *GOD*, the *Author* of all *Truth* and *Life*, profpering our Endeavors. For though the *Life* of *Man* be nothing elfe but a mafs and accumulation of fins and forrows, and they that look for an Eternal Life fet but light by a Temporary : Yet the continuation of VVorks of Charity ought not to be contemned, even by us *Chriftians*. Befides, the beloved *Difciple* of our *Lord* furvived the other *Difciples*; and many of the Fathers o the Church, efpecially of the holy Monks and Hermits, were long-lived. VVhich fhews, that this blefing of long life, fo often promifed in the Old Law, had lefs abatement after our *Saviours* days then other earthly blefsings had ; but to efteem of this as the chiefeft good, we are but too prone. Onely the enquiry is difficult how to attain the fame ; and fo much the rather, becaufe it is corrupted with falfe opinions and vain reports : For both thofe things which the vulgar *Phyfitians* talk of, *Radical Moifture* and *Natural Heat*, are but meer Fictions ; and the immoderate

B

praifes

praifes of *Chymical Medicines*, firft puff up with vain hopes, and then fail their admirers.

And as for that *Death* which is caufed by Suffocation, Putrefaction, and feveral Difeafes, we fpeak not of it now, for that pertains to an *Hiftory* of *Phyfick*; but onely of that *Death* which comes by a total decay of the Body, and the Inconcoction of old Age. Neverthelefs the laft act of *Death*, and the very extinguifhing of *Life* it felf, which may fo many ways be wrought outwardly and inwardly (which notwithftanding have, as it were, one common Porch before it comes to the point of death) will be pertinent to be inquired of in this Treatife; but we referve that for the laft place.

That which may be repaired by degrees, without a total wafte of the firft ftock, is potentially eternal, as the *Veftal Fire*. Therefore when *Phyficians* and *Philofophers* faw that living Creatures were nourifhed and their Bodies repaired, but that this did laft onely for a time, and afterwards came old age, and in the end diffolution; they fought Death in fomewhat which could not properly be repaired, fuppofing a *Radical Moifture* incapable of folid réparation, and which, from the firft infancy, received a fpurious addition, but no true reparation, whereby it grew daily worfe and worfe, and, in the end, brought the bad to none at all. This conceit of theirs was both ignorant and vain; for all things in living Creatures are in their youth repaired entirely; nay, they are for a time increafed in quantity, bettered in quality, fo as the Matter of reparation might be eternal, if the Manner of reparation did not fail. But this is the truth of it, There is in the declining of age an unequal reparation; fome parts are repaired eafily, others with difficulty and to their lofs; fo as from that time the Bodies of Men begin to endure the torments of *Mezentius, That the living die in the embraces of the dead*; and the parts eafily repairable, through their conjunction with the parts hardly repairable, do decay: For the *Spirits, Blood, Flesh*, and *Fat* are, even after the decline of years, eafily repaired; but the drier and more porous parts (as the *Membranes*, all the *Tunicles*, the *Sinews, Arteries, Veins, Bones, Cartilages*, moft of the *Bowels*, in a word, almoft all the *Organical Parts*) are hardly repairable, and to their lofs. Now thefe hardly-repairable parts, when they come to their office of repairing the other which are eafily repairable, finding themfelves deprived of their wonted ability and ftrength, ceafe to perform any longer their proper Functions: By which means it comes to pafs, that in procefs of time the whole tends to diffolution; and even thofe very parts which in their own nature are with much eafe repairable, yet through the decay of the Organs of reparation can no more receive reparation, but decline, and in the end utterly fail. And the caufe of the termination of Life is this, for that the *Spirits*, like a gentle flame, continually preying upon Bodies, confpiring with the outward *Air*, which is ever fucking and drying of them, do, in time, deftroy the whole Fabrick of the Body, as alfo the particular Engines and Organs thereof, and make them unable for the work of Reparation. Thefe are the true ways of *Natural Death*, well and faithfully to be revolved in our mindes; for he that knows not the ways of *Nature*, how can he fuccor her, or turn her about?

Therefore the *Inquifition* ought to be twofold; the one touching the *Confumption* or *Depredation* of the Body of Man; the other touching the *Reparation* and *Renovation* of the fame: To the end, that the former may, as much as is possible, be forbidden and restrained, and the latter comforted. The former of these pertains, especially to the *Spirits* and outward *Air*, by which the Depredation and Waste is committed; the latter to the whole race of *Alimentation* or *Nourishment*, whereby the Renovation or Restitution is made. And as for the former part touching *Consumption*, this hath many things common with *Bodies Inanimate*, or without life. For such things as the *Native Spirit* (which is in all tangible Bodies, whether living or without life) and the ambient or external Air worketh upon Bodies Inanimate, the same it attempteth upon Animate or Living Bodies; although the *Vital Spirit* superadded, doth partly break and bridle those operations, partly exalt and advance them wonderfully. For it is most manifest that Inanimate Bodies (most of them) will endure a long time without any Reparation; but Bodies Animate without Food and Reparation suddenly fall and are extinguished, as the Fire is. So then, our *Inquisition* shall be double. First, we will consider the Body of Man as Inanimate, and not repaired by *Nourishment*: Secondly, as *Animate* and repaired by *Nourishment*. Thus having Prefaced these things, we come now to the *Topick* places of *Inquisition*.

THE

THE
Particular Topick Places;
OR,
ARTICLES of INQUISITION
TOUCHING
LIFE and DEATH.

Irſt, inquire of *Nature durable*, and *Not durable*, in Bodies Inanimate or without Life, as alſo in Vegetables ; but that not in a
large or juſt Treatiſe, but as in a Brief or Summary onely.

Alſo inquire diligently of *Deſiccation*, *Arefaction*, and *Conſumption* of *Bodies Inanimate*, and of *Vegetables* ; and of the
ways and proceſſes, by which they are done ; and further, of
Inhibiting and Delaying of *Deſiccation*, *Arefaction*, and *Conſumption*, and of the *Conſervation of Bodies*, in their proper ſtate ;
and again, of the *Inteneration*, *Emollition*, and *Recovery of bodies* to their former freſhneſs, after they be once dryed and withered.

Neither need the *Inquiſition* touching theſe things, to be full or exact, ſeeing they
pertain rather to their proper Title of *Nature durable* ; ſeeing alſo, they are not Principals in this *Inquiſition*, but ſerve onely to give light to the *Prolongation* and *Inſtauration*
of *Life* in *Living Creatures*. In which (as was ſaid before) the ſame things come to paſs,
but in a particular manner. So from the *Inquiſition* touching *Bodies Inanimate* and *Vegetables*, let the *Inquiſition* paſs on to other *Living Creatures* beſides *Man*.

Inquire touching the *length* and *ſhortneſs of Life* in *Living Creatures*, with the due
circumſtances which make moſt for their long or ſhort lives.

But becauſe the *Duration of Bodies* is twofold, One in *Identity*, or the ſelf-ſame
ſubſtance, the other by a *Renovation* or *Reparation* ; whereof the former hath place onely
in *Bodies Inanimate*, the latter in *Vegetables* and *Living Creatures*, and is perfected by
Alimentation or *Nouriſhment* ; therefore it will be ſit to inquire of *Alimentation*, and
of the ways and progreſſes thereof ; yet this not exactly, (becauſe it pertains properly
to the Titles of *Aſſimilation* and *Alimentation*) but, as the reſt, in progreſs onely.

From the *Inquiſition* touching *Living Creatures*, and *Bodies* repaired by *Nouriſhment*, paſs on to the *Inquiſition* touching *Man*. And now being come to the principal
ſubject of *Inquiſition*, the *Inquiſition* ought to be in all points more preciſe and accurate.

Inquire touching the *length* and *ſhortneſs of Life* in *Men*, according to the *Ages* of
the *World*, the ſeveral *Regions*, *Climates*, and *Places* of their *Nativity* and *Habitation*.

Inquire touching the *length* and *ſhortneſs of Life* in *Men*, according to their *Races*
and *Families*, as if it were a thing hereditary ; alſo according to their *Complexions*, *Con-
ſtitutions*, and *Habits of Body*, their *Statures*, the manner and time of their growth, and
the making and compoſition of their *Members*.

Inquire touching the *length* and *ſhortneſs of Life* in *Men*, according to the times of
their *Nativity* ; but ſo, as you omit for the preſent all *Aſtrological* obſervations, and the
Figures of Heaven, under which they were born ; onely inſiſt upon the vulgar and

1.

2.

3.

4.

5.

6.

7.

C

manifeſt

manifeſt Obſervations ; as whether they were born in the Seventh, Eighth, Ninth, or Tenth Moneth ; alſo, whether by Night or by Day, and in what Moneth of the Year.

8.   Inquire touching the *Length* and *Shortneſs of Life in Men,* according to their *Fare, Diet, Government* of their *Life, Exerciſes,* and the like. For as for the *Air,* in which Men live and make their abode, we account that proper to be inquired of in the above-ſaid *Article,* touching the places of their *Habitation.*

9.   Inquire touching the *Length* and *Shortneſs of Life in Men,* according to their *Studies,* their ſeveral *Courſes of Life,* the *Affections* of the *Minde,* and divers *Accidents* befalling them.

10.   Inquire apart touching thoſe *Medicines* which are thought to prolong *Life.*

11.   Inquire touching the *Signs* and *Prognoſticks of long and ſhort life* ; not thoſe which betoken *Death* at hand, (for they belong to an *Hiſtory of Phyſick*) but thoſe which are ſeen and may be obſerved even in Health, whether they be Phyſiognomical ſigns, or any other.

Hitherto have been propounded *Inquiſitions* touching *Length* and *Shortneſs of Life,* beſides the *Rules of Art,* and in a confuſed manner ; now we think to add ſome, which ſhall be more *Art-like,* and tending to practice, under the name of *Intentions.* Thoſe *Intentions* are generally three : As for the particular *Diſtributions* of them, we will propound them when we come to the *Inquiſition* it ſelf. The three general *Intentions* are, the *Forbidding of Waſte and Conſumption,* the *Perfecting of Reparation,* and the *Renewing of Oldneſs.*

11.   Inquire touching thoſe things which conſerve and exempt the Body of Man from *Arefaction* and *Conſumption,* at leaſt which put off and protract the inclination thereunto.

13.   Inquire touching thoſe things which pertain to the whole proceſs of *Alimentation,* (by which the Body of Man is repaired) that it may be good, and with the beſt improvement.

14.   Inquire touching thoſe things which purge out the *old Matter,* and ſupply with new ; as alſo which do Intenerate and Moiſten thoſe parts which are already dried and hardned.

.   But becauſe it will be hard to know the Ways of Death, unleſs we ſearch out and diſcover the *Seat,* or *Houſe,* or rather *Den of Death,* it will be convenient to make Inquiſition of this thing ; yet not of every kinde of *Death,* but of thoſe *Deaths* which are cauſed by want and indigence of Nouriſhment, not by violence ; for they are thoſe *Deaths* onely which pertain to a decay of Nature, and meer old Age.

15.   Inquire touching the Point of Death, and the Porches of Death, leading thereunto from all parts, ſo as that Death be cauſed by a decay of Nature, and not by Violence.

Laſtly, becauſe it is behoveful to know the Character and Form of *Old Age,* which will then beſt be done, if you make a *Collection* of all the *Differences,* both in the State and Functions of the Body, betwixt *Youth* and *Old Age,* that by them you may obſerve what it is that produceth ſuch manifold *Effects;* let not this Inquiſition be omitted.

16.   Inquire diligently touching the *Differences* in the *State* of the *Body* and *Faculties* of

17.   the *Minde* in *Youth* and *Old Age;* and whether there be any that remain the ſame without alteration or abatement in *Old Age.*

Nature Durable, and not Durable.

The Hiſtory.

To the firſt Article.

1.

2.

MEtals are of that long laſting, that Men cannot trace the beginnings of them ; and when they do decay, they decay through *Ruſt,* not through perſpiration into Air ; yet *Gold* decays neither way.

Quick-ſilver, though it be an humid and fluid Body, and eaſily made volatile by Fire ; yet (as far as we have obſerved) by Age alone, without Fire, it neither waſteth nor gathereth Ruſt.

3.   *Stones,* eſpecially the harder ſort of them, and many other Foſſiles, are of long laſting

ing, and that though they be exposed to the open air; much more if they be buried in the earth. Notwithstanding *Stones* gather a kind of *Nitre*, which is to them instead of *Rust*. *Precious Stones* and *Crystals* exceed *Metalls* in long lasting; but then they grow dimmer and less Orient, if they be very old.

It is observed, that *Stones* lying towards the North do sooner decay with age than those that lie toward the South; and that appears manifestly in *Pyramids*, and *Churches*, and other ancient *Buildings*: contrariwise, in *Iron*, that exposed to the South, gathers *Rust* sooner, and that to the North later; as may be seen in the *iron-bars* of windows. And no marvel, seeing in all putrefaction (as *Rust* is) Moisture hastens Dissolutions; in all simple Arefaction, Driness.

In *Vegetables*, (we speak of such as are fell'd, not growing) the Stocks or Bodies of harder *Trees*, and the Timber made of them, last divers ages. But then there is difference in the bodies of Trees: some Trees are in a manner spongy, as the *Elder*, in which the pith in the midst is soft, and the outward part harder; but in Timber-trees, as the *Oak*, the inner part (which they call *Heart of Oak*) lasteth longer.

The *Leaves*, and *Flowers*, and *Stalks* of *Plants* are but of short lasting, but dissolve into dust, unless they putrefie: the *Roots* are more durable.

The *Bones* of living Creatures last long, as we may see it of mens bones in Charnelhouses: *Horns* also last very long; so do *Teeth*, as it is seen in *Ivory*, and the *Sea-horse* Teeth.

Hides also and *Skins* endure very long, as is evident in old *Parchment-books*: *Paper* likewise will last many ages, though not so long as *Parchment*.

Such *things* as have *passed the Fire* last long, as *Glass* and *Bricks*; likewise *Flesh* and *Fruits* that have *passed the Fire* last longer than *Raw*: and that not onely because the Baking in the Fire forbids putrefaction; but also because the watry humour being drawn forth, the oily humour supports it self the longer.

Water of all Liquors is soonest drunk up by *Air*, contrariwise *Oil* latest; which we may see not onely in the *Liquors* themselves, but in the *Liquors* mixt with other Bodies: for *Paper* wet with water, and so getting some degree of transparency, will soon after wax white, and lose the transparency again, the watry vapour exhaling; but oiled *Paper* will keep the transparency long, the *Oil* not being apt to exhale: And therefore they that counterfeit mens hands, will lay the oiled paper upon the writing they mean to counterfeit, and then assay to draw the lines.

Gums all of them last very long; the like do *Wax* and *Honey*.

But the *equal* or *unequal* use of things conduceth no less to long lasting or short lasting, than the things themselves; for *Timber*, and *Stones*, and other *Bodies*, standing continually in the *water*, or continually in the *air*, last longer than if they were sometimes wet, sometimes dry: and so *Stones* continue longer, if they be laid towards the same coast of Heaven in the Building that they lay in the Mine. The same is of *Plants* removed, if they be coasted just as they were before.

4.
5.
6.
7.
8.
9.
10.
11.
12.

Observations.

*L*ET this be laid for a Foundation, *which is most sure, That there is in every Tangible body a Spirit, or body Pneumatical, enclosed and covered with the Tangible parts; And that from this Spirit is the beginning of all Dissolution and Consumption, so as the Antidote against them is the detaining of this Spirit.*

This Spirit is detained two ways: either by a streight 'nclosure, as it were in a Prison: or by a kind of free and voluntary Detention Again, this voluntary stay is perswaded two ways: either if the Spirit it self be not too moveable or eager to depart; or if the external Air importune it not too much to come forth. So then, two sorts of Substances are durable, Hard Substances, and Oily: Hard Substance binds in the Spirits close; Oily partly enticeth the Spirit to stay, partly is of that nature that it is not importuned by Air; for Air is consubstantial to Water, and Flame to Oil. And touching Nature Durable and not Durable in Bodies Insinimate, thus much.

1.
2.

The History.

*H*ERBS of the *colder sort* die yearly both in Root and Stalk; as *Lettice*, *Purslane*; also *Wheat* and all kind of *Corn*: yet there are some *cold Herbs* which will last

13.

three or four years ; as the *Violet, Straw-berry, Burnet, Prim-rose,* and *Sorrel.* But *Borage* and *Buglos,* which seem so alike when they are alive, differ in their deaths; for *Borage* will last but one year, *Buglos* will last more.

14. But many *Hot Herbs* bear their age and years better; *Hyssop, Thyme, Savory, Pot-marjoram, Balm, Wormwood, Germander, Sage,* and the like. *Fennel* dies yearly in the stalk, buds again from the root : but *Pulse* and *Sweet-marjoram* can better endure age than winter ; for being set in a very warm place and wel-fenced, they will live more than one year. It is known, that a knot of *Hyssop* twice a year shorn hath continued forty years.

15. *Bushes* and *Shrubs* live threescore years, and some double as much. A *Vine* may attain to threescore years, and continue fruitful in the old age. *Rose-mary* well placed will come also to threescore years ; but *white Thorn* and *Ivy* endure above an hundred years. As for the *Bramble,* the age thereof is not certainly known, because bowing the head to the ground it gets new roots, so as you cannot distinguish the old from the new.

16. Amongst great *Trees* the longest livers are the *Oak,* the *Holm, Wild-ash,* the *Elm,* the *Beech-tree,* the *Ches-nut,* the *Plane-tree, Ficus Ruminalis,* the *Lote-tree,* the *Wild-Olive,* the *Palm-tree* and the *Mulberry-tree,* Of these, some have come to the age of eight hundred years ; but the least livers of them do attain to two hundred.

17. But *Trees Odorate,* or that have sweet woods, and *Trees Rozennie,* last longer in their Woods or Timber than those above-said, but they are not so long-liv'd ; as the *Cypress-tree, Maple, Pine, Box, Juniper.* The *Cedar* being born out by the vastness of his body, lives well near as long as the former.

18. The *Ash,* fertile and forward in bearing, reacheth to an hundred years and somewhat better ; which also the *Birch, Maple,* and *Sirvice-tree* sometimes do : but the *Poplar, Lime-tree, Willow,* and that which they call the *Sycomore,* and *Walnut-tree,* live not so long.

19. The *Apple-tree, Pear-tree, Plum-tree, Pomegranate-tree, Citron-tree, Medl-r-tree, Black-cherry-tree, Cherry-tree,* may attain to fifty or sixty years ; especially if they be cleansed from the Moss wherewith some of them are cloathed.

20. Generally, greatness of body in trees, if other things be equal, hath some congruity with *length* of *life* ; so hath *hardness* of *substance :* and trees bearing *Mast* or *Nuts* are commonly longer livers than trees bearing *Fruit* or *Berries* : likewise trees putting forth their leaves late, and shedding them late again, live longer than those that are early either in leaves or fruit : the like is of *Wild-trees* in comparison of *Orchard-trees* And lastly, in the same kind, trees that bear a *sowr fruit* out-live those that bear a *sweet fruit.*

An Observation.

ARistotle *noted well the difference between* Plants *and* living Creatures, *in respect of their* Nourishment *and* Reparation : *Namely, that the* bodies *of* living Creatures *are confined within certain* bounds, *and that after they be come to their full* growth *they are continued and preserved by* Nourishment, *but they put forth nothing new except* Hair *and* Nails, *which are counted for no better than* Excrements ; *so as the juice of living creatures must of necessity sooner wax old: but in* Trees, *which put forth yearly new* boughs, *new* shoots, *new leaves, and new* fruits, *it comes to pass that all these parts in* Trees *are once a year young and renewed. Now it being so, that whatsoever is fresh and young draws the* Nourishment *more lively and chearfully to it than that which is decayed and old, it happens withall, that the* stock *and body of the tree, through which the sap passeth to the branches, is refreshed and cheared with a more bountiful and vigorous* nourishment *in the passage than otherwise it would have been. And this appears manifest (though* Aristotle *noted it not, neither hath he expressed these things so clearly and perspicuously) in* Hedges, Copses, *and* Pollards, *when the* plashing, shedding, *or lopping* comforteth the old Stem or *stock, and maketh it more flourishing and longer-liv'd.*

Desiccation, Prohibiting of Desiccation, and In-teneration of that which is desiccated and dried.

The History.

Fire and strong Heats dry some things, and *melt* others.

Limus ut hic durescit, & hæc ut Cera liquescit, Uno eodemque Igne ?

How this Clay is hardned, and how this wax is melted, with one and the same thing, Fire ? It drieth *Earth, Stones, wood, Cloth,* and *Skins,* and whatsoever is not *liquefiable;* and it melteth *Metalls, wax, Gums, Butter, Tallow,* and the like.

Notwithstanding, even in those things which the *fire* melteth, if it be very vehement and continueth, it doth at last dry them. For *metal* in a strong *fire,* (*Gold* onely excepted) the *volatile* part being gone forth, will become less ponderous and more brittle; and those *oily* and *fat substances* in the like *fire* will burn up, and be dried and parched.

Air, especially *open Air,* doth manifestly *dry,* but not *melt* : as *High ways,* and the upper part of the Earth, moistned with showers, are *dried; linnen clothes* washed, if they be hang'd out in the *air,* are likewise *dried ; herbs,* and *leaves,* and *flowers,* laid forth in the shade, are *dried.* But much more suddenly doth the *air* this, if it be either en lightned with the *Sun-beams,* (so that they cause no putrefaction) or if the *air* be stirred, as when the *wind* bloweth, or in *rooms* open on all sides.

Age most of all, but yet slowest of all, *drieth;* as in all bodies which (if they be not prevented by putrefaction) are *drie* with *Age.* But *age* is nothing of it self, being onely the measure of *time ;* that which causeth the *effect* is the *native Spirit* of bodies, which sucketh up the moisture of the body, and then, together with it, flieth forth; and the *air ambient,* which multiplieth it self upon the *native spirits* and *juices* of the body, and preyeth upon them.

Cold of all things most properly *drieth* : for *drying* is not caused but by *contraction ;* now *contraction* is the proper work of *cold.* But because we *Men* have *heat* in a high degree, namely, that of *Fire,* but *cold* in a very low degree, no other than that of *VVinter,* or perhaps of *Ice,* or of *snow,* or of *Nitre ;* therefore the *drying* caused by *cold* is but weak, and easily resolved. Notwithstanding we see the *surface* of the *earth* to be more *dried* by *Frost,* or by *March-winds,* than by the *sun,* seeing the same *wind* both licketh up the *moisture* and affecteth with *coldness.*

Smoak is a *drier;* as in *Bacon* and *Neats tongues* which are hanged up in the chimneys: and *Perfumes* of *Olibanum,* or *Lignum Aloes,* and the like, dry the *Brain,* and cure *Catarrhs.*

Salt, after some reasonable continuance, *drieth,* not onely on the out-side, but in the inside also; as in *Flesh* and *Fish* salted, which if they have continued any long time have a manifest hardness within.

Hot Gums applied to the skin dry and wrinkle it; and some *astringent waters* also do the same.

Spirit of *strong waters* imitateth the *fire* in *drying* : for it will both potch an Egg put into it, and toast Bread.

Powders dry like *Sponges* by drinking up the moisture, as it is in Sand thrown upon Lines new written : also *smoothness* and *politeness* of bodies, (which suffer not the vapour of moisture to go in by the pores) *dry* by accident, because it exposeth it to the *air ;* as it is seen in *precious Stones, Looking glasses,* and *Blades* of *Swords,* upon which if you breath, you shall see at first a little mist, but soon after it vanisheth like a cloud. And thus much for *Desiccation* or *Drying.*

They use at this day in the *East* parts of *Germany Garners* in *Vaults* under ground, wherein they keep *VVheat* and other *grains,* laying a good quantity of straw both under the *grains* and about them, to save them from the dampness of the *Vault* : by which device they keep their grains 20 or 30 years. And this doth not onely preserve them from fustiness, but (that which pertains more to the present *inquisition*) preserves them also in that greenness that they are fit and serviceable to make *bread.* The same is reported to have been in use in *Cappadocia* and *Thracia,* and some parts of *Spain.*

The placing of *Garners* on the tops of houses, with windows towards the East and North, is very commodious. Some also make two *Sollars,* an upper and a lower; and the upper *sollar* hath an hole it, through which the grain continually descendeth, like *sand* in an *hour-glass,* and after a few dayes they throw it up again with shovels, that so it may be in continual motion. Now it is to be noted

  that

To the second Article.

1.

2.

3.

4.

5.

6.

7.

8.

9.

10.

11.

12.

that this doth not only prevent the Fustiness, but conserveth the Greeness, and slacketh the Desiccation of it. The Cause is that which we noted before, That the discharge-ing of the *Watry humour,* which is quickned by the *Motion* and the *Winds,* preserves the *Oily humour* in his being, which otherwise would fly out together with the *Watry humour.* Also in some Mountains, where the *Air* is very pure, *dead Carkases* may be kept for a good while without any great decay.

13.   *Fruits,* as *Pomegranates, Citrons, Apples, Pears,* and the like; also *Flowers,* as *Roses* and *Lilies,* may be kept a long time in Earthen Vessels close stopped : howsoever, they are not free from the injuries of the outward *Air,* which will affect them with his unequal Temper through the sides of the Vessel, as it is manifest in heat and cold. Therefore it will be good to stop the mouths of the Vessels carefully, and to bury them within the *Earth* ; and it will be as good not to bury them in the *Earth,* but to sink them in the *Water,* so as the place be shady, as in *Wells* or *Cisterns* placed within doors : but those that be sunk in *Water* will do better in Glass vessels than in Earthen.

14.   Generally those things which are kept in the *Earth,* or in *Vaults* under *ground,* or in the *bottom* of a *Well,* will preserve their freshness longer than those things that are kept above *ground.*

15.   They say it hath been observed, that in *Conservatories* of *snow* (whether they were in Mountains, in natural Pits, or in Wells made by Art for that purpose) an *Apple,* or *Chef-nut,* or *Nut,* by chance falling in, after many months, when the *Snow* hath melted, hath been found in the *snow* as fresh and fair as if it had been gathered the day before.

16.   Country people keep *Clusters* of *Grapes* in *Meal,* which though it makes them less pleasant to the taste, yet it preserves their moisture and freshness. Also the harder sort of *Fruits* may be kept long, not onely in *Meal,* but also in *Saw-dust,* and in *heaps* of *Corn.*

17.   There is an opinion held, that *Bodies* may be preserved fresh in *Liquors* of their own kind, as in their proper *Menstrua*; as, to keep *Grapes* in *Wine, Olives* in *Oil.*

18.   *Pomegranates* and *Quinces* are kept long, being lightly dipped in *Sea-water* or *Salt-water,* and soon after taken out again, and then dried in the open *Air,* so it be in the Shade.

19.   Bodies put in *Wine, Oil,* or the *Lees* of *oil,* keep long; much more in *Hony* or *Spirit* of *Wine*; but most of all, as some say, in *Quick-silver.*

20.   *Fruits* inclosed in *Wax, Pitch, Plaister, Paste,* or any the like Case or Covering, keep green very long.

21.   It is manifest that *Flies, Spiders, Ants,* or the like small *creatures,* falling by chance into *Amber,* or the *Gums* of *Trees,* and so finding a burial in them, do never after corrupt or rot, although they be soft and tender Bodies.

22.   *Grapes* are kept long by being hanged up in *bunches* : the same is of other *Fruits.* For there is a two-fold Commodity of this thing : the one, that they are kept without *pressing* or *bruising,* which they must needs suffer if they were laid upon any hard substance; the other, that the *Air* doth encompass them on every side alike.

23.   It is observed that *Putrefaction,* no less than *Desiccation* in *Vegetables,* doth not begin in every part alike, but chiefly in that part where, being alive, it did attract nourishment. Therefore some advise to cover the *stalks* of *Apples* or other *Fruits* with *Wax* or *Pitch.*

24.   Great *Wicks* of *Candles* or *Lamps* do sooner consume the *Tallow* or *Oil* than lesser *Wicks*; also *Wicks* of *Cotton* sooner than those of *Rush,* or *Straw,* or small *Twigs* : and in *Staves* of *Torches,* those of *Juniper* or *Firre* sooner than those of *Ash* : likewise *Flame moved* and *fanned* with the *Wind* sooner than that which is *still* : And therefore *Candles* set in a *Lanthorn* will last longer than in the *open Air.* There is a Tradition, that *Lamps* set in *Sepulchres* will last an incredible time.

25.   The *Nature* also and *Preparation* of the *Nourishment* conduceth no less to the *Lasting* of *Lamps* and *Candles,* than the nature of the *Flame* ; for *Wax* will last longer than *Tallow,* and *Tallow* a little wet longer t'an *Tallow* dry, and *Wax candles* old made longer than *Wax-candles* new made.

26.   *Trees,* if you stir the *Earth* about their *Root every year,* will continue less time ; if once in four, or perhaps in ten years, much longer : also *cutting* off the *Suckers* and *young Shoots* will make them live the longer : but *Dunging* them, or laying of *Marl* about their Roots, or much *Watering* them, adds to their fertility, but cuts off from their long lasting. And thus much touching the *Prohibiting* of *Desiccation* or *Consumption.*

The

The Inteneration or making tender of that which is dried (which is the chief Matter) affords but a small number of *Experiments*. And therefore some few *Experiments* which are found in Living Creatures, and also in *Man* shall be joyned together.　27.

Bands of willow, wherewith they use to binde Trees, laid in Water, grow more flexible ; likewise they put Boughs of Birch (the ends of them) in Earthen Pots filled with Water, to keep them from withering ; and Bowls cleft with dryness, steep'd in Water, close again.　28.

Boots grown hard and obstinate with age, by greasing them before the Fire with Tallow, wax soft, or being onely held before the Fire get some softness. *Bladders* and *Parchments* hardned also become tender with warm Water, mixed with Tallow or any Fat thing ; but much the better, if they be a little chafed.　29.

Trees grown very old, that have stood long without any culture, by digging and opening the Earth about the Roots of them, seem to grow young again, and put forth young Branches.　30.

Old Draught Oxen worn out with labor, being taken from the yoak, and put into fresh Pasture, will get young and tender flesh again, insomuch, that they will eat as fresh and tender as a *Steer*.　31.

A strict Emaciating Diet of *Guaiacum, Bisket*, and the like, (wherewith they use to cure the *French-Pox, Old catarrhs*, and some kinde of *Dropsies*) doth first bring men to great poverty and leanness, by wasting the Juices and Humors of the Body ; which after they begin to be repaired again, seem manifestly more vigorous and young. Nay, and I am of opinion, that Emaciating Diseases afterwards well cured, have advanced many in the way of long life.　32.

Observations.

MEn *see clearly, like Owls, in the Night of their own Notions; but in Experience, as in the Day-light they wink, and are but half sighted. They speak much of the Elementary quality of Siccity or Dryness, and of things Desiccating, and of the Natural Periods of Bodies, in which they are corrupted and consumed: But mean while, either in the beginnings, or middle passages, or last acts of Desiccation and Consumption, they observe nothing that is of moment.*　1.

Desiccation or Consumption in the process thereof, is finished by three Actions ; and all these (as was said before) have their original from the Native Spirit of Bodies.　2.

The first Action is, the Attenuation of the Moisture into Spirit · the second is, the Issuing forth or flight of the Spirit ; the third is, the Contraction of the grosser parts of the Body immediately after the Spirit issued forth. And this last is, that Desiccation and Induration which we chiefly handle ; the former two consume onely.　3.

Touching Attenuation, the matter is manifest. For the Spirit which is inclosed in every Tangible Body forgets not its nature, but whatsoever it meets withal in the Body (in which it is inclosed) that it can digest and master, and turn into it self, that it plainly alters and subdues, and multiplies it self upon it, and begets new Spirit. And this evicted by one proof, instead of many; for that those things which are throughly dryed are lessened in their weight, and become hollow, porous, and resounding from within. Now it is most certain, that the inward Spirit of any thing, confers nothing to the weight, but rather lightens it; and therefore it must needs be, that the same Spirit hath turned into it the moisture and juyce of the Body which weighed before, by which means the weight is lessened. And this is the first Action, the Attenuation of the Moisture, and converting it into Spirit.　4.

The second Action, which is the Issuing forth or Flight of the Spirit, is as manifest also. For that issuing forth, when it is in throngs, is apparent even to the sense ; in Vapors to the sight, in Odors to the smelling ; but if it issueth forth slowly, (as when a thing is decayed by age) then it is not apparent to the sense; but the matter is the same. Again, where the composure of the Body is either so streight or so tenacious, that the Spirit can finde no pores or passages by which to depart, then, in the striving to get out, it drives before it the grosser parts of the Body, and protrudes them beyond the superficies or surface of the Body: as it is in the rust of Metals, and mould of all Fat things. And this is the second Action, the Issuing forth or Flight of the Spirit.　5.

The third Action is somewhat more obscure, but full as certain ; that is, the Contraction of the grosser parts after the Spirit issued forth. And this appears, first, in that Bodies after the Spirit issued forth, do manifestly shrink, and fill a less room ; as it is in　6.
the

the Kernels of Nuts, which after they are dried, are too little for the Shells ; and in Beams and Planchers of Houses, which at first lay close together, but after they are dried, give ; and likewise in Bowls, which through drought, grow full of cranies, the parts of the Bowl contracting themselves together, and after contraction must needs be empty spaces. *Secondly*, It appears by the wrinkles of Bodies dryed : For the endeavor of contracting it self is such, that by the contraction it brings the parts nearer together, and so lifts them up ; for whatsoever is contracted on the sides, is lifted up in the midst : *And* this is to be seen in Papers and old Parchments, and in the Skins of Living Creatures, and in the Coats of soft Cheeses, all which, with age, gather wrinkles. *Thirdly*, This Contraction shews it self most in those things, which by heat are not onely wrinkled, but ruffled, and plighted, and, as it were, rouled together ; as it is in Papers, and Parchments, and Leaves, brought near the fire : For Contraction by Age, which is more slow, commonly causeth wrinkles ; but Contraction by the Fire, which is more speedy, causeth plighting. Now in most things where it comes not to wrinkling or plighting, there is simple Contraction, and angustiation or streightning, and induration or hardning, and desiccation, as was shewed in the first place. But if the issuing forth of the Spirit, and absumption or waste of the Moisture be so great, that there is not left body sufficient to unite and contract it self, then of necessity Contraction must cease, and the Body become putrid, and nothing else but a little dust cleaving together, which with a light touch is dispersed and falleth asunder ; as it is in Bodies that are rotten, and in Paper burnt, and Linnen made into Tinder, and Carkases embalmed after many ages. And this is the third Action, the Contraction of the grosser parts after the Spirit issueth forth.

7.   It is to be noted, that Fire and Heat dry onely by accident ; for their proper work is to attenuate and dilate the Spirit and Moisture ; and then it follows by accident, that the other parts should contract themselves, either for the flying of Vacuum alone, or for some other motion withal, whereof we now speak not.

8.   It is certain, that Putrefaction taketh its original from the Native Spirit, no less then Arefaction ; but it goeth on a far different way : For in Putrefaction, the Spirit is not simply vapored forth, but being detained in part, works strange garboils ; and the grosser parts are not so much locally contracted, as they congregate themselves to parts of the same nature.

Length and Shortness of Life in Living Creatures.

The History.

To the first Article.

TOuching the Length and Shortness of Life in Living Creatures, *the Information which may be had, is but slender, Observation is negligent, and Tradition fabulous. In* Tame Creatures, *their degenerate life corrupteth them ; in* Wilde Creatures, *their exposing to all weathers, often intercepteth them. Neither do those things which may seem concomitants, give any furtherance to this Information, (the greatness of their Bodies, their time of Bearing in the* Womb, *the number of their young ones, the time of their growth, and the rest) in regard that these things are intermixed, and sometimes they concur, sometimes they sever.*

1.   Mans age (as far as can be gathered by any certain Narration) doth exceed the age of all other *Living Creatures*, except it be of a very few onely ; and the *Concomitants* in him are very equally disposed, his *stature* and *proportion* large, his *bearing* in the *womb* nine moneths, his *fruit* commonly one at a birth, his *puberty* at the age of fourteen years, his *time* of *growing* till twenty.

2.   The *Elephant* by undoubted relation, exceeds the ordinary race of *Mans* life ; but his bearing in the Womb the space of Ten years, is fabulous ; of two years, or at least above one, is certain. Now his bulk is great, his time of growth until the thirtieth year, his teeth exceeding hard ; neither hath it been observed, that his blood is the coldest of all Creatures : His age hath sometimes reached to Two hundred years.

3.   *Lions* are accounted long livers, because many of them have been found Toothless, a sign not so certain, for that may be caused by their strong breath.

4.   The *Bear* is a great sleeper, a dull beast, and given to ease ; and yet not noted
for

for long life : nay, he hath this sign of short life, that his *bearing* in the *womb* is but short, scarce full forty days.

The *Fox* seems to be well disposed in many things for long life ; he is well skinned, feeds on flesh, lives in Dens ; and yet he is noted not to have that property.   Certainly he is a kind of *Dog*, and that kind is but short-liv'd.   5.

The *Camel* is a long liver, a lean Creature, and sinewy, so that he doth ordinarily attain to fifty, and sometimes to an hundred years.   6.

The *Horse* lives but to a moderate age, scarce to forty years, his ordinary period   7. is twenty years : but perhaps he is beholden for this shortness of life to *Man* ; for we have now no *Horses* of the *Sun*, that live freely, and at pleasure, in good pastures. Notwithstanding the *Horse* grows till he be six years old, and is able for generation in his old age.   Besides, the *Mare* goeth longer with her young one than a *Woman*, and brings forth two at a burthen more rarely.   The *Ass* lives commonly to the *Horse's* age ; but the *Mule* out-lives them both.

The *Hart* is famous amongst men for long life, yet not upon any relation that   8. is undoubted.   They tell of a certain *Hart* that was found with a Collar about his neck, and that Collar hidden with *Fat*.   The long life of the *Hart* is the less credible, because he comes to his perfection at the fifth year ; and not long after his *Horns* (which he sheds and renews yearly) grow more narrow at the Root, and less branched.

The *Dog* is but a short liver, he exceeds not the age of twenty years, and for the   9. most part lives not to fourteen years: a Creature of the hottest temper, and living in extreams ; for he is commonly either in vehement motion, or sleeping : besides, the *Bitch* bringeth forth many at a Burden, and goeth nine weeks.

The *Ox* likewise, for the greatness of his body and strength, is but a short liver, about   10. some sixteen years, and the *Males* live longer than the *Females* ; notwithstanding they bear usually but one at a burden, and go nine months : a Creature dull, fleshy, and soon fatted, and living onely upon Herby substances, without Grain.

The *Sheep* seldom lives to ten years, though he be a creature of a moderate size, and   11. excellently clad ; and, that which may seem a wonder, being a creature with so little a Gall, yet he hath the most curled Coat of any other, for the *Hair* of no Creature is so much curled as *Wool* is.   The *Rams* generate not before the third year, and continue able for generation until the eighth.   The *Ewes* bear young as long as they live.   The *Sheep* is a diseased Creature, and rarely lives to his full age.

The *Goat* lives to the same age with the *Sheep*, and is not much unlike in other   12. things ; though he be a Creature more nimble, and of somewhat a firmer flesh, and so should be longer-liv'd ; but then he is much more lascivious, and that shortens his life.

The *Sow* lives to fifteen years, sometimes to twenty : and though it be a Creature   13. of the moistest flesh, yet that seems to make nothing to *Length* of *Life*.   Of the *Wild Boar* or *Sow* we have nothing certain.

The *Cat's* age is betwixt six and ten years: a creature nimble and full of spirit, whose   14. seed (as *Ælian* reports) burneth the Female ; whereupon it is said, *That the Cat conceives with pain, and brings forth with ease :*   A Creature ravenous in eating, rather swallowing down his meat whole than feeding.

Hares and *Conies* attain scarce to seven years, being both Creatures generative, and   15. with young ones of several conceptions in their bellies.   In this they are unlike, that the *Coney* lives under ground ; and the *Hare* above ground ; and again, that the *Hare* is of a more duskish flesh.

Birds for the size of their bodies are much lesser than *Beasts* ; for an *Eagle* or *Swan*   16. is but a small thing in comparison of an *Ox* or *Horse*, and so is an *Estrich* to an *Elephant*.

Birds are excellently well-clad : for *Feathers*, for warmth and close sitting to the   17. body, exceed *Wool* and *Hairs*.

Birds, though they hatch many young ones together, yet they bear them not all in   18. their bodies at once, but lay their Eggs by turns, whereby their Fruit hath the more plentiful nourishment whilst it is in their bodies.

Birds chew little or nothing, but their meat is found whole in their crops, notwith-   19. standing they will break the shells of Fruits, and pick out the Kernels : they are thought to be of a very hot and strong concoction.

D

The

20. The motion of *Birds* in their flying is a mixt motion, consisting of a moving of the limbs, and of a kind of carriage; which is the most wholsome kind of Exercise.

21. *Aristotle* noted well touching the generation of *Birds*, (but he transferred it ill to other *living Creatures*) that the feed of the *Male* confers less to generation than the *Female*, but that it rather affords Activity than Matter; so that fruitful *Eggs* and unfruitful *Eggs* are hardly distinguished.

22. *Birds* (almost all of them) come to their full growth the first year, or a little after. It is true, that their Feathers in some kinds, and their Bills in others, shew their years, but for the growth of their Bodies it is not so.

23. The *Eagle* is accounted a long liver, yet his years are not set down; and it is alledged as a sign of his long life, that he casts his Bill, whereby he grows young again: from whence comes that old Proverb, *The old age of an Eagle*. Notwithstanding perchance the matter may be thus, That the renewing of the *Eagle* doth not cast his bill, but the casting of his bill is the renewing of the *Eagle*, for after that his bill is grown to a great crookedness, the *Eagle* feeds with much difficulty.

24. *Vultures* are also affirmed to be long livers, insomuch that they extend their life well near to an hundred years. *Kites* likewise, and so all *Birds* that feed upon flesh, and *Birds* of prey live long. As for *Hawks*, because they lead a degenerate and servile life for the delight of men, the term of their natural life is not certainly known: notwithstanding amongst *Mewed Hawks* some have been found to have lived thirty years, and amongst *wild Hawks* forty years.

25. The *Raven* likewise is reported to live long, sometimes to an hundred years: he feeds on Carrion, and flies not often, but rather is a sedentry and malanchollick *Bird*, and hath very black flesh. But the *Crow*, like unto him in most things, (except in greatness and voice) lives not altogether so long, and yet is reckoned amongst the long livers.

26. The *Swan* is certainly found to be a long liver, and exceeds not unfrequently an hundred years. He is a *Bird* excellently plumed, a feeder upon fish, and is always carried, and that in running waters.

27. The *Goose* also may pass amongst the long livers, though his food be commonly grass, and such kind of nourishment; especially the *Wild-Goose*; whereupon this Proverb grew amongst the *Germans, Magis senex quam Anser nivalis, Older than a Wild-Goose*.

28. *Storks* must needs be long livers, if that be true which was anciently observed of them, that they never came to *Thebes*, because that City was often sacked. This if it were so, then either they must have the knowledge of more ages than one, or else 'the old ones must tell their young the History. But there is nothing more frequent than *Fables*.

29. For *Fables* do so abound touching the *Phœnix*, that the truth is utterly lost if any such *Bird* there be. As for that which was so much admired, That she was ever seen abroad with a great troop of *Birds* about her, it is no such wonder; for the same is usually seen about an *Owl* flying in the day-time, or a *Parrot* let out of a Cage.

30. The *Parrot* hath been certainly known to have lived threescore years in *England*, how old soever he was before he was brought over: a *Bird* eating almost all kind of meats, chewing his meat, and renewing his bill; likewise curst and mischievous, and of a black flesh.

31. The *Peacock* lives twenty years; but he comes not forth with his *Argus Eyes* before he be three years old; a *Bird* slow of pace, having whitish flesh.

32. The *Dunghill-Cock* is venerious, martial, and but of a short life; a crank *Bird*, having also white flesh.

33. The *Indian-Cock*, commonly called the *Turkey Cock*, lives not much longer than the *Dunghill-Cock*: an angry *Bird*, and hath exceeding white flesh.

34. The *Ring-Doves* are of the longest sort of livers, insomuch that they attain sometimes to fifty years of age: an aiery *Bird*, and both builds and sits on high. But *Doves* and *Turtles* are but short liv'd, not exceeding eight years.

35. But *Pheasants* and *Partiges* may live to sixteen years. They are great breeders, but not so white of flesh as the ordinary *Pullen*.

The

The *Black bird* is reported to be, amongst the lesser birds, one of the longest livers ; an unhappy bird, and a good singer.   36.

The *Sparrow* is noted to be of a very short life; and it is imputed in the Males to their lasciviousness.   But the *Linnet*, no bigger in body than the *Sparrow*, hath been observed to have lived twenty years.   37.

Of the *Estrich* we have nothing certain : those that were kept here have been so unfortunate, that no long life appeared by them.   Of the bird *Ibis* we find onely that he liveth long, but his years are not recorded.   38.

The age of *Fishes* is more uncertain than that of terrestrial Creatures, because living under the water they are the less observed : many of them breath not, by which means their vital spirit is more closed in ; and therefore though they receive some refrigeration by their Gills, yet that refrigeration is not so continual as when it is by breathing.   39.

They are free from the *Desiccation* and *Depredation* of the *Air ambient*, because they live in the water : yet there is no doubt but the *water ambient*, and piercing, and received into the pores of the body, doth more hurt to long life than the Air doth.   40.

It is affirmed too that their blood is not warm.   Some of them are great devourers, even of their own kind.   Their flesh is softer and more tender than that of terrestrial creatures : they grow exceedingly fat, insomuch that an incredible quantity of Oyl will be extracted out of one *Whale*.   41.

Dolphins are reported to live about thirty years ; of which thing a trial was taken in some of them by cutting off their tails : they grow untill ten years of age.   42.

That which they report of some *Fishes* is strange, that after a certain age their bodies will waste and grow very slender , onely their head and tail retaining their former greatness.   43.

There were found in *Cæsar's* Fish ponds *Lampreys* to have lived threescore years : they were grown so familiar with long use, that *Crassus* the Orator solemnly lamented one of them.   44.

The *Pike* amongst Fishes living in fresh water is found to last longest, sometimes to forty years : he is a Ravener, of a flesh somewhat dry and firm.   45.

But the *Carp*, *Bream*, *Tench*, *Eel*, and the like, are not held to live above ten years.   46.

Salmons are quick of growth, short of life ; so are *Trouts* : but the *Pearch* is slow of growth, long of life.   47.

Touching that monstrous bulk of the *Whale* or *Ork*, how long it is veiled by vital spirit, we have received nothing certain ; neither yet touching the *Sea-calf*, and *Sea-hog*, and other innumerable *Fishes*.   48.

Crocodiles are reported to be exceeding long-liv'd, and are famous for the time of their growth, for that they, amongst all other Creatures, are thought to grow during their whole life.   They are of those Creatures that lay Eggs, ravenous, cruel, and well-fenced against the waters,   Touching the other kinds of *Shell-fish*, we find nothing certain how long they live.   49.

Observations.

TO find out a *Rule* touching Length and Shortness of Life in Living Creatures is very difficult, by reason of the negligence of *Observations*, and the intermixing of *Causes*. A few things we will set down.

There are more kinds of Birds found to be long liv'd than of Beasts ; as the Eagle, the Vulture, the Kite, the Pelican, the Raven, the Crow, the Swan, the Goose, the Stork, the Crane, the Bird called the Ibis, the Parrot, the Ring dove, with the rest, though they come to their full growth within a year, and are less of bodies : surely their cloathing is excellent good against the distemperatures of the weather ; and besides, living for the most part in the open Air, they are like the Inhabitants of pure Mountains, which are long-liv'd. Again, their Motion, which (as I else-where said) is a mixt Motion, compounded of a moving of their Limbs and of a carriage in the Air, doth less weary and wear them, and 'tis more wholsome. Neither do they suffer any compression or want of nourishment in their mother's bellies, because the Eggs are laid by turns. But the chiefest cause of all I take to be this, that Birds are made more of the substance of the Mother than of the Father, whereby their Spirits are not so eager and hot.   1.

2. t may be a Position, that Creatures which partake more of the substance of their Mother than of their Father are longer-liv'd, as Birds are; which was said before. Also that those which have a longer time of bearing in the womb, do partake more of the substance of their Mother, less of the Father, and so are longer-liv'd: Insomuch that I am of opinion, that even amongst Men, (which I have noted in some) those that resemble their Mothers most are longest-liv'd; and so are the Children of Old men begotten of young Wives, if the Fathers be sound, not diseased.

3. The first breeding of Creatures is ever material, either to their hurt or benefit. And therefore it stands with reason, that the lesser Compression, and the more liberal Alimentation of the Young one in the womb, should confer much to Long Life. Now this happens when either the young ones are brought forth successively, as in Birds; or when they are single Births, as in Creatures bearing but one at a Burthen

4. But long Bearing in the Womb makes for Length of Life three ways First, for that the young one partakes more of the substance of the Mother, as hath been said. Secondly, that it comes forth more strong and able. Thirdly, that it undergoes the predatory force of the Air later. Besides, it shews that Nature intendeth to finish her periods by larger Circles. Now though Oxen and Sheep, which are born in the womb about six months, are but short-liv'd, that happens for other causes

5. Feeders upon Grass and mere Herbs are but short livers, and Creatures feeding upon Flesh, or Seeds, or Fruits, long livers, as some Birds are. As for Harts, which are long-liv'd, they take the one half of their meat (as men use to say) from above their heads; and the Goose, besides Grass, findeth something in the water, and stubble to feed upon.

6. We suppose that a good Cloathing of the Body maketh much to long life; for it fenceth and armeth against the intemperances of the Air, which do wonderfully assail and decay the body: which benefit Birds especially have. Now that Sheep, which have so good Fleeces, should be so short-liv'd, that is to be imputed to Diseases, whereof that Creature is full, and to the bare eating of Grass.

7. The seat of the Spirits, without doubt, is principally the Head; which though it be usually understood of the Animal Spirits onely, yet this is all in all. Again, it is not to be doubted but the Spirits do most of all waste and prey upon the Body, so that when they are either in greater plenty, or in greater Inflamation and Acrimony, there the life is much shortned. And therefore I conceive a great cause of long life in Birds to be the smalness of their Heads in comparison of their Bodies; for even Men which have very great Heads I suppose to be the shorter livers.

8. I am of opinion that Carriage is of all other motions the most helpful to long life; which I also noted before. Now there are carried Water-fowls upon the water, as Swans; all Birds in their flying, but with a strong endeavour of their limbs; and Fishes, of the length of whose live we have no certninty.

9. Those Creatures which are long before they come to their perfection (not speaking of growth in stature onely, but of other steps to maturity; as Man puts forth, first, his Teeth, next the signs of Puberty, then his beard, and so forward) are long-liv'd, for it shews that Nature finished her Periods by larger Circles.

10. Milder Creatures are not long-liv'd, as the Sheep and Dove; for Choler is as the whetstone and Spur to many Functions in the Body.

11. Creatures whose Flesh is more duskish are longer-liv'd than those that have white Flesh; for it sheweth that the juice of the body is more firm, and less apt to dissipate.

12. In every corruptible Body Quantity maketh much to the conservation of the whole: for a great Fire is longer in quenching, a small portion of Water is sooner evaporated, the Body of a Tree withereth not so fast as a Twig. And therefore generally (I speak it of Species, not of Individuals) Creatures that are large in body are longer-liv'd than those that are small, unless there be some other potent cause to hinder it.

Alimentation, or Nourishment: and the way of Nourishing.

The History.

NOurishment ought to be of an inferiour nature, and more simple substance than the thing nourished. *Plants* are nourished with the Earth and Water, *Living Creatures* with Plants, *Man* with living Creatures. There are also certain *Creatures* feeding upon Flesh, and *Man* himself takes Plants into a part of his Nourishment ; but *Man* and *Creatures* feeding upon Flesh are scarcely nourished with Plants alone : perhaps *Fruit* or *Grains*, baked or boiled, may, with long use, nourish them ; but *Leaves* or *Plants* or *Herbs* will not do it, as the *Order* of the *Foliatanes* shewed by Experience.

Over-great *Affinity* or *Consubstantiality* of the *Nourishment* to the thing nourished proveth not well : Creatures feeding upon Herbs touch no Flesh ; and of Creatures feeding upon Flesh, few of them eat their own kind : As for *Men*, which are *Cannibals*, they feed not ordinarily upon *Mens* flesh, but reserve it as a Dainty, either to serve their reveng upon their enemies, or to satisfie their appetite at some times. So the *Ground* is best sown with *Seed* growing elsewhere, and *Men* do not use to *Graft* or *Inoculate* upon the same Stock.

By how much the more the *Nourishment* is better *prepared*, and approacheth nearer in likeness to the thing nourished, by so much the more are *Plants* more fruitful, and *living Creatures* in better liking and plight : for a young *Slip* or *cion* is not so well nourished if it be pricked into the ground, as if it be grafted into a Stock agreeing with it in Nature, and where it finds the nourishment already digested and prepared : neither (as is reported, will the *Seed* of an *Onion*, or some such like, sown in the bare earth, bring forth so large a fruit as if it be put into another *Onion*, which is a new kind of *Grafting*, into the root, or under ground. Again, it hath been found out lately, that a *Slip* of a *Wild Tree*, as of an *Elm*, *Oak*, *Ash*, or such like, grafted into a Stock of the same kind, will bring forth larger leaves then those that grow without grafting: Also Men are not nourished so well with raw flesh as with that which hath passed the fire.

Living Creatures are nourished by the *Mouth*, *Plants* by the *Root*, *Young ones* in the womb by the *Navel*: *Birds* for a while are nourished with the *Yolk* in the Egge, whereof some is found in their Crops after they are hatched.

All *Nourishment* moveth from the *centre* to the *Circumference*, or from the Inward to the outward : yet it is to be noted, that in *Trees* and *Plants* the Nourishment passeth rather by the Bark and Outward parts then by the Pith and Inward parts ; for if the Bark be pilled off, though but for a small breadth, round, they live no more : and the Bloud in the Veins of living Creatures doth no less nourish the Flesh beneath it then the Flesh above it.

In all *Alimentation* or *Nourishment* there is a two-fold Action, *Extrusion* and *Attraction* ; whereof the former proceeds from the Inward Function, the latter from the Outward.

Vegetables assimulate their Nourishment simply, without Excerning: For Gums and Tears of Trees are rather Exuberances then Excrements, and Knots or knobs are nothing but Diseases. But the substance of living Creatures is more perceptible of the like ; and therefore it is conjoyned with a kind of disdain, whereby it rejecteth the bad, and assimulateth the good.

It is a strange thing of the *stalks* of *Fruits*, that all the Nourishment which produceth sometimes such great Fruits, should be forced to pass through so narrow necks ; for the Fruit is never joyn'd to the Stock without some stalk.

It is to be noted, that the Seeds of living Creatures will not be fruitful but when they are new shed, but the Seeds of Plants will be fruitful a long time after they are gathered ; yet the Slips or Cions of Trees will not grow unless they be grafted green ; neither will the roots keep long fresh unless they be covered with earth.

In *living creatures* there are degrees of Nourishment according to their Age: in the womb, the young one is nourished with the Mother's blood ; when it is new-born, with Milk ; afterwards with Meats and Drinks ; and in old age the most nourishing and savoury Meats please best.

To the fourth Article.

1.

2.

3.

4.

5.

6.

7.

8.

9.

10.

Above all it maketh to the prefent *Inquifition*, to inquire diligently and attentively whether a man may not receive *Nourifhment* from without, at leaft fome other way befide the Mouth. We know that Baths of Milk are ufed in fome *Hectick Fevers*, and when the body is brought extream low, and *Phyficians* do provide *Nourifhing clyfters*. This matter would be well ftudied; for if *Nourifhment* may be made either from without, or fome other way than by the ftomach, then the weaknefs of Concoction, which is incident to old men, might be recompenced by thefe helps, and Concoction reftored to them intire.

Length and Shortnefs of Life in Man.

The Hiftory.

To the 5, 6, 7, 8, 9, and 11 Articles.

1.

BEfore the *Floud*, as the *Sacred Scriptures* relate, *Men* lived many hundred years; yet none of the *Fathers* attained to a full thoufand. Neither was this *Length* of *Life* peculiar onely to *Grace*, or the *Holy Line*; for there are reckoned of the *Fathers* until the *Floud* eleven Generations; but of the fons of *Adam* by *Cain* onely eight Generations; fo as the pofterity of *Cain* may feem the longer-liv'd. But this *Length of Life* immediately after the *Floud* was reduced to a moiety, but in the *Poft-nati*; for *Noah*, who was born before, equalled the age of his Anceftors, and *Sem* faw the fix hundredth year of his life. Afterwards, three Generations being run from the *Floud*, the *Life* of *Man* was brought down to a fourth part of the primative *Age*, that was, to about two hundred years.

2.

Abraham lived an hundred feventy and five years: a man of an high courage, and profperous in all things. *Ifaac* came to an hundred and eighty years of age: a chafte man, and enjoying more quietnefs than his Father. But *Jacob*, after many croffes and a numerous progeny, lafted to the hundred forty feventh year of his life: a patient, gentle, and wife man. *Ifmael*, a military man, lived an hundred thirty and feven years. *Sarah* (whofe years onely amongft women are recorded) died in the hundred twenty feventh year of her age: a beautifull and magnanimous woman: a fingular good Mother and Wife; and yet no lefs famous for her Liberty, than Obfequioufnefs towards her husband. *Jofeph* alfo, a prudent and politick man, paffing his youth in affliction, afterwards advanced to the height of honour and profperity, lived an hundred and ten years. But his brother *Levi*, elder than himfelf, attained to an hundred thirty feven years: a man impatient of contumely and revengeful. Near unto the fame age attained the *fon* of *Levi*; alfo his *grand-child*, the *father* of *Aaron* and *Mofes*.

3.

Mofes lived an hundred and twenty years: a ftout man, and yet the *meekeft upon the earth*, and of a very *flow tongue*. Howfoever *Mofes* in his *Pfalm* pronounceth that the life of man is but feventy years, and if a man have ftrength, then eighty; which term of man's life ftandeth firm in many particulars even at this day. *Aaron*, who was three years the elder, died the fame year with his *Brother*: a man of a readier fpeech, of a more facile difpofition, and lefs conftant. But *Phineas, grandchild* of *Aaron*, (perhaps out of extraordinary grace) may be collected to have lived three hundred years; if fo be the *War* of the *Ifraelites* againft the *Tribe* of *Benjamin* (in which Expedition *Phineas* was confulted with) were performed in the fame order of time in which the *Hiftory* hath ranked it: He was a man of a moft eminent Zeal. *Jofhua*, a martial man, and an excellent Leader, and evermore victorious, lived to the hundred and tenth year of his life. *Caleb* was his Contemporary, and feemeth to have been of as great years. *Ehud* the Judge feems to have been no lefs than an hundred years old, in regard that after the Victory over the *Moabites* the *Holy Land* had reft under his Government eighty years: He was a man fierce and undaunted, and one that in a fort neglected his life for the good of his People.

4.

Job lived, after the reftauration of his happinefs, an hundred and forty years, being before his afflictions of that age that he had fons at man's eftate: a man politick,

litick, eloquent, charitable, and the *Example of Patience.* *Eli* the Priest lived ninety eight years ; a corpulent man, calm of disposition, and indulgent to his children. But *Elizeus* the *Prophet* may seem to have died when he was above an hundred years old ; for he is found to have lived after the *assumption* of *Elias* sixty years ; and at the time of that *assumption* he was of those years, that the boys mocked him by the name of *Bald-head* : a man vehement and severe, and of an austere life, and a contemner of riches. Also *Isaiah* the *Prophet* seemeth to have been an hundred years old ; for he is found to have exercised the Function of a *Prophet* seventy years together, the years both of his beginning to prophesie and of his death being uncertain ; a man of an admirable eloquence, an *Evangelical Prophet*, full of the promises of God of the *New Testament*, as a Bottle with sweet Wine.

Tob*ias* the Elder lived an hundred fifty eight years, the Younger, an hundred twenty seven : merciful men, and great alms-givers. It seems, in the time of the *Captivity*, many of the *Jews* who returned out of *Babylon* were of great years, seeing they could remember both *Temples*, (there being no less than seventy years betwixt them) and wept for the unlikeness of them. Many ages after that, in the time of our *Saviour*, lived old *Simeon*, to the age of ninety ; a devout man, and full both of hope and expectation. Into the same time also fell *Anna* the *Prophetess*, who could not possibly be less than an hundred years old ; for she had been seven years a wife, about eighty four years a widow, besides the years of her virginity, and the time that she lived after her Prophecy of our Saviour : She was an holy woman, and passed her days in fastings and prayers.

5.

The *long Lives* of *Men* mentioned in *Heathen Authors* have no great certainty in them ; both for the intermixture of Fables, whereunto those kind of relations were very prone, and for their false calculation of years. Certainly of the *Ægyptians* we find nothing of moment in those works that are extant as touching *long Life*, for their *Kings* which reigned longest did not exceed fifty or five and fifty years, which is no great matter, seeing many at this day attain to those years. But the *Arcadian Kings* are fabulously reported to have lived very long. Surely that Country was Mountainous, full of flocks of Sheep, and brought forth most wholsome food ; notwithstanding, seeing *Pan* was their god, we may conceive that all things about them were *Panick* and vain, and subject to fables.

6.

Numa King of the *Romans* lived to eighty years : a man peaceable, contemplative, and much devoted to Religion. *Marcus Valerius Corvinus* saw an hundred years complete, there being betwixt his first and sixth *Consulship* forty six years : a man valorous, affable, popular, and always fortunate.

7.

Solon of *Athens*, the *Law-giver*, and one of the seven *Wise-men*, lived above eighty years : a man of an high courage, but popular, and affected to his Country ; also learned, given to pleasures and a soft kind of life. *Epimenides* the *Cretian* is reported to have lived an hundred fifty seven years : the matter is mix'd with a *prodigious Relation* ; for fifty seven of those years he is said to have slept in a *Cave*. Half an age after *Xenophon* the *Colophonian* lived an hundred and two years, or rather more : for at the age of twenty five years he left his Country, seventy seven complete years he travelled, and after that returned ; but how long he lived after his return appears not ; a man no less wandring in mind than in body, for his name was changed for the madness of his opinions from *Xenophanes* to *Xenomanes* : a man no doubt of a vast conceit, and that minded nothing but *Infinitum*.

8.

Anacreon the Poet lived eighty years and somewhat better : a man lascivious, voluptuous, and given to drink. *Pindarus* the *Theban* lived to eighty years : a Poet of an high fancy, singular in his conceits, and a great adorer of the god. *Sophocles* the *Athenian* attained to the like age : a lofty Tragick Poet, given over wholly to Writing, and neglectful of his Family.

9.

Artaxerxes King of *Persia* lived ninety four years : a man of a dull wit, averse to the dispatch of business, desirous of glory, but rather of ease. At the same time lived *Agesilaus* King of *Sparta* to eighty four years of age : a moderate Prince, as being a *Philosopher* among *Kings* ; but notwithstanding ambitious, and a Warriour, and no less stout in war than in business.

10.

Gorgias the *Sicilian* was an hundred and eight years old ; a *Rhetorician*, and a great boaster of his faculty, one that taught Youth for profit : he had seen many
Countries,

11.

Countries, and a little before his death said, That he had done nothing worthy of blame since he was an old man. *Protagoras* of *Abdera* saw ninety years of age: this man was likewise a *Rhetorician*, but professed not so much to teach the Liberal Arts, as the Art of Governing Common-wealths and States: notwithstanding he was a great wanderer in the world, no less than *Gorgias*. *Isocrates* the *Athenian* lived ninety eight years: he was a *Rhetorician* also, but an exceeding modest man; one that shunned the publick light, and opened his School onely in his own house. *Democritus* of *Abdera* reached to an hundred and nine years: he was a great *Philosopher*, and, if ever any man amongst the *Grecians*, a true *Naturalist*; a Surveyor of many Countries, but much more of Nature; also a diligent searcher into Experiments, and (as *Aristotle* objected against him) one that followed Similitudes more than the Laws of Arguments. *Diogenes* the *Sinopean* lived ninety years: a man that used liberty towards others, but tyranny over himself: a course diet, and of much patience. *Zeno* of *Citium* lacked but two years of an hundred: a man of an high mind, and a contemner of other mens opinions; also of a great acuteness, but yet not troublesome, chusing rather to take mens minds than to enforce them: The like whereof afterward was in *Seneca*. *Plato* the *Athenian* attained to eighty one years: a man of a great courage, but yet a lover of ease; in his Notions sublimed, and of a fancy, neat and delicate in his life, rather calm than merry, and one that carried a kind of Majesty in his countenance. *Theophrastus* the *Eressian* arrived at eighty five years of age; a man sweet for his eloquence, sweet for the variety of his matters, and who selected the pleasant things of Philosophy, and let the bitter and harsh go. *Carneades* of *Cyrene* many years after came to the like age of eighty five years: a man of a fluent eloquence, and one who by the acceptable and pleasant variety of his knowledge delighted both himself and others. But *Orbilius*, who lived in *Cicero*'s time, no *Philosopher* or *Rhetorician*, but a *Grammarian*, attained to an hundred years of age, he was first a Souldier, then a Schoolmaster; a man by nature tart both in his Tongue and Pen, and severe towards his Scholars.

12. *Quintus Fabius Maximus* was *Augur* sixty three years, which shewed him to be above eighty years of age at his death; though it be true, that in the *Augurship* Nobility was more respected then age: a wise man, and a great *Deliberator*, and in all his proceedings moderate, and not without affability severe. *Masinissa* King of *Numidia* lived ninety years, and being more than eighty five got a son: a daring man, and trusting upon his fortune, who in his youth had tasted of the inconstancy of Fortune but in his succeeding age was constantly happy. But *Marcus Porcius Cato* lived above ninety years of age: a man of an Iron body and mind; he had a bitter tongue, and loved to cherish factions; he was given to Husbandry, and was to himself and his Family a Physician.

13. *Terentia Cicero*'s wife, lived an hundred and three years: a woman afflicted with many crosses; first, with the banishment of her Husband; then with the difference betwixt them; lastly, with his last fatal misfortune: She was also oftentimes vexed with the Gout. *Luceia* must needs exceed an hundred by many years; for it is said that she acted an whole hundred years upon the Stage, at first perhaps representing the person of some young Girl, at last of some decrepit old Woman. But *Galeria Copiola*, a Player also and a Dancer, was brought upon the Stage as a Novice, in what year of her age is not known; but ninety nine years after, at the *Dedication* of the *Theatre* by *Pompey* the *Great*, she was shewn upon the Stage, not now for an Actress, but for a Wonder: neither was this all, for after that, in the *Solemnities* for the health and life of *Augustus*, she was shewn upon the Stage the third time.

14. There was another *Actress*, somewhat inferiour in age, but much superiour in dignity, which lived well-near ninety years, I mean *Livia Julia Augusta*, wife to *Augustus Cæsar*, and mother to *Tiberius*. For if *Augustus* his life were a Play, (as himself would have it, whenas upon his death-bed he charged his friends they should give him a *Plaudite* after he was dead) certainly this *Lady* was an excellent *Actress*, who could carry it so well with her husband by a dissembled obedience, and with her son by power and authority: a woman affable, and yet of a Matronal carriage, pragmatical, and upholding her power. But *Junia*, the wife of *Caius Cassius*, and sister of *Marcus Brutus*, was also ninety years old; for she survived the *Philippick Battel* sixty four years: a magnanimous woman, in her great wealth

happy:

happy in the calamity of her husband and near kinsfolks, and in a long widow-hood
unhappy; notwithstanding much honoured of all.

    The *year* of our *Lord* seventy six, falling into the time of *Vespasian*, is memorable;   15.
in which we shall find, as it were, a *calendar* of long-liv'd men: For that year there
was a *Taxing*, (now a *Taxing* is the most Authentical and truest Informer touching
the ages of men;) and in that part of *Italy* which lieth betwixt the *Apennine Mountains* and the *River Po*, there were found an hundred and four and twenty persons that
either equalled or exceeded an hundred years of age: namely, of an hundred years
just, fifty four persons; of an hundred and ten, fifty seven persons; of an hundred
and five and twenty, two onely; of an hundred and thirty, four men; of an hundred
and five and thirty, or seven and thirty, four more; of an hundred and forty, three
men. Besides these, *Parma* in particular afforded five; whereof three fulfilled an hundred and twenty years, and two an hundred and thirty: *Bruxels* afforded one of an hundred and twenty five years old; *Placentia* one, aged an hundred thirty and one; *Fa-
ventia* one woman, aged one hundred thirty and two: a certain Town, then called
Velleiatium, situate in the *Hills* about *Placentia*, afforded ten, whereof six fulfilled an
hundred and ten years of age; four, an hundred and twenty: Lastly, *Rimini* one of an
hundred and fifty years, whose name was *Marcus Aponius*.

    *That our catalogue might not be extended too much in length, we have thought fit,
as well in those whom we have rehearsed, as in those whom we shall rehearse, to offer
none under eighty years of age. Now we have affixed to every one a true and short
Character or Elogy; but of that sort whereunto, in our judgment, Length of Life
(which is not a little subject to the Manners and Fortunes of men) hath some relation,
and that in a two-fold respect: either that such kind of men are for the most part long-
liv'd; or that such men may sometimes be of long life, though otherwise not well disposed
for it.*

    Amongst the *Roman* and *Grecian Emperors*, also the *French* and *Almain*, to these   16.
our dayes, which make up the number of well-near two hundred *Princes*, there
are onely four found that lived to eighty years of age: unto whom we may adde the
two first Emperors, *Augustus* and *Tiberius*; whereof the latter fulfilled the seventy
and eighth year, the former the seventy and sixth year of his age, and might both perhaps have lived to fourscore, if *Livia* and *Caius* had been pleased. *Augustus* (as was
said) lived seventy and six years: a man of moderate disposition; in accomplishing
his designs vehement; but otherwise calm and serene; in meat and drink sober,
in Venery intemperate, through all his life-time happy; and who about the thirtieth year of his life had a great and dangerous sickness, insomuch as they despaired of life in him; whom *Antonius Musa* the Physician, when other Physicians
had applied hot Medicines, as most agreeable to his disease, on the contrary cured
with cold Medicines, which perchance might be some help to the prolonging of his
life. *Tiberius* lived to be two years older: *A man with lean chaps*, as *Augustus*
was wont to say, for his speech stuck within his jaws, but was weighty. He was
bloudy, a drinker, and one that took Lust into a part of his diet; notwithstanding
a great observer of his health, insomuch that he used to say, That he was a fool
that after thirty years of age took advice of a *Physician*. *Gordian* the elder lived
eighty years, and yet died a violent death when he was scarce warm in his *Empire*:
a man of an high spirit and renowned, learned, and a Poet, and constantly happy throughout the whole course of his life, save onely that he ended his dayes by a
violent death. *Valerian* the *Emperour* was seventy six years of age before he was
taken prisoner by *Sapor* King of *Persia*, after his Captivity he lived seven years in
reproaches, and then died a violent death also: a man of a poor mind, and not va-
liant; notwithstanding lifted up in his own and the opinion of men, but falling
short in the performance. *Anastasius*, surnamed *Dicorus*, lived eighty eight years: he
was of a setled mind, but too abject, and superstitious, and fearful. *Anicius Justi-
nianus* lived to eighty three years: a man greedy of glory, performing nothing in his
own person, but in the valour of his Captains happy and renowned; uxorious, and not
his own man, but suffering others to lead him. *Helena of Britain*, mother of *Constantine* the *Great*, was fourscore years old: a woman that intermedled not in matters of
State neither in her Husband's nor sons Reign, but devoted her self wholly to Religion:
magnanimous, and perpetually flourishing. *Theodora* the *Empress* (who was sister to *Zoes*,

E

wife

wife of *Monomachus,* and reigned alone after her decease) lived above eighty years : a pragmatical woman, and one that took delight in Governing ; fortunate in the highest degree, and through her good fortunes credulous,

17.   We will proceed now from these *Secular Princes* to the *Princes* in the *Church.* St. *John,* an Apostle of our *Saviour,* and the *Beloved Disciple,* lived ninety three years. He was rightly denoted under the *Emblem* of the *Eagle,* for his piercing sight into the *Divinity*; and was a *seraph* amongst the *Apostles* in respect of his burning Love. St. *Luke* the *Evangelist* fulfilled fourscore and four years : an eloquent man, and a Traveller, St. *Paul's* inseparable Companion, and a *Physician.* *Simeon* the son of *Cleophas,* called the *Brother of our Lord,* and Bishop of *Jerusalem,* lived an hundred and twenty years though he was cut short by Martyrdom : a stout man, and constant, and full of good works. *Polycarpus, Disciple* unto the *Apostles,* and Bishop of *Smyrna,* seemeth to have extended his age to an hundred years and more ; though he were also cut off by Martyrdom : a man of an high mind, of an heroical patience, and unwearied with labours. *Dyonisius Areopagita,* Contemporary to the Apostle St. *Paul,* lived ninety years : he was called the *Bird of Heaven* for his high flying Divinity, and was famous as well for his holy life as for his Meditations. *Aquilla* and *Priscilla,* first St. *Paul* the Apostle's Hosts. Afterward his Fellow-helpers, lived together in a happy and famous Wedlock at least to an hundred years of age a piece ; for they were both alive under Pope *Xistus* the first : a noble Pair, and prone to all kind of charity, who amongst other their comforts (which no doubt were great unto the first *Founders* of the *Church*) had this added, to enjoy each other so long in an happy marriage. St. *Paul* the *Hermite* lived an hundred and thirteen years : now he lived in a Cave ; his diet was so slender and strict, that it was thought almost impossible to support humane nature therewithal : he passed his years onely in Meditations and Soliloquies ; yet he was not illiterate or an Idiot, but learned. St. *Anthony,* the first Founder of *Monks,* or (as some will have it) the Restorer onely, attained to an hundred and five years of age : a man devout and contemplative, though not unfit for Civil affairs ; his life was austere and mortifying, notwithstanding he lived in a kind of glorious solitude ; and exercised a command, for he had his *Monks* under him. And besides, many *Christians* and *Philosophers* came to visit him as a living Image, from which they parted not without some adoration. St. *Athanasius* exceeded the term of eighty years : a man of an invincible constancy, commanding fame, and not yielding to Fortune : he was free towards the Great ones, with the People gracious and acceptable, beaten and practised to oppositions, and in delivering himself from them stout and wise. St. *Hierom,* by the consent of most Writers, exceeded ninety years of age : a man powerful in his Pen, and of a manly Eloquence, variously learned both in the Tongues and Sciences, also a Traveller, and that lived strictly towards his old age, in an estate private, and not dignified ; he bore high Spirits, and shined far out of obscurity.

18.   The *Popes* of *Rome* are in number to this day two hundred forty and one. Of so great a number five onely have attained to the age of fourscore years, or upwards. But in many of the first *Popes* their full age was intercepted by the Prerogative and Crown of *Martyrdom.* *John* the twenty third, *Pope of Rome,* fulfilled the ninetieth year of his age : a man of an unquiet disposition, and one that studied novelty : he altered many things, some to the better, others onely to the new, a great accumulator of Riches and Treasures. *Gregory,* called the twelfth, created in Schism, and not fully acknowledged *Pope,* died at ninety years : of him, in respect of his short *Papacy,* we find nothing to make a judgment upon. *Paul* the third lived eighty years and one : a temperate man, and of a profound wisdom : he was Learned, an Astrologer, and one that tended his health carefully ; but, after the example of old *Eli* the Priest, over-indulgent to his Family. *Paul* the fourth attained to the age of eighty three years : a man of an harsh nature and severe, of an haughty mind and imperious, prone to anger ; his speech was eloquent and ready. *Gregory* the thirteenth fulfilled the like age of eighty three years : an absolute good man, sound in mind and body, politick, temperate, full of good works, and an alms-giver.

19.   Those that follow are to be more promiscuous in their order, more doubtful in their faith, and more barren of observation. King *Arganthenius,* who reigned at *Cadiz* in

Spain lived an hundred and thirty, or (as some would have it) an hundred and forty years, of which he reigned eighty. Concerning his Manners, Institution of his Life, and the time wherein he reigned, there is a general silence. *Cyntras* King of *Cyprus*, living in the *Island* then termed the *Happy* and *Pleasant Island*, is affirmed to have attained to an hundred and fifty or sixty years. Two *Latin Kings* in *Italy*, the Father and the Son, are reported to have lived, the one eight hundred, the other six hundred years: but this is delivered unto us by certain *Philologists*, who though otherwise credulous enough, yet themselves have suspected the truth of this matter, or rather condemned it. Others record some *Arcadian Kings* to have lived three hundred years : the Country, no doubt, is a place apt for long life ; but the Relation I suspect to be fabulous. They tell of one *Dando* in *Illyrium*, that lived without the inconveniences of old age to five hundred years. They tell also of the *Epians*, a part of *Ætolia*, that the whole Nation of them were exceeding long liv'd, insomuch that many of them were two hundred years old : and that one principal man amongst them, named *Litorius*, a man of a Giant-like stature, could have told three hundred years. It is recorded, that on the top of the Mountain *Timolus*, anciently called *Tempsis*, many of the Inhabitants lived to an hundred and fifty years. We read that the *Sect* of the *Esseans* amongst the *Jews* did usually extend their life to an hundred years : Now that *Sect* used a single or abstemious diet, after the rule of *Pythagoras*. *Apollonius Tyaneus* exceeded an hundred years, his face bewraying no such age : he was an admirable man, of the *Heathens* reputed to have something Divine in him, of the *christians* held for a Sorcerer ; in his diet *Pythagorical*, a great traveller, much renowned, and by some adored as a *god* : notwithstanding, towards the end of his life he was subject to many complaints against him, and reproaches, all which he made shift to escape. But lest his long life should be imputed to his *Pythagorical* diet, and not rather that it was hereditary, his *Grandfather* before him lived an hundred and thirty years. It is undoubted that *Quintus Metellus* lived above an hundred years, and that after several *Consulships* happily administred, in his old age he was made *Pontifex Maximus*, and exercised those holy duties full two and twenty years ; in the performance of which Rites his voice never failed, nor his hand trembled. It is most certain that *Appius cæcus* was very old, but his years are not extant, the most part whereof he passed after he was blind ; yet this misfortune no whit softned him, but that he was able to govern a numerous Family, a great Retinue and Dependance, yea, even the Commonwealth it self, with great stoutness. In his extream old age he was brought in a Litter into the *senate-house*, and vehemently disswaded the Peace with *Pyrrhus* : the beginning of his Oration was very memorable, shewing an invincible spirit and strength of mind ; *I have with great grief of mind (Fathers conscript) these many years born my blindness, but now I could wish that I were deaf also, when I hear you speak to such dishonourable Treaties.* *Marcus Perpenna* lived ninety eight years, surviving all those whose Suffrages he had gathered in the *senate-house*, being *Consul*, I mean, all the *Senators* at that time ; as also all those whom a little after, being *Consul*, he chose into the *Senate*, seven onely being excepted. *Hiero* King of *Sicily*, in the time of the second *Punick War*, lived almost an hundred years : a man moderate both in his Government and in his Life ; a worshiper of the *gods*, and a religious conserver of Friendship : liberal, and constantly fortunate. *Statilia*, descended of a noble Family in the days of *Claudius*, lived ninety nine years. *Clodia*, the daughter of *Ofilius*, an hundred and fifteen. *Xenephilus*, an ancient Philosopher, of the *Sect* of *Pythagoras*, attained to an hundred and six years, remaining healthful and vigorous in his old age, and famous amongst the vulgar for his learning. The *Islanders* of *Corcyra* were anciently accounted long liv'd, but now they live after the rate of other men, *Hipocrates Cous*, the famous *Physician*, lived an hundred and four years, and approved and credited his own Art by so long a life : a man that coupled Learning and Wisdom together, very conversant in Experience and Observation ; one that haunted not after Words or Methods, but severed the very Nerves of Science, and so propounded them. *Demonax* a Philosoper, not onely in Profession but Practice, lived in the dayes of *Adrian* almost to an hundred years : a man of an high mind, and a vanquisher of his own mind, and that truly and without affectation ; a contemner of the world, and yet civil and courteous. When his friends spake to him about his Burial, he said, *Take no care for my Burial, for Stench will bury a Carcase.* They replied, *Is it your*

                                                                 mind

mind than to be caft out to Birds and Dogs? He faid again, *Seeing in my life-time I endeavoured to my uttermoft to benefit Men, what hurt is it if when I am dead I benefit Beafts?* Certain *Indian* People called *Pandora* are exceedingly long-liv'd, even to no lefs than two hundred years. They adde a thing more marvellous, That having, when they are boys, an hair fomewhat whitifh, in their old age, before their gray hairs, they grow coal black, though indeed this be every where to be feen, that they which have white hair whilft they are boys, in their man's eftate change their hairs into a darker colour. The *Seres*, another people of *India*, with their Wine of Palms are accounted long livers, even to an hundred and thirty years. *Euphranor* the *Grammarian* grew old in his School, and taught Scholars when he was above an hundred years old. The elder *Ovid*, father to the *Poet*, lived ninety years, differing much from the difpofition of his fon, for he contemned the *Mufes*, and diffwaded his fon from Poetry. *Afinius Pollio*, intimate with *Auguftus*, exceeded the age of an hundred years : a man of an unreafonable Profufenefs, Eloquent, and a lover of Learning ; but vehement, proud, cruel, and one that made his private ends the centre of his thoughts. There was an opinion, that *Seneca* was an extream old man, no lefs than an hundred and fourteen years of age : which could not poffibly be, it being as improbable that a decrepit old man fhould be fet over *Nero*'s Youth, as, on the contrary, it was true, that he was able to manage with great dexterity the affairs of State : befides, a little before, in the midft of *Claudius* his Reign, he was banifhed *Rome* for Adulteries committed with fome *Noble Ladies*, which was a Crime no way compatible with fo extreme old age. *Johannes de Temporibus*, among all the men of our later Ages, out of a common fame and vulgar opinion, was reputed long-liv'd, even to a miracle, or rather, even to a fable ; his age hath been counted above three hundred years : He was by Nation a *French-man*, and followed the Wars under *Charls* the *Great*. *Garcius Aretine*, Great Grand-father to *Petrarch*, arrived at the age of an hundred and four years : he had ever enjoyed the benefit of good health ; befides, at the laft, he felt rather a decay of his ftrength, than any ficknefs or malady, which is the true Fefolution by old age. Amongft the *Venetians* there have been found not a few long livers, and thofe of the more eminent fort : *Francifcus Donatus*, Duke ; *Thomas Contarenus*, Procurator of St. *Mark* ; *Francifcus Molinus*, Procurator alfo of St. *Mark*, and others. But moft memorable is that of *cornarus* the *Venetian*, who being in his youth of a fickly body, began firft to eat and drink by meafure to a certain weight, thereby to recover his health : this Cure turned by ufe into a Diet, that Diet to an extraordinary long Life, even of an hundred years and better, without any decay in his fenfes, and with a conftant enjoying of his health. In our age *William Poftel*, a *French-man*, lived to an hundred and well-nigh twenty years, the top of his beard on the upper-lip being black, and not gray at all : a man crazed in his brain, and of a fancy not altogether found, a great Traveller, Mathematician, and fomewhat ftained with *Herefie*.

20. I fuppofe there is fcarce a *Village* with us in *England*, if it be any whit populous, but it affords fome Man or Woman of fourfcore years of age : nay, a few years fince there was in the County of *Hereford* a May-game or Morrice dance, confifting of eight men, whofe age computed together made up eight hundred years, infomuch that what fome of them wanted of an hundred, others exceeded as much.

21. In the *Hofpital* of *Bethlehem*, corruptly called *Bedlam*, in the *Suburbs* of *London*, there are found from time to time many mad perfons that live to a great age.

22. The ages of *Nymphs*, *Fauns*, and *Satyrs*, whom they make to be indeed mortal, but yet exceedingly long-liv'd, (a thing which ancient Superftition and the late Credulity of fome have admitted) we account but for *Fables* and *Dreams* ; efpecially being that which hath neither confent with *Philofophy* nor with *Divinity*. And as touching the *Hiftory* of *Long Life* in *Man* by *Individuals*, or next unto *Individuals*, thus much. Now we will pafs on to *Obfervations* by certain Heads.

23. The *Running* on of *Ages*, and *Succeffion* of *Generations*, feem to have no whit abated from the length of Life ; for we fee that from the time of *Mofes* unto thefe our dayes, the term of man's life hath ftood about fourfcore years of age, neither hath it declined (as a man would have thought) by little and little. No doubt there are times in every Country wherein men are longer or fhorter liv'd.

Longer.

Longer, for the moſt part when the times are barbarous, and men fare leſs delici-
ouſly, and are more given to bodily exerciſes : Shorter, when the times are more
civil, and men abandon themſelves to luxury and eaſe. But theſe things paſs on by
their turns, the ſucceſſion of Generations alters is not. The ſame, no doubt, is in
other living Creatures ; for neither Oxen, nor Horſes, nor Sheep, nor any the
like, are abridged of their wonted ages at this day. And therefore the Great
Abridger of Age was the *Floud* ; and perhaps ſome ſuch notable accidents (as
particular *Inundations*, *long Droughts*, *Earthquakes*, or the like) may do the ſame
again. And the like reaſon is in the dimenſion and ſtature of Bodies ; for neither
are they leſſened by ſucceſſion of Generations, howſoever *Virgil* (following the
vulgar opinion) divined, that after Ages would bring forth leſſer Bodies than the
then preſent : whereupon ſpeaking of ploughing up the *Æmathian* and *Æmonen-
ſian* Fields, he ſaith, *Grandiáq; effoſſis mirabitur oſſa ſepulchris, That after-ages ſhall
admire the great bones digged up in ancient ſepulchres.* For whereas it is manifeſted that
there were heretofore men of Gigantine Statures, (ſuch as for certain have been found
in *Sicily*, and elſe-where, in ancient Sepulchres and Caves) yet within theſe laſt
three thouſand years, a time whereof we have ſure memory, thoſe very places have
produced none ſuch: although this thing alſo hath certain turns and changes, by the
Civilizing of a Nation, no leſs than the former. And this is the rather to be noted,
becauſe men are wholly carried away with an opinion, that there is a continual
decay by Succeſſion of Ages, as well in the term of man's Life as in the
ſtature and ſtrength of his Body ; and that all things decline and change to the
worſe.

In *Cold* and *Northern Countries* men live longer commonly than in *Hot* : which
muſt needs be in reſpect the skin is more compact and cloſe, and the juices of
the body leſs diſſipable, and the Spirits themſelves leſs eager to conſume, and in
better diſpoſition to repair, and the Air (as being little heated by the Sun-beams)
leſs predatory: And yet under the *Æquinoctial Line*, where the Sun paſſeth to and
fro, and cauſeth a double Summer and double Winter, and where the Days and
Nights are more equal, (if other things be concurring) they live alſo very long;
as in *Peru* and *Taprobane*.

Iſlanders are, for the moſt part, longer-liv'd than thoſe that live in *Continents*: for
they live not ſo long in *Ruſſia* as in the *Orcades* ; nor ſo long in *Africa*, though
under the ſame *Parallel*, as in the *Canaries* and *Tercera's* ; and the *Japonians* are
longer-liv'd than the *Chineſes*, though the *Chineſes* are made upon long life. And this
thing is no marvel, ſeeing the Air of the Sea doth heat and cheriſh in cooler Regions, and cool in hotter.

High Situations do rather afford long-livers than *Low*, eſpecially if they be not Tops
of Mountains, but Riſing Grounds, as to their general Situations ; ſuch as was *Arcadia* in *Greece*, and that part of *Ætolia* where we related them to have lived ſo long.
Now there would be the ſame reaſon for *Mountains* themſelves, becauſe of the pureneſs
and clearneſs of the Air, but that they are corrupted by accident, namely, by the
Vapours riſing thither out of the Valleys, and reſting there ; and therefore in Snowy
Mountains there is not found any notable long life, not in the *Alps*, not in the *Pyre-
nean Mountains*, not in the *Apennine* : yet in the tops of the *Mountains* running
along towards *Æthiopia* and the *Abyſſines*, where by reaſon of the Sands beneath little
or no Vapour riſeth to the *Mountains*, they live long, even at this very day, attaining many times to an hundred and fifty years.

Marſhes and *Fens* are propitious to the Natives, and malignant to Strangers, as touching the lengthning and ſhortning of their lives : and that which may ſeem more marvellous, *Salt-Marſhes*, where the Sea Ebbs and Flows, are leſs wholſome than thoſe of
Freſh water.

The *Countries* which have been obſerved to produce long-livers are theſe ; *Arcadia,
Ætolia, India* on this ſide *Ganges, Braſil, Taprobane, Britain, Ireland*, with the Iſlands of
the *Orcades* and *Hebrides* : for as for *Æthiopia*, which by one of the Ancients is reported to bring forth long-Livers, 'tis but a toy.

It is a Secret ; The *healthfulneſs of Air*, eſpecially in any perfection, is better
found by *Experiment* than by *Diſcourſe* or *Conjecture*. You may make a trial by
a lock of Wool expoſed for a few dayes in the open Air, if the weight be not much

24.

25.

26.

27.

28.

29.

E 3   increaſed

increased ; another by a piece of flesh exposed likewise, if it corrupt not over-soon ; another by a Weather-glass, if the Water interchange not too suddenly. Of these and the like enquire further.

30. Not onely the *Goodness* or *Pureness* of the *Air*, but also the *Equality* of the *Air*, is material to long life. Intermixture of Hills and Dales is pleasant to the sight, but suspected for long life. A Plain, moderately drie, but yet not over-barren or sandy, nor altogether without Trees and Shade, is very convenient for length of life.

31. *Inequality* of *Air* (as was even now said) in the place of our dwelling is naught ; but *Change* of *Air* by travelling, after one be used unto it, is good ; and therefore great Travellers have been long liv'd. Also those that have lived perpetually in a little Cottage, in the same place, have been long-livers : for air accustomed consumeth less ; but air changed nourisheth and repaireth more.

32. As the continuation and number of Successions (which we said before) makes nothing to the Length and Shortness of Life ; so the *immediate condition* of the *Parents*, (as well the Father as the Mother) without doubt availeth much. For some are begotten of old men, some of young men, some of men of middle age ; again, some are begotten of fathers healthful and well-disposed, others of diseased and languishing ; again, some of fathers immediately after repletion, or when they are drunk, others after sleeping, or in the morning ; again, some after a long intermission of *Venus*, others upon the act repeated ; again, some in the fervency of the father's love, (as it is commonly in Bastards) others after the cooling of it, as in long-married couples. The same things may be considered on the part of the Mother : unto which must be added the condition of the Mother whilst she is with child, as touching her health, as touching her diet, the time of her bearing in the womb, to the tenth month, or earlier. To reduce these things to a Rule, how far they may concern *Long Life*, is hard ; and so much the harder, for that those things which a man would conceive to be the best, will fall out to the contrary : For that alacrity in the Generation which begets lusty and lively children, will be less profitable to long-life, because of the Acrimony and inflaming of the Spirits. We said before, That to partake more of the mother's bloud conduceth to long life : also we suppose all things in moderation to be best ; rather Conjugal love than Meretricious ; the hour for Generation to be the morning ; a state of body not too lusty or full, and such like. It ought to be well observed, that a strong Constitution in the Parents is rather good for them then for the Child, especially in the Mother : And therefore *Plato* thought, ignorantly enough, that the virtue of Generations halted, because the Woman used not the same exercise both of mind and body with the Men. The contrary is rather true ; for the difference of virtue betwixt the Male and the Female is most profitable for the Child ; and the thinner Women yield more towards the nourishment of the Child ; which also holds in Nurses. Neither did the *Spartan Women*, which married not before twenty two, or, as some say, twenty five, (and therefore were called *Man-like women*) bring forth a more generous or long-liv'd Progeny than the *Roman* or *Athenian*, or *Theban women* did, which were ripe for Marriage at twelve or fourteen years ; and if there were any thing eminent in the *Spartans*, that was rather to be imputed to the Parsimony of their Diet than to the late Marriages of their Women. But this we are taught by experience, that there are some Races which are long liv'd for a few Descents ; so that Life is like some Diseases, a thing hereditary within certain bounds.

33. *Fair* in *Face*, or *Skin*, or *Hair*, are shorter livers ; *Black*, or *Red*, or *Freckled*, longer. Also too fresh a colour in Youth doth less promise long life than paleness. A *hard skin* is a sign of long life rather that a *soft* ; but we understand not this of a *rugged skin*, such as they call the *Goose skin*, which is as it were spongy, but of that which is hard and close. A *Fore-head* with deep furrows and wrinkles is a better sign than a smooth and plain *Forehead*.

34. The *Hairs* of the *Head* hard and like bristles, do betoken longer life than those that are soft and delicate. *Curled Hairs* betoken the same thing, if they be hard withal ; but the contrary if they be soft and shining : the like if the *curling* be rather thick than in large bunches.

35. Early or late *Baldness* is an indifferent thing, seeing many which have been

Bald

Bald betimes have lived long.   Also early *gray hairs* (howſoever they may ſeem fore-runners of old age approaching) are no ſure ſigns; for many that have grown *gray* betimes have lived to great years: nay, haſty *gray hairs* without *Baldneſs* is a token of long life : contrarily, if they be accompanied with *Baldneſs*.

Hairineſs of the *upper parts* is a ſign of ſhort life, and they that have extraordinary much *hair* on their breaſts live not long: but *Hairineſs* of the *lower parts*, as of the Thighes and Legs, is a ſign of long life.   56.

Talneſs of *Stature* (if it be not immoderate) with convenient making, and not too ſlender, eſpecially if the body be active withal, is a ſign of long life : Alſo on the contrary, men of low ſtature live long, if they be not too active and ſtirring.   37.

In the proportion of the body they which are *ſhort* to the *waſtes*, with *long Leggs*, are longer-liv'd than they which are *long* to the *waſtes*, and have *ſhort Leggs*: alſo they which are large in the *neather parts*, and ſtreight in the *upper*, (the making of their body riſing, as it were, into a ſharp figure) are longer-liv'd than they that have *broad ſhoulders*, and are ſlender downwards.   38.

Leanneſs, where the affections are ſetled, calm, and peaceable ; alſo a more *fat habit of body*, joyned with Choler, and a diſpoſition ſtirring and peremptory, ſignifie long life : but *Corpulency* in Youth foreſhews ſhort life, In Age it is a thing more indifferent.   39.

To be *long* and *ſlow* in *growing* is a ſign of long life; if to a greater ſtature, the greater ſign, if to a leſſer ſtature, yet a ſign though: contrarily, to *grow* quickly to a great ſtature is an evil ſign; if to a ſmall ſtature, the leſs evil.   40.

Firm Fleſh, a raw bone body, and veins lying higher than the fleſh, betoken long life ; the contrary to theſe, ſhort life.   41.

A *Head* ſomewhat leſſer than to the proportion of the body ; a moderate *Neck*, not long, nor ſlender, nor flat, nor too ſhort ; wide *Noſtrils*, whatſoever the form of the Noſe be ; a large *Mouth*; and *Ear* griſtly, not fleſhy; *Teeth* ſtrong and contiguous, ſmall, or thin-ſet, fore-token long life ; and much more if ſome new *Teeth* put forth in our elder years.   42.

A broad *Breaſt*; yet not bearing out, but rather bending inwards ; *Shoulders* ſomewhat crooked, and (as they call ſuch perſons) round-back'd ; a flat *Belly* ; a *Hand* large, and with few lines in the Palm ; a ſhort and round *Foot*, *Thighs* not fleſhy, and *ulver* of the *Leggs* not hanging over, but neat, are ſigns of long life.   43.

Eyes ſomewhat large, and the *Circles* of them inclined to greenneſs ; *ſenſes* not too quick ; the *Pulſe* in youth ſlower, towards old age quicker ; *Facility of holding* the *Breath*, and longer than uſual; the body in youth inclined to be bound, in the decline of years more laxative, are alſo ſigns of long life.   44.

Concerning the *Times of Nativity*, as they refer to long life, nothing hath been obſerved worthy the ſetting down, ſave onely *Aſtrological Obſervations*, which we rejected in our *opicks*.   A *Birth* at the eighth month is not onely long liv'd, but not likely to live   Alſo *winter births* are accounted the longer-liv'd.   45.

A *Pythagorical* or *Monaſtical Diet*, according to ſtrict rules, and always exactly equal, (as that of *Cornarus* was) ſeemeth to be very effectual for long life.   Yet on the contrary, amongſt thoſe that live freely and after the common ſort, ſuch as have *good ſtomachs*, and *feed more plentifully*, are often the longeſt-liv'd.   The *middle diet*, which we account the temperate, is commended, and conduceth to good health, but not to long life : for the *ſpare diet* begets few *Spirits*, and dull, and ſo waſteth the body leſs; and the *liberal diet* yieldeth more ample nouriſhment, and ſo repaireth more : but the *middle diet* doth neither of both, for where the Extreams are hurtful, there the Mean is beſt ; but where the Extreams are helpful, there the Mean is nothing worth.   46.

Now to that *ſpare diet* there are requiſite *Watching*, leſt the Spirits being few ſhould be oppreſſed with much ſleep; *little Exerciſe*, leſt they ſhould exhale ; *abſtinence* from *Venery*, leſt they ſhould be exhauſted : but to the *liberal diet*, on the other ſide, are requiſite much *Sleep*, frequent *Exerciſes*, and a ſeaſonable uſe of *Venery*. *Baths* and *Anointings* (ſuch as were anciently in uſe) did rather tend to deliciouſneſs than to prolonging of life.   But of all theſe things we ſhall ſpeak more exactly when we come to the *Inquiſition* according to *Intentions*.   Mean while that of *Celſus*, who was not onely a learned Phyſician, but a wiſe man, is not to be omitted, who adviſeth interchanging and alternation of the diet, but ſtill with an inclination to the more benign : as that a man ſhould ſometimes accuſtom himſelf to

watching,

watching, sometimes to sleep; but to sleep oftnest: again, that he should sometimes give himself to fasting, sometimes to feasting; but to feasting oftnest: that he should sometimes inure himself to great labours of the mind, sometimes to relaxations of the same; but to relaxations oftnest. Certainly this is without all question, that *Diet* well ordered bears the greatest part in the prolongation of life: neither did I ever meet an extream long-liv'd man, but being asked of his course, he observed something peculiar; some one thing, some another. I remember an *old man,* above an hundred years of age, who was produced as witness touching an ancient Prescription. When he had finished his testimony the *Judge* familiarly asked him how he came to live so long. He answered, beside expectation, and not without the laughter of the hearers, *by eating before I was hungry, and drinking before I was dry.* But of these things we shall speak hereafter.

47. A *Life* led in *Religion* and in *Holy Exercises* seemeth to conduce to long life. There are in this kind of life these things, Leisure, Admiration and Contemplation of heavenly things, Joyes not sensual, noble hopes, wholsome Fear, sweet Sorrows; lastly, continual Renovations by Observances, Penances, Expiations: all which are very powerful to the prolongation of life. Unto which if you add that austere diet which hardneth the mass of the Body, and humbleth the Spirits, no marvel if an extraordinary length of life do follow; such was that of *Paul* the *Hermite, Simeon Stelita* the *Columnar Anchorite,* and of many other *Hermites* and *Anchorites.*

48. Next unto this is the life led in good Letters, such as was that of Philosophers, Rhetoricians, Grammarians. This life is also led in leisure, and in those thoughts, which, seeing they are severed from the affairs of the world, bite not, but rather delight through their Variety and Impertinency: They live also at their pleasure, spending their time in such things as like them best, and for the most part in the company of young men, which is ever the most chearful. But in Philosophies there is great difference betwixt the Sects as touching long life: For those Philosophies which have in them a touch of Superstition, and are conversant in high Contemplations, are the best; as the *Pythagorical* and *Platonick*: also those which did institute a perambulation of the world, and considered the variety of natural things, and had reachless, and high, and magnanimous thoughts, (as of *Infinitum,* of the Stars, of the Heroical Vertues, and such like) were good for lengthning of life; such were those of *Democritus Philolaus, Xenophanes,* the Astrologians and Stoicks: also those which had no profound Speculation in them, but discoursed calmly on both sides, out of common Sense, and there received Opinions, without any sharp Inquisitions, were likewise good; such were those of *Carneades* and the *Academicks,* also of the Rhetoricians and Grammarians. But contrary, Philosophies conversant in perplexing Subtilties, and which pronounced peremptorily, and which examined and wrested all things to the Scale of Principles, lastly, which were thorny and narrow, were evil: such were those commonly of the *Peripateticks,* and of the *School-men.*

49. The *Country life* also is well fitted for long life: it is much abroad, and in the open air, it is not slothful, but ever in employment; it feedeth upon fresh Cates, and unbought; It is without Cares and Envy.

50. For the *Military life,* we have a good opinion of that whilst a man is young. Certainly many excellent *Warriors* have been long-liv'd; *Corvinus, Camillus, Xenophon, Agesilaus,* with others both ancient and modern. No doubt it furthereth long life to have all things from our youth to our elder age mend, and grow to the better, that a Youth full of crosses may minister sweetness to our Old age. We conceive also that *Military affections,* inflamed with a desire of Fighting, and hope of Victory, do infuse such a heat into the *Spirits,* as may be profitable for long life.

Medicines for Long Life.

To the tenth Article.

*T*He Art of Physick, *which we now have, looks no farther commonly than to Conservation of Health and Cure of Diseases : As for those things which tend properly to* Long Life, *there is but slight mention, and by the way onely.* Notwithstanding we will propound those Medicines *which are notable in this kind, I mean, those which are* Cordials. *For it is consonant to reason, that those things which being taken in Cures do defend and fortifie the Heart, or, more truly, the Spirits, against Poysons and Diseases, being transferred with judgment and choice into Diet, should have a good effect, in some sort, towards the Prolonging of Life. This we will do, not heaping them promiscuously together, (as the manner is) but selecting the best.*

1.

Gold is given in three forms ; either in that which they call *Aurum potabile* , or in *Wine* wherein *Gold* hath been *quenched,* or in *Gold* in the *Substance,* such as are *Leaf-gold,* and the *Filings of Gold.* As for *Aurum potabile,* it is used to be given in desperate or dangerous diseases, and that not without good success. But we suppose that the Spirits of the *Salt,* by which the *Gold* is dissolved, do rather minister that vertue which is found in it, than the *Gold* it self; though this secret be wholly suppressed. Now if the body of *Gold* could be opened with these *Corrosive waters,* or by these *Corrosive waters* (so the venomous quality were wanting) well washed, we conceive it would be no unprofitable Medicine.

2.

Pearls are taken either in a fine Powder, or in a certain Mass, or Dissolution by the juice of sour and new Limons: and they are given sometimes in Aromatical Confections, sometimes in Liquor. The *Pearl,* no doubt, hath some affinity with the Shell in which it groweth, and may be of the same quality with the Shels of *Cra-fishes.*

3.

Amongst the *transparent precious Stones,* two onely are accounted *Cordial,* the *Emerauld* and the *Jacinth,* which are given under the same forms that the *Pearls* are ; save only that the dissolutions of them, as far as we know, are not in use. But we suspect these *Glassie jewels,* lest they should be cutting.

Of these which we have mentioned, how far and in what manner they are helpful, shall be spoken hereafter.

4.

Bezoar-Stone is of approved vertue for refreshing the Spirits, and procuring a gentle Sweat. As for the *Unicorn's Horn,* it hath lost the credit with us ; yet so, as it may keep rank with *Hart's Horn,* and the *Bone* in the heart of a *Hart,* and *Ivory,* and such like.

5.

Amber-griece is one of the best to appease and comfort the Spirits.

Hereafter follow the names only of the *simple Cordials,* seeing their Vertues are sufficiently known.

Hot.	Hot.	Cold.	Cold.
Saffron.	Clove-Gilly-flowers.	Nitre.	Juice of sweet
Folium Indum.	Orenge-flowers.	Roses. Violets.	Orenges.
Lignum Aloes.	Rosemary.	Strawberry-	Juice of Pearmains.
Citron Pill or	Mint.	Leaves.	Borage.
Rind.	Betony.	Straw-berries.	Buglofs.
Balm.	Carduus Benedi-	Juice of sweet	Burnet. Sanders.
Basil.	Etus.	Limons.	Camphire.

Seeing our speech now is of those things which may be transferred into Diet, all hot Waters *and* Chymical Oiles, *(which, as a certain Trisler saith, are under the Planet* Mars *, and have a furious and destructive force) as also all hot and biting Spices are to be rejected, and a Consideration to be had, how waters and Liquors may be made of the former Simples : not those phlegmatick distilled waters, nor again those burning waters of Spirits of Wine ; but such as may be more temperate, and yet lively, and sending forth a benign Vapour.*

6.

I make some question touching the frequent letting of *Bloud,* whether it conduceth to long life nor no ; and I am rather in the opinion that it doth, if it be turned into a habit, and other things be well disposed : for it letteth out the old Juice of the body, and bringeth in new.

I suppose also, that some *Emaciating Diseases* well cured, do profit to long life, for they yield new Juice, the old being consumed; and, as (as he saith) *To recover a sickness is to renew youth :* Therefore it were good to make some *Artificial Diseases,* which is done by strict and *Emaciating Diets,* of which I shall speak hereafter.

The Intentions.

To the 12, 13, and 14 Articles.

*H*Aving finished the Inquisition *according to the Subjects, as namely, of* Inanimate Bodies *,* Vegetables *,* Living Creatures *,* Man *; I will now come nearer to the matter, and order mine* Inquisitions *by certain* Intentions, *such as are true and proper, (as I am wholly perswaded) and which are the very paths to* Mortal Life. *For in this part, nothing that is of worth hath hitherto been inquired, but the contemplations of men have been but simple, and* non-proficients. *For when I hear men on the one side speak of comforting* Natural heat, *and the* Radical moisture, *and of* Meats *which breed good* Blood, *such as may neither be burnt nor phlegmatick ; and of the chearing and recreating the* Spirits ; *I suppose them to be no bad men which speak these things: but none of these worketh effectually towards the end. But when on the other side I hear several discourses touching* Medicines *made of* Gold, *because* Gold *is not subject to corruption ; and touching* Precious stones *to refresh the spirits by their hidden properties and lustre, and that if they could be taken and retained in* Vessels, *the* Balsoms, *and* Quintessences *of* living Creatures, *would make men conceive a proud hope of Immortality : And that the* Flesh *of* Serpents *and* Harts, *by a certain consent, are powerful to the* Renovation *of* Life, *because the one casteth his* Skin, *the other his* Horns : *(they should also have added the* Flesh *of* Eagles, *because the* Eagle *changes his* Bill) *And that a certain* Man, *when he had found an* Oyntment *hidden under the ground, and had anointed himself therewith from head to foot, (excepting onely the soles of his feet) did, by his anointing, live three hundred years, without any disease, save onely some* Tumors *in the soles of his feet : and of* Artesius, *who when he found his* Spirit *ready to depart, drew into his body the spirit of a certain young man, and thereby made him breathless, but himself lived many years by another mans* Spirit : *And of* Fortunate Hours *according to the* Figures of Heaven, *in which* Medicines *are to be gathered and compounded for the prolongation of* Life : *And of the* Seales of Planets, *by which vertues may be drawn and fetcked down from* Heaven *to prolong* Life : *and such like fabulous and superstitious vanities : I wonder exceedingly that men should so much doat, as to suffer themselves to be deluded with these things. And again, I do pity* Mankind *that they should have the hard fortune to be besieged with such frivolous and senceless apprehensions. But mine* Intentions *do both come home to the* Matter, *and are far from vain and credulous* Imaginations *; being also such, as I conceive, posterity may adde much to the matters which satisfie these* Intentions *; but to the* Intentions *themselves, but a little. Notwithstanding there are a few things, and those of very great moment, of which I would have men to be forewarned*

First, we are of that opinion, that we esteem the Offices *of* Life *to be more worthy than* Life *it self. Therefore if there be any thing of that kind that may indeed exactly answer our* Intentions, *yet so, that the* Offices *and* Duties *of* Life *be thereby hindred ; whatsoever it be of this kind, we reject it. Perhaps we may make some light mention of some things, but we insist not upon them. For we make no serious nor diligent discourse, either of leading the life in* Caves, *where the* Sunbeams *and several changes of the* Air *pierce not, like* Epimenides *his* Cave *; or of perpetual* baths, *made of* Liquors *prepared ; or of* Shirts, *and* Sear-cloths *so applied, that the body should be always as it were in a* Box *; or of thick paintings of the body, after the manner of some* Barbarous *Nations ; or of an exact ordering of our* Life *and* Diet, *which aimeth onely at this, and mindeth nothing else but that a man live, (as was that of* Herodicus *amongst the Antients, and of* Cornarus *the* Venetian *in our days, but with greater moderation ;) or of any such* Prodigy, *Tediousness, or* Inconvenience *: but we propound such* Remedies *and* Precepts, *by which the* Offices *of* Life *may neither be deserted, nor receive any great interruptions or molestations.*

Secondly,

Secondly, on the other side we denounce unto men that they will give over trifling, and not imagine that so great a work as the stopping and turning back the powerful course of nature, can be brought to pass by some Morning-draught, or the taking of some precious Drug, but that they would be assured that it must needs be, that this is a work of labour, and consisteth of many Remedies, and a fit connexion of them amongst themselves ; for no man can be so stupid as to imagine, that what was never yet done, can be done, but by such ways as were never yet attempted.

Thirdly, we ingeniously profess, that some of those things which we shall propound have not been tried by us by way of Experiment, (for our course of life doth not permit that) but are derived (as we suppose) upon good reason, out of our Principles and Grounds , (of which some we set down, others we reserve in our mind) and are, as it were, cut and digged out of the Rock *and Mine of Nature her self.* Nevertheless *we have been careful, and that with all providence and circumspection, (seeing the* Scripture *saith of the* Body of Man, *that it is more worth than* Raiment) *to propound such Remedies, as may at least be safe, if peradventure they be not fruitful.*

Fourthly, we would have men rightly to observe and distinguish, that those things which are good for an Healthful Life, *are not always good for a* Long Life ; *for there are some things which do further the alacrity of the* Spirits, *and, the strength and vigour of the Functions, which, notwithstanding, do cut off from the sums of Life ; and there are other things which are profitable to prolongation of Life, which are not without some peril of health, unless this matter be salved by fit Remedies ; of which, notwithstanding, as occasion shall be offered, we will not omit to give some Cautions and Monitions.*

Lastly we have thought good to propound sundry Remedies, *according to the several* Intentions ; *but the choice of those* Remedies, *and the order of them, to leave to Discretion : for to set down exactly which of them agreeth best, with which* Constitution *of* Body, *which with the several courses of Life, which with each Mans particular* Age, *and how they are to be taken one after another, and how the whole Practique of these things is to be administred and governed, would be too long, neither is it fit to be published.*

In the Topicks *we propounded three* Intentions : *The* Prohibiting *of* Consumption, *The* Perfecting *of* Reparation, *and the* Renewing *of* Oldness. *But seeing those things which shall be said are nothing less than words, we will deduce these three* Intentions *to ten* Operations.

The first is, the Operation *upon the* Spirits *that they may renew their vigour.*   1.
The second Operation *is upon the* Exclusion *of* Air.   2.
The third Operation *is upon the* Bloud, *and the* Sanguifying Heat.   3.
The fourth Operation *is upon the* Juices *of the* Body.   4.
The fifth Operation *is upon the* Bowels, *for their* Extrusion *of* Aliment.   5.
The sixth Operation *is upon the* Outward Parts, *for their* Attraction *of* Aliment.   6.
The seventh Operation *is upon the* Aliment *it self, for the* Insinuation *thereof.*   7.
The eighth Operation *is upon the last* Act *of* Assimilation.   8.
The ninth Operation *is upon the* Inteneration *of the* Parts, *after they begin to be dried.*   9
The tenth Operation *is upon the* Purging away *of* Old Juice, *and* Supplying *of* New Juice.   10.

Of these Operations, *the four first belong to the* First Intention, *the four next to the* Second Intention, *and the two last to the* Third Intention.

But because this part touching the Intentions *doth tend to* Practice, *under the name of* History, *we will not onely comprise* Experiments *and* Observations, *but also* Counsels, Remedies, Explications *of* Causes, Assumptions, *and whatsoever hath reference hereunto.*

                                          The

The Operation upon the Spirits that they may remain Youthful, and renew their Vigour.

The History.

1. THE *Spirits* are the Master-workmen of all effects in the *Body*. This is manifest by Consent, and by infinite instances.

2. If any man could procure that a young man's *Spirit* could be conveyed into an old man's *Body*, it is not unlikely but this great Wheel of the *Spirits* might turn about the lesser Wheel of the *Parts*, and so the course of Nature become retrogade.

3. In every Consumption, whether it be by Fire or by Age, the more the *Spirit* of the Body, or the Heat, preyeth upon the Moisture, the lesser is the duration of that thing. This occurs every where, and is manifest.

4. The *Spirits* are to be put into such a temperament and degree of activity, that they should not (as he saith) *drink* and *guzzle* the juices of the Body, but *sip them onely.*

5. There are two kinds of *Flames :* the one eager and weak, which consumes slight substances but hath little power over the harder ; as the flame of straw, or small Sticks : the other strong and constant, which converts hard and obstinate substances; as the flame of hard wood, and such like.

6. The eager flames, and yet less robust, do dry Bodies, and render them exhaust and sapless ; but the stronger flames do intenerate and melt them.

7. Also in *Dissipating Medicines*, some vapour forth the thin part of the tumors or swellings, and these harden the tumour ; others potently discuss, and these soften it.

8. Also in *Purging* and *Absterging Medicines*, some carry away the fluid humors violently, others draw the more obstinate and viscous.

9. The *Spirits* ought to be invested and armed with such a heat, that they may chuse rather to stir and undermine hard and obstinate matters, than to discharge and carry away the thin and prepared ; for by that means the Body becomes green and solid.

10. The Spirits *are so to be wrought and tempered, that they may be in* Substance Dense, *not* Rare ; *in* Heat Strong, *not* Eager ; *in* Quantity Sufficient *for the offices of Life, not* Redundant *or* Turgid ; *in* Motion Appeased, *not* Dancing *or* Unequal.

11. That *Vapours* work powerfully upon the *Spirits*, it is manifest by Sleep, by Drunkenness, by Melancholick Passions, by letificant Medicines, by Odours, calling the Spirits back again in Swoonings and Faintings.

12. The *Spirits* are condensed four ways ; either by *putting them to flight*, or by *refrigerating* and *cooling* them, or by *stroaking* them, or by *quieting* them. And first of their *Condensation* by *putting them to flight*.

13. Whatsoever putteth to flight on all parts, driveth the body into his Centre, and so *Condenseth.*

14. To the *Condensation* of the *spirits* by flight, the most powerful and effectual is Opium, and next Opiates, and generally all *Soporiferous things.*

15. The force of *Opium* to the *condensation* of the *spirits* is exceeding strong, whenas perhaps three grains thereof will in a short time so coagulate the *Spirits*, that they return no more, but are extinguished, and become immoveable.

16. *Opium*, and the like, put not the *Spirits* to flight by their coldness, for they have parts manifestly hot ; but, on the contrary, cool by their putting the *Spirits* to flight.

17. The *Flight* of the *Spirits* by *Opium* and *Opiate Medicines* is best seen by applying the same outwardly; for the *Spirits* straight with-draw themselves, and will return no more, but the part is mortified, and turns to a *Gangrene.*

18. *Opiates*, in grievous pains, as in the Stone, or the cutting off of a Limb, mitigate pains most of all, by putting the *spirits* to flight.

19. *Opiates* obtain a good effect from a bad cause ; for the *Flight* of the *Spirits* is evil, but the *Condensation* of them through their flight is good.

The

The *Grecians* attributed much, both for health and for prolongation of life, as O-
piates: but the *Arabians* much more, insomuch that their *grand Medicines* (which they
called the *gods Hands*) had *Opium* for their Basis and principal ingredient, other things
being mixed to abate and correct the noxious qualities thereof; such were *Treacle*,
Methridate, and the rest. *20.*

Whatsoever is given with good success in the curing of *Pestilential* and *Malignant
Diseases*, to stop and bridle the *Spirits*, lest they grow turbulent and tumultuate, may
very happily be transferred to the prolongation of life; for one thing is effectual unto
both, namely, the *condensation* of the *Spirits*: now there is nothing better for that
than *Opiates*. *21.*

The *Turks* find *Opium*, even in a reasonable good quantity, harmless and comfortable,
insomuch that they take it before their Battel to excite courage: but to us, unless it be
in a very small quantity, and with good Correctives, it is mortal. *22.*

Opium and *Opiates* are manifestly found to excite *Venus*; which shews them to have
force to corroborate the Spirits. *23.*

Distilled Water of wilde Poppy is given with good success in Surfeits, Agues, and divers
diseases; which no doubt is a temperate kind of *Opiate*. Neither let any man wonder
at the various use of it; for that is familiar to *Opiates*, in regard that the Spirits, cor-
roborated and condensed, will rise up against any disease. *24.*

The *Turks* use a kind of Herb which they call *Capke*, which they dry and powder,
and then drink in warm water; which, they say, doth not a little sharpen them, both
in their Courage, and in their Wits; notwithstanding, if it be taken in a large quantity,
it affects and disturbs the mind: whereby it is manifest, that it is of the same nature
with *Opiates*. *25.*

There is a Root much renowned in all the *Eastern parts*, which they call *Betel*, which
the *Indians* and others use to carry in their mouths, and to champ it, and by that
champing they are wonderfully enabled both to endure labours, and to overcome
sicknesses, and to the act of carnal copulation: It seems to be a kind of *Stupefactive*,
because it exceedingly blacks the Teeth. *26.*

Tobacco in our age is immoderately grown into use, and it affects men with a secret kind of delight, insomuch that they who have once inured themselves unto it can
hardly afterwards leave it: and no doubt it hath power to lighten the body, and to
shake off weariness. Now the vertue of it is commonly thought to be, because it
opens the passages, and voids humors: but it may more rightly be referred to the *condensation* of the Spirits; for it is a kind of *Henbane*, and manifestly troubles the
Head, as *Opiates* do. *27.*

There are sometimes *Humors* engendred in the body, which are, as it were, *Opiate*
themselves; as it is in some kind of *Melancholies*, with which if a man be affected, it
is a sign of very long life. *28.*

The *simple Opiates* (which are also called *stupefactives*) are these: *Opium* it self,
which is the juice of *Poppy*; both the *Poppies*, as well in the Herb as in the Seed; *Henbane*, *Mandrake*, *Hemlock*, *Tobacco*, *Night-shade*. *29.*

The compound *Opiates* are, *Treacle*, *Methridate*, *Trisera*, *Ladanum*, *Paracelsi*, *Disco-
nium*, *Diascordium*, *Philonium*, *Pills of Hounds-tongue*. *30.*

From this which hath been said, certain Designations or Counsels may be deduced
for the prolongation of life, according to the present intension; namely, of *condensing*
the *Spirits* by *Opiates*. *31.*

Let there be therefore every year, from Adult years of Youth, an *Opiate* diet; let it
be taken about the end of *May*, because the Spirits in the Summer are more loose and
attenuated, and there are less dangers from cold humours; let it be some *Magistral
Opiate*, weaker than those that are commonly in use, both in respect of a smaller quantity of *Opium*, and of a more sparing mixture of extreme hot things; let it be taken in
the morning betwixt sleeps. The fare for that time would be more simple and sparing than ordinary, without Wine, or Spices, or Vapourous things. This Medicine to
be taken onely each other day, and to be continued for a fortnight. This Designation in
our judgment comes home to the intension. *32.*

Opiates also may be taken, not onely by the mouth, but also by *Fumes*; but the
Fumes must be such as may not move the expulsive Faculty too strongly, nor force
down humours, but onely taken in a West, may work upon the Spirits within the
brain. And therefore a *Suffumigation* of *Tobacco*, *Lignum-Aloes*, *Rosemary-leaves*
dried, *33.*

dried, and a little *Myrrhe* snuffed up in the morning at the mouth and nostrils, would be very good.

34.   In *Grand Opiates*, such as are *Treacle*, *Methridate*, and the rest, it would not be amiss (especially in youth) to take rather the *distilled waters* of them than themselves in their bodies ; for the vapour in distilling doth rise, but the heat of the Medicine commonly setleth. Now *distilled waters* are good in those vertues which are conveyed by Vapours, in other things but weak.

35.   There are Medicines which have a certain weak and hidden degree, and therefore safe to an *Opiate* vertue ; these send forth a slow and copious vapour, but not malignant as *Opiates* do, therefore they put not the Spirits to *flight* ; notwithstanding they congregate them, and somewhat thicken them.

36.   Medicines in order to *Opiates* are principally *Saffron*, next *Folium Indum*, *Amber-greese*, *Coriander-seed prepared*, *Amomum*, *Pseuda-momum*, *Lignum-Rhodium*, *Orenge-flower water*, and much more the *Infusion* of the same *Flowers* new gathered in the *Oil* of *Almonds* ; *Nutmegs* pricked full of holes, and macerated in Rose-water.

37.   As *Opiates* are to be taken very sparingly, and at certain times, as was said, so these secondaries may be taken familiarly, and in our daily diet, and they will be very effectual to prolongation of life. Certainly an *Apothecary of Calecute*, by the use of *Amber*, is said to have lived an hundred and sixty years ; and the *Noble-men* of *Barbary*, through the use thereof, are certifi'd to be very long liv'd, whereas the mean people are but of short life. And our *Ancestors*, who were longer-liv'd than we, did use *Saffron* much in their Cakes, Broths, and the like. And touching the first way of condensing the Spirits of *Opiates* and the *Subordinates* thereto, thus much.

38.   Now we will enquire of the second way of condensing the *Spirits* by *Cold*. For the proper work of *Cold* is *Condensation*, and it is done without any malignity, or adverse quality ; and therefore it is a safer operation than by *Opiates*, though somewhat less powerful, if it be done by turns onely, as *Opiates* are. But then again, because it may be used familiarly, and in our daily diet with moderation, it is much more powerful for the prolongation of life than by *Opiates*.

39.   The *Refrigeration* of the Spirits is effected three ways, either by *Respiration*, or by *Vapours*, or by *Aliment*. The first is the best, but, in a sort, out of our power ; the second is potent, but yet ready, and at hand ; the third is weak, and somewhat about.

40.   *Air clear* and *pure*, and which hath no fogginess in it, before it be received into the Lungs, and which is least exposed to the Sun-beams, condenseth the Spirits best. Such is found either on the tops of dry Mountains, or in Champagnes open to the wind, and yet not without some shade.

41.   As for the *Refrigeration* and *Condensation* of the *Spirits* by *Vapours*, the Root of this operation we place in *Nitre*, as a Creature purposely made and chosen for this end, being thereunto led, and perswaded by these Arguments.

42.   *Nitre* is a kind of cool Spice : this is apparent to the sense it self, for it bites the Tongue and Palate with *cold*, as Spices do with *heat*, and it is the onely thing, as far as we know, that hath this property.

43.   Almost all *cold things* (which are cold properly, and not by accident, as *Opium* is) are poor and jejune of Spirit ; contrarily, things full of *spirit* are almost all hot, onely *Nitre* is found amongst Vegetables, which aboundeth with *Spirit*, and yet is cold. As for *Camphire*, which is full of Spirit, and yet performeth the actions of cold, it cooleth by accident onely ; as namely, for that by the thinness thereof, without *Acrimony*, it helpeth perspiration in inflammations.

44.   In *congealing* and *freezing* of *Liquors*, (which is lately grown into use) by laying Snow and Ice on the out-side of the Vessel, *Nitre* is also added, and no doubt it exciteth and fortifieth the *Congelation*. It is true, that they use also for this work ordinary Bay-Salt, which doth rather give activity to the coldness of the Snow, than cool by it self : But, as I have heard, in the hotter Regions, where Snow falls not, the congealing is wrought by *Nitre* alone ; but this I cannot certainly affirm.

45.   It is affirmed that *Gun powder*, which consisteth principally of *Nitre*, being taken in drink, doth conduce to valour, and that it is used oftentimes by Mariners and Souldiers before they begin their Battels, as the *Turks* do *Opium*.

Nitre

Nitre is given with good success in burning Agues, and Pestilential Fevers, to mitigate and bridle their pernicious heats. 46.

It is manifest, that *Nitre* in *Gun-powder* doth mightily abhor the Flame, from whence is caused that horrible Crack and puffing. 47.

Nitre is found to be, as it were, the *Spirit* of the Earth : for this is most certain, that any Earth, though pure and unmixt with Nitrous matter, if it be so laid up and covered, that it be free from the Sun-beams, and putteth forth no Vegetable, will gather *Nitre*, even in good abundance. By which it is clear, that the Spirit of *Nitre* is not onely inferiour to the *Spirit* of living Creatures, but also to the *Spirit* of Vegetables. 48.

Cattle which drink of *Nitrous* water do manifestly grow fat, which is a sign of the cold in *Nitre*. 49.

The manuring of the Soil is chiefly by *Nitrous substances*; for all Dung is *Nitrous*, and this is a sign of the Spirit in *Nitre*. 50.

From hence it appears, that the Spirits of Man may be cooled and condensed by the Spirit of *Nitre*, and be made more crude, and less eager. And therefore, as strong Wines, and Spices, and the like, do burn the Spirits, and shorten life ; so on the contrary side, *Nitre* doth compose and repress them, and furthereth to life. 51.

Nitre may be used with meat, mixed with our Salt, to the tenth part of the Salt ; in Broths taken in the morning, for three grains to ten, also in Beer : but howsoever it be used, with moderation, it is of prime force to long life 52.

As *Opium* holds the preheminence in *condensing* the Spirits, by putting them to *flight*, and hath withal his *Subordinates*, less potent, but more safe, which may be taken both in greater quantity, and in more frequent use, of which we have formerly spoken : so also *Nitre*, which condenseth the Spirits by cold, and by a kind of Frescoor, (as we now a-days speak) hath also his *Subordinates*. 53.

Subordinates to *Nitre* are, all those things which yield an Odour somewhat Earthy, like the smell of Earth, pure and good, newly digged or turned up ; of this sort the chief are, *Borage, Buglass, Langue de Bœuf, Burnet, Strawberry leaves* and *Strawberries, Frambois* or *Raspis,* raw *Cucumers,* raw *Pearmains, Vine leaves,* and *Buds* ; also *Violets*. 54.

The next in order are those which have a certain freshness of smell, but somewhat more inclined to heat ; yet not altogether void of that vertue of refreshing by coolness ; such as are *Balm, green Citrons, green Orenges, Rose-water distilled, roasted Wardens* ; also the *Damask, Red,* and *Musk Roses*. 55.

This is to be noted, that *Subordinates* to *Nitre* do commonly confer more to this *Intension*, *Raw*, then having passed the Fire, because that the Spirit of Cooling is dissipated by the Fire ; therefore they are best taken, either infused in some liquor, or raw. 56.

As the condensation of the Spirits by *Subordinates to Opium* is, in some sort, performed by *Odours*, so also that which is by *Subordinates to Nitre* : therefore the smell of new and pure *Earth*, taken either by following the Plough, or by digging, or by weeding, excellently refresheth the Spirits. Also the Leaves of Trees in Woods, or Hedges, falling towards the middle of Autumn, yield a good refreshing to the Spirits, but none so good as *Strawberry-leaves* dying. Likewise the smell of *Violets*, or *Wall-flowers*, or *Bean-flowers*, or *Sweet-briar*, or *Hony-suckles*, taken as they grow, in passing by them onely, is of the same nature. 57.

Nay, and we know a certain great Lord who lived long, that had every morning immediately after sleep, a *Clod* of fresh *Earth* laid in a fair Napkin under his Nose, that he might take the smell thereof. 58.

There is no doubt, but the cooling and tempering of the blood by cool things, such as are *Endive, Succory, Liver-wort, Purslain*, and the like, do also by consequent cool the Spirits ; but this is about, whereas vapours cool immediately. 59.

And as touching the condensing of the Spirits by *Cold*, thus much : The third way of condensing the Spirits, we said to be by that which we call *stroaking* the *Spirits* : The fourth, by *quieting* the *alacrity* and *unruliness* of them. 60.

Such things *stroke* the *Spirits* as are pleasing and friendly to them, yet they allure them not to go abroad ; but rather prevail, that the Spirits contented, as it were, 61.

in

in their own society, do enjoy themselves, and betake themselves into their proper Centre.

61. For these, if you recollect those things which were formerly set down, as *Subordinates* to *Opium* and *Nitre*, there will need no other *Inquisition*.

62. As for the quieting of the *unruliness* of the Spirits, we shall presently speak of that, when we enquire touching their *Motion*. Now then, seeing we have spoken of that *Condensation* of the *Spirits* which pertaineth to their substance, we will come to the *temper* of *Heat* in them.

63. The *Heat* of the *spirits*, as we said, ought to be of that kind that it may be *robust*, not *eager*, and may delight rather to master the tough and obstinate, than to carry away the thin and light humors.

64. We must beware of *Spices*, *wine*, and strong *Drinks*, that our use of them be very temperate, and sometimes discontinued; also of *Savory*, *Wild marjoram*, *Penny-royal*, and all such as bite and heat the tongue; for they yield unto the *Spirits* an heat not *Operative*, but *Predatory*.

65. These yield a *robust heat*, especially *Elecampane*, *Garlick*, *Carduus Benedictus*, *Water-cresses* while they are young, *Germander*, *Angelica*, *Zedoary*, *Vervin*, *Valerian*, *Myrrhe*, *Pepper-wort*, *Elder flowers*, *Garden-Chervile*: The use of these things with choice and judgement, sometimes in Sallads, sometimes in Medicines, will satisfie this *Operation*.

66. It falls out well that the *Grand Opiates* will also serve excellently for this *Operation*, in respect that they yield such an *heat* by composition, which is wished, but not to be found, in Simples. For the mixing of those excessive hot things (such as are *Euphorbium*, *Pellitory of Spain*, *Stavis-acre*, *Dragon-wort*, *Anacordi*, *Castoreum*, *Aristolochium*, *Opponax*, *Ammoniachum*, *Galbanum*, and the like, which of themselves cannot be taken inwardly) to qualifie and abate the *Stupefactive* virtue of the *Opium*, they do make such a constitution of a Medicament as we now require; which is excellently seen in this, That *Treacle* and *Methridate*, and the rest, are not sharp, nor bite the tongue, but are onely somewhat bitter, and of strong scent, and at last manifest their heat when they come into the stomach, and in their subsequent operations.

67. There conduce also to the *robust heat* of the Spirits *Venus* often excited, rarely performed; and no less some of the affections, of which shall be spoken hereafter. So touching the heat of the Spirits, Analogical to the prolongation of Life, thus much.

68. Touching the *Quantity* of the Spirits, that they be not *exuberant* and *boiling*, but rather *sparing*, and within a mean, (seeing a small flame doth not devour so much as a great flame) the *Inquisition* will be short.

69. It seems to be approved by experience, that a *Spare Diet*, and almost a *Pythagorical*, such as is either prescribed by the strict Rules of a *Monastical life*, or practised by *Hermites*, which have Necessity and Poverty for their Rule, rendreth a man long-liv'd.

70. Hitherto appertain *drinking of water*, a hard *Bed*, *abstinence from Fire*, a slender *Diet*, (as namely, of *Herbs*, *Fruits*, *Flesh*, and *Fish*, rather *powdred* and *salted* than *fresh* and *hot*) an *Hair-shirt*, frequent *Fastings*, frequent *Watchings*, few *sensual Pleasures*, and such like; for all these diminish the Spirits, and reduce them to such a *quantity* as may be sufficient onely for the Functions of Life, whereby the depredation is the less.

71. But if the *Diet* shall not be altogether so *rigorous* and *mortifying*, yet notwithstanding shall be always *equal* and *constant* to it self, it worketh the same effect. We see it in *Flames*, that a *Flame* somewhat bigger (so it be always alike and quiet) consumeth less of the fuel than a lesser Flame blown with Bellows, and by Gusts stronger or weaker: That which the *Regiment* and *Diet* of *Cornarus* the *Venetian* shewed plainly, who did eat and drink so many years together by a just weight, whereby he exceeded an hundred years of age, strong in limbs, and intire in his senses.

72. Care also must be taken, that a body plentifully nourished, and not emaciated by any of these aforesaid Diets, omitteth not a seasonable use of *Venus*, lest the Spirits increase too fast, and soften and destroy the body. So then, touching a moderate *quantity* of Spirits, and (as we may say) Frugal, thus much.

73. The *Inquisition* touching *bridling* the *motions* of the *Spirits* followeth next.

Motion doth manifestly attenuate and inflame them.   This bridling is done by three
means: by *Sleep*; by *avoiding* of *vehement Labours, immoderate Exercise,* and, in a word,
all *Lassitude*; and by refraining *irksome Affections.*   And first, touching *Sleep.*

The Fable tells us, that *Epimenides slept* many years together in a Cave, and all that
time needed no meat, because the *Spirits* waste not much in *sleep.*   74.

Experience teacheth us that certain Creatures, as *Dormice* and *Bats, sleep* in some
close places an whole Winter together ; such is the force of *sleep* to restrain all vital
Consumption.   That which *Bees* and *Drones* are also thought to do, though sometimes
destitute of *Honey*; and likewise *Butter-flies,* and other *Flies.*   75.

Sleep after *Dinner* (the stomach sending up no unpleasing Vapours to the head, as
being the first Dews of our Meat) is good for the *spirits,* but derogatory and hurtful
to all other points of health.   Notwithstanding in extream old age there is the same
reason of Meat and *Sleep,* for both our meals and our *sleeps* should be then frequent,
but short and little ; nay, and towards the last period of old age, a mere *Rest,* and, as
it were, a perpetual *Reposing* doth best, especially in Winter-time.   76.

But as moderate *sleep* conferreth to long life, so much more if it be *quiet* and not
disturbed.   77.

These procure *quiet sleep, Violets, Lettuce,* especially boiled, *Sirrup* of *dried Roses,*
Saffron, Balm, Apples, at our going to bed ; a *sop* of *Bread* in *Malmsey,* especially
where *Musk-Roses* have been first *infused*: therefore it would not be amiss to make
some *Pill,* or a small Draught of these things, and to use it familiarly.   Also those
things which shut the mouth of the stomach close, as *Coriander-seed* prepared, *Quinces*
and *Wardens* roasted, do induce sound sleep ; but above all things in youth, and for
those that have sufficient strong stomacks, it will be best to take a good draught of *clear*
cold Water when they go to bed.   78.

Touching voluntary and procured Trances, *as also* fixed *and* profound Thoughts, *so*
as they be without irksomness, I have nothing certain : no doubt they make to this Intention,
and condense *the* Spirits, *and that more potently than* Sleep, *seeing they lay a?eep , and*
suspend the senses as much or more. Touching *them, let further inquiry be made. So far*
touching Sleep.

As for *Motion* and *Exercise,* Lassitude hurteth, and so doth all Motion and Exer-   79.
cise which is too nimble and swift; as Running, Tennis, Fencing, and the like ; and
again, when our strength is extended and strained to the uttermost, as Dancing, Wrestling, and such like : for it is certain, that the *spirits* being driven into streights, either by
the swiftness of the motion, or by the straining of the forces, do afterward become
more eager and predatory.   On the other side, *Exercises* which stir up a good strong
motion, but not over-swift, or to our utmost strength, (such as are Leaping, Shooting,
Riding, Bowling, and the like) do not hurt, but rather benefit.

We must come now to the *Affections* and *Passions* of the *Mind,* and see which of them
are hurtful to long life, which profitable.

Great Joys attenuate and diffuse the *spirits,* and shorten life ; *familiar Chearfulness*   80.
strengthens the *spirits,* by calling them forth, and yet not resolving them.

Impressions of *Joy* in the sense are naught ; ruminations of *Joy* in the memory, or   81.
apprehensions of them in hope or fancy, are good.

Joy suppressed, or communicated sparingly, doth more comfort the *spirits* than *Joy*   82.
poured forth and published.

Grief and *Sadness,* if it be void of *Fear,* and afflict not too much, doth rather pro-   83.
long life ; for it contracteth the *spirits,* and is a kind of *condensation.*

Great Fears shorten the life : for though *Grief* and *Fear* do both streighten the *spirit,*   84.
yet in *Grief* there is a simple contraction ; but in *Fear,* by reason of the cares taken
for the remedy, and hopes intermixed, there is a turmoil and vexing of the *spirits.*

Anger suppressed is also a kind of vexation, and causeth the *spirit* to feed upon the   85.
juices of the body; but let loose and breaking forth, it helpeth: as those *Medicines* do
which induce a *robust heat.*

Envy is the worst of all *Passions,* and feedeth upon the *spirits,* and they again   86.
upon the *body* ; and so much the more because it is perpetual, and, as it is said, *keepeth*
no holidays.

Pity of another man's misfortune, which is not likely to befall our selves, is good: 87.

but *Pity*, which may reflect with some similitude upon the party pitying, is naught, because it exciteth *Fear*.

88.   *Light Shame* hurteth not, seeing it contracteth the *spirits* a little, and then straight diffuseth them: insomuch that *shamefac'd* persons commonly live long: but *Shame* for some great ignominy, and which afflicteth the mind long, contracteth the *spirits* even to suffocation, and is pernicious.

89.   *Love*, if it be not unfortunate, and too deeply wounding, is a kind of *Joy*, and is subject to the same Laws which we have set down touching *Joy*.

90.   *Hope* is the most beneficial of all the *Affections*, and doth much to the prolongation of life, if it be not too often frustrated, but entertaineth the Fancy with an expectation of good: therefore they which fix and propound to themselves some end, as the mark and scope of their life, and continually and by degrees go forward in the same, are, for the most part, long-liv'd; in so much that when they are come to the top of their hope, and can go no higher therein, they commonly droop, and live not long after: So that *Hope* is a *Leaf-joy*, which may be beaten out to a great extension, like *Gold*.

91.   *Admiration* and *light Contemplation* are very powerful to the prolonging of life; for they hold the *spirits* in such things as delight them, and suffer them not to tumultuate, or to carry themselves unquietly and waywardly. And therefore all the *Contemplators* of *Natural things*, which had so many and eminent Objects to admire, (as *Democritus, Plato, Parmedides, Apollonius*) were long liv'd: also *Rhetoricians*, which tasted but lightly of things, and studied rather Exornation of speech than profundity of matters, were also long liv'd; as *Gorgias, Protagoras, Isocrates, Seneca*. And certainly, as old men are for the most part talkative, so talkative men do often grow very old; for it shews a *light contemplation*, and such as doth not much stain the *spirits*, or vex them: but subtil, and acute, and eager inquision shortens life; for it tireth the *spirit*, and wasteth it.

And as touching the *motion* of the *spirits* by the *Affections* of the *Mind*, thus much. Now we will adde certain other general *Observations* touching the *Spirits*, beside the former, which fall not into the precedent distribution.

92.   *Especial* care must be taken that the *Spirits* be not too often *resolved*; for attenuation goeth before resolution, and the *spirit* once attenuated doth not very easily retire, or is *condensed*. Now *Resolution* is caused by over-great labours, over-vehement affections of the mind, over great sweats, over great evacuations, hot Baths, and an untemperate and unseasonable use of *Venus*; also by over-great cares and carpings, and anxious expectations; lastly, by malignant diseases, and intolerable pains and torments of the body: all which, as much as may be, (which our vulgar *Physicians* also advise) must be avoided .

93.   The *spirits* are delighted both with *wonted* things, and with *new*. Now it maketh wonderfully to the conservation of the *spirits* in vigour, that we neither use *wonted* things to a satiety and glutting; nor *new* things, before a quick and strong appetite. And therfore both *customs* are to be broken off with judgment and care, before they breed a fulness; and the *appetite* after new things to be restrained for a time until it grow more sharp and jocond: and moreover, the *life*, as much as may be, so to be ordered, that it may have many *renovations*, and the *spirits* by perpetual conversing in the same actions may not wax dull. For though it were no ill saying of *Seneca's*, *The fool doth ever begin to live*; yet this folly, and many more such, are good for long life.

94.   It is to be observed touching the *spirits*, (though the contrary used to be done) That when men perceive their *spirits* to be in good, placid, and healthful state, (that which will be seen by the tranquility of their Mind, and cheatful disposition) that they cherish them, and not change them: but when, in a turbulent and untoward state, (which will also appear by their sadness, lumpishness, and other indisposition of their mind) that then they straight overwhelm them, and alter them. Now the *spirits* are contained in the same state, by a restraining of the affections, temperateness of diet, abstinence from *Venus*, moderation in labour, indifferent rest and repose: and the contrary to these do alter and overwhelm the *spirits*; as namely, vehement affections, profuse feastings, immoderate *Venus*, difficult labours, earnest studies, and prosecution of business. Yet men are wont, when they are merriest and best disposed, then to apply themselves to feastings,

Venus.

Venus, Labours, Endeavours, Businesses, whereas if they have a regard to long life, (which may seem strange) they should rather practise the contrary. For we ought to cherish and preserve good *spirits,* and for the evil-disposed *spirits* to discharge and alter them.

Ficinus saith not unwisely, That *old men,* for the comforting of their spirits, ought often to remember and ruminate upon the *Acts* of their *Childhood* and *Youth.* Certainly such a remembrance is a kind of peculiar Recreation to every *old man :* and therefore it is a delight to men to enjoy the society of them which have been brought up together with them, and to visit the places of their education. *Vespasian* did attribute so much to this matter, that when he was *Emperour* he would by no means be perswaded to leave his Father's house, though but mean, lest he should lose the wonted object of his eyes, and the memory of his childhood ; and besides, he would drink in a *wooden Cup,* tipped with silver, which was his *Grandmother's,* upon *Festival dayes.*   95.

One thing above all is grateful to the *Spirits,* that there be a *continual progress* to the more *benign ;* therefore we should lead such a Youth and Manhood, that our Old age should find new Solaces , whereof the chief is *moderate ease :* And therefore old men in honourable places lay violent hands upon themselves, who retire not to their ease *:* whereof may be found an eminent Example in *Cassiodorus,* who was of that reputation amongst the *Gothish Kings* of *Italy,* that he was as the soul of their affairs ; afterwards, being near eighty years of age, he betook himself to a Monastery, where he ended not his dayes before he was an hundred years old. But this thing doth require two Cautions *:* one, that they drive not off till their bodies be utterly worn out and diseased : for in such bodies all mutation, though to the more *benign,* hasteneth death : the other, that they surrender not themselves to a *sluggish ease,* but that they embrace something which may entertain their thoughts and mind with contentation ; in which kind the chief delights are Reading and Contemplation ; and then the desires of Building and Planting.   96.

Lastly, the same *Action, Endeavour* and *Labour* undertaken *chearfully* and with a *good will* doth refresh the *spirits ;* but with an *aversation* and *unwillingness,* doth fret and deject them. And therefore it conferreth to long life, either that a man hath the art to institute his life so as it may be free and suitable to his own humour ; or else to lay such a command upon his mind, that whatsoever is imposed by Fortune, it may rather lead him than drag him.   97.

Neither is that to be omitted towards the government of the *Affections,* that especial care be taken of the *mouth* of the *Stomach,* especially that it be not too much relaxed ; for that part hath a greater dominion over the affections, especially the daily affections, than either the Heart or Brain ; onely those things excepted which are wrought by potent vapours, as in Drunkenness and Melancholly.   98.

Touching the *Operation* upon the *spirits ,* that they may *remain youthful,* and renew their *vigours,* thus much : which we have done the more accurately, for that there is, for the most part, amongst *Physicians* and other Authors touching these *Operations* a deep silence ; but especially, because the *Operation* upon the *spirits,* and their *waxing green again,* is the most ready and compendious way to long life ; and that for a two-fold compendiousness : one, because the *Spirits* work compendiously upon the body ; the other, because *Vapours* and the *Affections* work compendiously upon the *spirits ;* so as these attain the end, as it were, in a right line, other things rather in lines circular.   99.

The Operation upon the Exclusion of the Air. 2.

The History.

THE *Exclusion* of the *Air ambient* tendeth to length of life two wayes : First for that the *External Air,* next unto the *Native spirit,* (howsoever the *Air* may be said to animate the Spirit of Man, and conferreth not a little to health) doth most of all prey upon the juices of the body,   1.

and haften the *Deficcation* thereof; and therefore the *Exclufion* of it is effectual to length of life.

2. Another effect which followeth the *Exclufion* of *Air* is much more fubtil and profound, namely, that the Body clofed up, and not perfpiring by the pores, detaineth the *fpirits* within, and turneth it upon the harder parts of the body, whereby the *Spirit* mollifies and intenerates them.

3. Of this thing the reafon is explained in the *Deficcation* of *Inanimate Bodies* ; and it is an Axiom almoft infallible, That the *Spirit* difcharged and iffuing forth, drieth Bodies ; detained, melteth and intenerateth them. And it is further to be affumed, That all Heat doth properly attenuate and moiften, and contracteth and drieth onely by Accident.

4. *Leading* the *Life* in *Dens* and *caves*, where the *Air* receives not the Sun-beams, may be effectual to long life. For the *Air* of it felf doth not much towards the depredation of the body, unlefs it be ftirred up by heat. Certainly, if a man fhall recal things paft to his memory, it will appear that the ftatures of men have been anciently much greater than thofe that fucceeded, as in *Sicily*, and fome other places : but this kind of men led their lives, for the moft part, in *Caves*. Now length of life and largenefs of limbs have fome affinity. The *cave* alfo of *Epimenides* walks among the Fables. I fuppofe likewife, that the life of *Columnar Anchorites* was a thing refembling the life in *Caves*, in refpect the Sun-beams could not much pierce thither, nor the *Air* receive any great changes or inequalities. This is certain, both the *Simeon Stelita*'s, as well *Daniel as Saba*, and other *Columnar Anchorites*, have been exceeding long-liv'd. Likewife the *Anchorites* in our dayes, clofed up and immured either within Walls or Pillars, are often found to be long-liv'd.

5. Next unto the life in *Caves* is the life on *Mountains* : for as the beams of the Sun do not penetrate into *Caves* ; fo on the tops of *Mountains*, being deftitute of Reflexion, they are of fmall force. But this is to be underftood of *Mountains* where the Air is clear and pure ; namely, whether by reafon of the drinefs of the Vallies Clouds and Vapours do not afcend ; as it is in the Mountains which encompafs *Barbary*, where, even at this day, they live many times to an hundred and fifty years, as hath been noted before.

6. And this kind of *Air* of *Caves* and *Mountains*, of its own proper nature, is little or nothing predatory ; but *Air*, fuch as ours is, which is predatory through the heat of the Sun, ought, as much as is poffible, to be excluded from the body.

7. But the *Air* is prohibited and excluded two ways : firft, by *clofing* the Pores : fecondly, by *filling* them up.

8. To the *clofing* of the Pores help coldnefs of the air, going naked, whereby the skin is made hard, wafhing in cold water, Aftringents applied to the skin, fuch as are *Maftick*, *Myrrhe*, *Myrtle*.

9. But much more may we fatisfie this *Operation* by *Baths*, yet thofe rarely ufed, (efpecially in Summer) which are made of *Aftringent Mineral waters*, fuch as may fafely be ufed, as Waters participating of Steel and Coperas ; for thefe do potently contract the skin.

10. As for *filling* up the *Pores*, *Paintings* and fuch like *Unctuous daubings*, and (which may moft commodioufly be ufed) *Oil* and *fat things*, do no lefs conferve the fubftance of the body, than Oil-colours and Varnifh do preferve Wood.

11. The ancient *Britains* painted their bodies with *woad*, and were exceeding long liv'd : the *Picts* alfo ufed paintings, and are thought by fome to have derived their name from thence.

12. The *Brafilians* and *Virginians* paint themfelves at this day, who are (efpecially the former) very long liv'd ; infomuch that five years ago the *French Jefuites* had fpeech with fome who remembred the building of *Fernambuck*, which was done an hundred and twenty years fince ; and they were then at Man's eftate.

13. *Joannes de temporibus*, who is reported to have extended his life to three hundred years, being asked how he preferved himfelf fo long, is faid to have anfwered, *by Oyl without, and by Honey within*.

14. The *Irifo*, efpecially the *wild-Irifh*, even at this day live very long : certainly they report, that within thefe few years the *countefs* of *Defmond* lived to an hundred and forty years of age, and bred Teeth three times. Now the *Irifh* have a fafhion to chafe, and, as it were, to bafte themfelves with old Salt-butter againft the fire.

The

The same *Irish* use to wear *Saffroned Linen* and *Shirts* : which though it were at first devised to prevent Vermin, yet howsoever I take it to be very useful for lengthning of life ; for *Saffron*, of all things that I know, is the best thing for the skin, and the comforting of the flesh, seeing it is both notably Astringent, and hath besides an Oleosity and subtle heat, without any Acrimony.   I remember a certain *Englishman*, who when he went to Sea carried a bagg of *Saffron* next his stomack, that he might conceal it, and so escape Custom ; and whereas he was wont to be always exceeding Sea-sick, at that time he continued very well, and felt no provocation to vomit. | **15.**

Hippocrates adviseth in Winter to wear clean Linen, and in Summer foul Linen and besmeared with Oil.   The reason may seem to be, because in Summer the *Spirits* exhale most, therefore the pores of the skin would be filled up. | **16.**

Hereupon we are of opinion, that the use of *Oil*, either of *Olives* or sweet *Almonds*, to anoint the skin therewith, would principally conduce to long life : The *anointing* would be done every morning when we rise out of bed, with Oil in which a little *bay-salt* and *Saffron* is mixed.   But this *anointing* must be lightly done with Wool, or some soft sponge, not laying it on thick, but gently touching and wetting the skin. | **17.**

It is certain that *Liquors*, even the Oily themselves, in great quantities draw somewhat from the body ; but contrarily, in small quantities are drunk in by the body : therefore the anointing would be but light, as we said, or rather the shirt it self would be besmeared with Oil. | **18.**

It may happily be objected, that this anointing with Oil, which we commend, (though it were never in use with us, and amongst the *Italians* is cast off again) was anciently very familiar amongst the *Grecians* and *Romans*, and a part of their Diet ; and yet men were not longer-liv'd in those dayes than now.   But it may rightly be answered, Oil was in use onely after Baths, unless it were perhaps amongst *Champions* : now hot Baths are as much contrary to our operation, as *Anointings* are congruous, seeing the one opens the passages, the other stops them up : therefore the Bath, without the anointing following, is utterly bad ; the anointing without the Bath is best of all.   Besides, the anointing amongst them was used onely for *delicacy*, or (if you take it at the best) for *health*, but by no means in order to long life ; and therefore they used them with all precious Ointments, which were good for deliciousness, but hurtful to our intention, in regard of their heat : So that *Virgil* seemeth not to have said amiss, | **19.**

> —— *Nec Casia liquidi corrumpitur usus Olivi,*
> *That odoriferous Casia hath not supplanted the use of neat Oil-Olive.*

Anointing with Oil conduceth to health, both in Winter, by the exclusion of the cold Air, and in Summer, by detaining the spirits within, and prohibiting the Resolution of them, and keeping off the force of the air which is then most predatory. | **20.**

Seeing the anointing with *Oil* is one of the most potent operations to long life, we have thought good to add some cautions, lest the health should be endangered. They are four, according to the four *Inconveniences* which may follow thereupon. | **21.**

The first *Inconvenience* is, that by *repressing sweats*, it may ingender diseases from those excrementitious humours.   To this a remedy must be given by *Purges* and *Clysters*, that evacuation may be duly performed.   This is certain, that evacuation by sweats commonly advanceth health, and derogateth from long life ; but gentle *Purgers* work upon the humours, not upon the spirits, as sweat doth. | **22.**

The second *Inconvenience* is, that it may *heat* the body, and in time inflame it ; for the spirits shut in, and not breathing forth acquire heat.   This inconvenience may be prevented, if the *Diet* most usually incline to the colder part, and that at times some proper cooling Medicines be taken, of which we shall straight speak in the operation upon the *Bloud*. | **23.**

The third is, that it may *annoy the head* ; for all *Oppletion* from without strikes back the vapours, and sends them up unto the head.   This inconvenience is remedied by *Purgers*, especially *Clysters*, and by shutting the mouth of the stomach strongly with Stipticks, and by combing and rubbing the head, and by washing it with convenient Lies, that something may exhale, and by not omitting competent and good exercises, that something also may perspire by the skin. | **24.**

G 3

The

25. The fourth *Inconvenience* is a more subtil Evil, namely, that the Spirit being detained by the closing up of the *Pores*, is likely to multiply it self too much; for when little iffueth forth, and new Spirit is continually ingendred, the Spirit increaseth too faft, and so preyeth upon the body more plentifully. But this is not altogether so; for all Spirit clofed up is dull, (for it is blown and excited with motion as Flame is) and therefore it is lefs active, and lefs generative of it self: Indeed it is thereby increafed in Heat, (as Flame is) but flow in Motion. And therefore the remedy to this inconvenience muft be by cold things, being fometimes mixed with Oil, fuch as are *Rofes* and *Myrtles*; for we muft altogether difclaim hot things, as we faid of *Caffia.*

26. Neither will it be unprofitable to wear next the body Garments that have in them fome *Unctuofity* or *Oleofity*, not *Aquofity*, for they will exhauft the body lefs; fuch as are thofe of Woollen rather than thofe of Linen. Certainly it is manifeft in the Spirits of Odours, that if you lay fweet powders amongft Linen, they will much fooner lofe their fmell than amongft Woollen. And therefore Linen is to be preferred for delicacy and neatnefs, but to be fufpected for our *Operation.*

27. The Wild *Irifh*, as foon as they fall fick, the firft thing they do is to take the fheets off their beds, and to wrap themfelves in the woollen cloaths.

28. Some report, that they have found great benefit in the confervation of their health by wearing *scarlet Wafcoats* next their skin, and under their fhirts, as well down to the neather parts as on the upper.

29. It is alfo to be obferved, that *Air* accuftomed to the body doth lefs prey upon it than new *Air* and often changed; and therefore poor people, in fmall Cottages, who live always within the fmell of the fame chimney, and change not their feats, are commonly longeft liv'd: notwithftanding, to other operations (efpecially for them whofe Spirits are not altogether dull) we judge change of air to be very profitable; but a mean muft be ufed, which may fatisfie on both fides. This may be done by removing our habitation four times a year, at conftant and fet times, unto convenient feats, that fo the body may neither be in too much peregrination, nor in too much ftation. And touching the *Operation* upon the *Exclufion* of *Air*, and avoiding the predatory force thereof, thus much.

The Operation upon the Bloud, and the Sanguifying Heat. 3.

The Hiftory.

1. THE following *Operations* anfwer to the two precedent, and are in the relation of *Paffives* and *Actives*: for the two precedent intend this, that the *Spirits* and *Air* in their actions may be the lefs depredatory; and the two latter, that the *Bloud* and *Juice* of the body may be the lefs depredable. But becaufe the Bloud is an irrigation or watering of the Juices and Members, and a preparation to them, therefore we will put the operation upon the *Bloud* in the firft place. Concerning this *Operation* we will propound certain Counfels, few in number, but very powerful in virtue. They are three.

2. Firft, there is no doubt, but that if the bloud be brought to a cold temper, it will be fo much the lefs diffipable. But becaufe the cold things which are taken by the mouth agree but ill with many other Intentions, therefore it will be beft to find out fome fuch things as may be free from thefe inconveniences. They are two.

3. The firft is this: Let there be brought into ufe, efpecially in youth, *Clyfters*, not *purging* at all, or *abfterging*, but onely cooling, and fomewhat opening: Thofe are approved which are made of the Juices of *Lettuce, Purflane, Liver-wort, Houfefleek*, and the *Mucilage* of the feed of *Flea-wort*, with fome temperate opening decoction, and a
little

little *Camphire* : but in the declining age let the *Housleek* and *Purslane* be left out, and the juices of *Borrage* and *Endive*, and the like, be put in their rooms. And let these *Clysters* be retained, if it may be, for an hour or more.

The other is this, Let there be in use, especially in Summer, *Baths* of fresh water, and but luke-warm, altogether without *Emollients*, as *Mallows*, *Mercury*, *Milk*, and the like; rather take new *Whey* in some good quantity, and *Roses*.

But (that which is the principal in this intention, and new) we advise that before the bathing of the body be anointed with Oil, with some *thickness*, whereby the quality of the cooling may be received, and the water excluded: yet let not the pores of the body be shut too close; for when the outward cold closeth up the body too strongly, it is so far from furthering coolness, that it rather forbids, and stirs up heat.

Like unto this is the use of *Bladders*, with some decoctions and cooling juices, applied to the interiour region of the body, namely, from the ribbs to the privy parts; for this also is a kind of *bathing*, where the body of the liquor is for the most part excluded, and the cooling quality admitted.

The third counsel remaineth, which belongeth not to the quality of the *blood*, but to the substance thereof, that it may be made more firm and less dissipable, and such, as the heat of the spirit may have the less power over it.

And as for the use of *Filings* of *Gold*, *Leaf-gold*, *Powder* of *Pearl*, *Precious stones*, *Coral*, and the like, we have no opinion of them at this day, unless it be onely as they may satisfie this present *Operation*. Certainly, seeing the *Arabians*, *Grecians*, and *modern Physicians* have attributed such virtues to these things, it cannot be altogether Nothing which so great men have observed of them. And therefore omitting all fantastical opinions about them, we do verily believe, that if there could be some such thing conveyed into the whole mass of the blood in minute and fine portions, over which the spirits and heat should have little or no power, absolutely it would not onely resist *Putrefaction*, but *Arefaction* also, and be a most effectual means to the prolongation of life. Nevertheless in this thing several cautions are to be given. First, that there be a most exact comminution. Secondly, that such hard and solid things be void of all malignant qualities, lest while they be dispersed and lurk in the veins, they breed some ill convenience Thirdly, that they be never taken together with meats, nor in any such manner as they may stick long, lest they beget dangerous obstructions about the Mesentery. Lastly, that they be taken very rarely, that they may not congregate and knot together in the veins.

Therefore let the manner of taking them be *fasting*, in *white wine*, a little *Oil* of *Almonds* mingled therewith, *Exercise* used immediately upon the taking of them.

The *Simples* which may satisfie this *Operation* are, in stead of all, *Gold*, *Pearls*, and *Coral* : for all *Metalls*, except *Gold*, are not without some malignant quality in the dissolutions of them, neither will they be beaten to that exquisite fineness that *Leaf-gold* hath. As for all *glassie* and *transparent Jewels*, we like them not, (as we said before) for fear of Corrosion.

But, in our judgment, the safer and more effectual way would be by the use of *Woods* in Infusions and Decoctions ; for there is in them sufficient to cause *firmness* of *blood*, and not the like danger for breeding obstructions ; but especially, because they may be taken in meat and drink, whereby they will find the more easie entrance into the veins, and not be avoided in excrements.

The *Woods* fit for this purpose are *Sanders*, the *Oak* and *Vine*. As for all *hot woods* or something *Rosennie*, we reject them : notwithstanding you may adde the *woody stalks* of *Rosemary* dried, for *Rosemary* is a Shrub, and exceedeth in age many Trees ; also the *woody stalks* of *Ivy*, but in such quantity as they may not yield an unpleasing taste.

Let the *Woods* be taken either boiled in *Broths*, or infused in *Must* or *Ale* before they leave working: but in *Broths* (as the custom is for *Guaiacum* and the like) they would be infused a good while before the boiling, that the firmer part of the *wood*, and not that onely which lieth loosely, may be drawn forth. As for *Ash*, though it be used for Cups, yet we like it not. And touching the *Operation* upon the *Blood* thus much.

The Operation upon the Juices of the Body. 4.

The History.

1.   THere are two kinds of *Bodies* (as was said before in the *Inquisition* touching *Inanimates*) which are hardly consumed, *Hard* things and *Fat* things ;   as is seen in *Metalls* and *Stones*, and in *Oil* and *Wax*.

2.   It must be ordered therefore, that the *juice* of the *body* be somewhat *hard*, and that it be *fatty* or *subroscid*.

3.   As for *hardness*, it is caused three ways: by *Aliment of a firm nature*, by *cold* condensing the skin and flesh, and by *Exercise*, binding and compacting the juices of the body, that they be not soft and frothy.

4.   As for the *Nature* of the *Aliment*, it ought to be such as is not easily *dissipable* ; such as are *Beef, Swine's-flesh, Dear, Goat, Kid, Swan, Goose, Ring-dove*, especially if they be a little powdred ; *Fish* likewise salted and dried, *Old Cheese*, and the like.

5.   As for the *Bread* ; *Oaten-bread*, or *bread* with some mixture of *Pease* in it, or *Rye-bread*, or *Barly-bread*, are more solid than *wheat-bread*, and in *wheat-bread*, the course *wheat-bread* is more solid than the pure *Manchet*.

6.   The Inhabitants of the *Orcades*, which live upon *salted fish*, and generally all *Fish-eaters*, are long-liv'd.

7.   The *Monks* and *Hermites* which fed sparingly, and upon dry *Aliment*, attained commonly to a great age.

8.   Also *pure water* usually drunk makes the juices of the body less frothy ? unto which if, for the dulness of the spirits, (which no doubt in *Water* are but a little penetrative) you shall adde a little *Nitre*, we conceive it would be very good.   And touching the firmness of the *Aliment* thus much.

9.   As for the *Condensation* of the *skin* and *flesh* by *cold* : They are longer-liv'd for the most part that live abroad in the *open air*, than they that live in *Houses* ; and the Inhabitants of the *cold Countries*, than the Inhabitants of the *hot*.

10.   Great store of *clothes*, either upon the bed or back, do resolve the body.

11.   Washing the *body* in *cold water* is good for length of life ; use of *hot Baths* is naught. Touching *Baths* of *Astringent Mineral Waters* we have spoken before.

12.   As for *Exercise* ; an *idle life* doth manifestly make the flesh soft and dissipable : *robust exercise* (so it be without over-much sweating or weariness) maketh it hard and compact.   Also *exercise* within cold Water, as swimming, is very good ; and generally *exercise* abroad is better than that within houses.

13.   Touching *Frications*, (which are a kind of *exercise*) because they do rather call forth the Aliment than harden the flesh, we will inquire hereafter in the due place.

14.   Having now spoken of *hardning* the *juices* of the *body*, we are to come next to the *Oleosity* and *Fattiness* of them, which is a more perfect and potent Intention than *Induration*, because it hath no inconvenience or evil annexed.   For all those things which pertain to the *hardning* of the *juices* are of that nature, that while they prohibit the absumption of the Aliment, they also hinder the operation of the same ;   whereby it happens, that the same things are both propitious and adverse to length of life : but those things which pertain to making the *Juices Oily* and *Roscid*, help on both sides, for they render the Aliment both less dissipable, and more reparable.

15.   But whereas we say that the *Juice* of the *body* ought to be *Roscid* and *Fat*, it is to be noted that we mean it not of a visible *Fat*, but of a *Dewiness* dispersed, or (if you will call it) *Radical* in the very substance of the body.

16.   Neither again let any man think, that *Oil* or the *Fat* of *Meats* or *Marrow* do engender the like, and satisfie our intention : for those things which are once perfect are not brought back again ; but the Aliments ought to be such, which after digestion and maturation do then in the end engender *Oleosity* in the *Juices*.

17.   Neither again let any man think, that *Oil* or *Fat* by it self and simple is hard of dissipation, but in mixture it doth not retain the same nature : for as *Oil* by it self is much more longer in consuming then *Water* ; so in Paper or Linnen it sticketh longer, and is later dried, as we noted before.

To

To the Irroration of the body, roasted meats or baked meats are more effectual than boiled meats, and all preparation of meat with water is inconvenient: besides, Oil is more plentifully extracted out of drie bodies than out of moist bodies. 18.

Generally, to the *Irroration* of the body much use of sweet things is profitable, as of *Sugar, Honey, sweet Almonds, Pine-Apples, Pistachio's, Dates, Raisins* of the *Sun, Corans, Figs,* and the like. Contrarily, all sour, and very salt, and very biting things are opposite to the generation of *Roscid Juice.* 19.

Neither would we be thought to favour the *Manichees,* or their diet, though we commend the frequent use of all kinds of Seeds, Kernels, and Roots, in Meats or Sauces, considering all Bread (and Bread is that which maketh the Meat firm) is made either of Seeds or Roots. 20.

But there is nothing makes so much to the *Irroration* of the body, as the quality of the Drink, which is the convoy of the Meat; therefore let there be in use such Drinks as without all acrimony or sowrness are notwithstanding subtil : such are those Wines which are (as the old woman said in *Plautus*) *vetustate edentula,* toothless with age, and *Ale* of the same kind. 21.

Mead (as we suppose) would not be ill if it were strong and old : but because all Honey hath in it some sharp parts, (as appears by that sharp water which the *Chymists* extract out of it, which will dissolve metals) it were better to take the same portion of Sugar, not lightly infused in it, but so incorporated as Honey useth to be in *Mead,* and to keep it to the age of a year, or at least six months, whereby the Water may lose the crudity, and the Sugar acquire subtilty. 22.

Now ancientness in Wine or Beer hath this in it, that it ingenders subtilty in the parts of the Liquor, and acrimony in the Spirits, whereof the first improfitable, and the second hurtful. Now to rectifie this evil commixture, let there be put into the vessel, before the Wine be separated from the Must, *Swines-flesh* or *Deers-flesh* well boiled, that the Spirits of the Wine may have whereupon to ruminate and feed, and so lay aside their mordacity. 23.

In like manner, if *Ale* should be made not only with the grains of Wheat, Barly, Oates, Pease, and the like ; but also should admit a part (suppose a third part to these grains) of some fat roots, such as are *Potado-roots, Pith* of *Artichokes, Burre-roots,* or some other sweet and esculent roots ; we suppose it would be a more useful drink for long life than *Ale* made of grains onely. 24.

Also such things as have very thin parts, yet notwithstanding are without all acrimony or mordacity, are very good Sallets : which vertue we find to be in some few of the Flowers : namely, Flowers of *Ivy,* which infused in Vinegar are pleasant even to the taste ; *Marigold leaves,* which are used in Broths ; and Flowers of *Betony.* And touching the operation upon the *Juices* of the *Body* thus much. 25.

The Operation upon the Bowels for their Extrusion of Aliment. 5.

The History.

WHat those things are which comfort the *Principal Bowels,* which are the fountains of Concoctions, namely, the *Stomack, Liver, Heart* and *Brain,* to perform their functions well, (whereby *Aliment* is distributed into the parts, *Spirits* are dispersed, and the *Reparation* of the whole body is accomplished) may be derived from *Physitians,* and from their Prescripts and Advices. 1.

Touching the *Spleen, Gall, Kidneys, Mesenteries, Guts* and *Lungs,* we speak not, for these are members ministring to the principal ; and whereas speech is made touching health, they require sometime a most special consideration, because each of these have their diseases, which unless they be cured, will have influence upon the *Principal Members.* But as touching the prolongation of life, and reparation by aliments, and retardation of the inconction of old age ; if the Concoctions and 2.

those

those *principal Bowels* be well disposed, the rest will commonly follow according to ones wish.

3.   And as for those things which, according to the different state of every man's body may be transferred into his Diet and the regiment of his life, he may collect them out of the Books of Physicians, which have written of the comforting and preserving the four *Principal Members* : For conservation of health hath commonly need of no more than some short courses of Physick ; but length of life cannot be hoped without an orderly diet, and a constant race of *soveraign Medicines*. But we will propound some few, and those the most select and prime directions.

4.   The *Stomach* (which, as they say, is the Master of the house, and whose strength and goodness is fundamental to the other concoctions) ought so to be guarded and confirmed, that it may be without *intemperateness* hot ; next *astricted* or *bound*, not *loose* ; furthermore *clean*, not surcharged with foul Humours , and yet (in regard it is nourished from it self, not from the veins) not altogether *empty* or *hungry* : lastly, it is to be kept ever in *appetite*, because *appetite* sharpens digestion.

5.   I wonder much how that same *Calidum bibere*, to drink warm drink, (which was in use amongst the Ancients) is laid down again. I knew a Physician that was very famous, who in the beginning of dinner and supper, would usually eat a few spoonfulls of very warm *broth* with much greediness, and then would presently wish that it were out again, saying, *He had no need of the broth, but only of the warmth.*

6.   I do verily conceive it good, that the first draught either of *Wine*, or *Ale*, or any other *drink*, (to which a man is most accustomed) be taken at supper *warm*.

7.   *Wine* in which *Gold* hath been quenched, I conceive, would be very good once in a meal ; not that I believe the *Gold* conferreth any vertue thereunto, but that I know that the quenching of all Metals in any kind of liquor doth leave a most potent *Astriction* : Now I chuse *Gold*, because besides that Astriction which I desire, it leaveth nothing else behind it of a metalline impression.

8.   I am of opinion, that the sops of bread dipped in wine, taken at the midst of the meal, are better than wine it self ; especially if there were infused into the wine in which the sops were dipped *Rosemary* and *Citron-pill*, and that with *Sugar*, that it may not slip too fast.

9.   It is certain that the use of *Quinces* is good to strengthen the stomach ; but we take them to be better if they be used in that which they call *Quiddeny* of *Quinces*, than in the bodies of the *Quinces* themselves, because they lie heavy in the stomach. But those *Quiddenies* are best taken after meals, alone ; before meals, dipped in Vinegar.

10.   Such things as are good for the stomach above other Simples are these, *Rosemary, Elecampane, Mastick, Wormwood, Sage, Mint.*

11.   I allow Pills of *Aloes*, *Mastick* and *Saffron* in Winter time, taken before dinner ; but so, as the *Aloes* be not only oftentimes washed in *Rose-water*, but also in *Vinegar* in which *Tragacanth* hath been infused, and after that be macerated for a few hours in Oil of sweet *Almonds* new drawn, before it be made into Pills.

12.   *Wine* or *Ale* wherein *Wormwood* hath been infused, with a little *Elecampane* and yellow *Sanders*, will do well, taken at times, and that especially in Winter.

13.   But in Summer, a draught of *White-wine* allayed with *strawberry-water*, in which Wine Powder of Pearls and of the shells of *cra-fishes* exquisitely beaten and (which may perhaps seem strange) a little *Chalk* have been infused, doth excellently refresh and strengthen the stomach.

14.   But generally, all *Draughts* in the morning (which are but too frequently used) of *cooling* things, as of Juices, Decoctions, Whey, Barly-waters, and the like) are to be avoided, and nothing is to be put into the stomach fasting which is purely *cold*. These things are better given, if need require, either at five in the afternoon, or else an hour after a light breakfast.

15.   Often fastings are bad for long life ; besides, all thirst is to be avoided, and the stomach is to be kept clean, but always moist.

16.   *Oil of Olives* new and good, in which a little *Mithridate* hath been dissolved, anointed upon the back-bone, just against the mouth of the stomach, doth wonderfully comfort the stomach.

17.   A small bag filled with locks of Scarlet-wool steeped in Red-wine, in which

Myrtle,

Myrtle, and *Citron-pill,* and a little *Saffron* have been infused, may be always worn upon the stomach. And touching those things wich comfort the stomach thus much, seeing many of those things also which serve for other operations are helpful to this.

The *Liver,* if it be preserved from *Torrefaction,* or *Desiccation,* and from *Obstruction,* it needeth no more; for that loosness of it which begets *Aquosities* is plainly a disease, but the other two old age approaching induceth.

Hereunto appertain most especially those things which are set down in the *Operation* upon the *Blood:* we will adde a very few things more, but those selected.

Principally let there be in use the Wine of sweet *Pomegranats,* or, if that cannot be had, the juice of them newly expressed; let it be taken in the morning with a little *Sugar,* and into the glass into which the Expression is made put a small piece of *Citron-pill* green, and three or four whole *Cloves :* let this be taken from *February* till the end of *April.*

Bring also into use above all other Herbs *Water-creßes,* but young, not old; they may be used either raw in Sallets, or in Broths, or in Drinks : and after that take *Spoon-wort.*

Aloes, however washed or corrected, is hurtful for the *Liver,* and therefore it is never to be taken ordinarily. Contrariwise, *Rhubarb* is sovereign for the *Liver,* so that these three cautions be interposed. First, that it be taken before meat, lest it dry the body too much, or leave some impressions of the *Stipticity* thereof. Secondly, that it be macerated an hour or two in Oil of sweet *Almonds* new drawn, with *Rose-water,* before it be infused in Liquor, or given in the proper substance. Thirdly, that it be taken by turns, one while simple, another while with *Tartar,* or a little *Bay-salt,* that it carry not away the lighter parts onely, and make the mass of the Humours more obstinate.

I allow *Wine,* or some decoction with *Steel,* to be taken three or four times in the year, to open the more strong obstructions; yet so, that a draught of two or three spoonfuls of Oil of sweet *Almonds* new drawn ever go before, and the motion of the Body, especially of the arms and sides, constantly follow.

Sweetned Liquors, and that with some fatness, are principally, and not a little effectual to prevent the *Arefaction,* and *Saltness,* and *Torrefaction,* and in a word, the *Oldness* of the *Liver,* especially if they be well incorporated with age. They are made of sweet Fruits and Roots, as namely, the Wines and Julips of *Raisins* of the *Sun* new, *Jujubaes, dried Figs, Dates, Parsnips, Potatoes,* and the like, with the mixture of *Licoris* sometimes : also a Julip of the *Indian* grain, (which they call *Maiz*) with the mixture of some sweet things, doth much to the same end. But it is to be noted, that the intention of preserving the *Liver* in a kind of softness and fatness, is much more powerful than that other which pertains to the opening of the *Liver,* which rather tendeth to health than to length of life, saving that that *Obstruction* which induceth *Torrefaction* is as opposite to long life as those other *Arefactions.*

I commend the Roots of *Succory, Spinage* and *Beets* cleared of their piths, and boiled till they be tender in Water, with a third part of *white-wine,* for ordinary Sallets, to be eaten with Oil and Vinegar : also *Asparagus,* pith of *Artichokes,* and *Burre-roots* boiled and served in after the same manner; also Broths in the Spring-time of *Vine-buds,* and the green blades of *wheat.* And touching the preserving of the *Liver* thus much.

The *Heart* receiveth benefit or harm most from the *Air* which we breath, from *Vapours,* and from the *Affections.* Now many of those things which have been formerly spoken touching the Spirits may be transferred hither; but that indigested mass of Cordials collected by Physicians avails little to our intention : notwithstanding those things which are found to be good against Poysons may with good judgment be given to strengthen and fortifie the *Heart,* especially if they be of that kind, that they do not so much resist the particular poysons as arm the heart and spirits against poyson in general. And touching the several Cordials, you may repair to the *Table* already set down.

The goodness of the *Air* is better known by experience than by signs. We hold that Air to be best where the Country is level and plain, and that lieth open on all sides, so that the soil be dry. and yet not barren or sandy; which puts forth

H 2

Wild

Wild Thyme, and *Eye-bright*, and a kind of *Marjoram*, and here and there stalks of *Calamints*; which is not altogether void of wood, but conveniently set with some Trees for shade ; where the *Sweet-briar-rose* smelleth something Musky and Aromatically. If there be *Rivers*, we suppose them rather hurtful than good, unless they be very small, and clear, and gravelly.

28.   It is certain that the *morning air* is more lively and refreshing than the *evening air*, though the latter be preferr'd out of delicacy.

29.   We conceive also, that the *air stirred* with a *gentle wind* is more wholesome than the *air* of a *serene* and *calm skie*; but the best is, the *wind* blowing from the *West* in the morning, and from the *North* in the afternoon.

30.   *Odours* are especially profitable for the comforting of the *heart*, yet not so as though a good *odour* were the prerogative of a good *air* : for it is certain, that as there are some *Pestilential airs* which smell not so ill as others that are less hurtful ; so, on the contrary, there are some *airs* most wholsome and friendly to the *spirits*, which either smell not at all, or are less pleasing and fragrant to the sense. And generally, where the *air* is good, *odours* should be taken but now and then ; for a continual *odour*, though never so good, is burthensome to the *spirits*.

31.   We commend above all others (as we have touched before) *odour* of *Plants, growing*, and not *plucked*, taken in the open *air* : the principal of that kind are *Violets*, *Gilliflowers, Pinks, Beau-flowers, Lime-tree-blossoms, Vine-buds, Honey-suckles*, yellow *Wall-flowers, Musk-Roses*, (for other *Roses* growing are fast of their smells) *Strawberry-leaves*, especially *dying, Sweet-briar*, principally in the early Spring, *wild Mint, Lavender flowered*; and in the hotter Countries, *Orenge-tree, Citron-tree, Myrtle, Laurel*: Therefore to walk or sit near the breath of these *Plants* would not be neglected.

32.   For the comforting of the *Heart*, we prefer cool smels before hot smells : therefore the best perfume is, either in the morning, or about the heat of the day, to take an equal portion of *Vinegar, Rose-water*, and *Claret-wine*, and to pour them upon a Fire-pan somewhat heated.

33.   Neither let us be thought to sacrifice to our Mother the *Earth*, though we advise, that in *digging* or *ploughing* the *Earth* for health, a quantity of *claret-wine* be poured thereon.

34.   *Orenge-flower-water*, pure and good, with a small portion of *Rose-water* and *brisk wine*, snuffed up into the nostrils, or put into the nostrills with a *syringe*, after the manner of an *Errhine*, (but not too frequently) is very good.

35.   But *champing* (though we have no *Betel*) or holding in the mouth onely of such things as cheer the Spirits, (even daily done) is exceeding comfortable. Therefore for that purpose make *Grains* or little *cakes* of *Amber-griece, Musk, Lignum-Aloes, Lignum Rhodium, Orrai Powder*, and *Roses*; and let those *Grains* or *Cakes* be made up with *Rose-water* which hath passed through a little *Indian Balsam*.

36.   The *Vapours* which arising from things inwardly taken do fortifie and cherish the *heart* ought to have these three properties, that they be Friendly, Clear, and Cooling; for hot *vapours* are naught, and *wine* it self, which is thought to have onely an heating *vapour*, is not altogether void of an *Opiate quality*. Now we call those *vapours* Clear which have more of the *vapour* than of the *exhalation*, and which are not smoaky, or fuliginous, or unctuous, but moist and equal.

37.   Out of that unprofitable rabble of *cordials*, a few ought to be taken into daily diet : instead of all, *Amber-griece, Saffron*, and the grain of *Kermes*, of the hotter sort; Roots of *Bugloss* and *Borrage, Citrons, Sweet Limons*, and *Pearmains*, of the colder sort. Also that way which we said, both *Gold* and *Pearls* work a good effect, not onely within the veins, but in their passage, and about the parts near the heart ; namely, by cooling, without any malignant quality.

38.   Of *Bezoar-stone* we believe well, because of many trials : but then the manner of taking it ought to be such, as the vertue thereof may more easily be communicated to the *spirits* : therefore we approve not the taking of it in *Broths* or *Syrups*, or in *Rose-water*, or any such like ; but onely in *wine, Cinnamon-water*, or the like distilled water, but that weak or small, not burning or strong.

39.   Of the *Affections* we have spoken before ; we onely adde this, That every *Noble*, and *Resolute*, and (as they call it) *Heroical Desire*, strengthneth and inlargeth the powers of the Heart. And touching the *Heart* thus much.

As for the *Brain*, where the Seat and Court of the *Animal Spirits* is kept, those things which were inquired before touching *Opium*, and *Nitre*, and the *subordinates* to them both, also touching the *procuring of placid sleep*, may likewise be referred hither. This also is most certain, that the *Brain* is in some sort in the custody of the *Stomach*; and therefore those things which comfort and strengthen the *Stomach* do help the *Brain* by consent, and may no less be transferred hither. We will adde a few Observations, three Outward, one Inward.   40.

We would have *bathing* of the *Feet* to be often used, at least once in a week: and the *Bath* to be made of *Lye* with *Bay-salt*, and a little *Sage*, *Chamomile*, *Fennel*, *Sweet-marjoram*, and *Pepper-wort*, with the leaves of *Angellica* green.   41.

We commend also a *Fume* or *Suffumigation* every morning of dried *Rosemary*, *Bay-leaves* dried, and *Lignum-Aloes*: for all sweet *Gums* oppress the head.   42.

Especially care must be taken that no *hot things* be applied to the *Head* outwardly; such are all kind of Spices, the very *Nutmeg* not excepted: for those hot things we debase them to the soles of the *Feet*, and would have them applied there onely; but a light anointing of the *Head* with *Oil*, mixed with *Roses*, *Myrtle*, and a little *Salt* and *Saffron*, we much commend.   43.

Not forgetting those things which we have before delivered touching *Opiates*, *Nitre*, and the like, which so much *condense* the *spirits*; we think it not impertinent to that effect, that once in fourteen days *broth* be taken in the morning with three or four grains of *Castoreum*, and a little *Angelica-seed*, and *Calamus*, which both fortifie the *Brain*, and in that aforesaid density of the substance of the *spirits*, (so necessary to long life) adde also a *vivacity* of *motion* and *vigour* to them.   44.

In handling the *Comforters* of the four *principal Bowels*, we have propounded those things which are both proper and choice, and may safely and conveniently be transferred into Diets and Regiment of Life: for variety of *Medicines* is the *Daughter of Ignorance*; and it is not more true, that *many Dishes have caused many Diseases*, as the *Proverb* is, than this is true, that *many Medicines have caused few Cures*. And touching the *Operation* upon the *principal Bowels* for their *Extrusion* of *Aliment*, thus much.   45.

The Operation upon the Outward Parts for their Attraction of Aliment. 6.

The History.

Although a good *Concoction* performed by the *Inward Parts* be the principal towards a perfect Alimentation; yet the Actions of the *Outward Parts* ought also to concur; that like as the *Inward Faculty* sendeth forth and extrudeth the Aliment, so the *Faculty* of the *Outward Parts* may call forth and attract the same: and the more weak the *Faculty of Concoction* shall be, the more need is there of a concurring help of the *Attractive Faculty*.   1.

A *strong Attraction* of the *outward parts* is chiefly caused by the motion of the Body, by which the parts being heated and comforted, do more chearfully call forth and attract the Aliment unto themselves.   2.

But this is most of all to be foreseen and avoided, that the same motion and heat which calls the new juice to the members, doth not again despoil the member of that juice wherewith it had been before refreshed.   3.

Frications used in the morning serve especially to this *Intention*: but this must evermore accompany them, that after the *Frication* the part be lightly anointed with Oil, lest the Attrition of the outward parts make them by Perspiration dry and juiceless.   4.

The next is *Exercise*, (by which the parts confricate and chafe themselves) so it   5.

be moderate, and which (as was noted before) is not swift, nor to the utmost strength, nor unto weariness. But in *Exercise* and *Frication* there is the same reason and caution, that the body may not perspire or exhale too much : Therefore *Exercise* is better in the open air than in the house, and better in Winter than in Summer ; and again, *Exercise* is not onely to be concluded with Unction, as *Frication* is , but in vehement *Exercises* Unction is to be used both in the beginning and in the end, as it was anciently to *Champions*.

6.   That *Exercise* may resolve either the spirits or the juices as little as may be, it is necessary that it be used when the stomach is not altogether empty : and therefore that it may not be used upon a full stomach, (which doth much concern health) nor yet upon an empty stomach, (which doth no less concern long life) it is best to take a breakfast in the morning, not of any Physical Drugs, or of any Liquors or of Raisins, or of Figs, or the like; but of plain Meat and Drink, yet that very light, and in moderate quantity.

7.   *Exercises* used for the irrigation of the members, ought to be equal to all the members ; not (as *Socrates* said) *that the Legs should move, and the Arms should rest*, or on the contrary ; but that all the parts may participate of the motion. And it is altogether requisite to long life, that the Body should never abide long in one posture, but that every half hour, at least, it change the posture, saving onely in sleep.

8.   Those things which are used to *Mortification* may be transferred to *Vivification* : for both Hair-shirts, and Scourgings, and all vexations of the outward parts, do fortifie the Attractive force of them.

9.   *Cardan* commends *Nettling*, even to let out *Melancholly* : but of this we have no experience ; and besides, we have no good opinion of it, lest, through the venemous quality of the *Nettle*, it may with often use breed Itches and other diseases of the skin. And touching the *Operation* upon the *Outward Parts* for their *Attraction* of *Aliment*, thus much.

The Operation upon the *Aliment* it self for the Insinuation thereof. 7.

The History.

1.   THe vulgar reproof touching many Dishes doth rather become a severe *Reformer* than a *Physician* : or howsoever it may be good for perservation of health, yet it is hurtful to length of life, by reason that a various mixture of Aliments, and somewhat heterogeneous, finds a passage into the veins and juices of the body more lively and chearfully than a simple and homogeneous diet doth : besides, it is more forcible to stir up *Appetite*, which is the spur of Digestion. Therefore we allow both a *full Table*, and a *continual changing of Dishes*, according to the Seasons of the year, or upon other occasions.

2.   Also that opinion of the *Simplicity* of *Meats* without *Sawces* is but a simplicity of judgment ; for good and well-chosen *Sawces* are the most wholesome preparation of *Meats*, and conduce both to health and to long life.

3.   It must be ordered, that with Meats hard of digestion be conjoyned strong Liquors and Sawces that may penetrate and make way ; but with Meats more easie of digestion, smaller Liquors and fat Sawces.

4.   Whereas we advised before, that the first *Draught* at *Supper* should be taken warm ; now we adde, that for the preparation of the stomach, a good draught of that Liquor (to which every man is most accustomed) be taken warm half an hour before meat also, but a little spiced, to please the taste.

5.   The preparation of Meats, and Bread, and Drinks, that they may be rightly handled, and in order to this Intention, is of exceeding great moment howsoever it may seem a Mechanical thing, and favouring of the Kitchin and Buttery; yet it is of more consequence than those Fables of Gold and precious Stones, and the like.

The

The moiftning of the juices of the body by a moift preparation of the aliment, is a childifh thing ; it may be fomewhat available againft the fervours of difeafes, but it is altogether averfe to rofcid alimentation.   Therefore boiling of meats, as concerning our Intention, is far inferiour to roafting, and baking, and the like.

Roafting ought to be with a quick fire, and foon difpatched ; not with a dull fire, and in long time.

All folid flefhes ought to be ferved in, not altogether frefh, but fomewhat powdered or corned ; the lefs Salt may be fpent at the table with them, or none at all : for Salt incorporated with the meat before is better diftributed in the body, then eaten with it at the table.

There would be brought into ufe feveral and good *Macerations*, and *Infufions* of *Meats* in convenient Liquors, before the roafting of them : the like whereof are fometime in ufe before they bake them, and in the Pickles of fome Fifhes.

But *beatings*, and as it were *fcourgings*, of flefh-meats before they be boiled, would work no fmall matter.   We fee it is confeffed that *Partridges* and *Pheafants* killed with an *Hawk*, alfo *Bucks* and *Stags* killed in *Hunting*, (if they ftand not out too long, eat better even to the tafte ; and fome *Fifhes* fcourged and beaten, become more tender and wholfome ; alfo hard and four *Pears*, and fome other Fruits, grow fweet with rowling them.   It were good to practife fome fuch beating and bruifing of the harder kinds of Flefhes before they be brought to the fire ; and this would be one of the beft preparations of all.

Bread a little levened, and very little falted, is beft, and which is baked in an Oven throughly heated, and not with a faint heat.

The preparation of Drinks in order to long life fhall not exceed one Precept.   And as touching *water-drinkers* we have nothing to fay ; fuch a diet (as we faid before) may prolong life to an indifferent term, but to no eminent length : but in other Drinks, that are full of fpirit, (fuch as are *Wine, Ale, Mead*, and the like) this one thing is to be obferved and purfued, as the fum of all, That the parts of the *Liquor* may be exceeding thin and fubtil, and the *Spirit* exceeding mild.   This is hard to be done by *Age* alone, for that makes the parts a little more fubtil, but the fpirits much more fharp and eager : therefore of the *Infufions* in the Veffels of fome fat fubftance, which may reftrain the acrimony of the fpirits, counfel hath been given before.   There is alfo another way without *Infufion* or *Mixture* : this is, that the Liquor might be continually agitated, either by carriage upon the Water, or by carriage by Land, or by hanging the veffels upon lines, and daily ftirring them, or fome fuch other way : for it is certain that this *local motion* doth both fubtilize the parts, and doth fo incorporate and compact the fpirits with the parts, that they have no leifure to turn to fowrnefs, which is a kind of *putrefaction*.

But in extream *old age* fuch a preparation of meats is to be made as may be almoft in the middle way to *chylus*.   And touching the *Diftillations of Meats*, they are mere toys ; for the Nutritive part, at leaft the beft of it, doth not afcend in *Vapours*.

The incorporating of meat and drink before they meet in the ftomach is a degree to *chylus* : therefore let *Chickens*, or *Partridges*, or *Pheafants*, or the like, be taken and boiled in water with a little falt, then let them be cleanfed and dried, afterward let them be infufed in *Muft* or *Ale* before it hath done working, with a little *Sugar*.

Alfo *Grazies* of meat, and the *mincings* of them fmall well feafon'd, are good for *old perfons* ; and the rather, for that they are deftituted of the office of their *Teeth* in chewing, which is a principal kind of preparation.

And as for the helps of that defect, (namely, of the ftrength of *Teeth* to grind the meat) there are three things which may conduce thereunto.   Firft, that new *Teeth* may put forth ; that which feems altogether difficult, and cannot be accomplifhed without an inward and powerful reftauration of the body.   Secondly, that the *Jaws* be fo confirmed by due *aftringents*, that they may in fome fort fupply the office of the *Teeth*; which may poffibly be effected.   Thirdly, that the meat be fo prepared, that there fhall be no need of chewing : which remedy is ready at hand.

We have fome thought alfo touching the *Quantity* of the meat and drink, that the fame taken in a larger *quantity* at fome times is good for the *irrigation* of the *body* : therefore both *great Feaftings* and *free Drinkings* are not altogether to be inhibited. And touching the *Operation* upon the *Aliments* and the *Preparation* of them, thus much.

The

6.

7.

8.

9.

10.

11.

12.

13.

14.

15.

16.

17.

The Operation upon the last *Act* of *Assimilation.* 8.

TOuching the last *Act* of Assimilation (*unto which the three* Operations *immediately preceeding chiefly tend*) *our advice shall be brief and single: and the thing it self rather needs Explication, than any various Rules.*

1. IT is certain, that all bodies are endued with some desire of *Assimilating* those things which are next them. This the rare and pneumatical bodies, as *Flame, Spirit, Air,* perform generously and with alacrity: on the contrary, those that carry a gross and tangible bulk about them, do but weakly, in regard that the desire of *assimilating* other things is bound in by a stronger desire of Rest, and containing themselves from *Motion.*

2. Again, it is certain that the desire of *assimilating* being bound, as we said, in a Gross body, and made uneffectual, is somewhat freed and stirred up by the *heat* and *neighbouring spirit,* so that it is then actuated: which is the onely cause why *Inanimates assimilate not,* and *Animates assimilate.*

3. This also is certain, that the harder the Consistence of the body is, the more doth that body stand in need of a greater heat to prick forward the *assimilation:* which falls out ill for old men, because in them the parts are more obstinate, and the heat weaker; and therefore either the obstinacy of their parts is to be softned, or their heat increased. And as touching the *Malacissation* or *mollifying* of the members, we shall speak afterward, having also formerly propounded many things which pertain to the prohibiting and preventing of this kind of hardness. For the other, touching the increasing of the heat, we will now deliver a single precept, after we have first assumed this *Axiom.*

4. The *Act* of *Assimilation* (which, as we said, is excited by the heat circumfused) is a motion exceeding accurate, subtile, and in little; now all such motions do then come to their vigour, when the *local Motion* wholly ceaseth which disturbeth it. For the *Motion of Separation* into *homogeneal* parts, which is in Milk, that the Cream should swim above, and the Whey sink to the bottom, will never work, if the Milk be never so little agitated; neither will any *Putrefaction* proceed in Water or mixt Bodies, if the same be in continual *Local Motion.* So then, from this *Assumption* we will conclude this for the present Inquisition.

5. The *Act* it self of *Assimilation* is chiefly accomplished in Sleep and Rest, especially towards the morning, the distribution being finished. Therefore we have nothing else to advise, but that men keep themselves hot in their sleep; and further, that towards the morning there be used some Anointing, or shirt tincted with Oil, such as may gently stir up heat, and after that to fall asleep again. And touching the last *Act* of *Assimilation* thus much.

The Operation upon the Inteneration of that which begins to be Arefied, or the *Malacissation* of the *Body.* 9.

VVE *have inquired formerly touching the* Inteneration *from within, which is done by many windings and Circuits, as well of* Alimentation *as of* Detaining *the Spirit from issuing forth, and therefore is accomplished slowly.* Now *we are to inquire touching that* Inteneration *which is from without, and is effected, as it were, suddenly; or touching the* Malacissation *and* Suppling *of the* Body.

The History.

1. IN the *Fable* of restoring *Pelias* to youth again, *Medea,* when she feigned to do it propounded this way of accomplishing the same, That the Old man's body should be cut into several pieces, and then boiled in a Cauldron with certain Medicaments. There may, perhaps, some boiling be required to this matter, but the cutting into pieces is not needful.

Notwithstanding, this cutting into pieces seems, in some sort, to be useful, not with a knife, but with judgment. For whereas the Consistence of the *Bowels* and *Parts* is very diverse, it is needfull that the *Inteneration* of them both be not effected the same way, but that there be a Cure designed of each in particular, besides those things which pertain to the Inteneration of the whole mass of the Body ; of which, notwithstanding, in the first place.

This *Operation* (if perhaps it be within our power) is most likely to be done by Baths, Unctions, and the like ; concerning which these things that follow are to be observed.

We must not be too forward in hoping to accomplish this matter from the Examples of those things which we see done in the *Imbibitions* and *Macerations* of *inanimates*, by which they are intenerated, whereof we introduced some instances before : For this kind of operation is more easie upon *Inanimates*, *because they attract and suck in the Liquor ; but upon the bodies of Living creatures it is harder, because in them the motion rather tendeth outward and to the *Circumference*.

Therefore the *Emollient Baths* which are in use do little good, but on the contrary hurt, because they rather draw forth than make entrance, and resolve the structure of the body rather than consolidate it.

The *Baths* and *Unctions* which may serve to the present *Operation* (namely, of *Intenerating* the *body* truly and really) ought to have three properties.

The first and principal is, That they consist of those *things* which in their whole substance are like unto the *body* and *flesh* of *man*, and which have a *feeding* and *nursing* virtue from without.

The second is, That they be mixed with such things as through the *subtilty* of their parts may *make entrance*, and so insinuate and conveigh their *nourishing virtue* into the *body*.

The third is, That they receive some *mixture* (though much inferiour to the rest) of such things as are *Astringent* ; I mean not sour or tart things , but unctuous and comforting ; that while the other two do operate, the exhaling out of the body, which destroyeth the virtue of the things *intenerating*, may (as much as is possible) be prohibited ; and the motion to the inward parts, by the *Astriction* of the skin and closing of the passages, may be promoted and furthered.

That which is most *consubstantial* to the body of man is *warm Bloud*, either of man, or of some other living creature : but the device of *Ficinus*, touching the sucking of *bloud* out of the arm of a wholesome young man, for the restauration of strength in old men, is very frivolous ; for that which nourisheth from within ought no way to be equal or homogeneal to the body nourished, but in some sort inferiour and subordinate, that it may be converted : but in things applied outwardly, by how much the *substance* is *liker*, by so much the *consent* is *better*.

It hath been anciently received, that a *Bath* made of the *bloud* of *Infants* will cure the *Leprosie*, and heal the flesh already putrefi'd ; insomuch that this thing hath begot envy towards some *Kings* from the common people.

It is reported that *Heraclitus*, for cure of the *Dropsie*, was put into the *warm belly* of an ox newly slain.

They use the *bloud* of *Kitlins* warm to cure the *disease* called St. *Anthony's Fire*, and to restore the flesh and skin.

An *Arm* or other *Member* newly cut off, or that upon some other occasion will not leave *bleeding*, is with good success put into the *belly* of some *creatures newly ripped up*, for it worketh potently to stanch the *bloud* ; the *bloud* of the member cut off by consent sucking in, and vehemently drawing to it self, the *warm bloud* of the creature slain, whereby it self is stopped and retireth.

It is much used in extreme and desperate *diseases* to cut in two *young Pigeons*, yet living , and apply them to the *soles* of the *feet*, and to shift them one after another, whereby sometime there followeth a wonderful ease. This is imputed vulgarly as if they should draw down the malignity of the disease ; but howsoever, this application goeth to the *Head*, and comforteth the *Animal Spirits*.

But these *bloudy Baths* and *Unctions* seem to us flattish and odious : let us search out some others, which perhaps have less loathsomeness in them, and yet no less benefit.

17. Next unto *warm Bloud, things alike in substance* to the Body of a man are *nutritives*: *fat fleshes* of *Oxen, Swine, Dear*; *oisters* amongst *Fishes*; *Milk, Butter, Yolks* of *Eggs, Flower* of *Wheat, sweet wine*, either Sugred, or before it be fined.

18. Such things as we would have mixed to make impression are, instead of all, *Salts*, especially *Bay salt*; also Wine (when it is full of spirit) maketh entrance, and is an excellent Convoy.

19. *Astringents* of that kind which we described, namely, unctuous and comfortable things, are *Saffron, Mastick, Myrrhe*, and *Myrtle berries*.

20. Of these parts, in our judgment, may very well be made such a *Bath* as we design: *Physicians* and *Posterity* will find out better things hereafter.

21. But the *Operation* will be much better and more powerful, if such a *Bath* as we have propounded (which we hold to be the principal matter) be attended with a fourfold *Course* and *Order*.

22. First, that there go before the *Bath* a *Frication* of the body, and an *Anointing* with *Oil*, with some thickning substance, that the virtue and moistning heat of the *Bath* may pierce the body, and not the watry part of the Liquor. Then let the *Bath* follow, for the space of some two hours. After the *Bath*, let the body be *Emplaistered* with *Mastick, Myrrhe, Tragacanth, Diapalma*, and *Saffron*; that the perspiration of the body may (as much as is possible) be inhibited, till the *supple matter* be by degrees turned into *solid*: This to be continued for the space of twenty four hours or more. Lastly, the *Emplaistering* being removed, let there be an *anointing* with *Oil* mixed with *Salt* and *Saffron*. And let this *Bath*, together with the *Emplaistering* and *Unction*, (as before) be renewed every fifth day. This *Malacissation* or *suppling* of the body be continued for one whole month.

23. Also during the time of this *Malacissation*, we hold it useful and proper, and according to our intention, that men nourish their bodies well, and keep out of the cold air, and drink nothing but warm drink.

24. Now this is one of those things (as we warned in general in the beginning) whereof we have made no trial by *Experiment*, but onely set it down out of our aiming and levelling at the end: For having set up the Mark, we deliver the Light to others.

25. Neither ought the *warmths* and *cherishings of living bodies* to be neglected. *Ficinus* faith, and that seriously enough, *That the laying of the young Maid in* David's *bosom was wholsome for him, but it came too late.* He should also have added, That the *young Maid*, after the manner of the *Persian Virgins*, ought to have been anointed with *Myrrhe*, and such like, not for deliciousness, but to increase the virtue of this cherishing by a living body.

26. *Barbarossa*, in his extream old age, by the advice of a *Physician*, a *Jew*, did continually apply young Boys to his stomach and belly, for warmth and cherishing: also some old men lay Whelps (creatures of the hottest kind) close to their stomachs every night.

27. There hath gone a report, almost undoubted, and that under several names, of certain men that had great *Noses*, who being weary of the derision of people, have cut off the bunches or hillocks of their *Noses*, and then making a wide gash in their arms, have held their *Noses* in the place for a certain time, and so brought forth fair and comely *Noses*: Which if it be true, it shews plainly the *consent of flesh* unto *flesh*, especially in *live fleshes*.

28. Touching the particular *Inteneration* of the *principal Bowels*, the *Stomach, Lungs, Liver, Heart, Brain, Marrow* of the *Back-bone, Guts, Reins, Gall, Veins, Arteries, Nerves, Cartilages, Bones*, the *Inquisition* and *Direction* would be too long seeing we now set not forth a *Practick*, but certain *Indications* to the *Practick*.

The

The Operation upon the Purging away of old Juice, and Supplying of new Juice; or of Renovation by Turns. 10.

The History.

ALthough those things which we shall here set down have been, for the most part, spoken of before; yet because this Operation is one of the principal, we will handle them over again more at large.

It is certain that *Draught-Oxen* which have been worn out with working, being put into fresh and rich pastures, will gather tender and young flesh again : and this will appear even to the taste and palat ; so that the *Inteneration* of flesh is no hard matter. Now it is likely that this *Inteneration* of the *flesh* being often repeated, will in time reach to the *Inteneration* of the *Bones* and *Membranes*, and like *parts* of the *body*.

It is certain that Diets which are now much in use, principally of *Guaiacum*, and of *Sarsaperilla*, *China*, and *Sassafras*, if they be continued for any time, and according to strict rules, do first *attenuate* the whole *juice* of the body, and after consume it and drink it up. Which is most manifest, because that by these Diets the *French-Pox*, when it is grown even to an hardness, and hath eaten up and corrupted the very marrow of the body, may be effectually cured. And further, because it is manifest that men who by these diets are brought to be extream lean, pale, and as it were ghosts, will soon after become fat, well-coloured, and apparently young again. Wherefore we are absolutely of opinion, that such kind of diets in the decline of age, being used every year, would be very useful to our Intention ; like the old skin or spoil of *Serpents*.

We do confidently affirm, (neither let any man reckon us among those *Hereticks* which were called *Cathari*) that often *Purges*, and made even familiar to the body, are more available to long life than *Exercises* and *Sweats* : and this must needs be so, if that be held, which is already laid for a ground, That Unctions of the body, and Oppletion of the passages from without, and Exclusion of air, and Detaining of the spirit within the mass of the body, do much conduce to long life. For it is most certain, that by Sweats and outward Perspirations not only the Humours and excrementitious vapours are exhaled and consumed, but together with them the juices also and good spirits, which are not so easily repaired: but in Purges (unless they be very immoderate) it is not so, seeing they work principally upon the Humors. But the best Purges for this Intention are those which are taken immediately before meat, because they dry the body less ; and therefore they must be of those Purgers which do least trouble the belly.

These Intentions *of the* Operations *which we have propounded (as we conceive) are most true, the* Remedies *faithful to the* Intentions. *Neither is it credible to be told (although not a few of these* Remedies *may seem but vulgar) with what care and choice they have been examined by us, that they might be (the* Intention *not at all impeached) both safe and effectual* Experience, *no doubt, will both verifie and promote these matters. And such, in all things, are the* works of every *prudent counsel, that they are* Admirable in *their* Effects, *Excellent also in their* Order, *but seeming* Vulgar in the Way *and* Means.

The Porches of Death.

WE are now to enquire touching the Porches of Death, that is, touching those things which happen unto men at the point of Death, both a little before and after : that seeing there are many Paths which lead to Death, it may be understood in what Common *way they all end, especially in those Deaths which are caused by Indigence of Nature rather than by Violence: although something of this latter also must be inserted, because of the connexion of things.*

The History.

1. THe living Spirit stands in need of three things that it may subsist; *Convenient Motion, Temperate Refrigeration,* and *Fit Aliment.* Flame seems to stand in need but of two of these, namely, *Motion* and *Aliment,* because Flame is a simple substance, the Spirit a compounded, insomuch that if it approach somewhat too near to a flamy nature, it overthroweth it self.

2. Also Flame by a greater and stronger Flame is extinguished and slain, as *Aristotle* well noted, much more the *Spirit.*

3. Flame, if it be much compressed and streightned, is extinguished: as we may see in a Candle having a Glass cast over it; for the Air being dilated by the heat, doth contrude and thrust together the Flame, and so lesseneth it, and in the end extinguisheth it; and fires on hearths will not flame if the fuel be thrust close together without any space for the flame to break forth.

4. Also things fired are extinguished with compression; as if you press a burning coal hard with the Tongs or the foot, it is streight extinguished.

5. But to come to the Spirit: if Bloud or Phlegm get into the Ventricles of the Brain, it causeth sudden death, because the Spirit hath no room to move it self.

6. Also a great blow on the head induceth sudden death, the Spirits being streightned within the Ventricles of the Brain.

7. *Opium* and other strong *Stupefactives* do coagulate the Spirit, and deprive it of the motion.

8. A *venemous Vapour,* totally abhorred by the spirit, causeth sudden death: as in deadly poisons, which work (as they call it) by a specifical malignity; for they strike a loathing into the Spirit, that the spirit will no more move it self, nor rise against a thing so much detested.

9. Also extreme Drunkenness or extreme Feeding sometime cause sudden death, seeing the spirit is not onely oppressed with over-much *condensing,* or the malignity of the vapour, (as in *Opium* and malignant poisons) but also with the abundance of the Vapours.

10. Extreme Grief or Fear, especially if they be sudden, (as it is in a sad and unexpected message) cause sudden death.

11. Not onely over-much Compression, but also over-much Dilatation of the spirit, is deadly.

12. Joys excessive and sudden have bereft many of their lives.

13. In greater Evacuations, as when they cut men for the *Dropsie,* the waters flow forth abundantly ; much more in great and sudden fluxes of bloud oftentimes present death followeth : and this happens by the mere flight of *Vacuum* within the body, all the parts moving to fill the empty places, and amongst the rest the spirits themselves. For as for slow fluxes of blood, this matter pertains to the indigence of nourishment, not to the diffusion of the spirits. And touching the motion of the spirit so far, either compressed or diffused, that it bringeth death, thus much.

14. We must come next to the want of Refrigeration. Stopping of the breath causeth sudden death, as in all suffocation or strangling. Now it seems this matter is not so much to be referred to the impediment of Motion, as to the impediment of Refrigeration; for air over-hot, though attracted freely, doth no less suffocate than if breathing were hindred; as it is in them who have been sometime suffocated with burning coals, or with char-coal, or with walls newly plaistered in close chambers where a fire is made: which kind of death is reported to have been the end of the Emperor *Jovinian.* The like happeneth from dry Baths over heated, which was practised in the killing of *Fausta,* wife to *Constantine* the Great.

15. It is a very small time which Nature taketh to repeat the breathing, and in

which

which she defireth to expel, the foggy air drawn into the *Lungs*, and to take in new, fcarce the third part of a minute.

Again, the beating of the *Pulfe*, and the motion of the *Syftole* and *Diaftole* of the heart, are three times quicker than that of breathing : infomuch that if it were poffible that that motion of the heart could be ftopped without ftopping the breath, death would follow more fpedily thereupon than by ftrangling.

Notwithftanding, ufe and cuftom prevail much in this natural action of breathing ; as it is in the *Delian* Divers and Fifhers for Pearl, who by long ufe can hold their breaths at leaft ten times longer than other men can do.

Amongft living Creatures, even of thofe that have *Lungs*, there are fome that are able to hold their breaths a long time, and others that cannot hold them fo long, according as they need more or lefs refrigeration.

Fifhes need lefs refrigeration than *Terreftrial Creatures*, yet fome they need, and take it by their Gills. And as *Terreftrial Creatures* cannot bear the air that is too hot or too clofe ; fo *Fifhes* are fuffocated in waters if they be totally and long frozen.

If the Spirit be affaulted by another *heat* greater than it felf, it is diffipated and deftroyed : for it cannot bear the proper *heat* without refrigeration, much lefs can it bear another heat which is far ftronger. This is to be feen in *burning-Fevers*, where the heat of the putrefied humours doth exceed the native heat, even to extinction or diffipation.

The want alfo and ufe of *Sleep* is referred to *Refrigeration*. For Motion doth attenuate and rarifie the fpirit, and doth fharpen and increafe the heat thereof; contrarily, *sleep* fetleth and reftraineth the motion and gadding of the fame : for though Sleep doth ftrengthen and advance the actions of the parts and of the livelefs fpirits, and all that motion which is to the circumference of the body ; yet it doth in great part quiet and ftill the proper motion of the *living Spirit*. Now fleep regularly is due unto humane nature once within four and twenty hours, and that for fix or five hours at the leaft : though there are, even in this kind, fometimes miracles of Nature ; as it is recorded of *Mecænas*, that he flept not for a long time before his death. And as touching the want of *Refrigeration* for conferving of the Spirit thus much.

As concerning the third *Indigence*, namely of *Aliment*, it feems to pertain rather to the *parts* than to the *living Spirit*; for a man may eafily believe that the *living Spirit* fubfifteth in Identity, not by fucceffion or renovation. And as for the *reafonable Soul* in man, it is above all queftion that it is not engendred of the Soul of the Parents, nor is repaired, nor can die. They fpeak of the *Natural Spirit* of living Creatures, and alfo of Vegetables, which differs from that other Soul effentially and formally. For out of the confufion of thefe that fame tranfmigration of Souls, and innumerable other devices of Heathens and Hereticks have proceeded.

The Body of man doth regularly require *Renovation* by *Aliment* every day, and a body in health can fcarce endure fafting three days together ; notwithftanding ufe and cuftome will do much even in this cafe : but in ficknefs fafting is lefs grievous to the body. Alfo *sleep* doth fupply fomewhat to nourifhment ; and on the other fide *Exercife* doth require it more abundantly. Likewife there have fome been found who fuftained themfelves (almoft to a miracle in nature) a very long time without meat or drink.

Dead bodies if they be not intercepted by *putrefaction*, will fubfift a long time without any notable *Abfumption* ; but *Living bodies* not above three days, (as we faid) unlefs they be repaired by nourifhment : which fheweth that quick *Abfumption* to be the work of the *living Spirit*, which either repairs it felf, or puts the parts into a neceffity of being repaired, or both. This is teftified by that alfo which was noted a little before, namely, that *living creatures* may fubfift fomewhat the longer without *Aliment* if they fleep: now fleep is nothing elfe but a reception and retirement of the *living Spirit* into it felf.

An abundant and continual *effluxion* of blood, which fometimes happeneth in the *Hæmorrhoides*, fometimes in vomitting of blood, the inward Veins being unlocked or broken, fometimes by wounds, caufeth fudden death, in regard that the bloud of the *Veins* miniftreth to the *Arteries*, and the bloud of the *Arteries* to the *Spirit*.

I 3

The

26.   The quantity of meat and drink which a man, eating two meals a day, receiveth into his body is not small; much more than he voideth again either by stool, or by urine, or by sweating. You will say, No marvel, seeing the remainder goeth into the juices and substance of the body. It is true; but consider then that this addition is made twice a day, and yet the body aboundeth not much. In like manner, though the spirit be re-paired, yet it grows not excessively in the quantity.

27.   It doth no good to have the Aliment ready, in a degree removed, but to have it of that kind, and so prepared and supplied that the spirit may work upon it: for the staff of a *Torch* alone will not maintain the flame, unless it be fed with wax, neither can men live upon herbs alone. And from thence comes the *Inconcoction* of old age, that though there be flesh and bloud, yet the spirit is become so penurious and thin, and the juices and bloud so heartless and obstinate, that they hold no proportion to *Alimentation.*

28.   Let us now cast up the *accounts* of the *Needs* and *Indigences*, according to the ordi-nary and usual course of nature. The Spirit hath need of opening and moving it self in the *Ventricles* of the Brain and Nerves even continually, of the motion of the *Heart* every third part of a moment, of breathing every moment, of sleep and nourishment once within three days, of the power of nourishment commonly till eighty years be past: And if any of these *Indigences* be neglected, *Death* ensueth. So there are plainly three *Porches* of *Death*; Destitution of the Spirit in the *Motion*, in the *Refrigeration*, in the *Aliment.*

    It is an error to think that the Living Spirit is perpetually generated and extinguished, as Flame *is, and abideth not any notable time: for even* Flame *it self is not thrust out of its own proper nature, but because it liveth amongst enemies, for* Flame *within* Flame *endureth. Now the Living Spirit liveth amongst friends, and all due obsequiousness. So then, as* Flame *is a momentany substance,* Air *is a fixed substance, the* Living Spirit *is betwixt both.*

    Touching the extinguishing *of the Spirit by the* destruction *of the Organs (which is caused by Diseases and Violence) we enquire not now, as we foretold in the beginning, al-though that also endeth in the same three* Porches. *And touching the* Form *of Death it self thus much.*

29.   There are two great *forerunners* of Death, the one sent from the *Head*, the other from the *Heart*; *Convulsion*, and the extreme labour of the *Pulse*; for, as for the deadly *Hiccough*, it is a kind of *Convulsion*. But the deadly labour of the *Pulse* hath that unusual swiftness, because the *Heart* at the point of death doth so tremble, that the *Systole* and *Diastole* thereof are almost confounded. There is also conjoyned in the *Pulse* a weakness and lowness, and oftentimes a great intermission, because the motion of the *Heart* faileth, and is not able to rise against the assault stoutly or constantly.

30.   The immediate proceeding signs of *Death* are, great unquietness and tossing in the bed, fumbling with the hands, catching and grasping hard, gnashing with the teeth, speaking hollow, trembling of the neather lip, paleness of the face, the memory con-fused, speechless, cold sweats, the body shooting in length, lifting up the white of the eye, changing of the whole visage, (as the nose sharp, eyes hollow, cheeks fallen) contraction and doubling of the coldness in the *extreme parts* of the body; in some, shedding of bloud or sperm, shrieking, breathing thick and short, falling of the nea-ther chap, and suchlike.

31.   There follow Death a privation of all sense and motion, as well of the Heart and Arteries as of the Nerves and Joynts, an inability of the body to support it self upright, stiffness of the Nerves and parts, extream coldness of the whole body; after a little while, putrefaction and stinking.

32.   *Eeles, serpents* and the *Insecta* will move a long time in every part after they are cut asunder, insomuch that Country people think that the parts strive to joyn together again. Also *birds* will flutter a great while after their heads are pulled off; and the hearts of living creatures will pant a long time after they are plucked out. I remem-ber I have seen the heart of one that was bowelled, as suffering for High Treason, that being cast into the fire, leaped at the first at least a foot and half in height, and after by degrees lower and lower, for the space, as I remember, of seven or eight minutes. There is also an ancient and credible Tradition of an *Ox* lowing after his bowels were plucked out. But there is a more certain tradition of a man, who being under the

Execu-

Executioner's hand for high Treason, after his *Heart* was plucked out and in the Executioner's hand, was heard to utter three or four words of prayer : which therefore we said to be more credible than that of the *Ox* in *Sacrifice*, because the friends of the party suffering do usually give a reward to the Executioner to dispatch his office with the more speed, that they may the sooner be rid of their pain ; but in *Sacrifices* we see no cause why the Priest should be so speedy in his office.

For *reviving* those again which fall into sudden *Swooning* and *Catalepses* of *astonishments*, (in which Fits many, without present help, would utterly expire) these things are used ; Putting into their mouths Water distilled of Wine , which they call *Hotwaters*, and *Cordial-waters*, bending the body forwards, stopping the mouth and nostrils hard, bending or wringing the fingers, pulling the hairs of the beard or head, rubbing of the parts, especially the face and legs, sudden casting of cold water upon the face, shrieking out aloud and suddenly ; putting *Rose-water* to the nostrills with *Vinegar* in faintings ; burning of Feathers or Cloth in the suffocation of the *Mother* : but especially a *Frying-pan* heated red hot is good in *Apoplexies* ; also a close embracing of the body hath helped some.

There have been many examples of men in shew dead, either laid out upon the cold floor, or carried forth to burial ; nay, of some buried in the earth, which notwithstanding have lived again, which hath been found in those that were buried (the earth being afterwards opened) by the bruising and wounding of their head, through the strugling of the body within the Coffin ; whereof the most recent and memorable example was that of *Joannes Scotus*, called the *Subtil*, and a *School-man*, who being digged up again by his Servant, (unfortunately absent at his burial, and who knew his Masters manner in such fits) was found in that state : And the like happened in our days in the person of a Player, buried at *Cambridge*. I remember to have heard of a certain *Gentleman*, that would needs make trial in curiosity what men did feel that were hanged ; so he fastened the Cord about his neck, raising himself upon a stool, and then letting himself fall, thinking it should be in his power to recover the stool at his pleasure, which he failed in, but was helped by a friend then present. He was asked afterward what he felt. He said he felt no pain, but first he thought he saw before his eyes a great fire and burning ; then he thought he saw all black and dark ; lastly it turned to a pale blew, or Sea-water green ; which colour is also often seen by them which fall into *Swoonings*. I have heard also of a Physician, yet living, who recovered a man to life which had hanged himself, and had hanged half an hour, by *Frications* and hot *Baths:* And the same Physician did profess, that he made no doubt to recover any man that had hanged so long, so his Neck were not broken with the first swing.

The Differences of Youth and Old Age.

THe Ladder of Man's Body is this, To be conceived, to be quickned in the womb, to be born, to suck, to be weaned, to feed upon Pap, to put forth Teeth the first time about the second year of age, to begin to go, to begin to speak, to put forth Teeth the second time about seven years of age, to come to *Puberty* about twelve or fourteen years of age, to be able for generation and the flowing of the *Menstrua*, to have hairs about the legs and arm-holes, to put forth a Beard ; and thus long, and sometimes later, to grow in stature, to come to full years of strength and agility, to grow gray and bald ; the *Menstrua* ceasing, and ability to generation, to grow decrepit and a monster with three legs, to die. Mean-while the Mind also hath certain periods, but they cannot be described by years, as to decay in the *Memory*, and the like ; of which hereafter.

The differences of *Youth* and *old Age* are these : A young man's skin is smooth and plain, an old man's dry and wrinkled, especially about the forehead and eyes : a young man's flesh is tender and soft, an old man's hard ; a young man hath strength and agility, an old man feels decay in his strength and is slow of motion ; a young man
hath

hath good digestion, an old man had; a young man's bowels are soft and succulent, an old man's salt and parched : a young man's body is erect and streight, an old man's bowing and crooked ; a young man's limbs are steady, an old man's weak and trembling ; the humours in a young man are cholerick, and his blond inclined to heat, in an old man phlegmatick and melancholick, and his blond inclined to coldness ; a young man ready for the act of *Venus*, an old man slow unto it : in a young man the juices of his body are more roscid, in an old man more crude and waterish ; the spirit in a young man plentiful and boiling, in an old man scarce and jejune : a young man's spirit is dense and vigorous, an old man's eager and rare ; a young man hath his senses quick and intire, an old man dull and decayed ; a young man's teeth are strong and entire, an old man's weak, worn, and faln out ; a young man's hair is coloured, an old man's (of what colour soever it were) gray : a young man hath hair, an old man baldness ; a young man's pulse is stronger and quicker, an old man's more confused and slower, the diseases of young men are more acute and curable, of old men longer and hard to cure; a young man's wounds soon close, an old man's later ; a young man's cheeks are of a fresh colour, an old man's pale, or with a black blond ; a young man is less troubled with rheums, an old man more. Neither do we know in what things old men do improve as touching their body, save onely sometime in fatness; whereof the reason is soon given, Because old men's bodies do neither perspire well, nor assimilate well : now Fatness is nothing else but an exuberance of nourishment above that which is voided by excrement, or which is perfectly assimilated. Also some old men improve in the appetite of feeding by reason of the *acid humors*, though old men digest worst. And all these things which we have said, *Physicians* negligently enough will refer to the *diminution* of the *Natural heat* and *Radical moisture*, which are things of no worth for use. This is certain, *Driness* in the coming on of years doth forego *Coldness* ; and bodies when they come to the top and strength of heat do decline in *Driness*, and after that follows *Coldness*.

3. Now we are to consider the *Affections* of the *Mind*. I remember when I was a young man, at *Poictiers* in *France* I conversed familiarly with a certain *French-man*, a witty young man, but something talkative, who afterwards grew to be a very eminent man : he was wont to inveigh against the manners of *old men*, and would say, That if their Minds could be seen as their Bodies are, they would appear no less deformed. Besides, being in love with his own wit, he would maintain, That the vices of old men's Minds have some correspondence and were parallel to the putrefactions of their Bodies : For the driness of their skin he would bring in *Impudence* ; for the hardness of their bowels, *unmercifulness* : for the *lippitude* of their eyes, an *evil Eye* and *Envy* : for the casting down of their eyes, and bowing their body towards the earth, *Atheism* ; (for, saith he, *they look no more up to Heaven as they are wont*) for the trembling of their members, *Irresolution* of their *decrees* and *light Inconstancy* ; for the bending of their fingers, as it were to catch, *Rapacity* and *covetousness* ; for the buckling of their knees, *Fearfulness*; for their wrinkles, *Craftiness* and *Obliquity*: and other things which I have forgotten. But to be serious, a young man is modest and shamefac'd, an old man's fore-head is hardned ; a young man is full of bounty and mercy, an old man's heart is brawny : a young man is affected with a laudable emulation, an old man with a malignant envy ; a young man is inclined to Religion and Devotion, by reason of his fervency and inexperience of evil, an old man cooleth in piety through the coldness of his charity, and long conversation in evil, and likewise through the difficulty of his belief ; a young man's desires are vehement, an old man's moderate ; a young man is light and moveable, an old man more grave and constant ; a young man is given to liberality, and beneficence, and humanity, an old man to covetousness, wisdom for his own self, and seeking his own ends ; a young man is confident and full of hope, an old man diffident and given to suspect most things ; a young man is gentle and obsequious, an old man froward and disdainful; a young man is sincere and open-hearted, an old man cautelous and close ; a young man is given to desire great things, an old man to regard things necessary ; a young man thinks well of the present times, an old man preferreth times past before them ; a young man reverenceth his Superiours, an old man is more forward to tax them : And many other things, which pertain rather to Manners than to the present Inquisition. Notwithstanding old men, as in some things they improve in their Bodies, so also in their Minds, unless they be altogether out of date : namely, that as they are less apt for invention,

tion, so they excel in judgment, and prefer safe things and sound things before specious; also they improve in Garrulity and Ostentation, for they seek the fruit of speech, while they are less able for action : So as it was not absurd that the *Poets* feigned old *Tithon* to be turned into a *Grashopper.*

Moveable Canons of the Duration of Life and Form of Death.

Canon I.

COnsumption *is not caused, unless that which is departed with by one body passeth into another.*

The Explication.

THere is in Nature no *Annihilating,* or *Reducing to Nothing :* therefore that which is consumed is either resolved into Air, or turned into some Body adjacent. So we see a *spider,* or *Fly,* or *Ant* in Amber, entombed in a more stately Monument than *Kings* are, to be laid up for Eternity, although they be but tender things, and soon dissipated : But the matter is this, that there is no air by, into which they should be resolved; and the *substance* of the *Amber* is so *heterogeneous,* that it receives nothing of them. The like we conceive would be if a Stick, or Root, or some such thing were buried in *Quick-silver :* also *Wax,* and *Honey,* and *Gums* have the same *Operation,* but in part onely.

Canon II.

THere is in every Tangible body *a* Spirit, *covered and encompassed with the grosser parts of the body, and from it all* Consumption *and* Dissolution *hath the beginning.*

The Explication.

NO Body known unto us here in the upper part of the Earth is without a Spirit, either by *Attenuation* and *Concoction* from the heat of the Heavenly Bodies, or by some other way : for the *Concavities* of *Tangible things* receive not *Vacuum,* but either Air, or the proper *Spirit* of the thing. And this *spirit* whereof we speak is not some *Virtue,* or *Energie,* or *Act,* or a *Trifle,* but plainly a *Body,* rare and invisible; notwithstanding circumscribed by Place, Quantitative, Real. Neither again is that Spirit Air, (no more than Wine is Water) but a body rarefied, of kin to Air, though much different from it. Now the grosser parts of bodies (being dull things, and not apt for motion) would last a long time ; but the Spirit is that which troubleth, and plucketh, and underminneth them, and converteth the moisture of the body, and whatsoever it is able to digest, into new Spirit ; and then as well the pre-existing Spirit of the body as that newly made flie away together by degrees This is best seen by the *Diminution* of the *weight* in bodies dried through *Perspiration :* for neither s" - hich is issued forth was Spirit when the body was ponderous, neither was it not hen it issued forth.

Canon III.

THe Spirit issuing forth Drieth; Detained *and working within either* Melteth, *or* Putrefieth, *or* Vivifieth.

The Explication.

THere are four Processes of the Spirit, to *Arefaction,* to *Colliquation,* *Putrefaction,* to *Generation* of bodies. *Arefaction* is not the proper work of the Spirit, but of the grosser parts after the Spirit issued forth : for then they contract themselves partly by their flight of *Vacuum,* partly by the *union* of the *Homogeneals :* as appears in all things which are arefied by age, and in the drier sort of bodies which have passed the fire, as *Bricks, Char-coal, Bread.* *Colliquation* is the mere work of the Spirit : neither is it done but when they are excited by heat : for when the Spirits dilating themselves, yet not getting forth, do insinuate and disperse themselves among the grosser parts, and so make them soft and apt to run, as it is in *Metalls* and *Wax :* for *Metalls* and all tenacious things are apt to inhibit the Spirit, that being

K

excited

excited it iſſueth not forth. *Putrefaction* is a mixed work of the *Spirits* and of the groſſer parts : for the Spirit (which before reſtrained and bridled the parts of the thing) being partly iſſued forth and partly infeebled, all things in the body do diſſolve and return to their *Homogeneſſies,* or (if you will) to their Elements : that which was *Spirit* in it is congregated to it ſelf, whereby things putreſied begin to have an ill ſavour : the *Oily* parts to themſelves, whereby things putreſied have that ſlipperineſs and unctuoſity ; the *watry* parts alſo to themſelves : the *Dregs* to themſelves : whence followeth that *confuſion* in *bodies putrefied.* But *Generation* or *Vivification* is a work alſo mixed of the Spirit and groſſer parts, but in a far different manner : for the Spirit is totally detained, but it ſwelleth and moveth locally : and the groſſer parts are not diſſolved, but follow the motion of the ſpirit, and are, as it were, blown out by it, and extruded into divers figures, from whence cometh that *Generation* and *Organizaion :* and therefore *Vivification* is always done in a matter tenacious and clammy, and again, yielding and ſoft, that there may be both a detention of the ſpirit, and alſo a gentle ceſſion of the parts, according as the ſpirit forms them. And this is ſeen in the matter as well of all Vegetables as of living Creatures, whether they be engendred of *Putrefaction* or of *Sperm* ; for in all theſe things there is manifeſtly ſeen a matter hard to break through, eaſie to yield.

Canon IV.

IN all living Creatures there are two kinds of Spirits : Liveleſs Spirits, ſuch as are in bodies Inanimate ; *and a* Vital Spirit *ſuperadded.*

The Explication.

IT was ſaid before, that to procure long life the Body of man muſt be conſidered, firſt, as *Inanimate,* and not repaired by nouriſhment : ſecondly, as *Animate,* and repaired by nouriſhment : for the former conſideration gives Laws touching *Conſumption,* the latter touching *Reparation.* Therefore we muſt know that there are in humane fleſh bones, Membranes, Organs : finally, in all the parts ſuch ſpirits diffuſed in the ſubſtance of them while they are alive, as there are in the ſame things (Fleſh, Bones, Membranes, and the reſt) ſeparated and dead : ſuch as alſo remain in a *Carkaſs :* but the *Vital Spirit,* although it ruleth them, and hath ſome conſent with them, yet it is far differing from them, being integral, and ſubſiſting by it ſelf. Now there are two ſpecial differences betwixt the *Liveleſs Spirits* and the *Vital Spirits.* The one, that the *Liveleſs ſpirits* are not continued to themſelves , but are , as it were, cut off, and encompaſſed with a groſs body which intercepts them ; as *Air* is mixed with *Snow* or *Froth :* but the *Vital Spirit* is all continued to it ſelf by certain Conduit-pipes through which it paſſeth, and is not totally intercepted. And this Spirit is two-fold alſo : the one branched, onely paſſing through ſmall pipes, and, as it were, ſtrings : the other hath a *Cell* alſo, ſo as it is not onely continued to it ſelf, but alſo congregated in an hollow ſpace in reaſonable good quantity, according to the Analogy of the body, and in that *Cell* is the fountain of the Rivulets which branch from thence. That *Cell* is chiefly in the Ventricles of the Brain, which in the ignobler ſort of creatures are but narrow, inſomuch that the ſpirits in them ſeem ſcattered over their whole body rather than Celled ; as may be ſeen in *Serpents, Eels* and *Flies,* whereof every of their parts move long after they are cut aſſunder. *Birds* alſo leap a good while after their heads are pulled off, becauſe they have little heads and little Cells. But the nobler ſort of creatures have thoſe Ventricles larger, and Man the largeſt of all. The other difference betwixt the Spirits is, that the Vital Spirit hath a kind of enkindling, and is like a Wind or Breath compounded of Flame and Air, as the Juices of living creatures have both *Oil* and *Water.* And this enkindling miniſtreth peculiar motions and faculties : for the ſmoke which is inflamable, even before the flame conceived, is hot, thin and movable, and yet it is quite another thing after it is become flame : but the enkindling of the vital ſpirits is by many degrees gentler than the ſofteſt flame, as of *Spirit* of *Wine,* or otherwiſe ; and beſides, it is in great part mixed with an *Aerial* ſubſtance, that it ſhould be a *Myſtery* or *Miracle,* both of a *Flammeous* and *Aereous* nature.

Canon V.

THe Natural Actions are proper to the ſeveral Parts, but it is the Vital Spirit *that excites and ſharpens them.*

The

The Explication.

THe *Actions* or *Functions* which are in the several *Members* follow the nature of the *Members* themselves, (*Attraction, Retention, Digestion, Assimilation, Separation, Excretion, Perspiration*, even *Sense* it self) according to the propriety of the several *Organs*, (the *Stomach, Liver, Heart, Spleen, Gall, Brain, Eye, Ear*, and the rest :) yet none of these *Actions* would ever have been actuated but by the vigour and presence of the *Vital spirit* and heat thereof : as one *Iron* would not have drawn another *iron*, unless it had been excited by the *Load stone*, nor an *Egge* would ever have brought forth a *Bird*, unless the substance of the *Hen* had been actuated by the treading of the *Cock.*

Canon VI.

THe liveless Spirits *are next Consubstantial to* Air ; *the* vital Spirits *approach more to the substance of* Flame.

The Explication.

THe Explication of the precedent fourth *Canon* is also a declaration of this present *Canon* : but yet further, from hence it is that all fat and oily things continue long in their Being ; For neither doth the *air* much pluck them , neither do they much desire to joyn themselves with *Air*. As for that conceit it is altogether vain, That Flame should be Air set on fire, seeing *Flame* and *Air* are no less *heterogeneal* than *Oil* and *water*. But whereas it is said in the *Canon*, that the *vital spirits* approach more to the substance of *Flame* ; it must be understood, that they do this more than the *liveless spirits*, not that they are more *Flamy* than *Airy*.

Canon VII.

THe Spirit *hath two* Desires ; *one of* multiplying *it* self, *the other of* flying forth *and congregating it self with the* Connaturals.

The Explication.

THe *Canon* is understood of the *liveless spirits* ; for as for the *second Desire* , the *vital spirit* doth most of all abhor flying forth of the body, for it finds no *Connatural* here below to joyn withal : Perhaps it may sometimes flie to the outward parts of the body, to meet that which it loveth ; but the flying forth, as I said, it abhorreth. But in the *liveless spirits* each of these two *Desires* holdeth. For to the former this belongeth, *Every spirit seated amongst the grosser parts dwelleth unhappily* ; and therefore when it finds not a *like* unto it self, it doth so much the more labour to create and make a like, as being in a great solitude, and endeavour earnestly to multiply it self, and to prey upon the *volatile* of the *grosser parts*, that it may be encreased in quantity. As for the *second Desire* of flying forth, and betaking it self to the *Air*, it is certain that all light things (which are ever movable) do willingly go unto their *likes* near unto them, as a *Drop* of water is carried to a *Drop*, *Flame* to *Flame* : but much more this is done in the flying forth of *spirit* into the *Air* ambient, because it is not carried to a particle like unto it self, but also as unto the *Globe* of the *connaturals*. Mean-while this is to be noted, That the *going forth* and *flight* of the *spirit* into *air* is a redoubled action, partly out of the *appetite* of the *spirit*, partly out of the *appetite* of the *air* ; for the *common air* is a needy thing, and receiveth all things speedily, as *Spirits, Odours, beams, sounds*, and the like.

Canon VIII.

SPirit detained, *if it have no possibility of begetting new* spirits, itenerateth *the grosser parts.*

The Explication.

GEneration of new Spirit is not accomplished but upon those things which are in some degree near to spirit, such as are humid bodies. And therefore if the grosser parts (amongst which the Spirit converseth) be in a remote degree, although the spirit cannot convert them, yet (as much as it can) it weakneth, and softneth, and subdueth them, that seeing it cannot increase in quantity, yet it will dwell more at large, and live amongst good neighbours and friends. Now this *Aphorism* is most useful to our End, because it tendeth to the Inteneration of the obstinate parts by the detention of the spirit.

Canon IX.

THe Inteneration *of the* harder parts *cometh to good effect, when the* Spirit *neither* flyeth forth, *nor* begetteth new Spirit.

K 2　　　　　　　　　*The*

The Explication.

THis *Canon* solveth the knot and difficulty in the Operation of Intenerating by the Detention of the *Spirit*: for if the *Spirit* not flying forth wasteth all within, there is nothing gotten to the *Inteneration* of the parts in their subsistence, but rather they are dissolved and corrupted. Therefore together with the *Detention* the *Spirits* ought to be cooled and restrained, that they may not be too active.

Canon X.

The heat of the Spirit *to keep the body fresh and green, ought to be* Robust, *not* Eager.

The Explication.

ALso this *Canon* pertaineth to the solving of the knot aforesaid, but it is of a much larger extent, for it setteth down of what *temperament* the *heat* in the body ought to be for the obtaining of Long life. Now this is useful, whether the *spirits* be detained, or whether they be not. For howsoever the *heat* of the *Spirits* must be such, as it may rather turn it self upon the hard parts than waste the soft; for the one Desiccateth, the other Intenerateth. Besides, the same thing is available to the well perfecting of *Assimilation*; for such an heat doth excellently excite the *faculty* of *Assimilation*, and withall doth excellently prepare the matter to be *Assimilated*. Now the properties of this kind of *heat* ought to be these. First, that it be *slow*, and heat not suddenly: Secondly, that it be not very *intense*, but *moderate*: Thirdly, that it be *equal*, not *incomposed*, namely, intending and remitting it self: Fourthly, that if this heat meet any thing to resist it, it be not easily suffocated or languish. This *Operation* is exceeding subtil, but seeing it is one of the most useful, it is not to be deserted. Now in those *Remedies* which we propounded to invest the spirits with a *Robust heat*, or that which we call *Operative*, not *Predatory*, we have in some sort satisfied this matter.

Canon XI.

The Condensing *of the Spirits in their* Substance *is available to Long life.*

The Explication.

THis *Canon* is subordinate to the next precedent : for the *Spirit condensed* receiveth all those four properties of heat whereof we speak; but the ways of *Condensing* them are set down in the first of the Ten *Operations*.

Canon XII.

The Spirit *in great quantity hastneth more to flying forth, and preyeth upon the body more, than in small quantity.*

The Explication.

THis *Canon* is clear of it self, seeing mere Quantity doth regularly increase virtue. And it is to be seen in flames, that the bigger they are, the stronger they break forth, and the more speedily they consume. And therefore over-great *plenty* or *exuberance* of the spirits is altogether hurtful to Long life; neither need one with a greater store of spirits than what is sufficient for the function of life, and the office of a good Reparation.

Canon XIII.

The Spirit *equally* dispersed *maketh less haste to flie forth, and preyeth less upon the body, than unequally placed.*

The Explication.

NOt onely abundance of spirits in respect of the whole is hurtful to the Duration of things, but also the same abundance unevenly placed is in like manner hurtful; and therefore the more the spirit is shred and inserted by small portions, the less it preyeth: for Dissolution ever beginneth at that part where the spirit is looser. And therefore both Exercise and Frications conduce much to long life, for Agitation doth fineliest diffuse and commix things by small portions.

Canon XIV.

The inordinate *and* subsultory *motion of the* spirits *doth more* hasten *to going forth, and doth prey upon the body more, than the* constant *and* equal.

The Explication.

IN *Inanimates* this *Canon* holds for certain; for Inequality is the Mother of Dissolution : but in *Animates* (because not onely the Consumption is considered, but the

Repara-

Reparation, and Reparation proceedeth by the Appetites of things, and Appetite is sharpned by variety) it holdeth not rigoroufly; but it is fo far forth to be received, that this variety be rather an alternation or enterchange than a confufion, and as it were conftant in inconftancy.

Canon XV.

The Spirit *in a Body of a folid compofure is detained, though unwillingly.*

The Explication.

ALl things do abhor a *Solution* of their *Continuity*, but yet in proportion to their *Denfity* or *Rarity* : for the more *rare* the *bodies* be, the more do they fuffer themfelves to be thruft into fmall and narrow paffages ; for *water* will go into a paffage which *duft* will not go into, and *air* which water will not go into, nay, *flame* and *fpirit* which *air* will not go into. Notwithftanding of this thing there are fome bounds : for the *fpirit* is not fo much tranfported with the defire of going forth, that it will fuffer it felf to be too much difcontinued, or be driven into over-ftreight pores and paffages ; and therefore if the fpirit be encompaffed with an *hard* body, or elfe with an *unctuous* and *tenacious*, (which is not eafily divided) it is plainly bound, and, as I may fay, imprifoned, and layeth down the appetite of going out : wherefore we fee that *Metalls* and *ftones* require a long time for their fpirit to go forth, unlefs either the fpirit be excited by the fire, or the groffer parts be diffevered with corroding and ftrong waters. The like reafon is there of *tenacious bodies*, fuch as are *Gums*, fave onely that they are melted by a more gentle heat : and therefore the *juices* of the body *hard*, a *clofe* and *compact* *skin*, and the like, (which are procured by the *drinefs* of the *Aliment*, and by *Exercife*, and by the *coldnefs* of the *air*) are good for long life, becaufe they detain the fpirit in clofe prifon that it goeth not forth.

Canon XVI.

In Oily *and* Fat *things the* Spirit *is detained willingly, though they be not* tenacious.

The Explication.

THe fpirit, if it be not irritated by the *antipathy* of the body enclofing it, nor fed by the over-much *likenefs* of that body, nor follicited nor invited by the *external body*, it makes no great ftir to get out : all which are wanting to *Oily bodies* ; for they are neither fo preffing upon the fpirits as *hard bodies*, nor fo *near* as *watry bodies*, neither have they any good *agreement* with the *air ambient*.

Canon XVII.

THe fpeedy flying forth *of the* Watry humor *conferves the* Oily *the longer in his being.*

The Explication.

WE faid before that the *Watry humors*, as being confubftantial to the *Air*, flie forth fooneft ; the *Oily* later, as having fmall agreement with the *Air*. Now whereas thefe two *humors* are in moft bodies, it comes to pafs that the *watry* doth in a fort betray the *Oily*, for that iffuing forth infenfibly carrieth this together with it. Therefore there is nothing more furthereth the confervation of bodies than a *gentle drying* of them, which caufeth the *watry humour* to expire, and inviteth not the *Oily* ; for then the *Oily* enjoyeth the proper nature. And this tendeth not onely to the inhibiting of *Putrefaction*, (though that alfo followeth) but to the confervation of *Greennefs*. Hence it is, that *gentle Frications* and *moderate Exercifes*, caufing rather *Perfpiration* than *Sweating*, conduce much to long life.

Canon XVIII.

Air excluded *conferreth to Long life, if other* inconveniences *be avoided.*

The Explication.

WE faid a little before, that the *flying forth* of the *fpirit* is a redoubled action, from the *appetite* of the *fpirit* and of the *air*, and therefore if either of thefe be taken out of the way, there is not a little gained. Notwithftanding divers *Inconveniences* follow hereupon, which how they may be prevented we have fhewed in the fecond of our *Operations*.

Canon XIX.

YOuthful Spirits *inferted into an old Body might foon turn* Nature's courfe *back again.*

The Explication.

THe *nature* of the *spirits* is as the uppermost *wheel,* which turneth about the other wheels in the body of man, and therefore in the *Intention* of Long life, that ought to be first placed. Hereunto may be added, that there is an easier and more expedite way to alter the *spirits,* than to other *Operations.* For the *Operation* upon the *spirits* is two-fold: the one by *Aliments,* which is flow, and, as it were, about; the other, (and that two fold) which is sudden, and goeth directly to the spirits, namely, by *Vapours,* or by the *Affections.*

Canon XX.

Juices *of the* Body hard *and* roscid *are good for Long life.*

The Explication.

THe reason is plain, seeing we shewed before, that *hard* things, and *oily* or *roscid* are hardly dissipated : notwithstanding there is difference, (as we also noted in the tenth *Operation*) That *juice* somewhat *hard* is indeed less *dissipable,* but then it is withal less *reparable* ; therefore a *convenience* is interlaced with an *inconvenience,* and for this cause no wonderful matter will be atchieved by this. But *roscid juice* will admit both *Operations* ; therefore this would be principally endeavoured.

Canon XXI.

VVhatsoever is *of* thin parts *to penetrate, and yet hath no* Acrimony *to* bite, *begetteth* Roscid Juices.

The Explication.

THis *Canon* is more hard to practise than to understand. For it is manifest, whatsoever *penetrateth* well, but yet with a *sting* or *tooth,* (as do all sharp and four things) it leaveth behind it wheresoever it goeth some mark or print of *driness* and *cleaving.* so that it hardneth the *juices,* and chappeth the *parts :* contrarily, whatsoever things *penetrate* through their *thinness* merely, as it were by stealth, and by way of insinuation, without violence, they *bedew* and *water* in their passage. Of which sort we have recounted many in the fourth and seventh *Operations.*

Canon XXII.

Assimilation *is best done when all* Local Motion *is expended.*

The Explication.

THis *Canon* we have sufficiently explained in our Discourse upon the eighth *Operation.*

Canon XXIII.

ALimentation from without, *at least some other way than by the* Stomach, *is most profitable for Long life, if it can be done.*

The Explication.

WE see that all things which are done by *Nutrition,* ask a long time, but those which are done by *embracing* of the *like* (as it is in *Infusions*) require no long time. And therefore *Alimentation* from without would be of principal use, and so much the more, because the *Faculties* of *Concoction* decay in old age : so that if there could be some auxiliary *Nutritions,* by *Bathings, Unctions,* or else by *Clysters,* these things in conjunction might do much, which single are less available.

Canon XXIV.

WHere the Concoction *is weak to thrust forth the* Aliment, *there the* Outward parts *should be strengthned to call forth the* Aliment.

The Explication.

THat which is propounded in this *Canon* is not the same thing with the former ; for it is one thing for the *outward Aliment* to be *attracted inward,* another for the *inward Aliment* to be *attracted outward :* yet herein they concur, that they both help the weakness of the *inward Concoctions,* though by divers ways.

Canon XXV.

ALL *sudden* Renovation *of the* Body *is wrought either by the* Spirit, *or by* Malacissations.

The Explication.

THere are two things in the body, *Spirits* and *Parts :* to both these the way by *Nutrition* is long and about ; but it is a short way to the *Spirits* by *Vapours* and by the *Affections,* and to the *Parts* by *Malacissations.* But this is diligently to be noted, that by no means we confound *Alimentation from without* with *Malacissation ;* for the intention of *Malacissation* is not to nourish the parts, but onely to make them more fit to be nourished.

                                                                         Canon

Canon XXVI.

MAlaciſſation *is wrought by* Conſubſtantials *,* by Imprinters, *and by* Cloſers up.

The Explication.

THe reaſon is manifeſt, for that *Conſubſtantials* do properly ſupple the body, *Imprinters* do carry in. *Cloſers up* do retain and bridle the *Perſpiration*, which is a motion oppoſite to *Malaciſſation*. And therefore (as we deſcribed in the ninth *Operation*) *Malaciſſation* cannot well be done at once, but in a courſe or order. Firſt, by *excluding* the *Liquor* by *Thickners* : for an outward and groſs Infuſion doth not well compact the body: that which entreth muſt be ſubtil, and a kind of vapour. Secondly, by *Inenerating* by the conſent of *Conſubſtantials* : for bodies upon the touch of thoſe things which have good agreement with them, open themſelves, and relax their pores. Thirdly, *Imprinters* are *Convoys*, and inſinuate into the parts the *Conſubſtantials*, and the mixture of gentle *Aſtringents* doth ſomewhat reſtrain the *Perſpiration*. But then, in the fourth place, follows that great *Aſtriction* and *Cloſure* up of the body by *Emplaiſtration*, and then afterward by *Inunction*, until the *ſupple* be turned into *Solid*, as we ſaid in the proper place.

Canon XXVII.

FRequent Renovation *of the* Parts Repairable *watereth and reneweth the leſs* Reparable *alſo*.

The Explication.

WE ſaid in the Preface to this Hiſtory, that the *way of Death* was this, That the *Parts Reparable* died in the fellowſhip of the *Parts leſs Reparable* : ſo that in the *Reparation* of theſe ſame *leſs Reparable Parts* all our forces would be employed. And therefore being admoniſhed by *Ariſtotle's* obſervation touching *Plants*, namely, *That the putting forth of new ſhoots and branches refreſheth the body of the Tree in the paſſage* ; we conceive the like reaſon might be, if the *fleſh* and *blood* in the body of man were often renewed, that thereby the *bones* themſelves, and *membranes*, and other parts which in their own nature are *leſs Reparable*, partly by the chearful paſſage of the *juices*, partly by that new cloathing of the young *fleſh* and *blood*, might be *watered* and renewed.

Canon XXVIII.

REfrigeration *or* Cooling *of the body, which paſſeth ſome other way than by the* Sto-mach, *is uſeful for Long life*.

The Explication.

THe reaſon is at hand : for ſeeing a *Refrigeration* not temperate, but powerful, (eſpecially of the *blood*) is above all things neceſſary to Long life : this can by no means be effected from within as much as is requiſite, without the deſtruction of the *ſtomach* and *Bowels*.

Canon XXIX.

THat Intermixing *or* Intangling, *that as well* Conſumption *as* Reparation *are the works of Heat, is the greateſt obſtacle to Long life*.

The Explication.

ALmoſt all great works are deſtroyed by the *Natures* of things *Intermixed*, whenas that which helpeth in one reſpect hurteth in another : therefore men muſt proceed herein by a ſound judgement, and a diſcreet practice. For our part, we have done ſo as far as the matter will bear, and our memory ſerveth us, by ſeparating *benign heats* from *hurtful*, and the *Remedies* which tend to both.

Canon XXX.

CUring *of Diſeaſes is effected by* Temporary Medicines ; *but* Lengthning *of Life requireth* Obſervation *of* Diets.

The Explication.

THoſe things which come by accident, as ſoon as the cauſes are removed ceaſe again ; but the continued courſe of nature, like a running River, requires a continual rowing and ſailing againſt the ſtream : therefore we muſt work regularly by Diets. Now Diets are of two kinds : *Set Diets*, which are to be obſerved at certain times; and *Familiar Diet*, which is to be admitted into our daily repaſt. But the *Set Diets* are the more potent, that is, a courſe of *Medicines* for a time : for thoſe things which are of ſo great virtue that they are able to turn Nature back again, are, for the moſt part, more ſtrong, and more ſpeedily altering, than thoſe which may without danger be received into a continual uſe. Now in the Remedies ſet down in our *Intentions* you ſhall

shall find onely three *Set Diets*, the *Opiate Diet*, the *Diet Malaciſſant* or *Suppling*, and the *Diet Emaciant* and *Renewing*. But amongſt thoſe which we preſcribed for *Familiar Diet*, and to be uſed daily, the moſt efficacious are theſe that follow, which alſo come not far ſhort of the vertue of *Set Diets* : *Nitre* and the *ſubordinates* to *Nitre*; the *Regiment* of the *Affections* and *Courſe* of our *Life* ; *Refrigeratours* which paſs not by the *Stomach* ; *Drinks Roſcidating*, or *ingendring Oily Juices* ; beſprinkling of the bloud with ſome *firmer Matter*, as *Pearls*, certain *woods*, competent *Unctions* to keep out the *Air*, and to keep in the *Spirit* ; *Heaters* from without, during the Aſſimilation after ſleep ; avoiding of thoſe things which inflame the Spirit, and put it into an *eager heat*, as *wine* and *Spices* ; laſtly, a moderate and ſeaſonable uſe of thoſe things which endue the Spirits with a *robuſt Heat*, as *Saffron*, *Croſſes*, *Garlick*, *Elecampane*, and *compound Opiates*.

Canon XXXI.

THe Living Spirit is inſtantly extinguiſhed if it be deprived either of Motion, or of Refrigeration, or of Aliment.

The Explication.

NAmely, theſe are thoſe three which before we called the *Porches of Death*, and they are the proper and immediate paſſions of the Spirit. For all the *Organs* of the principal parts ſerve hereunto, that theſe three *offices* be performed ; and again, all deſtruction of the *Organs* which is deadly brings the matter to this point, that one or more of theſe three fail. Therefore all other things are the divers ways to *Death*, but they end in theſe three. Now the *whole Fabrick* of the *Parts* is the *Organ* of the *Spirit*, as the *Spirit* is the *Organ* of the *Reaſonable Soul*, which is *Incorporeous* and *Divine*.

Canon XXXII.

FLame is a Momentany Subſtance, Air a Fixed ; the Living Spirit in Creatures is of a middle Nature.

The Explication.

THis matter ſtands in need both of an higher Indagation and of a longer Explication than is pertinent to the preſent Inquiſition. Mean-while we muſt know this, that *Flame* is almoſt every moment generated and extinguiſhed ; ſo that it is continued only by ſucceſſion : but *Air* is a *fixed body*, and is not diſſolved ; for though Air begets new Air out of watery moiſture, yet notwithſtanding the old Air ſtill remains ; whence cometh that Super-oneration of the Air whereof we have ſpoken in the Title *De Ventis*. But *Spirit* is participant of both Natures, both of *Flame* and *Air*, even as the nouriſhments thereof are, as well *Oil*, which is homogeneous to *Flame*, as *Water*, which is homogeneous to *Air* : for the Spirit is not nouriſhed either of *Oily* alone, or of *watry* alone, but of both together ; and though *Air* doth not agree well with *Flame*, nor *Oil* with *water*, yet in a *mix'd body* they agree well enough. Alſo the *Spirit* hath from the *Air* his eaſie and delicate impreſſions and yieldings, and from the *Flame* his noble and potent motions and activities. In like manner the *Duration* of ſpirit is a *mixed thing*, being neither ſo *momentany* as that of *Flame*, nor ſo *fixed* as that of *Air* : And ſo much the rather it followeth not the condition of *Flame*, for that *Flame* it ſelf is extinguiſhed by accident, namely, by Contraries and Enemies environing it ; but *Spirit* is not ſubject to the like conditions and neceſſities. Now the *Spirit* is repaired from the lively and florid bloud of the ſmall *Arteries* which are inſerted into the *Brain*; but this Reparation is done by a peculiar manner, of which we ſpeak not now.

FINIS.